D1742705

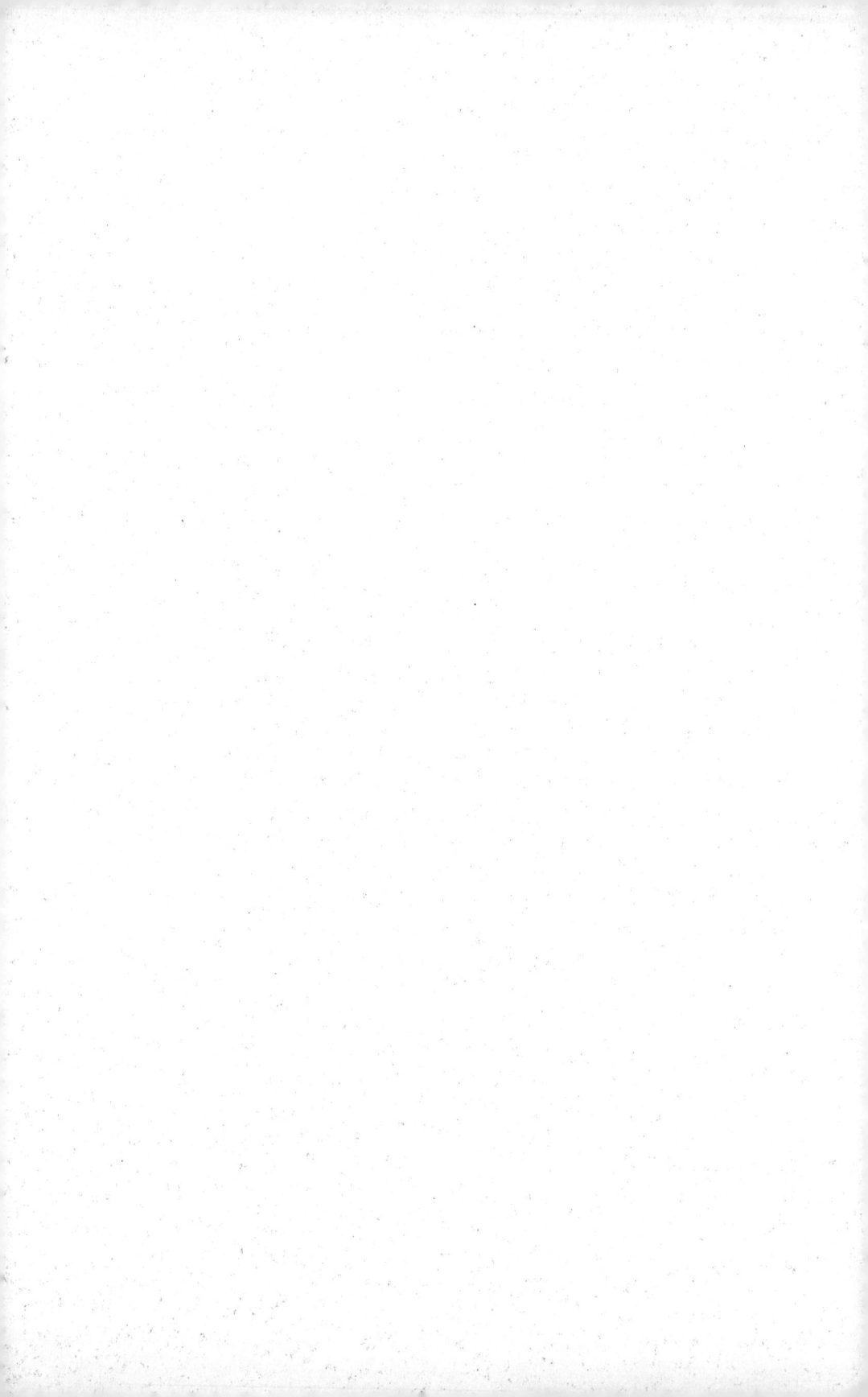

Geoffrey Dutton

OUT IN THE OPEN

Geoffrey Dutton

OUT IN THE OPEN

An Autobiography

University of Queensland Press

First published 1994 by University of Queensland Press
Box 42, St Lucia, Queensland 4067 Australia

Designed by Paul Rendle
Part-title illustrations by Brian Sadgrove

Indexed by Susan Rintoul, Professional Editing Services, SA
Typeset by University of Queensland Press
Printed in Australia by McPherson's Printing Group

Distributed in the USA and Canada by
International Specialized Book Services, Inc.,
5804 N.E. Hassalo Street, Portland, Oregon 97213–3640

Sponsored by the Queensland Office of Arts and Cultural Development.

Cataloguing in Publication Data
National Library of Australia

Dutton, Geoffrey, 1922– .
Out in the open.

Includes index.

1. Dutton, Geoffrey, 1922– . 2. Poets, Australian — 20th century — Biography. 3. Editors — Australia — Biography. I. Title.

A821.3

ISBN 0 7022 2681 5

For Robin, my wife
Found, after nearly sixty years
and
Chibs, my sister
My first companion

I speake truth, not my belly-full, but as much as I dare: and I dare the more, the more I grow into yeares: for it seemeth, custome alloweth old age more liberty to babbel, and indiscretion to talk of it selfe ... I excuse me not unto my selfe.

Michel de Montaigne, Essayes

Contents

List of Illustrations

following page 178

following page 418

Acknowledgments

My thanks are due to the Literature Board of the Australia Council for having awarded me an Emeritus Fellowship, which enabled me to give all the time I needed to write this book.

I would also like to thank those of my friends who, in various ways, helped me in the preparatory work for this book: Colin Angas; Helen Blackburn; Arthur and Yvonne Boyd; Rosemary Brissenden; Ed Campion; Judy Campbell; Wally and Georgie Campbell; Dymphna Clark; Tim Curnow; Lawrence and Edit Daws; Donald and Myfanwy Horne; Bob Hughes; Barry Humphries; Derry and Jeanne Jeffares; Margaret Jones; Alister Kershaw; Robin Lucas; Igor Mezhakoff-Koriakin; Harri Peccinotti; Ross Porteus; Nicholas Pounder; Michael and Mary Rasmussen; Barrett Reid; Brian Sadgrove; Rob Shrapnell; Jeffrey Smart; George Smith; Bob Southey; Wesley Stacey; Brian and Noel Stonier; Mark Strizic; Ian Templeman; Greg Vitiello; Patsy Zeppel; Philip Ziegler.

I also thank Barbara Mobbs for granting permission to quote from Patrick White's letters.

I am particularly grateful to Judy MacDonald, Craig Munro and Florence Reye for their meticulous, inspiring and sympathetic editing.

I would also like to thank Warren Horton and the staff of the National Library, Canberra, where my papers are deposited, for their assistance in research.

PART ONE
Early Years
1922–41

No maps are needed, when I move in darkness
Through the gentle valley of my journey home,
Where still unchanged, my childhood secrets
Move like foxes, furred in fable,
From daytime hiding to the night's release.

"Anlaby"

One

I was born in a house of books.

Outside the house the garden stretched in all directions, rose garden and rose-arches below Grandfather's decaying conservatories and shade-houses, and the aviary big enough to have trees in it, fenced sides and top against foxes and hawks. At the bottom of the garden there were vegetables and the orchard. Beyond that were the endless paddocks, at night whispering, rustling, thumping and coughing with lizards, snakes, rabbits, hares, foxes and possums, hooting and wailing with owls, mopokes and curlews; and in daytime carking and swearing and chattering with crows, galahs and rosellas, the cries of sheep and the ordering barks of sheepdogs, and from the station hands the whistles and the yells of "Git behind, Dan!".

My father was a collector, my mother an omnivorous reader. There were many thousands of books, around the corridor outside our rooms, on shelves by the entrance to the library, which itself held about five thousand books. My sister and I laid its two foundation stones early in 1928, when I was five and she was nine. There were hundreds more books in the little smoking room, and many more in the old billiard room that was now a guest room. There were no bookshelves in my mother's bedroom, but always books by her bed: no modern novels, but *Esther Waters* or *Ethan Frome*; biographies of Lord Curzon or Catherine the Great of Russia; histories, Thucydides or Gibbon. Scarcely ever an Australian book.

Mine was an Edwardian childhood, even though my ancestors were Australian pioneers, and I had come into the world twelve years after King Edward VII left it. I was born on 2 August 1922 in my mother's brass bed in her bedroom in the old house at Anlaby in South Australia. I was an enormous baby, twelve and a half pounds.

Later I would hop into that same bed, with its shining rails and curved ends, and she would read me Greek or Norse myths and legends. There was a very appealing if rather mysterious little window high in the wall by the bed, which showed the treetops and the sky.

Below the marble stairs outside that went down to the lawn was a grotto full of ferns, and behind it was a mirror. Every morning, when we were in bed with Pallas Athene or Thor, a thrush would sing from the grotto to the bird in the mirror which exactly mimicked everything it did, except sing. So my mother would whistle to it, in a melodious and accurate rendering of that call, marvellous in its purity, of three repeated notes followed by a glissando, down and up. Answer and call, answer and call, until the thrush decided to settle for a worm and flew off into the garden.

On other mornings I could also snuggle up with my father; his bedroom was twenty yards around the corridor from my mother's, and opened onto plane trees, oaks and ilex. He would read to me and offer me delicious Bournville dark chocolate, each piece separately wrapped in white paper with gold lettering. I imagined all parents had separate bedrooms. I did not know that my father was an alcoholic, nor that he was eating chocolate to disguise the whisky on his breath. I thought all old men — he was in his forties — smelled like that. He would read me Kipling's *Jungle Books* or *Uncle Remus*; he had been to the southern states of the USA, and had a lifelong passion for music-hall and "nigger minstrels", so he could do an artistic rendering of Uncle Remus's yarns about Brer Rabbit and Brer Fox. I can still hear Dad reading, like Uncle Remus yarning to the listening boy: "Brer Fox ain't never kotch 'im yet, en w'at's mo, honey, he ain't gwineter".

My father, Harry, was short, witty and jolly, with brown eyes in a genial round face, smoking cigarettes and cigars incessantly. He always wore a suit, with a waistcoat and white collar and tie. He loved the vulgarity of music-hall jokes and songs, and French ashtrays in the shape of a little wooden lavatory with a polished seat, and around the outside of the bowl the inscription *"Vos cendres, s.v.p."*. Many years after his death, I found in a book of sermons half a dozen exquisitely engraved French naughty postcards; he must have bought them in Paris in 1899 when he was an undergraduate at Oxford. He liked to sing "Alfonso Spigoni the Toreador", or "Take a Pair of Sparkling Eyes", while my mother grimly played the piano accompaniment for the thousandth time.

I never knew about his terrifying attacks of the DTs, or about the time he took an axe to the locked door of my mother's bedroom, although I always wondered about the .22 bullet hole in one of the diamond-shaped panes of the window by his bed, which was never mended. I don't suppose I saw that much of him, anyway.

Both my mother and my father came from pioneering stock in Australia, but my mother always hated her name Emily as it was too often pronounced in Australia, "Emly". She wanted to hear it fall in three syllables like clear, cold water, in an English voice, "Em-i-ly". She was blue-eyed with the most delicate skin, tall and beautiful; worse, she was A Beauty. W.B. Yeats's lines in "A Prayer for my Daughter" could have been written for my mother.

May she be granted beauty and yet not
Beauty to make a stranger's eye distraught,
Or hers before a looking-glass, for such,
Being made beautiful overmuch,
Consider beauty a sufficient end,

Lose natural kindness and maybe
The heart-revealing intimacy
That chooses right, and never find a friend.

She was cursed as well as distinguished by her beauty. When she was young, and with her younger sister Jean, her mother used to introduce the girls as "My beautiful Emily and my clever Jean".

To keep such a beauty in suitable state, my father bought her jewels and clothes and shoes from London and Paris; my mother never threw anything away, and in one of the innumerable cupboards at Anlaby she would show me the black dress by Worth which she wore for her portrait by George Lambert, or the incredibly slender shoes which she wore at her wedding. No wonder she had bunions.

For eight years, until we went to school, my sister was my only home companion. We had two much older brothers, but they were living away from home and we almost never saw them. My sister, christened Bryony Helen Carola, was publicly known as Bryony until she was about eight, when she was always being teased by other girls about her odd name. So she banned the hated first name, calling herself Helen ever afterwards. But at home and among her friends she was, and still is, called Chibs or Chibby. The name obscurely originated from my father's first sight of her.

In the course of each year we lived in several, or all, of four houses. If I describe the excessive style in which my parents lived, it is not to boast about it, but to indicate its absurd irrelevance to the provincial boundaries of South Australia in the 1920s and 1930s.

Anlaby was "home", to which we always returned. Kalimna was a large, two-storeyed house on the edge of the east parklands of Adelaide. Ooraminna was a long, low house on the seafront at Victor Harbor, some fifty miles south of Adelaide. Rocky Point was the wild one, a limestone house on a cliff over the sea at Kangaroo Island, the virgin bush behind it.

We had an English nurse, Nertie (Miss Bain), and a German governess, Heckie (Miss Ada Hechler). Nertie was kind, dim and quiet; of her I chiefly remember a green overcoat. She and Heckie discussed their private affairs, and us, in French, without realising how quickly we came to understand the language.

I seem to have taken a liking to French. When my parents were away overseas for a year or so in 1928–29, my mother's cousin Cora, a redoubtable but likeable woman who was a nursing sister with the Australian Inland Mission at Innamincka, came to live with us for a while. When I was five she wrote to my mother in England: "Geoff has taken to settling himself on the nursery sofa and tucking the shawl snugly around his legs. I was convulsed when I noticed his final tuck-in and heard the murmured 'Voilà'."

Heckie was a stern woman with hair like iron filings on her papery skull.

She was a demanding, unremitting teacher, and we learned German as well as French. Although she was German-speaking, she did not teach us the language systematically, as she did with French. She would make us learn poems off by heart, preferably songs like "*Die Lorelei*" or "*Heiden-Röslein*", or give us slabs of dictation. This we had to take down in the old German script, using our left hand; this was supposed to develop that side of the brain — or perhaps it was the other.

Our hours were long and arduous, beginning at 7.30 a.m. with piano practice. There was a short break for lunch, then more lessons until 4. Tea was at 6.30, so there wasn't much time for play. After tea, Chibs had to do two hours homework; fortunately I was too young for this duty.

Heckie was, as my sister remembers it, "free with her ruler on our knuckles". A far worse torture, if we had been naughty, was to be read to for at least half an hour from a deadly, lachrymose, moral tale called *Eric, or Little by Little*. This introduced us to apparently simple, short words like "virtue", "vice" and "purity", of the meaning of which we were of course entirely ignorant. "Virtue is strong and beautiful, Eric, and vice is downcast in her awful presence. Lose your purity of heart, Eric, and you have lost a jewel which the whole world, if it were 'one entire and perfect chrysolite', cannot replace."

Heckie used to stop and explain some of the long words in our wide reading, but mostly she just charged along, like my mother with the myths and legends she read to me. I don't think this does children any harm at all, but sometimes incomprehension is painful. On one occasion I was rude to Heckie. She said she would not continue with the lesson until I apologized. I did nothing, so she barked at me "Apologize!". I rushed from the room and found my friend Violet, the parlourmaid, dusting in the corridor. I hugged her. "Violet, Heckie says I have to apologize. What does 'apologize' mean?" "Heck now!" (Her favourite expression, nothing to do with Heckie.) "That's a problem, Geppie. Just go and say you're sorry."

Heckie also taught us arithmetic and Latin, and English in which we learned more long poems by heart. One of my more bizarre memories is of the German Miss Hechler chanting the relentless trochees of Longfellow's *Hiawatha*:

By the shores of Gitche Gumee,
By the shining Big-Sea-Water,
Stood the wigwam of Nokomis,
Daughter of the Moon, Nokomis ...

Not a word did we learn about our own native peoples, but then, no white poet had written an epic about them.

Heckie certainly taught us how to read. At six I was reading *Gulliver's Travels* which my godmother Lily Waite had sent for my birthday. Heckie was reading us *Westward Ho!* and *Hereward the Wake.* At this time Chibs was reading A.A. Milne and writing poems, one of which was called "The Story of Cap'n Cutlass Bold" — "I wrote it for Dads it's about pirates in the time of Charles I". In another letter to our parents, who were away in England or somewhere, she said, "Mr Byard sent me Pollyanna by Eleanor H. Porter, it's ripper".

I am grateful to Heckie for teaching me to read and how to work, and for making me learn poems off by heart which have stuck with me for ever, but those years with her were mostly joyless, as was her pinched face with the steel-rimmed spectacles under the iron-grey hair.

She also gave us piano lessons, and the ruler was used again, for wrong notes. Chibs hated the piano as much as I loved it. Oh the agony of rattling out a duet, one of Schubert's "Marches Militaires" — dum-didi-dum-dum, dum-didi-dum-dum — sitting up side by side in the library, playing the Steinway instead of the usual upright in the schoolroom. My mother, who was a good musician, would listen with a suspiciously soft smile. My father stayed firmly in the smoking room with Kipling or Thackeray and a cigarette from a tin of a hundred called The Greys, or a cigar from a sleek, cedar box with a label of tropical palms and Cuban damsels.

My mother played the violin and the piano well enough to have, earlier in her life, given public performances, but now she was always officially "out of practice" when I asked her to play Chopin or Beethoven. She would storm through a Chopin Etude saying "Faking, faking"; I thought it sounded wonderful. Later I was to find drawers full of Bach and Mozart, Debussy and Ravel, which she seldom played, apart from "*La Cathédrale Engloutie*" or "*La Fille aux Cheveux de Lin*". Debussy and Ravel were very modern for an Australian like her, born in 1884.

We hardly ever saw any other children. There were six families, apart from single men, living on the station, but I never played with any of the children, of whom there were in any case few of my generation. Chibs used to ride bikes with Joan, the daughter of the bookkeeper, Mr Brewster. They and Chibs' other friend, Janet Winser, would whizz fearlessly by, no hands, down the path from the top sheds, a skid turn on the drive and through the cypress arch. They persecuted Hugh, the son of the manager, Mr Lucas. One day Hugh, trying to keep up with them, no hands, couldn't make the corner by the cypress hedge and went straight on into the kitchen wall, breaking his arm.

But mostly we were solitary children, and kept that way. My mother was fiercely ambitious for us. She was a dreadful snob, though she always preserved the ability not only to get on well with all sorts of people but to command respect. However, she was implacable in her plans for us. She would have liked Chibs to be the wife of the Governor-General or, perhaps preferably, a rich English aristocrat. There was no doubt of what she had in mind for me: Sir Geoffrey Dutton, Australian Ambassador to Washington or Paris. (There weren't at that time any Australian Ambassadors, not even a Department of Foreign Affairs, but she was sure there would be.) Maybe she sowed the seeds of my republicanism.

Chibs was allowed to join the Brownies and go to meetings in Kapunda, but when she asked whether she could bring a friend from Kapunda home for the weekend she was refused. She was allowed her friend Janet Winser, but then Janet's father was the Private Secretary to the Governor. Even at that early age Janet was a strikingly beautiful blonde. But she and Chibs went riding horses or bikes all day and giggled in their room in the evening, so I never really talked to her; she, in any case, wouldn't have had anything to say to me.

I had no idea, of course, that my upbringing was odd. Children who are kept solitary have no basis for comparison. I did not even know any of my grandparents. Three of them were long dead by the time I was born, and my mother's mother and my only aunt, Jean, lived in Brussels. (My brother John, who often visited them there, said they were tremendous fun, "Much more fun than Mum".) Jean died before her mother, in 1929. For many years my father paid for the family's upkeep and the education of Jean's two girls, Eileen and Leueen. Leueen became a successful stage and film actress, and had a remarkable married career: five marriages, two of them to the playwright George S. Kaufman. When I first met her, she and Kaufman were staying at the Ritz in London. She had just had the pictures rearranged, and hanging over the fireplace was a lovely little Renoir her first husband had just given her for her fortieth birthday. My mother's two brothers lived in Western Australia and I never met either of them. My father had no brothers, and his sister drowned as a girl.

Moreover, we were never visited by families, so I had no idea how other parents behaved, how they treated their children and how their children regarded them. Up until my late teens the only family I knew were the Angases who lived near Angaston, thirty miles away, and at their home the parents were very formal with me. My first introduction to real family life was not until my first year at Adelaide University.

Being unable to make any contrast between our family life, such as it was, and that of others meant that my ability to understand society was acutely impaired. The knockabout quality of ordinary family life would have done me the world of good, but I knew nothing of it. Although there was no lack of conversation with my father, in the short time I knew him, or with my mother, there was a certain code of behaviour to be adhered to. Certain subjects were never discussed. No doubt this surface equanimity was partly occasioned by my mother's determination to preserve me from knowledge of my father's alcoholism. If I had mingled with other, more worldly, children, no doubt some kid would have told me my father was a pisspot. As it was, I never knew.

Our parents were often away. In 1921 my father, who had driven the first motor car across Australia from south to north in 1907-1908, repeated the trip in two Dodges, one of which was driven by my mother, making her the first woman to drive a car across Australia. In 1924 my father was asked to accompany the expedition of the famous Arctic explorer Vilhjalmur Stefansson and the Australian geologist Sir Edgeworth David in a motorised expedition to Central Australia, from Adelaide to Alice Springs. My mother again accompanied him, driving the station's Dodge light truck.

Then in 1928-29 they went to Britain, Europe and other parts — including Egypt, Turkey and Greece — for a year or so. Somewhere over the years they also went to Japan. My mother went to Britain and Europe in 1931-32, taking my unfortunate sister with her, to be educated at schools in England, Paris and Rome, with a stay in Austria as paying guest of some indigent aristocrats.

For about ten years, from 1927 to 1937, my most reliable source of affection, apart from Chibs, was the parlourmaid, Violet Poole. An orphan, she had come out from England, as a girl of 18 and, by an odd coincidence, worked for a year for the Holden family who eventually bought Kalimna from my father. She had a soft voice with a slight county accent; there was something distinguished about her carriage and her manner, although she was always modest, never superior. My father said darkly that Violet's mother had been a maid at the Duke of Roxburghe's castle, and that explained why she was an orphan.

I always called her Wiolet, because that is what her good friend, the old Dutch vegetable gardener, Harry West, called her. Violet was such a happy person it was always a delight to be with her, especially after Heckie. She loved living at Anlaby, and was genuinely fond of my mother, whose snobberies did not extend to those who worked for her. She really enjoyed setting the silver and china for afternoon tea, and if my mother was away, and my father by himself, she would take me down to the garden with her to pick roses for the dining-room table, different colours for lunch and for dinner. My father would eat on his own in the dining room, while Chibs and I had our tea in the nursery.

I never quite knew how many women there were in the house, but Violet later told me that when she arrived there was Nertie, Heckie, a nursery maid, a housemaid, a cook and a kitchen maid, and Violet herself as parlourmaid; her duties were also to look after the men's clothing. "Your mother never bothered us," she said, "she was out in the garden working most of the day."

She was very fond of Harry West, who was so old he didn't know how old he was. He had been a sailor, and had jumped ship at Adelaide. There was some story that as a young man he had been with a party that went to the Crimea gathering bones for fertilizer; the cracks in his huge old hands I was sure were filled with the dust of the dead soldiers' bones. He was the only gardener allowed in to morning and afternoon tea in the servants' sitting room. If no one else was there to talk to, he would talk to himself. He could express himself very well, and was an avid reader, but he could not write. Violet used to pass on to him all her copies of the overseas edition of the *Daily Mail*. "Harry cottoned on to me," said Violet. "One day he said to me, 'Wylet, you're not like these Osstrilians, they don't go over the hill to see what's on the other side'." She used to do all his shopping for him when she went to Adelaide.

Chibs and I were allowed to have a patch of vegetable garden each, and Harry used to supervise our efforts. He also kept the enormous kitchen wood stove and the house fires in wood. I remember Harry sitting by the woodshed, which he kept full of chopped wood, plucking quail shot by my father and brothers. "Them bloody feathered mice", he would say in his thick Dutch accent as he chucked another pink, plucked body into the kitchen basket. Harry had no relations, and when he died he left about ten thousand pounds to the Mission for Seamen and the Kapunda Hospital.

Violet, when I saw her in later years, could always remember little details of Chibs' and my childhood. She recalled one occasion at Rocky Point, when the family and guests were seated for lunch and she brought in a large leg of ham off Rosy, in its former life the pig that ate up the scraps at Anlaby. Aged about six, I said in a loud voice to Janet Winser, "There's Rosy. She's blowflied underneath but she's all right on top." I can still clearly see the maggots seething under Rosy's massive thigh.

All Violet ever said to me, and that was years later, about my father's alcoholism was "It used to sadden me about Mr Dutton, the truth". When my daughter Tisi made a tape with her about her ten years at Anlaby, Violet finally asked her to turn it off, and spoke about the painful business of looking after my father (which she did up to the time of his death) when my mother was away in Europe. He used to have bad attacks of the DTs, and after his binges she used to have to clear up the awful messes in his room. "And all the rest of the time," she said, "he was such a lovely gentleman."

In the late 1930s Violet married a local storekeeper and landowner, John Prior, at the church my grandfather had built at Hamilton; my mother gave her away.

If Violet was, apart from Chibs, the source of the affection so often not supplied by my absent mother, the one constant for the first fifty years of my life, to which I could always return and find much the same, was Anlaby — the house, the garden, the sheep station itself. One odd feature of the house's architecture was that there were connecting doors between all the living rooms and bedrooms in the central and east wings. This was a legacy of the original building of the 1850s, which had three separate wings, for cooking and eating, for living and for sleeping. The doors were never used; most of them had wardrobes or bookcases in front of and behind them. In a way they represented the separate lives of my dysfunctional family, basically connected but never opened.

There was also another station, Uno, out in the saltbush country to the west, beyond Port Augusta and Iron Knob, where the measurements were not in acres but square miles; Uno, not large by those standards, was 350 square miles. That was a vague but exciting presence.

Some of the scents of childhood stay with one for life, and irrevocably fix certain environments. The sharp yet sticky scent of fig leaves, close to the white juice that oozes when you break one from its stem, a juice which witches say will remove warts. The witch who told me this (my first mother-in-law) was right; the juice did remove my warts, although not as dramatically as when at school I put some sulphuric acid on a couple of them. There were three enormous fig trees at the bottom of the garden, which would release a cloud of starlings as we came for the purple figs with their glinting red seeds. Alongside them was a smaller tree which produced very sweet golden figs. You couldn't climb up inside it, as you could with the big trees.

The dry, acrid scent of rosemary. There were rosemary hedges beside the brick paths of the garden at Victor Harbor; they led to the tamarisks around the tennis court, with the scaly, salty smell of seaweed wafting over the brush fence from the beach.

In the Anlaby garden, there was the cloudy brew of sweetness coming from the creamy flowers of the two magnolias. Although planted at the same time in the early 1920s, on either side of the pergola below the front lawn, one was already thirty feet high and the other, unaccountably, half the size. The pungent smell of oil and grease from the bench and pit for servicing the cars, behind the arch under the clock at the centre of the buildings around the Anlaby stable yard. The suffocatingly tight smell of the red and green feathers of a dead rosella. The shock of the stink of the guts of a rabbit when you slit it from chest to tail. The warm scents of the hayshed, the soothing lanolin scent of the woolshed, the scent of the first drops of rain after hot, dry days. These remain.

Only one scent was to die, forever, not to be recalled, though if it were distilled again it would be instantly recognizable. That was the scent of my mother as she sat in front of the triple mirror, at her dressing table, with the embossed silver hand mirror face down on the glass, and, all around, the pots and jars whose unguents and powders combined with her own body to make her unique scent. The silver cask, knobbly with fruit and flowers, that contained her face powder and that catlike creature, the powder puff. The pink jars of Elizabeth Arden creams and liquids, the vanishing fragrance of eau-de-cologne. Despite all these ingredients, that scent of her was so delicate, so light. It was painful to be embraced by other women who reeked of assertive perfumes.

Over the years, running into each other in memory, were Important Visitors, most of whom I had never heard of. The table set for the lunch to which Chibs and I were not invited. Grandfather's best silver and the Royal Worcester plates (I always thought them rather vulgar, with his initials, H.D., in the centre, inside the gold and navy blue rim). The perfectly ironed napkins seemed much too good for gravy-smeared mouths.

These Important People were subjected to regular rituals. Before lunch, a walk in the garden, the slow admiring of roses, the homage to delphiniums. When I was about six the Governor and his Lady (the Hore-Ruthvens, later Lord and Lady Gowrie) were on one of these processions, from which my father, with a variety of excuses, always absented himself. I thought I was a dead shot with a bow and arrow at the time, and laid an ambush as the party emerged from behind the cypress hedge by the mulberry trees. My mother came out first; I certainly was not going to take a shot at her. Then came Zara, Lady Hore-Ruthven. I let fly. It was a fine shot, scoring a bull on her bottom. Despite her appeals for clemency, my father was summoned. A branch of tamarisk was snapped off, and I was whisked stingingly across the backs of my legs and knees.

There were other visitors, and time to observe them at afternoon tea in the library, the ritual that followed the drive around the station and up to the woolshed, which was usually a vast, empty cathedral awaiting its compulsory congregation of noisy sheep. Chibs and I were allowed to perch on the edge of afternoon tea and have a sandwich or a little cream cake with wings, while the guests drank from the generous Copeland cups with the blue and pink flowers and gold rims. "More tea?" and my mother would top up silver from silver; the water was always boiling in the spirit-kettle with the wooden handle that sat on its frame above the blue flame of methylated spirits.

There were visitors who yielded gracefully when asked by my mother to perform, artists like Jascha Heifetz or Artur Schnabel.

When Lotte Lehmann came to Anlaby, my mother and John took two cars (I was allowed to squeeze into the second one) up to the woolshed because the rams were being shorn and the great soprano wanted to meet these famous Australian merino rams. She was somewhat dismayed to see these majestic creatures, once ruffed like monarchs while they stood stiff as generals, now heaved over onto their backs and shorn to a bony white, creased body and a horribly vulnerable, enormous bag of balls. They were shoved down the chute into the sunlight and stood in the yards waiting for their next humiliation. “The poor darlings!” cried soft-hearted Lotte, and leaned on the wooden rail of the yards and sang them a soothing aria of the Marschallin's from *Rosenkavalier*.

This was one of the rare occasions my mother was definitely upstaged. In the house, in her grey silk dress and the large hat which she did not remove, she was undoubted queen, and exercised a gracious power. Dame Sybil Thorndike and her husband Lewis Casson came for the usual rituals. Two old friends of our family, Bill and Ursula Hayward, had driven them up from Adelaide. When the car was brought around for them to leave, my mother farewelled the guests with a raised hand and a slight curve to her tall figure. As they drove down the avenue Sybil turned to Ursula and said, “Oh, I would love to play that part!”

Other guests were obviously distinguished, but treated more like family. Hans Heysen, so clean that his face and forehead seemed polished, stumped around like a genial peasant in his gaitered trousers, and his wife was especially nice to Chibs and me. On one visit, after lunch, Heysen excused himself and went down below the terrace and did a pencil drawing of the house, which he gave to my mother for Christmas. He used to send her a little drawing or etching every Christmas.

Distinguished guests apart, various friends of my parents used to visit Anlaby, but my mother and father seemed to have few really close friends. In their way, they were as lonely as we were.

Two

The house at Victor Harbor sprawled along the seafront behind a brush fence, angled oddly to face Granite Island, a small outcrop of giant boulders, walks of grass and the gaunt outlines of Norfolk Island pines. The island was connected to the mainland half a mile away by a double-decker tram drawn by an old horse that clip-clopped and clattered out over a wooden jetty.

There was a rumour that the house was built to face the spot where my aunt had met her death in 1892. My father's elder sister by four years, Ethel was just sixteen when she went out to Granite Island to paint with a friend, sitting on one of the rocks facing the shore. It was time for lunch, so the girls scrambled up the boulders to the path. Then Ethel remembered she had left her brushes on the rock, and went back for them. Just as she picked them up a huge wave swept her off the rock into the surf. She was never seen alive again. Her body was found some days later on the beach by the blacks' camp at the mouth of the Inman River.

When I was about the same age as Ethel had been, I mentioned this rumour of the angled site of the house to my mother. "Rubbish!" she said, and went back to reading *The Illustrated London News*.

January 1927. The scent of rosemary hedges by the brick paths, the great heads of bronze and golden dahlias leaning down, wistaria trailing over the pergola, and beyond the formal garden the open grass and tall stone-pines of what was called The Wilds. I had a rabbit hutch there with a couple of lolloping white rabbits. I was feeding them lettuce leaves, talking to my old godfather, a schoolmaster at St Peter's College called Buck Wyatt. Suddenly he hissed, "Keep absolutely still, Geppie." I thought he was going to knock me down as his open hand came at the back of my neck. But he had brushed off an enormous scorpion, which scuttled to the side of the cage and glared at us, its venomous tail curved over its back.

These Wilds were a place for adventure. Wandering back to the house one day I went over to the mulberry tree and realized it was covered with ripe fruit. I climbed up the thick, rough trunk and sat on a branch and gorged myself. On the way to the house I saw a bush gleaming with dark-purple berries. I picked a branch to show my mother, who was ill in bed after being bitten by a redback spider. I came into her bedroom bearing my branch. She looked at it and my spattered face and shirt, her hand flew to her mouth and her face went stiff with terror. "What have you been eating, tell me, what?" Like all small children faced with apparent wrongdoing I lied. "Nothing." "You must tell me." Her voice changed, soft and loving, there were tears in her eyes. "Mulberries," I gasped. "Shouldn't I have?" She began to laugh and held out her arms to hug me; she took the branch from my hands and threw it across the room. She explained that the bush was called Deadly Nightshade, and that two children at Victor Harbour had died from eating the berries only a week before.

As well as mulberries, there were other safe, good things to eat in the wilds, and not as messy. Chibs and I would collect the freshly fallen cones of the stone-pines that towered over the back fence by the road, and extract the milky nuts by cracking the smooth, brown shells. There were so many that we set ourselves up in business, filling ice-cream dixies and selling them for a penny each, or else striking them and selling the seedlings, also in dixies. No doubt we were the curse of visitors who politely felt obliged to buy our stock.

Near the house, but hidden behind some fig trees, was a rubbish bin, built on a grand scale with stone walls and a curved galvanized-iron roof. An oblong door with a steel hand grip was slid up when rubbish was to be thrown into the bin. I had a recurring dream about this. It concerned an Afghan in a turban and long robes (harmless hawkers, the Afghans used to come around houses with exotic items for sale). This dream Afghan carried a long, ancient rifle with the stock inlaid with mother-of-pearl. (There was a rifle like this at Anlaby, brought back from Morocco by my father in the 1890s.) He seized me by the arm and made me sit on the stone wall at the mouth of the rubbish bin, with the lid slid up. Then he walked back a few yards, raised the rifle and shot me so I fell backwards into the rubbish dump.

In waking hours Victor Harbor was a happy place where my mother was at her best, perhaps because my father always had something to do. He had his yacht, the *Wyruna*, a 36-foot sloop, anchored towards the end of the jetty in the lee of Granite Island. An old sailor, a master mariner called Walter Jeffrey, lived on her. Every day my father and Walter would go fishing around the reefs and islands, and bring back sweep and whiting, supplemented by crayfish from the pots Walter put out from his own boat. I loved Walter, with his soft voice and gentle manner, and was fascinated by his toes; always bare, they were like another set of fingers. These miraculous toes could pick up stones and throw them accurately; they kept the mainsheet fast while his hands adjusted a halyard when out sailing; if both hands were busy he would tie a knot in a rope with his toes in a flash.

Walter was later appointed Harbour Master, and a house was built for him on the island. One night his son was driving him home from Adelaide and went over the edge of the jetty. After a lifetime at sea, the old master mariner Walter was drowned in a foot of water, trapped beneath the inverted car.

My mother never went out in the boats, not caring to be on the sea unless she had to, when she was invariably seasick. She was content with the land; she loved working in the garden and playing tennis with neighbours on the grass court behind the tamarisks.

Near the tennis court there was a flagpole, and my father taught my mother how to signal by flags. When my father and Walter came in from fishing, the *Wyruna* would be anchored a few hundred yards out in front of the house, and my father would run up the signal flags for "Lots of fish". My mother would dash to the flagpole and hoist the flags for "Liar". They seemed to have lots more fun together at Victor Harbor than they did at Anlaby.

The comfortable, white, L-shaped house had only one flaw, that its walls were finished, after a deplorable fashion of the time, in some technique where pebbles were thrown into the concrete that covered the brick. They not only looked ugly and collected dust, but were very painful if you fell against them when playing chasey. All the doors were of dark, stained wood, with big round handles of black, twisted iron, very pleasing to turn. The rooms, unlike those at Anlaby, were full of light. In the living and dining rooms the house had polished jarrah floors with rugs on them; in our nursery there were pale untreated pine floors.

In 1927 I was madly in love with Saint Cecilia, really erotically, although of course I had not as yet been introduced to Eros. I cannot imagine where this passion came from, although I vaguely remember a reproduction of some painting of the patron saint of music, with an elegant Botticelli-like figure playing a tiny little pipe organ. When Chibs and I were put down for our rest after lunch, I was full of exciting fantasies about Saint Cecilia. One day, thinking longingly about her, I leaned over the edge of the bed and dropped a few large mouthfuls of spit onto the floor, where they spread out most interestingly into the unsurfaced, pale, dry wood. When Nertie came in to get us up she was horrified by these wet splodges, and I was told I was a dirty little boy. But it had all been in homage to Saint Cecilia.

Perhaps the most flagrant example of my parents' extravagance, and one of the proofs that they spoiled my brothers, was Kalimna, the house they bought in the early 1920s in Adelaide. Nowadays this house, in Dequetteville Terrace, Kent Town, is the headquarters of the Country Women's Association.

At the time my parents acquired Kalimna, John and Dick were at school at St Peter's College in Adelaide. My father had painful memories of living with two aunts when he was at the same school — they were frozen relics of Victorian piety, without any sense of humour, and used to starve him — so he bought the Adelaide house for John and Dick. Now they would not have to board at school or be farmed out to relatives. All the furniture from the unused "cottage" at Anlaby was brought down to Kalimna, and my mother indulged herself in magnificent curtains.

Chibs and I used to go for regular walks across the park in front of the house with the rather alarming and very modern American governess we had at the time. Cows used to graze in the parks in those days, placid red Shorthorns, not like the sleek but evil-tempered little Jerseys at Anlaby which would chase you like bulls. One day we were walking across the short, summer-yellow grass and I was looking up at a pair of kookaburras in a tall gum tree laughing at the state of the world. Suddenly I felt a horrible warm wetness all around my right leg almost up to my knee (I was only just three), and found I had walked into an enormous, fresh cow pat. Nanny, much ashamed, had to lead me shrieking back to Kalimna, leaving a trail of cow dung across the street, to have my shoe and sock removed and be washed under a garden tap.

When we were living at Kalimna my mother had to be taken to hospital with appendicitis. Adelaide's most famous surgeon, Sir Henry Newland, removed the appendix. When she was allowed home again I was brought to see her in her bed in the upstairs bedroom, which looked out across the veranda to the park. I was allowed to kiss her, but told to be very careful not to jolt her. With the smile of an accomplice my mother asked would I like to see the scar. I was amazed, as I had never seen any part of my mother's anatomy exposed bare, except her face, shoulders and arms. I imagined that when an appendix was removed it would involve lifting off the top of the whole tummy, an oval shape like the top of an apple pie. My mother pushed down the bedclothes a little way and lifted her voluminous nightie to show a pink scar several inches long across her beautiful skin. I was amazed, if rather disappointed. Many years later she was to tell me that another surgeon, seeing this enormous scar, had declared that old Newland must have been drunk when he operated, chasing her appendix up and down her tummy.

Of the four houses around which our lives revolved, the most exciting was down at Kangaroo Island. This long, low house, built in 1913, which my father had bought in 1918 together with 35 acres of bush and a mile of foreshore, stood on the edge of a cliff giving on to the sloping rocky point. This was the only rock in the white sandy curve that forms part of the bay. Flinders called it Rocky Point and marked it in his chart. Behind, there was the green and bronze sea of the mallee, stretching to the South Coast four or five miles away; in front was the blue, blue sea, usually calm because of prevailing southerly winds, with its wonderful rim of green and pure-white sand. I have never anywhere seen clearer water. For two miles to the east, and four miles to the west, only one other house was visible. There was no electric light and no running water; the lavatories were the long-drop variety down in the scrub, one for the ladies, one for the gents, and one for the maids. In the main limestone house behind the deep veranda with its square concrete posts there were eleven rooms, and out the back a building known as the tin hut where the maid and the cook slept; Nanny slept with us.

Going to Kangaroo Island was an immense operation. We would leave Anlaby in two cars followed by the station truck, which was laden with huge laundry baskets full of linen and clothes, and a large wooden box marked "BOOKS". My father had a permanent library at Rocky Point of several hundred of the classics of English prose and verse, reference books, including Greek and Latin dictionaries and *Everyman's Encyclopaedia*, biographies and modern novels. Beside the fireplace in the sitting room were the modern English and American humorists he loved so much, Harry Graham and Jerome K. Jerome. I could seldom get a laugh out of them. But in the wooden box marked "BOOKS" there were lots of new purchases to be looked at, and the irresistible rare-book catalogues of Maggs, Francis Edwards, Quaritch and Dobell.

Our procession would make its way from Anlaby to Second Valley, a tiny town in a cleft in the cliffs about forty miles south of Adelaide. From there, it was only a short voyage to Kangaroo Island. On the sand by the jetty rugs would be laid, and out of wicker baskets would come a picnic, thermoses of tea and hot water, and enamel mugs and plates. Already there was smoke on the horizon, and soon the *Karatta*, the little coastal steamer with her one mast and tall funnel, would tie up at the jetty. The two cars would bump down the alarmingly narrow jetty and be winched aboard, and the truck would be unloaded of its boxes and baskets.

For my mother, this journey was a trial; I once saw her being seasick on the jetty at Kangaroo Island, just from watching the *Karatta*, tied up to the jetty, lurching up and down in the swell. The Captain would lead her to his cabin, where she would be settled in with rugs and cushions, maintaining a faint, martyred smile. Meanwhile my father, who was never seasick in his life, would repair to the oval saloon with its lovely golden panelling, and tuck into a roast lunch. After half an hour the ship would start to stir as we came into Backstairs Passage, where it was nearly always rough, with a nasty cross swell caused by the tide running counter to the wind. A couple of hours later we would be tying up at the jetty at Penneshaw, and Jack Jones would be waiting with his Ford truck to take the baskets and boxes to Rocky Point. Jack was tall and always wore a waistcoat over his collarless white shirt; he had a straggly moustache and a neck like a turkey gobbler. We always called him J-J-J-Jack Jones because he had such a stutter.

There were enormous family parties, when my brothers would invite their friends and their flapper girlfriends over. John and Dick roared across the blue bay at 45 knots in their hydroplane (as speedboats were called then) the *Jolly Roger*. My father sometimes brought the *Wyruna* down, but usually we went out fishing (when I was allowed, which was seldom) in the *Lyria*, a 22 ft half-decked cutter that could seat a dozen or so in comfort. As well as the *Lyria* there were a couple of dinghies, and a solid little flat-bottomed boat, about five feet long, called the *Chipmunk*, in which Chibs and I learned to row, as our brothers had before us. Rowing was one of my father's passions; he had been in the Oxford Eight. I modelled myself on his crisp, precise style, always feathering the oars as they passed the rowlocks as if I were rowing in a racing scull or an eight.

I loved Rocky Point, and continued to do so for the next sixty-five years, finally selling my share to my niece. But it remained an unspoiled paradise to return to. At Rocky Point my father was always happy, and as far as I know did not drink. Even in the summer he wore a tweed suit and waistcoat, collar and tie, or a suit of stiff twill, but dispensed with shoes and socks. My mother wore sweeping dresses she had made from cretonne, and always her large hats. She did not like the sea any better at Kangaroo Island, except to watch its colours and moods, and never went fishing or swimming. She did not expose herself to the sun, and as a result had the skin of a child up to her death. She was kind to everyone in the large parties, but really longed for the day when we would move to Victor Harbor, where she had her garden.

Only one of the four houses, Rocky Point, now belongs to the family. How quickly fortunes come and go in Australia! The land is so ancient, and despite our maltreatment of it, continues, outside the cities, to assert a presence indifferent to man. This presence, both of the bush or desert and the sea, makes a perennial, muted, ironic comment on the scrambling and the spending, the abandonment of a seemly modesty, that drives the life on the outer rim on the edge of the sea. The Aborigines, who built nothing and wandered in peace with their environment, were regarded as ignorant savages. The civilized conquerors preferred to model themselves on the follies of the Great Britain from which most of them had migrated.

Neither branch of my ancestors, the Duttons and the Martins, had any capital when they came to Australia. But within a mere fifty years, the owner of Anlaby and all the other stations was a millionaire; James Martin and his son and nephew, while not quite so rich, were running a large and very succesful business. The Martin works made mining equipment for Kalgoorlie and Coolgardie, the railway bridge at Murray Bridge in South Australia, and rolling stock for states as far away as Queensland. Ten years later the Martin business was bankrupt.

My Dutton grandfather, on the other hand, had become richer and richer, and considered it an obligation to live like an English gentleman. He was known as the Squire of Anlaby, and rejoiced in the pompous honorary title. He died in 1914. An extra ingredient in that fateful year was the worst drought in South Australian history, when millions of sheep died. Lawyers were writing to Grandfather's many legatees saying that his bequests would be paid, but only after assets had been sold. The wily trustees bought the best assets themselves, and my father was left with little cash and eight stations of various productivity, some of them enormous, others quite small, which were finally whittled away to two. Yet he still, unchecked and indeed urged on by my mother, continued to live like a rich man.

"Don't forget," my mother said to me not long before her death, "if you go to live at Anlaby everybody will think you are rich." It had already occurred to me that it was my parents who thought they were rich, even though a brief look at Elder, Smith & Co.'s statements would have told them they were not.

The relativity of provincial notions of domestic grandeur, especially in any involvement with age or size, was brought home to me very early, when I was six or seven years old. When Important Visitors came to lunch, Chibs and I usually took our meal in the nursery. However, when the visitors came with children, we were sometimes allowed into the dining room, where we sat at a separate table with a white tablecloth, while the rest of the party lunched on glistening mahogany. On this occasion the visitors were English county, the sort of people Chibs and I disliked from the moment they opened their mouths, with their characteristic English vowels, and began to patronize us.

We were seated at our little table with a buxom blonde girl of about fourteen, perhaps a couple of years older than Chibs, afflicted with the name Pandora. Thinking I ought to say something, I pathetically began with "This is a very old house, almost a hundred years old, and it has 28 rooms." "Oh really?" Pandora fixed me with a withering but pitying look. "Our house in Warwickshire was built in 1420 and has 130 rooms." She turned to my sister. "It's such a thrill to be in Orstralia, as at last I'll be able to jump a horse over a barbed-wire fence." "Not on my horse you won't," answered Chibs, indignant at her beloved white Dawn being subjected to such dangers. After lunch the girls did go for a ride, and Chibs put Pandora on old Pompey, who would have had trouble jumping a teapot.

Not long after this, Pompey died, out in the Gums paddock where, I heard from one of the men, he was to be incinerated; this was safe, as it was winter. Chibs was too soft-hearted to attend the ceremony, but I was not going to miss it. Pompey's carcase was heaped with dead boughs and then liberally doused with kerosene. In no time there was a roaring blaze, black smoke ascending far above the gum trees, and to my riveted gaze Pompey's guts began to burst from his belly and burn fiercely as his fat dripped into the flames. A few days later only Pompey's white bones remained and I wondered why they were white when fire usually blackens. Portions of the biggest bones were still there fifty years later.

In 1926 my brother John went to Magdalen College, Oxford, the same college where my father had been. He was followed in 1929 by my brother Dick, who went to University College. Neither of them took a degree; they did nothing but row in the College First Eight, drink and drive their Bentleys. What a waste.

I have often wondered why they had no conscience, with all their advantages in life, in making so little of themselves. Both of them were intelligent, although Dick had more imagination and zest than John. John, on the other hand, was more cultured than Dick, with a deep love of music and books. An old school friend of mine, who saw a lot of John, described him after his death as a fine example of that vanishing breed, an educated gentleman. Perhaps that was the trouble. The only role model they had when young, apart from our parents, was of our paternal grandfather, who died when John was eight and Dick five. He was rich and, to his credit, performed many good works with his money. He continued the beneficence of his uncle Fred, founder of Anlaby, who had built the Kapunda hospital. Grandfather endowed the Kapunda Showgrounds with its various buildings, and made many personal benefactions; on one occasion he bought an attractive small property not far from Anlaby for an impecunious friend of my father's at Oxford, who was best man at my parents' wedding. But his life was like a slow movement from an Elgar symphony, dignified, boring and long-winded; he did nothing but supervise his estates in a vague way.

My father was the same, except that he was not rich, although he didn't let on and acted as if he were. He built a new wing on the Kapunda Hospital when he could ill afford to, keeping up his forebears' traditions without their resources. Perhaps my mother, so full of moral fervour and exhortations to work at every stage of my life, saw her two elder sons as ornaments in her splendid life rather than as developing individuals. She was, in fact, despite her frequent protestations of deep affection for the boys, a very neglectful and thoughtless mother.

John would never talk to me about Dad's drinking, except to say that he would never live in the big house because of the terrible things he had seen there. It was all part of the tradition in which I grew up. Certain things were never talked about.

In 1926 my father sold Kalimna, for 8500 pounds, and his interest in Corona, an enormous sheep station out of Broken Hill, and in June 1928 my parents embarked on a long tour of Britain, Europe and the Middle East. These voyages were torture for my mother. When they reached Marseilles she wrote, "How I hate the sea!" There was nothing my father loved more.

At first my mother's letters to Chibs and me begin with lamentations, how much she is missing us, how she will never go away again. Then that theme fades as she goes into great detail, of no possible interest to us small children, about palaces or statues or gardens or the opening of Parliament. At first they are coming home in October. Then she promises they will be home in February. They finally make it in April.

My mother writes to us every week, my father never. One of her letters ends, "Dads is telling me to stop writing and turn the light off and come to bed".

My mother has the absurd idea that it will help Dick settle in to Oxford if she and my father spend a month there with him. This month in Oxford not surprisingly drives my father to drink. This is, of course, not mentioned in the letters, but we are told that poor Dads has such a bad cold that he has to go to a private hospital for a week. My mother seizes the opportunity of freedom, and settles in at Claridge's for a week. "This is the nicest place in London — and the most expensive." She is never in bed before 3.30 a.m. but doesn't mention what she has been doing. The account book reveals that the week at Claridge's in December cost 60 pounds 13 shillings and 11 pence. (Roughly speaking, 100 pounds sterling in 1930 would be worth about 6000 dollars today.) My mother's bill for dresses and evening gowns from Maison Alexander is 229 pounds 11 shillings and 6 pence. My father's tailor's bill from Radford, Jones & Co., which includes a jacket, suits and overcoats, plus a morning coat and dress coat (which he will never wear) comes to 133 pounds thirteen shillings and sixpence. A pretty little .20 bore shotgun which he buys for my mother costs 50 pounds, complete with a case on which, for some reason, his own initials instead of hers are stamped in gold.

The Anlaby library was being built while they were away, and much the most interesting item they bought in London was a group of four oil paintings, all set together in a lovely gold frame, to hang above the fireplace in the new library. These were by Thomas Baines, who accompanied Augustus Gregory on his expedition to Northern Australia in 1855; the paintings are mostly of activities around the Victoria River, of the men digging for water by the beach, or of cattle stampeding from the spears of Aborigines. Baines was a very talented artist and altogether a most attractive character; he later went to South Africa and was the first person to paint the Victoria Falls. The four oils that used to hang in the library are now in the collection of the National Gallery of Australia. In 1928 in London, complete with frame, they cost my father 32 pounds, about a seventh of what he paid for my mother's dresses.

He also bought more books for the library. He had been buying Australiana with a very keen eye since he was at Oxford at the turn of the century. When I went to England in 1946 I called on old Mr Maggs at his wonderful bookshop in Berkeley Square. He remembered my father well, and took me down to the cellar to look up in the account books what sort of prices he had paid for what are now the most valuable items of Australiana. In 1905 he had bought a complete set of Cook's *Voyages* for less than 20 pounds, and Gould's majestic *Mammals of Australia* for about 30 pounds. And so the list went on. Mr Maggs showed me about six sets of Cook, which he had not yet sold, but which he had rescued from junk shops. Almost no one cared for books about Australia in the first two decades of the twentieth century. The literature of the colonies, like the colonies themselves, was an inferior item, although the primary products of the colonies were extremely useful to the Mother Country.

People like my grandfather, rich from Australia's wool, modelled themselves on landholders in the Mother Country, which of course was always called Home. They surrounded their large houses with conservatories and shadehouses and were driven by the chauffeur in the Daimler to their large houses in the city, or to the steam-yacht at the Port. The steam-yacht (the *Adèle*, 140 ft long, 350 tons), which had cost Grandfather 20,000 pounds in 1906, was sold on his death for much less, but my father and mother still lived in South Australia as if they were the gentry at Home. It was not to last for long.

Adelaide in my boyhood was much like a provincial city in a story or play by Chekhov. Melbourne and Sydney loomed in the distance like Moscow and St Petersburg, but an ambitious, beautiful woman like my mother really longed for London, as her equivalent in Chekhov longed for Paris. My father, stifled by the boredom of Adelaide, hid himself away in the country or by the sea, and drank himself to death.

Three

The Anlaby house had grown almost like something in nature, which was one reason it never met with the approval of National Trust purists. The original 1850s house, built in three separate sections around a courtyard, was enlarged by the addition of more and more bedrooms and bathrooms, a large kitchen and servants' wing, the marble terrace with its columns, the library. It was its own story. So I grew up in a world threaded and webbed with Australian history.

Everything around the house and station buildings spoke of the past. But my present time was a solitary one, except when I was with my sister. Other kids bounced off each other in primary school, burned round the town on bikes, played footy in the streets, dodged cars or trams. Country kids were enmeshed with families and festivals. I rode my bike alone (too slow for Chibs), or trailed after her; she was mounted far higher than me on Pompey or Dawn, while I straddled a vile-tempered Shetland pony called Di. Di tried again and again to scrape me off against a barbed-wire fence, or she would stop dead and hope I would continue, over her neck. My only satisfaction with Di was that I never fell off.

Sometimes Charlie Campbell, the overseer, would let us ride with him. He was a bluff, solid man with a splendid moustache yellow with nicotine, who, like J-J-J-Jack Jones, always wore a waistcoat, and a white shirt without a collar.

In the station office, a fine two-storey stone building with a huge cellar containing a disused freezing-plant, Mr Lucas, the manager, and Mr Brewster, the bookkeeper, sat at their desks in their offices on opposite sides of the corridor. Mr Lucas, even when the temperature was over 100 degrees Fahrenheit, always wore a tweed suit with waistcoat, and a white stiff collar and tie. I never saw him touch a sheep, let alone get his hands dirty. I have no idea what his qualifications were to be manager, not only of Anlaby but of four or five other stations. No doubt the fact that one by one most of them were sold indicated his abilities.

Mr Brewster, equally immaculate but in clothes of a lighter weight, was a skinny man with a bird-like face and thin, brushed and oiled down hair. He was a champion golfer. His ledgers were as neat as himself, and his handwriting, with a variety of steel nibs, was unfailingly elegant.

I saw Mr Brewster discomfited only once. I was in his office talking to him when one of the sharefarmers, a huge Barossa-German called Schubert, came in to collect his cheque. When Mr Brewster handed it to him he asked, in his perky-sparrow way, "Any relation to the famous composer?" Schubert leaned over him. "Ach, so you have heard of him also?"

Barossa-German humour is understated; you have to be listening for it. One day I accompanied my brother John to visit another sharefarmer, called Pfitzner. As we walked in from the garden gate there were animals and birds everywhere — turkeys, ducks, chickens, pet lambs, dogs and cats. Mr Pfitzner came out to greet us, and John said jovially, waving at all these creatures, "I suppose you have lots of children?" "Well, Mr Dutton," he replied thoughtfully, "sometimes a girl, sometimes a boy, and tausends of times nothing."

My parents did not spend much time with us; that was for Nertie or, when lessons started, Heckie the governess. But at weekends, freed from lessons, there was always plenty to do, sometimes dangerously so. If fate, or whoever, means one to survive, one does, although for what end remains obscure.

One day Chibs and I, then perhaps four and eight, wandered through the picket gate leading to the rubbish bins and the vegetable garden. By the gate there was a big galvanized-iron shed in which all sorts of garden junk was stored, the home of mice and spiders whose thick webs sang in the breeze by a broken window. Here on a bench we found a jar containing some sort of paste with a most appetising smell; I now realize this spice was fenugreek, and every time I make a curry it evokes this memory. There were several other fresh jars in the cupboard above the bench. One of us had the idea that this paste would be delicious mixed with bran and pollard into little cakes.

We were just finishing moulding the cakes with an old spoon rich in verdigris when Nertie burst through the door saying, "Children, what are you doing?" She seized the cakes, lifted up the jar with its torn label, and took a fresh jar from the cupboard. As soon as she read the label she screamed (we had never heard her scream before; it was a scary noise like a horse in pain). "Oh my God! Oh God! RAT POISON! Oh God in heaven, have you eaten any?" "No," we replied, for once not telling a lie when under pressure. "Oh dear God, I thank thee." She shepherded us back into the house and made us promise never to go near that shed again.

Country children may not be streetwise, but if they grow up at all it will be because they have avoided drowning in a dam, falling down a well, being bitten by a snake, or succumbing to one of the dozens of other hazards that surround a house in the country.

On the other hand, country children, in the words of Randolph Stow's poem, "know more than they know". The so-called facts of life are soon old hat to them.

When I was four or five I was accompanying my mother on one of her drives around the station with Distinguished Guests. As we drove past the stables, there in the holding yard was one of the station hands with a stallion serving a mare. "What's that huge thing? Why's that horse being beastly to that other horse?" I asked my mother, and couldn't think why everyone laughed. But from then on I knew what was hidden under a stallion's tummy and what it was useful for.

Country children are also trained in some areas much earlier and more thoroughly than their city cousins. This is especially true of driving cars, trucks and tractors. Like most other country boys I was a competent driver well before the age of ten, and what is more, knew how to control skids, get out of bogs and across river fords, and change a tyre. I was also beginning to know how to service a vehicle.

Mick Ridge, the mechanic who looked after the station vehicles and machinery and drove daily into Kapunda for the mail and stores, was very kind to me, and taught me to drive. Mick was tall, skinny, and red-haired, with a very long nose. Once when he was driving us back from Kapunda, a bee bit him right on the end of his nose. It was fortunate I was there to grab the wheel of the Morris, because Mick let it go with a torrent of oaths, clapping his hands to swat the bee, roaring with pain.

The best times I spent with my father were when we went out shooting rabbits. This was of course in pre-myxomatosis days, and there were thousands of rabbits in the paddocks, despite programs of trapping, and poisoning their burrows.

The horrors of rabbit plagues in Australia were almost beyond belief. In the station office there was a notebook bound in red leather, with "Here It Is" on the cover, containing records of rabbit scalps brought in by the twenty rabbiters employed on Anlaby. In 1904-5 the total was 111,851.

In 1929 the numbers of rabbits on Anlaby became so alarming that in summer all the dams were fenced in, with a gate to let the stock in to drink during the day. In the fence were tunnels of wire with a flap on the end; at night the gates were closed, so the rabbits could run in through the tunnels but not get out again, because of the flaps. In the mornings four or five of the men, armed with clubs, would go out in the truck round the dams. I went with them once and was astonished at what I saw. Inside the fence around each dam were four or five hundred rabbits. Dogs rounded them up in a squirming mass and the men waded in with their clubs in clouds of fur and dust. A typically bloodthirsty boy, I joined in with the Aboriginal waddy my father had brought back from Central Australia, a lethal weapon made from mulga, heavy as iron. Then the dead rabbits were piled in a heap on some bare ground; kerosene was poured over them and they were burnt. For a week or so about two thousand rabbits were destroyed each day. Even after that, there were still plenty of rabbits about.

My father and I would walk out through the garden, past the long windbreak row of osage oranges, a thorny tree with pale-green leaves, about twenty feet high, from the southern United States. These trees produced hundreds of useless, wrinkled, knobbly fruit, the size of a large orange and the colour of a ripe lemon. My father, as always an encyclopaedia of information, told me that the Osage Indians used to make their bows from the very flexible, yellow-orange wood. Across the cow paddock, keeping a wary eye out for the bad-tempered Jersey cows, then we were in the big paddock, The Gums. My father told me he had given orders that the trees in The Gums were never to be cut, nor the land ploughed; he wanted it to be preserved as a token of the original Australia, which, when our ancestors first came to Anlaby in the 1830s, they declared to be of "a park-like aspect". Other portions of Anlaby had been thick scrub; my father said that when he was a boy of my age in the 1870s, he needed a compass to walk back to the homestead from Mt Waterloo, the big hill a couple of miles to the north.

Once out in The Gums we were soon bowling the rabbits over. I was a good shot. It was one thing my father taught me well, along with fishing and boating. For my eighth birthday he gave me a beautiful little Ithaca double-barrelled .410 shotgun. One day after rain I tripped and fell. A few moments later I fired both barrels at a running rabbit and realized that the gun looked odd. When I had fallen I had unwittingly jammed both barrels into the earth, and the two shots had made them bulge at the muzzle like fat grapes. If the barrels had not been made of good steel they would have burst and probably severely injured both of us.

My father was very strict about shooting. One day I fired towards the house. Although it was far out of range, he made me walk back home immediately, by myself.

On another occasion he stumbled and fell, and lay on the ground moaning, rolling from side to side. He put his gun down and pulled up the left leg of his trousers. I had never before seen the white skin of his leg and the swollen blue veins. His left kneecap had swivelled around and now lay behind his knee. With a grunt of pain he heaved it back and it clicked into its normal position. He pulled down his trouser leg, picked up his gun and got to his feet. He explained that when he was a young man he had had a riding accident which had permanently damaged his knee, although normally he walked without a limp.

If it had not been for that riding accident, Chibs and I might never have been born. He was in London at the outbreak of World War I, and the day after war was declared he went to a recruiting centre to enlist. Because of his knee, he was rejected on medical grounds. If he had been accepted he would undoubtedly have become an officer, as he had served many years in the cadet corps at school; about eighty per cent of those original officers were killed in the first year or two. He attempted to enlist again after returning to Australia, but was again rejected. That explained the lapel badge, "Rejected Volunteer", pinned to the blue silk of a small glass case in the library.

The only time I ever spent more than a few hours with my father was in 1928, when, for some unaccountable reason, he took me with him in the Essex tourer on a trip to Uno, our sheep station a couple of hundred miles north-west of Anlaby. I loved Harry Edkins, the manager, and Jack Learmonth, the overseer, and his wife Pearl; they were the first real bush people I had met.

There was a timeless quality about Uno, as there always is in the outside country. At Anlaby the past was all about me, sometimes seeming of such weight that the present could not balance it. Some of it, however, was very romantic for a small boy. I loved to heave back the rusty bolt on the door of one of the sheds and open the doors onto the 1908 Talbot, with its brass radiator and acetylene lamps, with the large four-cylinder engine cast in two separate blocks, with the valves and springs exposed at the side. It was in this car that my father, with Murray Aunger as co-driver and mechanic, drove from Adelaide to Darwin in 1907–8.

What I did not realize as a child was that the past, this personal history, was patrilinear, all about Duttons. Anlaby, taken up by my great-grand uncle Frederick in 1839, was the oldest stud sheep station in South Australia. Another great-grand-uncle, Francis Stacker, had discovered copper in 1842 with Charles Bagot and then established the first copper mine in Australia, at what became the town of Kapunda. And so it went.

My mother seldom spoke about her family, the Martins, although every time we drove through the beautiful town of Gawler on our way to Adelaide, there was Martindale, her old home, designed by George Kingston in the 1850s, with its high white arches, on the top of the hill above the river. Much later I found out why she was so reticent.

My mother's family was Scottish and Cornish, an interesting mix with the Duttons, who were Sephardic Jewish from Spain, Portuguese, English and Welsh. James Martin was a mechanic, engineer and inventor from Foundry in Cornwall, who arrived in South Australia in 1847 and set up as a blacksmith and wheelwright in the settlement of Gawler. Within 25 years Martin & Co. was one of the biggest engineering works in Australia. They built the first locomotive in South Australia.

My mother probably owed her ability to get on with all sorts of people to her childhood acquaintance with the men at the Works. In 1907, for various complicated reasons, but mainly because the South Australian Government had set up its own locomotive and rolling stock works at Islington, Martin & Co. went into liquidation. The general engineering business had been bought by my grandfather, Henry Dutton, in 1905. As my father and mother had only just been married, this must have been very humiliating for her. So the Martins, whose history was just as interesting as that of the Duttons, were hardly ever mentioned.

Whatever the past, it was still the past, like Grandfather's conservatories and shadehouses, mushroom house and apple house and grape house, built long before Chibs and I were born. My mother had opened up this formal garden which Grandfather had maintained with no fewer than fourteen gardeners. Now with a mere four gardeners — one of whom was my hardworking mother — she transformed it into something much more beautiful than it used to be. However enthusiastic my parents were about the Australian trees in their plantations, natives were excluded from the inner garden; as Miles Franklin said of her mother's garden, it was like a ring around the house to keep Australia out.

A mile-long avenue of great red gums led to the front gate of the garden, where an avenue of oaks took over and led to the house. Outside this were three vast peppertrees dating back to the 1850s (the false pepper, formerly *Schinus molle*, now *Schinus areira* from California), with their rough bark, slim, feathery, drooping leaves and hundreds of "peppers" in crackly, rose-pink shells. The green flames of tall cypresses stood around the front lawn, and below the terrace and stone wall were magnolias and crab-apples. Outside my bedroom were lilacs, white, pink and one deep-purple, with an achingly delectable scent which floated in through my window.

This oasis of scents and delicate petals was, of course, not impregnable, and never less so than on what was known as a North Wind Day. As soon as you woke in the morning, you knew that not only was it going to be a scorcher but that a dust storm was on the way. Under every shaded veranda and ledge of the house, and under the terrace where on happier mornings the thrush sang to himself in the mirror, a million blowflies were vibrating like double-basses, with a terrifying sforzando if you were foolish enough to walk out, when you would be enveloped by them. There was a mustardy tinge to the morning light, and a boding threat in the air. There was an ominous stillness, the conversations of leaves were silenced, even the delicate peppertree leaves hung dead down.

Your skull felt boomingly empty, and a headache started to grow. A few hours later, red clouds began to swirl to the north, then lurch towards us. All the windows and doors in the house had long since been closed tight, and most of the blinds pulled down. One such day, Chibs and my mother and I were watching the red clouds from the terrace, rolling above and beyond the rose garden, the grape house and Harry West's rows of vegetables. "Here she comes," said my mother like the Delphic oracle, and we fled into the house as twigs and leaves began to snap at the windows like wildcats' claws, and the branches of the peppertrees, that usually hung down so gracefully, streamed out horizontally. The cypresses, once still and vertical as candle flames, now thrashed like whips, and all the leaves of the waterlilies on the lily-pond flipped over from dark-green to grey. A magpie or a crow flapped squawking downwind.

And then the dust arrived, mustard turned to ochre to umber, the sun was extinguished, the rose-arches and the cypresses disappeared and dust was all.

The lightning split the curtains of dust, thunder rolled and cracked, and down came the rain in balls of mud. "Oh my roses, my lovely roses," wailed my mother. Even she was sweating, although that was not a word used about ladies in those days. I always wondered what happened to the blowflies, because when the dust storm had gone by, and the air was clean again, there was not a fly to be seen or heard.

My mother was passionate about her roses. She did not care for modern varieties, oversized, vulgar colours and no scent. She preferred old-fashioned roses with scents you could bury your face in, and the tight little moss-roses with their fuzzy branches and curly leaves. She had a long-standing feud with the rosellas. These parrots, handsome in their green, blue and red, seemingly for sheer joy of destruction would sway up and down on the branches of the rosebushes, nipping off the buds. One day towards the end of her life she was taking some friends of mine around the garden. When they reached the rose garden she said with a snort, "What with the rats, the rosellas and the Labor Government, you can't grow a decent rose nowadays."

She often used to go round the garden with my little .410 gun, with which she was a dead shot. On one occasion Lady Spencer (whose son John Althorp, Princess Diana's father, was an ADC at Adelaide's Government House) was visiting Anlaby. They had taken the ritual walk around the garden, and were having tea under the peppertrees, the .410 lying on a seat nearby, when a cloud of rosellas descended on the roses in front of the house, chattering like schoolgirls. Unable to bear another bud falling, my mother grabbed the gun and strode out onto the drive. The rosellas all took off. She shot one on the wing, and it landed exactly in the centre of Lady Spencer's full teacup.

There were actually a few Australian plants in the garden, like the 30 foot-high lagunaria outside the kitchen, in fact a species of hibiscus from western Queensland (and Norfolk Island), with pink flowers that lasted all summer and, its terrible trap, seeds the size of walnuts which were lined with hundreds of fine hairs that pierced the skin of unwary children.

And then there was the pandorea, the wonga-wonga vine, which scrambled all over the old furnace shed for heating the hothouses. This produced lots of pods like little canoes, polished brown and pale lemon inside, three or four inches long, bow and stern pointed and flaring; they could safely navigate rapids. Chibs and I used to launch them in the ponds of one of the old shadehouses, and send them through the waterlilies. In the rocks held together with brown cement there was hollowed out, at the water's edge, a perfect little smooth harbour, twice the size of a man's hand, where we could leave our canoes safe from storms.

When, years later, I first walked in a rainforest, I immediately remembered the thick, warm air and the scents of jostling greenery that were so characteristic of the conservatories at Anlaby. There were ferns and palms and those lilies through which our canoes floated like pirogues in some backwater of the Amazon. A rubber tree grew in the middle of the hothouse; we would dig a knife into the bark, smooth as brown skin, and out would ooze the milky fluid. You could squeeze a few drops between thumb and forefinger, then open them out and watch it expand into a thread and finally snap.

In the long area in the middle of the building was a concrete humidity tank the size of a swimming pool, with tiers of slats on which sat pots of orchids and other plants, with their roots dangling in the water. Sometimes, on nights when there was a full moon, there would be a crash of glass from one of the conservatories, a sign that a duck had landed on it, thinking the glass to be a pool of water reflected in the moonlight. In the morning the dead bird would be lying amidst the ferns.

For some reason Chibs and I had no pets, although John and Dick had had plenty of them. This was yet another odd thing about our upbringing.

One day when I was four or five I found a little, skinny, wild kitten in the apple house, a fairytale building walled and roofed with orange Marseilles tiles, with long racks in the cool interior where the apples were kept. The kitten didn't seem to mind being caught until I brought it inside the house, when it began to struggle violently and dig its very sharp claws into me. I threw the kitten as hard as I could down a stairway onto the stone steps at the bottom. It lost a few of its nine lives, but was still quite active, so I rushed down, picked it up, ran up the stairs and threw it down again. At this Violet came round the corner and asked what was going on. "The poor kitty fell down the stairs," I answered innocently. She took it away and Harry West put it out of its misery.

Perhaps this ugly episode led to the pet which I was to love more than any other animal. In one of the old shadehouses near the fig trees I heard something yowling; I went in and found a sturdy, tabby wild kitten. This time I wrapped it in my sweater, but even when I took it inside the house it did not struggle. In fact it purred. My mother, surprisingly, said I could keep it.

Many years later Violet told me that I came with it to her and said, "Tigs is Tiger and Tiger is my cat." Tigs, devoted as a dog, followed me out into the paddocks. He found a way to get onto the roof of the downstairs room below my bedroom window, where he would sit on the bed of wistaria leaves and wash himself. I took him down to Rocky Point; unlike most cats, which hate travelling, he settled in happily. Then one day I went out fishing with Chibs in the little wooden dinghy, to what we called the "blue line", where the sand gives way to weed, about a hundred yards out from the beach. After we had been fishing for a while, Chibs said, "Look, there's a baby seal", pointing to a grey whiskery head. But it wasn't a seal, it was Tigs, swimming out to the dinghy. I hauled him over the edge, his fine fur now like an old dishcloth.

The only boring event in our weeks at Anlaby was on Sundays, when we had to accompany my mother to church. She was not particularly devout, but she played the organ at the services.

Grandfather had been very devout, Church of England. In the early 1900s he had built the handsome church, designed by an English architect in the Norman style, at the tiny village of Hamilton, about six miles from Anlaby. He built it there because Hamilton was on the old coach road to the north, and it would be easier for the congregation to get to the church than if it were at Anlaby. It was built in memory of my grandmother, Helen Elizabeth, who died in 1901, and my Aunt Ethel, who was drowned in 1892.

The woodwork, of English oak, the blue painted ceilings, the stained-glass windows and the silver-gilt candlesticks were very fine. But its most notable feature was a magnificent three-manual pipe organ which my mother played with bravura. Its bellows were pumped by a long handle hidden behind the organ, worked by an old man. Occasionally the clink of bottles could be heard between hymns, and at the end of the service the organ blower's face was red, and not only from his exertions.

The images of my childhood which really impressed me were a diverse lot. They certainly did not include the pallid saints in the Hamilton church. One of the first, out of my mother's readings to me from the myths of ancient Greece, was of Pallas Athene coming down from the sky with her robes streaming, spear in hand and the Gorgon's head on her shield. When I heard of her severe beauty and her blue eyes I identified her with my mother, who could be very severe.

All the images of *Struwwelpeter*, a book which Hecky read and read to us with relish, are unforgettable, beginning with Shock-headed Peter on the cover, with his "nasty hair and hands" and the tapering nails over a foot long. Then there were Cruel Frederick having his foot bitten by faithful Tray; the two pussycats weeping over the little mound of ashes and the two shoes that are all that remain of naughty Harriet who played with matches; the terrible story of Augustus who would not have any soup, who in consequence shrinks in four drawings from a fat boy to a stick figure to a cross on a grave; and little Johnny Head-in-Air who strides into the river alongside three watching fishes. Chibs and I loved both stories and images. It is a delicious commentary that under the title, below the drawing of

Shock-headed Peter, is the byline, "Pretty Stories and Funny Pictures for Little Children".

There were many reminders of sudden death in the big house at Anlaby. My father, the mildest of men, had been an indefatigable hunter in his youth, and had slaughtered beautiful animals in Morocco, Newfoundland, Canada, Wyoming and the Rocky Mountains. The skull and antlers of an elk, over the cabinet of the Ericsson telephone, confronted you as you walked in the front door. In the dining room the stuffed heads of three wapiti with many-pointed antlers looked down on the diners, joined by an avuncular moose and a couple of mountain sheep.

Between the heads were wondrously incongruous paintings. In the place of honour, in a superb gold frame, was the sweeping Lambert portrait of my mother in her Worth dress on her honeymoon in London. She was the first woman Lambert painted on commission. On either side of this romantic gesture were Grandfather and Grandmother Dutton, in boring Victorian rectitude. Over the fireplace was a noble eighteenth-century horse painting by Sartorius, and to the left of the fireplace a Tom Roberts oil of the bush in the hills near Melbourne. Outside the dining room in the corridor was the coloured lithograph of Colonel Light's sketch of the first settlement at Adelaide.

In the corridor outside the smoking room my father came into his own with two marine studies of sailing ships (another of his passions), a big oil by Somerscales of two clippers hove-to exchanging mail, and a watercolour by Joseph Spurling of a clipper under full sail. My father had commissioned this painting of the *Torrens*, in which Joseph Conrad made two trips to Adelaide in 1891 and 1893.

There were deceptively tender pictures in my mother's bedroom, a coloured engraving of one of Romney's paintings of soft-eyed, delectable Emma Hamilton, and a lovely, rhythmic red conté study of the Three Graces by Angelica Kauffmann.

There were lots of other paintings and engravings, including those by Heysen and Lambert (one of his only two flower oil paintings), and some Dutch flower painter whose circular offering in a complex frame hung over the drawing room fireplace, facing two Rowlandson watercolours of village scenes. (What was the point of a drawing room, I always wondered; it was never used, but was the most elegant room in the house. Perhaps my mother felt the same — about 1929 she converted it into her bedroom.)

I particularly loved the birds in glass cases in the corridor outside our bedrooms, pheasants and grouse and an exquisite white owl which had flown into Grandfather's flagpole and killed itself.

What a mixture it was of Australian and exotic!

Four

When I was eight my parents sent me to Wykeham, a small preparatory boarding school for boys in the Adelaide hills near Belair. There were also two brave girls at the school, my sister's friend Janet Winser and her young sister Ruth.

My mother had bought me a very smart grey-flannel suit at Harrods when she was in London, and it had long trousers. The first thing I noticed when we arrived at Wykeham was that all the boys were wearing short trousers. It was not a good start. My sister had suffered a similar handicap at Victor Harbor, where we used to swim in the baths alongside the causeway to Granite Island. My mother insisted on her wearing dresses with bows for swimming, which of course meant that she was mocked by the other kids, who also pounced on her unusual name, and chanted "She's called Bryony, she's called Bryony" when we appeared at the baths. That was one reason why Chibs hated the name, and abandoned it for her second name, Helen, as soon as she could.

Wykeham was run by Stuart Hutchinson, a tall, cadaverous classical scholar from Oxford. His wife, Rica, a comfortable woman with much more drive than him, was a member of the famous Western Australian Drake-Brockman family. She was also an old friend of Sybil Thorndike; she had considerable knowledge and love of the theatre, and directed the school in some quite bearable productions of Shakespeare. She also had a passion for Persian cats.

These cats at least seem to have lessened my alarm at arriving at Wykeham. Writing the next day to Chibs, who had been installed at Stawell school at Mount Lofty, my mother said, "Gep and I arrived quite safely at Wykeham — his face looked only half its size when I said goodbye to him, but he was very brave. It was so funny to see such lots of small boys. Gep was twice their size tho in 2 or 3 cases he was years younger. Mrs Hutch has 13 kittens in the house! Gep made friends with them at once. I had tea with the Governor today ..." The cats certainly were a bonus.

Before my mother left I made her promise to send me some short trousers as soon as possible. The other boys seemed amiable enough after they had tired of laughing at my long trousers, and at least I knew one of them, Colin Angas, and the two girls (although they hardly mixed with us, and did not board).

Wykeham was a pleasant, roomy old house, in a couple of acres of scrub which made up for the rather dreary garden. I was with a number of boys wandering about in the scrub one day when, to my surprise, one of them produced a length of rope, three or four others grabbed me, and I was tied to a tree. It was a she-oak and had very rough bark which dug into the backs of my arms. One of the boys then poked me in the ribs with a large stick and said, "What's the worst word you know?"

I looked around the semi-circle of grinning faces, all waiting for appalling swear-words or obscene slang, and in my pathetic innocence I tried to make up my mind which was worse, "hell" or "damnation". I settled for "damnation". This produced hoots of derision and more pokes with more sticks. "Garn, you've gotta know something worse than that!" I shook my head, fortunately too scared to cry. "Ar shit," said the boy with the big stick, "he's stupid, cut him loose."

Apart from this episode, there was surprisingly little bullying at Wykeham. The unpleasant coercions came from the Hutchinsons. We had to eat everything that was set in front of us. I had never seen porridge before, and this grey, glutinous gunk made me retch. "Put more sugar on it," suggested Colin Angas. I just managed to get it down, half an inch deep in sugar. And that happened every morning. But I was not nearly as badly off as one boy, Barrett, who simply could not eat lamb's fry, that absurd euphemism for sheep's liver. I knew about this aversion, because Chibs was completely allergic to any form of offal. Once when confronted with liver at Anlaby, and Nertie saying "Don't be silly, Chibby, it's lovely, eat it up", Chibs took a mouthful and was promptly sick all over the tablecloth. This is exactly what happened to Barrett at Wykeham, unfortunately more than once; the liver would arrive, wearing its overcoat of brown gravy. Barrett would pick at the gravy, obviously with extreme revulsion, and then Hutch would be standing over him saying "Eat up, boy, come on, eat up", and Barrett would eat up and promptly throw up.

I found the lessons in Latin, English and French absurdly easy, thanks to all that Heckie had taught me, so speedily earned a reputation for carelessness and lack of seriousness. Writing to Chibs, my mother said her reports were much better than mine.

As part of the old English public school tradition that we should grow up manly and cruel, we were taught boxing. I hated pulling on the fat gloves, which had an acrid smell, especially when one of them hit you on the end of the nose. I was put up against Peter Anderson, a boy of about my own height, although of slighter build and eighteen months older than me. I liked Peter, a gentle and humorous boy, and didn't see any point in hitting his delicate, pampered face. We sparred away without really touching each other, until old Hutch came over and barked, "Come on, you boys, let's see some boxing, straight left there, Anderson, uppercut, Dutton." I was a lot stronger than Peter, and couldn't bear to put any force into my unstylish blows. Suddenly Peter, taunted by Hutch, let fly a straight left into my solar plexus. Infuriated out of reason, I hit him as hard as I could on the side of the jaw, knocking him to the ground. As I was picking him up and apologizing, Hutch was saying, "That's it, boys, that's it, now you're getting the idea!"

Remaining good friends, Peter and I worked out a system whereby any bystander would think we were knocking hell out of each other, without in fact doing any damage at all.

Early in my career at Wykeham, it was announced that Mrs Hutch would be directing us in a performance of Shakespeare's *Julius Caesar*. Colin Angas was cast as Mark Antony, and turned in a splendid performance, admired by us all. Mrs Hutch was hard put to find a part for anyone as lacking in talent as I was, and finally settled for Artemidorus, "a sophist of Cnidos". After sixty and more years I can still recite the pregnant but unbeautiful words of my one and only speech:

> Caesar, beware of Brutus; take heed of Cassius, mark well Metellus Cimber; Decius Brutus loves thee not ...
>
> Here will I stand till Caesar pass along,
> And as a suitor will I give him this ...

I was such a feeble performer that my schoolmates percipiently dubbed me "Ah-timid-dormouse".

My letters home contained endless hints such as "You can come up and take me out for the day if you want to", but all that happened was that the terms went by and my brother John took me back to Anlaby in our father's Buick; neither my mother nor my father ever came.

At Kangaroo Island in summer my mother suddenly announced that she was taking Chibs to school in England and that I was being sent to Geelong Grammar School, Corio, Victoria. Of course neither of us, being brought up as we had been, and the time being what it was, said anything more than "Yes Mum".

My mother explained to me that I was not being sent to St Peter's College in Adelaide, where my grandfather, father and brothers had gone, because it was too easy, and I would just be accepted as another Dutton. At Geelong nobody would know me and my character would be moulded. She didn't of course mention that, being over five hundred miles from Anlaby, I would be well and truly out of the way. And she was right in wanting me to be kept from the easy family traditions of St Peter's, a very conventional school. And also, by 1931, with both her elder boys sent down from Oxford without taking a degree, it was maybe at last dawning on her that I would have to be brought up differently from my spoiled brothers. The new headmaster at Geelong, J.R. Darling, was reputed to be full of good ideas on education. My father remained silent on that subject, inscrutable and jolly as always, on the occasions when I saw him.

My mother and Chibs sailed for England, and in 1932, aged nine, I set off for Geelong. Fortunately there were half a dozen South Australian boys also travelling to the school, two of them, Bob Angas and David Hawker, being about five years older than me — and Colin Angas and Billy Wills, the other boys I knew, one or two years older. Off we went in the famous Melbourne Express, the big boys promising to take good care of Billy and me — which they did, and not only on the journey. It was to turn out that bullying was rife at the Junior School of Geelong Grammar. Bob and David, who were not only older but very powerful boys, let it be known that anybody belting Wills or Dutton would have the bejesus belted out of them in return. We were very soon let alone.

Everything around Geelong was totally foreign to me. I had spent my country life on red soil, among hills and thousands of old gum trees. Here the soil was a dirty grey, there were windbreaks of cypresses, not the slender green flames around the front lawn, but flattened, stunted trees with their boughs growing into each other, in themselves a promise of bitter winds. There were hardly any gum trees, and they stuck up straight like posts. The landscape was flat without any sheltering hills, and the houses were built of wood and the churches of a black, prison-like stone mysteriously called bluestone. Being the time of the Depression, most of the wooden houses had not been painted for years, and this made them look even more dismal.

The school itself was built of a glaring brick; I had never seen large brick buildings before, except for the Hamilton Church. They stood in a semi-circle overlooking football and cricket ovals, more cypresses, and the lagoon, a dreary inlet in the smelly bay, where there was a rickety wooden construction, the school baths, fifty yards square. The wooden piles were encrusted with big mussels; if you were pushed off the walkways, a favourite sport, you were liable to receive deep gashes down your legs or backside from the razor edges of the mussels. No bathers were worn in the baths, so you were particularly vulnerable.

Beyond the powdery dust of the cypress windbreaks, and the paddocks of grey grass and boxthorn with its bitter smell, were the industrial areas of Geelong, an oil refinery, a whisky distillery, the Ford works.

It was a prison, without locks or bars, but from which there was no escape. Every now and then a boy would run away, but he would always be brought back, looking sheepish, to be caned before being cast back into the mob.

The Headmaster of the Junior School, Mr Jennings, inspired instant distrust in me. Although almost totally ignorant of strangers in authority, I sensed immediately from his slippery smile and the few grey hairs separately greased down over the dome of his head, that he was not to be trusted. I was to learn that he was very popular with parents, and hated by the boys.

When we were at our first assembly, he gave us some invaluable advice about our lives at Geelong Grammar Junior School. On Sundays we wore Eton collars, huge stiffly starched affairs that sat down to our shoulders; they were, mysteriously, called "bomb-proofs". Inside the collar, and down our chests, was a light-blue tie — "Light blue for purity, boys". We were told that we would be good sailors as long as Captain Will Power was on the bridge. We were told never to do anything that we would not do in front of our sisters; I thought this would give me plenty of latitude, not knowing, of course, what he really meant.

At tea in the dining hall I was appalled to find that a boy was rostered to stand behind Jennings' chair and scratch his head with a quill. Fortunately I was never one of the favoured boys elected for this disgusting duty.

We had been shown our beds in the dormitory, and the rug each boy had brought as part of his equipment was folded on the blanket, giving the bed a vestige of individuality. Lights were put out early in our dormitory. On the first night my resolve that all these mysterious happenings must be borne without complaint was shattered as I began to be aware that strangled sobs were emerging from most of the beds. In no time I was sobbing too, at the same time as thinking it was ridiculous and not at all what my mother would expect of a lucky boy sent to this lovely school.

We were put down for a rest after lunch in the dorm, and some ingenious boy demonstrated that by tying the tassels of our rugs to the curved metal ends of the beds a private tent could be made. This was most consoling. A chance to be alone was one thing never available at boarding school.

This pleasure did not last long. One day we heard someone burst in the door and then Jennings' voice shouting "You horrible little boys, you beastly boys", as he rushed along tearing down our rug tents. I had no idea what we were supposed to be doing that was beastly or why he was so worked up, but there were no more rug tents in the dorm.

At school a bike was a boy's best friend. Behind the school buildings were the thick cypress plantations generically known as The Planny. In the one nearest the Junior School a banked mud track had been made through the trees, and we would spend hours racing our bikes around this track. Best of all, on our bikes, in groups of three or four, we could go for Saturday parties (called a Rarridy), riding fifteen to thirty miles to places like Batesford, or the You Yangs, where there were hills with great boulders, or Anakie. Each group would be given a sugar bag containing a billy and tea, bread, butter, chops, tomato sauce, oranges and apples. It was glorious peace, away from the school all day, even if the winds always blew against you going out (two hours to get to Batesford) and against you coming home.

Just sometimes the first wind held, and you could get home from Batesford in forty minutes.

My constant companion, Teddy, was a kindly boy, plump but not porky, serviceable and dull as unpolished pewter, with a snorting laugh like a surprised horse. When I was nine, and he was ten, he nearly killed me.

At recess we would play chasey or kick a ball. One day Teddy and I decided on a new game. Standing at either end of a deserted patch of grass, maybe twenty yards apart, we would throw each other a pair of brass, steel-tipped dividers from our geometry sets. Whoever threw it so the end stuck in the grass the most times won the game. We had a few throws, and then Teddy threw a very high one. I gaped up into the sun to see where it would land. It landed like a bullet in the side of my nose half an inch from my eye. The force of the blow knocked me down, and blood spurted out of my nose. Teddy and the other boys who rushed to me thought at first that the dividers had gone through my eye into my brain, but then someone realized that the steel point was still buried in my face. By this time a master arrived, and pulled the dividers out; he had to pull really hard, and it felt as if half of my face was going with them. Matron by this time had appeared with a wet towel and I was taken off to be cleaned up. Poor Teddy, he looked sicker than I did.

School seemed to me an infinitely depressing place. What was perhaps worse, there seemed no point to it. In fact there seemed to be no point to life at all. One night I took to bed with me the dividers that Teddy had thrown and which had lodged by my eye. Somebody had said to me I was lucky, they could have killed me if they had gone into my eye. So I intended now to stick them in between my ribs and pierce my heart, which I was naive enough to think would put an end to it all. When everyone was asleep I unfolded the dividers, lifted the sheet and blanket, and placed the point against my chest. I pressed. It hurt like hell. Sanity took over, and I said to myself that there must be some less unpleasant way of dying.

One of the painful duties at Geelong was the weekly letter to one's parents. I found it impossible not to be boring. "Dear Mum. We had a cross-country run on Friday and I came last. I just run out of puff and I don't like the boxthorn." "Dear Mum. My house, Barwon, played Barrabool at cricket on Wednesday. I think we won but am not sure as I don't know much about cricket. There are three house teams but I'm not in any of them."

Another problem was that my father was at Anlaby and my mother in London. I thought I should write now and then to my father, but as he never wrote to me I didn't know quite how to put things. When we were together, which was not all that often, he was full of jokes. I thought I would try some jokes in a letter. I remembered the first letter I had ever written, when I was seven, from Rocky Point to my mother at Victor Harbor. She thought it was a hoot, and kept it. Here it is, my first literary effort.

> One day on a heatwaved old Friday, Janet, Chibs, Erny, Caliph and Wilks, went out a-fishing in the leaking old Cutty Sark.
>
> When they were half a mile out to sea, suddenly the rusty old engine stopped. Meanwhile fat Pa at the beach had turned the Greenwich telescope on them. By gosh! Their playing the yankidoodle out there, said Pa.
>
> Out at sea Chibs said to Janet, and Janet said to the rest of them "Wake up, you iron fisted spalpeens!"

So I attempted something jovial, playing with words, for my father. It was along the lines of "Hi ho, old fruit! How's your cock crowing, you tough old rooster? I hope you're well and dingling your dangle and banging your bungle."

A furious letter came back from my father. "I am shocked and appalled at your letter. I have shown it to your two brothers and they agree with me. I cannot think what got into you to write such stuff ..."

Not long after this disaster, early in the second term, when I was still nine, a boy came up to me at recess and said Mr Jennings wanted to see me in his study. Guilt struck me immediately, in classic schoolboy style, but I could not think of any recent misdeed, although I was sure that Jenno would have uncovered one. To my surprise he stood up when I came into his study and asked me to sit down in an armchair. With his most unctuous smile, he told me he had some bad news for me, "I'm afraid, Dutton, very bad news. Your father has died. Your brother John rang a few minutes ago to tell me. He had a heart attack."

After a few platitudes he suggested that it was best to carry on on such occasions, and I should go into my Latin class which would start, let me see, in about five minutes. His attitude was: "Play up, play up, and play the game, Captain Will Power on the Bridge".

I went out to the lawn. Teddy came up and immediately said, "What's wrong, Dutt?" I told him, and he let me bawl on his shoulder, for which I have always been grateful. He told the Latin master what had happened, and he said I could be excused the lesson, but I didn't know what else to do, so stuck with "*Omnis Gallia*".

I didn't really know how to feel about my father's death. Apart from the time he had made me walk home, after I'd fired my gun towards the house, and the episode of the letter, he had always been very friendly to me. He was more fun than my mother, who rarely let go. But I hardly knew him. He had never driven me to Wykeham, or come to see me, or picked me up at the end of term. I had learned nothing from him about life, although he did teach me how to fish and manage a boat, a gun or rifle. He had read to me — that was important and always enjoyable. But he was like his vast library of first and limited editions, mostly not to be opened.

Shortly after my father's death Jennings had a cable from London to say that my mother was coming home.

It must have been a bitter blow for her to have to abandon her exciting life in London and in Europe, just when her long-frustrated career in high society was really taking off. I don't think I was any bonus in exchange.

Not long after my mother's return to Australia my brother Dick was married to Margaret Newland. Margie was very pretty indeed, and expert at conveying a slightly languorous charm. She was also considered very brainy, as she had won the coveted Tennyson Medal for coming top of the state in Leaving English. She and Dick both liked reading and always had the very latest novels, and American magazines I had never seen before. My mother and father subscribed to lots of magazines, but they all came from London: *The Illustrated London News, Britannia and Eve, The Connoisseur, The Cornhill, The Tatler, The Bystander, John o' London's Weekly, The Times Literary Supplement, Country Life. L'Illustration* was a French exception. My mother would sigh over the advertisements for manor houses and castles in *Country Life* and the articles on the luxuriant gardens of the British Isles. "What you can do with plenty of rain", she would say plaintively, not mentioning the number of gardeners required. My preference was for the superbly stylish advertisements in *L'Illustration* for cars as glamorous as the women stepping out of them in front of the Ritz: Delage, Isotta-Fraschini, Hispano-Suiza, Delahaye, Bugatti. Dick and Margaret's wedding was, of course, The Social Event of the Year. The Adelaide *Advertiser* used to run a full page or more of local gossip, the tone slyly bitchy, written appropriately enough by "Lady Kitty". My mother, seemingly unaware of the rancour she had incurred, sent me Lady Kitty on the Dutton-Newland wedding, with the heading "Bridegroom's Mother Eclipses Bride".

Dick and Margaret went off on a prolonged honeymoon in the USA, where Dick had a number of friends he had made at Oxford before failing to pass his exams and being sent down. Once again, as with *Time, Fortune, The Saturday Evening Post, Esquire,* his favourite magazines, it was characteristic that Dick was more interested in America than Home.

At the end of the second term at Geelong my brother John arrived to take me back, in a car he had just bought, a 1928 four and a half litre Bentley. Nothing was said about our father, but we discussed the Bentley with great enthusiasm. With him he had an old friend I liked very much, Hurtle Morphett, who had been a star oarsman at Oxford; he looked a bit like John, and also sported a moustache. He had a highly individual chuckle, indicating his good nature. A few years before, at Kangaroo Island, I had unwittingly strained his amiability by asking him to take me out whiting fishing at dawn, when I had been told the fish would be biting at their best. He valiantly did so, and years later he told me it had nearly killed him, as he had been out in the sandhills till 3 a.m. with the prettiest girl at Rocky Point, whom he later married.

So off we went in the Bentley, John and Hurtle in the front and myself in the back, with the hood up as it was May and cold. We were roaring across the plains of the Western District when there was a tremendous bang, like a piece of artillery being fired. "Hold the road jolly well, these Bentleys," said John, thinking that it was a blowout. He walked all around the car and pronounced it a rum go; all the tyres were still blown up. I pointed to the hole in the back of the hood, near my head, and to the other in the roof. "Have you had a look at the spare?" I suggested, pointing at the back of the Bentley, where the spare was mounted behind the petrol tank. It was indeed the spare that had blown, and a piece of rubber had whizzed past my head. I have often wondered whether anybody's spare tyre has ever blown out, before or since.

We spent the night at a hotel in Portland; there was a delicious bed, which had a soft mattress into which I disappeared. In the morning I turned up all sprightly for breakfast, which I had finished when John and Hurtle appeared, not looking at all well. They drank some coffee but said they could not face bacon and eggs.

After a few minutes John, with some hesitation, said, "I say, Gep old chap, I don't suppose you could lend us some money?" I still had the fiver which, very generously, my dear old godmother Lily Waite had sent me when I went to school. It not only paid for the hotel but bought enough petrol to get us back to Adelaide.

We arrived at Hurtle's house, one of the oldest in Adelaide, at about three in the morning, and I was told to doss down on the sofa in the sitting room. I was woken at about eight by a ferocious old gentleman demanding to know what the hell I thought I was doing and who was I anyway. It was my first encounter with Hurtle's father, George, whom I was to meet again, under very different circumstances, about eight years later.

My mother had originally left for Home with Chibs in the *Otranto* at the beginning of February 1932. My father died on 15 June 1932, but my mother said it was very difficult to find a berth on a ship to Australia, and did not sail until the end of July, arriving in Adelaide in September.

Her last letter to my father, which was found in his coat pocket by Violet after his death, is an embarrassingly fulsome declaration of how much she loves him and the two dear wonderful boys, and of how she is staying away so they can all be together "and find themselves". There is no mention of the third son, safely tucked away at Geelong. In the letter she thanks my father profusely for all the good things he has given her, the Anlaby house and Victor Harbor, the gardens, and all the jewels and clothes — of these last items she writes "I know these are all tosh to you". The tone of the letter changes rapidly when she says that at last she has got Chibs off to school (to Belstead, a boarding school near Aldeburgh), and that she is going to exercise classes because she is about to be Presented at Court. This seems to be very important. She has a flat in Sloane Street. There is a note from my father in the same envelope saying that of course she may draw on his Elder, Smith account for anything she wants.

It is obvious that at last she is all set to enjoy herself in high society, genuine high society, not the spurious version in provincial Adelaide. Fiercely ambitious, she must have been exasperated for years by my father's lack of interest in high or any other society — especially when he had such grand friends with whom he had been at Oxford. And of course it was not only a question of my father's modesty. There was his Problem. It was best for him to stay at home. As for Adelaide, she may have been queen of it but she was bored stiff by it. So one can't grudge her a fling.

She returned to England to continue her fling as soon as was decent, sailing for Home again early in April "in order to look after Chibby". While she was in Australia she did not visit me at school, although of course we spent the Christmas holidays together.

My hundreds of letters to my mother (she kept most of them) make depressingly tedious reading. They prove two things: one, that despite my very extensive reading no one had succeeded in teaching me how to express myself; second, that I seldom told her what was really happening to me at school.

My reading was omnivorous. After the first long vacation, our English master (whom I liked), Kewpie Dart (after Cupid's Dart), asked us to write down how many books we had read during the holidays, if any. I truthfully wrote that I had read about thirty-six. He held my paper up and said to the class, "Splotton's exaggerating again." He had christened me Splotton because I had a bad stammer. I didn't stutter, but instead of saying "We had an egg for breakfast" I would say "We-we-we-we-we had an egg for breakfast", as if I were the last little piggy.

At the time of Kewpie's question, when I was ten, I was reading Kipling's *Jungle Books* and *Just So Stories*, everything of Edgar Wallace I could get my hands on, *Gulliver's Travels* and, my first taste of Australiana, the outback and Pacific Island true tales of Ion L. Idriess. I despised school stories and children's books. My sister had the Mary Grant Bruce books and *Seven Little Australians* and A.A. Milne, but I never read them, let alone *The Magic Pudding*, of which in any case there was not a copy in the Anlaby library. I read lots of the books that had been read to me, like the Greek, Roman and Norse myths and legends and Kipling, but *Uncle Remus* was far too difficult for me. I was always happy to reread *Struwwelpeter* and the tales of Grimm and Hans Andersen.

The nine years of my life at boarding school correspond to the dictionary definition of "past imperfect": "the past tense of incomplete action". There seemed to be no point or climax to life; it simply went on and slid into the past which insisted on going on as before.

Competitiveness was dinned into us, in class, in sport, in the hierarchy of power. I came about twelfth in the class in most subjects, and bottom in mathematics. I was hopeless at all sports except swimming and, later, rowing. Apart from being inept at catching, throwing, hitting or kicking little hard balls or bigger, tough leather ones, I was the slowest of runners and every hurdle fell before my big feet. In the gym I landed in the middle of the horse on my developing genitals, fell off ropes and couldn't stand on my head. Football and other contact sports seemed to me like boxing at Wykeham; I didn't want to bash into other bodies. But hours of every afternoon were devoted to one or other of these so-called sports, and on Saturdays we who were not in a team were told to go and yell encouragement to those who were, and insults at the other team, especially if they were from Roman Catholic Xavier. Sectarianism was alive and well. So was racism. There was a boy called Johns from somewhere up in Queensland who was called Dago simply because his father owned sugar farms, and these were worked by Italians. He got sick of this, and one term came south with a cane-knife, which terrified us.

Music was both a relief and a disappointment. I was tremendously looking forward to piano lessons until my first one with Mr McKinnon, the music master, who had the bristly hair and sharp commands of a drill sergeant. He asked me how long I had been playing the piano; I replied, "Since I was five." He told me to play something, so I chose Schumann's "*Träumerei*" and a Nocturne of Chopin's. He shoved a study by Czerny in front of me and told me to play it. I was never much good at sight-reading, but battled through it. He then told me that I had been taught very badly, and that I would play nothing but Czerny exercises for a term at least. He nearly put me off playing the piano for life.

But there was also the school choir and for all my years at Geelong I sang in it, as treble, then as alto and finally as bass. It was one of the best things at school, especially when the wonderful William McKie, who later became organist and choirmaster of Westminster Abbey, took over from McKinnon. Willie, as we all disrespectfully called him, was one of my greatest influences at Geelong, and I will come back to him.

Past imperfect. A few episodes remain in a perpetual present.

One day at general assembly Jenno gives us a lecture about buying and selling, about things he calls commerce and industry. "Your fathers," he says, "are graziers and lawyers, surgeons and captains of industry." I haven't got a father, but I put down "Grazier" all the same; definitely not "Farmer". "Now all these things are bound together by commerce and industry, by selling what you have to sell, whether it's wool or skills, and other people paying for it. Profit is what makes the world go round. It's called capitalism. Don't be taken in by evil people like communists who don't like capitalism. Capitalism is the best system because it is based on the profit motive."

My friend Bob shoots up his hand. Bob is skinny, with a face like a frog and big round glasses, and his own way of looking at things, though he can hardly see the school tower without his glasses. He is also a very good long-distance runner, but I don't hold this against him. I like Bob. "Sir," says Bob, "what about the Depression?" "A very good point, boy," says Jenno. "But it would take far too long to explain just now." Bob grins at me.

Jenno goes on to explain that he is launching something called The Industrial Scheme. Instead of going to the tuckshop to buy whatever you want you'll buy it off another person. You have to have a licence to sell whatever you want to, and if you do anything wrong you are imprisoned for half an hour in the telephone box. You can also perform services for other people, such as cleaning their bikes or polishing their shoes, and charge a fee for it, like a surgeon or a lawyer.

But the aim of the whole show is to teach us about commerce and industry, not to make a profit. Bob gives me a nudge in the ribs.

Bob suggests we go into the shoe-polishing business. We don't have to buy brushes or polish because we already have them, and if we look like running out of polish Bob'll get his parents to send over some more. We'll charge a penny a pair of shoes, and it'll be all profit.

So we make a big sign, "Shoes polished. One penny a pair", and sit in the back corridor where all the kids run out to their bikes, but no one wants to pay a penny to have their shoes polished, when all you need do is give them a rub with your hanky before Inspection. (In Inspection we all line up, the housemaster goes along the row saying to each boy "Hands. Thumbs. Palms". If they're dirty you get detention. He also looks at your shoes.)

We give the shoe-cleaning business away and set up in the Marmite and Cheese business. We make a new sign: "Purveyors of Marmite and Cheese to the Gentry. Under Vice-Regal Patronage". Jenno is not sure about this sign. We get all the marmite and cheese free from home in food parcels, so we make lots and lots of profit, fifty-five bob in the winter term, but we don't tell Jenno how much we've made.

It's winter and I've got terrible chilblains, red and itchy on my ears and all my fingers and toes. Some of my fingers are so swollen and weepy I have to have bandages on them which I can't resist twirling around for the itch, but that only makes them worse. "You look so horrible, Dutt, it's a wonder anybody buys our Marmite and Cheese." But they do.

In the summer term we decide to set up outside, on the edge of the Planny, in the toffee business. Our only expense is for patty pans, the little paper cake containers to hold the toffee. We make the toffee, just from butter and sugar, in a saucepan on a little fire between some bricks. We pinch the butter and sugar from the dining table. The butter is placed on the tables in big rolls. "Pass the butter, please, Bob," I say, and he hands the dish to me, but he clumsily tips it so the roll of butter, about a pound of it, falls into my lap where I have my hanky waiting to catch it. "Pass the sugar, please, Dutt," Bob says to me, and just as he's about to take it I let the bowl slip and down goes the sugar into his hanky. Thus we get all our ingredients for nothing.

Then, after a few mistakes when the toffee turns into black rock, we get it just right. We put a thin smear of golden toffee in each patty pan and then charge one penny for it. The kids love it, and queue up for it by our sign which reads "Quality Toffee. From an old London Recipe, as supplied to His Majesty King George V". One day when we are pouring the toffee into the patty pans Jenno comes along and asks how much we are charging for it. We tell him. "What? A penny each? No one will pay that much. Now remember, boys, the object of the Industrial Scheme is not to make profits." He must be blind not to see the queue of kids with their pennies at the ready. At the end of the term we have made two pounds each. All profit, apart from two bob for patty pans.

The school is going up to Melbourne for something called the Combined Sports, the annual athletic contest between the Victorian so-called Public Schools. We are to be there to cheer for our team and hurl curses at the other teams.

Mum has written to two old friends of hers, Dicky and Ida Dickson, and they have said I'm more than welcome to come and see them at their home, The Moorings, in Toorak. Just give a ring. So I do, and I am told Dicky will pick me up at Menzies Hotel.

Dicky is an immediate hit, as he says "Call me Dicky", which, despite his age, I do, and he has a 1927 three litre Bentley. We rumble out to Toorak by the longest possible route through the Gardens and along the river Yarra. The house is lovely and dark with big cushions; Ida gives me a fantastic tea, and they ask me to stay the night. "No point you going back just to be at school on Sunday," says Dicky. Lots of kids are staying overnight with friends and relations, so I say yes.

In the morning we drive out to Healesville and I see the koalas and we have a huge lunch. Then they put me on the train, with pots of jam and honey and a box of chocolates.

Back at school the Welcome mat is definitely not out. Jenno says my crime is so bad that I'll have to go and see the Boss, Mr Darling, and I'll be lucky not to be expelled.

I've never been so frightened in my life. The Boss!

Darling is much nicer than I thought he was going to be, and I can tell right off that I'm not going to be belted, though all the kids had been telling me that the Boss always belts on a bare bum, and I might even get twelve.

The Boss explains to me that you can't just not come back to school and stay away a night without telling anyone. Poor Mr Jennings was really worried. Mr Darling obviously thinks this is much more important than having a good time with Dicky and Ida.

"The Dicksons were awfully nice," I say weakly.

"Run along, Dutton, and apologize to Mr Jennings." Thanks to Violet, I know what apologize means.

So Jenno accepts my apology, and then belts me.

One term a daggy little bloke called Leigh Falkiner comes to the school, into our house. His father owns a whole lot of stud sheep stations up in the Riverina. Leigh becomes quite a mate of mine, and asks me out when his parents come down one Sunday. They have a beautiful black Talbot 105, with the most fantastic upholstery, big cushions of yellow leather that have this superb smell.

Leigh and I and a couple of other kids put our names down for a Rarridy party. At the last minute one of the other kids gets sick and is carted off to the Sanny, and the other cops a detention. There are supposed to be at least three on a Rarridy party, but Leigh and I go all the same.

We slog out to Batesford against a head wind, and then have a terrific day, including gutsing all the chops the other kids would have eaten. We climb up to the viaduct and put pennies on the rails and then wait for the train, which flattens them, then we hop over the fence into the farmer's orchard and nick a few apples. We're just climbing the fence again when there's a roar and a yell of "Thieving little buggers" and an almighty bang and my bum and the back of my legs sting like hell, just as I'm getting through the fence. We sprint off, Leigh is shaking with laughter. So the rumour is true, the old bastard does load cartidges with saltpeter and let fly. My legs really sting, especially in that tender patch behind the knees.

"This'll make you feel better, Dutt," says Leigh and gets out a packet of Balkan Sobranie cigarettes he's pinched from his father. They are black with gold tips and are tremendously strong and smell quite different from ordinary fags.

Believe it or not, the wind doesn't change and after plugging up the hill from the valley we fairly fly home in thirty-five minutes. It's one of the best Rarridy parties I've ever had.

We're just putting our bikes away when the housemaster, Noggs Newman, comes round the corner looking really wild. Noggs is not a nice person, and we all hate him, but he's never looked less nice than he does now. He grabs me by the ear and jerks it, hard. "Report to me in my study, Dutton," he says and stumps off.

"Shut the door." I do. He sits behind his desk and I stand to attention. He glares at me.

"You know the rules, Dutton. No fewer than three on a Saturday party?"

"Yes, sir."

"What passed between you and Falkiner today?" I can't make out what he means. He couldn't have found out about the Balkan Sobranies. Perhaps it was pinching the apples? Maybe the farmer has rung the school?

"I said," he speaks very slowly, as if I were a bit dumb, "what passed between you and Falkiner today?"

"Nothing," I say.

Noggs gets up out of his chair, goes over to a cupboard, and grabs an extra long cane.

"You're a beastly, dirty little boy, Dutton. Falkiner is a new boy, and already you're corrupting him."

I haven't a clue what he means, though I do know I wouldn't be in the race to teach Leigh anything, he's as smart as they come.

"Bend down." I've never had such a hard belting. The six blows seem to go right in my bum and out my eyes.

"Now get out!" he yells.

I head for the bike shed. I stand alongside my old blue bike and squeeze the rubber grips on the handlebars.

"Hey Dutt." It's Leigh. "Did he belt you?" I nod, trying not to blub out loud. I can't stop the stupid tears.

"What'd Noggs belt you for?"

I answer, truthfully, "I don't know. I don't know."

You could say there's a lot of school in those three words. Half the time you don't know what they're trying to teach you. You don't know why you have to stand around a cricket pitch while other kids bowl and bat. You don't know why you drop the catch when the ball comes your way.

You don't know why your mother doesn't come home, but writes you letters saying how wonderful it was to stay with the Earl and Countess of Pembroke and be Presented at Court. Then she sends you an awful photograph by someone called Lenare of her looking like Greta Garbo with feathers in her hair, with "This is my Presentation Dress" written on the back. It doesn't look like her at all.

Then one day, a weekday, one of the kids says, "Holy cow, look at that", and there's the most beautiful car I've ever seen, an enormous black drophead coupe with white canvas roof and white-wall tyres. It stops in front of the house, and out gets my brother Dick, and Margie looking really pretty. I can't believe it. They give me a hug and Dick says, "I bought her in Chicago. She's a Vee Twelve Packard. Come on, hop in." There's only one door on each side of the black leather seats, and I'm squeezing into the back when Margie says, "No Gep, hop in the front, you'll see better."

There are instruments everywhere on a polished wood dashboard, and the ridge of the bonnet goes out for about a hundred yards, and there's a sort of swan or something on the radiator cap, with its wings down.

Dick swings around and we head off down the school drive towards the railway line. "Feel this!" says Dick and puts his foot down. My head nearly jerks off my neck and I look, I can't stop looking, at the speedometer. Half way to the railway line we're doing a hundred miles an hour. A hundred miles an hour! And the engine is as quiet as if we were doing thirty.

Back at school Jennings is waiting outside the house. I've never seen him smarmier, all over Margie and Dick. Finally Dick says they'll have to go, and slips me a fiver. "What a nice headmaster you've got," says Margie. They turn and drive off. The other kids seem to love that Packard almost as much as I do. "You beauty, Dutt!" says Wal and slaps me on the back.

Jenno calls out sharply, "Dutton, come to my study immediately."

Now what's Jenno want? I can't think of anything I've done wrong. What the hell have I done wrong?

In his study Jenno starts off with a long lecture about it being the Depression, a time of great hardship for many people, and how it's wrong for rich people to be driving around in expensive motor cars.

I don't see how this is my fault, and I can't help interrupting here. "Dick's not rich, and he bought the car secondhand in Chicago."

"Be quiet, boy." Jenno continues with his speech, which seems to be along the lines of how I ought to be ashamed of myself having a brother like that, with a beautifully dressed wife, and an enormous car, and how such a display of wealth as that car will antagonize the other kids and make them hate me.

I wait to be belted, but he just tells me to go and to think about what he's said to me.

Months later I get a letter from Mum, on a cruise ship in the Adriatic, wherever that is, saying she had a lovely letter from Mr Jennings, what a nice man he is, so interested in you, and he had just met your delightful brother and his charming wife, and dear little John, he writes ("He seems to think your name is John," says Mum), was so bucked by their visit. "I'm so glad," Mum continues, "that you're so happy at school."

Five

My family always kept letters, and my letters to my mother, which I was forced to write every week from Geelong Grammar, are even more boring than her letters to me, which she faithfully wrote every week. But neither of us told the other much of what was really going on in our hearts or bodies.

I cannot pardon her neglect of Chibs and me, but I cannot help sympathize with her in her longing to see the beauties of the old world, and to fly high in society. When she was away with my father in 1928, and while he was having one of his spells in hospital with "a bad cold", she went to stay with the 70-year old Earl of Lonsdale at Lowther Castle in Northumberland. Lonsdale was the most famous patron of sport in England; in one of his manifestations, as yachtsman, he had befriended my grandfather, in the days of the *Adèle*. The Lonsdales had been immmensely rich for generations, and my mother wrote Chibs and me one of her longest letters, enumerating many of the formidable treasures of Lowther Castle, descriptions which could not have been more irrevelant to two Australian children of six and ten, but about which she cared passionately.

What she did not mention was that a fellow guest was King George II of the Hellenes, who had been deposed from the throne of Greece in 1923. KG, as my mother always called him, was a small, elegant man of great charm to women. He and my mother were immediately attracted to each other. From then until his death in 1947 they exchanged letters, photographs and presents; after his death my mother sent Australian wildflowers every year to his former equerry, Colonel Levidis, to be laid on his grave.

Incidentally, KG was six years younger than my mother.

A photo in a leather frame of his portrait by Philip de Laszlo, looking very Germanic and rather like a smaller version of his first cousin the Duke of Edinburgh (they were of course not Greek), used to stand at the front of the dozen or so photos of Famous People on the Steinway at Anlaby.

What happened at Lowther Castle in 1928 no one knows, but it is interesting that a few months later, when my father was again in hospital with that infernal recurring "bad cold", my mother had her fling at Claridge's, and was never in bed before 3 or 3.30 a.m. KG had a permanent suite at Claridge's; my mother usually stayed at Brown's Hotel.

Their friendship was resumed in 1932 and 1933. Chibs remembers being taken to supper at the Savoy with KG — (one can imagine how peeved he must have been to have his inamorata turn up with her thirteen-year-old daughter). Chibs' knife slipped on her plate and she sloshed scrambled egg over him. "He fairly danced with rage and said to me 'You dirty little messer'."

Before and after my father's death there are odd phrases in my trite lettters to my mother which, if she had been a diffferent person, might have given her pause. A recurring theme is of various illnesses, not confined to myself — "Wills is covered in boils" — which are probably due to bad diet. I sound a wreck in letters to both parents. "I seem to be hurt everywhere, I've got a bad thumb, a bad face, a bad arm, a bad knee!" Three weeks before my father's death I am writing to him to thank him for the hamper. "I'm not allowed to have it so I hid it. Will you send me a case of fruit — if you like you can put a pot of Marmite in it too — because I am getting so many things wrong with me that matron says I must have more fruit. My thumb's been bad for a month but it's better now."

At the same time I am writing to my mother in sentiments that could have been directed by Jennings, but in the obvious accents of a small boy: "There is NO teasing at Geelong. We had great fun at Easter. I was not a bit lonely." I cannot imagine why I should have written giving her this (mis)information in a letter written so long after Easter; it must have suddenly occurred to her in London to wonder what I had done for Easter. What did in fact happen was that all the boys who were able to went home; others who lived too far away, in the days before jets, were billeted with friends or relations in Victoria. The dregs, such as myself, spent Easter at school.

One phrase in this letter is identical to one in a letter to my father at much the same time: "We have great fun here".

My mother had arrived back in Australia in September 1932. In the summer holidays she had announced her intention of returning to London "to look after dear Chibby". In March 1933 I am writing apprehensively: "I won't think any more about you going away. What is going to happen to me at Easter? Shall I stay here or what shall I do? I am 19th in my form." I stayed at school again for Easter.

Early in May, when her ship is somewhere between Colombo and Port Said, I am writing: "The school breaks up on the 12th of May. I wish I could find you at home!" On 7 July, when she has settled into the flat in Lord North Street which she is renting from Katharine Elliott (wife of a well-known M.P., Walter Elliott), and has booked cabins for Chibs and herself for a Scandinavian cruise in the *Empress of Australia*, I am writing: "When [underlined four times] you do [underlined three times] come back do you think you could get one of of these things for me and take them out here, the Hornby cabin-cruiser motor-boat No. 5, or the Meccano motor Car Construction No. 2?" A week later, I follow up with a drawing: "You in a murderous mood".

In August she and Chibs take a train to Venice to embark on a Hellenic

Cruise, down the Adriatic, across to Athens — "Fancy Athens — Greece the home of the Gods — Pericles & Hypasia & dozens of wonderful people" — then Constantinople and Rhodes and many other places from which I am bombarded with postcards.

On 1 October, when she is back in London and has at last been Presented at Court, my comment is succinct: "It must be horrible bowing in front of the King and Queen".

On 1 November I am told by Dick and Margie the sort of news she does not put in my letters. "I do wish [underlined five times] you would come back again, darling, because I got a letter from Margaret saying that you would not be home for Christmas." As a result I was to spend the summer holidays at the cottage at Anlaby with Dick and Margie and thoroughly enjoyed myself; whether they enjoyed having the eleven-year-old brother for six weeks is another matter.

They had already had me and Billy Wills for the September holidays. Margie wrote to my mother: "They both arrived complete with several dozen septic sores, but I've been practising first aid to some effect and they are completely cured by now ... In case you are worrying about him at all — don't — because he is quite well and happy, although he often asks when you are coming home ..."

Margie is an expert at daughter-in-law diplomacy, if you don't read too hard between the lines, for the Tennyson Medallist has a good grip of irony:

> Thank you for your darling postcard, dear one — and now I must go and play my nightly game of draughts with Geoff — (someone thought he was my son the other day!!!)
>
> Very much love to you — and don't break too many hearts! ... P.S. Dickie is an angel and I adore him.

It did at that time seem a very happy household. Dick was rumbustious, inventive, affectionate and talked to me about all sorts of things, from the principle of the fulcrum to being taught how to drive a racing car at Brooklands by Sir Henry Seagrave. Margie was the essence of everything feminine in a female-starved life. Violet, on the other hand, although she got on well enough with both Dick and Margie, said the hours were very different from the regular ones they had been used to in the big house, where the evening clearing away and washing up was always done by eight o'clock. Here Dick and Margaret and their friends sat a long time over coffee and drinks, and often asked for more coffee, while Violet and the other maid sat in the kitchen, and often did not finish until after eleven.

Dick, with his usual enthusiasm and lack of follow-up, had put in a swimming pool at the cottage; the outlet was at the shallow end of the pool, so draining it was always a great problem. There was no filter and the application of chlorine was rather vague. Perhaps because of the pool water

I had a series of excruciating abscesses in my ears, which had to be opened. I missed about six weeks of school at the beginning of 1934. In April I wrote to my mother to say I had dropped to twentieth in the form, "but Jenno says it's all right because I had been away so long".

Later in November, when she is staying with the Pembrokes at Wilton, I am in the Sanny (the school sanitarium, i.e. hospital) with one of the childhood diseases which flash through the school until you've had them all, whooping cough, measles (German and ordinary), chicken-pox, etc. I write: "Last week as I would have been left by myself for a week in the San (I'm quite all right now), a boy called Wood, who also had whooping-cough asked me to stay with him for a week, isn't it nice of them?" This was a wonderful week. David Wood's father was the vet in charge of Caulfield racecourse; they lived in a big house right amongst the horses and we spent all day with jockeys and trainers and watching gallops. It was the only time in my life when I have really enjoyed horses.

Things looked up at school. "John Masefield came down — He was wonderful." There were stimulating extracurricular talks. "There was a very good lecture last night on 'Big Game Hunting in British East Africa'."

Kind parents of other children took me out on occasional Sundays. "I went to the You Yangs with Fisher and his parents. We had great fun throwing she-oak nuts at each other, and catching (???) lizards."

In the meantime, J.R.D., The Boss, tried to make us aware of the hard times the world was suffering with the Great Depression. Darling had as a young man been intensely influenced by Victor Gollancz and those associated with the Left Book Club. At heart he was a kind of Christian Socialist, who wanted us to share his awareness of the injustices of the world.

By no means all the boys at Geelong Grammar were from rich families; many parents had skimped and saved and borrowed to send their children there. But, like millions of other Australians, most of us had had no personal contact with the miseries of the unemployed. In the 1930s in Australia, the egalitarian land of opportunity, there were horrendous gaps between rich and poor. The best way of seeing how the fortunate in Australia lived then is to look at issues from the 1930s of *The Home*, the finest glossy magazine ever produced in Australia. It not only has advertisements (of superlative quality of design) for Orient liners about to sail for Europe, for Packard and other luxury cars, and for imported furniture or glass, but articles on the arts and architecture, a gossip column from each state of grand balls or receptions, and a regular London and Paris letter that is a gem of intricate snobbery. You would never suspect from the pages of *The Home* that there were homeless people living in caves around Sydney Harbour, as reported on by Kenneth Slessor for the *Sun*.

I knew the world of *The Home*; in fact, in one of the regular pages, on

"The Rising Generation", there is a repulsive photo of Chibs and myself in our best clothes, looking very uncomfortable. But I had also met men on the track humping their swag, who came in to Anlaby and asked for a job cutting wood. This was not really needed, but to save their dignity something was always found for them to work at for a few hours, so they could be given a sugar bag of meat, flour and sugar. In Adelaide I had seen, on the north bank of the Torrens, the humpies and hessian huts where evicted families lived until they were moved on.

To give us some contact with what it meant to be poor, and to give poor boys a treat, a number of boys from a church orphanage in Geelong were brought out for the day to play sport with us and swim in the baths and have lunch with us. Even at the age I was then, I thought this well-meaning activity must surely be deeply resented by the poor kids. On other days, we would go into Geelong in buses and do useful jobs for widows or women bringing up children on their own. Perhaps this was more worthwhile.

J.R.D. had been taking an interest in me, after our initial encounter over my staying a night with the Dicksons. Incidentally, I never saw them again, though in mid-1934 Ida is writing to "Darling Emmelina" and saying "We've heard nothing of Geoffrey for ages".

In the middle of the first term of 1934, Darling wrote a long letter to my mother, who was now in America, saying, tactfully but firmly, that he thought I needed her presence in Australia. "He's obviously had a very difficult year … I do hope that next year you will be able to come over and see him at least one or two times."

When she eventually returned from America to London, my mother decided to go back to Australia, and arranged for Chibs to attend finishing schools in Paris and Rome. She flew with Chibs to Brussels (where her mother was still living), and then travelled on to Germany and Austria. They arrived in Vienna the day after the premier, Dr Dolfuss, was assassinated on Hitler's orders. My mother then went on to Naples, leaving Chibs to stay as a paying guest with impoverished Austrian aristocrats, and caught a ship to Australia in August. My last letter had just reached her in London: "I'm so glad that you are coming home, won't we have fun together, it's so long since I've seen you, and I could dance with joy". Actually I have always been a terribly bad dancer.

She arrived in Adelaide late in September, so I did not see her in the holidays, but she more than made up for that by actually coming to school in the 1931 Buick in December at the beginning of the summer holidays, and we went off together for a couple of weeks which were the best I had ever spent with her.

She had a friend in Melbourne, a rather mysterious, awesome financier called Edward Dyason, who lent us his cottage up in the mountains, near a village called Wandiligong, between Mount Buffalo and Mount Feathertop. I had never seen mountains, and never been in a house with a clear mountain stream rushing past the back door. There were wildflowers everywhere and strange bird-calls clanged through the shaggy trees. It was cool and crisp, and there was even some snow left on Mount Buffalo, which I scrunched in my hands. And of course I had my mother all to myself, although she did talk endlessly of the treasures in huge country houses, and how the Duchess of York's dear sister, with whom she had had lunch more than once, was ever so much nicer than the Duchess, who did fancy the young men rather too much. I preferred her tales of Hollywood, where she had dined at a restaurant with two film stars of the time, Elissa Landi and George Arliss, and when Elissa got into her limousine to go home she took out a little pearl-handled pistol from her handbag and waved goodbye with it.

1935, Senior School, Cuthbertson House. It was a new world. No more Jenno. Willie McKie as Music Master and Joe Pinner as Housemaster; Joe appeared to have no educational qualifications except an extraordinary capacity to deal with boys. He lived like an amiable spider in a time-web, never forgetting what had already happened, and somehow or other aware in advance of what was going to happen. He could hear through shut doors, and see round corners. One boy, who had been head prefect, came to pay his respects to Joe some ten years after he had left school. When he knocked, Joe called out, "Come in, Lewis."

Willie McKie, with his domed head and flashing eyes, and ferocious discipline at choir practice, was no less demanding but human and humorous at piano lessons. Although one of the greatest of Bach organists, he did not restrict me to Bach nor collapse with exasperation at my mistakes, and when I brought some of my mother's sheet music he allowed me to learn Ravel and Debussy. Not only that, he would ask two or three of us to tea in his rooms, where there were reproductions of Cézanne on the walls. Suddenly there seemed to be a future to school instead of that past imperfect.

There were still far too many hours devoted to compulsory sports. However, although I was as bad as ever at ball games and running and jumping, I won my first and only cup, Under 15 Swimming Champion.

I rowed in crews with success, and on Saturdays we would row for ten miles or so up the Barwon, tying up by willow trees and eating sandwiches and the wonderful apple pies and cream to be bought from a bakery near the boatsheds. One day we were walking in from the willows for a pee when a big, raw-boned boy called Dobber Dobson leaned down very quickly and straightened up with a four-foot brown snake in his hand. He cracked it like a whip and broke its back. "Always wondered if you could do that," he said slowly.

(To my utter astonishment, some thirty years later I received a letter from Brian Dobson, asking me to comment on some translations, enclosed, which he had made from poems by the German poet Erich Kästner, written at the time of the *Neue Sachlichkeit* movement of the 1920s. Thirty years on, you find that head prefects have disappeared into nothingness, and boys everyone had thought boring and insignificant have become famous scientists or Captains of Industry. I can think of three of the latter breed immediately, one of them being Teddy who showed us younger boys how to pull our dicks.)

Darling in the 1930s was a great headmaster, who taught us how to think, and not necessarily to accept either conservative politics or the conventions of provincial Australia. Darling offered us the opportunity to change our opinions without lapsing into anarchy. I was delighted when I found in William Blake's *Poems* the aphorism: "The man who never alters his opinions is like standing water, and breeds reptiles of the mind".

I don't know how Darling got away with his radicalism, having a deeply conservative School Council sitting on top of him. Perhaps it was at the Council's insistence that Ned Austin, a wealthy old (very old) boy, was programmed every now and then to preach the sermon in chapel. Ned was not there to talk, in his gravelly voice which every boy in the school delighted in imitating, about religion, but about the relation of Christianity to capitalism. It seemed that Christ was a kind of upwardly mobile executive who had the misfortune to fall foul of an evil cartel. Being such a Fine Chap, so brave and good, he would not stoop to using Influence; after all, his Old Man could have bust the cartel without any trouble. No, he took it on the chin and died for us all on the Cross as an Example.

There was of course that awkward episode when he drove the money changers out of the Temple, and that idea of his that you should sell everything and give it to the poor, and, worst of all, that "It is easier for a camel to go through the eye of a needle than for a rich man to enter into the kingdom of God".

Ned gamely tackled this one head on, regularly every year. It used to amuse me, even at my early age, to watch Darling wince as Ned continued with his exegesis of this thorny aphorism. Knowing that there were a number of sons of rich men in the school, rich men who should in no way be alienated from subscribing to the Building Fund for the much-needed new House, Ned said that what Jesus really meant was a compliment to rich men. The poor, it seemed, in their simple way would have no trouble in going through the eyes of needles. But for a rich man there were temptations to be overcome, possessions and luxuries to be handled in the right way. Despite all this, with the good grease of Christian humility, a rich man twice the size of a camel would have no trouble with the eye of a needle, all through self-discipline. Ned wound up with the greatest of all advertising slogans: "It's not just a question of faith, boys, but good works as well". At that stage he might almost have put in a plug for the Building Fund, but forced himself to sit down. Or perhaps he caught Darling's eye.

Darling did not only suggest that we question the social system, but he, with considerable skill, also took the risk of regularly mocking the school's sporting heroes, instead of holding them up as desirable models. It was no handicap to be bad at sport. I was such a hopeless footballer that I could not even get into the third house team. With the others who were down at my level, we played a desultory game on what was called the Cowpatch; among my fellow Cowpatch footballers were two of the cleverest boys in the school and one of the most athletic, all of whom nowadays have long entries in *Who's Who*.

But I still couldn't write English essays, although I was reading more than ever. I could never think what to say when I sat down to write those accursed essays, especially given inspiring subjects such as "The Advantages of Being Tall", or, on a higher intellectual level, "Heredity versus Environment". Then, when I was about fourteen, our class was given a new English master, a lumbering man with a squashed nose, who we called Basher Neild because of his nose, not because he ever hit anyone. He told us that he came from a very poor family, and his nose had been flattened from years of pushing it against shop windows looking at all the good things he could not have.

Basher told us to write a story for our English essay, on any subject we liked, a fictional one if possible, but if not, a true one would do. He grinned at us and said in his slow voice, "But how would I know whether it was true or not?" Then he added, "You mightn't know yourselves."

For no reason at all, I made up a story about a railway-engine driver and his mate who were attacked by a swarm of bees; perhaps it had something to do with the day Mick Ridge was bitten on the end of the nose when we were driving back from Kapunda in the Morris. Various adventures then followed. Basher gave me nine out of ten, the best mark in the class. He also offended me deeply by writing at the bottom "Excellent. Original?" I indignantly assured him it was original.

My English marks started to look up. With Basher, whatever the subject, our own or his, there seemed to be some point to essays. Then Darling himself took us for a while. I am eternally grateful for one piece of advice he gave us, which was of course really very simple. He said that when we were given a subject for an essay we shouldn't just start thinking about it when we sat down to write it. We should mull it over when we were having a shave (some of us had achieved this landmark, more or less), when we were walking down to the school baths, when we were polishing our shoes, even when we were sitting on the lavatory (the word "toilet" was not then in approved use; my Edwardian father had always called it the thunder-box). Thus thinking became a part of life, and not a part-time duty.

We were very lucky to have so many good masters. Colin Gordon, later headmaster of St Peter's College in Adelaide, also took us for English. He came from British Guiana, was very tall, and had been an Olympic high-jumper. He had also been at Oxford with my brothers — "Oh, they were so lazy. Mind you, they were fun." He had also been a friend at Oxford of W.H. Auden, he told me when he noticed I was reading a book of Auden's poems. In his drawling voice he said, "Such a pity he and his friends were homosexuals." I didn't really know what a homosexual was, and didn't like to display my ignorance by asking, or ask why it was a pity to be one.

Col, as we called him (of course never to his face), was very elegant, and often wore suede shoes. I at least knew about them, because my brother Dick wore them. In about 1937 I was in a bank at Adelaide cashing a cheque for my mother; on seeing the name "Dutton" the teller asked if I were any relation to Richard Dutton. I told him he was my brother, and he said, "He's a really wild one, that one. He wears suede shoes."

One day we were queueing up in class to be handed our essays back by Col Gordon. In front of me was Allen, a pleasant enough boy, if not exactly a very thoughtful one. "Oh, yes, Allen," said Col in an ominously sarcastic tone. "Listen, boys, listen to this." He picked up the essay with extended fingers, as if it had come out of a rubbish-bin. "I will read you the opening sentence: "Now that I have reached the age when I am able to distinguish between right and wrong ...'." He tore the essay in two and dropped it on the floor.

It was a cruel thing to do to Allen, but the moral went home.

I studied Latin and Greek among my subjects for the Leaving Exam. A lugubrious and amiably ugly man called Polkinghorne taught Greek; our text for study was a speech by Demosthenes about a dispute over drains. When I passed the public exam Polkinghorne said to me, "I don't know who's more surprised, Dutton, you or me." Latin, on the other hand, was the domain of a brilliant teacher, Chauncy Masterman, whose sentences emerged rather floridly above his twitching moustache, but whose enthusiasm for Latin poetry as very much still a living language came across to all of us.

He and his wife also lent their house and her cooking to meetings of the Literary Society, where challenging papers were read, some of them by another likeable master, Barney Hutton, to be followed by a sumptuous supper. However lofty a boarding-school boy's thoughts, they can always be elevated a little more by food. It was at one of those meetings I first heard, from Hutton, about Gerard Manley Hopkins, and began to drive my friends mad by reciting "Glory be to God for dappled things", or "I saw this morning morning's minion".

God, of course, dominated everything at Geelong Grammar School, even J.R. Darling who when not called The Boss was frequently referred to, with reason, as God. We went twice to chapel every day, to morning service and to evensong; the school was small enough in those days for us all to be able to fit into the chapel. When we were old enough to be confirmed we could also go to early morning communion and feel very holy.

For a couple of years, about the time of adolescence, I suffered from a severe bout of holiness, before becoming one of Alexander Pope's mob who "to church repair, / Not for the doctrine but the music there". My cure for this holiness was accelerated by my disillusionnent with the school chaplain, Joey Allen, who struck us all as being quite insincere, as well as vulgar. At one stage it was announced that Joey would give us classes in something called "elocution", the object being for us to develop "naice" voices. I particularly loathed affected boys with "naice" voices. But Joey's voice was irredeemably that of a bookmaker or football commentator.

A miasma of religion and sex hung over the school, even though we didn't know what either of them meant. Darling was obsessed by sin. Religion was all about sin, and life in some inexplicable way was constantly threatened by sin. In my first year in senior school, when I was twelve, Darling was thundering away in a sermon about the sin of lasciviousness. I had never heard of this word, and interpreted what he was saying as "lassy-viciousness". It was obviously a very bad thing to suffer from. It never occurred to me that I was unconsciously indulging in it when I was reading some of my favourite novels, the romances of Jeffery Farnol. These, at thirteen, provided something of the same stimuli as St Cecilia had when I was five.

These dreadful books were about highwaymen who were really gentlemen, aristocrats with names like Sir Marmaduke who said "Good morrow" or "ejaculated 'Deuce take him!' "; rustics who said "dang 'im" or "'osses be wonderful wise"; and, of course, devilish pretty women who "can't be bought".

If only I had known, I was being driven into a frenzy of lassy-viciousness by women like Charmian:

> Tall she was, and nobly shaped, for her wet gown clung, disclosing the sinuous lines of her waist and the bold, full curves of hip and thigh. Her dress, too, had been wrenched and torn at the neck, and, through the shadow of her fallen hair, I caught the ivory gleam of her shoulder, and the heave and tumult of her bosom.

Jeffery Farnol was of course unheard of in the steamy, pre-confirmation evening discussions at Darling's house, with a delicious supper brought in by his patient wife Margaret. Sir Marmaduke and Charmian were off limits. We officially had a new hero: Jenno's Captain Will Power at the Bridge had metamorphosed into Jesus Christ, who seemed to be a cross between Parsifal and Albert Schweitzer, between a purity we could not reach and an intellect we could not understand. Christ of course had no trouble with lassy-viciousness.

Fortunately my reading was not restricted to Jeffrey Farnol, for I was devouring — there is no other word for the voracity of it — all the adventures of Bulldog Drummond and, somewhat more sophisticated, The Saint. Edgar Wallace was also a favourite. But of course these books were of the surface and did not provoke the mysteries of imagination, either in the darker worlds of unexplained symbols, like fairy stories, or in the ivory gleams of untouched skin.

There were dark rumours when a boy was expelled (an event rivalling a hanging in awful finality) that he had been doing unmentionable things with small boys in the Planny. There were other rumours that two boys had just escaped being caught in a foray into the maids' quarters. (The maids were always known as bids; we were appallingly spoiled and unappreciative boys, being waited on at table and having our beds made and dormitories swept out.) This episode in the maids' quarters did not seem to compete in awfulness with the goings on in the Planny.

Of course we all masturbated, and it was murkily proposed that communion, with a regular intake of sanctified bread and wine, would keep us safe from this sin, although it was never mentioned by name; nor was sex. Actually, given that there were some four hundred boys cooped up for months on end without any contact with the other sex, it was amazing that we were so innocent. In my eight years at Geelong I had another boy's hand on my cock only once. It was in 1938, and I was having a pee when Alex, a tough little Sydney kid, finished his pee, and then, as I was flicking off the last drips, he grabbed my cock. "Fuck off," I said. "All right, shithead," he replied, and we both walked out cheerily into the yard.

But there was that catch about the sin in the mind being just as bad as the one in the hand, or wherever. You couldn't win, either way. It was no wonder, then, that when on one occasion a group of boys and masters were reading their favourite poems, Darling's was John Donne's "Wilt thou forgive that sin, where I begun ...".

The insulation from female contact was absolute, except for the bids and the matron in each house; in my day these were of a great age, probably all of forty. Maybe a sister or two of the boys came down with parents in cars on Sunday, but that was all.

There were dancing classes for those who enrolled in them, but we had to take it in turns to dance the girl. My regular dancing partner was Peter Anderson, with whom I had fake-boxed at Wykeham. I can still waltz backwards, and heartily agree with those who think Ginger Rogers had a much more difficult job than Fred Astaire.

If there was a school play the girls were of course always played by boys; it was explained to us that Shakespeare would have approved of this arrangement. There were usually one or two pretty boys who were given these parts, but no lover took them to bed. For years I was in love with the most beautiful boy in the school, and carved his initials on my rubber eraser. I had daydreams in which he always turned into a girl; I would have died rather than attempt to kiss him, let alone any further contact. In the course of this passion I also fell madly in love with Susanne, the willowy sister of my friends Bob and Colin Angas. For her, I had another rubber with MSA carved on it. But I was never game to confess my love to her, although I did so to my mother, in a letter, and begged her to ask Susanne down to Kangaroo Island in the summer. She did not. I have often wondered why; Susanne was eminently "suitable", coming from "an old family" and being rich enough. Perhaps it was because she was only fifteen.

I never talked about either of my loves, the boy or the girl, to any other boy, not even to my friend Deasey, at least not until after we had left school.

Denison Deasey was the most original and subversive boy at Geelong. His father was the Anglican Archdeacon of Geelong, and an Old Boy famous for athletic and academic prowess. He was a nasty old bully; his wife was an invalid with arthritis. There were two elder brothers at school, much older than me, and Denison was two years older than me; one of the brothers became a clergyman; the other, a long-distance runner, drank himself to death at an early age.

One day Dease ran away from school with a boy called Goldie. They hitched a ride to Melbourne, where, by this time, the Reverend Deasey was living in Toorak and was Rector of a fashionable church. Dease, making the best of his newly acquired bass voice, rang the garage where the car had been serviced, saying he was the Reverend Deasey and he was sending his son to pick up the car. They headed for Sydney, but ran out of petrol and money at Albury.

Other runaways looked glum when they were brought back to school, but Dease just looked cheerfully defiant. We realized, with admiration, that he and Goldie had had a great adventure.

Dease was a good musician, and he and I won the Musical Competition for our House with a clarinet and piano sonata by Mozart. Being madly Irish, he persuaded me that the House choir should sing an impossible song called "The Bold, Unbiddable Child". We did not win that section of the Competition. His Irishness had also led to a passion, which I soon shared, for the poetry of Yeats and the plays of Synge.

Dease was the only boy in the school who was excused from the detestable Cadet Corps. He had managed to convince Darling that he was a conscientious objector. While we paraded up and down, or charged over the You Yangs on the manoeuvre called Field Day, he was playing records of the *Eroica* in the Music School.

On one Field Day I was demoted from corporal to private for instructing my men to fire on a platoon we had ambushed; they turned out to be on our own side. After this battle, when we marched down the road into the school, we were led by the School Band. Just inside the front gate was a dais on which stood Darling and the visiting General who was to take the salute. As the Band approached the gates, Dease ran swiftly (he was an excellent runner) out of the Planny and into the middle of the Band. In amongst the khaki in his blue shirt and grey trousers he then provided a splendid clarinet obbligato to the turgid strains of "Colonel Bogey".

Dease was very nearly expelled for this effort, but Joe Pinner persuaded Darling not only to let him stay, but to make him a prefect. Dease was so astonished that he became quite wellbehaved for a while. Alas, my life of comparative virtue never led to my being made a prefect.

Dease, being so much older, left school a year before I did, and I sorely missed his iconoclastic but wildly enthusiastic company. There was no one else I could have such deep talks with, about Life, Art, Love and Death. Very sportingly, he came down one Sunday in his father's car (with permission, this time) and took Bob Fisher and me to lunch in Geelong. I wrote to my mother, "He really is one of the few interesting boys who have ever been here ... He's wonderfully vital and full of interest."

Dease was to become my closest confidant and to remain a friend for the rest of his stormy life.

Six

One miracle of Senior School was that I began to enjoy Easter. Before Easter there was a hymn we used to sing, which I thought not only a travesty of the truth but an insult to those about to be left at school. It began: "This joyful Eastertide, away with sin and sorrow".

Three very friendly and interesting masters, Ponder (whom we called Percy), Priestman and Wallace, completely changed Easter for me and some other boys. They used to take a cottage on the back beach at Sorrento, and they invited two Sydney boys, Bruce Sinclair-Smith (who later edited the school magazine) and Peter Lawrence, and Peter Anderson and myself from South Australia. Priesty had a nifty little Standard roadster, and Wallace hired an old Rugby tourer; its huge wheels ploughed through the sandy tracks rather better than the smart Standard's. The cottages were amidst tea-trees instead of stunted cypresses, there was a surf beach at the door, and there was no talk of sin. We owed the holiday to Jesus, but no one gave him a thought; we had already paid our respects in Chapel.

The other miracle was my mother. Despite Darling's letter, she had only visited me at school that one time, when she arrived in the Buick and we went to Wandiligong. But now, instead of her being on the other side of the world, I could go home to her for the three long holidays; Easter was too short a break to get to South Australia and back in time. She often took over from Bella, the good-natured but not very brilliant cook, to whip up a special treat, like toheroa soup or whitebait from New Zealand; she played the piano with me and went yabbying or shooting.

She had been well-trained in watercolours and oils by an artist in Adelaide, and had a natural talent for drawing. She was now busy painting oils of her beloved flowers from the garden. She was quite a talented painter, but slow, so the flowers usually died before she could finish painting them, but her efforts were really very presentable. Now she taught me to paint in oils (Heckie having introduced me to watercolour), and I spent most of a spring holiday painting, especially wrestling with the view from the drawing room across the garden to Grandfather's Folly, the water-tower. It took several holidays to finish this large painting.

I also at last had a local friend, Jimmy Riddell, the son of the Kapunda doctor who had brought Chibs and me into the world. Doc Riddell had rimless rectangular glasses and a fresh-scrubbed pink face, and always drove the latest model Packard tourer. Those were the days when country doctors went out in all weathers and on every apology for a road to visit their patients. Jimmy's mother had died, and the Doc had married a widow with two girls, and then he and the new wife had a son, so Jimmy's family consisted of mine, yours and ours.

Jimmy was three years older than me, a wiry, cheerful little bloke, on for anything, but all the same, very conscientious. He didn't care for books or paintings, but it was enough to share a passion for Bing Crosby and Fred Astaire. We were true friends, although I used to strain his good nature by insisting that both of us should do useful deeds on the place, like digging out rabbits or hoeing thistles. There was no pleasure at all to be had out of thistles, but there was a strange excitement in locating a rabbit's nest, and pulling out the little kittens from their warm straw in the cool earth. It was an effort to do the right thing and knock them on the head.

Jimmy and I also used to drive out into the paddocks and smoke, deliberately and with insouciance, in the style of Maurice Chevalier or George Sanders. I even managed to buy some Balkan Sobranies, like those Leigh Falkiner had introduced me to. The Buick must have reeked of exotic smoke, but my mother never seemed to notice.

One of the first V-8 Fords had been bought as the station's utility, or buckboard as they were still called. This was an incredibly powerful machine, and very sporty, because it had a collapsible canvas hood. When I was thirteen and Jimmy had just got his license at sixteen, my mother allowed us to go up to Uno by ourselves. The only stipulations were that I was not to drive through any towns, and that we would not go over 50 m.p.h. I was immensely excited at the prospect of Uno, as I had not been there since the trip with my father in 1928, before he and my mother went to England and Europe. It was both generous and trusting of her to allow us to go, and we religiously observed her instructions.

The best present she was ever to give me was the old Morris, the van that used to run into Kapunda for the mail. In no time, with Mick's help, I had removed the old blue van body, leaving nothing but the bonnet, front mudguards and running boards. I cut off the drooping ends of the front mudguards, giving her what I thought was a racy look, and then set about building a dashing new character for the Morris.

Mick showed me how to work the forge, and I became familiar with the joys of winding the handle of the blower in a rising scream until the flames were leaping out of the coke in the forge. Then came the heating of the black steel into a pulsing red, and the ringing zing of the hammer as I banged the steel into shape on the anvil. Then came the big drill, worked off a long belt from one of the pulleys driven by a huge old electric motor that crackled when you turned it on. The drill sighed as it curled out the shining steel ribbons from the hole, and the oil smoked at the tip of the drill. Sometimes, to my dismay, I would press down too hard as the drill was emerging, and it would catch and snap. Mick would scratch his nose and say, yes, such things did happen if you were a bit careless, and get out a new drill for me to fit into the bit.

The first pieces of steel were bent to give a more modern, streamlined look to the old vertical windscreen. Then one length of steel was shaped into an oblong U, and drilled and fitted to the front of the Morris's chassis, and along the top I bolted on the old lights, which had crouched miserably down below the mudguards, together with a large third light which I had found in the workshop. I then painted everything British racing green. The Morris's top speed was about 45 m.p.h.

Going by back tracks because I was too young to have a license, I took the Morris over to Collingrove to show Bob and Colin Angas. They were enchanted, and immediately began to lobby their parents for an old car so they could race me in the Morris. Meanwhile Ron Angas, their handsome father, who Chibs and I always thought the next thing to Clark Gable, sawed me a heavy slab of red gum for a backrest; I found the back of a seat in a wrecker's yard and bolted it on to the red gum.

In the next holidays the boys arrived, with their most desirable sister Susanne, in a 1928 14/40 Bean, which they had beautified with new front mudguards and a superb V windscreen which had originally belonged to a Delage. By this time I had built a wooden tray with sides on the back of the Morris, which meant that someone could sit in the back holding the spotlight when we went out for rabbits, and for foxes whose eyes would suddenly glow out of the darkness in the beam of the spotlight. It was bitterly cold careering around the paddocks on a winter's night at Anlaby or Collingrove, and we would swathe ourselves in scarves and woollen balaclavas, come home with aching fingertips and drink cup after cup of hot Bournvita.

In the long vacation at the end of 1938 I was one of a group of boys from Melbourne Grammar School, Scotch College and Geelong Grammar who went on a six-week trip to India. The British Raj was then in full sway, and we were staggered by the power of Imperialism, that a few British civil servants and soldiers could rule millions of so many peoples, as if it were by the nature of things. The Melbourne Grammar parson, known to us as Dingo Clark, who was in charge of our group, had spent many years in India and had very good contacts. We were often billeted out to the British, some of whom lived in astonishing luxury. When we were in Calcutta, one lucky boy slept in satin sheets and had two servants and a Rolls-Royce at his disposal.

We learned about colour and racism; of course, at home none of us had questioned the White Australia Policy. We were amazed that so many Indians accepted the British caste system as well as their own. In Delhi we were given a sumptuous lunch by a famous Maharaja. We then went to afternoon tea at a British club. There was a fleet of the Maharaja's cars to take us to the club; another boy and I were told by the Maharaja to come with him in his Rolls-Royce. When we arrived at the club, a servant opened the door of the car and we waited for the Maharaja to get out. But he sat tight, and waved us to the door, saying, "I'm a coloured chappie, don't you know, I'm not allowed in the club." But he said it with a smile, as if he didn't mind.

In various places we met Indian writers and intellectuals who talked at enormous speed about the infamies of Imperialism. We wondered how safe they were, taking such risks, when so many of their leaders were in gaol. The benign British Empire began to look a bit different.

What appalled me most about India was not Imperialism but the poverty and the Indian caste system. I had never seen so many millions of people, and half of them seemed to be missing an arm or a leg and to be out in the streets begging. We were told that the sweeper who cleaned the lavatories was an Untouchable. The British class system was mild compared with this.

This journey was invaluable for my development, although it took many years for me to absorb all that I had learned. In the face of this world, our Australia seemed remote and its emptiness alarming. What if a few millions of these people decided to populate our millions of acres? The British Navy would protect us, of course.

In the other world, of school, although I found history (always European, never Australian) and Latin interesting, I was on the trail of never-failing new discoveries in music and English. Not that I had much talent as a pianist; I had to practise hard in the little soundproof rooms of the magnificent new music school, but it was worth it. What I glimpsed in my own efforts, and in singing in the choir, opened into the huge landscapes of the works of the great composers, where you could look again and again at the same entrancing view, or hike over the hill and find a new river, valley or mountain. Dvorak's New World Symphony had exactly the right name. And every Sunday evening, after chapel, Willie McKie would give an organ recital, always beginning with Bach, and then going on to a more modern composer.

As a reader I raced all over the place like a hunting dog in a paddock full of rabbits. The commonplace book, which I began in 1938 to fill with poems or extracts from prose works or plays, veers widely from *Peer Gynt* to Stephen Spender's "The Express", from Helen Waddell's *Peter Abelard* to *Lust for Life*, from Sir Walter Ralegh's "Even Such is Time" to Richard Aldington's "Dream in the Luxembourg", from Dorothy Parker's *Not So Deep as a Well* to Hans Andersen's *Fairy Tales*, which I read with new insights, in the beautiful Cobden-Sanderson edition illustrated by Rex Whistler.

I was completely bowled over by the discovery of modern poetry, and it was encapsulated in Michael Roberts' *Faber Book of Modern Verse*; one pleasing aspect of this book was that it included American poets like Marianne Moore, Wallace Stevens and Richard Eberhart, whose work was very hard to come by in Australia. For the next few years Roberts' anthology was to remain my bible. Not only mine; I remember an earnest boy, although I have forgotten his name, who brandished the book under my nose and said that he was going to have read and understood every poem in the book by the end of the holidays. I wished him luck. I couldn't understand half of them, but they still excited me and I thought that some day enlightenment would dawn.

Once again, nothing Australian; in all my years at Geelong not an hour was spent on Australian history or literature. In my own reading were lots of books by Ion L. Idriess, like *Lasseter's Last Ride* which at last filled in the back country and desert landscape which I had approached at Uno, and roused my imagination with adventure and dreams of gold. On a different literary level I discovered *Robbery Under Arms*. For the first time I found the true, unselfconscious Australian idiom in a book.

> It took us an hour's hard dinkum to get near the peak. Sometimes it was awful rocky, as well as scrubby, and the poor devils of cattle got as sore-footed as babies — blood up to the knee, some of 'em; but we crowded 'em on; there was no help for it.

The Marstons reminded me of the Learmonth family at Uno, although Jack and the boys were not into bushranging. (Not quite; I remember over a few years small numbers of sheep kept disappearing without trace, and Jack's explanation to my brother John was "They just run away into the hills and died, Mr Dutton".) *Robbery Under Arms* also brought the bush and my imagination together, in Terrible Hollow where the cattle were hidden. In a notable development from Jeffery Farnol's Sir Marmadukes, there was a gentleman who was as tough as an Australian, Captain Starlight, with the mystery of his past and what drove him to the bushranger's life. His devoted companion, the half-caste Warrigal, with his natural grace and humour, was the first Aborigine I had met in a book until I read *We of the Never-Never* a few years later. The decency of the Marstons, despite their life, struck me, and still does, as being quintessentially Australian; in addition, there was nothing mealy-mouthed about them, and Dick's sense of sin was comprehensible.

Other books interpreted a world of which the foundations were shaking, like foreign correspondent Douglas Reed's *Insanity Fair*, which detailed exactly what Hitler had done. I remembered my mother and Chibs arriving in Austria in time for the murder of Dr Dollfuss. Reed predicted what Hitler was going to do. Reed was not impressed by what he called the "British do-lets-try-and-get-together trips to dictators". My copy of *Insanity Fair* was the thirteenth edition in two months; the book had been first published in April 1938. Why didn't anybody listen? Why should Australia be dragged into this insanity? Why did we have to be implicated in British and French pusillanimity?

There was an unexpected incidental interest in reading *Insanity Fair*. I discovered that Douglas Reed had covered the story of KG's restoration to the throne of Greece. And I had not realized that KG's mother was the sister of Kaiser Wilhelm of Germany. Reed's description was exactly like the photos my mother had shown me: "How Prussian he looks, I thought ... His bottle-green uniform was on the French model, but his monocle, his features and his bearing all reminded me strongly of a Prussian officer."

Everything to do with reading and writing accelerated in my last two years at school, 1938 and 1939. No English master after Basher Neild encouraged us to write fiction, although once I wrote a play instead of an essay and then decided it was no good. But I did discover that English essays could be about art or music or literature as well as the ethical pseudo-profundities of "Heroes and Hero-Worship". Darling set us a subject for an essay, a quotation from Shakespeare, which at first reduced me to indignation. It was simply: "Thoughts all confused, my Lord". I wrote to my mother: "How in the name of fortune one can write an essay about that I don't know". A few weeks later I was writing: "I was amazed last week, because I wrote a few pages about modern art and music for that essay on 'Thoughts all confused', not seeing myself that it had much to do with the point, and yet I was informed that it was an excellent essay, well developed on a good theme!!!!! I'm regaining confidence."

In 1939 Russel Ward took over Sixth Form English. I was electrified by this young (he was 24) man who urged us to read *The Waste Land*, saying he was not sure what it meant himself, but it was a poem we just had to read. He told us about the Spanish Civil War and Picasso's *Guernica*, painted in 1937. He seemed to know Auden and Spender backwards, and wrote poetry himself. And he was a good rowing coach.

A week after my birthday in August I was writing to my mother: "Mr Ward said my last essay was the best he'd seen. I came 1st with 89, the next was 61, on Modern Poetry. As you perhaps know, to have come 1st in the School in English pleases me far more than to have come 1st in anything else. It makes you feel that perhaps you might be able to become something after all."

What this indicated, of course, was that for some time I had been writing for myself, mostly poems, well aware of their deficiencies, but at least learning more about looking at the world, by the difficulties of the art of using words. I wrote in a letter home: "Writing poetry, however bad and prosaic, at least teaches you, like painting, to be more observant. I've just finished a book (in French) on Degas. He was really most interesting. He says, I hope I've translated correctly, 'There is an immense difference between seeing a thing without a pencil in your hand, and seeing it when you are drawing it'. He also has a marvellous description of a horse, 'All nervously naked in its robe of silk'." To have come upon that last image was worth more to me than hours of those early English lessons at school.

I had begun, in an incongruous school book with the school badge and motto on the front cover, to write down poems, stories and "deep thoughts". The first poem is headed "Imagination"; somewhat later, and very reasonably, I had written "BALLS" in huge letters up the page. A similar message on another poem comes with a translation: "Balls ... i.e.bloody awful".

The thoughts are often more interesting than the poems. "Dreadful, shocking, demoralizing dullness of the middle class explained by complete lack of imagination— it's been killed." "The man who lives in realism cannot in this age of sordid and disinterested [I suppose I meant "uninterested"] despair, help becoming hopeless and disinterested himself."

I remember wondering at the time, and still do, how the minds of children can ever develop on a diet of facts. Darling and a handful of masters had been the first to stimulate my imagination in my long years at school. But perhaps this is too much to ask of teachers, and one could vary Marie Antoinette and say "Let them read books".

The influence of Auden and Spender, and a rapidly accelerating exasperation with orthodox religion, fume out of a poem inscribed "To The Faithful", which ends:

Pray for God's grace not to see the misery
Choking down potentialities of beauty
But the joy and glory of the heavens
Where as honest churchman you must finish,
Knees worn out, eyeballs rooted upwards.

Joey Allen set us an essay: "On what do you think the authority of a church should be based?". I copied this down, and then wrote underneath: "ON NOTHING, my dear Holy Joe. So stuff that." I cannot remember what Joey thought of the finished essay. It ends: "The church should be there as a vehicle for outward observance only, a handy officiating machine, not as an authoritative body. By this I mean that a church should have no authority and consequently nothing to rest it upon."

I could be doctrinaire and forceful about religion, but not about love. A poem to Susanne, intertwined with her initials and her name written in swan's-neck languishing letters, says that I fear madness at her touch, but that is not likely to happen because "At her sight / I lose my might". The page has a crude but correct comment in the margin: "Slops of the mind".

I was friendly with the two cleverest boys in the school, Bob Southey and Jim Gardiner, who came top of the state in various subjects in Leaving

Honours; Bob was a classicist, Jim a scientist. Rather to my chagrin, Bob won the poetry prize with a batch of well-turned sonnets. Barney Hutton, one of the judges, said that he thought I would turn out to be the poet rather than Bob; Bob was generous enough to agree.

Jim was also the most beautiful boy in the school; he was always given the girl's part in plays. In *Alpha and Omega,* one of the school pageants, enormous spectacles where boys like myself who were too dumb to act were given appropriate non-speaking parts, Jim was a Babylonian princess. He/she was carried in a litter by two black slaves, while I, another slave, walked in front carrying a huge fan. We were blackened by boot polish; it is a wonder that we did not expire. The slave carrying the front of the litter was Stephen Murray-Smith. Steve was one of those fat boys who are teased, but so good-natured he never complained. He was thoroughly likeable, but at that stage, as far as I ever knew, displayed none of that passion for Australian literature that was to make him one of the best-known editors and writers in Australia.

J.R. Darling, The Boss, had left for England early in March 1939 and did not return in my school days. The Acting Headmaster was Charlie Cameron, a dry, boring, second-rate physics and maths teacher. I felt that all the free-thinking and reforming zeal that Darling had encouraged had vanished from the direction of the school. There is one quite interesting poem, not too badly written and rhyming and scanning correctly, headed "On the Absence of J.R.D.", in which I lament this decay.

I rediscovered this poem only recently, after 53 years, and sent it to Darling, then aged 93. He wrote back, in his excellent, unchanging hand, to thank me and said "I enjoyed the time up to 1939 but it was a mistake to leave you in that year ... It was never quite the same again."

There were also comings and goings in my family during the 1930s. The best news was Chibs' return to Australia. She was at school in Rome at the time of the war in Abyssinia, when there were sanctions against Italy. Fascists spat in the faces of English-speaking people and stones were thrown. Chibs made up her own mind to get out of Italy. So there she was, sitting beside me in the Morris, or driving us out spotlight-shooting, and getting hopelessly lost in the dark paddocks she knew so well by day. One night, urged on by us in pursuit of a fox, she drove us into a dry creek bed. We had to walk home, as the Morris's front wheels were facing each other. But cars were simple in those days, and Mick and I removed the front axle and took it into Hawke & Co, the engineeers in Kapunda, who swiftly straightened it.

My brother John, who had been jackerooing at Hartwood in the Riverina, returned to manage Anlaby and Uno. He also bought a property,

Burleigh, near Mt Gambier, where land at that time was cheap if drab, but very productive, with a reliable rainfall. The house was not very beautiful, built in the 1920s of dreary Mt Gambier limestone, which is so soft you can saw it into building blocks. If you wanted hot water in the shower you stuffed a newspaper into the chip heater and applied a match.

For a while John installed a manager at Burleigh, and continued to live at Anlaby. It was a tricky situation, with the two brothers at home. I remember coming back for the holidays and finding John with his ankle in plaster. He had broken it, allegedly by falling out of the Packard when Dick was driving them back to the cottage. It did not seem very plausible; Dick and he were very stiff together for a while.

But John had further plans. He had become engaged to a Melbourne girl, Peggy Horn, pretty and unrelentingly vivacious, quite unlike slow-moving, introverted John. He cunningly made a secret rendezvous with her in London, and in 1936 they were married there, so my mother was unable to upstage the bride. But when they returned to South Australia, they were foolish enough to go to live at Anlaby, where my mother had done up the downstairs rooms for them. It was not suggested that they move into either of the big spare rooms, each of which had a bathroom attached. From where they were, the nearest bathroom was a long walk. After a while they could stand it no longer, and moved to Burleigh, where they were a good two hundred and fifty miles from my mother at Anlaby.

Not so Dick and Margaret, living in the cottage on the other side of the courtyard. About this time, Dick learned to fly, and with typical over-confidence, when he had only done about ten hours solo, he flew up to Anlaby in a Gipsy Moth. He swooped over the houses and roared up into the sky above the half-dozen people waving to him from the courtyard. Coming back towards them in a steep turn, he was too busy looking at them to watch his airspeed, and he spun in and crashed into the ninety-foot-square courtyard. When the dust had settled, there was the aircraft, right side up, Dick still in the cockpit, the nose and propellor a couple of feet from the office wall and the port wing touching the door of the workshop. The faithful Gipsy Moth did not catch fire, and Dick broke only a small bone in his wrist. One of his guests was severely bruised when a wing hit her upraised arm. Never mind about Dick, it was a miracle none of the spectators was killed.

Dick was now supposed to be managing Anlaby and supervising Harry Edkins, who was managing Uno; this was a highly complex job for which he had no qualifications. At least John had done his training as a jackeroo, under one of the best and toughest sheep men in Australia, Hunter Patterson, and he had developed a very good eye for breeding strains. Dick knew nothing, and gave no time to learning. Dick should have gone into politics, with his intelligence and his curiosity about the world, his easy way with people and his flow of talk. And Margie would have been a great asset. His interest in all things American could have been a corrective to Australia's fixation on Britain. But he was too lazy, and Anlaby too comfortable a berth.

Always a heavy drinker, he was now following in his father's disastrous footsteps. We would be driving through Kapunda on the way back from Adelaide, and there would be the Packard outside the Sir John Franklin Hotel, looking like a grandee from another world between the Dodges and the Fords. Chibs and I and a girlfriend of hers, out shooting one day, saw the Packard in a dry creek bed and drove over to find out what had happened. The car was undamaged, but not so its owner, who, to our acute embarrassment in front of the visitor, had passed out in a sprawl across the front seat.

It seemed that Dick, like my father, was a binge drinker, for he was his usual affectionate, good-hearted self in between bouts. He had seemed particularly happy when Margie had a daughter, Léonie, whom he adored. On one occasion he built her a beautiful big fenced-in playpen, complete with a couple of tons of sand from the Waterloo Creek, where she could play in safety from dogs or snakes. Léonie was an enchanting child; I taught her how to swim. Fortunately she had a steady person always near her, a Nanny who remained a close friend for life.

When John first came back from London to Anlaby, he brought with him two magnificent cars: a 1927 Vauxhall 30/98 tourer, and a 1934 supercharged Monthlery MG racing car. Between them, they cost him less than 300 pounds; they would be worth a fortune today. He raced the MG in the 1936 Grand Prix at Victor Harbor.

One day when Colin Angas was staying with me, he and I went into Kapunda in the Vauxhall with John. We were seated in the back, the wind blowing our hair and the exhaust roaring behind us. It was dry, and the dirt track good, and John was doing about eighty miles an hour down one straight and forgot about a drain in the road. When we hit it, Colin and I shot up into the air but the car of course went on. We landed, rather painfully, just on the very back curve of the body, and, fortunately, fell forward into the seat again.

This rear half of the car's body unbolted for racing, and a pointed tail was fitted. I was allowed to go as "mechanic" in the speed trials at Sellick's Beach; my duties were to work a brass pump madly to keep up a strong petrol supply to the engine. John broke the Australian B Class record in the Vauxhall, at about 100 m.p.h., on Sellick's Beach. One time the Packard and the Vauxhall were raced by the two brothers; the Packard, with its enormous V12 engine, accelerated faster, but the Vauxhall reached a higher speed, being lighter on the slightly damp beach.

A year or so after John's departure for Burleigh I was having breakfast at school, sitting next to the master at the head of the table, a man whose name I forget, but I remember that we all disliked him. He was reading the paper, and he turned to me and said in a matter-of-fact voice, "Have you got any relations in South Australia? A chap called John Dutton went into the Blue Lake at Mt Gambier in his Vauxhall racing car, and is not expected to live." I was never particularly close to John, but this did seem a bit abrupt.

It was some time before I could find out whether he was alive or dead, as my mother had flown with Dick and Margaret to Mt Gambier, where John was in the hospital. He had been driving home to Burleigh on a wet night, round the rim of the Blue Lake, which is an extinct volcano crater. The local vet came skidding round the corner on the wrong side, and forced John over the edge. Fortunately the Vauxhall did not have a hood, and John was thrown out, to land on the only substantial bush, about halfway down the precipitous 200-foot slope to the water. The car then ran over him, breaking most of his ribs and sticking some of them into his liver and spleen, and went on down to the bottom, in 260 feet of water. John's last sight, before he passed out, was of the lemon rays of light from the still-burning headlamps, swivelling down through the lake as the car sank.

The vet continued on his way into Mt Gambier, had a couple more drinks and then remembered about John. A heroic policeman descended on a rope, tied another around John, and they were then pulled to the top. John survived, and never suffered any after-effects.

A year later a man called Howard bought the rights to the car from the insurance company for one pound, launched a pontoon on the lake, located the Vauxhall electrically, and winched it all 260 feet up to the surface. It was hardly damaged, and all its tyres were still blown up. Some forty years later, the then owner of the Vauxhall told me that it was still good for a comfortable 100 m.p.h. He let me drive the old charger. In the early 1990s it was being meticulously restored by a new owner in Sydney.

By late 1938 Dick was in a bad way, and a manager had been appointed to take charge of Anlaby, with Harry Edkins running Uno. In a fit of sheer madness Dick suddenly took a ship to Europe, got off in Marseilles, hired a Rolls-Royce and drove to London to see his old friends.

He had borrowed money from my mother and John, and Margaret could not afford to run the Packard any more (not surprisingly, as it did about eight miles to the gallon), and it was decided to sell it, in Melbourne, where a better price would be likely. I knew nothing of all this, but was very suprised one afternoon to see the Packard sweep round in front of the school to stop at Cuthbertson House. Out stepped Chibs, who had agreed to take the car to Melbourne. I went for a last drive, this time at the wheel myself, when we reached 100 m.p.h. well before the railway-line crossing.

In my last year at school, World War II broke out in September, and Australia immediately and obediently followed Britain. John and Dick joined up in the army, and in 1940 John sailed for the Middle East with the 9th Division AIF, as a gunner in the 2nd 7th Artillery.

My mother, who had always been involved with the Red Cross, was put in charge of training country people in first aid. When caught in London by the outbreak of the First World War, she had trained in the famous classes on emergency nursing given by Sir James Cantlie. Now there was a selfless outlet for her energies and knowledge and she stormed into it, travelling thousands of miles all over South Australia in the new Buick and addressing meetings.

Writing to Dease in September 1939, I was complaining that I had been alone for a fortnight. My mother had never made me work on the station in my holidays, as Ron Angas made his boys. I was grateful for the freedom, but with typical teenage crankiness used to throw myself into some sort of activity, as with Jimmy Riddell and the rabbits and thistles. But being left alone at home meant many hours of uninterrupted reading. With a splendid eclecticism I urged Dease to read, as soon as possible, Voltaire's *Candide* and *Zadig*, Tolstoy, Dante, Synge, Marlowe and Apuleius. At last I could make free of my father's library, although I concentrated on international literature and did not open the books of the history of my own country in his superb collection of Australiana.

Now I could lift out and open books like the Nonesuch edition of Dante with Botticelli's drawings, each illustration cleverly bound so that it could spread out without being jammed in the binding. Apuleius' *Golden Asse* was in a Golden Cockerell Press edition with sexy woodcuts by Eric Gill. There was a William Morris's Kelmscott Press edition of Spenser's *Faerie Queene,* and an edition, by the Ashendene Press, of Spenser's shorter poems, which was so big I could only just lay it open on the Steinway.

These limited editions, with their beautifully firm paper, elegant print, and gleaming leather or sleek vellum bindings, stimulated the senses as well as the mind. The library, in which my mother had had her afternoon tea parties and drinks before lunch for Important Visitors, had been a room for me in which I played the piano to a mute audience of unopened books. It now became what my father had created but not laid open, a wonderful library of books to be read. But it was still significant that there was no reading table in the library, an indication of its peculiar role in my parents' lives. There was the Cromwellian oak table on which afternoon tea was laid out, with its ancient waxed wood that glowed darkly, and my mother's wicker-backed high chair with the tapestry cushion, and other leather chairs, but neither chairs nor table were suitable for reading. So I laid Spenser's sonnets out on the Steinway and read standing up, or else lay on the carpet.

Another revelation in these September holidays was the Melbourne *Herald* touring exhibition of modern art, an exhibition which changed the course of the history of Australian art, and drove the guardians of orthodoxy into frenzy. It seemed impossible, but it was true, that here in front of our eyes were 215 works including 9 Picassos, 8 Van Goghs, 7 Cézannes and 6 Bonnards. Gum trees at dusk and southern aspects of cows looking north had never been like this. I came back again and again, wandering for hours among these marvels. My mother approved of my enthusiasm, although she did not altogether share it, but to her eternal credit went to Mr Preece's bookshop and bought me Phaidon Press, Skira and other books about Cézanne, Van Gogh, Renoir and the Impressionists. For the first time both books about modern art and the actual paintings themselves impinged on the Australian consciousness. But, alas, it was typical of the aesthetically timid yet brashly boorish conservatism of art institutions in Australia that this unparalleled exhibition, in which many of the paintings were for sale, was to remain in storage for the rest of the war. A very few, mostly minor, paintings were bought for Australian galleries.

Meanwhile, at the time when John's regiment was preparing to go overseas, Dick went to the army camp at Puckapunyal in Victoria. But he was too far gone, and was soon discharged for medical reasons. By this time Margie, Léonie and the nanny had moved to Adelaide. Most of the time no one knew just where Dick was; sometimes a letter would come from Sydney, where he seemed to have fallen into the clutches of a man described by my mother's Sydney friends as really evil. The last time I saw Dick was when he returned briefly to Adelaide. Once so handsome, he had become very fleshy and red-faced. He borrowed more money from my mother, and with it bought her a very expensive silver and pigskin writing case, and gave me ten pounds, before disappearing back to Sydney.

On Friday 13 December 1940, when Chibs and I were both at home at Anlaby, the phone rang early one morning. A few minutes later my mother came round the corridor with a white face. She said to Chibs and me: "Darling Dickie is at rest. Thank God." The circumstances of his death have always remained unsatisfyingly obscure; the official story was that he had slipped in the bath, and since he was such a heavy man, the fall had broken his neck. The official report said there was no suspicion of foul play or suicide. But it seems a very odd death. What a wasted life, the second in my immediate family.

Seven

This year 1940 was a tragic one for much of the world, but for me it was the happiest and most productive of my first eighteen years. I joined St Mark's College in Adelaide, and enrolled for English, History and French at the University, and arranged to continue my piano lessons with Brewster Jones, a talented composer and brilliant pianist.

Before the term started I went to stay with Dease in the gloomy house in Lansell Road, Toorak. Dease was like me, the youngest; his two brothers and two sisters were in and out of the house, while his mother lay in bed, crippled with arthritis, but like Pope's spider her touch was "exquisitely fine! Feels at each thread, and lives along the line". She not only knew everything her five children were doing but where everything in the house could be found. Randall would come in to her bedroom and complain that he couldn't find his tennis racket. "Don't you remember, dear, when you were tidying your room you put it in the cupboard under the stairs." Denison would complain that we wanted to play the recording of Schumann's "*Dichterliebe*", but some ratbag had pinched it. "But, dear, you were going to take it in to play at Max Nicholson's, and you put it in your briefcase."

Just round the corner Yehudi Menuhin was staying with the Nicholas family (he later married a Nicholas daughter, and his sister Hepzibah a Nicholas son). We slipped in through the gates and hid in the shrubbery and heard him play a Bach chaconne, the most exciting musical event of my life until then.

Then the whole family, except the Reverend Deasey — a blessed relief — moved up to Mount Macedon in the cool hills, where a large house with an English garden had been rented. There we would walk through the splendidly towering bush, by the arching tree ferns, all so different from sparse South Australia, or sit in the house in peace and comfort. Unconscious of the incongruity, we would play German songs and read German poetry and agonize over our *Weltschmerz*, our *Sehnsucht*, our *grossen Schmerzen*. From our sighs arose a choir of nightingales, although of course we had never seen, let alone heard, a nightingale.

Why did two healthy, cheerful, well-fed and comfortably housed boys go on like this in Australia? I suppose, apart from the usual adolescent longings, it was a surge of the romanticism we had missed at school and in the pragmatic world of Australia in the 1930s. Unrequited love was naturally the main cause, in both our cases the object of love being like a lady in the strict rules of medieval courtly love, totally unattainable, although in fact all we had to do was declare ourselves and our loves might have been requited.

Dease later wrote about his adored Ailsa: "Do I bore you? Let us make a compact to eliminate this phrase ... I have never touched her — I doubt whether my reason would survive it — seriously. Have we ever discussed the extent to which pure love thinks of the body of the beloved? No woman has attracted me more in her fleshly being." Dease was dismayed that she was enjoying herself in the fleshpots of fashionable Portsea. "Why oh why do the most desirable women have such an unfortunate upbringing?"

We had long discussions of poetry, and he was carried away when I introduced him to Hopkins. "I walk about roaring out 'dapple-dawn-drawn Falcon' at the top of my voice!" In the throes of aesthetic pleasure Dease always had to explode into action; he drove me mad when we were playing our favourites of the time, like the *Eroica* or the Sibelius Second Symphony, by leaping to his feet, striding around the room conducting a vast orchestra.

He read my own poems with great interest and useful comment, sometimes even being kind about them. "I wish I could write poetry as you do, old bean. Whatever you may lack, you know how to cut a statue clean. Not so me. (Yes, me!)"

The times did genuinely intrude on our romanticism. We both knew we could not avoid the war. In one letter he tackled this gnawing problem: "Has it occurred to you that we have perhaps two years in which to read all the books, write all the poetry, live all the love, hear all the music? What space does this leave for History or English courses? One cannot define sin, but I know that not to live the fullest life possible in this short space would be a real sin. The poem that most returns to me these days is Marvell, 'Had we but world enough ...' " Of course Dease was also using the war as an excuse for not going to the University; those courses were a potential threat to his freedom.

In Melbourne Dease introduced me to Arthur Boyd, one of whose lovely early Rosebud landscapes, painted when Arthur was about sixteen, hung on his bedroom wall. Arthur, with his shambly walk, lopsided grin and lock of hair falling across his forehead, was (and has remained) a true original; he is now Australia's greatest living painter. At the time he was temporarily abandoning landscape and painting Melbourne streets and buildings or foreshores, populated with dancing gargoyles or tormented lovers. He too, however far away we were in Australia, was afflicted by the war, by the basic unease of the times.

Dease had met Arthur through Max Nicholson, a great supporter of Arthur's. Dease had written about Max before I met him, speaking of "the necessity of broadening one's acquaintance to include rather dirty intellectuals — such as Max Nicholson, who lives in a garret in Carlton. The curse of it seems to me that they have not grown out of the homosexual stage." What an innocent remark! Max was rewardingly sophisticated, and had a highly idiosyncratic appearance and manner. Everything was pointed up and exquisitely shaped with Max, from his nose to his cupid's bow mouth to the extended tips of his fingers. He bowed slightly to you as he talked in his mellifluous voice about the latest in art or music or drama, always the delighted entrepreneur, not at all dismayed that he was not a creator himself.

His loft in Carlton was much in demand with lovers. If Max was sympathetic to a pair of lovers with nowhere to go to do the deed, he would lend them the loft, which could only be entered through a trapdoor at the top of a ladder. There was a heavy trunk on the floor, which could be slid across the trapdoor, making the garret impregnable to rivals or wowsers. If the lucky couple stayed too long, Max would hammer on the trap from below with a broom handle, calling out "Time's up, time's up".

Dease took me to Little Collins Street and introduced me to Gino Nibbi at his Leonardo Art Shop (so often incorrectly called "Leonardo Book Shop" by later historians). I had never met an Italian, let alone one who had known Modigliani and de Chirico. In this sanctuary in Little Collins Street, which meant more to us than any cathedral, art and literature lived side by side, bulging out into the street.

Gino, sturdy but sleek, with brushed-back hair, treated us like favourite students, although we had known no teachers like him, as he talked with equal zestful fluency about Rimbaud or Rilke, Goethe or Dante, Braque or Piero di Cosimo. On the walls of the shop, battling for space with the books, were prints of Modigliani, Matisse, Breughel, Piero della Francesca, Chagall, Cézanne, and postcards which we bought by the dozen. On an early visit I bought a postcard and wrote to Dease: "I sent a Christmas card, a Cézanne Mont something or other, to Willie McKie today. I hope he gets it, as he was very keen on Cézanne." (Willie had been appointed organist and choir master at Magdalen College, Oxford.)

At the Leonardo Art Shop young painters like Bert Tucker, Sid Nolan and Arthur Boyd learned about modern art (and a lot of classical art) through Gino, his books, his reproductions and his conversation, for there were almost no great originals in Australia for them to see. Gino Nibbi's name should be enshrined in all histories of modern art and literature in Australia.

I was a bit nervous of being disappointed when the term started in Adelaide. Who in little Adelaide would not seem dull after Nibbi, Dease, Arthur Boyd and Max Nicholson?

My mother had long since introduced me to her old friend John Preece, who with his brother ran a remarkable Adelaide bookshop; upstairs there was a French department run by another man, who was an expert in

French literature. Preece himself, of course, unlike Nibbi, was orientated to England, and he had all the advance notices of new books airmailed to him from London; thus, even though they had to make a six-week sea voyage, he had the latest novel or book of poems very close to the date of their publication in London. The most exciting books I bought from him were those Faber & Faber poets, handsomely printed even in wartime, volumes of Eliot, Auden, Spender and MacNeice. Preece was also an enthusiast for Roy Campbell and the very young poets like Dylan Thomas and the New Apocalypse writers, most of them forgotten now, like Henry Treece, J.F. Hendry and David Gascoyne. Despite their obscurity, there was a vitality of fresh imagery and personal involvement in their work. I also came across some wiry but sensuous poems by a poet called Alex Comfort which appealed to me very much; there was one in Michael Roberts' anthology which began: "There is a white mare that my love keeps / unridden in a hillside meadow". I too wanted to ride "her thighs' white horses". Comfort, who was also a medical man, later became famous for his books about the joys of sex.

Between Preece and Nibbi I collected and immersed myself in German poets like Rilke, Novalis and Hölderlin, as well as the French poets like Baudelaire and Rimbaud. I corresponded with Dease about them, and of course his favourite, W.B. Yeats, also one of mine. In the little smoking room at Anlaby was a remarkable collection of first editions of all Yeats' books up to my father's death in 1932. Preece had all the later volumes.

At the University, I had as English Professor J.I.M. Stewart (who also wrote detective stories under the name of Michael Innes), a man of formidable learning and contemporary discrimination, who introduced us to William Dunbar and James Joyce with equal sparkle. Despite the handicap of rather a high, squeaky voice, and a face like a mouse with glasses, he read poetry beautifully, and could cope with the Scots dialect of Dunbar, and, in Dunbar's greatest poem, with that refrain that rings out like a funeral bell, "*Timor mortis conturbat me*".

Stewart urged me to read James Joyce's *Ulysses*; thanks to Dease I was already familiar with *Dubliners* and *Portrait of the Artist*. I had my first brush with Australian censorship when I attempted to borrow *Ulysses* from the Barr Smith Library. The book was banned in Australia, along with a generous selection of the world's masterpieces, and the Barr Smith Library's copy, kept in the strongroom, was only handed over on receipt of a letter from Professor Stewart authorizing it for purposes of study.

My History Professor was Gerry Portus, whose *History of Australia* was a standard text, never used by Gerry at the University because there was no course in Australian history, any more than there was one on Australian literature. Gerry would have liked to have written D.H. Lawrence's poem "How beastly the bourgeois is!". He never lost an opportunity of reminding us of the inadequacies of bourgeois society as it was worshipped in Adelaide, and the gross inequities of capitalism. He particularly hated what he called "two-car families", a phrase he would roll out with a sarcastic smile and a flash of his round glasses. (To have two cars in Adelaide in 1940 was a parade of opulence.) He got our measure in his first lecture, for my friends and I had all seated ourselves in the back row, which made it easier to comment to each other, and clearly indicated that we did not wish to be teacher's pets. He would pause in an elucidation of feudalism and lift his chin and say in a specially loud but mock-pleading voice: "Perhaps one of the scholars in the back row could tell us about *droit de seigneur*?"

I never knew Gerry give a dull lecture. He had been in the priesthood, but couldn't stand the religious life. He was also an international rugby footballer. Some enlightened member of the Adelaide Club put him up for membership, but he was blackballed, being considered by Club members to be undoubtedly a Communist. Many years later, one of the most eminent (by Adelaide standards) members of the Club said to me: "Pity Gerry Portus went in for that socialist nonsense. If he hadn't, he'd have been a member of the Club and really got to the top."

The only lecturer at Adelaide who had any knowledge of Australian literature was Brian Elliott, but without any Australian Literature course his advice could be taken only marginally. Brian was an amiable enthusiast; he urged me to read a writer I had never heard of, Patrick White. White's only published novel then was *Happy Valley*; at least it was not stuck fast in Australian realism, but it was dominated by James Joyce, and I was deep in the master himself, and found *Happy Valley* a bit mannered and flimsy. I think more of it now, and regret that White would never allow it to be republished.

There was a profusion of brilliant scholars and teachers at Adelaide University in 1940: Antarctic explorer Sir Douglas Mawson in Geology, Kerr Grant in Physics, my father's friend Stanton Hicks in Pathology and many others, quite remarkable in such a small university.

I was equally lucky at St Mark's. The Master, Archibald Grenfell Price, bald and beaming with a chirpy manner easy to imitate, was a pioneer of Australian history and geography. He also, unlike those in power, was acutely aware of the dangers emanating from Japan, and gave us many informal talks of warning on the subject. What was so good for one's self-esteem was that he treated us as men, and always referred to the college members as men. As well, he told us about the difference between university and school, how we were now our own masters. What bliss it was not to have any of the compulsory idiocies of school, like the Cadet Corps and sport every afternoon, and not to be fettered in a repressive framework of sin and punishment.

If we wanted to make fools of ourselves we could. One night Mrs Price had organized a dance in the big upstairs room of the old house in which several of us had rooms. After the dance, we found what seemed to be some superfluous bottles in the corridor, and purloined a bottle of dry vermouth. We had no idea what that was, but piled into my Morris and drove down to the river-bank, where three of us drank the bottle neat. Somehow or other I drove us all back to the College and we climbed the outside steps to the room where the dance had been held. There were Mrs Price and her daughter Betty clearing up. I saw them swaying in the bright distance, as indeed the not-so-upright piano and some chairs were doing a polka, and set off across the floor. Unfortunately this had been freshly waxed for the dance, and I found myself sitting on the smooth wood. Mrs Price helped me up, saying, "Poor Geoffrey, the floor is slippery, isn't it?" She guided me to the door. I rushed to my room, threw open the window and spewed all over her roses. Not a word was ever said.

This was my first drunken spree. Had my mother known about it, she would have had a heart attack. She had warned me again and again about the horrors of alcohol, and I knew it was with good reason. All her men had been failures; even John, she told me, had been so drunk when his troopship sailed that he had hardly been able to say goodbye. "Think," she said, "that might have been the last time I ever saw him." Poor old John, I thought, why shouldn't he get pissed on his last night in Australia before going off to the war. But my mother feared terribly for me. Had she only known, the horrible experience of getting so drunk was very good for me. Apart from that, to this day I still cannot drink neat dry vermouth.

My English tutor at St Mark's was Paul Pfeiffer, a poet, a soft-spoken but clear-minded lover of literature who kept me from waffling and encouraged every enthusiasm. He introduced me to Sam (really Donald) Kerr, a third-year student. Sam had been editor of the University literary magazine, *Phoenix*, a handsomely produced collection of radical new work of far from negligible standard. Sam, curly-headed with lips and nose like a Greek statue of a satyr, an ardent rugby player (an unusual game in South Australia), was a very good poet indeed. He became a close friend, recipient and donor of endless confidences about love and poetry.

My closest friend was Sandy Dey, a science student whose father was manager of the B.H.P. works at Port Pirie. Engineering and science were in his blood, but he was also a great reader and had a most appealing capacity for enjoying all the things which made life zestful. He was the ideal friend to have to stay at Kangaroo Island.

Bob Fisher was another friend; he had been at school with me, my partner in the toffee-making business, and was studying law. Although not a literary man, he used to read my poems and browse among the books in my room. St Mark's was right next to the Anglican Cathedral. "My, my," he said one day, reading Stephen Spender, " 'Religion stands, the church blocking the sun'." Bob was one of those rare people who can combine a generally conservative outlook with an undying and healthy scepticism.

Another good friend was a distant cousin, Peter Rudall. Peter was a kind of Australian renaissance man in the making, extraordinarily good-looking, a brilliant tennis and golf player, who had been editor of the St Peter's school magazine and School Librarian. He also had an uninhibited sense of humour.

Peter had a girlfriend, Suzie Bowen, and three or four of us used to pile into the Morris and go out to the Bowens for supper. This was the first time I had ever known the joys of family life. (I am well aware that they can also be hell.) On the walls of the comfortable but not grand house at Glenunga were a number of oil paintings that particularly appealed to me. I was told that they were by Stella, sister of Suzie's father Tom, and that she lived in England and had been appointed an official war artist. I was later to discover that she was one of the most interesting women of the 1920s and 1930s; for many years she lived with Ford Madox Ford and was friends with most of the famous artists and writers of the time. She wrote an autobiography, *Drawn from Life*, which has an acute and entertaining description of the provincial capital of Adelaide.

But art was only one of many subjects of discussion at the Bowens. Molly was a most spirited woman, despite being the daughter of an archdeacon, and had the same sweet nature as her daughter Suzie. Suzie had had the unbelievable misfortune to contract poliomyelitis twice, and as a result she was, to put it ungallantly, not exactly tall and willowy. But she had a perfect complexion, and above all this winning nature. Dances in those days were usually programme dances, where everybody had a programme, and you rushed to sign up your favourite girl before someone else grabbed her. Suzie's programme was always filled first of all the girls.

Molly Bowen would bring in a large supper and lots of tea and coffee (I don't think we ever drank beer or wine), and we would start talking. The Bowens were miraculously patient with our endless stories of university life, and open to the deepest discussions of the meaning of life and death, politics and the war. I had never realized that the generations could have such an equal give and take in conversation, that families could make so many people so happy. We used to stay much too late, before rolling down the hill to St Mark's in the Morris.

In the blissful absence of organized sport, I gave up rowing in a crew, and taught myself to scull, with many a wobble. When I was proficient I was allowed to take out the ultra-light racing scull and fly down the River Torrens, this delicately responsive craft almost lifting right out of the water with the stroke of the two oars.

Then I fell in love, abandoning the unreachable Susanne for the very-present Nancy Oxlade who was sharing all my classes with me. Nancy was fair and very pretty, with curly hair of a reddish-gold colour called in those days Titian, and a round, laughing face. She was an orphan who lived with that grim old tyrant Cousin George Morphett, the one who had found me sleeping on his couch when John, his son Hurtle and I returned from Geelong. Nancy hated Cousin George but loved his wife, Cousin Vi.

Whenever I called to take Nancy out, Cousin George would cast a disapproving eye over the ancient and open Morris, and bark that she must be returned by midnight, "AT THE LATEST". "Yes, sir", and I would open the creaky door for Nancy in her evening dress and off we would go under the stars (for the Morris had no hood) up to Adelaide for the dance.

One of Nancy's few pleasures at Cummins was to play the lovely, very old grand piano. Nancy was brisker than me with Bach and Mozart, but had not graduated to the sonorities and implications of Ravel and Debussy. We had much to offer each other, principally our bodies. Casting Dease's fears aside, I kissed her and did not die, and she responded with ardour, not even resisting when my tremulous hand slid down her dress and found her perfect breasts. I couldn't believe my luck. After all these years of monastic seclusion! I didn't know what came next, but she did. If my hand strayed further down it was firmly restrained. But I was more than happy to live within those limits.

As soon as we had an opportunity after lectures, we would hurry past the zoo, through the pine trees of the park, and down to the river bank, which in those peaceful days we seemed to have all to ourselves. One afternoon we were locked in a passionate embrace on the pine needles of the slope down to the river and the incurious swans, when we suddenly heard a shout of "Platoon, CHARGE", and there was Corporal Ken Price, Archie's younger son, and his brave platoon from the St Peter's College Cadet Corps, about to capture the River Torrens. Clamping Nancy even tighter to me and thrusting our heads into the pine needles, I stayed still on top of her while the putteed legs and army issue boots thundered past us. We waited. "Platoon, form fours!" ordered the heroic corporal, and the troops were marched up the bank.

The next time we made for the Torrens, we went along the edge of the bank, below the galvanized-iron fence of the zoo, and found a delicious spot under the willows, where no military clods would intrude. We were even sheltered from passing boats.

I later found out that this was a favourite spot for such diversions. Max Harris used to take his girlfriend to this green shelter behind the zoo, and he wrote a good poem about love-making there, beginning "Granted the water-rats, scuttling their ecstatic thoughts amidst the reeds", and ending "We weren't lovers. We hadn't time."

Sam Kerr had told me about Max, the *enfant terrible* of the University, who was also closely associated with *Phoenix*. A letter of mine at the time to Dease gives quite a percipient description: "There is a bloke here at the Varsity called Max Harris who has just had a book of poems published ... He is an amazing self-advertiser, horribly pleased with himself and believing in the fact that nobody has anything compared to him, but he has a high percentage of the works, I think."

Max always made an impressive entry into the Refectory, the big hall where we had our meals and talked endlessly over coffee or milk-shakes. He would sweep in, wearing a white tie and a black shirt with his sportscoat and grey trousers, his slave Mary Martin carrying his notebooks and texts a couple of paces behind. He would select an unoccupied table and open a book, while Mary scuttled off to get coffee.

I was much in favour of Max's first book of poems, *The Gift of Blood*. The long and impenetrably obscure title poem had something to do with Jews, Germany and the war; we did not know then about his Jewish blood, but the poems undoubtedly were influenced by it. I cannot imagine anywhere in the world in 1940, except perhaps the land of the Eskimos, where there was less anti-Semitism than in Adelaide. No one ever worried about who were Jews and who were not; I never even thought about my own Jewish blood. One of the most respectable families in Adelaide were the Jacobs; it never occurred to anyone that it was a Jewish name. The Jews in Germany were much more real to us than any Jews in Australia.

Max's poems were undoubtedly "modern", and denounced as such in the daily newspaper, the *Advertiser*, where the poetry reviewer, Talbot Smith, was a gentleman in his eighties. Max in those days had a lovely lyrical gift, which he later tended to smother in turgid profundities or tangles of surrealist imagery. He also, as always, had a lot of energy and a restless enjoyment of intrigue and ways to power. Max, at that time, was very good-looking, with dark hair and big, intent eyes. Hal Porter, meaning to be unkind, likened him to "a Syrian sweets vendor". He was slim and had been athletic; he was always proud of the fact that, when he was playing football for St Peters College, the *Advertiser* had referred to him as "a nifty little rover".

Max was then genuinely interested in the work of young writers, and he read my poems and made helpful criticisms in his abrupt way. "This is crap, Dutts", he would say about one offering, and then talk for ten minutes about the next one. He and I shared passions for the same poets, especially Rilke and Hölderlin. He had long been studying German, and was enrolled for German at the University; a year ahead of me, he had done well in English and was a favourite of Professor Stewart's. He did not read French, but was deep in translations of Baudelaire; he was delighted when a drunken friend introduced him to a newcomer as "Max Hashish".

What was appealing about Max was his enthusiasm for the *avant garde* in art and literature, although *En avant!* or *Plus avant!* would better describe his attitude. *Avant garde* has become a dirty expression in post-modernist days, but something new, modern, out front was desperately needed at that dead time in Australian art and literature. The word *garde* exactly describes the intolerant, authoritarian attitudes of those who controlled, or wished to control, the arts in Australia — people like Robert Menzies, with his Australian Academy, J.S. McDonald, Professor Cowling or even pathetic old Talbot Smith. "*Garde:* safe-keeping, protection, guard, custody, charge, watch". Their idea of art or poetry was that of a prisoner in custody, to be guarded against those who might smuggle in a rope and a file.

Until 1940, *Phoenix* then had been published with funds from the University Union; a philistine, sporting group took over the Union, and cancelled *Phoenix*'s grant, despite protests from Professor Stewart and Charles Jury, a well-off bachelor aesthete who lived across North Terrace, not far from the University, and did much to assist literature in Adelaide. So Sam Kerr and Max decided to approach sponsors and bring out a new literary magazine, which would appear as published by the Arts Association, where there was a small cache of funds available over which they both had some influence. A lot of us dobbed in with money, Jury and Stewart substantially, others with what they could. I put in my ever-faithful godmother's birthday present of five pounds, which was a lot of money for an impoverished undergraduate. The magazine was called *Angry Penguins*, a title chosen by Sam from a phrase in one of Max's poems, "as drunks, the angry penguins of the night". It sounded suitably surrealistic, the art and literature of that movement being a particular enthusiasm of Max's; there had been an unforgettable Salvador Dali in the *Herald* exhibition.

I happened to have a copy of the first issue of *Angry Penguins* in my hand when I passed Sir Douglas Mawson, near the Barr Smith Library. He had often met me with my parents, and greeted me with "What have you got there, Geoffrey?". I showed him. Modern poetry and art had no great appeal for him, but he looked through it politely and handed it back saying, "Obviously you chaps don't know much about penguins. Never seen an angry one yet."

From the first, the magazine encompassed modern Australian art as well as literature. Arthur Boyd, John Perceval and Sidney Nolan were among the earliest contributors. I was very excited to see my first poems in print.

A second issue of the magazine followed, appearing about the same time as Sam departed to the RAAF. Max then secured the patronage of John and Sunday Reed in Melbourne, and transferred his headquarters to that city.

Much of the work in *Angry Penguins* is immature, but it is interesting to look back on what we were trying to do. We were all for internationalism and detested Australian nationalism. The other literary movement emanating from Adelaide was that of the Jindyworobaks, led by Rex Ingamells and supported by Flexmore Hudson, Ian Mudie and many others. We poured scorn on their fake Aboriginality, although most of us appeared in the Jindy collections. James McAuley also appeared there, so he and Max were in print together long before Ern Malley.

For us internationalists, gum trees in poetry or art were a noxious weed. Magpies and kookaburras were shot at sight. It was not that we wanted to substitute oaks or nightingales, though we liked reading about them in English or German poetry, but that we wanted to speak an international language in an idiom untainted by local imagery or conventional form and poetic diction.

Actually, of course, we could have learned much from the Jindys, as they from us. But in the meantime, we stayed with Yeats and Eliot and Auden, Rimbaud and Baudelaire, Rilke and Lorca, and left Lawson and Paterson to the Jindys. I don't think any of us had ever even read a poem by the greatest Australian poet, Kenneth Slessor, whose *Five Bells* had been published in 1939, and whose verse was distinctively Australian, yet international in its evocations and sensibility, and of supreme technical virtuosity.

On my eighteenth birthday, 2 August, my mother took me to lunch at the Covent Garden Cafe, which was our favourite eating place. There was not a restaurant worthy of being dignified by the name in Adelaide in 1940. The swishest place to eat was in the dining room of the South Australian Hotel, where Lewy Coton the head waiter ruled tyrannically, insisting that no man should appear without a tie. He once refused entrance to the dining room to Norman Hartnell, the Queen's dressmaker, who was wearing an exquisite cravat. The next day a group of students, all wearing collars and ties, but nothing else except underpants, stormed the South Australian Hotel's dining room waving a placard which read "Phooey to Louis". "They can't even spell my name right," said the unamused Lewy as he shepherded them outside.

Now, at the Covent Garden, my mother and I settled in for a huge plate of deliciously fresh crayfish (still correctly named, before the demands of the American market imposed the erroneous name of "lobster", which is a creature with claws, unlike the crayfish). This crayfish salad cost two shillings and sixpence, for which you got half a large cray each.

I had news for my unfortunate mother. I waited until we had finished the crayfish. "Now that I'm eighteen, I'm going to join the RAAF as a pilot." She put down her cup of tea. "I suppose you must", was all she said. "Yes", was all I said.

She already had two sons in the AIF (Dick had not yet been discharged for medical reasons). She was liable to lose all three of us, but she never asked my reasons for enlisting. I wouldn't have been able to tell her anyway. I knew that Hitler and what he stood for was evil, thanks to Douglas Reed and Russel Ward in particular. Yet I had in fact been going to go to Freiburg University in Germany if it had not been for the war. Various friends of my mother, and J.R. Darling, thought that apart from studying the German culture and language it would be good for me to be studying in a country that was obviously going to be one of the most powerful and influential in the world. It was for these reasons that Darling had made German the main modern foreign language to be studied at Geelong. We had a new text-book, freshly imported from Germany, *Wir Lesen Deutsch*, which I later realized was oozing Nazi propaganda about healthy Nordic blonds and the joys of youth hostels.

But I was dead against militarism and its symbols in Australia. I had written a priggish poem about Anzac Day in 1940, when I watched the old Diggers march and then proceed to the pubs to get pissed, and, in the words of my poem, "forget the monster still standing".

There was no doubt that Nazism was a monster, even looking at it from Australia. What was also monstrous was that, through no fault of our own, and with no say of our own, fatuous British politicians had dragged us into a war that might have been prevented by more courageous action earlier on. And it was not as if Australia had not suffered enough, for the same reasons, in the First World War which, incredibly, had only ended in the year in which Chibs was born, twenty-one years before.

At much the same time Dease joined the commandos in the AIF, a typically offbeat thing to do. I wrote to him about much that was on my mind:

> I have joined the Air Force. I am terrified of the mathematics and physics and pretty confident that I will never be trained in time to commit murder.
>
> I am again reading *Ulysses*, entranced, it's marvellous.
>
> I am torn in a way you couldn't be between two lives — the life I lead with you and my friends here, and the life at home, where windmill shafts, sheeps' stomachs, and weeds attain equal if not superior importance to wars and plagues and fires and deaths. I find it almost impossible to be idle during the day at Anlaby and consequently only during the night can I think. And yet I love the extraordinary simplicity which underlies all country people's lives, although it makes one gnash one's teeth to think that Beethoven will never mean as much to them as a Merino ewe.
>
> I am writing an essay for the Sanderson Essay Prize (of five pounds!) on Wordsworth's view of childhod. I'm afraid a child's life, though attractive, never seems much more than a bloody waste of time to me. [Despite this disinclination to trail clouds of glory, I did win the five pounds.]

My long letter ended: "I can scarcely envisage the extent of the happiness that might have been ours but for the war. This bloody war is getting more and more depressing, isn't it."

But it seemed inevitable that I should go. And the same applied to my friends at St Mark's. Sam Kerr, Sandy Dey and Paul Pfeiffer joined up as aircrew in the RAAF, Peter Rudall joined the RAN and Bob Fisher joined the AIF. As Bob was almost blind and would be rejected if this were found out, he had spies bring him the reading charts from the recruiting office and learned them all by heart. It's a wonder that the doctor, just by looking at his owlish blink without glasses, did not realize how abysmal his eyesight was. I joined the RAAF as aircrew. I was selected to become a pilot, and was told that there would be a delay because of shortage of training aircraft, and that I would probably be called up next May.

Of my St Mark's friends, Sam was shot down in a Hudson over the Timor Sea. Sandy and Paul were killed in Europe in Bomber Command; Sandy's only brother, George, was also killed in the RAAF. Peter was killed when the *Sydney* was sunk; Peter's only brother, Jake, in the AIF, was also killed. Out of us eight young men, only two survived — Bob and myself.

Those who did not expose themselves to the war not only did not risk their lives, but gained four or five years, in the most valuable period of training in one's life, over those who did go and who were lucky enough to survive. They were the ones who became university lecturers while their ex-service contemporaries were beginning again as undergraduates. The American writer Gore Vidal expressed the situation very well when he said in an interview: "For those of us who enlisted in the war at about 17, our youth was cut short, and by the time we were out of the army in our early twenties, something hadn't been completed between 17 and 21. And what would it have been? I don't know."

The year ended well for me, with lots of poems (gradually improving) written and some even published, and the top place in the University exams in English and History. St Mark's closed down and was handed over to the RAAF.

My mother, Chibs, Sandy Dey and I went down to Rocky Point; it was in many ways the best holiday I ever had there. My mother was happy looking after us, making herself dresses on an ancient, turn-the-handle Singer sewing machine, or making charcoal drawings of the twisting boughs of her beloved tea-tree. On other days she would set off in the Buick to the hill above American River and work on a big oil painting of Flinders' Pelican Lagoon.

The 18-foot clinker-built sailing boat, in which Walter Jeffrey had taught me how to sail at Victor Harbor, was brought down on the *Karatta* to Hog

Bay. Chibs and Sandy and I then sailed her around the twelve miles of coast to Rocky Point. The only trouble was that, having been years out of the water, her planks had dried out, and she leaked furiously. We lost our only bailing can overboard, and then had to bail with our sandshoes.

Her planks soon took up, and we sailed endlessly around the bay, scorning to take in reefs, although she carried a very large mainsail and our gunwale was often lapping the water. Sometimes we would load up the little dinghy and with the outboard buzz across the bay to Sapphire Point and catch prodigious quantities of King George whiting, the island's greatest fish. I don't think any fish tastes better than fresh whiting fillets you have caught yourself.

We spent days restoring my father's beautiful old 12-foot dinghy. It was clinker-built, and double-ended for getting in to the beach on rough days at Victor Harbor; the pointed stern would divide the waves instead of receiving them with a wet slap. She was built of red cedar, and varnished. When we had finished sanding her down and revarnishing her, she glowed; she was light as a scull to row.

There was also sweep fishing from the reefs on the South Coast on north-wind days. Old scrawny-necked Mr Goebbels who ran a litle farm by the salt lagoon, and trapped wallabies for the skins, offered to take us to a new spot. We walked miles across the sandhills and came to a cliff, scrambled down, assembled our rods and baited up our hooks with fresh cockles. In the meantime Goebbels had baited up his decrepit hand line with chunks of wallaby, thrown it in and was pulling out bigger sweep than we ever caught.

Our only visitor at Rocky Point was Lady Barclay-Harvey, the Governor's wife, a huge, bossy woman known to us kids as Lady Mew, because she was burdened with the name of Muriel. She had come down to inspire the island girls to join the Voluntary Aid Detachments of the Red Cross, of which my mother was Country Controller. There was a frightful storm when she was with us, and that night, as Sandy and I were lying in bed enjoying the thunder and lightning, there was a timid knock on the door. In came shivering Lady Mew in a pink dressing gown, saying she was absolutely terrified of thunder storms, and begging us to let her spend the night with us. She would not get into either of our beds (thank God), but lay on the end of mine enclosed in a blanket, like some sort of gift-wrapped crocodile.

At Rocky Point I suddenly realized I no longer loved Nancy, and wrote and told her so, after long struggles to find the best words. She was, she said in her reply, shattered and bewildered. What had she done wrong? I could not reply. She had done nothing "wrong"; I simply realized, with rare honesty instead of my usual excuse-making, and my training in not disturbing the status quo, that she was the wrong girl for me.

A few weeks later I was writing to Dease: "Nancy is engaged to Bob Angas!!! Within a month of protesting her undying love for me she is engaged to someone she hardly knew before. I no longer care for anything of her except the power of her breasts and the drug of her skin. And just that alone is no good."

I was not turning into a Platonist; I was already ardently in search of more skin and breasts, but having no success at all. Susanne was even more out of reach. I wrote to Dease: "Susanne has been in hospital for two months and nobody allowed to see her, write to her, or send her books or flowers. Mrs Angas calls it a rest cure. It would have driven me barmy." This mysterious incarceration was never explained.

At the beginning of the university year in 1941 Chibs and I took a flat in an old house facing the park in North Adelaide, and I went back to take the second year in the same subjects. But it was not the same without St Mark's, although Stewart and Portus were still lecturing. One day a notice went up saying that Professor Stewart would be giving the inaugural lecture on Australian Literature, sponsored by the Commonwealth Literary Fund. We all went along to enjoy this new experience. Stewart took his place in the lecture theatre and said in his high voice: "I am most grateful to the Commonwealth Literary Fund for providing the funds to give this lecture on Australian Literature, but unfortunately they have neglected to provide any Literature — I will lecture therefore on *Kangaroo* by D.H. Lawrence."

The seats in the Barr Smith Library were rather oddly arranged; those on the right of the main doors faced those on the left. While working in the Library in this first term, I noticed an attractive dark-haired girl facing me, a few rows back in the other rows of seats. Then I realized that I had seen her before.

In 1940, when we were at St Mark's, Sam Kerr and another student and I were asked to represent the University in a debate with the girls of Woodlands School at Glenelg. When I went round to Sam's room to collect him, I found him in great pain, as he had twisted his ankle playing rugby. He was endeavouring to alleviate the pain with a glass of whisky. By the time he had had another one, and was saying that only a third would make him able to face the girls of Woodlands, I realized that we would be late for the debate if we did not leave immediately. I put my foot down going along the Anzac highway in the Morris, and we might almost have reached 48 m.p.h., but by the time we arrived at the school hall, the Head Mistress, the adjudicator, who was the Lord Mayor, and all the girls were already seated and waiting. The President of the Debating Society was a legitimately cross and anxious girl called Ninette Trott. This was the girl sitting oppposite me in the Library. (Needless to say, Sam and I had lost the debate.)

She obviously would not want to talk with me. I consulted Sam who said like an old roué, "Go on, Geoff, she's probably sitting there so you'll have to look at her." Some time later she confessed to me that this indeed was the truth.

She agreed to have coffee in the Refectory with me. After she had left, Max came over to me and said, "You're wasting your time with the British Virgin, Dutts, though she does look pretty good." "I bet you I'll have her in bed within a month," was my retort, delivered with all the confidence and expertise of an 18-year-old virgin. "Poor old Dutts, I wouldn't take your money," Max replied, and signalled to Mary Martin that it was time for them to leave the Refectory.

Thus began a mutual pursuit; lustful and short-term on my part, but with further aims on hers.

In May, after completing the first term, I was called up for training. With the others who were to be on the same training course, I was told we would have to march through the city to raise more volunteers for the armed forces. With Bruce Cowell, who was tall like me, I had to carry a banner which stretched across the street, proclaiming "WE JOINED UP TODAY, WHAT ABOUT YOU?". This enraged us, as we had joined up, that is, volunteered, some seven months ago. It was a windy day, and we had to struggle with our long, phallic poles and flapping banner. A drunken spectator yelled out, "Watchit, mate, yer cock's getting away with yer."

We left in the evening on the Melbourne Express for Somers Initial Training School in Victoria. My fellow-trainees, a lively bunch of lads, immediately set up a game of poker. They asked me to join in. I had no idea how to play, but thought they would despise me if I admitted it, so I joined the game. I made a fool of myself a few times, but soon got the hang of it, and suddenly Beginner's Luck smiled on me and I kept on winning. It looked like a good omen for ultimate survival.

PART TWO
Wartime
1941–45

A few : Frank, Sandy, Sam, Paul, Geoff and Leigh.
Some shot or burnt in air, some hit by sea
As hard as land. What's left is left to me.
And when our friends go solo, we sing with all our might
"Per Ardua Ad Astra, up you, Jack, I'm all right."

"Abandoned Airstrip, Northern Territory"

Eight

I became a number — 416329, Aircraftman Second Class Geoffrey Piers Henry Dutton, Royal Australian Air Force. This, with ranks both ascending and descending, was to be my identity for the next four and half years.

Nine years of boarding school had been worth it for this alone, that I was inured to discomfort, bad food and the necessity for getting on with a lot of people who were more or less contemporaries. As well, I was used to authority that was often stupid and unjust. The only obvious difference from boarding school was that, for the privilege of defending our country, we would be paid five shillings a day. I remember the communists, who in the infamous days of the Stalin-Hitler pact were ordered to oppose the war, calling all us volunteers five-bob-a-day murderers.

As we threw our new kitbags on the floor of the hut, by the metal stretchers that were to be our beds, and went off to fill our palliasses with straw, I resigned myself to the boredom of six weeks of drill and "education", before I could begin to learn to fly. "Don't fill it too full," a sandy-haired AC2 said to me, "you bloody keep rolling off if you do." I pulled out a few handfuls of straw from the hessian palliasse. This, I was to find, was typical of the RAAF. People actually wanted to help each other, and there was no ganging up or bullying as at school. There were of course drill sergeants who roared at you and certain officers who thought it added to their dignity to treat ordinary ranks like shit, but that was only to be expected.

I was an eighteen-year-old boy, or man, in Archie Price's terminology, who had had a very sheltered life, economically if not emotionally. And from my isolated upbringing the only different people I had met were station hands and country people, and they were not all that different, as we shared the same background if not the same upbringing. At school and at university my fellow students and I were not remote in our interests or our origins. Now I was plunged into a new world. Around me in the hut were my new poker-playing friends and others of like kinds of expertise, a printer, a bank clerk, a schoolteacher and a speed cop. The latter, an iron-handshake man with a jaw of solid rock, asked me if I was any relation of a John Dutton who had a Vauxhall 30/98. When told John was my brother he said: "Good bloke, that. I was parked behind a tree on the north road when he goes past me at about 80 m.p.h. I roared after him, and was just catching up when the bugger puts his foot down and disappears into the distance. The old Norton was flat at about 90, and he just left me for dead. Well, I slowed down, and after a few miles saw him parked outside the Old

Spot Hotel. When I pulled up alongside him he said, 'Hi! Thought you might like a drink.' Well, I couldn't give a bloke like that a ticket. And yes, duty or not, I did have a glass of beer."

At Initial Training School (ITS) I learned about life faster than I mastered Theory of Flight and Navigation and other subjects which sorely tested a brain so weak in Mathematics and Physics and Geometry. English and History were no use to me at all, though German might come in handy later.

We had a day off, and all piled into buses to go to Frankston and the pub. Here was a problem. I had faithfully promised my nervous mother that I would not drink beer, that I would not be drawn into the terrible drinking sessions that she knew went on in the armed forces. Think of Dad and Dick, was the unspoken message. But I could not possibly leave all the blokes and not go into the pub. So I said, no thanks, I wouldn't have a beer, but — an anguished look around the bar. Near me was a tall glass that seemed to be full of some sort of soft drink, with a bit of cucumber sticking out of it. "I'll have one of them." "What, a Pimms Number One?" The barman looked at me a bit curiously. "Yes, that's right," I said, as if I'd been socking them back for years.

So for every beer the others drank, I swallowed a Pimms, which tasted harmless enough until my mate Les said, "D'you realize those things are about three times as powerful as a beer?" "And three times as expensive," said the bloke who'd just done the last shout. I switched to beer, and thought God would pardon me the broken promise.

After a couple of weeks of cold and boredom — Somers was near the sea, but it was not the time of year for swimming — we were allowed a night's leave in Melbourne. Dease was up north somewhere with the Commandos, so I went along with the boys, and somehow or another we met some girls at St Kilda, and had a few drinks with them, and somehow or other I lost my virginity on St Kilda beach on the rather chilly sand, which infiltrated some inconvenient places. She was a nice, jolly, comfortable girl who was a secretary with Shell. I didn't think I'd given much of a performance or done anything sizzling for her, but as we were getting dressed she said "Thank you very much," and gave me a big kiss. At least now I knew how everything worked, even without nightingales or tears. So much for romanticism. It was good to give sensibility and soul a rest, and the body would surely improve its performance.

There was no past imperfect in the RAAF, only a present indicative of soulless days and unimaginative instruction, with bursts of grog, girls (not called women in those days), and the roaring of bawdy songs, with the girls joining in. With great and typical generosity, Chibs had insisted on lending me her beautiful, new, little blue Vauxhall tourer; she had driven it over to Melbourne and left it there for me. So four or five of us could hop into the Vauxhall and get away to Frankston or Sorrento whenever we had a leave pass.

But I was fatally bitten with the venom and the elixir of poetry; even in the hut amongst the mob, with several radios going full blast, I had to keep writing. On one occasion I came into the hut and found I was the only person there. I turned on the radio to different station from the usual ones, and there was some pianist playing a Bach prelude and fugue. I couldn't believe my luck. I thought of Willie McKie, now in the Royal Air Force himself. Halfway through the fugue a bunch of my mates charged in the door and said "Shit, Dutts, what's this crap", and it was back to Glenn Miller.

Not that I didn't like Glenn Miller, Benny Goodman, Artie Shaw and the rest of them with their big rhythms, sweet saxes and weaving clarinets. And their music was made for dancing. Terrible dancer though I was, "In The Mood" brought me straight onto the floor with an arm around a girl. It was a new life, all right.

As for my writing poetry, the lads in the hut didn't seem to mind, after the initial "Shit, what's that stuff you're writing? You OK Dutt?"

As for swearing, I had come up in the world since the day I was tied to the tree at Wykeham. I knew all the words by now, but I had never heard them used so relentlessly. Some of the men couldn't get through a sentence without interlarding every two words, sometimes even two syllables, with a word beginning with "f" or "c". Some of the more elaborate swearing was new to me, and I thought it splendidly ingenious, for example, "Why don't ya pull a cow's cunt over yer head, sport, and get a bull to fuck some sense into ya".

It didn't seem to affect their attitude to women that everything from a stuck nut to a problem in navigation could be called a cunt. In fact, their treatment of women was amazingly chivalrous. And they laid off another man's "squarey" (steady girlfriend); otherwise it was every man for the woman of his choice, and vice versa, for another thing I learned was that women had a great deal of skill in latching on to the man they wanted. In my innocence I had thought that although women might be intellectually independent, sexually they meekly waited their turn. But I was already leading a double life, for these women were diversions, or I was a diversion for them, whereas at home I was firmly hooked. I had a squarey in Ninette Trott.

Elementary Flying Training School took me back to South Australia in July 1941, to the grass aerodrome at Parafield, ten miles north of Adelaide, where I went solo in a Gipsy Moth biplane. Gipsy Moths were the forerunners of the incomparable Tiger Moth, and looked much the same except that the upper wing was directly above the lower, giving the aircraft a rather stodgy look compared with the Tiger, where the lower wing was raked back. One snag about the Gipsy was that the exhaust pipe ran back outside the fuselage, and if you weren't careful you could rest your arm on red-hot metal. Every evening the ground staff pulled out a kind of safety pin from the place where the wings joined the fuselage, folded back the wings and wheeled the Gipsies into the hangar. My instructor assured me that the pins never dropped out.

Going solo was like your first fuck. You were sure you had the equipment to do it, and it was a bit clumsy, but the exciting bit, the flying, couldn't go on for ever. You had to come back to earth. On my first solo the grass of the aerodrome came up a bit suddenly and I bounced high in the air, but came down again more gently. I was now a genuine pilot.

Aerobatics, though rather scary and sick-making at first, were the entry into a new dimension. You could roll sky and land around, fly up into the sky and go over and down again towards earth in a loop, or send everything into a crazy whirl in a spin. An aerobatic aircraft, you learned, was almost a living creature, waiting to be liberated from boring straight and level flight, as well as from the ground. But with flying you had to learn never to be careless. My father's early training with the sea, which he said you must always respect, always watch, stood me in good stead, as did his training with a gun and rifle. I knew about not tensing up, how to aim steady. And my years with the Morris made me responsive to the sounds and inclinations of a machine, always listening, knowing when the revs were building up too high, always feeling, knowing in the seat of your pants when a skid was developing or your airspeed was too low. Even to have ridden a bicycle was a help. But there was one vital difference between sailing or riding a bike and flying. You had to watch your instruments — not that a Gypsy had many. The instructor dinned into me that the seat of the pants was all very well, but you must also be in constant touch with your instruments, which would never lie. The proof of this was in learning blind flying. A hood was pulled over you and suddenly you didn't know which was up and which was down. You just had to concentrate on the arrow and the ball in a bubble in front of you, the turn and bank indicator, the airspeed indicator and the altimeter. Flying under the hood was the prelude to night flying or flying in cloud, although the latter was avoided wherever possible, as of course we had no radar or sophisticated instruments. Gipsies had no landing lights, so when night flying and coming in to land, you judged your height from the ground by a flare-path; the closer you were to the ground, the more the space between the flares seemed to diminish until finally there you were, rather surprisingly, on the ground and the flares were rushing past alongside you, while the tail-skid rattled on the ground. Gipsies had no brakes.

In one sense, however, it was a regression to be doing my elementary training in South Australia. Ninette and I were now officially girlfriend and boyfriend, and my mother seemed to approve of the arrangement. So my taste of freedom was over, and I was back in the land of parental authority, for Ninette was very much in awe of my mother.

And now, as well, there were her parents to consider. If I had a leave pass I would have to pick her up at her parents', who were the essence of everything rigidly bourgeois in Adelaide. Gerry Portus would have snorted at them, although in those days they had only one car, a Pontiac. I would ring to say I was coming. If he was at home, Ninette's father Leonard would answer the phone and always say the same thing: "Hello. Are you there?" I had a screaming urge to say "No!", but was too polite. They had a dignified old two-storeyed house in Gilberton, surrounded by other large houses, with a spacious garden and a separate ballroom. The inside of the house was stiff with her mother Clarice's knick-knacks, and everywhere on the heavily wallpapered walls were oil paintings by Clarice's father, George Webb, principally of subjects like kangaroos in Scottish glens, or cattle under gum trees that looked like oaks. He had come out from England as a young man, and his eye had never adjusted to the Australian light or landscape. He was an irascible old brute who did not approve of me, especially when I said how excited I had been by the *Herald* exhibition, which he considered to be rubbish.

We would go out to dinner with the Trotts to the South, as the South Australian Hotel was always called, where Clarice and Leonard treated Lewy with unctuous respect and patronising hauteur, all at once. The little band, a trio of violin, cello and piano, would have a signature tune for favourite regulars; at a signal from Lewy as the Trotts, Ninette and I in my blue uniform came into the dining room, the band would strike up with Clarice's signature tune (I have forgotten the name) and she would bend a wrist gracefully towards them. Being an Air Force Man I was allowed a glass of wine, but with the licensing laws as they were, all drinks had to be off the table by eight o'clock. So we dined at six. That, incidentally, was the hour the bars closed, the famous six o'clock swill, when schooners of beer were gulped down with the barmaid chanting "Time, please, time".

If I had a weekend leave we would go to Anlaby, where my mother would leave us alone for most of the time, to encourage the young lovers, although she thought Trott *père* and *mère* were awful. It was all very different from being off with the boys. I could not see, having been brought up as I was, that my life, which until recently had known no other women but my mother and Chibs, was now being firmly guided by my mother, not to mention my girlfriend, away from dangerous regions beyond their control.

Towards the end of the course at Parafield a couple of my fellow trainees caught mumps and were sent to the hospital. One morning I woke up with a swelling on one side of my neck by my jaw. Fearful of going to hospital and missing the passout of my course, and thus not going on with my friends to, so rumour had it, Canada, I rolled the long blue scarf Ninette had knitted me around my neck and went on flying. But a couple of days later my left testicle began to swell up; in no time it was the size of a lemon, or perhaps a grapefruit, it felt so huge and painful, and I could no longer disguise my symptoms. I was sent to hospital. While I was still there, nearly all my course was posted to Canada for advanced training. And nearly all of them, sent to Britain as bomber pilots, were shot down or killed in accidents. I probably owe my life to a swollen ball.

I was posted to Point Cook, near Melbourne, where as a single-engine pilot I trained on Wirraways. This aircraft was an Australian version of the American Harvard trainer; it had a radial engine and, although heavy, it was a lot of fun to fly, and very responsive. Its perfomance, moderate enough, was tremendous after a Gipsy Moth. It seemed that I was turning out to be a good pilot, and I was graded Above Average.

At this time my mother kept on urging me, when I had some leave, to go to Melbourne and look up some dear old friends who had a charming daughter. I was rather puzzled, after all the encouragement she had given Ninette and me. But I dutifully obeyed, and found myself at the Toorak mansion of a Captain of Industry. The daughter was tall, gawky and very stupid. I was sent with her down to the Village to shop for luxuries. At dinner my hosts talked of the disgraceful state of labour and the unions in Australia. "Hitler wouldn't stand for it," said the lady of the manor, "he'd put those strikers up against a wall and shoot them, those Bolsheviks." She was quite unconscious of the irony of what she was saying, that we were fighting a war against that kind of thinking.

I resisted the temptation my mother was offering me of securing a rich wife. When I told her that I would refuse all further invitations from that family she didn't seem surprised; but she had obviously thought it was worth a try.

At last the Advanced Training course ended and we had our wings pinned to our manly chests, and we all went and took photographs of each other. There was nothing to do while the RAAF decided our future, but we were supposed to keep our hand in by flying a couple of hours each day.

I had noticed that there was an army camp under canvas across the bay near Barwon Heads, so I suggested to my friends that we pay the brave soldiers a visit. Five of us took off, with five illegal passengers along for the fun, the other pilots in a V formation behind my aircraft, and I led them down to the camp. I signalled, peeled off and dived down to the level of the tea-trees, flattened out and crossed the camp; looking back I saw to my satisfaction that I had blown a couple of tents down, and that my companions were on my tail. Roaring up on full throttle I looked back from about two thousand feet and saw the last aircraft do a climbing slow roll. To my horror, it began a second roll. You just can't do two climbing rolls in a

Wirraway, there isn't enough power. While I watched, the aircraft suddenly flipped and went straight down into the ground, crumpling like yellow foil and bursting into flames, black smoke surging up above the drab green of the tea-tree to the blue sky.

The other three aircraft were almost out of sight, heading back towards Point Cook. I felt, however idiotically, that I ought to do something for Bruce and Doug; I knew from the aircraft number as it rolled that it was them. I lowered my undercariage and flaps and attempted to land in the little paddock where the flames were still leaping from the wreck, and dozens of soldiers were running from the trees. No one could possibly still be alive; they would both have been killed on contact with the ground. I realized there wasn't room to land, and that I could do nothing even if I could land, so flew back to Point Cook.

My passenger and the other three vanished, and we four pilots had a conference. Obviously nothing could be done for Bruce and Doug, so we decided to keep quiet. It did not seem a very honourable thing to do, but any other course of action would have been uselessly quixotic.

An Air Force team of enquiry went down to the camp, and unfortunately the innocent soldiers said yes, there were about half a dozen planes, they had put on a wonderful show, blown a number of tents down they had flown so low, all most enjoyable till the dreadful crash. No, they had not seen any numbers on the planes.

We were grilled by a legal team sent down from Air Board. They had no clear evidence that it was us, but lack of evidence never stopped the armed forces. We were committed to be court-martialled. In the meantime we were all promoted to Sergeant Pilot, and our pay increased to a princely seventeen shillings and sixpence a day.

My mother hired a K.C. to defend us; he told me that in a court of law he would get us off without any trouble, but that the Air Force was determined to make an example of us, and he feared the worst. He was right. We were all found guilty of Low Flying, and reduced to the ranks. The others were sentenced to thirty days detention; I, considered the ringleader, was sentenced to forty-two days, to be served in the old Geelong Gaol, which had been taken over by the armed forces.

The WAAAF driver of the tender, a plump and pretty girl from a famous South Australian wine-making family, burst into tears as she stopped outside the huge gates in the black stone walls of the prison. "You poor boys," she sobbed as we filed past, under the guard of two neanderthal Service Policemen with revolvers on their hips. A few minutes later we were shut in solitary cells. The gaol was still exactly as it was when it was built in the 1870s. The solitary cells were about ten feet by six. A barred window about the size of a shoe-box was eight feet above the floor. Through it you could see sky or cloud, but nothing else. There was a wooden bed with a thin palliasse and a couple of blankets, and a shit-bucket. The same slightly sweet, sickly smell, of shit and disinfectant, was in the cell and through the whole gaol.

There is no experience like the first time you are shut in a cell. The big steel door clangs shut, one key is turned, then another, and then a bolt banged to. There is a peep-hole in the door, for looking in, not for looking out. The hollow interior of the gaol echoes with the boots of the warders on the metal catwalks.

I think that every judge who sentences anyone to gaol ought to be locked up for a night, just to know what it is like. John Bray, who is, amazingly, both a good poet and an ex-Chief Justice, tells me this is ridiculous, that a doctor doesn't have to have had appendicitis or a brain tumour to operate on a patient. But I still think it would do judges good to know what it is like to be in gaol.

The gaol of course was not a gaol; it was a detention camp. The warders were not warders or screws but guards, and were all sergeants. They were, in fact, the old civil warders; Sergeant Green, the head warder, sorry, guard, was a likeable, even kindly man, with a deadly eye for those in his charge. He took a very poor view of the armed services riffraff in the gaol. "The old lifers," he said to me, "were gentlemen compared with this mob."

For those locked up in it, the establishment was known as neither gaol nor detention camp, but as The Boob. For breakfast we had burgoo, which is porridge without milk or sugar. Lunch was a stew, mainly of old sheep bones. Tea was a chunk of bread and a hunk of cheese. A long-term prisoner showed me how to cut several slices as thin as possible, put a few shreds of cheese between them, then place the sandwiches in your handkerchief and wet it. If you were friendly with a trusty slushy, that is, a prisoner working in the kitchen, you might score a tomato or onion, in which case you would slice them and add them to the sandwich. Then you could have something to assuage the pangs of hunger which began to gnaw after you were locked in your cell at 5 p.m. You were not allowed books; the Commandant seemed to think they were dangerous. You just lay on your bunk and watched the darkness come on, and tried not to think about anything desirable in life. You were allowed to write a letter once a week, which of course was censored.

During the day most prisoners sat around in the yards doing nothing. We were not allowed to talk, although of course we soon became expert at talking out of the sides of our mouths, without seeming to move our lips. Some prisoners were detailed every day to build walls in the yard; every evening they knocked them down again, in order to let other prisoners build them up again the next day. Lucky prisoners were given duties, such as washing up in the kitchens, or cleaning. These jobs were much sought after.

In one of the yards there was a sort of cage of wire and steel, with a galvanized-iron roof to keep off the sun. In fact, it intensified its heat. In this cage was incarcerated, like a wild beast, a handsome young man. I was told he had led a mutiny at Benalla, and had escaped from two other gaols.

After a couple of days I was paraded in front of Sergeant Green and told that I was to be moved to a community cell, and because of my education I would be put to work each day in the library. I was astonished to hear that there was a library. Imagine my joy when I found that my co-worker there was an old school acquaintance, Geoff Cornfoot. He was in gaol for, allegedly, stealing aviation fuel. So we were members of that exclusive club, Old Boys of both Geelong Grammar School and Geelong Gaol.

Geoff was a brilliant pilot who should have been away in a fighter squadron. Instead, because he was always in trouble with the authorities, he was kept in Australia performing menial tasks like towing the drogue (a conical, canvas target for air-to-air gunnnery) behind an antiquated Westland Wapiti aircraft.

Geoff was about the same height and build as me, although he was very athletic, a champion squash and tennis player. When amused with life, as mostly he was, his possum nose would twitch and the skin wrinkle around his brown eyes. When I was sent to work with him in the library I was rather a glum fellow; being in the boob when you are nineteen years old seems rather a waste of life. Besides, I had to eat burgoo every morning or else go even hungrier than I was already. But for Geoff the whole drama, somehow, was comedy. Everything and everyone made him laugh, not only because he could detect individual absurdities, but because he thought that life, and especially all authority, was absurd. It is interesting that Camus was writing *L'Etranger* in the same year as we were in gaol.

Geoff was logical in a way that seemed absurd to authority. He was in The Boob because, when he was stationed at Laverton outside Melbourne, he used to push the old Wapiti into the hangar every evening, instead of taxying it in. This saved about a gallon of petrol, which he would then milk out and pour into the tank of his Austin Seven. Thus he would be able to drive into Melbourne, see his girlfriend, and be back for flying in the morning. Aircraft fuel had a very distinctive smell. A service policeman happened to walk past the Austin Seven, and he noticed that it was fairly reeking of aircraft fuel. Geoff's defence at the court-martial was that he had never stolen a drop of petrol; he had only used what he had saved. Such logic was beyond the court, and he, like me, was sentenced to forty-two days, and yet again be demoted to AC1. He pointed out to me that this was a very distinguished rank for a pilot. AC2s were of course mere trainees, but there were no more than a handful of AC1s with wings on their chests.

The library housed several hundred books, mostly Bibles, with a number of collections of nineteenth century tracts and sermons, and books about phrenology or astrology. The prisoners were not allowed to read them. Our job was to keep the books clean, and rearrange them according to the whim of the Commandant, a bulky moron who regularly regaled us with moral homilies. Outside the library window, yes, a real, full-sized window, was the Commandant's garden; our other duty was to keep it weeded. This, Geoff showed me, enabled us to steal tomatoes, slip them inside our overalls, and then put them to ripen behind the Bibles. Sometimes the Commandant would cause us acute anguish by pulling out a Bible or two in the course of a moral lecture. We would look anxiously to see if a tomato was coyly peeping out. But we were spared. For tomatoes we could swap onions, sugar and even sometimes butter with the trusties who worked in the kitchen. We also lent out books to some trusties, who seemed prepared to read anything.

After working a few days with Geoff, The Boob did not become any more attractive, but I found it much more bearable.

After release, I had a few days leave, so went back to South Australia. In those years my mother, whenever she went to Melbourne, always stayed at Menzies Hotel (never "The" Menzies), where General MacArthur and his staff were now installed. The Americans had not entirely taken over the hotel, and the head porter, Harry, a good friend of my mother's, was still at his desk in the front hall. Harry could arrange almost anything, including the miracle of a sleeping berth in the Melbourne-Adelaide express. These were of course normally reserved for high-ranking officers. Harry arranged a berth for me; a fiver changed hands.

I was sitting in the compartment reading D.H. Lawrence's *Fantasia of the Unconscious*, wondering who my fellow-passenger would be, when in came an army General, in full splendour of uniform. He gruffly said hello, and sat down. I saw him glance at my wings and the absence of any rank on my arms or shoulders. After a while he said, "What rank are you, Airman?" Remembering Geoff Cornfoot, I snapped out, like a good salute, "Aircraftman Pilot, Sir." "Oh, yes, yes, I see." Obviously baffled, but not intending to demean himself to enquiry, he went back to his newspaper. "I'll take the top bunk, of course, Sir," I could not resist following up.

Now some of my fellow-felons and I were sent up to Tamworth in New South Wales to Central Flying School, to do a conversion course on a horrid little aircraft called a Wackett Trainer. For our sins, we were to be sent to the Wireless and Air Gunners' School (WAGS), at Ballarat. There we passed a bitterly cold winter. Our duties were unbelievably boring and uncomfortable. In our noisy and unheated Wacketts we had to fly for half an hour over the bare Western District, turn left and fly for another half hour, then turn again and fly for half an hour back to the aerodrome. All this time the WAG student in the back seat would be tapping and receiving messages in Morse code. The only compensation for all this was that we were given our stripes back again.

Early on I worked out a relief for this boredom, if not from the cold which I felt even inside the enormous white sweater dear Chibs had knitted me from greasy wool. Books were the answer.

I found that a book could be balanced on the cowl above the instruments, and propped against the windscreen. My favourite reading at the time was D.H. Lawrence, and Gino Nibbi sent me volume after volume of the fiction, in that lovely little red Heinemann edition with a phoenix on the jacket. I think I may be the only person who has read the collected fiction of D.H. Lawrence while flying an aircraft. The only snag was that it is a little difficult to read and look where you are going at the same time. The Wackett was not the problem — if properly trimmed it would fly straight and level on course; the problems were other aircraft, and remembering to turn when half an hour was up. Years later, I opened my copy of *Sons and Lovers* and out fell a note from a trainee WAG: "Sarge — cannot hear base any longer". The feeble signal from Ballarat could only be picked up inside a radius of a little over half an hour's flying from base; absorbed in Lawrence, I had flown on for another twenty minutes or more.

For many years I was not very interested in politics, but the thread of my reading ran through the pattern of my views about politics. Reading Lawrence, and poets like Auden and Spender, let alone Rimbaud or Lorca, meant that I could never vote for a political party serving money and middle-class interests. Menzies was for me the epitome of these predilections. All my life I have never voted for any party but Labor. My Australian common sense and humanity stopped me following Lawrence into the idiocies of a kind of Fascism. In *Kangaroo* Lawrence was incredibly percipient to have detected the seeds of militant organizations like the New Guard in Australia, but he did not know enough about Australians to realise that nothing more than some wretched sprouts would come from these seeds. Only a few contemptible individuals or misguided idealists have espoused Fascism in Australia.

Four of us — Ken McRae and Fred Lethbridge who had been in The Boob with me, and Alan Michie who was six feet eight and a half inches tall, and I — bought a 1926 Morris tourer for ten pounds. One day, having some leave, we drove out to Beaufort, a neighbouring town. We stopped outside the pub and were just going in when a well-dressed gentleman asked us if we would let him buy us a drink. It seems impossible to believe now, in this cynical age, but in 1942 civilians in country towns would do such things for the brave boys in blue.

After a couple of beers he said that we should be driving a better car than "that old Morris". By this time we had found out that Mr Wotherspoon more or less owned Beaufort, including the hotel, several shops and the garage. "What do you suggest?" I asked. "What about a Rolls-Royce?" was his reply. We all laughed at the jest, and followed him across the road to a large, locked wooden shed. He produced a key and opened the double doors. Inside were at least five Rolls-Royces.

"Which one would you like, boys?" he asked, and went on to explain that with petrol rationing he could only occasionally use them. I said I thought it was a fine jest, and explained how impecunious we were.

He did not say anything, but walked over to a huge grey sedan, with the inimitable radiator and naked-lady mascot, and said, "Surely you could afford a hundred pounds? I'll give you twenty pounds for the Morris, so that's only twenty pounds each." He explained that the 40/50 engine and chassis were about 1920 vintage, and the body was built in Melbourne in about 1930. It was in perfect condition; there were even silver-plated flower vases on either side of the back seat. So we drove the Rolls back to Ballarat and parked her alongside the Commanding Officer's Ford Ten. The Rolls had the most wonderful effect on the Ballarat girls, and the back seat was the size of a double bed.

When the spring began to arrive, and the Ballarat snow and ice were melting, Ken and I were posted back to Central Flying School, where we were to learn how to become Flying Instructors on Tiger Moths. A month later I received a money order for twenty-five pounds and a sad letter to say that Michie, Lethbridge and another pilot called Peacock, who had been at school with me, had flown down to Geelong Grammar School and beaten it up. The boys enjoyed the display of low flying, but the aircraft registration numbers were taken and the pilots were court-martialled and sent off to The Boob, poor Fred Lethbridge, the mildest of men, for the second time. They had made a rush sale of the Rolls for a hundred pounds. So I had made five pounds profit. I wonder what that might have grown to, had the Rolls been salted away. But life is in the present in the Air Force.

Nine

I was to spend sixteen months of 1943 and 1944 at No. 7 Elementary Flying Training School, teaching pupils how to fly Tiger Moths. Instructing was boring and repetitive, but the Tiger is one of the most delightful aircraft ever built, infinitely responsive and patient of maltreatment, with no vices, except the no-fault one of being open and thus very cold to fly in a Tasmanian winter. One could always take over for a few minutes and dive and roll around the sky, or low-fly between the trees, for The Boob had not cured us of this pleasure.

I had wondered when I was training to be an instructor whether I would be able to cope with issuing instructions, in a steady, clear voice, into the rubber cup of the speaking tube which was connected with the earphones in the trainee's helmet. The trouble was that I still had the embarrassing stammer that had induced Kewpie Dart to call me Splotton. It would hardly inspire confidence in a pupil if his instructor told him to "Pull-pull-pull-pull back the stick now". By this time the Tiger would have buried its nose in the ground.

To my surprise, and relief, I had no difficulty at all in speaking my instructions. I also began to stammer less in conversation, and before long did not stammer at all.

I often wondered what caused that stammer, why one word would suddenly start to repeat itself like a machine-gun, instead of emerging neatly and cleanly by itself. Max Nicholson had a favourite phrase by which he used to explain almost anything defective in another person's behaviour: "Fear of the world, my dear, fear of the world". I certainly had been afraid when I first went to school, but I had stammered long before that. Otherwise I didn't think I suffered from Max's fear. It was all very mysterious, but, whatever it was, it was now in the past.

The aerodrome was a few miles south of Launceston, in some of the prettiest country in Australia. Some of my fellow-instructors were remarkable people. My two best friends were Frank Maughan, a schoolteacher from Byron Bay in New South Wales, and a law student from Brisbane called Wally Campbell. Frank was killed in 1944.

Frank saw the world and people very clearly. His brains and energy had lifted him out of an impoverished background, but he was never bitter about the past. I most remember him saying, in his dry voice, "There are two sorts of people in the world, Geoff, those with soul and those without". Ever afterwards I have thought of people in terms of Frank's judgment.

Wally was studying Law at the University of Queensland. He was to become Sir Walter Campbell, Chief Justice and then Governor of Queensland. Both Frank and Wally had been political radicals in their student days. They were good friends, and could not have looked more different. Frank was bony and curly-haired and his chin stuck out like his opinions; he loved reading and understood poetry. Wally was rounded in face, with a moustache, and a smile that was as easy-going as Frank's was quizzical. He loved to argue, with such skill and anticipation that it did not surprise me when he rose to the top of his profession, nor that he was to outwit Joh Bjelke-Petersen on several noteworthy occasions.

Ken McRae, our other friend, was also a Queenslander. A photo-lithographer, Ken had worked for the *Courier-Mail*. He was lithe and quick in speech and movement, one of those dark Scots, very old and experienced in matters of women and booze. (He would have been about 28.)

We each dobbed in five pounds and bought a 1926 Dodge tourer. The advantage of this sturdy machine, apart from its capacious seats and excellent leather uphostery, was that after being started on a carburettor-full of petrol, it would run on neat kerosene. This of course was in the days of petrol rationing; strictly speaking, it was illegal to run cars on kerosene, which was unrationed, but the Launceston police would hold their noses as we drove by in a cloud of blue smoke. As long as you changed the oil every two hundred miles, the Dodge didn't mind this treatment. I set about teaching Frank to drive, for although he was a flying instructor, he had never learned how to drive a car.

This Dodge was a faithful friend. Late one night, or rather early one morning, I had to return to camp alone, leaving the other lucky lads with their girls, as I was on duty in the morning. About four miles from the station I went to sleep, and awoke with the Dodge upside down, leaning against a stout strainer post a few yards down a steep slope. Just above my head, the big twelve-volt battery was swinging to and fro on the ends of its terminals. Once again luck had been good to me. As I walked the four miles home in the freezing dark I wondered what I was being saved up for.

By the time we got back to the Dodge, all four wheels and the spare had been stolen, not to mention the battery, so we left her there and she gradually disappeared until just the dark-blue of the body shell remained. We bought another similar model, also for twenty pounds. This one survived Frank's head-on encounter with a cow, in which the cow's horn went right through the radiator.

In matters of love, or rather, love-making, we enjoyed a unique advantage. We were the only station of the armed forces near Launceston, and thus had the complete cooperation in the war effort of the girls of the city. Whenever we could get away from the station, we would drive in to the Brisbane Hotel and drink beer to excess, then be joined by several girls and have dinner at the Brisbane, where the landlady kept a strict eye on us. If we stayed the night and had a room, there was no sneaking a girl upstairs. Instead, four pilots and four girls would pile into the Dodge and go to a night club at St Leonard's, and dance to "In the Mood" or "Elmer's Tune".

When the club closed we would drive up to the river pool in the hills above Launceston for a swim, trailing blue wisps of kerosene smoke.

The Basin, as it was called, was a beautiful deep pool created by a dam in the Tamar river. A lawn ran down to it, and across this ran our naked white figures, to splash white foam in the cold, dark, shock of the pool. It was a wonder we did not drown ourselves, but we were all, the girls included, strong swimmers. Then we would run shivering back to the Dodge, dry ourselves on our clothes, and drink some more beer.

What happened next was what I had been denied for so many years, except for that brief sandy interlude at St Kilda. I knew all about it from poetry:

Licence my roving hands, and let them go
Before, behind, between, above, below.
O my America, my new-found land
My kingdom, safeliest when with one man manned …

I thought I knew all about it from being a country boy and watching stallions and rams about their business. But of course I knew nothing.

These wonderful Tasmanian girls were happy to make their knowledge mine. Frank, alone of us, might have been heading towards marriage, with his pretty, dark Betty. The rest of us never invoked the future or pretended to permanence. The present was indicative of happiness enough.

Our boozing and lechery were rituals as harmless as the songs we roared out one after another, "The Ball of Kirriemuir", "Cats on the Rooftops", "Abdul A-Bul-Bul Emir", "The Good Ship Venus", "The Harlot of Jerusalem" and all the rest of them. One test of erudition was to take it in turns to sing limericks to a standard tune, with a chorus ending "Sing us another one, do". We could keep this up all the way back to Western Junction. Some of the limericks are still dear to me:

There once was a Bishop of Birmingham
Who would use his young boys while confirming 'em.
At the end of each clause
He would whip down their drawers
And insert his episcopal worm in 'em.

The filthiness of some of these songs is prodigious, but it never seemed to stick. As with *Struwwelpeter* all those years ago, when we did not become cruel by reading about cruelty, now we did not become depraved by singing about the most frightful depravities. The songs made fun of both man and woman, prick and cunt, and the women weren't just victims; look at Eskimo Nell. The verses were often subtly witty. The imagery was often metaphysical in its ingenuity; Donne would have enjoyed Eskimo Nell who took on the famous fucker Red-Eye Dick and "gripped his cock like a Chatswood lock in the National Safe Deposit". The verses of most of the ballads were as practical and straight-shooting as Chaucer, as in the exhausted end to the alphabet song to the tune of "Heigh ho, says Anthony Rowley": "W is the whore who thought fucking a farce / and X, Y and Z you can shove up your arse".

When I was in Adelaide on leave before coming to Tasmania, I was having a drink with Max Harris and discussing the future of *Angry Penguins*; the new issue, which would have a colour reproduction of a surrealist painting by James Gleeson on the cover, would contain some poems of mine. Max was a loyal supporter. When he heard that I would be stationed near Launceston, he said "You lucky bastard, Dutton, do you realize who lives in Launceston?" I didn't. "Magda von Horch." Magda's poems in *Angry Penguins* and other magazines were sultry sizzlers. "I bare my breasts to the fingers of the sun / My belly receives the benediction of the moon." That kind of thing. "It's just bloody not fair," sighed Max, "and you are actually being paid to wear that blue uniform and then take it off to fuck Magda." He stubbed out one of his inevitable cigarettes. "But I suppose I'll do my bit for the war effort, and give you her address." He looked in his book. "Christ, I even have her phone number."

As soon as possible after arriving at Western Junction I rang Magda. A husky voice, not with a German accent, but definitely husky, answered. "Geoffrey Dutton!" she exclaimed, as if she were connected to Dylan Thomas. It was arranged that I should meet her at the Public Library. I begged the Dodge off the other owners; I wasn't going to have Campbell's crudities interfere with my idyll.

I went in the doors to the dowdy interior of the Launceston Public Library. There was no one there who could possibly be Magda. I sat in a corner from which I could see anyone entering the room, and pretended to read a magazine. After a quarter of an hour I was getting desperate, so I went up to the beaky little middle-aged woman at the desk, who was wearing a green-and-white tennis shade to shield her obviously weak eyes, and asked her if by any chance she knew Magda von Horch. "Oh!" She took off the tennis-shade. "You must be Geoffrey Dutton!"

We went to her flat for "real coffee"; while she was making it she put on a record of the slow movement of Rachmaninov's Second Piano Concerto. There were embarrassing paintings of nudes in Rousseauish jungles on the walls. "They're mine," she said with a proprietorial sigh, "they mean so much to me."

As soon as I decently could, before the onset of any indecency, I sprang to my feet and said: "I'm so sorry, Magda, but I have to be back on duty. Night-flying tonight, you know." She believed me, with a slightly different sigh. It was wartime, of course.

When I next saw Max, he swore he knew nothing of the real Magda. I wonder. There are occasions when life does not imitate art ...

Western Junction was also good for more conventional forms of literature. There were, as always in the Air Force when you were not actually flying, endless periods of doing nothing. This was ideal for anyone who loved reading, and a perfect opportunity for anyone like myself, trying to become a writer. Being sergeants, we were privileged to share a room, instead of being thrown into the noise and scrimmage, with twenty-three other young men, of an open hut. I shared a room with Frank, who liked reading as much as I did, and was particularly pleased to find himself with a constant supply of books he had not read. Frank's educational opportunities had been limited. But he had fought his way up and loved the climb, neither alarmed by the cliffs of mind above him, nor fearing the cliffs of fall below him, to borrow from Hopkins. His comments on my poems were invaluable, as was his immunity to fashionable jargon. When in a new issue of *Angry Penguins* Max Harris described me as being a poet of tight, internal cohesion, Frank said, "Christ, Dutt, I didn't know you suffered from the consty. My old Grandma always swore by syrup of figs. Try it."

I had a selection of my favourite books with me, mostly poetry; by now I knew most of the *Faber Book of Modern Verse* off by heart. Poetry, my own or that of others, was always intruding into my Air Force life, a great force for sanity as well as an outlet for the starved imagination. On night flying we used to operate from a paddock which functioned as our little satellite aerodrome. As the trainee in the rear seat one night, flew the Tiger in a left-hand circuit around the jewels of the flare-path a thousand feet below, I looked up and repeated "Cold shuttered loveless star, skulker in clouds / Streetwalker of the sky / Where can you hide?" "Eh? What was that, Sarge?" The voice of the trainee in my earphones brought me back to my duties. "What's up, are you deaf?" I barked. "Keep your left wing up, you bloody drongo." "Thanks, Sarge."

In our room Frank would lie on his stretcher, knees up, smoking a cigarette he had just rolled. "Can't nut this out at all, Dutt, it's too bloody obscure, this stuff."

A candle in the thighs
Warms youth and seed and burns the seeds of age;
Where no seed stirs,
The fruit of man unwrinkles in the stars,
Bright as a fig;
Where no wax is, the candle shows its hairs.

Dawn breaks behind the eyes;
From poles of skull and toe the windy blood
Slides like a sea;
Nor fenced, nor staked, the gushers of the sky
Spout to the rod
Divining in a smile the oil of tears.

I was not going to be drawn into explication of Dylan Thomas with pragmatic Frank. "Just roll with the images, Maughan, let yourself go. Think of the times you tell those trainees that they'll never learn unless they relax."

Frank was used to me and let it roll over.

"Hey, but I really like this:

Down the road someone is practising scales,
The notes like little fishes vanish with a wink
  of tails.
Man's heart expands to tinker with his car
For this is Sunday morning, Fate's great bazaar.

We agreed that we both liked Louis MacNeice, but Frank said that I could have Dylan Thomas. I tried both approaches in my own poems; I could have done with more clarity and less explosive imagery, but I wanted the poems to be supercharged, not just to putter quietly along in top gear.

I sent my poems off to my mother. She was supportive but obviously baffled. When night flying I had been watching the moonlight in the blue valleys of the mountain range east of the aerodrome. I wrote in a poem: "The light froths like blue juice in a bitten apple". She commented that she had never seen a blue apple. Well, fair enough.

Max Harris and John Reed were now the publishers of *Angry Penguins*, which had moved to Melbourne, although Max at this stage was still living in Adelaide. Reed was a lawyer from a rich Tasmanian family, who had married an even richer wife, Sunday Baillieu, from Melbourne. Reed had been much involved in the Melbourne battles between the defenders of the orthodox in art and the Contemporary Art Society. The Reeds were already generous patrons of modern Australian art, although fiercely regional. Nolan, Arthur Boyd, Joy Hester and Tucker were essential, but Drysdale or Margaret Preston were scorned. Reed, mainly through Max's influence, had a more eclectic view of literature. *Angry Penguins* published Dylan Thomas, American servicemen in the South Pacific like Karl Shapiro and Harry Roskolenko, and the Western Australian short-story writer Peter Cowan.

In 1943 Max had spoken of the immensely exciting possibility of Reed & Harris publishing a book of my poems. In early 1944 he wrote to say that this offer was now definite; the writing paper he used, of Reed & Harris,

Publishers, gave addresses in Adelaide, Melbourne and New York. "No cracks!" Max's letter started. In it he warned me not to write to Reed, but to do everything through him. The letter ended: "Don't forget the urgency of this letter and work through me, not Reed. All of which is mysterious, but necessary." I didn't care what manipulations Max was up to; my book of poems was what mattered. It was to be called *Night Flight and Sunrise*, a title reminiscent of Saint-Exupéry, whose books on flying over the desert and South America I had been devouring.

Before long a wash-and-ink painting for the jacket arrived; it was by Sid Nolan, his first effort at a book cover. Frank sat beside me on the bench outside the flight office as I opened the packet. It showed an aerodrome with some stick-insect aircraft on it; on each side was a windsock, one pointing east, the other west. "Jesus!" said Frank, "two fucking winds blowing at once! You'd better watch this Nolan bloke."

I sent the art work back to Max, saying that my life in the Air Force would not be worth living if this jacket was printed. Sid seemed to bear no ill-will, and before long back came a pleasing design of a tree with some birds, based on a line from one of the poems, "What wind flowered the dead branches with galahs". Typical of the carelessness of Reed & Harris, this was to appear on the jacket of the book, misquoted as "dead trees".

I had been promoted to Pilot Officer in 1943, and was now a Flying Officer, which meant that I was paid a dizzying eighteen shillings and eightpence, from which tax of one shilling and eightpence was deducted. It seemed hardly the action of a grateful nation, to pay us so little in the first place, and then to deduct tax.

Teaching trainees to fly was of course very boring, endless repetition, calling for patience when some ham-handed lad pushed the Tiger out of its natural tendency to fly straight and level, or jammed his great foot on the rudder so that the Tiger slid out of what should have been a neat turn. Landings were the worst. The trainees would either fly into the ground as if the Tiger were a harpoon and they were trying to stick it into the hide of the earth, or else they would level off, some ten feet above the ground, onto which they hoped some fairy parachute would lower them. In either case, the undercarriage would take a severe jolt as the wheels hit the ground, and one could almost hear a moan of pain as the Tiger bounced into the air.

If we were interested, the ground staff would let us have our own aircraft, and I grew as fond of A17-686 as if she were a pet. But it was a pet you had to treat with great respect; however friendly, it could still kill you. Occasionally, to beat the boredom, one would take over from the trainee and chase the clouds and do aerobatics, including forbidden antics like inverted spins and attempts at outside loops, where one's eyeballs would bulge against one's goggles.

I spent months looking at a railway bridge over a river and wondering whether I could fly under it. One day my trainee, who was a natural flyer and on for anything, read my thoughts and said, "Go on, have a go, Sir." So down we went and flew up the river, the wheels almost touching the water, until there was the bridge and it was too late to pull up over it. For a second the sky was steel girders, and we were through. There was silence from the back seat. "Are you OK?" I called down the communication tube. There was no answer. My tough trainee had fainted.

For practising night flying, we would often go down to a so-called auxiliary aerodrome, which was in fact just a big paddock. We would arrive in a flurry of illegal low aerobatics, which would cause strong complaints from the Flight Commander, Ian Johnson, who later became a famous cricketer. What gave me most pleasure in the soft, still air of evening was to roll the Tiger onto its back at five hundred feet on the final approach to the field, and glide down inverted, the motor popping as we dropped. The trick was to make sure you had enough speed up to roll level before landing, as the Tiger's carburettor was gravity-fed from the tank between the top wings, and you could not rely on the engine revving up again. Ian Johnson would stride over, eyes glowering beneath the tight waves of his red hair, and shout, "Next time you do that, Dutton, you're on a charge!"

The sweetest stint of all was when we had to take the train down to Hobart, where there was a Tiger Moth kept for cooperation with the Army in anti-aircraft procedure at night. We were supposed to fly up and down the Derwent at five thousand feet, so that the anti-aircraft units could fix us in their searchlights and pretend they were about to shoot us down. We had been told that we were allowed to take evasive action, but the heroes on the searchlights were so hopeless that we used to try to fly into their beams in order to help them. It was beautiful, all alone above the city and river, with the white beams poking about in the dark sky, and the black mass of Mount Wellington faintly but threateningly visible on the western horizon.

We lived in luxury at the old Wrest Point Hotel, looking out over the river, and, apart from the night flying, our time was our own. Whether we flew or not was up to us. After a sticky start, I had made friends with a blonde girl of splendid appearance (she was later to become Miss Tasmania) if not great brain. The initial difficulty had arisen on my first meeting with her family, at their perfect Thirties white house above Sandy Bay. Her genial father had poured me a whisky and asked, inevitably, what I thought of Hobart. "It's really beautiful," I replied truthfully, and with equal honesty went on to say that the only disappointment was the railway station, which was like the wheat siding at Woop-Woop; there wasn't even a platform. You just jumped down into the mud. Judy's father stiffened, and she said, "Daddy is Commissioner of Railways."

The advantage of being your own boss was that it was up to you whether or not you flew. Hobart is no place to be flying around at night in bad weather; we, of course, had no radar or any other means of getting in touch with Mount Wellington. Every afternoon we had to ring the Army Major in charge of the anti-aircraft unit and tell him whether it was safe for us to fly that night. He was always touchingly respectful (however much he outranked us), and would agree instantly with our judgement. So, when Judy begged me to come to a dinner-dance with her one night, I read the weather report with particular care, and told the Major there would be no flying that night. "Of course, if you say so, you're the boss", was his gratifying reply.

At the end of March 1943 I was posted to Central Flying School (CFS), which had moved to Parkes in New South Wales, to become an instructor of instructors and go on the staff. It was an honour, I suppose, but with the lack of good sense typical of youth, I was all the time wanting to be sent up to the shooting war as a fighter pilot, instead of being grateful that my life was reasonably secure as an instructor. At one stage Ken, Frank and I tried to join the Chinese Air Force, with General Chennault's Flying Tigers; we were told we would be paid a hundred dollars for every Japanese plane we shot down. It was the adventure, not the money, that we really wanted. We seemed to be making quite good progress, when suddenly we received a letter from Air Board, saying that on no account would we be allowed to leave the RAAF, which had invested a great deal of money and time in training us, etc. etc. So we stayed with another sort of Tiger.

Parkes is in western New South Wales, about 230 miles from Sydney, in rolling sheep and wheat country, not unlike Anlaby. It had a population of about 7000, and was a sleepy country town compared with Launceston with its 40,000 people. We had an English Commanding Officer, Royal Air Force, who was determined to busy idle hands and put some smartness into us easy-going Australians. When not flying, instead of being able to laze around in our rooms or the mess and do what we wanted to — in my case read and write — we were driven out into the sun to build ourselves a new mess. The old corrugated-iron hut suited us well enough, but this accursed martinet set us to building a sort of log cabin with polished floors of cypress pine, which grew all about Parkes. When finished, it looked like a country club, but the beer tasted the same, and I had not been able to write a word.

Some of my old friends turned up at Parkes, and I made some new ones, but life was not as it had been at Western Junction. The town itself was devoid of attractions comparable to those of Launceston; most importantly, although we sought them out, there were no girls like the Tasmanian ones. Our camp life was persecuted by the CO, and our town life consisted in drinking at one of the pubs, and I was bored with that.

While I was at Parkes a fat envelope arrived from Max Harris. In it were carbon copies of some poems he wanted me to read and comment on, poems that had been sent to him by the sister of a dead poet called Ern Malley. I thought many of them were very fine indeed, tying many of the intricate knots I was attempting myself, using a great variety of diction, formally strong. I urged him to publish them.

I have not changed my opinion of the poems. "Ern" was of course to be the most famous literary hoax of the twentieth century, and the repercussions almost ruined Max's career as a poet and entrepreneur. Because it was revealed that the poems were a hoax, the poems were assumed by most readers to be worthless; there was an unholy alliance in mocking them between those who detested any poetry and those whose taste in poetry was conservative. The philistine and the reactionary triumphed. But Ern Malley has never been out of print since 1944, and his poems have been acclaimed by some of the best judges around the world. There is now a fine book about the whole story, by Michael Heyward.

The worst aspects of provincial Adelaide were encouraged by the hoax. Max had already antagonized some of the authorities in Adelaide, notably a religious bigot called "Tacky" Hannan, the Crown Prosecutor, and they were waiting for an opportunity to get him. He was prosecuted under the South Australian *Police Offences Act* for publishing seven poems that were an "indecent advertisement" and other items that were "indecent, immoral or obscene". Among these was an expression from one of Peter Cowan's stories, "You can stick it". Literary merit was no defence; the Prosecution did not mind that the seven poems were by a poet who did not exist.

I happened to be home on leave at the time of Max's trial, and he asked me to appear as a witness, my respectability being guaranteed by my Flight Lieutenant's uniform (I had recently been promoted). In the event I was not called, but I was present in the court when Detective Sergeant Vogelsang, spearhead of the prosecution, said that he didn't know what "incestuous" meant, but he knew it was dirty. Max was found guilty and fined; he was not the only editor of the magazine, but he was the one who was prosecuted, because he was a South Australian. John Reed was a very influential lawyer, albeit in Melbourne, and I have always thought he behaved very feebly in this disgraceful episode of triumphant philistinism.

About this time, my book of poems was published. I have always treasured the review in the Adelaide *Advertiser* by Talbot Smith, then well into his eighties. He wrote along the lines of: "The photograph in the front of this book shows a cheerful, healthy young man in a flying suit. Some day he will look back, like many of us, to the follies of his youth."

In 1944 Ninette Trott and I were married. I had proposed to her in a romantic setting behind the cypress hedge on the front lawn at Anlaby, on a moonlit night. I told her, with all the brutality of youth, not to expect the marriage to last all that long, because I didn't.

I was very young for a prospective husband, just twenty-one; she was twenty. For nearly three years she had been, in Air Force parlance, my squarey, although I was faithful to her only when in Adelaide. Marriage had not been on my agenda. I had rejoiced in my sexual freedom in Tasmania and elsewhere, and now I was going to surrender it. But my relationship with Ninette had been a genuinely romantic one; I was in love with her, as I never even pretended to be with the Tasmanian girls (nor they with me). I think I was also like a lot of men who marry very young; they desperately need permanent sexual company. There had been plenty of it in Tasmania, but Parkes was a desert. And after all, Ninette was very pretty, I was in love with her, she was in love with me and desperate to escape from her bourgeois background, and I expected to be killed anyway, so what the hell. The marriage was not then, in my mind at least, the monument it finally became.

The wedding was painfully bourgeois, albeit the service was sonorously performed by Suzie Bowen's grandfather, Archdeacon Clampett. Nearly all my friends were either far away or dead; only my brother John was at hand, having survived the battle of El Alamein and returned to a life on the land. My mother had no difficulty in upstaging Clarice; the contest was hopelessly uneven.

Ninette returned with me to Parkes, where we had to begin married life in one of the hotels. Next to us was the Link Trainer instructor — the Link simulated blind flying — and his newly married wife. He was a man of great appetite, and every morning at 3 a.m. his alarm clock would go off, waking him to pounce again on his unfortunate wife.

The worst aspect of CFS was the tyrannical RAF Commanding Officer; the best was that we had almost every aircraft in the RAAF, and it was our duty to fly them from time to time. So I got to fly the most beautiful aircraft I have ever flown, a Spitfire, and many others such a Kittyhawk and a Vultee Vengeance dive-bomber. The rarest example was Australia's own bulbous-nosed fighter, the Boomerang, which we all tried to avoid flying.

I had a new friend, an enigmatic, very intelligent, odd character called Paul Burton, a brilliant pilot. Paul was also a highly skilled mechanic. He had a Triumph motor-bike which would comfortably exceed 100 m.p.h. I knew this, because the first time he let me ride it, I, who knew nothing about motor-bikes, found it going faster and faster down the straight road into Parkes. When I suddenly saw from the speedometer that we were doing over 100 m.p.h., I tried turning the handlebar grip-throttle the other way.

Together, in Tiger Moths, Paul and I had a battle one day with a wedge-tailed eagle. The eagle made fools of us for some time, but finally we out-manoeuvred the bird and my right-hand wing, at the tip where the metal flap comes over the fabric, accidentally cut off one of the bird's wings.

In acute misery at what we had done, I landed, followed by Paul, in the paddock where the bird's body lay. We united it with its missing wing, and buried it under a cairn of stones.

In Melbourne, not long before my marriage, I had acquired a treasure from Deasey, who was back on leave from the Commandos. This was a 1926 three litre Red Label Bentley, one of the greatest cars ever built; we agreed on the price of two hundred pounds and my 1938 Dodge sedan. Dease disappeared somewhere up north, and Paul and I drove the Bentley back to Parkes.

Not long after we had finished building the much-hated new officers' mess, C.F.S. was shifted to Point Cook, where I had done my advanced training. Ninette and I had the good luck to find a perfect flat, on the top floor of a little white house on the corner of Domain Road and Domain Street, South Yarra. I lived there most of the time, and rode out to Point Cook, some twenty miles away, leaving at 5 a.m., on a DKW two-stroke motor-bike. This would have been impossible had I not, somehow or other, found a source of black-market petrol from a man who owned a garage in Footscray. I exchanged beer or whisky from the mess for the more precious fluid; fortunately the little DKW did about eighty miles to the gallon. Athough I used to wear my entire winter flying gear of suit and boots over my uniform, it was cruelly cold in winter chugging along the Prince's Highway.

I also used to get sleepy at about midnight, much to the vexation of friends like Max Harris, Alister Kershaw, Max Nicholson and Arthur and Yvonne Boyd. Caustically, Kershaw would be saying, "Look at bloody Dutton, asleep again", seemingly unaware that I rose at 4.30 a.m. while he slept in till nine or ten when he strolled down to the ABC to become the golden-voiced broadcaster.

I had first heard of Alister Kershaw from Dease, when I was at St Mark's in 1940. "Have I mentioned Alister Kershaw? Met him a day ago. A poet, very weak, very strong, very stimulating, in quantities fatiguing." We were fellow-contributors to *Angry Penguins* and a Bohemian little magazine, printed on brown paper and edited by Cecily Crozier, called *A Comment*. Alister's first book, *The Lonely Verge*, had appeared in 1943, and it was a matter of great prestige that *Excellent Stranger*, which, with a jacket by Bert Tucker, appeared at the same time as my book, was his second published volume. Alister did not care for the Reed establishment, although he was not too proud to be published by it. We made up a long scatological poem about the goings on at Heide, where Nolan and Sunday and John Reed formed a *ménage à trois*; they were to be joined by Reed's sister Cynthia, with whom Nolan left Heide. Cynthia became both Nolan's wife and his watchdog.

Alister had written a number of delicate lyrics of a precise individuality, yet not to be pinned down to a stiff structure of meaning. His personal myth-making did not operate in the bang-crash style of Dylan Thomas or George Barker, or in the use of packed images like Harris's or mine, but more in the style of the French symbolists, perhaps foreshadowing the move to France, where he was to spend most of his adult life. His two other achievements were a swingeing satire of the contemporary cultural scene, "The Denunciad", and a poem of elemental energy, with lines that struck like gongs, called "Lands in Force". I still admire that poem, although to this day I don't know quite what it means.

Dease was now back in Melbourne, mysteriously still in the Army, but seemingly free of onerous duties. Perhaps he was doing some course or other. He now had a supercharged four and a half litre Bentley roadster. Despite my alarmed protests, he drove us down deserted Toorak Road at 100 m.p.h. at 3 a.m. one morning. Dease and Kershaw were now good friends, and he had kept up his old friendship with Max Nicholson and Arthur Boyd.

Arthur invited Dease and us down to the Boyd family house at Murrumbeena. This was indeed a family house, but of a most astonishing family. They were all artists: Merric, the father, a pioneer of modern pottery, and Doris, his wife, who decorated a lot of his work as well as being an artist herself; Arthur, the genius among them; his young brothers, David, both artist and potter, and sculptor Guy; his sister Mary, at that time a talented painter; and her husband, painter and potter John Perceval. The house was architecturally rather odd, but made more so by the fact that every square inch of it had a painting or piece of pottery on the floor or leaning against or hanging on the walls, amongst them some lovely domestic scenes by Arthur's grandmother, Emma Minnie Boyd.

Max Nicholson had warned me that Merric was "absolutely brilliant and charming, but, my dear, rather eccentric". So now when we knocked on the door it was Merric who answered, an old gentleman with wisps of white hair, wearing a dressing-gown and carpet slippers. Without any other greeting he chanted in a high voice, "Kiss the cats, kiss the cats." Arthur motioned to me to do what he said. "Kiss the cats," he called again, as we went down on all fours and awoke a selection of sleeping cats around the big room and kissed them on the whiskers. This task completed, Merric became utterly courteous and charming, the Earl of Beaumaris welcoming some fellow-aristocrats from across the Channel, and Doris was despatched to bring us tea. After spending a few hours at Murrumbeena it was clear why Arthur did not need to attend art school or become involved in art politics. He and the family lived art, and he had learned every aspect of it from earliest childhood.

Not long after this I ran into Sid Nolan at the Contemporary Art Society's exhibition. He took me around the show, where he had several paintings hanging, notably a particularly fine view of Heidelberg at night, expatiating on the various paintings with all his fluency and warmth.

Hearing of my enthusiasm for Arthur's work, he asked me to write an article about Arthur for *Angry Penguins*, for Sid was now a member of the editorial board of the magazine. It would have been the first article ever written about Arthur. I did so, and although well aware that I was no art critic, I was quite pleased with it. I posted it off to Sid and John Reed and Max. There was an ominous silence. Max had gone back to Adelaide, so I rang Reed, who in icy tones said he did not see why I had taken the opportunity of this article to insult *Angry Penguins* and all it stood for. I could be assured that they had no intention of printing the article.

Having been associated with the magazine for several more years than Reed, since its inception, I was baffled by the accusation. Later on, I found out from Max that Reed had expected me to praise him and I had not mentioned him, except indirectly at the end of my article when I said that Arthur was not a member of an *Angry Penguins* or any other school, and that the only school he belonged to was that of the Boyd family.

Soon after this I was told by various friends that Sid was denouncing me around Melbourne as "that Air Force moron". Kershaw and Dease were of course delighted to hear this, and from then on always addressed me by that title. Sid and I did not see each other again for about ten years, when we amiably began again, and never had another falling out, although in private I could never altogether forgive him for deserting from the Army.

At this time Arthur had been called up by the Army, and was shambling around in a private's uniform, driving the authorities to despair by his inability to understand the rigid world of army discipline. One afternoon, after drinking at our flat, we went into Domain Road to catch a tram into Melbourne. Trams were always very crowded in wartime — perhaps there were not so many of them — and we were resigned to not getting a seat, and having to straphang. But as the tram approached, Dease, who had that marvellous capacity to be outrageous without getting the giggles as I always did, suggested that we pose as service police and Arthur as a raving lunatic whom we were getting to hospital. "We'll get seats," he assured us.

Arthur accordingly pulled his hair down over his face (he had already lost his hat) and began to gibber most convincingly. Dease and I, each about eight inches taller than Arthur, lifted him under the armpits onto the tram, with Dease saying: "Steady there, lad, steady there. No need to be alarmed, ladies and gents, he's not really violent." In no time three passengers had jumped up and motioned us to their seats, while Arthur continued to twist and grunt.

A regular visitor to the South Yarra flat was a young Dutchman who looked rather like Arthur pretending to be a maniac. His name was Erik Schwimmer. He had a snub face with a mild, perpetual smile, and arms that continually thrashed. He had an amazing brain, and could talk in several languages about Spinoza or the theory of relativity, Bach's "Art of the Fugue" or the politics of the Dutch East Indies, as Indonesia then was. He introduced us to smoked eel, arriving with one about three feet long, wrapped in newspaper, which he laid on the table-cloth in the midst of our first attempt at a formal dinner party for some friends of my mother's.

On another occasion he forgot that we lived upstairs, and walked through the open french windows into our landlady's bedroom. It was a very hot day. She was extremely pregnant, and was lying naked on her bed moaning and stroking her distended belly. "Oh I am sorry to intrude," said Schwimmer, advancing to the edge of the bed, "I am looking for some friends of mine called Dutton, and I thought they resided here. Would you like some of these excellent fish and chips?"

Erik, like Arthur, was too much for the Army, Dutch or Australian, which in both cases simply gave up and discharged them. Erik's final torture of his drill sergeant was his inability to understand the basic movements of marching. "Left, right, Left, right!" he took to mean that you should shoot out your left arm and leg simultaneously, and follow with right arm and leg.

Altogether in 1944–45 I led a schizophrenic life, talking about poetry or music or philosophy or art or airy nothings to all these highly individual people, and then riding my little motor-bike out to spend the day in airy discipline.

The European war ended, and we flew over Melbourne in formation as part of the Victory Celebrations. The Air Force then staged some sort of carnival at Point Cook, of which the highlight was the sight of three of us in Wirraways doing formation aerobatics close to the ground, the sort of thing I had been sent to The Boob for. The climax of our thrill-giving was a dive in line astern down to just above the tarmac in front of the crowd, and then up in a barrel roll in formation. Harry Wharf, our leader, kept us in the dive for so long that Reggie Adsett, behind me as number three, missed the ground by such a small margin that two women in the crowd fainted. In an article *The Age* gave our effort a headline "Wirraways Steal Show", and went on to say it was "one of the most spectacular demonstrations of formation flying ever seen at 'The Point'. The Wirraways looped and rolled and dived and climbed as one machine. WAAAFs and ground staff downed tools and came out of hangars, even seasoned pilots deigned to step outside and watch. They stole the show completely, even from the streamlined Spitfires and Kittyhawks."

Shortly after this, three of us were told that we had been posted to Bougainville, to fly a little high-wing monoplane called an Auster, as artillery spotters for the AIF. The idea was for us to fly over the jungle until we could see the Japanese, and then radio back their position to the soldiers on the ground. It was pretty demeaning work for pilots like us, with more than two thousand hours up, expert in flying every aircraft in the RAAF. We should have been given Spitfires, we considered, but we were only too happy to go and do anything. At last we would be Up North, where the war was, with a better chance of being killed.

Towards the end of July 1945 it was time to leave Melbourne. I met Kershaw, with his friend John Morgan, at the ABC, where, with the help of a technician in an empty studio, Kershaw and Morgan made a record for me of a farewell poem from Kershaw, and then of them singing "The Minstrel Boy to the war has gone".

Ten

The Army and Air Force at Torokina was surrounded by tropical jungle. I had never known such dense vegetation. If you walked into it from one of the tracks around the base you were in a green prison, from the green tops of the tall, still trees down to the huge green flaps that hung like elephants' ears, from the stumpy trees and the green bamboos with spines on their shafts — even the spiders were green. I had brought a copy of Lorca's poems with me. I used to love his "*Romance Sonambulo*", "Sleepwalking Ballad", with its refrain that sounds so much more beautiful in Spanish than in translation: "*Verde que te quiero verde / Verde viento. Verdes ramas*" ("Green how I love you green./ Green wind. Green boughs"). It was a poem from a pale, dusty landscape, whether of Spain or Australia did not matter. In New Guinea it had a different translation: "Green how I hate you green".

Every day for a couple of hours green would turn to grey as solid sheets of rain crashed onto the tents. Then the sun would come out hotter than ever, and the sweat run into your eyes and down the channel of your back. And amidst the green and the grey we were all yellow from taking anti-malarial Atebrin tablets. No one had ever told us about skin cancer, and we would spend as much of the day as possible with our shirts off.

The other grey that sometimes floated over us was ash from the plume of smoke drifting from Mount Bagana, the volcano that lifted its distant cone some five thousand feet over the jungle. From the distance the plume was a glittering white cloud twisting and turning, rolling with the wind.

The war still existed, but by this time it was a quiet war on Bougainville; neither the Japanese nor the allies wished to provoke each other. It could have been quiet for a long time, had it not been for the insane ambition of the commander of the Australian Army, General Blamey, who, against General MacArthur's wishes, had insisted on attacking Japanese forces in the south and north of the island, to show that he was a General who could deploy troops on his own. The ferocity and waste of this little war has recently been fully documented; it had already been exposed in Tom Hungerford's powerful novel *The Ridge and the River*. Now, in late July 1945, it seemed that we and the Japanese would be there for ever, with no prospect of an ending of the Pacific War until Japan itself could be invaded.

In the meantime we flew our ridiculous little Austers, and learned about our duties as aerial observation posts for the Army. The Auster was a frail, sluggish plane with a very low stalling speed. This made it difficult to land on the tiny strips in the jungle which the Army had carved out for us. They cut down the tall trees at only one end of the strip, so you always had to land and take off in opposite directions. This meant that if a wind was blowing, you either landed or took off downwind. If you were landing downwind the infuriating Auster would just keep on floating; when it finally touched down you had to belt on the brakes to stop it running on into the jungle.

Taking off presented other problems, particularly when we flew up to the island where the Americans had an officers' rest camp. The Australians and the New Zealanders (who were flying Corsair fighters) were not allowed in this camp unless on duty. One day I flew up to the island to collect an American Colonel and bring him back to Torokina. It was like a movie set, a perfect little tropical island ringed with white sand, and in amongst the jungle there were luxuriously appointed huts, and meals of fresh crayfish, oysters and reef fish, with unlimited supplies of bourbon and beer. There also seemed to be a lot of pretty girls about in khaki dresses; I was told that the poor sick officers needed a lot of nursing.

Before leaving Torokina our flight commander had told me that I was to bring back a sack of oysters; I was not to mention this, but the sack would be placed in the Auster while I was at lunch. After a sumptuous meal, the portly Colonel and I were driven in a jeep to the airstrip, which was the usual one-ended type. A brisk breeze was blowing down the strip in the direction in which I would have to take off. I placed the Colonel's elegant leather bag on top of the sack of oysters, and taxied out. I ran the Auster up to full revs, standing on the brakes. I let them go and the wretched little machine lumbered down the strip while the sweat poured down my face. I thought about the fifteen or sixteen stone of the Colonel, my own thirteen stone, and the several hundred pounds of oysters. By this time we were just airborne, but the trees beyond the cleared area, a good hundred feet high, were towering in front of us. For once I was grateful for the Auster's slow stalling speed. With the airspeed at about 45 m.p.h. we just managed to rise above the branches.

It was worth it for the oysters. They were enormous, and could only be prised open after being bashed insensible by a jungle knife. I was reminded of the times we used to fly from Western Junction over to the east coast of Tasmania, to the little town of St Helen's, where a sack full of crayfish for our mess would be lowered into the front seat of the Tiger, and the belt done up over it, in case of bad weather. The Chief Flying Officer used to look the other way in the matter of these flights, because he enjoyed crayfish. Then one careless pilot crashed into the mountain side coming home, and crayfish were scattered down the slope, after which such flights were no longer allowed.

I had been in Bougainville little more than a fortnight when the camp's loudspeakers gave out the incredible news that the Emperor Hirohito had instructed the Japanese to surrender. The war was over. Apparently something called an "atomic bomb" had made this miracle happen; a miracle indeed, for we had all believed it was impossible for the Japanese to dishonour themselves by surrendering, and that an invasion of Japan would have cost tens of thousands of lives. We didn't know what the bomb was, or what it had done to Hiroshima or Nagasaki. All we knew was that the war was over. We could all keep on living and do what we wanted with our lives. After years of trying, I had made it to the war just as it ended. I could not complain.

We all got drunk and then roared off down to the beach to sober up in the surf. Someone had brought a Very signal pistol and shot flares into the sky. Whoever was driving our jeep swung off the track and down the airstrip, the tyres clattering on the steel-covered runway, and we had a Very light duel with the duty pilot in the control tower. The beach at Torokina was black, the waves were black in the moonless night, only the white foam was our guide. Naked and wet on the beach again, we downed more beer. The war was over.

That, of course, did not mean we could go home. It was up to Air Board to decide when that would be. My Flight Commander, an amiable Western Australian, urged me to put in a request for priority demobilization, so that I could return to the University. I did so. I wanted to write more than to return there, but I knew that poetry would not provide me, let alone me and a wife, with enough money to live on.

Another pilot and I were told to fly down to the south of the island, to the Japanese base at Buin, to take some documents to the Japanese commanding officer. We landed and taxied in to what seemed to be the tarmac. There were several hundred Japanese troops clearing grass around the huts. As we got out of the Auster, we did not feel like conquering heroes; we were too aware of the fact that we didn't even have a revolver between us. What if these Japanese had not heard the Emperor's command? A Sergeant came up and saluted. Some of the men waved at us and smiled. So these short, wiry men, who were much the same colour, thanks to the Atebrin, as us, were the ex-enemy. The total absence of enmity, on either side, was very strange.

A few days later I was told to fly down to Buin again, and pick up a Japanese Major and fly him up to a conference at the northern end of the island. He was tall and elegant, with a black moustache, and he wore beautiful gloves and soft suede boots. He spoke perfect English, and told me he had been at Oxford. He was puzzled that I wore no sidearms, and obviously thought my jungle greens were hardly smart enough for a Flight-Lieutenant pilot. As we flew over the jungle he asked me if I admired Tennyson, and how remarkable it was that in 1850 Tennyson, in "Locksley Hall", had anticipated the air battles of warring nations. "And now," he asked, "do you think we shall have 'the Parliament of man, the Federation of the world?' " The Auster roared on, the green landscape unrolled.

Below us was Buka passage, the slender channel between the islands of Bougainville and Buka, with an airstrip in the distance. I flew low over the water, between the two islands. Suddenly there was a sharp crack and the aircraft shuddered slightly. A steel cable across the Passage, carrying a telegraph cable, had snapped off our radio mast. If I had been flying two feet higher it would have taken off both our heads. The Major did not seem to be alarmed at what had happened. When we had landed he shook my hand and told me he had enjoyed our conversation about Tennyson, and that I was a very good pilot.

A day or two later my friend Geoff Tuck and I decided to fly over to Mount Bagana, the volcano, and take some photos of it. Geoff's delicate, high-boned features and fair, curling hair made him look more like an angel in a Renaissance painting than an Australian carpet salesman. He did not intend to return to selling carpets; he was going to stay on in the RAAF as a pilot, and later, perhaps, transfer to a civil airline as captain of a passenger plane.

The day was fine and clear as we took off. Half an hour later, as we came near the volcano, the green jungle shrivelled away to a bald, lifeless grey of pumice, of frozen lava that had spewed out of the fires within the cone. At the base of this last slope there was a bilious green lake; two streams of water cascaded down from the slope, not lacy like waterfalls but rushing dirtily, as if they were trying to escape. The cloud-plume that had looked so brilliantly white from Torokina now showed a base of smudgy grey as it emerged from the crater. The volcano was obscene rather than grand. Geoff and I smiled at each other in a kind of relief, as we turned to fly back to base.

We were now at about three thousand feet. We basked in the sun coming down through the perspex roof, the air blowing cool around our faces. We were about five miles from the volcano, and below us a wide river snaked into the distance towards the sea.

There was no warning, nothing threatening in the blue sky. Then it was like hitting a cliff, except that we went up and the aircraft went down. Our bare heads split the perspex roof and we fell back onto the seats, nearly stunned. Neither of us had his safety straps done up. Geoff had been flying, but he had now lost control, as we spun towards the jungle. I tried to apply the usual remedies of forward stick and opposite rudder, and realized he was trying to do the same thing. We both shoved and heaved but nothing answered. The Auster had ceased to be obedient.

Suddenly Geoff jerked his thumb at the window. I turned and looked out. The starboard wing was pointing upwards like a bent arm. The spar was broken. Some belch of hot air from the volcano, some invisible trap in the clear sky, had hit us.

Neither of us had any doubt at all that we would be killed. Parachutes were never worn in Austers. We just had to sit there and wait as the green disc of jungle spun around us. It was a very long wait, spinning in from three thousand feet.

The rotating jungle was now all we could see, and I wondered how long it would take to die. Then we were into it, with a crashing of metal and ripping of fabric and a final terrible thud. But we were still alive. The good wing had hit the top of a tall tree, and we had spun around and landed right side up. I shook myself like a dog, flicking blood onto my face from a cut in my hand. But apart from that small cut I seemed to be in one piece, uninjured.

I could smell petrol. I tore away the remnants of the broken door and began to get out before the fire started. I thought Geoff was doing the same thing, when I suddenly realized that he was trapped between his seat and the instrument panel. His face was grey. "I can't move," he said.

Waiting for the crackle of flames I heaved at his seat with my arms and pushed with my feet on the instrument panel. Nothing happened. We did not even have a jungle knife that I could use as a lever. I could see that Geoff was in acute pain, but even so, he began to wriggle a little. I was getting him free. One last heave, and the frame of the instrument panel buckled. I got out, ran around through the crushed vegetation and dragged him out his door as gently as I could. The second miracle had happened. The aircraft had not burned.

Now a third miracle was called for, as the jungle was all around and over us, level after level of greenness, and there was no distance, no landmark visible, nothing but trunks and branches and leaves of trees and bushes. We could not even see the volcano. I looked in the Auster; the compass was shattered. I looked up to try to catch a glimpse of the sun through the layers of vegetation, to see where it was in the sky. It was still morning, and when I could see the sun I could get an idea where west was, where lay the sea and the safety of a world with direction. Perhaps we might even strike that river we had seen. But almost every day it rained for a couple of hours, obliterating everything except the leaves in front of your face; I did not know what we could do when it started to rain.

"Can you walk?" I asked Geoff. He was standing by the crumpled engine cowl, hanging on to a strut. He said he thought he could, although something seemed to be broken in his back. He took a few steps and winced. He said he would be able to make it. If he stayed, and I managed to get out of the jungle and went for help, neither of us thought I could ever find him again. The jungle had let us in, and now had closed its green roof over us.

We set off. Without a jungle knife to hack through creepers or leaves, we had to push our way in what seemed to be the right direction. Since childhood I had had an absurd fear of spiders; now they were scuttling across my face, and we were wreathed and wound with spiders' webs. There was one spider with a green body and enormously long red legs, and hundreds of others in all colours and sizes.

Every now and then the fallen debris we were walking on would give way. As I fell the first time it happened, I grabbed a bough and my hand closed on a cluster of inch-long spines. Such jolts were cruel to Geoff's back. It took extraordinary courage for him to walk at all.

There were no streams, let alone a river, to give us a path to freedom. Sometimes there would be a gully and we would have to crawl across it on fallen bamboo. In another place those plants with elephant-ear leaves closed all around us. There were enormous butterflies, and birds whistled and screeched in the distance. Once I thought I heard water, at last, but it was only a fresh breeze through the bamboo leaves.

Hours went by, and it became a little easier to steer by the sun. It still had not rained, the first fine day for a week.

Suddenly we heard it, no mistake this time. I ran forward. It was a little creek, making the sweetest sound in the world, a little creek that would join a river which would lead us to the sea. Geoff and I sat down on a rock and cupped our hands in cool water, drank it, washed our faces in it, sloshed it down our shirts.

It was still very difficult going, dangerous at times when the creek dived down a cliff, and always painful for Geoff, but we knew we would live. The creek was our saviour. It took a turn, the jungle opened, and there was our big river. We stumbled out into the sunlight and in front of us were a dozen naked men swimming in a pool. "Been out for a stroll?" one of them shouted. They were New Zealanders. They put us into the front seat of their truck and drove us to the Torokina hospital. A nurse bound up my hand while a doctor examined Geoff and then took him off for an X-ray.

I waited for half an hour, and then the doctor came out to me and said Geoff had several crushed vertebrae in his spine, but it was not broken. "Did you say you were walking for six hours?" I nodded. "Christ, how did the poor bastard stand it?"

Geoff spent a few days in hospital, and then was flown back to hospital in Australia. He made a complete recovery. He was to stay on in the Air Force, break the England-Australia record in one of the early jets, for which he was given the Air Force Cross, and then die of leukemia at the age of thirty-three.

One day I was lying on my stretcher in the tent, reading Lorca, when Ken McRae walked in laughing. He was now captain of a Liberator. "G'day,

Dutt, want a lift to Brisbane?" It sounded as if he were saying to hop into the Dodge and we would drive into Launceston to the Brisbane Hotel.

I bundled my possessions into a kitbag, signed a form disposing of myself, and in a few minutes was clambering into the nearly empty cavern of Ken's Liberator. Liberator indeed. Ken disappeared into the front of the aircraft, and half a dozen soldiers and I sat down on some sacks and leaned against our kitbags. All we were wearing was our jungle green shorts and shirts. As Ken reached cruising height we began to shiver. When we reached Brisbane about six hours later we were nearly insensible with cold. But I knew the warmth of Australia would soon cure me. After four and a half years of being RAAF/416329 I was on the way to being a civilian again.

PART THREE
Oxford and Europe
1946–51

Ah life! Ah life, which none can reach
Or understand, save those who teach!

"Our Academics"

Eleven

I went back to Adelaide University, but it was only temporary. While I had been away I had been accepted by Magdalen College, Oxford, to take up residence at the beginning of the academic year in October 1946. Willie McKie had now left Magdalen to take up the post of organist and choir master of Westminster Abbey, but he and Archie Price and J.R. Darling had all helped to get me into the College. Several other South Australians were also going, continuing the association with the College that had begun with my father in 1899; Archie Price had also been at Magdalen. So of course had my brother John, but I was glad that the College did not assume that I would also have to be sent down.

The months went by in a kind of limbo, beginning with an almost daily thanksgiving at no longer being in the Air Force. I missed my friends who had been killed: Sam, Sandy, Peter and many others from school. Leigh, with whom I had gone on that ill-fated Saturday party, had been shot down by some rabid Nazi pilot in a Messerschmitt while on a training flight in England in a Tiger Moth. Pilots on opposite sides still usually respected each other; this atrocity, comparable to the murder of a child, was a reminder that there was nothing chivalrous about World War Two.

I picked up again with those who had managed to avoid the war. *Angry Penguins* had fizzled out an issue or two after the Ern Malley number. Max had lost his zest, and sat alternately jesting and glowering in Mary Martin's Bookshop, which, despite its cramped quarters in a side street, at least provided coffee and conversation for its old customers. I saw Bruce Williams there; Bruce had been tutor in Economics at St Mark's when I was there, and had now been appointed Lecturer in Economics at Belfast University. He was later to become Vice-Chancellor of Sydney University, be knighted and have the honour of being Margaret Thatcher's economics adviser — a far cry from the room he and Roma shared in the tatty old Liberal Club building high over North Terrace. In that scruffy room Adelaide's struggling Bohemia gathered, trying to be intellectual, moral and immoral all at once, and Bruce would pretend to be drunk after one glass of sherry. Perhaps he was; after all, he was the son of a Methodist parson. He was a fluent and engaging conversationalist, with a formidable knowledge of many things, especially music, although he did not play an instrument. He told me I would have no musical discrimination until I could unfailingly tell the difference between Mozart and Haydn. While trying to acquire these skills, I took up the piano again with Brewster Jones, but was woefully out of practice.

Professor Stewart had left Adelaide, also going to Belfast, where he had been appointed to the Chair in English. His place had been temporarily taken by Charles Jury, who still had his smoky salon on North Terrace, and was still writing poetry about beautiful classical Greeks. It was understood that Charles was keeping the professorial chair warm for Herbert Piper, who was also going to Magdalen, to take an advanced degree.

Charles loved literature, especially poetry, but he was far too emotional to be a good lecturer or teacher. To our intense embarrassment he wept when lecturing on Shelley. When he asked me to read my essay on Byron he sat twitching, smoking more and more cigarettes quicker and quicker, until he burst out with "But Geoffrey, Byron was a cad!" No, it was not like the Stewart days.

It was very difficult to secure a passage to Britain in 1946. Finally we managed to obtain one on the *Rhexenor*, a 10,000 ton cargo ship with six cabins. The owners, the Blue Funnel Line, had installed three berths in each formerly single cabin, and women were ordered to sleep on the port side, and men on the starboard. Ninette was sharing a cabin with Roma Williams and a married woman with a baby. I was sharing with Bruce Williams and Andrew Wells, a law graduate who was also going to Magdalen, to do an advanced degree.

Conditions on the *Rhexenor* were obviously very difficult for couples who wanted to sleep together, married or not. The ship's Doctor, fortunately a good-natured man, was much in demand because there were no patients in his hospital, but four serviceable beds. Some, not able to borrow the hospital keys, climbed into lifeboats; one couple thought they had found a safe refuge at the very bow of the ship, hidden behind the bollards by the anchor chains. The First Mate, with whom I was on amiable drinking terms, invited me one night up on to the ship's bridge. "And they think nobody can see them, poor things." He pointed up to the bow; from the elevation of the bridge, two figures were plainly visible in the moonlight, *in flagrante delicto*.

The voyage took six long weeks. We finally docked at Liverpool on a grey autumn morning. It was my first sight of Britain and the British and it was unbearably depressing. Everything was grey-black, the bomb-damaged stone buildings, the asphalt and wood of the wharves, the faces and the clothes and the caps of the dockers who looked up at us with undisguised loathing, their faces ravaged by a shadowed, inverted V running down from inside their cheekbones to the sides of their mouths. It was like an image of a frown of the soul. No wonder. Those poor devils had survived all those years of bombing and rationing, and here were we passengers, brown and glowing and well-fed, who had been living it up on the other side of the world while Britain Stood Alone. I was to find that most of the British were hardly aware that there had been a war in the Pacific, even though they had suffered thousands of casualties in it. In the European and North African campaigns, many of them considered that Britain had fought it out alone, ignoring the contribution and deaths of thousands of men from Canada, South Africa, New Zealand, Australia and the other Colonies, as they were still called. I thought of the deaths of my friends in Bomber and Fighter Command and other squadrons, flying with the RAF.

The obverse of this pattern was to be found in the kindness of many British who, sometimes rather patronizingly, regarded us Australians as members of the family. They really believed in what we cynically thought of as a joke, the Bonds of Empire. Also, a great boon for impoverished students, various organizations existed through which, if we wanted to, we could be invited to stay with people all over the British Isles, and even in Eire.

But despite the atmosphere in which many of us had been brought up, by parents who regarded Britain as Home, the Mother Country, I found it irretrievably foreign. The climate was vile, the dinginess and overcrowding depressing, and, worst of all, despite hopes raised by the comradeship of war, the class system was entrenched as strongly as it had ever been.

It was immediately apparent in the private hotel in Bayswater, where we stayed when we arrived in London. In that prim building, with its perpetual faint smell of gas, overcooked cabbage and kippers, there was exactly the atmosphere re-created so wonderfully in Angus Wilson's short stories. I had never suspected, although Adelaide should have alerted me, that there were so many divisions even in one area, the middle class. Despite the fact that these people were obviously interchangeable in their customs and prejudices, retired army officers were far above people who had owned shops, an aged spinster living on a tiny bequest looked down on the jolly young wife of a student doctor, a bumptious caricature of a man "in the City" could scarcely bear to be seen talking to a Colonial. All of them kowtowed to a wizened old lady who sat by herself, who was the widow of a Baronet.

And then there was the food, for which, of course, the war was to blame and not the British people. Rationing was even worse than during the war, and nothing we were given to eat tasted or looked like real food. No doubt there was game and all sorts of delicious things to eat in my mother's old haunts like Claridge's or Brown's, but I could not afford anything in her former lifestyle.

As it was, she was doing all she could to help us, although in 1946 very little money was coming in from Anlaby and Uno, and all of her own funds had been lent to Anlaby many years ago. But she sent small sums when she could. Fortunately when I reached twenty-one I had inherited a lump sum from my grandfather's will, modest enough, but having grown since he died, twenty-nine years before my twenty-first birthday, it now provided an income of about a thousand pounds a year. This enabled me to pay for my fees at Oxford, and for my wife's expenses.

For some years, with other ex-servicemen, I fought a battle with the Australian authorities over the ex-serviceman's grant, which was paid to students at Australian universities, but not to those who were studying overseas. It still makes my blood boil that those bureaucrats in Canberra were so chauvinistic that they could not see the advantage for Australia in students studying at overseas universities, not only for the knowledge they could bring back, but for the pressure that would be taken off the Australian universities, which were crowded with ex-servicemen. And then there was the plain injustice of it; we had spent as long in the services as had our comrades who were studying at home, and so should have been equally entitled to the grant. That grant would have made a great deal of difference to all of us.

Oxford was quite different from London or Liverpool. Amazingly enough, given the proximity of the Morris works, it had never been bombed. Not only were all those marvellous buildings still intact, but so were the trees and gardens, and I had never seen anything like an English garden. No wonder my mother never stopped talking about them. The climate might have been a trial to human beings, but it was kind to flowers. I began to love green again, because in England it did not imprison you. "Annihilating all that's made / To a green thought in a green shade" was not a threat but a blessing.

Archie Price had urged me, despite being married, to live in College for my first year; otherwise I would not taste the full flavour and derive the full benefit from Magdalen. At first Ninette had to live in lodgings, but eventually we found a basement flat in North Oxford, on the Banbury Road, and I went there for weekends; it was an odd arrangement. I was not the only one — other married undergraduates lived in College for their first year while their wives lived elsewhere. Once when I asked the head porter, at the College's gate, whether I could go to the flat for the night, he said, "Honestly, I don't know, sir."

The aftermath of war had strange impacts on Oxford University society. I was an old married man of twenty-five; someone like Ken Tynan, who was in his second year at Magdalen, also doing English, seemed like a school kid, albeit a most entertaining one. Old fuddy-duddy ex-servicemen could never have worn his purple shirts and yellow ties, or let their hair fall to their shoulders. One of my friends had been a Group-Captain in the RAF, a Pathfinder, and he had been awarded the DSO and two DFCs. One of his tutors, now in stern charge of his academic advancement, had been a humble Sergeant.

The College rules, as everywhere in Oxford, were strict and absurd to those like us who had just been liberated from rules. We had to be back in College by 10 p.m., when the great iron-bound, wooden gate onto the High was closed. The Dean at Magdalen, responsible for discipline, made unofficial allowances for those who wanted to stay out late. The College wall ran alongside a small side street off the High, called Longwall, and there was a lamp post beside it. On this lamp post there were three collars of steel spikes to prevent students climbing the wall. In fact, these were perfectly spaced to provide footholds as you climbed the wall; once on top, it was not a very long jump onto the bicycle-shed roof. When this roof developed too great a sag, the Dean would order it to be resurfaced with fresh galvanized iron.

I was given a room on the first floor of the wing that ran along the High. Unfortunately the old arrangements, by which undergraduates had two rooms, a sitting room and a bedroom, no longer applied. Postwar crowding meant that each set of rooms was now shared. I was sharing with a classic ex-army Major from the Rifle Brigade, a lanky, long-jawed friendly man who was doing Law. He had the best room, the old sitting room. Both of us, as with all men in College, were protected from outside by double doors; if the outer one was closed, it signified that you were working and did not wish to be disturbed. This was called "sporting your oak".

Each staircase was looked after by a college servant called a scout; many of them had been working for the College for decades. They cleaned the rooms, made the beds and polished your shoes, and brought you a cup of tea in the morning. They also had a duty to report to the Dean if they found any of their young gentlemen with a girl in his bed in the morning, an offence that was taken very seriously, by both the Dean and the scouts. One friend of mine, with a handsome room in the New Buildings (so called because they had been built in the eighteenth century), was caught by his scout with a girl in bed, both of them naked. The scout promptly disappeared and my friend sat with his head in his hands, fearing the end of his College career, while the girl frantically dressed. There was a knock on the door. It was the scout, with two cups of tea. But such kindness was very unusual.

One day Pat Donovan, a friend from Queensland, whom I had first met in my tent at Torokina, came to see me; he was obviously upset about something. "It's this business of the scout cleaning my bloody shoes," he explained, "it's just not bloody right for an old man to have to clean a perfectly healthy young bugger's shoes. And it's no good my not putting them out to be cleaned, the old fox always finds them." I tried to explain that the scout would be most distressed if one of his charges cleaned his own shoes, but it was no use. Australian democracy continued to be distressed.

Before I left home my brother John urged me to look up old Hancock, who had been my father's scout at the turn of the century, and John's in the late 1920s. John had been told that old Hancock, although retired as a scout, pottered around the grounds, helping to keep them tidy. John gave me a precise description of old Hancock. On my first day of exploration I walked out between the main buildings and the New to reach Addison's Walk, which runs around the meadow, a unique advantage for Magdalen. Near the tall iron gates between the gardens I saw Hancock unmistakably pottering along. I came up to him and said, "Hello, Hancock. You were my father's scout in 1899 and my brother John's in 1926." "And who are you, young man?" He glared at me. "I am Emeritus Professor Fenwick. Good day to you."

My tutors were C.S. Lewis, most famous for *The Allegory of Love* and *A Preface to Paradise Lost*, not to mention his popular religious works such as *The Screwtape Letters*, and J.A.W. Bennett, who was an expert on Old and Middle English and language studies. For Oxford in 1946 English Literature stopped at 1832. Lewis thoroughly approved of this, and many times at Faculty meetings defended the exclusion of the nineteenth century, against the protests of many other dons, such as Helen Gardner. So we spent long hours pummelling our out-of-practice brains learning Old English, which was almost like a foreign language, and in studying boring texts, not only in Old and Middle English, which were of no literary merit whatsoever. We were taught nothing of Victorian prose and poetry, let alone modern literature.

In later life I often wished I had studied History with A.J.P. Taylor, another Magdalen don, instead of English. Why didn't I?

I once mentioned *Ulysses* to Lewis, and he snorted and said he had never read it. Jack Bennett, on the other hand, knew it backwards, and in addition the Old English scholar had all of Eliot, Auden, Whitman, Henry James, Hemingway and Wallace Stevens on his shelves; he had also spent several years teaching in the United States. Jack had a lovely self-deprecating sense of humour; as he said about himself, he looked like a don, with his big glasses and white hair, although he was only about forty, ten years younger than the balding Lewis. Lewis sat still and went chop into literature, his words like a butcher's cleaver. Jack Bennett would wriggle around, gesturing, his voice sliding around a concept, phrasing a possibility rather than a conclusion. He was to become a friend; he knew where there were treasures in remote villages as well as gems in some of the rockiest literature.

Some years later a small group of us were playing that game where each person says what she or he would like to be in another life. Jack had no hesitation in saying he would like to be the world's greatest expert on medieval water-wheels.

Jack was a New Zealander and could also talk with authority about Katherine Mansfield and the other extraordinary writers who have come from that country. He had been co-editor of the university magazine at Auckland, and had nearly been expelled from university for publishing an article on *Lady Chatterley's Lover*, so he also knew about antipodean censorship.

Lewis, oddly enough also called Jack by his friends (never, of course, by us), was like a jolly, thick-lipped, red-faced butcher, only that he was not really jolly. He would open a door on his idea of jollity, and then close it again; his whole attitude to students was managed on the principle of the open and closed door. You felt that he resented you, he would rather be doing his own work, although while you were with him, in his elegant rooms in the New Building, he would give you the full attention of a first-class brain and of his profound knowledge of the literature within his range. Of course he also knew medieval and Renaissance French and Italian literature in great detail, but as with literature in English, if he had read modern French or Italian writers he kept it to himself. And "modern" would include Rimbaud and Leopardi.

You felt with Lewis that if you dropped dead as you went out through his door, after the tutorial, he would not notice. After three years he was still confusing me with my American friend George Bailey; our only resemblance was that we were both about the same height. In my third year Lewis set me an essay on Dr Johnson's political pamphlets. As I was noting down the names of those he particularly wanted me to read, he mentioned "Taxation No Tyranny" (1775) in which Johnson develops his case against the American colonists. Suddenly he said, "Oh dear, Mr Bailey, I'm afraid you will be offended by Dr Johnson's scorn for you Americans."

The tutorial system, one of Oxford's incomparable advantages, had before the war meant that each student had an hour's weekly session with his tutor, during which he had to read an essay of a length which would take about twenty minutes to read. Because of the postwar rush, there were now two students to each tutorial. But it was still of enormous value to have to complete a fortnighly essay, and after it had been read, have the benefit of Lewis's or Bennett's comments on it. Lewis generously, and accurately, told us that Bennett was a better scholar than he was. He also told us, with his bar-room laugh, that the term was for play and the vacation for work. In other words, as long as we presented our essays we could do silly things in the rest of our time like drinking, talking, acting in plays or even rowing or playing football. In the vacation we could do what we liked as long as we read all the books for the next term. It was excellent advice, but of course most of us had not the moral fibre to stick to it.

My tutorial partner was Alan Skempton, an ex-RAF pilot; he was tall and of regular features, with curly fair hair and a vacuous expression. He would have been an ideal support actor in a Hollywood movie about England. He had a beautiful voice; after he left Oxford he joined the BBC and was, I believe, known as "the golden voice of the BBC". I could not imagine why he was doing English, he had read scarcely anything and was not interested in any of the works we were studying. He had to do the first essay, and after a day or two he came to me in great distress, saying he simply did not know what to do.

I felt sorry for him, as the essay was on *The Faerie Queene*, on which Lewis was perhaps the world's greatest authority; as for the poem itself, it would reduce most essay writers to impotence. I tried my best to help him, and suggested some critical works to study. When the day came he read out, in his splendid voice, a very inept piece, reeking with platitudes, only redeemed by a number of passages stolen from other critics, all of which Lewis clearly recognized. When Skempton came near the end of his essay he said that Spenser's vision of the poet and of God reminded him of the great poem "High Flight", by a young Canadian pilot called McGee. I saw Lewis stiffen in his chair.

McGee had been killed in action in 1941. "High Flight" was perhaps the most popular bad poem of the war, reprinted in countless women's magazines. It begins:

Oh, I have slipped the surly bonds of earth
And danced the skies on laughter-silvered wings ...

and ends:

Up, up, the long, delirious, burning blue
I've topped the windswept heights with easy grace
Where never lark, or even eagle flew;
And while with silent, lifting mind I've trod
The high untrespassed sanctity of space,
Put out my hand, and touched the face of God.

Skempton lowered the text, with the gravity of a statesman who has given the oration at a funeral service for a hero. Lewis coughed. "You have me at an advantage, Mr Skempton. I'm afraid I do not know my McGee very thoroughly."

A year or so later, I was reading Lewis an essay on Malory. I had a passion for Malory and his telling of the tales of King Arthur, Sir Lancelot and the rest. I thought I should try to find something to criticize with less enthusiasm than I had been showing, so picked on the catalogues which might have bored even his contemporary readers, passages along the lines of "And then Sir Mordred smote Sir Gawayne, and Sir Agravain smote Sir Ector, and Sir Lancelot ..." I followed with what I suggested might be a rare example of humour: "And then Sir Bors smote Sir Mordred in the buttocks so that he could not sit his horse for a week".

Lewis jumped to his feet. "And what's funny about that, young man?" He moved to his private door and grabbed his chamber pot. His lower lip thrust out and his eyes turned piggy. "Is it not as painful to be wounded in the posterior as anywhere else?" He slammed the door behind him and had what sounded like a very long pee.

Later I was to be told that Lewis had been wounded in the buttocks, as well as elsewhere, by a shell explosion in the First World War. A wound in the buttocks was often quite unjustly taken as a token that the soldier who sufffered it had been running away.

Lewis and Bennett were at one in demanding that we write clear prose, free of jargon; they were excellent exemplars themselves in this. Early in my career at Magdalen I introduced the phrase "objective correlative" into an essay, thinking to be showing myself familiar with a key concept of the time. Lewis made it clear that he did not care for T.S. Eliot, either as poet, critic, or writer on religious matters. He also suggested that it was better to try to put concepts into my own words, rather than use those of other people.

Literary theory and its deathly jargon sprays over critical writing nowadays like acid rain. Its undermining of the ordinary and extraordinary life of literature reminds me of W.H. Auden's poem "Gare du Midi", where the agent arrives, and "Clutching a little case / He walks out briskly to infect a city ..." When I was at Magdalen war had been declared between F.R. Leavis in Cambridge and scholars like Lewis in Oxford. Leavis had some good ideas, and his Great Tradition extended into the modern era, unlike anything at Oxford, but Leavis not only had an ugly prose style but, like many literary theorists today, put fences around books by being exclusive. What wasn't in his Great Tradition didn't rate. I admired Lewis, and of course Jack Bennett, for their dislike of fences. They did try to be open-minded.

From Lewis and Bennett I learned that there was nothing new about literary theory, that a network of theory, literary, political, philosophical and religious, supported every great writer from Chaucer to Coleridge. The aim for us students was to be aware of it but not to be dominated by it, just like the writers. I also learned how serious poetry was, more serious for a poet than anything except love.

The lyf so short, the craft so long to lerne,
Th'assay so hard, so sharp the conquering.

From that I also learned that the practice of pinching from other writers had not been invented by T.S. Eliot and Ezra Pound. Chaucer had stolen these words from Hippocrates, who wrote some fourteen hundred years before Chaucer's day. Most things had already been thought of.

But while one should acknowledge the major figures — Shakespeare with a full theatre, Milton with his "fit audience find, though few", polished Pope with his lady admirers — there was no major or minor in poetry itself. There was simply great poetry and lesser. Marvell, with his tiny output, was as fine as any poet in English. Whoever it was among the tribe of Anon. remains a mystery, but there is no doubt of the perfection of these four lines:

Western wind, when wilt thou blow,
The small rain down can rain?
Christ, if my love were in my arms
And I in my bed again!

Sex, however, was a problem. At that time both Lewis and Bennett were bachelors; you knew it was safe to talk about sex with Bennett, but not with Lewis. Lewis would give a bar-room laugh at Chaucer's or Shakespeare's bawdy, but it was not advisable, in an essay on Donne, to linger too long on some of the elegies. He congratulated me on my essay on Byron — "Ah, Mr Dutton" (getting my name right for once), "I can see you are a Byronist". But it was clear that, like dear old Charles Jury in Adelaide, he thought Byron was a cad.

Although he was a muscular Christian in his official attitude to sex, which of course he considered should be a business between married couples, I also recognized in him the familiar symptoms of a sucker for sin, like J.R. Darling. Sin and evil were seductive, of course, but there were clear rules for handling them. In an essay on Milton, I was foolish enough to quote William Blake: "The reason Milton wrote in fetters when he wrote of Angels and God, and at liberty when of Devils and Hell, is because he was a true Poet, and of the Devil's party without knowing it". Lewis explained that there was not time to go into such an important matter in a tutorial, but he referred me to his book on Milton, where the matter was satisfactorily explained. I did not let on that I had already read it.

In another essay on Malory, not the disastrous one about arrows in buttocks, I tried to speculate about the mystery, the wonderful mixture of sex, joy, and the clouds and darkness of wrong in the love between Lancelot and Guinevere. When I had finished, Lewis switched on the searchlight of reason, blasted the mystery into white light and put the guilty lovers in their destructive place.

The cruel rumour was that when Lewis had been wounded by an exploding shell in the war a piece of shrapnel had also damaged some vital portion of his sexual equipment, and that was why he had to pee so often. Be that as it may, Lewis just did not have the temperament to believe

Blake, or to understand Lancelot and Guinevere or Tristan and Isolde. He had two attitudes to sex. In one he thought of sex as funny, which of course it can be, but it was the sort of funny that produces the bar-room laugh without the sequel of fucking.

I could not help comparing Lewis's bawdry with that which I had known in the Air Force. He also liked the bawdy ballads we pilots would sing so lustily; indeed, some of them were surely written by Oxford dons. But in Tasmania they were part of the life of a bunch of young fuckers, male and female; the bawdy was real, even if we didn't quite attain the ingenuity of some of the deeds in the songs.

In another mood, the one in which Lewis had written a major book, *The Allegory of Love*, he was able, by writing about the intricacies of medieval courtly love, to avoid the realities of both sex and love. D.H. Lawrence would have accused him of sex-in-the-head. For Lewis, books were genuinely more real than life; if he wanted to know about lust, it was all in Catullus, if about the subtleties of love, it was all in Spenser.

One lesson of deep and enduring significance to my own attitudes came, somewhat unexpectedly, from Lewis. I was reading him one of my essays, in which there was a rather patronizing remark about old maids, typical of a hearty, young, Australian male. Lewis stopped me. "You have no right to talk like that about what you call old maids. Why shouldn't such women have a profound knowledge of life, women like Jane Austen and the Brontes?" I continued to read my essay, considerably (and permanently) chastened. It was surprising that such a comment should come from Lewis, a man who did not usually spring to the defence of women.

In addition, or perhaps I should say in contrast, he was also cursed with an overriding, vulgar common sense, and had the brain to apply it with devastation in an argument in a tutorial, when his thick lower lip would jut out at you and his small, triumphant eyes betray his jolly face. His vulgarity was not congenial, it was hiding an inadequacy. There was, in the end, something repulsive about Lewis.

Twelve

It was a great disadvantage to be a married undergraduate at Oxford; there were quite a number of us. We could concentrate fully neither on our studies, nor on our marriages. It was even harder for the wives, particularly those who, like Ninette, had accompanied their husbands from overseas. If their husbands were living in College, as I was, the wives had to exist in poky rooms or tiny flats, at a time when food and heating were at an even lower ebb than during the war, and during the week there was nothing much for them to do.

My parents' old friends, Bentley and May Osborn, had long been living in Oxford, where Bentley was Professor of Botany and May a brilliant assistant to Sir Howard Florey. They always made Ninette welcome, and Bentley gave her a job in the Botany Library. She also enrolled for drawing classes at the Slade; they turned out to be pathetically basic, just hours spent in front of plaster casts of classical statues.

Meanwhile, for us in College, the term, as Lewis had said, was for enjoying ourselves (and also for getting our essays done). As a married undergraduate you felt guilty for enjoying yourself, while your wife had no community life. There were innumerable openings for undergraduates, Oxford offering every activity: sport, drama, societies devoted to the most obscure subjects, and the grand debates of the Oxford Union.

Drinking, of course, could be a major occupation, in one or several of the many pubs, which gave you an opportunity to talk to members of other Colleges, or in the bar of the Junior Common Room. This was a very special place, normally out of bounds to freshmen, but we ex-servicemen were allowed immediate access. The little room was always known as Bond's Room, being overseen by Bond, a man of infinite knowlege about wine and spirits, and infinite sagacity in handling undergraduates. Bond, with his dark clothes and gravity, looked like the manager of a very select funeral parlour; his thin hair was oiled down across his head, and his voice was low, extremely respectful, but absolutely not to be argued with.

He was a frightful snob, which could be to your advantage if he approved of you. On principle he approved of those who had been officers in the services, even colonials; I don't think it occurred to him that some of these colonial ex-servicemen had not had commissions. The undergraduate cellar had the most amazing stocks of fine wine, available at purchase price plus some trifling charge for corkage each year, so we could buy the most expensive wine, a 1929 Chateau Haut Brion, for example, for fifteen shillings or so. Because of there being so few undergraduates in College during the war, stocks were high, unlike those in the Senior Common Room, where the dons had been guzzling the wines all through the war. I can remember Lewis coming to me and saying that he was having a very special dinner party, and, please, perhaps I could get him a couple of bottles of a good burgundy ...

When my friend Bob Southey's wife Val had their first child, a son, I asked Bond if I could buy something special in the way of champagne to wet the boy's head. (Bob, although an Australian, had been a Captain in the Coldstream Guards.) "Certainly, sir," he said and vanished to his sanctum. He returned with two bottles of 1937 Veuve Clicquot. I noticed an undergraduate called Moulds sitting by the window taking in this scene. Moulds was unpalatably *nouveau riche*, and unbearably bumptious. He was the only undergraduate in Magdalen to have a new car, a most desirable example of a new marque, a Healey tourer, which he used as often as possible to leave in an obvious position close to the College. For some reason I can still remember how much it cost: 1598 pounds. He probably got it at a discount.

As Bond was wrapping the champagne for me, Moulds came over and said he would like a couple of bottles too. "I'm so sorry, sir, but that's the end of the run. They were the last two bottles."

The Veuve Clicquot was duly drunk, and delicious it was. Next time I was in Bond's Room I thanked him for giving me such fine wine, and said I had been sorry to hear that was the end of the run. "Oh, plenty more for *gentlemen*, sir," said Bond, and returned to polishing a glass. Such subtleties of snobbery were certainly something new for a simple Australian.

There was one activity which was not permitted to undergraduates. We were not allowed to go to dances in the town, which made life very difficult for single men, especially those who had been in the services. The women undergraduates were fiercely ambitious and very few of them wanted to waste their time with male undergraduates; it was a bit like Lewis, if you wanted sex, read Catullus.

It was dangerous to break the rules and go to town dances. Pat Donovan was caught enjoying himself at one by the bulldogs (as the university police were called), and was severely admonished by the Senior Proctor.

I compounded my difficulties by following in the family tradition of spending an inordinate amount of time on the river, rowing. My father had been in the University Eight, and in several Magdalen crews which were Head of the River. John had stroked the Magdalen Eight which also went Head. So I yielded once again to foolish tradition when I could have been doing better things.

The Thames, known as the Isis where it flows through Oxford, is too narrow there for crews to race abreast, so there are bumping races instead.

The crews, in several divisions, are lined up, a length apart, and each tries to catch the crew in front, and bump it. (There is a knob on the bow of the boat to prevent damage.)

I was, with a number of other Australians, in the Magdalen First Eight. In my first year we bumped our way up to second place, but could not catch New College, the leading crew. Nor could we the next year, though we were so exhausted from trying so hard that we were nearly bumped ourselves.

After rowing in the University Trial Eights, I was selected for the University crew. Some weeks of practice later, the Coach, Pat Mallam, took me aside and told me that he and the selectors did not think that I — ahem, as a married man, ahem — would be able to give my all to the crew.

There were of course engaging aspects to this rowing business, although it was hardly like 1900 when the Magdalen crew would take a house at Henley for the great week of the Regatta and train on caviar and champagne. We were given horsemeat to build us up.

But I had put myself back into a prison again, with endless hours of training and, in the winter, acute discomfort. I can remember rowing at Henley when it was so cold that ice formed on the loom of the oar, and spray set solid in our hair. On one occasion all was temporarily redeemed when we were rowing through a snowstorm, and suddenly two white swans swept out of a cloud, banked and landed on the leaden grey river.

In my last year, when I had given up rowing to concentrate on my final exams, I went back to Henley during the Regatta. I wrote in my diary that night: "It was all not only another world but a world that had once contained an entirely strange human being — myself. At least, it had never contained me, but even to have fitted in seems incredible. The appalling dullness was the worst — even the RAAF had something more, some élan and sense of danger that strict training and the will to win don't have much of."

Why was I so docile, so given to doing the traditional thing? Was I still trying to please my mother? I don't know. But of course it was difficult for us old men to join in the frolics of the young, like Ken Tynan. His gaunt, white face, like that of a baby dinosaur, emerged as awkwardly as his stammer from his plumage. In a cartoon in one issue of the University magazine, the *Cherwell*, Ken's face appeared above a well-known slogan of the times: "Keep Death Off The Roads".

His clothing was worthy of an eighteenth century dandy, if rather untidy. His second name was Peacock, and he liked to quote Blake: "The pride of the peacock is the glory of God". He was also one of Lewis's pupils; his stammer was so bad that Lewis had to read his essays. (My stammer had returned, but not as badly as Ken's.) For Tynan, Lewis was a kind of father-figure and Magdalen a surrogate home; he asked to be buried in the grounds, but the Fellows would not allow it. It was much to Lewis's credit that he saw the talent in this extravagant young man. One of the greatest advantages of Oxford was its tradition of not only tolerating but encouraging eccentricity. At Adelaide Tynan would have been judged by the reigning bourgeois standards as being outrageously "affected" (Clarice Trott's favourite word of denigration), and the football hearties would have thrown him into the river.

Ken, the Magdalen Dramatic Society and other groups put on some wonderful shows. The best and most surprising was a dramatic version of Milton's *Samson Agonistes*, produced and directed by Tynan. It was the first time that I realized that Milton pronounced Dalila's name "DAH-lee-la".

The various College gardens, each of an individual beauty, were ideal settings as long as the rain held off. One of the best performances of *The Tempest* I have ever seen was directed by Nevill Coghill, of Chaucerian translation fame, in the garden of Worcester College, which contains a little lake. When Ariel made his first entrance he ran across the water to Prospero, sheer magic. Coghill had installed a plank just above water level, which could not be seen in the darkness, the spotlight being on Ariel's body.

I played no part in such activities, rowing instead. I knotted more ropes of orthodoxy and boredom around myself by taking Ninette,who loved going there, to spend holiday after holiday with friends of my mother's in Northern Ireland. Sir Basil Brooke (later Lord Brookeborough) was Prime Minister of Northern Ireland, and he and Cynthia had stayed at Anlaby on a prewar visit of Commonwealth Prime Ministers. They lived on the estate of Colebrooke in a typical eighteenth century mansion near Brookeborough, close to the border with Eire.

Whenever we walked around the property we were accompanied by two enormous policemen, making it obvious to the IRA that the Prime Minister was out for a stroll. But those were milder days, and no shots were exchanged. One day Cynthia opened for us the lid of an enormous chest on the upstairs landing. It was full of Schneider rifles and ammunition, from the days of The Troubles. There had of course been no real healing. The expression used about a Catholic was "He digs with the wrong foot".

Basil's father had been a ruthless hunter, and a huge tiger stood at the first bend of the stone staircase, and about a hundred heads of every kind of slaughtered horned beast covered every square inch of the walls of the great dining room, which was never used.

We sat by a big and permanent log fire in the "little" library. The diamond-latticed doors in front of the books in this and the main library were never unlocked. I asked one day if I could have a look around the books and was amazed at what I found — great leather-bound first editions going back to the sixteenth century, complete sets of all the literary, sporting and natural-history classics, most of them never opened.

Basil, with his black moustache, curved nose and sensual lips, looked exactly like the portrait of the first Sir Basil Brooke, one of the thousands of settlers introduced to Ulster by King James I. This was the action which caused the "Irish problem" which still so disastrously divides that distressful country. Cynthia was a rangy, very plain, good-natured English aristocrat with a face like a horse; when I later met Vita Sackville-West I thought how alike she and Cynthia were in body if not in mind, although they both shared a passion for gardens.

I suppose we made a surrogate Anlaby out of Colebrooke, and we went back there again and again. Ninette, as if she were my mother all over again, and yet also as if Cynthia were my mother-in-absentia, was Presented at Court by Cynthia and Basil.

I went along with it. (Why?) I had to hire a morning suit from Moss Brothers. I said jokingly to the gentleman's gentleman who was fitting me, "I suppose there'll be lots of men wearing your suits at the Palace." "All the *well-dressed* ones, sir."

At the Palace we walked through endless glittering, red-carpeted, gold-spattered rooms, and finally came to the enormous ballroom, where red-coated bandsmen were playing "The Donkey Serenade" against the backdrop of a great gold and cream organ. Attlee and his wife entered, and we shook hands, and followed them into the reserve for Prime Ministers and friends, where we looked down on the polloi of Lords and Countesses and suchlike folk.

The diplomats started off the procession past the two thrones, half of them knowing what to do and when to bow, the others falling over one another. The Turkish Ambassador was especially impressive, all twenty-five stone of him in grey satin. The Indian women, swirling their gorgeous saris, carried themselves with a grace mostly lost by their equivalents in the West.

Cynthia told me afterwards that I had suddenly seen a RAAF Air Marshall being presented to the King, and said in a highly audible whisper, "Christ, that's the bastard who sent me to gaol." So it was, a man called Knox-Knight who was head of Air Board when I was committed to The Boob.

The royal intelligence network is extraordinary. While we were talking the Queen (now the Queen Mother) came up; we shook hands and she asked me how Anlaby was. She had heard about it from Lady Spencer, her Lady-in-Waiting. The Queen was round, plump and girlish in her face and perfect skin; I could imagine her making sponge cakes, though I don't suppose she ever indulged in such activities.

Basil and Cynthia were very kind to us and other colonials, and it would have been fascinating to go once — or perhaps twice — and see how the Ulster aristocracy lived, but that would have been enough. There was so much else to do. At Oxford a new friend, the one-armed Australian zoologist and pamphleteer Jock Marshall, had invited me to lunch to meet his old friend Tom Harrisson, anthropologist, Keeper of the Museum at Sarawak, one-time co-founder with Charles Madge of Mass Observation. This was a prewar activity in which hundreds of volunteers collected information about, and interviews with, the British poor, which were then published. They were horrifying documents. Subsequently, Tom had parachuted into Borneo and worked behind the Japanese lines.

At one stage Tom Harrisson had been in Melbourne for a while, and had been very attracted to *Angry Penguins*. He had written a number of articles for the Melbourne *Age*, or perhaps the *Argus*, under the tongue-in-cheek pseudonym of "Lt. Col. I.M. English". In one of them he had said very kind things about my book of poems, *Night Flight and Sunrise*. He very much disapproved of my going to stay at Colebrooke. "All right to go once and find out what those sort of people are like, but not again!" If I really wanted to go back to Ireland, and liked aristocrats, he had a friend, a radical Earl, who was a lover of poetry and wine. But like a fool, I went back to the Brookes, who both had ulcers and drank very little, and ate almost nothing of the fabulous heap of game birds which came in from the kitchen for meals, and was always sent out again before we could have a second helping.

Jock was a lot older than me, and was doing a Doctorate at Merton College. He and his wife Jane, who drew most of the meticulous bird drawings which illustrated Jock's articles and books, lived in a wooden house amongst the trees, just out of Oxford. The first time I went there it was mid-winter; the house was high above the ground, on stilts, and as we came up the path there was a young man on his hands and knees, licking an icicle of beer which had formed from the drips falling from a keg in the sitting room. The young man was a son of Sir Julian Huxley, another friend of Jock's.

Jock was a remarkable man who a few years later became the first Dean of Science at Monash University, amongst many other distinctions. These included the founding at Oxford of an annual race called the Pint to Pint, in which the entrants had to ride a bicycle from pub to pub around Oxford, drinking a pint of beer at each pub. Jock, despite having only one arm, was a winner.

As well as working reasonably hard, and wasting my time doing conventional things, I was also trying to write poetry, but not finding it easy. Of course, it never is easy, but learning about so much dull writing, which never emerged into anything contemporary, seemed to drain my imagination and inventiveness. My poems were adequate enough to be included in the annual anthology, *Oxford Poetry*, with others by writers like Kingsley

Amis and Elizabeth Jennings, but they make dull reading compared with the often erratic but at least lively poems of the *Angry Penguins* days.

I liked a poet and magazine editor, Arthur Boyars, who was a stirrer and full of ideas and ambitions for new magazines, but did not care much for my other fellow-poets. Amis, with his tight blond curly hair that looked as if it had been freshly permed, was cocky and condescending; he no doubt thought I was a boring colonial. It amuses me to read that Amis detests English snobbery.

My best poetic encounter at Oxford was not with an undergraduate, but with the South African poet Roy Campbell, who came to talk to the University Poetry Society.

An amazing variety of distinguished people in all fields would take the trouble of giving talks at these University clubs and societies. Thomas Mann was one of my heroes of the 1940s; *The Magic Mountain* was certainly magic for me. I went to hear him talk; there was standing room only, and by a fluke I found myself standing very close to him. He looked like a neat and efficient businessman, with a slight paunch obviously held in by a surgical belt. He read his entire "talk", eyes down, but gesticulating all the time, wagging his forefinger, throwing his arms out, talking in a slightly hoarse voice and gobbling his words. I wished I hadn't gone.

Not so with Roy Campbell. I liked the look of him immediately. He was no longer slim and haughtily handsome as in the Augustus John portrait, but he was clearly himself, if now lame and a bit heavy, and he had made no attempt, over many years away from the land of his birth, to accommodate his South African accent to approved English. He had a face like a tortoise, the features seemed to thrust forwards from the shell of the head, and there was a wrinkled heaviness about his skin, and his eyes were wide but strongly lidded.

Roy was the star turn, kept till last. Various very solemn undergraduates read their own poems or those by other poets. One willowy youth who attended some of the same English lectures as I did, thoroughly bourgeois in style and dress, got up and read D.H. Lawrence's "How Beastly the Bourgeois is —". He enunciated the words with an almost squealing conviction, obviously reading about his own background.

How beastly the bourgeois is
especially the male of the species —
Presentable eminently presentable —

Shall I make you a present of him? ...
Nicely groomed, like a mushroom

standing there so sleek and erect and eyeable — ...
sucking his life out of the dead leaves of greater life
than his own, ...

Standing in their thousands, these appearances
in damp England ...

Then it was Roy's turn, his voice very blunt after the last reader's drawn-out vowels. He said that *épater les bourgeois* was, he thought, a bit out of date. "Man, what I always try to do is *épater les bohemiens*." Of course that didn't stop him coming out with a story of when he was living in the south of France and working in a circus. He and another attendant had to bring in the tub for the elephant to stand on, and help it up, when it would slowly raise itself onto its front legs on the tub and stand. Suddenly a drench of something scalding hot came over him, and the audience began to roar with laughter. He quickly realized that he and the other attendant were standing beneath a shower of shit. The elephant had diarrhoea.

I had introduced myself to Roy before his talk as a fellow-colonial, and now he made his way over to me, jerking his thumb at the tea and buns which were being brought in, and saying, "Come on, man, quick, where's the nearest pub." He only just caught the last train back to London.

Roy was working as a producer with the BBC at this time, in company with other poets like Louis MacNeice and Dylan Thomas. He told me that one night when Thomas was supposed to read some poems in his beautiful voice, he arrived so drunk that Roy had to read the poems himself. Half way through his reading he heard the controller shouting into his ear-phones, "Campbell, get that drunken Welshman off the air."

Not long after our meeting in Oxford I wrote to Roy at the BBC, suggesting we meet again. He replied promptly, beginning very formally with "Dear Mr Dutton", and continuing "Thanks for your letter. I am always at Broadcasting House (Room 207) if you would care to call around. If you don't find me in, then you will be sure to find me at 'The George' between 12 and 1. 'The George' is in Mortimer Street, close by. All the best/ Yours ever/ Roy Campbell."

Roy was to remain a loyal friend until his death, and I spent happier hours at the George with him and his poet mates than in three years at Oxford. MacNeice, who was often present, seemed to bear no grudge for Roy's swingeing satire of Auden, Spender, Day Lewis and himself in the character of McSpaunday.

Why didn't I get the message, and instead of rowing or traipsing over to Colebrooke, spend my time with those who were on the same wavelength? I can hear Max Nicholson: "Fear of the world, my dear, fear of the world".

Perhaps the trouble was rather that I was insecurely unable to see my own possibilities. I was like the "I" of Lorca's prose poem "In the Forest of the Lunar Grapefruits": "Poor and peaceful, I want to visit the ecstatic world, where all my possibilities live & all my lost landscapes". Roy was translating Lorca and read me some lovely, singing pieces in his hopelessly unmelodious voice.

How is it that so many great poets, masters of the musical cadence, have such unsuitable voices? — tone-deaf Yeats chanting away, Eliot sounding like a dry lay-preacher, Kenneth Slessor droning on like a subeditor dictating copy. But I would still rather hear them than the exquisitely modulated vocables of some actor emoting someone else's poem.

In 1947, when I had moved out of College to our flat in Banbury Road, Alister Kershaw of the beautiful radio voice arrived after an appalling voyage from Melbourne. We made him a bed on the floor on the huge Anlaby sheepskin we had brought with us, and he stayed for several weeks, enlivening Oxford life and abusing me for wasting my time rowing. He made it clear that he thought the whole business of studying for a degree was also pretty much a waste of time.

We would divert ourselves composing parodies. I can still remember a couple.

Sound, sound the clarion, fill the fife
Throughout the sensual world proclaim
This poem is not by Walter Scott
But someone of another name.

Herrick also got a doing over.

TO JULIA, IN A CHASTITY BELT
Whenas in chains my Julia pranks
Why then, methinks, how quaintly clanks
The ambulation of her shanks.

In the time when Alister was sleeping on the sheepskin I entered a short story competition sponsored by the BBC. The final prizewinner would be chosen from three finalists, all of whose stories would be broadcast. I submitted a story called "The Volcano", which was really not much more than an account of Geoff Tuck's and my crash in the jungle when flying back from Mt Bagana. To my surprise, as there were over a thousand entrants, I received a letter telling me that I was a finalist, and was told to report to the BBC to read my story myself.

Alister was pleased for me, but declared it would be impossible for me, with my stammer, to read the story. However, I was determined to do so, especially as there was an extra fee for reading your story yourself. With a groan, saying that perhaps something could be salvaged from the shambles, Alister set out to coach me in the art of fronting up to the microphone. He patiently heard me read and reread "The Volcano", until I knew the whole five thousand words by heart. I finally set off for London. I was shown into a producer's room, and to my delight found Roy Campbell seated at the desk.

He explained that I was to have an hour practising with another producer. “Man,” said Roy in his South African accent, “they'd never let me at you.” I have made hundreds of broadcasts since then, and it amazes me to think that the BBC would take the time and trouble to coach a young tyro as this very professional producer coached me.

“The Volcano” was repeated twice and published in *The Listener* and made me more than fifty pounds. Fifty pounds! It was the first money I had ever earned as a writer. (No one was ever paid by *Angry Penguins* or Reed & Harris.) What's more, I was asked for more contributions, and during the next four years made many broadcasts. So much for stammering.

At much the same time, I had my first short story accepted for a national magazine, a glossy monthly called *Courier*, which was owned by the father of my Magdalen friend Austen Kark and edited by his Uncle Leslie. Austen warned me that Uncle Leslie was very tough indeed, and that Nephew's recommendation would mean nothing more than that the story might possibly be nearer the top of the first batch eligible for rejection. But Uncle liked “The Devil has Wings”, an imaginary story based on a very real Kangaroo Island. *Courier* paid a princely twenty-five pounds, and later took other stories, as did some other magazines.

I introduced Alister to some of my fellow-students. He particularly liked my American friend George Bailey. George was one of the most remarkable people at Oxford. He had the build of a heavyweight boxer, which indeed he had once been, fighting under the name of Bearcat Bailey, and big hands which he could not keep still. If there was a delicate ornament lying around, in no time George would have picked it up and absent-mindedly broken it, which would send him into torrents of apology.

Although born in the state of Washington, the son of an engine driver and a cook, and holding an American passport, George was a mixture of several European origins, and was a phenomenal linguist. He spoke Russian, German and Hungarian perfectly, and was fluent in another dozen languages. At Columbia University he had studied classical Greek, and also while in New York had attended the Union Theological Seminary to learn Hebrew. The difficulty of this for George was that sometimes on waking up in the morning he could not think which language he was supposed to be speaking in.

When we took our final exams, George and I were waiting for the Viva Voce, which was an alarming experience in front of some of the most distinguished scholars of English Literature in the world — people like J.R. Tolkien, Neville Coghill, C.T. Onions and Lord David Cecil — and including, of course, Lewis and Bennett. One of this terrifying group would ask the hapless undergraduate to comment on some answer in one of his papers. George's name was called. A few minutes later he emerged, his face, never too well-shaven anyhow, as black as thunder. “Ignorant bunch of bums," he was saying, "ignorant bunch of bums." I asked him what had happened. Apparently they had decided to question him on his answer in the general essay paper, in which we were asked to write for three hours on any one topic out of the nine in the paper. George had chosen: "Who do you consider to be the greatest modern poet?". (It was an odd question for our pre-1832 course.) George had elected to write on the Russian symbolist poet Alexander Blok. "D'you know, none of those bastards know anything about Blok? Absolutely ignorant!" "But George," I protested, "we are supposed to be doing English Language and Literature". "Well," George snorted, "it didn't say *English* poet."

Ken Tynan considered George to be the most original undergraduate in Magdalen. George had an endless fund of stories about his career in the US Army, when he was commanding a Russian Liaison outfit. Under him he had a Russian ex-Count who was a Corporal, and a Russian ex-Prince who was a Private. The Prince would never accept an order from the Count, saying that that man's ancestors had been his family's serfs. Apparently the Prince was the best of all the linguists, and included Chinese amongst his range of tongues. (He claimed to have learned Chinese because he had had trouble with his laundry in New York.) There were some amazing developments when they all met up with the Soviet Army towards the end of the war.

George also had a superb bass voice; he could have been an opera singer. With it he had an endless repertoire of songs in all his languages, especially American and Russian.

Together with our other friends, we would ride bicycles out to places like the Trout Inn at Godstow, an enchanting old building by an idyllic curved bridge over a stream. If we felt bold enough, we would park the bikes and dive off the parapet of the bridge into the river; Jock Marshall, despite having only one arm, was an expert diver.

It seemed to me that with such a variety of places to visit around Oxford I ought to buy a car. My range was strictly limited; perhaps I could raise a hundred and fifty pounds, but only just. Not looking for anything in my price range, I used to amuse myself sitting on the lavatory in the mornings by reading the car advertisements in the London *Times*, a mouth-watering selection of famous marques. If only one had a thousand pounds or so. Then one day I spotted: "1926 Alvis 12/50 tourer. Has been up on blocks since 1939. What offers?"

As soon as I could I went to the address in Henley-on-Thames. The owner turned out to be an old lady called Lady Eardley-Wilmot. It seemed that her late husband had been an Indian civil servant of distinction, Controller of Oudh or something like that. She pointed to the garage. Her gardener showed me the car, and assured me that it had been up on blocks all those years, and that he had regularly turned over the engine to keep it free. The four-seater body was in perfect condition, complete with hood and side-curtains, leather upholstery and a fine array of instruments. I could just remember my mother's Alvis 12/50, and what an excellent car it had been.

When I returned to the crowded sitting room the old lady said, "Well, young man, what do you offer?" I had consulted the proprietor of the garage near our flat in Banbury Road, and he had suggested that I try for one hundred pounds, but if the car was in good condition I could go up to one hundred and fifty with prudence. I offered one hundred.

"Good Heavens!" Lady Eardley-Wilmot put down her teacup. "How absurd! You Australians have pots of money! No income tax out there."

I explained our taxation regulations and asked her how much she wanted for the Alvis. She suggested one hundred and fifty. I suggested one hundred and twenty.

"Why not?" she said. "Done!" She rose to her feet and we shook hands on it. "I wouldn't want to charge you too much, after all, you're only a student at Oxford and must be quite poor."

The Alvis was to take us all over Britain and half a dozen countries of Europe with only one hitch. It was half way up a mountain pass in the Pyrenees, when the crown wheel lost contact with the pinion in the differential. After a hair-raising descent, backwards, down the pass, a French mechanic took the differential to pieces, heated up the crown wheel, straightened it and away we went.

On my visits to London I had been seeing something of two old Australian friends, Nigel and Betty. Nigel was an easygoing, engaging character who worked for a London publisher. Betty took a job when their financial situtation became desperate, which often happened, but she preferred to do as little as she could; she was like Byron's Dudu in the Sultan's harem in *Don Juan*, whose form:

> Look'd more adapted to be put to bed,
> Being somewhat large, and languishing, and lazy,
> Yet of a beauty that would drive you crazy.

"Somewhat large" is somewhat unkind for Betty, who was quite small, and divinely plump, but otherwise the description fits her perfectly. The trap about Betty was that she was also extremely intelligent. She had a PhD in late nineteenth century French poetry. But just when someone had placed her as a highbrow, she would reveal a passion for the novels of Pamela Frankau or for romantic movies. She was, in fact, a delight to be with on every level, and I always envied Nigel.

It was an odd marriage; their frequent rows were nearly always about poetry. Voices would be raised, threats made of a speedy exit from the marriage, all because Nigel had quoted:

A drainless shower
Of light is poesy; 'tis the height of power
'Tis might half slumbr'ing on his own right arm.

"Nigel!" shouted Betty, "you have no ear, and you are nothing but a vulgarian! As if Keats would have talked about drains! What he said, if you are capable of recollection, was:

An exhaustless shower
Of light is poesy; 'tis the supreme of power;
'Tis might half-slumbering on its own right arm.

"Betty! Exhaustless! The internal combustion engine hadn't been invented in Keats' day! And as if 'might' would be followed by 'its'! Think of Michelangelo!"

There was one thing of which I was certain, as they argued on ever more heatedly, namely that they were both wrong. I had just written an essay on Keats' "Sleep and Poetry" for Lewis.

Now, as I was alone in the Oxford flat one afternoon, Betty rang to urge me to come to London, as there was a ravishing woman who had met me somewhere and was longing to see me again. Utterly bored with Oxford and everything there, and having the excuse of another broadcast to make on the BBC, I took the train to London and went to Nigel and Betty's flat in Mayfair. They loved to have an expensive address, even when broke. I was disappointed when they told me that their ravishing friend had got the flu. We had a pleasant dinner together and later on I retired to their spare room.

In the morning I heard Nigel slam the door as he went off to work, and thought about getting up for breakfast. Just then the door opened, and in came Betty in her most seductive nightgown. "Dutty darling!" she cried and in a second was beside me in the bed. In the last fraction of time in which I could still think, I realized that she herself was the "ravishing woman" of whom she had spoken.

Thus began my career as an adulterer. I feel neither proud of it, nor ashamed. Over many later years I tried to understand why I was a compulsively unfaithful husband in my first marriage. When I had asked Ninette whether she would marry me, I told her that probably it wouldn't last many years, and that I did not think I could be faithful, remembering my recent life in Tasmania. She accepted this. But we never had what later on came to be called "an open marriage". My infidelities were always kept secret, although by "not knowing" she retained a moral advantage, whatever her strong suspicions.

I think I was, for whatever reasons, always searching for Donne's "O my America, my new found land". Like Donne, I always believed that "change is the nursery / Of music, joy, life and eternity", and "The heavens rejoice in motion, why should I / Abjure my so much loved variety?" Oh the poets, how they can be quoted for one's own purposes.

I felt I had been virtuous too long, as my own cramped poetry showed. It was not only Betty's body that transported me, but her wit and ingenuity and love of poetry; her infinitely superior knowledge to mine of the French poets I most admired. And I also admired the element of intelligent trickery in her, something she shared with Shakespeare's Cleopatra. Betty (perhaps — who knows? — in tandem with Nigel) had engineered my quest, and we were both happy about the outcome.

Thirteen

The most important event of 1947 for me was crossing the English Channel. With my fellow student Herbert Piper, always known as Pip, and his wife Marie, Ninette and I drove in the Alvis through France, Belgium and Germany to Switzerland. There, in that orderly little enclave of four language groups peacefully coexisting, was an image, unmarked by war, of all that I had imagined Europe would be. Switzerland! Its inadequacies soon became apparent, but at first there it all was, sparkling with paint and wildflowers, mountains reflected in the lakes (which then were unpolluted), breakfasts of rolls and butter and cherry jam and REAL coffee under the plane trees. Then we went on into Italy, and came back through France, being away for about six weeks. We lived very simply and amazingly cheaply, and, after Britain, it was a revelation.

Despite my passion for English literature, which was being sorely tested at Oxford, wading through *Ancrene Riwle* or Gower or the essays of Addison, I had always longed to go to Europe, far more than to Britain. Perhaps it had something to do with the Brothers Grimm and Hans Andersen, the myths and legends of Greece and Rome, the Song of Roland, Schubert and Goethe, above all, Italy, that fountain of civilization that gave sustenance not only to Italian culture, but to Milton, Byron, Shelley, Keats and many others.

Nevertheless, I first experienced a new generosity of nature in England, a shock to a dry-country Australian. It didn't hem you in, like the Bougainville jungle, it opened out before you. The first spring and summer in Oxfordshire were amazing; green erupted from the grey blankets of drizzle, the woods were filled with bluebells. Even the sad ruins of London gave birth to stands of pink willow-herb, which flowers after fire, and came up everywhere in the bomb craters. I was told it was really a weed; maybe, but it seemed a promise of sanity. Another amazement was that in the English spring Eros flew up from Piccadilly Circus and shot his arrows into thousands of hitherto stodgy people. The lush Oxford meadows were alive with lovers. Pat came back from a walk along the river and said he had never seen so many bare bums in his life as he saw amidst the swaying grass. In punts along the Cher behind Magdalen, girls in big hats reclined gracefully on cushions, while undergraduates wobbled at the end of punt-poles.

But I wrote in my on-and-off diary that underneath it all there was still "an obliterating, inescapable greyness and gloom", adding "It has got into the bones of the people so that, while they are not reserved, as they are alleged to be, you never get to know them simply because inside there is nothing but greyness and gloom." This was obviously an absurd exaggeration; all I had to do was look at someone like Ken Tynan.

But there was some truth in it, and it was not solely because of those dispiriting years of war and shortages. Food rationing was worse than it had been during the war; the winter of 1946–47 was particularly severe, and there were terrible shortages of fuel for heating. But the English, rather than the Scots or Irish, seemed frozen in a perpetual queue for something better, each watching the other for a breach of decorum. Shaw's Mr Doolittle's hated middle-class morality ruled, a class tyranny within the class structure.

I found that the undergraduates I liked best all came from somewhere else but England. George Bailey, of course, was from America and most of Europe. Charles Monteith, also studying under Lewis, large, oracular, owlish and very funny, was from Ulster. Austen Kark, lean and gently stuttering, was (improbably) from South Africa. Clever, quick little Gunther Treitel was from prewar Germany. Open-hearted Harry Keith was from Scotland. Shura Shivarg, a bit sinister but highly entertaining, was from Harbin, and had the distinction of being the only Soviet citizen at Oxford on a British war grant; he had at one time been working behind the lines for the British Army. Kolya Rhiazanowsky was an American Russian who argued ceaselessly with Shura about communism; I always thought Shura was defending a system he did not believe in. There was a Frenchman, Philippe Giffard, whose family made liqueurs; he used to write the French essays for an English-speaking friend studying French at Magdalen, until the tutor (an Englishman) handed an essay back with "No Frenchman would ever write this" scrawled in the margin. And then there were all the Australians.

In 1947, when we came ashore in France, we found as we drove across France, Belgium and Germany that the war damage had been shattering, from invading armies as well as the bombing. But from the first meal in France, and even in Germany, life seemed more hopeful and less virtuously grim. Although I had eaten burgoo in The Boob, and had hungered after good food in Britain, I had never realized how important to life food is in itself, not only in the quality of it, but in the enjoyment of both the preparation and the eating of it. No English waitress beamed at you and said any equivalent of "*Bon appetit!*" The true democracy of food had not been presented to me before. In France, everyone from peasant to banker expected food to be a celebration; cost had nothing to do with it. In Britain and in its former colonies, food was an extension of the class system. The rich expected to eat well, and did; moreover, in Claridge's, the waiter (who was probably French anyway), would wish you enjoyment of the dish he was bringing you. The Oxford and Cambridge dons, and the clubmen of London, all ate very well indeed, often in the admirable plain style of old-fashioned English food. And they were still able, like Fortnum & Mason's, to get good materials; even at the worst times of rationing, Magdalen had ample game from its immense estates. But the poor in Britain ate poorly, and did not expect anything else.

Life was in many ways worse in most of Europe than it was in England, but no one seemed glum about it. In France you could live by day on tomatoes and baguettes and feel cheerful, and then for dinner you could have chicken or an omelette and haricots verts. I could not understand why there were chickens and eggs and fresh vegetables in France and not in England, where what little you could buy of anything from the shops always seemed stale.

As for rationing, everyone in France preferred the black market, which in England would have been be considered downright unpatriotic. Tourists with a car were given a generous allowance of petrol coupons in France. The Alvis used very little petrol, and by the time we reached the South of France, after Italy, I realized I would have quite a number of coupons left over. A consultation with the local patron at the cafe ended with the advice that I should go to Hyères, quite a large town, and sell my surplus coupons to a taxi-driver; the patron told me what was the going price.

So I went to the large square in Hyères, where there were a number of taxis parked. As I walked over to one I realized that there was a gendarme standing nearby. I thought it would look suspicious if I suddenly turned about and hurried off, so I went to the taxi driver in the Peugeot and whispered that I had some petrol coupons for sale. He replied in a loud voice, in his gravelly Midi accent, "*Ah merci, merci, monsieur, mais je n'en ai pas besoin.*" He put his head out the window and yelled across the square to the driver of a Renault taxi, "*Alphonse, vous voudrais des bons d'essence? Monsieur ici a beaucoup à vendre.*" The gendarme shifted his weight to the other foot and scratched his balls. The money I got for the tickets paid for the rest of the trip.

Particularly in Germany, the war damage was even worse than I had imagined. I could not envisage how they would be able to rebuild after such devastation. And, like the British, they must have been so tired.

Amidst all the sad aftermath of war, we had, in 1947, one immense advantage, a really prodigious advantage, as I realized more and more over the coming years. It was that there were almost no tourists. That meant that the proprietors of whatever inns or little restaurants were left standing were delighted to see some custom. Even more important was that the great monuments and galleries were almost empty. You could walk around the Sistine Chapel and actually see it all, without six guides in six different languages screaming at their victims.

You could go to the grandly named Palazzo Communale, which was really the poky Town Hall of the little town of Borgo San Sepolcro, where a few clerks were mouldering away, and find your own way to the wall on which Piero della Francesca had painted his *Resurrection*, which in an excellent essay in *Along the Road* Aldous Huxley simply calls "The Best Picture".

There were wonderful things to buy, especially in Italy, for very little money. Unfortunately, we didn't even have that much. But it was good to look.

From then on, in almost every vacation, we fled to Europe, and especially to France.

Alister Kershaw had remained in our Banbury Road flat when we went to Europe. At last he was able to leave the sheepskin and sleep in a real bed. He had spent only one night in it when there was a thump on the door, and in came, or rather, fell, Denison Deasey. Dease had just arrived by ship, and was suffering severely from pneumonia. Alister had to go back to the sheepskin.

Alister had four idols who dominated much of his thinking: D.H. Lawrence, T.E. Lawrence, Roy Campbell and Richard Aldington. The two Lawrences were dead. Alister met Roy with me in London and found him to be everything he had hoped for. The three of us got drunk in the Cafe Royal in Regent Street, which Roy assured us was not what it used to be in his youth, when every famous writer in London would be eating or drinking there. Alister suggested, although it was 11 p.m., that we should invite a famous writer to join us. We decided on Osbert Sitwell, but his phone did not answer. "I know," said Alister, "Noel Coward." "Man, oh my God, man, I'm leaving." Roy rose to his feet, plonked his wide grey Spanish sombrero on his head, and left. But Coward did not answer. I suggested, lowering our sights a little, Alex Comfort. He was very polite, said it was a bit late to go out, but would we have lunch with him the next day. We did, and I liked him very much, thin, bespectacled, rather earnest, but eloquent and direct, like his poetry. Alister did not care for him at all.

Alister's greatest success was with Richard Aldington. Shortly after our return from Europe he had written to Aldington, who was then living in Paris, asking if he might call to pay his respects. With typical generosity, Richard asked him to stay with him and his wife Netta. The meeting went so well that Alister stayed on, and became Richard's secretary.

Aldington, whose work has been out of favour for some years, is now being republished and reassessed. In the 1940s his reputation seemed secure; he was already famous, with his first wife H.D. (Hilda Doolittle) and Ezra Pound, as one of the original Imagist poets; he had achieved great popularity in the 1920s and 1930s as a novelist, with books like *Death of a Hero* and *The Colonel's Daughter* (banned in Australia); he was an accomplished essayist; and he had recently published a biography of the Duke of Wellington which was admired by Basil and Cynthia Brooke, an ironic accolade for someone who detested the British aristocracy.

By 1948 he had taken a villa at St Clair, near Le Lavandou in the South of France, and he and Netta invited us to stay. The Villa Aucassin was set in a grove of Australian wattle trees in which, in summer, the nightingales sang so loudly they kept you awake. It belonged to an American millionaire, and was of two storeys in white stone, with capacious rooms. The light was soft and flickered grey on the olive-bearing hills. When you walked up them, the soap-soft, glittering mica crumbled; there was pink cistus and dry-crackling leaves, and the trunks of the cork-oaks, stripped of their cork, were wine-red, then dark as dried blood, and the cracks in the new cork were gold to pink. The air was scented with herbs, sharp, aromatic, and there was wild lavender and strawberry-studded arbutus. The ancient Mediterranean ambience was unspoiled in the hills, whatever was happening on the coast, which was very little in those days.

At the long table in the dining room Richard would sit in massive, but soft-voiced, domination, his leonine head suggesting not Africa but Trafalgar Square. Despite his disillusion with the England he had satirized in his novels, he was essentially English of the old style, in the company of Dr Johnson, Byron, Thackeray, the Duke of Wellington and eccentrics like the naturalist Charles Waterton. In his opinion (second-hand, for he refused to go back) their England was gone for ever. He asked me searching questions about the state of the country and when I answered said, nodding, and lifting the wine glass to his lips, "I thought so." He could not understand why I was wasting my time reading English at Oxford. "My dear boy, anyone can read English. It is something we all do. Now why aren't you studying something really useful, like medieval French?"

His knowledge of medieval and Renaissance French and Italian was greater than C.S. Lewis's, but he didn't want to bully anybody with it. Instead, he translated all sorts of texts, from medieval, Renaissance and later literature; amongst his major translations were the *Decameron* and *Les Liaisons Dangereuses*, for a long time the only English version of the latter. Richard was a professional writer, someone expert in the literatures of the past, but always concerned with the present. In Oxford the present was always exiled. With Richard, the past existed to fertilize the present.

At that time Richard was in his late fifties; his wife Netta, tall, dark and languid, was in her forties. She had been married to the actor Michael Wilding. She and Richard had an enchanting daughter, about twelve, called Catherine but always known as Catha. Netta obviously welcomed some company; you felt that she was too isolated at the Villa Aucassin. It was all very well for Richard, who worked every day, but she had too much spare time. She was a mixture of self-control and no control. You couldn't shock her or surprise her, she was far too sophisticated, but she undermined her own poise. There would be sudden changes, demoniacal laughter, intense, big-eyed stares that made you feel you must quickly say something profound. Then there would be flashes of genuine insight and intelligence. She was drinking too much. Her idleness gave her a need for jabs of self-assurance, when she would tell you (and herself) that she was really rather good at painting and drawing, or that she was reading Proust for the third time.

Life at the Villa Aucassin was very different from Oxford. Richard's conversation was not to make a point or to score a tick for knowledge, he simply wanted to share with you and hear what you had to say, however unimportant you were. At first it seemed as if he might be making fun of you: "Oh, so you've just been in Pisa. Now, did you realize that Antonio Pisanello was born in 1395 in Pisa, hence his name. Of course, since you're in England," pause for another sip of wine, "you will be familiar with his *St Eustace* in the National Gallery, but next time you're in the Louvre" — as if you popped in there regularly — "don't whatever you do miss the portrait of Margherita Gonzaga." It was not showing off, or making fun of you, but simply longing to share what he loved.

Of course he could also be bitchy and harsh, especially about writers whose later careers had disappointed him, like T.S. Eliot (from whom he had many letters). He could also be funny about those he had always respected, like W.B. Yeats. He told me about the first time he had met the great poet, at Rapallo in Northern Italy. He was only a young writer himself, in awe of Yeats and very nervous. They went to a trattoria and Yeats ordered spaghetti. He was talking and gesticulating, his long hair flying as he tossed his head. The spaghetti came, and then to Richard's horror he saw that several locks of Yeats' hair had become entwined with the spaghetti he was trying to eat.

"What should I do?" Richard re-created his dilemma. "Should I say 'Mr Yeats, you're trying to eat your hair', or should I look the other way?" Fortunately at that moment Yeats gave a tug, hair and spaghetti parted, and without any introduction he said, "How do you account for Ezra?"

Richard's collection of letters was extraordinary, especially from people he had worked with on magazines, or helped in their writing careers. He would not bring them out to show you, but quietly retire to his study and come back with something that illustated a point in the conversation. But he did not mind Kershaw showing the letters to me. There was a huge pile from Ezra Pound, going back thirty years to their Imagist days. Pound's rummaging in the bowels of the typewriter, spelling words his own way, punning his way into a new paragraph, were wonderfully dotty, long before he was officially declared to be so. T.S. Eliot's were as orderly as Pound's were erratic. Richard had been responsible for getting Eliot his first job as reviewer for *The Times Literary Supplement*, and he had been heavily involved in Pound's scheme for providing Eliot with a pension so he could leave his job at the bank and concentrate on writing poetry. There were many letters from Ford Madox Ford, with whom Richard had worked on the *New English Review*, and from many others. Here was a life lived for literature in a way not understood by the dons of Oxford.

Richard continued to receive a lot of letters. One bizarre one arrived when we were in St Clair, staying with Dease at the little *auberge*, Les Sables d'Or, run by an amusingly eccentric White Russian, Serge Berkaloff, whose father had been an Admiral in the Black Sea Fleet. Dease at the time was attempting to disguise the extent of his affair with a blonde Belgian grass widow, but their mutual discretion was shattered one morning when we were all eating our *croissants* under the plane trees. Madame's little boy, aged about eight, came down after his mother. When he saw M. Denison Deasey he called out in a piping treble heard by all having breakfast, "*Monsieur Deni, qu'est-ce-que tu faisais dans notre chambre hier soir?*"

Now, as we were up at the Villa drinking one of Richard's *vins mousseux* (an odd taste for such an epicure), he was opening his mail. He laughed and handed over a letter. It was from a British Army Lieutenant-Colonel (Retd.), who said that he was a fan of Richard's, especially of his World War I novel, *Death of a Hero.* At the time it was published, in 1929, the publisher said it was impossible to print the soldiers' language as truthfully reported by Richard, who of course had been on the Western Front. Richard refused to bowdlerise his novel, and insisted that every deleted word be replaced by an equivalent number of asterisks. Thus "fucking shit" became " ******* **** ". The old soldier wrote that he had amused himself over the twenty years since the book was first published by filling in all the asterisks. He said he realized that most of the four-letter words were interchangeable, but his problem lay in two words printed thus: " ***** ******** ". He considered that after forty years service in India, Africa and Europe he had a fair knowledge of the language of his men, but these two words had him baffled.

Richard had already written his reply by the time we had finished reading the letter. It was simple. "Dear Lt. Col X. Thank you for your letter and your kind remarks about my books. However, and alas, unto the filthy-minded all things are filthy. The words in question are 'Queen Victoria'."

I couldn't help thinking of Richard later on, when my old Adelaide Professor, J.I.M. Stewart, now a Fellow of Christ Church, asked me to dinner at High Table. After dinner we repaired to the Senior Common Room, where we sat around a big table and the port and the snuff went round. I took some port but declined the snuff. The old don beside me, a famous scholar who looked like an Airedale dog gone grey, shouted at me:

"Our snuff not good enough for you, young man? Come on, take some, take some, and don't dribble it down your bib like that old Canon alongside you." Indeed, the venerable Canon had taken the snuff off the back of his hand and blown it all over his chin, lips, nose and waistcoat, or whatever the garment is that Canons wear below their dog-collars. Next to me, Lord Pakenham made nasty remarks about the Magdalen dons, a very inferior lot, while another don was busy on Evelyn Waugh, a disgusting fellow whose *Brideshead Revisited* was a travesty of Oxford; indeed it is, but to me Waugh was a writer to be treated with respect, and not as an unruly undergraduate who should be failed in his exams. The wit-sharpening continued around the table. There was none of Richard's geniality and love of knowledge in their determination to score off someone. Stewart, who was not taken in by any of it, remarked to me as he saw me to the gate afterwards, "In England there are three varieties of people — nice, very nice and frightfully nice. Dons, on the other hand, are mostly nasty."

Jack Bennett took me to dinner at the Magdalen High Table, which provided better food and drink, but the conversation was again disappointing. New books were strenuously discussed by the dons and you were impressed by the knowledge displayed, until suddenly you realized that they had taken all their opinions from the Sunday papers, and that the argument was really between Cyril Connolly and Desmond McCarthy. None of them had actually read the books.

After dinner we repaired to the small common room, where leather chairs were arranged in an oval, with the fireplace at one end and a table laden with fruit and decanters at the other. Guests and hosts were separated. I was seated between a young history don and Professor Young, who sat down and said, "I am the Professor of Anatomy." I didn't quite know how to follow up this opening. The only anatomy I could cope with was Robert Burton's *Anatomy of Melancholy*, but I didn't risk that.

In front of our chairs there was a little railway that ran in an oval from one side of the fireplace and back to the other. Along it trundled a decanter of sherry, which no one touched. Then one of claret, which was also ignored. Then one of port (a very good port) which was soon emptied. The decanter was finished when I picked it up. I was told to hold it up, whereupon a fresh one was brought, and I got a full glass extra. The port went around about three times.

It was the usual dons' conversation, one ear cocked for adjacent conversations, to place a quotation, correct an error, supply a reference. The young don asked me about Rhodes Scholars, and said he was only interested in their intellectual attainments. I agreed, saying it was ridiculous to do as the Rhodes selectors did, and place any importance on whether a candidate had been a school prefect or good at games. Whereupon Aranyi, the Arab don next along (whose guest was a lineal descendant of Mohammed) said he had never got over being a nothing at school, not even a prefect. Whereupon the young don admitted to having been head prefect of his schoool, Stowe, and captain of the cricket eleven.

We then moved to the larger common room, for bad coffee and general chat. Everyone had left by 10 p.m. Old Professor Chapman, the great linguistic scholar, bewailed this exodus; he said that at this hour everyone in the old days would be settling in with beer or whisky for prolonged argument.

Jack and I retired to his rooms for a beer and a long talk about the colonial worlds in which we had been brought up, and how as those values fell away we had had to think out a new set and start all over again. I remembered my (or was it George Bailey's?) essay on Dr Johnson's "Taxation No Tyranny"; Johnson had a low opinion of colonials, who were to him either discontented sectarians or mercenary adventurers.

Nevertheless, despite my disillusionment with many of the dons, there were amongst them some of the wisest, most kindly and thoughtful people I have ever met. One of them was Tom Boase, the President of Magdalen. An art scholar of international renown, former head of the Courtauld Institute of Fine Art in London, Tom, with his white hair and youthful-pink face, and his soft voice, took the trouble to be hospitable not only to us, his undergraduates, but to wives or girlfriends as well. In the President's Lodgings he had some very fine works of art, some of them from Sir Kenneth Clark's collection, amongst which there was a unicorn's horn. Actually, it was from a narwhal, but it looked exactly as if it had come out of the great French tapestry, "The Lady and the Unicorn". Clark had brought back from Australia a number of paintings, and he was particularly enthusiastic about Nolan and Drysdale.

We had arrived in Oxford with some icons from home: my Bokhara rug which I had bought for eight pounds in Peshawar on my schoolboy trip to India; a lot of books; and two early landscapes by Arthur Boyd. One of them Arthur had rolled up, tied with a piece of string around it, and given us for a wedding present. The other I had bought for ten pounds. The first time Tom Boase came to dinner he stopped in front of these paintings and declared them to be, in his opinion, quite remarkable. He asked who had painted them; he had heard of Arthur from Clark, but these were the first paintings of his that Tom had seen. I was pleased that from this encounter came a good friendship; the scholar and the painter later collaborated in a book on Nebuchadnezzar.

Tom was one of the Governors of the Shakespeare theatre at Stratford-on-Avon, and many times went with us in the old Alvis to see a play there. He had long nourished a passion for Peggy Ashcroft, unrequited, he sighed, but they were very good friends. We often had suppers with her after a play; on these occasions she was the least actressy actor I have ever known, unlike some others Tom took us backstage to meet.

By now I was no longer living in College, and we had secured much better accommodation in Oxford; we had left Banbury Road for St John's Street, where we had the top two floors of a house overlooking Worcester College garden. I had a piano there, and began to practice again. Max Nicholson arrived from Melbourne and came to stay. "A song, Geoffrey, a song!" he would demand. I would find something suitable and play the accompaniment, while Max sat beside me reading the music and singing in his melodious but not always tuneful tenor. "My dear, I think you played a wrong note there." "No, Max, look, it's a D not an E." "Oh, if you insist." Max's hands were busy as he sang. He simultaneously stroked Ninette's bottom with one hand and my leg with the other.

Dease stayed, after a visit to Ireland, mostly spent in a hospital in Dublin where it was feared he had tuberculosis; fortunately he recovered. He departed for Vienna, to write a book about Schubert.

From Vienna came Beate Ross, frail but not to be intimidated by life, speaking perfect English, whom George Bailey was courting. Her extended family had owned the famous German publishers, Ullstein Verlag; being Jewish, they had lost everything. But Beate's father, with his Scottish name (it came from one of those Scots who settled in Germany in the eighteenth century), had survived and Ullstein was beginning again.

George had a favourite shirt, of some thick green material, which he had had in the army; he never washed it, but amazingly enough it never smelled, although the collar had taken on the consistency and shine of leather. Beate, elegant and fastidious, insisted that George have a bath and that the shirt should be burned. After some argument, George agreed. He went upstairs to our bathroom. A few moments later there was a deep bass roar. George had got into the bath still wearing his shirt. It was now unburnable, so I picked it up with the fire tongs and took it down to the rubbish bin.

George was, despite his distinguished war service, his accumulation of degrees and languages, the most disorganized person I have ever known. One day I wrote down in my diary "A Day in the Life of George Bailey". He set off in Oxford with his friend Norsky to catch the 12.30 train to London. They stopped to have a beer and missed the train. George went back to get some money from his bank before catching the 2.05. They missed that; Norsky then deserted. George missed the fast 4.45, but caught a slow train, and when it reached Didcot remembered that he had forgotten his money and his G.I. Bill of Rights, which he had left at the bank. He got off to catch a train back to Oxford and found he had left his passport, tickets and so on in the train. He hailed a taxi and drove at 60 m.p.h. to Pangbourne, where he missed the train by a minute. He then rang Reading, to find out whether anyone had handed in his passport; it was not there. He rang Didcot. Yes, it was there all the time. So he went back to Oxford to collect his money and the Bill of Rights, and never got to London after all.

In my last term at Oxford I began to feel very depressed but put it down to the usual appalling weather. I kept feeling worse and worse, really suicidal; then I noticed one morning that my pee was a strange colour, like cheap orangeade. I went to the doctor, and found myself in hospital with a bad attack of what was known in those days as jaundice, now called hepatitis.

I was kept in hospital for three weeks, and told I was not to work, not that I felt like it. The snag about this was that, being a typical undergraduate, I had left all my revision till the last minute. Now I would be even more behind than I was already. In hospital the only consolation was that the weather had improved, although it was still very cold, and my bed was for some of the day in sunlight. It appeared that there was no treatment for jaundice but to be given a gallon of water to drink, four pills and a dose of salts every day. I wore a canyon between my room and the lavatory across the corridor.

A month or so after my release from hospital it was time for Schools, our final exams of nine papers. As I had expected, I turned in poor papers on Old English and the study of language. Jack had hoped I would get a 1st, but I got a 2/1. George, to general disappointment, got a 3rd; no doubt his essay on Alexander Blok contributed to this. Austen got a 2nd, Gunther, of course, a 1st. The four of us took half a dozen bottles of champagne from Bond's Room to St John's Street, still wearing our caps and gowns. At the College Ball one of the scouts had demonstrated to me how to open a champagne bottle without extracting the cork. You simply removed the foil and wire, and gave the top rim of the bottle a smart tap with a heavy carving knife, when it fell off with the cork inside it. In the back yard at St John's Street I attempted this method, but the trick would not work. Perhaps the carving knife was not heavy enough. When I did open the bottle, by the conventional method, the champagne was so shaken up that most of the bottle spouted over our lettuces. Fortunately Bond had not given us any of his finest.

My one aim now was to cross the Channel as quickly as possible. The plan was to have a holiday, and then drive to the South of France, where I had taken, sight unseen, a flat at the little seaside town of Sanary, where I intended to write my first novel. By this time I had sold the Alvis, and bought my first new car, a Morris Minor tourer. I was allowed to buy it only when I signed a form saying I would export it to Australia within a year. There were so few in England then that crowds used to gather around it in the street.

But first, we would meet Dease in Strasbourg, then George in Salzburg, where we would hope to see some of the Festival. By sheer luck we got tickets for a superlative concert, Bruno Walter conducting and Kathleen Ferrier singing Mahler's *Song of the Earth*. Nights in Salzburg became mornings as we all discussed whether or not George should propose to Beate. He still had not made up his mind when we arrived in Vienna. We went out through the Russian zone of occupation to her father's estate on the banks of the Danube. It had been unpillaged because, whereas most landowners had fled as the Russians approached towards the end of the war, Herr Ross and his wife had stayed and welcomed the Russians as liberators. Nothing was stolen except all the watches and clocks, and Herr Ross's dinner jacket.

It had taken two and a half hours to travel the twenty miles by train to Herr Ross's estate; we had been told we would not be allowed to drive in the car. Herr Ross said this was nonsense, so the next time we went in the Morris. At the check point a Russian soldier waved us through. But on the way back a Mongolian soldier sprang out with a submachine gun and ordered us to halt. George explained in his impeccable Russian that he was an American, and that we were bringing him back from the airport which was in the Russian zone. This only made the soldier more suspicious. He ordered me to drive to the Kommandantura, and climbed in the back with Ninette, poking her in the ribs with his machine gun and laughing. At the Kommandantura a scruffy Corporal told me that the car would be confiscated and that we would have to make our own way back to Vienna. George was then removed as he began to plead for me not to have my beautiful new car taken away from me. The situation was desperate.

Laboriously in longhand the Corporal made out a huge form, which seemed to include everything from my grandfather's first name down. He communicated with me in rudimentary German. He had just finished his toil when the door burst open and in strode New Russian Man, an extremely smart Sergeant, with George behind him. He glared at the Corporal, picked up the form and slowly tore it in half and threw the pieces onto the floor. Then he turned to us and said, in good English, "I apologize for my country. We were allies in the war. We should be still. Please take your car and go to Vienna, with my apologies."

What genuine goodwill between nations was to be dissipated by the Cold War!

Fourteen

After Vienna, we took a long loop down through Italy and up again and into the South of France. In Rome we called on Gino Nibbi, now back from Australia, who with his son Tristano was just moving into a new, large bookshop. Nibbi was in fine embonpoint, once again enjoying the cuisine of his ancestors, and he sat in a huge armchair like a Renaissance Pope on his throne. His hefty arms would sweep out in a gesture, his grey mane tossed back, with his handsome face making full use of his native tongue, "that liquid bastard Latin/ Soft melting in the mouth", as Byron put it.

He expatiated on Australia. "Someone said they're like the Attic Greeks, but surely the Attic Greeks created something more than record cricket scores?" He asked after mutual friends, particularly Max Nicholson, and then sighed and began a long recital about the woes of returning to Italy, the corruption, the bureaucracy. Australia was so free, so honest! He sighed again. "Life is a deception of magnitude. It is impossible to live anywhere!"

When we returned to France, Les Sables d'Or and the Villa Aucassin, Richard's despair with life was sharper and harsher than Gino's. He was fuming with the interruption of a visit from two of his English publishers and their dreadful wives who were wearing silk stockings and high heels. One of them said to Netta, "I expect Catherine absolutely adores Enid Blyton?" "Who is Enid Blyton?" Netta asked innocently.

Richard was very vulnerable to visitors from Britain. There were still acute currency restrictions, and all sorts of people from across the Channel would unmercifully renew tenuous friendships in order to eat the Aldingtons' food and drink their wine. At first Richard and Netta used to have them to stay, but now they sent them down the hill to Serge Berkaloff. Serge was a meticulous cook, and his menu (there was no à la carte) always a joy. One day when the publishers were there he brought us beautifully fresh oysters for lunch. Mrs Publisher sent hers back. "He should have asked us. Oysters are so personal, don't you agree?" Another Englishman asked for a bottle of tomato sauce, which he squirted over a sauce Serge had spent an hour making. After this, Serge always referred to him as "Monsieur Sauce de Tomate".

Richard, when expansive and relaxed, was as wonderful company as ever. But the world, that deception of magnitude, wounded him too easily. Even in the South of France there was certainly plenty of evidence of man's folly and cruelty, from the wreckage of the war, which could be found in a peaceful corner of the coast, to the growing frenzy of the Cold War. He took it all personally, and seethed with a Swiftian loathing, not of individuals, but of man and his works.

However, Richard's worst wounds came not from the jagged world but from himself. The bearings of the love-hate seesaw screeched in his soul. For all his profound personal culture, he lacked the nurturing of nature, the fertile simplicity of water and manure on a garden. For him, the manure remained shit, the compost did not meld with the soil.

Catha could always take him out of himself; Netta was too languid, and there were ominous signs of terminal exasperation between them. I think that is why he enjoyed our group of Australians so much; we came from a less overbuilt land and, however sophisticated we thought we were, retained a certain freshness, if not naiveté.

Richard moaned when he heard we were going to Sanary. "Oh, my God, my dear boy, Aldous and Maria used to live there. All the Toulon drains flow out there. For God's sake don't eat any local oysters or mussels." "Listen to him," laughed Catha, "Daddy loves to say things like that." He relaxed, and laughed at himself.

Sanary turned out to be a pretty little port, with the Mediterranean lapping against the pavement outside the cafes, and shops full of delicious and very cheap things to eat, and the proprietors all interested in our welfare.

I settled in to write my novel, which poured out at prodigious speed. It was set in Melbourne, about European migrants and Australians, about battered civilization and unspoiled nature. After nearly four years away from Australia, I had a hunger for nature and space. Netta had said to me, "Surely the best thing about Australia is that you have so few people there?"

I finished the first draft in five weeks and four days. We returned to England, and I set about revision, and finding whether anyone would publish it.

Dickens' publishers, the venerable firm of Chapman & Hall, were now the publishers of Evelyn Waugh; his father had been Director of the firm. But they also published fiction by new authors, so I sent them *The Mortal and the Marble.* (The title came from a passage in Byron about Pygmalion and Galatea, "The mortal and the marble still at strife / And timidly expanding into life".)

Before long I had a summons from the Managing Director, Jack McDougall. I took the train to London and then a cab to Nigel and Betty's flat, where they had asked me to stay. They wished me luck, and I went to the rather dilapidated building with the Chapman & Hall sign outside it. The lift was a survival from Dickens' day; you gave a tug on a thick rope, smooth from the passage of a thousand hands, which ran through the roof and the floor of the cage you stood in. This started the lift, and as you approached your floor you squeezed the rope till the lift stopped. I told myself to hope for nothing.

Jack was tall and bony and genial, with that rosy complexion that speaks more of another bottle of port than of walks over the downs at dawn. As charmingly as if he were offering me a whisky or a gin, he said, "If you want to, I'll publish it, if you'd rather not, then we'll wait for the next one." He obviously knew he wasn't going to make any money out of it. He produced his reader's report, by a woman, which said that I was "a born writer", and then gave a brilliant summary of the book. "Oh hang it," said Jack, "let's publish, then we can celebrate by having a spot of lunch at my club." His club turned out to be Brooks's in St James', where with delicious food we had sherry, Beaujolais, four ports and a cigar in a beautiful, barrel-ceiling room upstairs, overlooking the street and Boodles Club opposite. "The best thing," said Jack, "is the view of the very pretty front of Boodles, and the best thing about that is that you can't see inside, never see the dreadful people that belong to it." The literary life looked all right to me.

I floated in euphoria a foot or two above the street back to the flat where Betty kissed and congratulated me. In thirty seconds we were in bed. She said that Nigel would not be home until late, and then, with a most fetching earnestness, both mocking and revealing of herself, she added: "Please give me an orgasm. I have never had an orgasm." No young lover could have been given a more irresistible task, but ignorance is not displaced by enthusiasm, and I swiftly pounded away on top of her instead of really being any help. Her moans subsided, but I didn't think they had been genuine. Just then we both heard the door of the building slam as someone came in from the street. "Christ, it's Nigel," she said, diving into her dress (with Betty, there was never much more than a dress to be put on). She shut the door, so I could pretend to be in the bathroom. But I could not find one of my socks. It was becoming more and more like a French farce. I finally had to go down wearing only one sock; when I sat on the sofa I had to drape my right trouser leg over my left ankle.

I excused myself and went to a nearby shop and bought a new pair of socks. The attendant, with a gravity befitting his ancient establishment, showed no surprise when I took off my one sock and put on the new pair. Betty later found the missing sock in the bottom of the bed.

About this time I began to see Willie McKie again, and go to Westminster Abbey to hear the choir and listen to his organ voluntaries. One day I achieved the summit of my musical career by playing the organ for a service in the Abbey. Actually, it was only the chord of D major. Sometimes Willie liked to go down from his organ loft and conduct the choir for an anthem; amazingly enough, it was impossible to see the choir from the organ seat. A fat little choirboy called Simpkins was detailed by Willie to lean over the edge of the loft and signal to me when to play my chord. I nervously sat there with my hands over the keys, watching Simpkins. Suddenly he swivelled round and hissed "NOW!" I nearly missed the chord.

About this time, Willie became the object of a middle-aged English lady's passion. She looked highly respectable, and no doubt was, but she yearned mercilessly for Willie. She used to station herself outside the door at the bottom of the ladder leading up to the organ loft; he was trapped, as there was no other way out. So he would ask me to head her off. I would go down the steps, open the door, and say blandly, "Oh, are you waiting for Dr McKie?" She would be forced to admit it. I would then say he had already left the Abbey to go to the dentist, and that I had been standing in for him at the organ.

Although Australian, Willie had a hatred of France typical of a certain sort of Englishman over the centuries. He was distressed when I said I was thinking of returning there. "It is a disgusting country and the French are a vile people."

We still had not decided whether or when to return to Australia, or where to live, England or France. I wanted to write another novel, and Richard offered to find a cottage near St Clair, so we kept on the St John Street flat in Oxford, and set off once again for the South of France.

The cottage was high on the hill above the Villa Aucassin, tiny but adequate, except that it had no plumbing as yet. While this was being installed we stayed chez Berkaloff at Les Sables d'Or.

While we were at St Clair Roy Campbell brought his family down to stay at a nearby hilltop village, Bormes, and we paid frequent visits to each other and, of course, to the Aldingtons. Mary Campbell was a splendid if alarming woman, like something out of Goya, dark, smouldering and abrupt; then, suddenly, she would become gentle and affectionate. She was one of the famous Garman sisters, of whom one was married to Jacob Epstein, the sculptor, another to Wishart, the Communist publisher, and Mary to Roy. The three brothers-in-law hated each other. Roy and Mary had two daughters, Anna in her early twenties, Tessa about nineteen. Anna was as beautiful and sophisticated, funny, cruel and kind, as Tessa — recovering from a nervous illness — was plain and saintly.

Roy and Richard, so different, had immense respect for each other's writing, although there were some silent areas between them. Richard had just finished *Portrait of a Genius But* ..., his biography of D.H. Lawrence; Roy did not care much for Lawrence. Roy's two mentors, T.S. Eliot, who published his poetry, and Edith Sitwell, who as far back as the early 1930s had acclaimed him as "a poetic tornado", were both on Richard's black list. What the two men had in common was a deep love and knowledge of Provençal and French poetry (Roy was translating Baudelaire), and a detestation of Bloomsbury. Richard quoted with relish Roy's lines "Home

Thoughts in Bloomsbury": "Of all the clever people round me here / I most delight in Me — / Mine is the only voice I care to hear / And mine the only face I like to see".

John Minton, a celebrated artist of the time, was a good friend of Ánna's, and he came down to stay at Le Lavandou with two blond boyfriends, Roy and Richard. Roy Campbell and Richard Aldington were not very amused at the coincidence of names.

At first I didn't know how to keep up with Johnny's zany wit, his hands, legs and long bony head waggling and dipping as he spoke, turning on a little world of tricks I could not possibly enter, although Anna was expert in it. There were those whip-flicks of wit between them in which the art is not to draw blood.

Johnny was very amusing in such moods, then suddenly very appealing in unpompous moments of seriousness, with a genuine humilility. He was as quick, witty and inventive as the blonds were beautiful and dumb. The blonds used to flex their rippling muscles and throw out their splendid chests doing handstands or balancing acts on the beach, while gangling Johnny tried to climb up or jump over them until he would fall onto the sand, collapsing with laughter, while the boys, solemn with relief, resumed their act.

In his spare moments he was working on those wonderfully evocative pen-and-ink drawings for Elizabeth David's *French Country Cooking*.

I had the urge to write a story before starting on the novel, so made my way up a hill to the west, through crackly scrub and cork trees loud with cicadas, and in the shade of an ilex wrote a story based on Paul Burton's and my aerial battle near Parkes with the eagle. I called it "The Wedge-Tailed Eagle", and it has been the most succesful work I ever wrote. First published by Clem Christesen in *Meanjin* in 1950, then read by me on the BBC, it has since been republished or rebroadcast somewhere around the world every year, and translated into many languages. As for my second novel, it was a flop. I finished it, put it away, rewrote it, but it never worked as a novel. I showed it to Jack, against my better judgement, and he politely said he would let this one slide, but of course I could try another publisher. I didn't.

The Mortal and the Marble was published shortly after our return to England, when we took a boringly bourgeois flat in Holland Park. The reviews were mixed. James Hanley, a notable but now forgotten novelist of the time, said that I was a "born writer, miles away from the Australian rough diamond school". I wondered what school this was. Marghanita Laski, a waspish reviewer for the *Sunday Times*, wrote (quite correctly) that it was not a good novel, and then went on to make some acid remarks about Australians. I was in hospital for a minor operation when Roy rang

Ninette and said, "I know Geoff's in hospital so can't do it himself, but d'you think he'd like me to go round and bop that Laski bitch?"

The Mortal and the Marble has, deservedly, disappeared from sight, but it is still interesting to look back at its reception in Australia in 1950. John Hetherington in the *Age* and Douglas Stewart in the *Bulletin* both welcomed it, Stewart saying, which was true, that it was the first novel about the European migrants who were making such changes to Australian society. Hetherington and Stewart were always encouraging to new Australian writers. (Stewart's views on Patrick White, who of course was not new, are a different story.) Wally Campbell sent me a review from the Brisbane *Telegraph* which, to my astonishment, praised the book, well beyond its deserts. The review in the *West Australian* sounded familiar, and then I realized it was a straight quote from the blurb; I was later told that the fiction reviewer was the regular football writer for the paper. In Adelaide, Max Harris, running Mary Martin's Bookshop, asked the publisher's traveller for an advance copy of the book. The traveller, who represented some fifteen English publishers, said, "Oh you wouldn't want that one, it's by an Australian author, it's at the bottom of the bag."

Alas, three years studying English at Oxford had done nothing for me as a writer of fiction. I had indeed, rather superficially, studied the fathers of the English novel, Defoe, Richardson, Fielding and Sterne, but had learned nothing from them to apply to contemporary use. My fault, I suppose.

I reread *The Mortal and the Marble* recently, for the first time for more than forty years, and was dismayed at the lost opportunities, although encouraged by the absence of clichés in the writing. The trouble was that I had simply not sorted myself out, nor what I wanted to say. I had spent my life in trying to please my mother and then my wife, to "do the right thing", although frequently doing the wrong thing, hiding my emotions and deeper thoughts so everything would run smoothly. I had liberated myself as a man and as a writer in Tasmania, making no attempt to please authority, only doing the bare minimum to placate it. My imagination had flown free, like an aerobatic Tiger Moth; since then I had been flying straight and level. In my writing I was tyrannized by "reality", by attempting always to be true to experience, not to let experience and imagination develop together.

I had read Keats' "Sleep and Poetry" and had underlined (bad student habit, but at least it was my own book and not a library's) the very passage that should have given me pause to apply to myself. The poet has had a vision of a chariot, "O'er sailing the blue cragginess, a car/ And steeds with streaming manes", and then he loses the vision, and instead

> A sense of real things comes doubly strong,
> And, like a muddy stream, would bear along

My soul to nothingness: but I will strive
Against all doubtings, and will keep alive
The thought of that same chariot, and the strange
Journey it went.

Years later, I was to be in a correspondence with Patrick White over the many meanings of the chariot; he was unfamiliar with Keats' lines, but delighted by them. In 1950, and for too long afterwards, I was obsessed by "A sense of real things".

My literary earnings for 1950 make an interesting comment on what it meant to be a young writer starting off, with sales in Britain and Australia. I was paid seventy-five pounds sterling advance for *The Mortal and the Marble*, of which ten per cent went to my agent, A.D. Peters. The B.B.C. paid me twelve guineas each for three broadcasts. Magazines and the old *Evening News* paid the best, from twenty to twenty five pounds for stories. *Meanjin* paid me two guineas for "The Wedge-Tailed Eagle", which went on to earn fifty pounds in reprints and broadcasts in England. My total literary earnings for 1950 were one hundred and fifty pounds nine shillings. It was just as well I had the small inheritance from Grandfather, with occasional top-ups from my mother and the always generous Chibs.

Through the Campbells I met a very odd man, more than a little mad, and with reason. He was a South African poet, Hugo van Steen, tall, bone-thin and vague, who had worked behind the lines in Europe during the war, for British Intelligence, speaking Dutch and German fluently. He was betrayed to the Gestapo, and sentenced to death; they actually took him out to a wall in the prison yard and the firing squad were given the orders to fire, but the cartridges were blank. He had already, unknown to him, been exchanged for a German prisoner in England, but for several months, until the exchange could go through, he was kept under sentence, expecting every day to be shot. He gave an interview on the BBC about his experiences in which he described how he had managed to bore a tiny hole through the wall of his windowless cell, through which he could watch the sun rise. The inane interviewer said, "That must have been frightfully nice for you?" Hugo answered, "Oh yes, indeed, I would have missed the sun dreadfully if it had not risen."

Hugo used to send me poems, always written on long, thin sheets of paper, sometimes ten feet long, with elongated drawings a little like those of John Minton. One day he invited Ninette and me down to the house where he lived in Surrey, for dinner. He "looked after" (it was his description) Lady Ashwood, a rich old lady in an eighteenth century house. He explained that she was a little odd, and asked us to do whatever she asked.

We arrived at about 6 p.m., and a butler in white gloves showed us into a charming pale-brick two-storeyed house. We were joined by Hugo, who introduced us to Lady Ashwood, who was just finishing her breakfast. She looked like a first cousin of Blanche du Bois or a drawing by Charles Addams. Hugo rang a bell, and a manservant called Goddard offered us a gin, and then poured us each a tumblerful, neat. When he left, Hugo explained that the butler and the two menservants were all called Goddard, because a firm of solicitors called Goddard, Goddard and Goddard had once attempted to swindle Lady Ashwood. Now her servants all answered to the name of Goddard. I soon managed to pour most of my gin into a pot-plant, but Lady Ashwood noticed, and the glass was promptly refilled. Hours went by, and I tried very hard not to get drunk, as I had to drive the car back to London that night.

A fat old Labrador called Baby waddled in; Lady Ashwood introduced her as Babykins. She then said it was too late for teakins, so perhaps we should have dinnerkins before too long.

As it was summer, it was still light outside, and Lady Ashwood said, "It is a beautiful evening, I think we shall all go for a little drive." Hugo led the way out to the big triple garage. There, in solitary splendour, was a 1928 Packard limousine, up on blocks. Hugo, as he ceremonially handed the two ladies into the grey velvet of the back seat, mentioned that the Packard had won the *Concours d'Elégance* at Monte Carlo in 1928. Now he took the wheel and I sat beside him.

He said "Broom, broom, broom", and then looked behind him as if he were backing out of the garage. "Away we go!" and he rocked from side to side so that the old car moved a little on its springs above the blocks. "Ah, look, Penelope, how beautifully the setting sun is lighting up the spire on the cathedral!" She sighed with pleasure. "Now turn out into the country, Hugo, you know how I love to see the trees."

There were a couple of minutes of silence, while we rocked, and Hugo murmured "Broom, broom, broom", and then Hugo said, "There are two deer coming out of the copse over there, can you see them, Penelope?" "Perfectly, my dear." We continued through a beech wood, admired the bluebells, and then returned home and parked in the garage.

With great dignity Hugo opened the door so that the ladies could descend. As Lady Ashwood took Hugo's arm she said graciously, "That was indeed a lovely drive, dear Hugo." We walked back into the house.

An old psychiatrist, who had been asked to dinner at the last minute, had just arrived, a spry old boy whom we were asked by Lady Ashwood to tease unmercifully. Dinner was announced. I was given Lady Ashwood's arm, the psychiatrist took Ninette's and Hugo followed with Baby. There were menu cards in front of us for four courses, which turned out to be miniscule. Our hostess ate nothing, but continued to drink gin, while we were given brandy instead of wine in the wine glasses, and nothing else to drink. I will never know how I got the car back to London.

Alister had come back from France to live in London, and had been reunited with his old Melbourne girlfriend Patsy. They kept on lurching towards marriage and then skidding back again to what was in those days called "living in sin". When they finally rang to say that this time they were definitely getting married, in the church where Robert Browning and Elizabeth Barrett had been married, we did not believe them, so missed the wedding. Alister and Patsy's marriage always reminded me of one of La Rochefoucauld's *Maxims*: "Some people are so self-centred that, when in love, they contrive to be intent on their own feelings and not on the object of their love". I thought they used other people like money to secure themselves the luxury of being unhappy.

Alister was brim-full of specious doctrines of futility. It was a time of fashionable pessimism, which was enough to turn Alister into an optimist, as he had always to be going against the swim, but in this case he had arrived there first, so was sticking to his muddy island in the joyous river of life. I found it difficult to understand this pessimism, when the horrible 1930s and the dreadful war of the 1940s were over, and there was a real possibility of starting anew. Maybe it was Australian naiveté on my part.

Alister, desperate for money, had taken a job with a small, steely Czech refugee called Paul Hamlyn. Paul's empire then consisted solely of a book-remainder warehouse in Camden Town. Alister's work consisted of lumping batches of books off and into trucks. His most entertaining, and unnerving, customers were several London spivs. So that they could not be arrested for loitering, they had an official occupation, which was selling books from barrows in places like Trafalgar Square; naturally they didn't care what the books were.

One night, in search of a drink after leaving a favourite Soho restaurant of ours, the Isola Bella, we passed a spiv Alister knew, standing near the Windmill Theatre. Alister went up to him and introduced himself as a friend of two other spivs, Johnny Gilbert and Johnny the One. "Hacky," the spiv held out his hand, "pleased to meet you, Geoff." He complained that London had gone to the dogs, he had travelled all over the world, and he didn't know what London was coming to, and then took us to a club, the Green Parrot. It was obviously also a pick-up joint; there were three young but not very attractive girls waiting for customers. The walls were painted with parrots in cages, and nudes with weirdly long nipples. As I was about to sit down on a couch one of the girls called out, "Watch your head, dearie." I looked up, but could not see anything, so sat down and hit my head with a crash on the wooden back of the couch, the springs of which were quite gone. The girls all laughed. In the couch beside us the felt covering was split, with a gaping hollow revealing pieces of fluff and cigarette butts and matches. Three American sailors came in, and chatted up the girls; and then they all left.

A few weeks later there was a party. Anna Campbell, in a black taffeta

Emily Dutton, by George Lambert, 1906

Emily Dutton, 1906, wearing the Worth dress in which she was painted by Lambert

Emily and Harry Dutton and Nell Wynyard, 1907

Emily and Harry Dutton, Victor Harbor, c. 1918

Harry Dutton, c. 1930

Harry Dutton and Geoff, c. 1930

Anlaby, by Hans Heysen, 1931

Anlaby, the terrace (Wesley Stacey)

Anlaby, the library
(Wesley Stacey)

Anlaby, from Henry Dutton's flagpole

John, Dick, Chibs and Geoff, 1923

The Grim Guardian: Emily, Chibs and Geoff, 1926

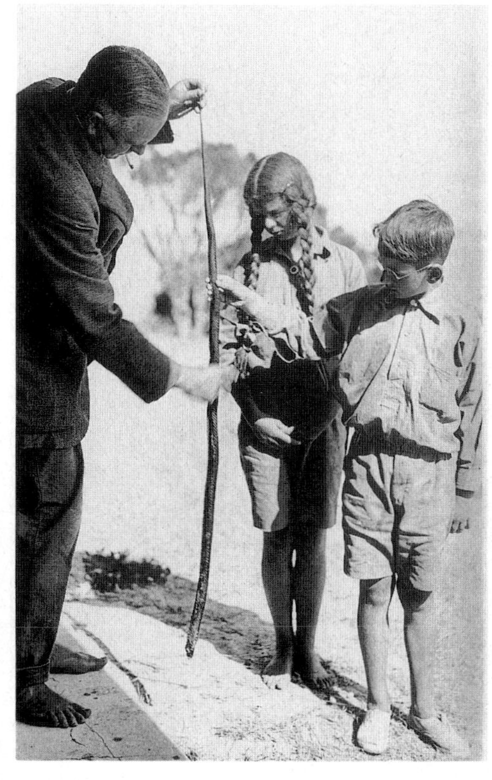

Harry, Chibs and Geoff, Rocky Point, 1930

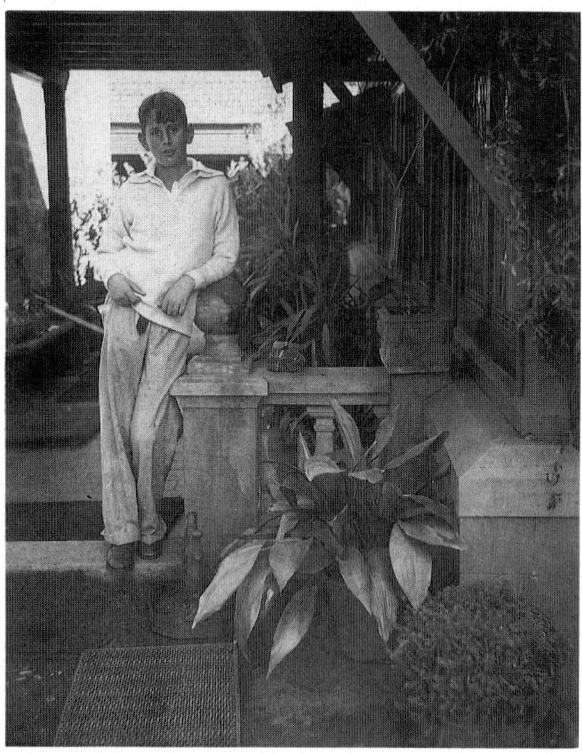

Geoff by the front door at Anlaby, 1933

The Gipsy Moth in which Dick crashed in the courtyard at Anlaby, 1935

John's 30/98 Vauxhall, after a year under 200 feet of water, Blue Lake, Mt Gambier, SA, at the bottom of a 200-foot cliff, 1935

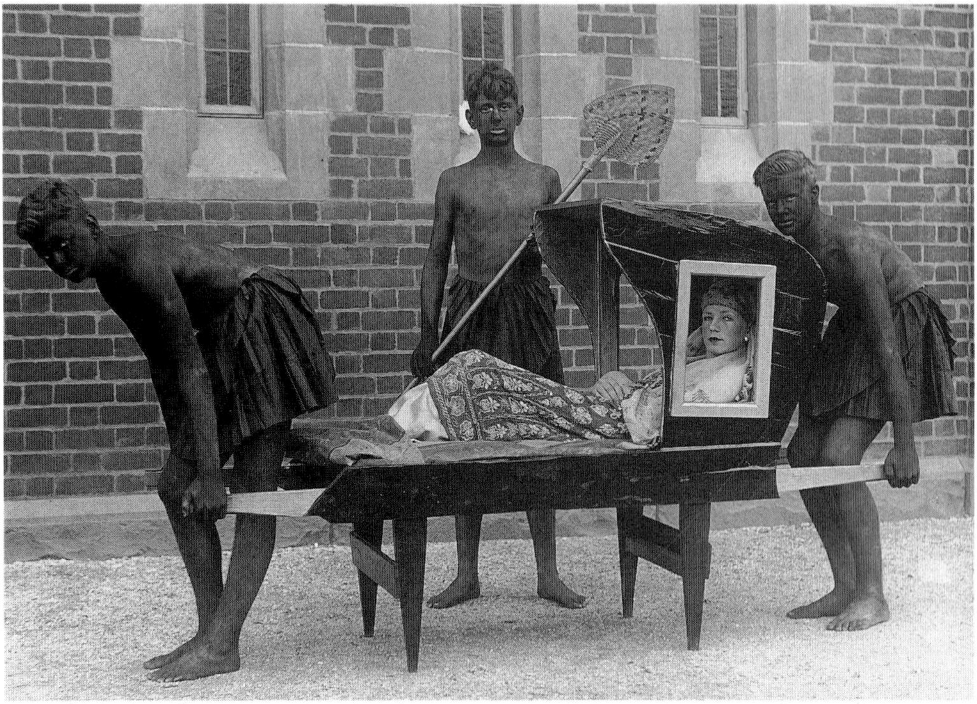

Alpha and Omega Pageant, Geelong Grammar School, 1936; left to right: Stephen Murray-Smith, Geoff, Jim Gardiner, John Ricketson

Chibs and Geoff, 1937

Rocky Point

Sandy Dey and Chibs, Kangaroo Island, 1940

The Gaolbirds, clockwise from left: Clive Bell, Ken McRae, David Martin, Fred Lethbridge; Geoff in centre

Our 100 pounds Rolls-Royce, Ballarat, 1942

Ken McRae, Geoff and Frank Maughan, Western Junction, 1943

Geoff and Ninette leaving for England on the *Rhexenor,* 1946

Alister Kershaw, Denison Deasey and Geoff, St Clair, 1948

George Bailey, Deasey sleeping, on the way to Les Iles d'Or, 1948

Bouillabaisse picnic, Les Iles d'Or: Deasey, Bailey, Ninette and the two fishermen

Richard and Catha Aldington and friend, 1949

Anna Campbell, St Clair, 1949

John Minton, St Clair, 1949

skirt with a mauve scarf in her hair, was with a Spaniard called Jesus. Johnny Minton was there with Ricky, the Richard of Le Lavandou. Johnny was in a blue suit of which the coat was too big, and this was accentuated by a floppy bow tie, so that with his padded shoulders sticking out high beside his thin, bony face, he looked like one of those carved wooden birds that sit with long beaks, their heads pressed down on hunched-up wings.

A young Australian artist was there with his wife and her sister. Jesus offered to translate *The Mortal and the Marble* into Spanish. I said that I was diffident about it. He said, shrewdly, as he had only just met me, "You cannot possibly be diffident about it if you have any faith in yourself as a novelist, your interest must be elsewhere if you're diffident about your work." If he had gone on to ask me where my interest really was, I could not have answered him then.

Johnny and Anna went into one of their routines, while the Australians (a national failing of Australians abroad) talked of home. Anna and Johnny were fanciful, unmeaning, witty-insulting, paradoxical, mock-serious in their chatter. The Australians talked, stodgy, sincere, not-going-to-be-made-a-fool-of, serious, worried talk.

We shed the Australians and Johnny took us on to a Slade students' party in a cellar, where they all jived in furious silence, and then to a homosexual club called Muriel's. Lucien Freud, then first becoming known for his extraordinary drawings, was there with a tough, baby-faced boy-friend. Lucien was a friend of Johnny's, and he came over to talk with us, but he was hesitant and often silent. With his long sideburns that would point towards you, and a manner where smile and gesture always seemed inseparable, he seemed to be reaching towards but never quite meeting you.

Johnny bought three bottles of champagne for us and told us all that he had just received a letter of instructions from the Festival of Britain, which had commissioned him to paint a mural. He was being told what his subject should be and how he should dispose the detail in his painting. It seems the Festival wanted, in the centre, a question-mark peering from a cloud. "My dears," said Johnny, "they're going to get a question-mark peeing from a cloud."

I suggested we go on to the Green Parrot. At the entrance there was a large Alsatian dog sitting alongside the doorman. "This 'ere dog is 'ere for a reason." When we climbed the stairs Johnny was deeply shocked. "My dear Geoffrey, I thought I knew every strata of London, but this is lower than any I've ever met before. The strangest thing about it is that it's a normal one. There are any amount of Lesbian and queer dives, but none like this."

A quiet and rather sober Dease arrived back from Vienna, where he had not written his book on Schubert, and had broken off his affair with Trixie, an awkward if *hochwohlgeboren* girl he had brought to Berky's at St Clair at the time when we had the cottage up the hill. However, it didn't take him long to revert to character. One evening when Ninette was away, Dease and I were walking towards Soho when he suddenly stopped me and said he had forgotten to have a piss, and immediately had one against the wall of a house. A blonde girl walking behind us stepped daintily over the stream; he quickly buttoned his fly, walked after her and asked her to dinner. She was lugubrious and told us she was recovering from an accident, and was going to cheer herself up by going to the Astoria, a dance-hall. We went with her. She disappeared.

I danced with another blonde; she was European, and I asked her if she was Austrian. Rather wearily she answered, "Why does one always have to be German or Austrian? I'm Latvian." Dease invited her and her girlfriend, who was Irish, to come home with us. They agreed, but the Irish girl grabbed my arm and said she was terrified of being followed by a man who had danced with her.

He did follow us, and Dease, typical Dease, walked up to him as the two girls and I piled into a taxi, and told him to piss off. The Irish girl was crossing herself and wailing, "Jesus Christ save me, Oh Holy Mary Mother of God make him go away." Dease was now raising his fists. I said to the girl, "Tell him to go away" and lowered the window. "Go away," she called, "I don't want to see you." "Oh well, that's all right then." No more. He just walked off. Dease got into the taxi, brushing his unused knuckles and snorting.

The Irish girl soon left, but the Latvian stayed, and for hours I could hear Dease tussling with Skygera, for that was her name.

Then, another night, Dease would ring up and suggest we all go to a Schubert recital in the Wigmore Hall. He could be a brilliant mimic or, as in the old days on the Melbourne tram with Arthur Boyd and me, do or say something quite outrageous and keep a straight face. We had to spend one evening with some slow-witted Australians, so slow-witted that they would simply accept whatever was said to them. So Dease would say to them, "Britain has the worst food in the world, and France the best". "Oh yes!" they would agree with alacrity. He would then pour himself another drink and say, "As a matter of fact, French food is really vile, too many sauces, give me honest British cooking every time." "Oh yes, yes, how true!" they would bleat.

Dease did not care for dogs, and the English habit of taking dogs everywhere and letting them crap on the footpath. So he worked out ways of annoying dog-owners. If a dog was not on a leash, he would whistle it up and talk to it. If it was, he would turn to me and say in a very loud voice how disgraceful it was to let a dog out with such frightful mange.

Poor Dease. He was, and remained for the rest of his life, in that tragic no man's land of those who have talents and knowledge in the arts, but not the ability to create anything. His life was littered with half-written books. He had, in those days, enough of a private income to support him in his attempts at creativity.

In 1951 my life in London was enlivened by the arrival of Chibs, complete with an American accent after some time in the USA. Since we left Australia we had managed to avoid visiting my mother's grand friends, but Chibs had been charged with the duty of getting us to see people like the Pembrokes at Wilton. They were as bored as we were, although the house was fabulous, literally. We also paid a ceremonial visit to the Spencers at Althorp. Their son John and Chibs were good friends, and he had often stayed with her at Rocky Point when he was ADC at Government House in Adelaide. His mother was very agreeable, but John was glum and silent as his square-headed father took us around some of his treasures, as he must have done with other guests a thousand times before; he certainly knew every detail about everything in the house, from the Chippendale chairs in the dining room to the Duke of Marlborough's enormous silver travelling bath and two-gallon wine bottles known as "pilgrims".

I could not see any future or any relevance for the monarchy or the aristocracy. On the other hand, the British class system, of which they were the apex, still seemed absolutely unshakeable.

Well, John Althorp, Earl Spencer, is now dead, and his daughter Diana has certainly shaken the monarchy if not the class system. This still seems to be impregnable, more than fifty years after we drove away from Althorp.

A few days later we took Chibs down to Heathrow. She was returning to Australia. Her parting words to me were, "Quick, can you tell me what some of the portraits are in the National Portrait Gallery, so I can pretend to Mum that I've been there?" Our mother always had to set us in her own conception of the world, which meant that we were always pretending to her.

Chibs was going home, and so were we. I had sold the busy little Morris and bought a truck-like four-door Ford sedan. It was a new English version of what was basically a 1936 American Ford V8, called a Pilot. We were going to drive out overland, through the Middle East, Iran and Afghanistan, Pakistan and India to Ceylon, where we would put the car and ourselves on a boat from Colombo to Perth, and then drive home across the Nullarbor.

It was in the days before TV, when people still read travel books in large quantities. Jack McDougall said he would publish an account of the journey, which would pay for a lot of it.

The journey was to be extraordinary, and sometimes dangerous, as when, in our stay in Jerusalem, King Abdullah was murdered and we were caught in a riot. The accursed car broke down incessantly, but that did mean we got to know the countries and inhabitants better than if it had swept us through them. We left on 22 May 1951 and arrived at Anlaby on 9 September.

I did write a book, *A Long Way South*, about the journey, and Jack McDougall did publish it, and it received some absurdly good reviews in Britain and Australia, but most of it is only of transient interest.

PART FOUR
New Directions
1951–64

All down the main street the Union Jacks are waving
Windy loyalty to the flag of another country ...

"Thoughts, Home from Abroad"

Fifteen

The most immediate surprise in coming home after five years away was to greet my mother, and see how much she had changed in physical appearance. Her face was just as beautiful, and her skin still perfect, but at sixty-seven she had shrunk from her five feet nine inches. She now seemed what could be called stocky. My brother John and Peg were living at Anlaby in the "cottage"; Margaret and Léonie had moved to Adelaide. John had been dragged back from Burleigh by my mother to be General Manager of Anlaby and Uno, which was good neither for him nor for the two stations.

There was precious little sustenance to be had from the provincial capital of Adelaide. There were, however, a few surprises. The ritual of agonizing dinners at the South Australian Hotel went on, with the theme tunes being played by the tired trio, and Lewy supervising it all, with his hand discreetly behind him for the tip from the departing diner. But there was more to Lewy than I realised.

A distinguished English publisher, Charles Prentice, an old friend of Richard Aldington's, was due to spend a day in Adelaide, and Richard wrote to ask if I could drive him up to Anlaby for lunch. I was happy to do this, and arranged to pick him up at the South the day after his arrival. Prentice turned out to be the most delightful type of quiet Englishman, with an enormous knowledge of books. As we were driving out of Adelaide he told me he had had "rather a surprise" towards the end of his dinner. He was sitting by himself, and Lewy, "that head waiter fellow", came up to chat with him. After a few banalities Lewy said that he thought Prentice looked lonely, but Lewy could arrange for a girl to be sent to his room. Thirty pounds was the usual price.

I was amazed, and was unable to answer Prentice when he said, "I'm sure it was very kind of him, and well-intentioned, but, I mean, does that sort of thing regularly go on?" Wickedness, or even naughtiness, was not a visible ingredient of Adelaide life. The rituals of society sufficed, with their variations in the University, or business, or whatever the little circle.

The happiest exception was at Carrick Hill, Ursula and Bill Hayward's house. Ursula was lastingly rich, a Barr Smith, the family who with their relations the Elders had founded Elder, Smith & Co, and given the Barr Smith Library, the Elder Conservatorium and many bequests to Adelaide University. As a young man, Bill Hayward had wanted to live on the land, which he loved, but on the death of his father was dragged in to run Adelaide's biggest department store, John Martin's.

There was a certain imperturbable quality about the old, authentic Adelaide rich. Ursula always relished the memory of her father giving her a four and a half litre Bentley coupé for her twenty-first birthday. Ursula drove it around to show to my godmother Lily Waite, who was a lover of fast cars; she had a three litre Sunbeam. Lily came out to admire it, walked all around it it, and said, "How nice, it's got an eight-day clock."

The Haywards lived in grandeur at Carrick Hill, which they willed, along with the contents, to the Art Gallery of South Australia. On the walls were paintings by Gauguin, Renoir, Boudin, Stanley Spencer, Gwen and Augustus John (Gwen's much better than Augustus's), and some horrible strident nudes by Matthew Smith; the nudes appealed to Bill, but I always suspected Ursula hated them. In the hall was the famous Dobell portrait of Joshua Smith, the subject of that infamous court case. In the cloak room there was a delicious little Dobell of a small boy having a pee, admiring his long, arching stream. Surreptitiously, on condition of silence, the Haywards were immensely helpful to young Adelaide artists like Jacqueline Hick and Jeffrey Smart.

Ursula used to sit, holding a glass of gin, in a deep chair in her little library, which had many books in common with my father's. There was something almost Chinese about the compactness of her face, like a nut, her eyes always bright with thoughts about the idiocies of the world, particularly of Adelaide, which kept her mouth in a perpetual smile of relish. Ursula was a joy at Adelaide "high society" parties. One evening, she and I were listening to a matron she called "Lady Nell", talking to a visiting Englishman about "Darling Dickie Mountbatten, oh I did know him so well". Ursie turned to me and whispered, "She met him for ten minutes in 1927."

Ursula used to call certain visitors, especially from Britain, and especially actors, "costly casuals" — "You give them drinks one day, dinner the next and on Sunday take them for lunch in the country. They beg you to ring them the instant you are next in London. When you do so they say they are frightfully sorry, but they are just leaving for a month in America."

The Britishness of Establishment Adelaide continued to amaze me. It thrived, of course, in the Adelaide Club; the atmosphere there was too rich in cigar smoke for me, but I used occasionally to go there to see some old school friends. The chief advantage of the place was that it had an excellent cellar. One vile north-wind, heatwave day, the dust so thick you could hardly see across North Terrace, the temperature at 110 degrees Fahrenheit, I saw emerging from the Government House gate opposite the Club, and advancing through the dust, the figure of Colin Duncan, the Governor's Private Secretary, clad in thick Scottish tweeds, with a waistcoat.

I was deeply dissatisfied with my life after my return to Australia. It was not as if I was altogether idle; in the first six months I wrote the travel book, *A Long Way South*, and a new novel. But the novel was another failure. I did not even send it to Jack McDougall.

I was unmistakably back home, and should have been able to draw sustenance as a writer from my roots, from all that experience of the land and Kangaroo Island, or distil satire from the inanities of Adelaide society. There was Uno and the wonderful, unique bush, and a trip overland to Darwin, and another to the Barrier Reef where a group of us hired a boat and went up the coast to the Whitsunday Islands. The only development at that time was a hotel on Hayman Island. The Australia of the 1950s was almost virgin for a writer with a fresh eye, as it was for the new artists, Drysdale, Boyd, Nolan and Perceval. But for me, as in the subject of that essay Darling had set us in the Sixth Form, it was a case of "Thoughts all confused, my Lord".

I did manage to write some tolerable poems. One, a mellifluous lyric, was the result of a new love affair, an ardent physical reality but in all other ways a fantasy that no Pygmalion of the spirit could bring to life. Kenneth Slessor surprised me, some years later, by reciting the first verse of this lyric:

O lovely, long-legged lazy blonde
Wandering down the sand to the sea,
Tell me what island lies beyond
The water that laps your flexing knee …

When my mother asked me what I wanted to do with my life I answered, "Write poetry." As tactfully as she could she suggested what was already obvious to me, that one could not survive economically as a poet. In those days there was no Literature Board, no grants and almost no prizes.

My first mistake was to live at Anlaby, albeit with many trips away, for the first fifteen months or so back in Australia. I wrote the travel book very quickly at Rocky Point, and then the novel at Anlaby. My mother regarded "my writing" as something almost holy, which nearly drove me crazy. She would tiptoe around the corridor and apologize for interrupting, but would I like some lime juice?

Yet it was she who came back from Adelaide one day with a pamphlet from a real estate agency, offering a subdivision of the Hawkers' old estate below Waverley Ridge at Mount Lofty, above Adelaide. She said she had always wanted to have some land in the hills, where all sorts of garden flowers and shrubs would grow that would find Anlaby too hot. We drove up to have a look at the land, which was very pretty indeed, nine acres with an old pisé and stone cottage going back to the 1860s. She had some ready cash, for once, as wool prices had soared, so bought it for nine thousand pounds. She suggested that we might like to live there, although it would need power and a bore and some plumbing. So we moved in to Nonsuch, as we called it, and only paid visits to Anlaby. I suppose I had been programmed once again, but it was a good effort on her part to ease me out of Anlaby, where she would have had us for company in the huge, empty house.

What I lacked, of course, was intellectual stimulation, not just the sparky kind I had enjoyed with Dease, Kershaw, Campbell and Aldington, but the kind which would help me to develop as an Australian writer. In the early 1950s we were all so isolated, there was so little communication. It was better for the artists; they either went for long visits to London and Paris, like Tucker in 1949, Drysdale in 1950 and Nolan in 1951, where they continued to paint primarily Australian subjects, or else, like Arthur Boyd and Perceval, worked in Melbourne in their own family artistic community of great integrity.

But the writers were all over the place. Max Harris and I got on well enough, but he was still recovering from Ern Malley, and living a life that did not stray far from his home and the bookshop. The Australian best seller was an Englishman who called himself "Nevil Shute", who had emigrated to Victoria. He published *A Town Like Alice* in 1950, the year in which Manning Clark published *Select Documents in Australian History*. Would that I had met Manning then and had not had to wait another five years!

There were certainly writers living in Adelaide at the time, like Flexmore Hudson and Ian Mudie, but although both of them had written good poems, in their thinking they were still Jindyworobaks, enmeshed in ideas that did not stimulate me. Max Harris, using a phrase of William Blake's, somewhat unkindly called Mudie "the serpent of mediocrity". The founder of the Jindies, Rex Ingamells, was then living in Melbourne. Colin Thiele, a much subtler thinker and writer, was living in South Australia, but I hardly knew him then, although he had been born on a farm that was once part of Anlaby, only eight miles from the house where I was born. Thiele and Hudson were teachers, while Mudie worked as copywriter for a real estate developer. Poor Ian, to his anguish, had to write a glowing prospectus for a new development on two or three hundred acres of unspoiled, beautiful coast, not far from Adelaide. His firm was developing it into housing lots for three hundred and fifty houses. It was now renamed Solitude Bay.

In Melbourne the Left certainly had a sense of solidarity and comradeship, although writers of every political persuasion rallied round Frank Hardy when he was prosecuted for criminal libel when he published *Power Without Glory* in 1950. Dymphna Cusack and Florence James published *Come In Spinner* in 1951, the year two Sydney poets, Nancy Keesing and Ray Mathew, made their debut, to be followed in 1952 by Francis Webb. There were some good war books, like Eric Lambert's *The Twenty Thou-*

sand Thieves and Tom Hungerford's *The Ridge and the River*, which was about the useless campaign in Bougainville. The Boyds were also active, Martin publishing the first volume of the Langton novels in 1952, and Robin *Australia's Home*. One of the old Left, Judah Waten, published one of the finest of all Australian books of short stories, *Alien Son,* in 1952.

But as a whole there was no whole, and there were few battles in Australian writing, either shared dreams or gang warfare. The only literary magazines of any account were *Southerly*, which seemed very boring, and *Meanjin*, heroically kept going by Clem Christesen, which to me lacked the excitement of *Angry Penguins*.

Honest country Australians had a deep distrust of what they called "intellectual snobs". But most Australian intellectuals and writers were neither snobs nor Bohemians nor rebels nor wild men of letters; they were just very, ploddingly, worthy.

On a visit to Melbourne it was a lift to the spirits to see Arthur and Yvonne Boyd again. They were just the same, very hardworking, modest, eager, humorous; Arthur was doing some of his best work. They had had their first child, Polly. Arthur had prepared for the day most carefully, knowing that the old Dodge did not always start when required to. He had booked a taxi for the hospital months in advance; a taxi was guaranteed to be ready whenever he phoned, day or night. The moment came, and he found that the taxi phone was disconnected; the firm had gone bust. It took Arthur so long to get the Dodge under way that Yvonne began to have the baby in the back seat. As she was being carried into the hospital Yvonne heard the nurse saying, "Poor Mr Boyd, oh poor Mr Boyd." She then turned to Yvonne. "Poor Mr Boyd was nearly fainting."

I longed to know what I was going to do, to have the confidence of Arthur in front of a canvas. I dithered, having no idea what to make of what little talent I had, except write poems.

Even in the early 1950s there were, of course, those who did a great deal to try to help Australian writers. I met three of them in Melbourne, John Hetherington, and Vance and Nettie Palmer. John, with his big, soft features and apologetic smile, was about forty-five; he had been a war correspondent in the Middle East with Kenneth Slessor. Many years later, when I was writing Slessor's biography, I was astonished to learn that Hetherington had been the lover of Slessor's wife Noela. He had returned to journalism in Melbourne, but had recently done a stint in Adelaide as editor of the *News*. He was particularly interested in the possibilities for Australian biography, which was still such a lean field.

Vance, who with his bow tie, his smoothly brushed white hair and steady gaze looked like a Professor in a Hollywood film, was the major all-rounder of Australian literature, essayist, fiction writer, biographer, broadcaster, as well as the key figure in the Commonwealth Literary Fund. He was a good friend to young writers, particularly in persuading the ABC to give time to Australian writing. Nettie was really more intelligent and percipient than Vance, and she kept up with writers in other countries. She was a champion of Christina Stead when hardly any Australians had heard of her.

In Sydney, I met Douglas Stewart for the first time, amidst the roar and rumble of the presses outside the *Bulletin* office. Doug was publishing more Australian writing of quality than anyone else, as well as reviewing prose and poetry on the Red Page. Despite the later canards put about by Vincent Buckley, which were to be refuted once and for all, with an accountant's precision, by Tom Shapcott, Doug did not favour country poets and Georgian themes as Literary Editor of the *Bulletin*.

Among the best of his poets, Judith Wright and David Campbell, the country was only one of their subjects, while others in their class, such as Rosemary Dobson and Francis Webb, were far removed from rural themes. In prose Stewart was as interested in Hal Porter as in E.O. Schlunke; he always kept that kind of balance. If he didn't like a poem you sent him he would tell you so, and why. He was dark and slight and very shy; he reminded me of one of those black cormorants whose eyes dart from side to side before they disappear under water and come up somewhere else. And Doug, like the cormorants, loved to fish. His favourite trout-fishing companion was David Campbell, and it was through Doug that I first met David, who was to be a lifelong friend, and stayed with him at his property, Wells, just outside Canberra.

David, then about thirty-five, tall and blond, with his easy grace of movement, his quiet, throwaway manner of talking, had a jaw and a squashed nose that hinted at trouble. He had, in fact, been heavyweight boxing champion of Cambridge, as well as an international footballer; he had won a DFC as a pilot in the RAAF. But when we met we talked of two poets he venerated, his namesake Roy and Herrick, and the one who was his master, W.B. Yeats. David's easy confidence came, not from being a kind of Australian Renaissance man, but from working the land and from being born on it; he belonged. When you got to know him well, of course, you found that like all good writers or artists, he was not confident at all, just determined to try to transcend his limitations. But most of the time, he didn't seem to have any. A few more fences might have been good for him at times, especially around the whisky bottle; but I suppose he would have jumped them. The most alarming drives in a motor car I have ever had were with David, although he was a pretty terrible driver even when sober.

We surged off to pay a visit to his friend Jo Gullett. At Jo's we swam in the river which was the colour of white wine; Jo, who was Government Whip, wished he could leave politics and write. He wasn't all that pleased that David had called his new sheepdog Gullett. "But, Jo," said David, "I've always wanted to be able to yell 'Down. Gullett', or 'Get behind, Gullett'." Later, Jo did write some books. A chapter in one of them, on the battle at Bardia in North Africa, is one of the finest pieces of Australian writing on war.

Returning to duller Adelaide, I was saved, more or less, by Archie Price, Master of St Mark's when I was a student. He suggested that I should write a biography of Colonel William Light, the Founder of Adelaide. Far from being some stuffy old retired colonel on a pedestal, Light was a most attractive, wild adventurer, who had been a hero of the Peninsular War, in which he served in more than forty actions without a wound. He left the British Army as a brevet major. In 1823 he joined an international force to fight in Spain for the liberals against King Ferdinand. He was given the rank of Lieutenant-Colonel and was badly wounded before the campaign fizzled out. So the Founder of Adelaide was a colonel only in a Spanish revolutionary army, fighting against the establishment.

As if this were not enough, respectable Adelaide was founded by a man who was an illegitimate son of a Malayan mother and an English father, Francis Light, who was himself illegitimate. William married an illegitimate daughter of the Duke of Richmond; she ran off with the poet Shelley's brother-in-law. William came to Adelaide with a mistress-housekeeper who after his death married the founder of one of the most eminent Adelaide families. No wonder he was such an appealing subject for a biography.

Archie said that of course I would have to do most of my research in London, for Light was only in Adelaide at the end of his life, when he was already suffering from tuberculosis. It would also be a help if I could go to Cairo, for he had been a captain of a warship in Mohamet Ali's navy, and to Spain and Portugal to follow his Peninsular War campaigns. This was the only snag; I did not see how I could quite manage all this.

Biography was an inspired option. Unconsciously I was obsessed by the past, and had been for much of my life. Coming back to live at Anlaby was a regression into this past. My first novel had the potential to use the past, of personal experience, in service of an idea, but I had allowed myself to be dragged down by "the sense of real things", by sticking too close to the facts. My second two novels, as far as I can remember, for I have never wanted to read them again, were re-creations of life with Dease, Kershaw and others, totally lacking in any vision of the chariot.

But a good biography requires imagination as well as the re-creation of the past. Coleridge and Wordsworth said that historians and biographers are of the second class of writers, because they are shackled to the facts, rather than liberated by the pleasures of the imagination. Nevertheless, there is plenty of room in a good biography for the shaping imagination, where the challenge is to divine, and then, as far as possible, prove various aspects of the truth. Unlike Francis Bacon's jesting Pilate, the biographer must ask, "What is truth?" and stay for an answer.

My novels had been too personal, too much involved with my own experience. However, on a deeper level, the biography of Light, and the ones I was to write later of Edward John Eyre and Ernest Giles, were personally challenging and rewarding to me because my own ancestors, on both sides of the family, had been Australian pioneers. And in the 1950s, the truth (or what can be offered as part of the truth) of the white settlement and development of Australia had hardly been scratched. About forty years later, Manning Clark, in his two autobiographical books, revealed himself to have been coping with some of the same troubles as I was, trying to find out how to handle the experience of being Australian. To come to terms with one's own country is the same as coming to terms with oneself, a battle of discovery and an asking of awkward and sometimes painful questions.

And in the case of William Light, it was symbolic, not of the cultural cringe but of our huge debt to the old world of Britain and Europe, that his greatest achievement, his guarantee of an enduring reputation, came only in the last three years of his life, from the age of fifty to his death at fifty-three.

On the subject of Light, I had an extraordinary stroke of luck, as the recipient of a most generous offer. David Elder, who worked for Oxford University Press in Melbourne, had been a prisoner of war of the Japanese in Changi and had developed a great interest in the history of Malaya, as it was then called. He was especially taken with Francis Light, William's father, in all practical respects the founder of the settlement of Penang. As a kind of therapy for his sufferings as a prisoner of war, David had begun twin biographies of Francis and William. When he heard that I had embarked on my biography he offered me all his own material, and to help me with further research. His generosity was not only in the obvious form of the research he made available to me, but in the comradeship I had with him while working on the book. I of course made full acknowledgement of all his help, but I am happy to say that this was followed up, more than thirty years after the publication of my biography, by an enlarged and updated version which bears both our names.

Those who are not writers do not know what a solitary business it is. Writers can seldom go out in a group and write together, as artists can paint together. Nevertheless, they still need friends or mentors with whom they can throw ideas around, and who can criticize their work without prejudice. Writers have dreary and dispiriting tools of trade, compared with painters and composers. Writers are trapped with their pen and ink and paper, their typewriters or word processors, while painters have the glorious colours of their palette, and musicians the whole repertoire of sound. I discussed this once with Patrick White, and then wrote a poem, "The Grey Medium"; Patrick said he liked the poem, but, oh dear, everyone would be calling him The Grey Medium.

The other person who helped raise me from the rut of non-doing was Derry Jeffares. Derry, now probably the world's greatest W.B. Yeats scholar, is known in such circles as A. Norman Jeffares. With his Scottish-Belgian wife Jeanne he came to Adelaide to take up the Chair of English Literature, which had been kept warm by Charles Jury for Herbert Piper, who was at Magdalen with me. But Piper was not appointed. Supporters of Piper, of whom there were many in Adelaide, cold-shouldered the unfortunate Jeffares when they arrived in Adelaide. Charles Jury, Derry's predecessor, refused to meet him. Derry had simply applied for the job and got it; he knew nothing of the background. The Jeffares became good friends of ours, and Derry asked me to do some tutoring in the English Department, which he hoped to expand into a lectureship. I did not really want an academic career, but it would bring in some money, and the association both with staff and students would be stimulating. There would also be access to the Barr Smith library, and to put it more crudely, I needed to get off my bum.

In 1953 my dear old godmother Lily Waite, who had all my life never missed sending me a birthday present, died and left me a thousand pounds. It was enough, together with the proceeds from the book I would write about the journey, to pay for the trip across Africa to Europe, in search of Colonel William Light.

Sixteen

I had bought a little blue Fiat 1100, half the size of the terrible Ford we had driven from London to Colombo. When I first brought it home to Anlaby, my mother looked at it and said, "But what if an elephant treads on it?" The Fiat took us, without any trouble at all, from Capetown to Cairo, then along the top of Africa to Tangier, and up through Spain and Portugal to Italy. As with the earlier journey, it would be impossible to do it today without becoming embroiled in some sort of violence.

Following *A Long Way South*, Jack McDougall published *Africa in Black and White* under the Chapman & Hall imprint. Roy Campbell wrote a Preface to it which (as Jack put it, some years later) was a lovely thing in itself but did the book a great deal of harm, as Roy was so unpopular with the reigning British literary pundits, several of whom he gaily insulted in the Preface.

Roy was thought of in London as a sort of wild man from the veldt, an image it amused him to cultivate. In fact, his family were some of the oldest and most distinguished of white settlers in Natal, and had been notable public benefactors. His brother George, a medical man, was Chancellor of the University of Natal. We stayed with George and his wife Agnes in Natal, and Roy received an Honorary Doctorate from the University while we were there; it was a touching moment when George capped his brother, South Africa's greatest poet.

Roy had just finished *Light on a Dark Horse*, which he referred to as his "autobuggeroffery". Robert Speaight had edited it for the publisher. "Man," Roy said to me, "he not only castrated it but circumcised it as well." My duty was to keep Roy sober for the day of the Degree ceremony. I took him into town in the little Fiat, and left him in the car while I ran a quick errand for Agnes. By the time I returned he was gone; on the car seat was a copy he had presented to me of his translation of Lorca's poems. Now across the jacket was scrawled, "Gone to have a quick one". By the time I found out which pub he was in he had drunk eight large glasses of beer. "Man," he said "I've been on the wagon for a month. Now I'm just having a few to get my health back."

He had recently been in America with Dylan Thomas, and had been with his sad Welsh friend towards the end of his life. " 'Roy,' Dylan said to me, 'You're the second best poet in the world'."

We had a few more. I said something about many writers being adrift nowadays. Roy said that of course that was true of him. I said I didn't agree with that, he'd always fitted in and worked, whether in Spain, France or Portugal. "Yes, man," Roy agreed, " you have to get a spade into the soil or a net into the sea before you can live in a place and feel you belong there." I thought of his namesake David.

Roy's romantic feeling about Catholicism and the political Right had led him to fight for Franco in what he thought of as a war against communism. This did not stop him from enlisting immediately in 1939 in the British Army in the fight against the Nazis and, later, the Fascists, unlike most of his fellow poets who had been so loud in their support of the Left.

Roy caused a considerable stir with the speech he made after the degree ceremony; a Natal newspaper said the next day that the noise of dropping bricks had echoed through the hall. He warmed up on the failings of South Africa which he had satirized in so many poems before he turned his attentions to England; T.S. Eliot called Roy the greatest satirist in English since Lord Byron. He ended with a resounding attack on apartheid, and sat down, mopping his forehead, to a remarkable amount of applause. After the ceremony, he swirled the scarlet-and-blue Doctor's robe through the air and murmured, "A lovely cape for a torero."

Later, after my return to Australia, it was Roy's speech as well as what I saw in South Africa that led to my becoming a subscriber to the South Africa Defence Aid Fund. The chilling newsletters from this organization were a perpetual condemnation of the evils of apartheid.

Roy said he wanted to come with us back to his farm in Portugal; we would go via Timbuctoo. But he hoped the Fiat had a high clearance, "otherwise the first geological specimen we come to will bust your car". I made enquiries about buying a second-hand jeep for Roy and the luggage, and he was very enthusiastic. But the timing was wrong; he had to be back at an impossible date for the publication of his autobuggeroffery. It still makes me sad. What adventures we would have had.

Four months after leaving the Campbell family in Durban we drove up to Roy and Mary's little pink farmhouse near Sintra in Portugal, set among vines, olives and fruit trees. Roy swept off his usual Spanish sombrero and clamped on his bald head the Kabyle hat we had brought him from Algeria, and the red wine flowed. Anna was still as beautiful as ever, but plumper and quiet and different. Tess was thin, pale, animated and different. Roy and Mary were the same. And there was a new arrival, Anna's baby, Impi. Anna had married the son of one of the premier Dukes of Spain. Before long, he had vanished to South America. Anna for a while endured the Oriental seclusion of a woman's life in aristocratic Spain, moving from palace to palace, enormous room to enormous room. Then she fled with Impi to Roy and Mary.

We drove on to Montpellier in France, where Richard Aldington was now living in poverty in a pension. After the publication of his biography of his old friend D.H. Lawrence he had been looking around for another subject for a biography, and Alister Kershaw, in his own words, ruined Richard's life by suggesting, in all innocence, that his next book should be a biography of T.E. Lawrence, another of Alister's heroes. But over the months of research (Dease was one of Richard's assistants, working in the British Museum Library), the truth began to emerge that Lawrence was a fraud and a liar. Richard, who had known the real war in the trenches, was incensed that this poseur should have been given the status of hero.

In dozens of his pungent letters, Richard had given me the whole melancholy story, which is too complex to be told here; Alister has given a brief account in his book *The Pleasure of their Company*. Suffice it to say that those who were exposed by the book as just plain foolish or deliberately falsifying — Liddell Hart, Robert Graves, Winston Churchill and many of the British literary establishment — ganged up and assassinated the book.

Richard and Alister both behaved very foolishly. Billy Collins, who published the book and later became my publisher, told me that Richard had in fact had a great deal of support in Britain. Billy had arranged for Richard to be given the opportunity of defending himself on the BBC and in the press. But Richard by this stage was so disillusioned by postwar Britain that he would not go. It was a kind of destructive pride, which Alister encouraged, to Richard's disadvantage. The Americans took their cue from London, although the French translation was well received in France.

It was a long time before Richard could find a publisher to take him on for another book. He had no income apart from his writing; he owned no house or property. Another blow was that his marriage to Netta was over; she had left to live in London. Now he and Catha were living in this poky pension in Montpellier and most of his excellent library was in storage.

When we arrived he was sitting under the pines in the garden of the pension, reading Provençal poetry. He was quiet, almost reserved. He knew all too well that the last time we had met he had been the genial host of the Villa Aucassin. But he soon cheered up and when Catha came back from the University, gay, grown-up and very French, he began to laugh. I went round the corner to get another bottle of champagne.

I asked where we could all have lunch the next day, and he guided me to a little village in the hills called St Guilhelm-le-Désert, where a channel diverted from the rushing mountain stream ran right through the restaurant and cooled the wine. There was a net at either end to keep in the trout which, when we gave our order to Madame, were scooped out and taken into the kitchen.

We drove on to Florence to find somewhere to live for a few months while I wrote my book about the African journey. There was an amazing estate agency, run by two old English ladies. They offered me a near-palace, the

Villa Diana, about which Alan Moorehead wrote a book. It was not outrageously expensive, but I settled for half a house up the hill behind San Miniato, owned by an Italian, Giulio Giuffrida, whose mother was English. Mina, a wonderful cook, and her idle husband Pinotto went with the house. Giulio lived in the other half of the building. It seemed most of his friends also had English mothers, and their English was perfect, which made it difficult to learn to speak Italian.

I found *Africa in Black and White* a very difficult book to write, not because of the book itself, but because Giulio and his delightful friends would always be suggesting an expedition for the next day, to Boccaccio's birthplace at Certaldo, or to the little village of Monterchi where Piero della Francesca's pregnant Virgin is in the Capella, or to Milton's Vallombrosa in the mountains. "Geoffrey, why do you come to Tuscany and sit all day inside writing that damn book? You are wasting your opportunities!" It was very difficult to resist.

It was impossible to resist Giulio's friends. Grato Maraini looked like a great blond condottiero in a Renaissance painting; he lived with his father in an immense villa. The two men never spoke, and at meals sat at opposite ends of a table the length of a cricket pitch, reading their separate copies of the London *Times*. The girl they were all in love with was the beautiful Lisabetta Ricasoli, whose family were famous makers of Chianti wine; they lived in a palace on the edge of the Arno. When we visited her there I could not take my eyes off an immense wedding chest which was entirely covered in paintings by Botticelli. Soft-spoken Didi (short for Dionysio) was another friend, who told me his soft speech came from being Sienese, and that all Florentines spoke dreadfully roughly. Then there was Carlo, who had a fiercely conservative old father. One evening, we were all going to hear a recital by the great Bulgarian bass, Boris Christoff. When I called for Carlo in the car I asked the old man if he was coming too. "Certainly not," he replied with disdain, "I would never listen to a man who wears black suede shoes with a white tie and tails."

I was pleased to find that the Italians had not lost the innocent bawdry and scatology of Boccaccio or Aretino. They could mock religion without losing belief, curse "*Porca Madonna*!" but still love the Holy Virgin, roar out songs even ruder than the ones we used to sing in the Air Force, about a priest fucking their sister, about their mama shitting in a chamber pot when the bottom falls out, or some such amiable fantasy. However filthy their songs, with these Italians there was a spontaneous gaiety, as if they were singing about the lambs in springtime.

I wanted to see where D.H. Lawrence and Frieda had lived when he was writing *Lady Chatterley's Lover*, so we drove to Scandicci and a helpful man, hearing me ask for directions to the Villa Mirenda, said "Follow me," jumped into his Topolino and drove at least three miles to show us the Villa.

It was up on a high hill, peasants with their oxen moving through the olives and vines, overlooking misty Florence in the warm October afternoon. A young man shovelling manure, dozens of chickens around his feet, said that the writer Lorenzo had lived there. Two little bells on a tower began to ring and then suddenly stopped. Around the edge of the house were hundreds of yellow crocuses, and the chestnuts were tumbling into the first fallen leaves. The peasants' voices sounded very clearly across the valley. At the Villa Mirenda Lawrence had been far from the beastly bourgeois, and I remembered how tender are his essays about Tuscany, and how lovely his poems about animals and flowers.

On seeing my photos of the Villa, Richard Aldington, who was in regular correspondence with Frieda, suggested I send her some copies. She wrote back thanking me, and said "Behind the Villa under the umbrella pines Lawrence wrote his *Lady Chatterley*; don't you agree, it's a very innocent setting for this book, that shocked people so much?" She asked me to look up her son in London, Montague Weekley, curator of the Bethnall Green Museum, and please to come and see her in Taos when I was in America. I did both. Weekley was pleasant enough, rather limply English, nothing like Frieda who, despite being born Baronin Richthofen, had the solidity and directness of a peasant, and seemed happiest by her handsome kitchen stove. She fulminated against Roosevelt and Churchill, who had sold the world to Stalin. "Vat does a grown man vant vith a name like Vinnie?" I was reminded of Roy Campbell on the same theme, calling Roosevelt a tittering zombie and Churchill a valiant but senile beefeater.

The worst mistake I made in five months in Florence was to ask my mother to join us and then go on with us to London. I thought, as she was now seventy, that this would be a last visit to all the places she had loved so much, even though most of her friends in Britain and Europe were dead.

Only a week after arriving in Florence, I drove over to Genoa where she was arriving by ship. Although she was officially in raptures over the beauties of Italy, I could soon tell that she was not enjoying herself. To all our Italian friends she was just my old mother, no one special; the Queen of Adelaide was nothing in Florence. She took a particular dislike to Giulio; she considered he was swindling us and that he and all his friends were freeloaders, although there was no evidence for this. "All Italian men are beasts," she confided in me.

She wanted to have painting lessons, and Giulio persuaded one of the best teachers in Florence, an artist called Colacicchi, to bend his rules and take her on for three months. She was outraged when I asked Christina, Colacicchi's model, to come to the opera with us. "There must be something very queer about a girl who'll pose with no clothes on."

A furious row erupted with her when Giulio explained to me that I was supposed to pay Mina separately; I had thought Mina was included with the rent. It was my error, and immediately and painlessly rectified. But as soon as Giulio withdrew, my mother accused him of being a swindler. And he hated her. She knew this because at one of our parties, she had heard Giulio refer to her as "*La vecchia*". She had enough Italian to know that it meant "the old woman". (Giulio had not meant it disrespectfully, but as a matter of fact.) "You know I never try to hide my age, it doesn't worry me." She launched another attack on Giulio, and how he was trying to come between us, and then, oblivious of the contradiction, reverted to those fatal words, "*la vecchia*". "I don't want all those people in the house knowing I'm seventy."

Then she was saying everybody here hated her, as everybody had hated her all her life, my father, John, Dick, Margaret, Ninette, and of course Chibs. Moreover, Chibs had told her that Ninette found it impossible to live at Anlaby with her. And now she didn't like her being here in Florence. She'd go home on the next boat to Australia. This row was punctuated by Mina coming in with the pasta, and later with the fruit, but my mother resolutely kept the theme going, like the soloist in a concerto. I tried to pacify her by telling her that I didn't hate her. I got up and went to her and stroked her head. There was a temporary calm, but not for long. A little later I tried again, holding her head to my chest. Her skin was as soft as a little girl's. Finally peace was declared.

Ten days later she tried to crank up the row again, after saying that her heart was giving her a lot of trouble, and that the pills for it gave her indigestion. "I was only sticking up for you against that swindler, but you said terrible things to me" etc. And then a complete change of direction: "Oh, if only you'd known Europe before the war. Everything has been ruined by the war, all that beauty. Beauty, it means so much to me." She reached for her heart pills and burped. "And now it's all gone." The trouble was, of course, that her old self was gone, the beautiful Emily who had cut such a swathe in London in the 1930s, and now KG was dead, and Lord Gowrie had just died. She was just the old mother of an Australian writer in a rented house in Florence.

My second mistake, which compounded the first, was to ask Richard and Catha to join us for Christmas and the New Year. I misguidedly thought that my mother and Richard, sharing a mutual passion for the ancient Greeks and Romans and Renaissance Italy, would get along well together.

Richard still corresponded amicably with H.D., who was now living in Zürich with the historical novelist who called herself Bryher, a millionaire whose money came from the Ellerman shipping line. Bryher had just sent Richard the money to buy himself a car. So Richard and Catha drove from Montpellier in their little white Simca, and moved into our spare room. It was a disaster.

My mother, speedily realizing Richard's immense erudition and, as always, being underconfident as a result of her own lack of education, decided instead to act the *grande dame*. This was precisely the tactic most certain to arouse Richard's ire and scorn. Many years later I was reading Caroline Zillboorg's excellently edited collection of Richard's and H.D.'s letters. In her Introduction she writes about Richard's mother: "A domineering woman who aspired to 'culture' as socially defined at the turn of the century, May Aldington seemed to her son throughout his life an affected, pretentious, and hollow person whose sentimentality and materialism came to represent all that he abhorred in England". Clearly, my mother was identified for Richard with his mother; but, really, my poor old Mum, infuriating enough, was not as bad as May seems to have been. And of course, in his perfect Italian Richard chatted away to all our Italian friends, complimenting them to me as absolutely delightful.

Richard and my mother had some fairly harmless disagreements about Italian life, and Italian men in particular, but I was dismayed when walking behind them in one of the Florentine streets to hear her disparaging Kershaw and Deasey. For many years she had considered them to be bad influences on me. Voices were being raised when I interrupted and suggested we stop for an ice-cream.

After returning to Montpellier Richard wrote to Deasey: "For dear old Geoff's sake I put up with Emily who struck me as exactly like the English female of the moneyed class — ignorant, snobbish, vain, purse-proud, domineering, fatuous and disagreeable. I'm sorry to say that about the old Geoff's Ma, but you know I'm right. I nearly had a sanguinary row with her in Firenze over you and Alister — I had to remind her you are my friends." Later on in the same letter, commenting on a query of Deasey's about whether some mushrooms (cèpes) were poisonous or not, he suggested "Why not try those dubious cèpes on Emily?"

In a later letter he replies to Deasey, who had made some derogatory comments on what he interpreted as my drive to have a "career". (Richard might have replied to Deasey, better some sort of career than none.) "Yes I wish Geoff wouldn't 'career' so much, but I blame *the women*. What a ghastly cow is Emily. She ought to be stuffed (I mean posthumously) and put in the Adelaide natural history museum. I suspect the old Geoff has to be a continual 'success' in order to keep the aspidistra flying."

Trouble erupted again in Florence when my mother saw Giulio holding Ninette's hand in the car; our Italian friends always held the neighbouring young woman's hand, if more of her were not available. My mother said it was disgusting. A few days later it was brought up again. She wasn't going to have Ninette holding Giulio's hand in *her* house. It wasn't done in her day. Some man in Greece had once attempted to hold her hand and she'd put him in his place. The worst of all the rows erupted when I defended Ninette.

This was still simmering on the drive up to London. We took several days over this, as she wanted to see her old friend Alvilde Bridges and her husband James Lees-Milne in the South of France, and then I wanted to show her the Camargue and Carcassonne. For days she remained absolutely silent, and resolutely remained in the car when I stopped for lunch. One day this was at one of the best restaurants in France, at Vienne (impossible to afford nowadays). I talked her into joining us for lunch, but she ruined it by trying to have a shouting match over the pheasant. She stayed dead silent throughout the whole dinner at Moulins. Then, the next day, driving into Paris, she suddenly became cheerful, and remained so for the rest of the journey to London.

Some years later, my sister Chibs gave me the letters our mother had written to her about this time. They are full of phrases like "We're having a lovely drive up through France. Carcassonne was superb" — three pages of description follow — "we had a wonderful meal at a place called Vienne".

Back again in London, by a fluke I found a cheap flat on the second and third floors of a brick building in Stratton Street, just off Piccadilly, in the very heart of London. The landlord was a Colombian, svelte and too polite, who conducted a mysterious business on the first floor.

Jack McDougall paid me an advance on the Africa book, and with that and the income from Grandfather's invaluable bequest and some freelance work for magazines and the BBC, we managed to survive. It was amazing in those days how cheaply you could live in London, if you were sensible. A short walk from our flat you could be at the Ritz and spending a fortune.

I was working in the marvellous London Library, one of the great institutions of England, a short walk down the slope from Stratton Street, researching my biography of William Light. The supreme advantage of the London Library to members is that you are allowed to borrow books, except from the excellent reference section.

On my way back in the evening the whores would be out on their beat. After a while they got to know me, and gave up soliciting me. Then for one evening there were no girls to be seen. The next day I asked one of them what had happened; I thought they all might have been arrested in the latest of those spasms of morality which shake Britain from time to time. The girl sniffed, and answered, "Millie died." She pulled a handkerchief from her dress and blew her nose. "We all went to her funeral."

The sight of London itself, after Florence and the Midi, was depressing. I was working hard on my book, and when I got up at 5 a.m. it was pitch dark. When dawn finally began to creep in, some hours later, it revealed slate roofs and walls of brick and concrete. By ten o'clock a few sparrows and some typists in offices were moving, and there were a few pigeons sitting on a television aerial. Everything was black and grey, what the Italians call the colour of a dog running away.

Jack McDougall invited me to lunch at Brooks's to meet Evelyn Waugh. I was terrified, having been told that Waugh ate colonials for breakfast. Waugh turned out to be a little, chubby man with a red face which matched the knitted tie he wore with a blue suit. He launched over the sherry into vituperations against a Lord Noel-Buxton who had been snooping around the Waugh country estate for some newspaper. When he came to the locked gates Waugh ordered him to fuck off. He indignantly replied that he was a member of the House of Lords and unaccustomed to hearing such language. "Typical of what's gone wrong with this bloody country," snorted Waugh, indicating to the steward that his glass was empty.

Whether Waugh was diverted from colonial-baiting by Lord Noel-Buxton, or whether (more likely) he would not risk offending Jack In Loco Parentis McDougall, he was perfectly charming to me, although not going so far as to say he would like to visit Australia. He did mention that I had wasted my time crossing Africa by not going to Abyssinia. And who could have been waspish with the wine flowing as it always did with Jack?

A few days later Jack came to lunch with us at Stratton Street. As a starter he brought a pot of Beluga caviar and a bottle of Krug 1947. We stayed with him and his wife May at their house in the country and Jack danced like a drunk spider to a record of a song called "This Old House", while beautiful, dark-eyed May looked on. May was American. We later stayed with her parents, Helen and Lydig Hoyt, in their house on the Hudson River. When we arrived I went to get our cases from the car. Lydig stopped me. "No guest of mine has ever carried his bags into my house."

They were very grand, like something out of an Edith Wharton novel, and rich, but not as rich as their neighbours along the Hudson who had names like Vanderbilt and Astor. Nevertheless the Hoyts' was the only house right on the river; it was sited, all alone, on a litle point. The other millionaires, with their capacious gardens rolling down to the Hudson, now had a giant two-track railroad between them and the river. The railway went around the back of the Hoyts on their little peninsula, so they alone had an unimpaired outlook. Helen took us to see Hyde Park, the home of Franklin D. Roosevelt. I opened the car door for her when we pulled up in the car park, but she said she would wait in the car; she would not enter the house of a traitor to his class.

These American experiences were of course still to come. In London Johnny Minton had dinner with us. It seemed that the Home Secretary was having a moral purge of the country, and concentrating on Male Vice. "My dear," said Johnny, waving his arms, "it's been *terrible*. We've all been burning our letters, and I've been throwing my very best drawings, all the pornographic ones, into the fire. My dear, the sky above Chelsea has been positively black with burning evidence."

Poor loveable Johnny, he later committed suicide.

Anna Campbell was now with Rob Lyle, a millionaire from the sugar empire, Tate & Lyle, who was sponsoring a literary magazine and the publication of Roy's collected poems. Rob took us to dinner at a very fashionable restaurant, La Popotte. Anna's dark good looks were flushed with a fever, and she was punning and improvising wildly. Roy had showed her some of my new poems, and the copy of my first book, *Night Flight and Sunrise*, which I had sent him. "Oh I didn't know you were a poet. What was your little book called? Nightlife at Sunset? Oh no, Nightlight before Sunrise. Oh, I am sorry, Gnatlife at Sunrise." After the main course she said she had to go home, and asked Ninette to go with her. Rob ordered another bottle and some cheese. The waiter refused to bring them. Rob demanded to see the willowy maître d'hôtel. He curtly said would we please hurry up, pay the bill and go. "You know you can only stay for an hour. There are other guests waiting for your table." "You didn't warn me. I wouldn't have come." Rob was getting angry; besides, he was rich. "Nowhere else in the world have I been told to leave the table after an hour." "Well, sir, you are here in London." Rob sat his ground. "In that case, as I said before, you should have warned me." The manager stamped his foot. "In that case, sir, you can stay." "Come on, Geoff, let's go," said Rob.

After months in Italy and France, it was unbelievable. But that was Britain in 1955.

Jack Bennett was getting a divorce from his American wife. He did not want his address to appear as Magdalen College, so asked if he could use the Stratton Street address and say that I was his brother-in-law. He was due to stay with us for the night before the court hearing, and said he would arrive about nine. At eleven he still had not arrived; I rang Magdalen and was told he had left on time. I began to ring the hospitals. He arrived at eleven thirty. He had got into the wrong bus at the station, opened a book and settled into it; suddenly it occurred to him that the bus had been stationary for some time, and he found that he was at the terminus somewhere in Kent.

When he went to court the next day the judge asked him where he lived. "With my brother-in-law." "What is his name?" Jack could not think what my name was. "Well, where does he live?" Jack simply could not remember. The judge, who must have been both patient and decent, asked, "Could it be Stratton Street?" "Of course, of course," said Jack gratefully. "And my brother-in-law's name is Geoffrey Dutton."

Jack got his divorce, and married Gwynneth, a Schools Inspector. I visited them at Oxford. Gwynneth was obviously of sterling character, but she was big and bossy, never letting gentle Jack alone, hurrying him when he was carving the roast or berating him for not having poured the wine, calling out "Jack, stop talking and eat up". As Jack, apart from being one of the greatest scholars of medieval English in the world, was a droll and witty talker, he might just have had something interesting to say.

I caught up again with Bobby Speaight. He asked me to lunch at the Garrick Club, which, although not as superb as Brooks's, had many more congenial members. Not content with that, Bobby invited Ninette and me down to Kent for the weekend, where his wife lived and he joined her for the weekends. They were very hospitable. We drank a 1904 port. They drove us over to afternoon tea with their neighbours at Sissinghurst, Vita Sackville-West and Harold Nicolson. Vita reminded me of Byron's description of his friend Madame de Staël: "frightful as a precipice". Harold wore a hideous tie and shirt in clashing colours, with a tweed overcoat which he wore all the time, thrown over his shoulder like an opera cloak. On arrival we were given sherry in the long room; Bobby later told me it was a great honour to have been offered sherry.

The many-chambered garden was as marvellous as it had appeared in photographs, and Vita a gentle but acute guide; Harold stayed inside reading. At afternoon tea Harold talked of his biography of George V. Edward VII's letters to his son always ended: "I must go now and dress for dinner. Hope this finds you as well as it leaves me."

It was time to return to Australia, via the United States. I proposed to Jack McDougall that I take the little Fiat and wander over a large number of the states of the union, and write about what I found. He generously offered to publish a book; he had already committed himself to the biography of William Light.

I had booked on the *Queen Mary*, but at the last minute the Cunard Line workers staged a strike. We had to transfer to the *United States*, and the only cabins available were in the first class. The advertisements for this ship read: "You enter the USA at Southampton". You certainly did.

The *United States*, the fastest ship on the Atlantic, zoomed across the Channel to Cherbourg and took on a lot more passengers. At dinner that night we found ourselves sitting with a Chicago millionaire and his faded blonde wife. He asked me if I could do him a favour. I could not think what I could do for anyone so much richer than me, but offered my services. "Wal," he said, "these friends of ours in France have arranged for us to be given a bottle of Verve Clicko every night for dinner, and we can't stand the stuff. Would you mind drinking it?" I accepted.

The luxury of the menu was far beyond the experience of most of the passengers, who, however rich, preferred hamburgers. The stewards were also ill at ease. At dinner I asked for the *Coquilles St Jacques*. The stewardess looked baffled, and had a look at the menu. "Oh, you mean the croquettes." A few minutes later she returned and said, "Hey, them croquettes is fish. You still want 'em?"

The Fourth of July was celebrated by a tremendous banquet. The *filets mignons* came with a whole cylinder of pâté de foie gras *bien truffé* sitting on top of the steak. Mrs Chicago Millionaire poked at it nervously with her fork. "Hey, honey," said her husband, "you don't have to eat the liver sausage."

Once again, it was all very different from life in France or Italy, where both poor and rich know how to eat and drink. Looking around my fellow passengers on the *United States* I wondered what was the point of having all that money and still preferring to eat hot dogs and drink Coca-Cola.

Yet the United States was to be an astonishing experience which helped to cure me of the already weakened Australian tendency to regard Britain as "Home". And it also severely modified my tendency to idealize Europe.

Four months and many thousands of miles later, on the ship from San Francisco to Sydney, I was reading D.H. Lawrence's letters, and came across these sentences: "Europe is like a dying pig uttering a long, infinitely conceited squeak. At least America isn't so depressing."

Seventeen

When Ninette and I returned to South Australia in 1956 we went back to live at Nonsuch in the Adelaide hills. A great joy was that Chibs had returned, after some years in America, and had married Dick Blackburn, who was at Magdalen with me and was now Professor of Law at the University of Adelaide. They lived only half a mile up the road from Nonsuch.

I was offered a Lectureship in English at Adelaide University, which I accepted; I was especially pleased to work with Derry Jeffares as Professor in charge of the English Department. He and Jeanne and their daughter Felicity lived in John Bray's rambling old house in Hutt Street; they also had the use of the fine old stone stables, where they fixed up a work-room for me so that I could escape the University between lectures and tutorials.

There were only eight on the English Department staff, of whom two, Brian Elliott and me, were Australians. Brian was on study leave when I took up my post, so I was the sole representative of the people who owned the University.

After Derry, by far the most interesting member of the Department was Bryn Davies, a limping, bearded, gesticulating, wild Welshman. Because of his tendency to stumble, and his convulsive manner, respectable Adelaide citizens thought he was a drunk. Actually Bryn had a type of epilepsy, and never touched a drop of alcohol. He and his wife Bel were genuine eccentrics; they never planned their eccentricities. I remember that at one stage Bryn decided to wear a magnificent opera cloak to Adelaide concerts, in which he stood out like a *torero* in a nonconformist church service. One evening he walked down the steps of the Town Hall in the interval, and inadvertently put one foot into one of those large, oblong, chromium floor ashtrays. Bryn clumped onwards with this boat-boot until he reached a window, and lit a cigarette. Then for the first time he seemed to become conscious of the ash-tray, and flicked his foot a few times like a cat with a wet paw. I knelt down and removed it.

Bryn and Bel were both also, unlike some academics and their wives, genuine readers of every sort of book, and not only in English. Bryn had been Professor of English at Cairo University until Nasser sacked all British staff. They had lived in great style, with cooks and servants, and Bel arrived in Adelaide totally unequipped to be a housewife. Nothing daunted, she would attempt the most difficult dishes at her dinner parties;

your spoon would ricochet off a soufflé, or your knife fail to make a dent in what was supposed to be a *sauce béarnaise*.

There were excellent people on the staff of Adelaide University at the time: Peter Karmel was Professor of Economics; Hugh Stretton, who had rowed with me at Oxford but managed his life more sensibly, Professor of History; and, as already mentioned, Dick Blackburn, Professor of Law; there were a number of scientists who were interested in the Humanities, and vice versa. I did not realise at the time that W.G.K. Duncan, the Professor of Politics and History, was the model for Jonathan Crow in sharp-tongued Christina Stead's novel, *For Love Alone*.

The Vice-Chancellor, A.P. Rowe, was a wartime scientist who knew nothing about universities, and was generally detested. His best asset was his wife, who had a genuine interest in collecting and encouraging Australian art, an interest in which Rowe followed her. Rowe considered that a university should be run like a business. He told us we should be in our "offices" from nine to five, apparently unconscious of the hours of tutorials and lectures, or the times spent in libraries. He started ringing staff members first thing in the morning. He could never, needless to say, manage to raise Bryn. One day I was having lunch with Bryn in the staff club when Rowe charged up and castigated Bryn for not being in his office at 9 a.m. Bryn put down his cigarette, looked coldly at Rowe, and said, "I was under the impression, Mr Vice-Chancellor, that you had hired my brains and not my arse."

Rowe's idea of efficiency meant that when Sir Douglas Mawson, Adelaide's most famous Professor, retired from the Geology Department, he was not allowed to keep on a room in the building named after him. Mawson by this time bitterly regretted that he had been instrumental in appointing Rowe. Not long after this, Rowe and his wife moved into a Vice-Chancellor's flat in the old Anatomy Building, which still smelled of formalin; it was in the centre of the University. New deep drains had to be dug, and there were large signs on the footpath warning pedestrians of these, with ropes across the footpath. I was walking into the University one morning and met Sir Douglas, who was obviously in very high spirits. I said, "You're looking very sprightly, Sir Douglas." He seized me by the arm, even at his age his grip still of iron. "Who wouldn't be, Geoffrey, haven't you heard that Rowe disregarded all the signs and ropes and contrived to fall down the drain and break his ankle? Splendid! But, oh dear, if only it had been a crevasse."

I was very nervous when I went to give my first lecture. It was on Restoration Comedy, and I wrote it out carefully from beginning to end. When I entered the lecture room I was dismayed to see three nuns in the front row; I had some very bawdy quotations to make. I ploughed on; the nuns seemed to understand the jokes better than the other students. But at the end of my hour I had only reached about halfway through my written script. Derry laughed when I told him, and advised me always to lecture from notes; in any case, this usually makes for a livelier lecture.

The students were the most rewarding part of my years lecturing at universities. The majority, of course, were not particularly interested in the subject, but the good ones were wonderfully responsive. And our tutorials, though not like those at Oxford, were small enough to allow personal contact to be made. One day one of my best students came to me, after attending a lecture by Bryn on Milton. It had become apparent to her, after the first couple of minutes, that Bryn had mistaken an English I class of a hundred and fifty for an English III class of twenty-five, and that he was delivering a lively lecture on D.H. Lawrence instead of one on *Paradise Lost*. My student was particularly amused, when she looked around the lecture room, to see that nearly all the students were assiduously taking notes, no doubt expecting a trick question in the exams.

Sometimes there was more going on in one's lectures than one realized. I was asked by the enlightened Professor Rogers of the Zoology Department to have lunch with him and his colleagues and talk about the study of literature. One of the tutors, a quiet and dignified woman called Miss Pilton, had brought a small, sick possum along to a lecture of mine on Spenser. In the course of my lecture she realized that the possum, hidden inside her dress, had died. "I felt it getting colder and colder," she told me, "and I just couldn't concentrate on *The Faerie Queene*."

Sometimes a student would give one a severe shock, as in a tutorial I was giving on Milton's Satan. I asked the half-dozen students if any of them believed in evil — did they understand Satan when he said "Evil be thou my Good". There was no response. So I asked them if they considered that Hitler was evil. "Please, Mr Dutton," asked one girl, "who exactly was Hitler?" And this was only a little more than ten years after the end of World War II.

There were some interludes of rich comedy in the petty tedium that occupies so much of university life. A distinguished scholar, Wallace Robson from Wadham College, Oxford, came to teach in the Adelaide English Department for a term. Wally was a delight to talk to, witty, erudite but not pompous; he was also a shambling wreck, the dirtiest and most untidy man I have ever known. Part of his trouble was that in Adelaide he was on his own; he had no scout to look after him. He told me he did not like his room at St Mark's, there was no hand-basin, no bath, and the showers had no curtains.

A friend of mine, Chris Legoe, had a room with its own bath and kitchen behind his house, and he agreed to take Wally in as a boarder. Chris, a lawyer, used to drive Wally in to the University on the way to his chambers in the morning. One day Wally was not waiting by the car as usual, so Chris went to his room. There he found Wally sitting on the bed in his dressing gown, his head in his hands. Chris asked him what was wrong. "I've nothing to wear," Wally wailed. He pointed to the door. Behind it was a pile of dirty clothes reaching up to the ceiling; no scout had come to take it away to be washed.

Wally asked me about the Adelaide Club, and obviously wanted to sample its cellar. I thought it would be good for him to see a different side of Adelaide life, so arranged to meet him at his room one day, and we would walk together up North Terrace to the Club. When I called I found that he was wearing a very dirty open-necked shirt and sandals. I explained that the old gentlemen in the Club were a bit stuffy, and insisted on a tie being worn. "Oh that's all right," said Wally brightly, "I want to get a new shirt, so I'll buy a tie as well." I took him to John Martin's where he was outfitted in new shirt and tie; I did not have the heart to suggest socks as well, to hide the horny toenails peeping out of his sandals.

It was a lovely warm Easter day, so I took him out to the balcony by the little garden at the back of the Club to have a drink before lunch. I was hailed by my friend from childhood, Hurtle Morphett, who was now President of the Club. Hurtle was seated in a cane chair by a drinks table, with two of the most dapper members of the Club, Lum Rymill (actually Sir Arthur Rymill, Lord Mayor of Adelaide), and Keith Lawson from Padthaway. "Join us, Geoff," said the genial Hurtle, "and introduce your guest." I did so, and Wally sat down between Hurtle and Lum, crossing his legs so that one set of toenails was just below Lum's nose, and the pile of dandruff on his jacket close to Hurtle. They talked of Oxford, where Hurtle had stroked the University Eight when he was up at Brasenose.

Wally, unconscious of course of the effect his toenails were having, was very conscious of the attitudes revealed when one of the older members, Hugh Giles, came over to join us. He had recently been in Oxford, and was shocked at the deterioration of standards in the two old universities. The captain of the Cambridge cricket team was from Ceylon, a dark chappie. "Couldn't have happened in my day." At Oxford Don Laidlaw had had the effrontery to introduce him to some dark fellow who was actually in the team. "In my day there were a few of them about, but of course nobody *met* them."

Later I apologized to Wally for my compatriot's racism; I then apologized to Hurtle for my guest's lack of socks. "That's all right, Geoff," said Hurtle, "if that's what they're wearing at Oxford nowadays I expect we'll catch up in a few years."

My mother had suggested that it would be friendly to invite all the staff members of the English Department up to Anlaby for a picnic, especially as none of them were Australians. Wally and Bryn and Bel also stayed the night. Wally ate a gigantic dinner, concentrating especially on the meringues and the thick fresh cream. The next morning he complained of frightful indigestion, and my mother gave him her special medicine for indigestion together with a lot of sympathy. When we went down later to clean up his room, we found that (as when he had stayed at Nonsuch) he had not used the towel, and in the wastepaper basket was a large, empty box of Haigh's chocolates, the chocolate papers everywhere. He had obviously eaten the whole box, which had been intended as a present for my mother. "The greedy brute," she said, "and I wasted my sympathy on his indigestion."

She was at her worst throughout the picnic, which was basically a jolly family affair, as the staff had brought wives and children. She was very suspicious of them all; perhaps she thought they would ask her questions about English literature.

Two of the women had collected some of the hundreds of fallen pine cones around the picnic spot, and piled them into a pusher and a basket. When they were about to put them into their car, my mother said, "Oh, if you don't mind, we use all the pine cones. Please leave them." I was appalled and said, "Oh come off it, Mum, there's millions of them." But the wives were already tipping them out onto the ground, and one said between tight lips, "No, Geoff, if Mrs Dutton needs her pine cones, then of course she must have them." This was one of the worst of the many occasions on which I simply could not understand my mother's thought processes.

She had been complaining about various aspects of her health, which she said had not been good ever since her attack of shingles in London after the dreadful drive up from Florence, which had no doubt contributed to her shingles. For a while she insisted she was suffering from indigestion; a friend who had given her crumpets with too much butter on them three months before was still being blamed as a cause of the indigestion. One day she was with me in the car when I stopped for petrol at Crafers. Mr Miller, as he filled the car, groaned and said he had had too good a night. My mother wound down her window and said, "Were you eating onions?" He replied, "I don't know what I was eating but I know what I was drinking, and the missus gave me hell this morning." "There you are," my mother continued, "I knew it was onions. President Eisenhower's last heart attack was caused, I'm sure, by eating spring onions; I was going to write and tell him so."

A specialist in Adelaide told her that her real trouble was her heart, and put her into hospital for a week. At first she had said she would go home to Anlaby. It was a Tuesday, and he told her bluntly that if she did she would be dead by Thursday.

When I drove her home from hospital she was undoubtedly feeling better. She immediately told me about a telephone conversation with my sister-in-law Peggy; John and Peg were still, foolishly, living in the cottage at Anlaby. “I didn’t lose my temper. I wasn’t a bit cross. I just said quietly, ‘Peggy, you are the most selfish, hard-hearted person I have ever met, and I think your behaviour to me has been absolutely disgusting’.”

At the University there was still, of course, no systematic study of Australian Literature, and none of my colleagues except Derry, Bryn and Brian Elliott were interested in any of its manifestations. The only time any writers visited the English Department was when some of us who were writers met in my room at the University for further discussion about setting up a branch of the Fellowship of Australian Writers (FAW) in Adelaide. The first meeting had been at Flexmore Hudson’s house, attended also by Max Harris, Ian Mudie, Nancy Cato and Colin Thiele. We drank iced claret and then cider; it all seemed worthy but dull. I wrote to David Campbell asking for his advice, as there was a very lively branch of the FAW in Canberra. I wrote: “Flexmore is one of those owlish twerps who like ‘Meet Your Author’ fiestas, and public poetry readings and similar farcical pastimes. Harris fancies a knockabout clown act in which he’d be star clown. I myself fancy no meetings at all.” That was four years before the first Adelaide Festival, by which time I had changed my ground about “farcical pastimes”.

The most pleasing thing was the vigorous development in my poetry. I had moved on from the clotted imagery and intense compression of my earlier poems, and the staid dullness of most of the poems written at Oxford. The death of Geoff Tuck, my companion in the crash at Bougainville, from leukaemia, led me to thoughts about the craziness of our appointments with death. My biography of William Light had also been going well; when we were in England we had visited Thebarton Hall in Suffolk, where he spent his childhood, and found that the hall was being demolished. This led to a longish poem.

I later sent this poem to Kenneth Slessor, who was then, in erratic fashion, editing *Southerly*, and he accepted it with a note that cheered me greatly. It was even better when a letter came from David Campbell, who also had liked “Thebarton Hall”. “I lunched with Ken Slessor the other day. He bored me to death right through the oysters, with his praises of ‘Thebarton Hall’. — ‘One of the best things’, harumph, ‘in recent years’. He’s sent it for the Penguin anthology.” David went on to say how excited he was by Randolph Stow’s *Act One*, “the best first book by a young poet since Judith Wright’s *Moving Image*”. The Melbourne neo-classic school did not appeal so much to him. “I’ve been getting sick and bored of the recent crop of neo-classic columns weighing down the little reviews lately: there’s no life in them, just marble.” It is an interesting further comment that David was later to marry the ex-wife of one of the leading neo-classicist poets.

David later came to stay at Rocky Point, eager to enjoy every aspect of life there. An Adelaide doctor friend, Jim Bonnin, and his wife Heather, were also staying. Jim and I were both very good swimmers and used to the cold water of the sea at Kangaroo Island. Our passion at the time was to snorkel, sometimes for a couple of hours, along a reef a couple of hundred yards off the beach at what we called Little Rocky. David was a big man, but skinny and bony, and not used to cold sea. We always used to wear sweaters (it was the days before wetsuits), but David scorned my offer of one. I hadn't been paying any attention to him, totally lost in the world of silent, swinging fish, diving for scallops, giving the dark shape with pointed wings of a stingray a wide berth, when suddenly I looked towards the shore, where Ninette had been lying on the beach reading a book: David was lurching along the sand with her, his arm around her neck. They then lay down beside each other on the sand. I was thinking they might at least have gone into the sandhills, when she began waving to us.

By the time we got ashore David was quite delirious. Fortunately Jim, being a doctor, realized immediately that David was suffering from severe hypothermia, and knew what to do. David later told me that all he could see was Ninette and the red roof of Rocky Point in the far distance. He thought he was going mad, and was far more afraid of madness than death. He was very ill, and had to spend a couple of days in bed. Being a poet, he took the opportunity to write a poem about the experience, which Douglas Stewart published in the *Bulletin* with an absurd drawing by an artist who must have thought Rocky Point was in Pittwater.

I was seeing quite a lot of Max Harris, who had partially recovered from his Ern Malley wounds and was writing good poems himself, such as "The Tantanoola Tiger" or "On Throwing a Copy of the *New Statesman* into the Coorong", and some delicate love poems.

Thinking of this last poem, I told Max that Kingsley Martin, Editor of the *New Statesman*, had recently been on a visit to South Australia, and I was asked if I could make arrangements for him to visit an Australian sheep station. The owner of one of our most famous Merino studs, north of Clare, agreed to have him to stay for the weekend. When I saw him in Adelaide after his return I asked him how the visit had gone. "Oh, the station was very interesting," he said, his white brush of hair twitching, "but I must say I was rather shocked by my hostess." Having known his hostess since I was a boy, I could not imagine how she could have offended him. "Well," he continued, "she woke me up in the morning, very early, by coming into my room in her very flimsy dressing gown, ostensibly to offer me a cup of tea." I suggested that that was exactly what she had in mind, but he was convinced she intended to seduce him, otherwise she would have sent the maid. "But," I pointed out, "like most Australians, they don't have any maids." Kingsley Martin shook his head. "How shocking." "That wasn't the only peculiar thing," he continued. "At lunch a sweaty young man in moleskins sat down alongside me. I mean, that's carrying democracy a bit far, inviting the gardener in for lunch." I explained that the young man was the jackeroo, son of one of the most famous Merino breeders in Australia. So much for the old Socialist.

Max was, and for many years remained, an excellent and honest critic of my poetry; he would take a lot of trouble over reading it. In 1957, we finally launched our literary quarterly, *Australian Letters*, with Bryn Davies as co-editor. We had no grant and no sponsor, nothing but a friendly printer who would give us credit, and the excellent launching pad of the Mary Martin Bookshop. To provide funds, I used my Adelaide Club connections to persuade half a dozen Adelaide businessmen, and Lloyd Dumas of the *Advertiser*, to take out advertisements. These were, of course, quite useless to them in furthering their sales; they were a kind of donation. I assured them that they would gain great personal prestige in supporting Australian literature, despite its being an unknown field for most of them.

I did not have such success with the Canberra-based, well-endowed Humanities Research Council. Max and I had made a preliminary Quarterly Bibliography of Australian Literature which would appear regularly in *Australian Letters* if we could find the funds for it. There was nothing like it then in Australia, and we thought this was the sort of thing the Humanities Research Council might well sponsor. The members of the board of the Council were having a meeting in Adelaide. Our sample Bibliography was printed at the back of our new issue, which contained what has become probably the most-quoted article in Australian literary history, Patrick White's "The Prodigal Son". This was the only article White ever wrote. I had asked him to write it, as one who had returned to Australia, in answer to Alister Kershaw's sparkling defence of his expatriate status. To my surprise, White had agreed.

When the Chairman of the Council, Professor Trendall, emerged from the morning's meeting he tripped up to me and said that the Council had turned down our application for support for the Bibliography. "And I don't see," he brandished the magazine, "what a naked female has to do with Australian letters." (On the cover of the magazine there was a beautiful photograph by Axel Poignant of an outback Aboriginal child.) I replied, "Letters are to do with life, and naked females of all ages have a lot to do with life." He was not amused. He and the members of his Council were, he said, off to do some field work; I happened to know that they were going to the Reynella vineyard for what would be a prolonged lunch. Their combined airfares from Canberra would have paid for our Bibliography for a year or more.

Our policy with *Australian Letters* was to avoid parochialism. As well as making sure our printed items came from all around Australia, we commissioned articles and reviews from writers such as Frank Kermode,

Lawrence Durrell, Richard Aldington, Roy Campbell and Philip Larkin. Max had suggested that Larkin should be asked to review my new book of poems *Antipodes in Shoes*, beautifully produced by Edwards & Shaw. I thought this rather dangerous, as at that time it was *de rigueur* in England to sling off at Australian poetry. In our very first issue of *Australian Letters* we had commissioned a symposium of Australian and overseas writers to comment on some of the fruitier criticisms of Australian writers, including some of the best, that had appeared in *The Times Literary Supplement* (which thought that Slessor was a bush poet), *Encounter* and the *London Magazine*. A couple of samples will indicate what Australian writers had to cope with in the 1950s. The first, from *Encounter*, refers to the great difficulty of writing poetry at all in the colonies: "While there are good men and true in Torrowangee, in Wanganui, and for that matter in Klerksdorp, they are unlikely to be those who are much concerned with what Ezra Pound calls the life of the mind". Or this, from the *London Magazine*: "There are quite a lot of reasonably competent figures on the Australian scene, but none who are outstanding. They all seem a thoroughly nice lot of cobbers who for some reason have decided to have a go at writing poetry." In hindsight, I have often wondered exactly what Max had in mind when he suggested that Larkin should review my book.

Derry Jeffares, who by now had moved from Adelaide to become Professor of English at the University of Leeds, agreed to act as middleman, since he knew Larkin, who lived a few miles away at Hull. (Andrew Marvell, incidentally, from whom my title was taken, lived for some time near Hull. Perhaps I was trespassing on Larkin's territory.) The review was a stinker; too bad, we published it. Derry wrote: "I thought Larkin was a shit. I had a pretty tart correspondence with him when he wrote to say that he wondered, as the review was unfavourable, if you'd (a) pay him the ten pounds fee offered and (b) publish his review. I said I thought you'd think both suggestions, as I did, insulting, and that I was sorry that his critical perception did not match his poetic ability."

I was happier with a letter from David Campbell, written on Christmas night 1958, saying how pleased he was with the book. "But you must forgive me, Geoff, if I do not wave flags immediately: it took me two years before anything of Slessor's came in — what he wrote was new. And I'm forming the same slow friendship with your book — surprises, awakenings, the learning of a language … So don't be too fast with your farmer friends."

I was pleased when *Antipodes in Shoes* was awarded the Grace Leven Prize for poetry, especially as with the hundred pounds prize money I bought a set of the *Australian Encyclopaedia* which has been in constant use ever since.

Vi Johns, who ran John Martin's Art Gallery for Bill Hayward, asked me if I would open an exhibition of Arthur Boyd's new paintings and large ceramic tiles. The paintings turned out to be those lovely, luminous ones, many of them in tempera, of Wimmera landscapes. These early ones remain among his finest paintings. The tiles were quite different, of harsh figures in strong colours, mostly of Biblical subjects. Arthur wrote to me about these tiles: "Judith Wright once wrote a poem about an old king. She said it had something to do with a tile painting she bought of mine, of David and Saul."

I bought one of the most beautiful landscapes, for fifty pounds, and for thirty pounds a tile of Jesus, most definitely not meek and mild, throwing the money-changers out of the Temple. Alas, the landscape was later sold to placate a bank that refused to be patient any longer.

A strange thing happened with these tiles. They were mounted on wooden five-ply and framed with lead, which was bent around them. Kym Bonython also bought one, and ten years later, to the day, both tiles fell out of their frames. His crashed onto a tiled floor and was shattered; mine, fortunately, fell on a carpet and was only cracked in a minor way.

In the mid-1950s I began an affair with a married woman which was to be one of the most important relationships of my life. I had always felt vaguely discontented and impatient with married life; I had had a few fleeting affairs, as with Betty in London, and the long-legged lazy blonde. But now I was deeply in love. I fooled myself that it was perfectly possible for anyone to love more than one person. I told myself I still loved Ninette. Why should I not love someone else too?

At a time when women wore girdles, makeup, stockings, gloves and other armour, Annie strode to our Adelaide meetings hatless, stockingless, definitely ungirdled. She never wore makeup and still doesn't.

Annie was no intellectual, but she was certainly not bourgeois. You would never catch her giving huge lunches for the right people, nor would she have had fitted into patterns like going for holiday after holiday to the Brookes in Northern Ireland, as I was weak enough to agree to do with Ninette. Annie opened my eyes — although she never once criticized my wife — to the way I had been burying my discontent by taking the line of least resistance and going along with whatever was planned. I had still not broken free of my childhood credulity, believing that whatever was happening was inevitable. Before Annie I had secretly thought of myself as a free agent — that is, free to pursue affairs. But I had congratulated myself too soon. Now I began to understand that I had allowed myself to become enclosed in just the sort of life I really least wanted.

Although there was so much fresh activity going on, with the University and my meetings with Max Harris, I had in some ways returned to the stupid social life that I had found so enervating after my last return to Australia. When we came back to Nonsuch, basically a most desirable if very simple place to live, we had enlarged the house with what turned out to be a regrettably ugly extension, and now behaved as if it were Anlaby, having large dinners, and huge parties in the courtyard for many people I did not care about at all. There was a constant building of a circle of acceptable friends around what should have been solitary walks into life, and I went along with it. Rocky Point parties were often for too many people, even though they were sometimes great fun, and Ninette managed them expertly. But they were not the sort of thing a writer should do too often. Fortunately, Rocky Point was also a refuge; I managed to write there, on the few occasions when there were no visitors, or hardly any.

Now for the first time I thought of ending my marriage. I went through periods of great and private depression, thinking more and more often of a break, but was too confused to know where to begin, how to go about it. I often thought that my marriage should have ended before I left for Oxford, regarding it as a typical wartime liaison, which in retrospect is what it was. I would have grown in all sorts of ways while in England and Europe had I been single, and not only in the ways I had begun to explore in Tasmania, and so thoughtlessly gave up at Parkes because I was temporarily sexually and emotionally lonely. Marriage at such a young age to a middle-class girl a year younger than me, who had learned much of her knowledge of "how to handle Geoffrey" from my mother, was not conducive to self-discovery or journeys of the intellect. I had often felt that Ninette herself, aware that I was no longer completely committed to our marriage, was determined, come what may and at whatever cost to herself, to "make it work". She would have been better off with someone else.

My discontent was nobody's *fault* — would that life and marriage were so simple. There were many happy times. There were also many times when I fell into black depression, my soul being borne along to nothingness. And there is no remedy for an underlying incompatability of spirit. You either part, or pretend. I went on pretending for another twenty-five years.

I tried to conform to what was expected of me, and there were many times when Ninette's priorities and behaviour angered or embarrassed me, and many times when she must have been fed up with me. I lurched between deep guilt over my heretical thoughts of ending my marriage, calmer passages of thankfulness when all was going well, and the ecstasies and laughter of my times with Annie.

I have said that Annie was no intellectual; she had only a sketchy formal education. She was, however, the first Australian I spoke to who seemed to understand instinctively and by personal experience the potential for change in our country. On almost the first time we talked together, in the hubbub of a huge party, Annie was saying to me how the New Australians (as migrants were called then) were helping to break down the idea of the strong-arm ideal Australian male; women were pleased to be treated, for a change, like intelligent and responsive creatures, and men would have to realize this. She also amused me about English men. "They are the only ones I know", she said, "who can be cold and lecherous at the same time." At the same time Annie had a vision of Australia's true relationship with Asia — a vision that was not to emerge generally, either to individuals or to government, for a long time. She had been brought up in Thailand, or Siam as it was called then, where her father was a forestry expert, and she had a profound bond with Asia. Yoga kept her trim and supple; she read the Buddha, Zen writings and Confucius without telling you it was virtuous to do so.

When I say that my relationship with Annie was important, I do not mean only in the way that all love affairs are important to the individuals involved. Annie was the first to set changes going in me, to modify my personality. She was the cause of a new burst of energy which gave my confidence a boost when I was unsure of my direction. One of the results was an outpouring of poems, and the first direct, passionate (and I think succesful) love poems of my life.

I was pleased to be writing such poetry, and the pattern she inspired endured. From the time of my affair with Annie, every burst of poetic energy which resulted in a new direction, in a new way of looking at the world, was the result of an extramarital affair. It was as if the poems in me had to be kick-started by a jolt to the inner self, and as if the respectable outer self had to be left to go about its own bland existence.

Annie was a kind woman with insight, devoid of snobbery and not afraid of the world, not a destroyer and never a manipulator. From her I learned what real sexual equality and companionship were. I had rented a small, condemned 1870s terrace house in Grenfell Street in the city, where I could work between lectures and tutorials, and it was there we met every Thursday. She used to come up the lane from the back, by a slum cottage raucous with a cocky screeching, a dog barking and two old women swearing. I used to sit at the top window, behind the flywire, and wait for the sight of her. She walked up the lane quickly and modestly, but even so, men in the street would stop to stare at her. She would look up at the wire blind. And then when she left, she would turn round to look at it again, and then walk firmly on.

She was not shy of the world, but amused by its ways. She could see the possibility of change in my attitude to it. She would question me about *my* direction, *my* needs. She asked me why I was so underconfident below my easy exterior. I was a bit miffed at first with this observation — me, underconfident? But Annie was right. I was still Ah-timid-dormouse, deferring to everyone, sure that my friends like Kershaw, Deasey and Harris were much more talented than I was; pathetically pleased to be getting away with a few affairs, very much under the thumbs of my mother and my wife. And yet I thought I was in charge.

Before Annie, I had always patronizingly thought that men had to pander to women's needs and their "more highly strung" emotions. This nonsense was because all the women I had known before Annie were like that. Or maybe my mother had trained me to look after her emotional life, and the pattern was set. Of course this leads to a self-neglect that nurtures self-distrust, and also to the possibility of being emotionally bullied and manipulated by those you are trying, albeit with unconscious superciliousness, to help. Annie showed me another, easier way of being.

Instead of allowing my life to roll along I began to think harder about what I wanted.

Annie told me that she would not leave her husband. I wonder now if she had hoped to open my eyes and release me from the wrong directions I so often blearily took. I was too naive to see that I could have left my marriage without another woman — Annie — to go to. After all her quiet demonstration that my life was wrong, I still could not change direction without a dramatic reason such as "the other woman".

After two years Annie and I decided to remain loving friends, but to end our affair. The way of life begun in my weekly meetings with her had become a necessary habit — I felt my sanity depended on such an outlet, and the secrecy of it all was essential. I desperately needed to keep something of myself away from my marriage and all those friends, and chose to do it through love affairs. After Annie, married life ran parallel to my affairs.

Eighteen

On the day after Anzac Day, 1957, I received a telegram from Douglas Stewart from the *Bulletin*. The woman at the Post Office read it out to me over the phone: "Could you please write 1000 word obitchery on Roy Campbell". She repeated the word: "obitchery". I thought how Roy would have loved it. I had heard nothing of Roy's death at the time, but soon found out that he had been killed in a car accident in Portugal. Mary, who was driving, was only slightly injured.

I thought, when writing the piece for Doug, that what shone through Roy's faults, his reactionary politics, the braggadocio, the occasional cruelties, the drunken impossible behaviour, was an extraordinary gentleness and courage, and a capacity for love and friendship. Above all, he was a true poet.

I love to see, when leaves depart,
The clear anatomy arrive ...

In Adelaide, the only poet I used to see was Max Harris. A welcome visitor was the young poet and novelist, Randolph Stow, who came to Adelaide from time to time, and for a while tutored in the English Department. His ancestors were pioneers in both South Australia and Western Australia, and he and the poet and jurist John Bray believed they shared a marvellously exotic ancestor in Pocahontas.

Mick, as Stow was always called, reminded me of the West Australian wildflowers around his native Geraldton, at home in the dry country, delicate, romantic, the stem thin and wiry. Often he was as silent as a wildflower. He would stand by himself, tall and slender, clutching a drink, his jutting head bent forward. Then, when he could no longer avoid talking to someone, launch into a conversation with a grunt. Australia had never had such a talented lad: by the age of twenty-three he had published (in England, and some of them in the USA) a book of poems and two novels. Fortunately, for the most part he was not a prophet scorned; his books were well received in Australia, and he won a number of major awards. The flagrant exception was Leonie Kramer, Nonie the Knocker, as Mick called her; Patrick White later gave her another name, Killer Kramer. In both cases she persistently failed to understand what Stow and White were trying to do in their work.

Some other well-meaning critics tried to link Stow with White, saying how he had been influenced by *Voss*. But *Voss* was published in 1957, while

Stow's *A Haunted Land* was published earlier, in 1956, and *The Bystander* in 1957. Stow was an admirer of White's work, but such comments understandably irritated him.

My mother asked me to bring Mick up to Anlaby for a weekend. I regaled him with stories of the ghost, whose presence had manifested itself to a number of people, in a number of different ways. One night John was by himself in the house, reading in the smoking room with the door shut, when suddenly his sheepdog woke up and howled. The front door closed and footsteps came around the corridor. When John opened the door there was no one there and the dog was still howling. Chibs and I had heard these footsteps. One night we rigged up a ghost trap, a piece of cord across the corridor, above a tray of sand for footprints. We were woken up by curses; we had caught Dad.

Mick slept in what had been the billiard room in Grandfather's day, and wrote a poem called "The Ghost at Anlaby", agreeably replete with rather raffish goings-on. My mother snorted when she read the poem: "Your grandfather was nothing like that. He was a very boring man."

Mick loved the bush, and came with us on a trip to Uno. Jack Learmonth, now manager, and his wife Pearl and the boys were just the same, and the country as beautiful as ever. The live myalls hung down silver-grey and the dead myalls' branches were like the necks of water-birds, in country far remote from water. Then on the red earth there was the amazing scarlet and black of the Sturt pea. There were blue wildflowers in the red rocks of the ranges, and a little mountain devil running in jerks with his tail up, like a clockwork toy.

When we arrived Jack said, "Your wife's looking nice and stout, Geoff old man." He meant it as a compliment; Ninette, somewhat naturally, thought otherwise. There were more ornaments than ever in the house, including two ashtrays, one in the shape of a very pink flamingo, the other a naked lady with her legs in the air.

Jack was making silver initials for a whip-handle. He bored tiny holes in the mulga and poured the metal, melted down from an old tea-pot. While he was doing it, Jack was giving Mick some advice about the bush, whether he needed it or not. "Always take a spare can of juice with you when you're out on the bike. I know, you'll say it does 75 m.p.g. and the tank holds one and a half gallons and you should be right, but you mightn't be right, old man. And if you're lost, never go out of a fenced paddock." Jack gave Mick the baffling instructions on how to catch a "roo in a snooze", if you were out of ammunition, until he realized that Jack meant "in a noose". Jack also showed us a most ingenious picker he had invented for extracting broken pump-rods from wells. "Now I was working down the 175 foot well the other day and I dropped the spanner. My word, now, that's a pickle. Some of them wells is getting real galapigated."

A mention of the words "east-west" set him off remembering the days when he worked as a fettler on the construction of the east-west railway line from Port Augusta to Perth. Every story was based on how many miles they were out of Port Augusta. "There was supposed to be a couple of Johns with us all the time, but these here Johns were putting their bit in about the two-up game, so the men just left 'em behind at the 350 mile when we moved out to the 400 mile." All the men working on the line were particularly keen to get to the Port Augusta races, so when the tea-and-sugar train arrived they got the driver drunk on whisky and persuaded him to head back to Port Augusta. "He's going along real fine but then we met the outgoing stores train at the points at the 200 mile. Well, there was a bit of an argument over the right of way, finally our bloke pushed the other train back over the points and away we go to the Port. My word, we were hauled over the coals for it, too."

That night there was music and singing. Jack's son Colin twanged his guitar and sang "Oh first you made me live and then you made me love and now you make me die". Then, red-faced, he took up his new saxophone and Will the squeeze-cordeen. They agreed on the key of F, but when they started it seemed more as if Col was in E and Will in A. I wished Willie McKie had been there. He had recently been on a visit to Australia and said he had not enjoyed himself so much for nine years, especially with the graziers at the Queensland Club, one of whom took him out west to his station. Jack gave a recitation: "Sure Ireland must be heaven because an angel [i.e. 'Mum'] came from there". Mick was enchanted by it all, and incidents later appeared in his poems.

Sometimes, back in Adelaide, Mick got very drunk, without becoming more talkative. We had a few drinks at the Sturt Arcade with Max Harris, a great admirer of Mick's work. This had followed a long, unscheduled lunch. Max was dolefully saying (much to my surprise) that he was trying to write a novel about Sam Kerr and Paul Pfeiffer, who had both been killed in the RAAF, and Michael Quinn-Young and me, who had survived, to exorcise his guilt at never having been on death row in the war. Nothing more was ever heard of this novel.

At a party Ninette and I gave for Mick later that week, he wandered around with a brandy bottle, sighing with love for Annie, whom he had just met. "The most beautiful girl in Adelaide." "Hardly a girl," I said, "she has five children." Mick could not believe it. When Bel Davies left she said, "Isn't Mick sweet when he's drunk, he's like a spot of candle-grease without a wick in it." Of Kylie Tennant, she said, "Why does she act so philistine, as if she's a bricklayer with a pen in her hands." Earlier in the evening Bryn had approached Nan, Rohan Rivett's wife, who had on a gold lamé dress with angels' wings over her breasts. Bryn peered at them, close up, and said: "What is this supposed to be? I mean, is it a protection or an invitation?"

In 1956 I first met the painter Lawrence Daws, at a time when he was temporarily teaching at St Peter's College. We met at Elaine Wreford's house; Elaine was dark and sculptured and grave, and quite a talented artist herself, in the Sydney Charm School style. She and her husband Bob were art patrons, and they had several paintings by Lawrence, one of which, *Mining Town Blacks*, particularly impressed me with its far-out-back red colours, its strict perspectives, its lean figures. Lawrence was dark, slight but with strong features, a soft, deep, slow voice and a way of rolling his cigarette across his mouth. He was to become, and remains, one of my best friends, but in the strange way that friendships often begin, neither of us did anything much about it for several years. This was partly because he went to Melbourne in 1957 where he won the Italian Government/Flotto Lauro-Dante Alighieri Prize and disappeared to Rome and then London.

Lawrence had had a show at the Royal Society of Artists Gallery in Adelaide, which I had urged Mick Stow to see. As I had hoped, Mick greatly admired the paintings. Both men were intensely ambitious, working beyond the surface but not losing the surety of aspects of Australia which had as yet been so little painted or written about. Their minds were filled with new visions of human experience and nature, and they had both been exposed to the remote Australian bush, and worked in Papua-New Guinea. In words or in paint they achieved rich tonalities of the spirit, seized from the pale shimmer or the red glow of the Australian landscape.

Soon afterwards, on a visit to Melbourne, I met Andrew Fabinyi of F.W. Cheshire, who was to become one of Australia's great publishers and an inventive enthusiast for all aspects of writing in Australia. He would emerge, sleek, gently charming and aware, from his book-filled burrow in the basement of Cheshire's bookshop, and you immediately felt that here was someone who took you seriously, even if by that time you hadn't written a great deal. He was married to Elizabeth, a cousin of Vance Palmer's, so his European sophistication was merged with a far-ranging consciousness of Australian issues.

He was keen to publish my biography of William Light, which at last was near completion. I told him that Jack McDougall had already offered to publish it; in the end Jack agreed to take part of the Cheshire printing for publication in Britain under the Chapman & Hall imprint. It came out in 1960 and was handsomely received, in both Australia and Britain, rather to my surprise because Light was hardly known outside South Australia. Andrew was also to publish two volumes of my poetry, a book of poetry for children, and a book in the series called *Australia Since the Camera*.

I had dinner with Steve and Nita Murray-Smith at the Oriental — "at the Paris end of Collins Street" — and congratulated Steve on the great job he was making of *Overland*. He had wrested that magazine away from the hardline communists of the Realist Writers' Group after the Hungarian revolution had failed. Steve, large, imposing and genial, was far from the fat boy we had teased at Geelong. Born in the same year as me, he had put away his Toorak background to slog away with Nita for literature for Australian everyman and everywoman. Steve was usually imperturbable, but he lost his cool a little when Nita ordered a dozen oysters. "Do you *have* to have a dozen?" he asked, and then followed up with "Have you got some money in the car?"

On another occasion we were performing with Max Harris and others in some literary symposium in the lower Town Hall. Steve was majestically enraged when journalists Stuart Sayers and Keith Dunstan (also old school colleagues) alleged in an answer to a question, that they did not read Australian poetry. Dunstan then said he had read an Australian poem, but it was by an Englishman. Anyhow, offered Sayers, did any Australian poets make a living out of it? Under the guise of humour, they were in fact pandering to the worst philistine members of the audience.

It was quite a literary visit to Melbourne. I met and had a long talk with Judah Waten, by then not a friend of Steve's, as they had fallen out over the hijack, as Judah called it, of *Overland*. Judah, large with black jowls and friendly eyes, was quite obviously a most humane and gentle man, but he lapsed into doctrinaire bursts about the Soviet Union. He was like a priest who rams God down your neck in case his good nature should make you think he was not a true believer.

Dease turned up in a battered Delage drophead coupe; only Dease could own such a desirable car and allow it to become a near-wreck. He had, of all surprising things, become a successful teacher in one of the toughest state schools in Melbourne. Most of his money was gone, a process in which he had been enthusiastically helped by Kershaw. This was probably the best thing that could have happened to him.

In 1957, after thirteen years of marriage, Ninette became pregnant. We had been told by various experts that we would not be able to have children, the main difficulty being that I was allegedly sterile, as a result of the attack of mumps I had had all those years ago in the RAAF. But, as so often in human affairs, the experts were proved wrong. I also have always believed that my affair with Annie had rejuvenated my mumps-damaged sperm. Ninette's doctor decreed that she should rest, staying in bed for most of the pregnancy, which she did, with great stoicism.

The worst part of it, for both of us, was when the doctor made us move down to Adelaide to stay with the Trotts, so we could be close to the hospital. The days dragged frigidly by. Ninette had been ordered to take long walks; after lectures, I was pleased to accompany her as it enabled us to leave the house. Clarice told us not to walk past Wilderness girls' school; the horrible sight of Ninette would revolt the children. Chibs came to call, with her little daughter Charlotte. After they left Clarice said, "Poor Charlotte, the sight of Ninette will give her complexes about having children."

Life was as boring and predictable as the accursed grandfather clock on the stairs, which chimed relentlessly through the long nights. By day "the maid", as Clarice called her although she did not live in, vacuumed all the carpets four times a week. The only diversion was the news of a friend of Ninette's sister Helen, who had dyed her poodle pink to match her new baby. Finally I begged the doctor to allow us to return to Nonsuch, and we did.

A week after our return a Landrover came down the hill and expired right outside the house, the petrol tank empty. It contained Tass (Russell) Drysdale, Jock Marshall, and Tass's twenty-year-old son Tim. They were on their way home after the long trip around the north-west of Australia, about which they wrote in *Journey Among Men*, with illustrations from Tass's drawings.

It was a great reunion; they were full of hilarious stories about Kimberley characters, such the barmaid No-Pants Nancy at Broome. Jock had noticed that she had had a baby since they last saw her, and asked her if she had married. She assured him she didn't even know who the father was. "Listen, mate, if you was nicked by a circular saw, would you know which tooth had done it?" We were all in high spirits before falling into bed.

At 4 a.m. the phone rang. It was the police in Adelaide. Tim had stolen our Peugeot and had been arrested for drink-driving. Fortunately he had not injured anyone nor crashed the car. Tass was distraught; Tim had already been in trouble twice in Sydney for doing the same thing with friends' cars, and in the Northern Territory he had gone off in the Landrover when Tass and Jock were asleep and had been arrested for drink-driving.

Poor Tass. I had to go with him to the Court. Bob Fisher and Chris Legoe defended Tim who was sentenced to a sixty-pound fine and the loss of his licence.

On 13 November, my mother's birthday, Francis was born, the first Dutton grandson. Friends and relations were touchingly pleased, and I finally crept up the stairs past the Trotts' grandfather clock as it was striking 3 a.m. At breakfast the next morning the temperature was way below zero. Leonard did not approve of the way the announcement in the *Advertiser* of the birth had been worded. It seemed that "daughter of Dr and Mrs Leonard Trott" was too far down the column. "Oh, here it is," said Leonard, "I see we got a mention. What a pity." I asked Clarice whether she had seen Ninette. "Yes. I was shocked at her appearance." "And the baby?" "Oh yes, a fine baby." She drank some more tea, as if it were neat prussic acid and her favourite brew, then continued, "His ears are too big, like his father's, and his mouth is open, which means he has a bad nose like his grandmother Dutton."

Francis was followed in 1961 by Teresa Rose, always called Tisi, and in 1963 by Sam. I could write hundreds of pages about the joys and anxieties of life with those three children; but however much they have enriched my life, I believe their stories are their own. And all parents have their own wonderful variations of the same experiences we shared with our children. I think Vaughan and Wordsworth were right about the magic of childhood, and most of all, perhaps, William Blake who wrote songs of experience as well as of innocence.

In these years I often used to see Rohan Rivett, who was Editor of the *News*. Rohan had been a prisoner of the Japanese in the Second World War, and was the author of a celebrated book about the experience, *Behind Bamboo*. At this time the *News* was the only newspaper owned by Rupert Murdoch, then in his mid-twenties. Rohan was a big, handsome man with blond hair, a high forehead and piercing blue eyes. He was a journalist of great experience and ability, and really much too good for the Adelaide *News*. Rohan came from one of the most distinguished families in Australia. His grandfather, Albert, was a clergyman, pacifist and socialist, who died in the Sydney Domain immediately after addressing a crowd of five thousand people on the Lyons Government's ban on the entry into Australia of Egon Kisch. His father, Sir David Rivett, was the first chief executive officer of the Council for Scientific and Industrial Research, one of the most influential posts in Australia. He had married Alfred Deakin's daughter.

Rohan asked me to dinner with Rupert and Malcolm Muggeridge. It was a sparkling evening which had long-term consequences for me. In the course of dinner Malcolm asked me if I was a monarchist or a republican. I had never really thought about the issue, while being no enthusiast for the monarchy, unlike my mother, who had once told me to take back the new stamps I had bought her at the Post Office. They had some Christmas picture on them. "Take them back," she said, "and tell the Postmaster to give me some proper stamps with the King's head on them."

So I confessed my feebleness to Malcolm, who roundly castigated me for kowtowing to a foreign monarch who did not live in Australia. Rohan and Rupert were already republicans. Afterwards, the more I thought about it, the more I realised how inappropriate it was for Australia to have a foreigner as head of state.

Of course the Adelaide Establishment was solidly monarchist and even more British than Menzies. It is hard now to realise just how narrow, inturned, smug and racist were those running South Australia. People like the Chief Justice, Sir Mellis Napier, and the Crown Prosecutor, Roderick Chamberlain, were reactionary bigots of the worst type. The Premier, Sir Thomas Playford, and Sir Lloyd Dumas of Adelaide's only morning paper, the *Advertiser*, were much more intelligent, but still chronically limited in their views. None of them was interested in Aboriginal people. Although Playford was never a member of the Adelaide Club, the power-brokering of South Australia was conducted behind its stone walls. It is very much to the young Don Dunstan's credit that after he became Premier the Adelaide Establishment's influence was never the same again. Moreover, his enthusiasm for the rights of Australia's indigenous people led to his state's pioneering Land Rights legislation. The old buzzards in the Club shook their heads and said it was all because he had a touch of the tar-brush; he was born in Fiji, you know ...

In 1958 Adelaide was convulsed by the trial of an Aboriginal, Rupert Max Stuart, for the murder of a white child at Ceduna in the far west of South Australia. The trial was a travesty of justice. Stuart was sentenced to death; appeals and even a Royal Commission failed to clear his name. Eventually the death sentence was commuted to life imprisonment. Two books and an ABC TV programme have been based on the infamies of the Stuart case.

Rohan Rivett had been instrumental in procuring further evidence that provided an alibi for Stuart. It was ignored. Rohan's condemnation of Napier in the *News* led to his being brought to court by Napier on a charge of criminal libel. This was extremely serious for Rohan, as criminal libel carries a jail sentence.

A daily comedy was enacted in the Adelaide Club. Sir Lloyd Dumas of the *Advertiser* would assemble his forces at one large, round table in the Club's dining room, and Rupert Murdoch's forces would glare from a rival table, his Chairman being another distinguished Adelaide knight.

Rohan had dinner with me the night before the verdict was to be announced. He was pale and shaking, he could hardly get his fork into his mouth, so convinced was he that he would be spending the next night in jail. But John Bray's brilliant defence won the day, and the vengeful old Napier was routed.

Rupert knew and approved of his Editor's idealism, but their relations were strained beyond endurance when Aneurin Bevan, one of Rohan's heroes, died on the same day as the news broke about a kidnapping in Sydney which had all Australia agog. Rohan's front page screamed in huge type "Nye Is Dead", and the kidnapping was relegated to page two. Most Australians, even those who had heard of Bevan, would not have known that he was called Nye.

Rupert sacked Rohan, but with a golden handshake; Rohan would never say a word about his dismissal.

I have already said that Lloyd Dumas, despite his backing of Napier, deserves credit for his encouragement of *Australian Letters*. His greatest contribution to Adelaide was to take up the cause of John Bishop's idea of an Adelaide Festival of Arts, and give it the support of the *Advertiser*, Adelaide's only morning daily paper. Bishop was a most remarkable man, easy to laugh at, with his prancing manner, his halo of white hair and his carefully modulated, "distinguished" voice. He was Professor of Music at Adelaide University.

I was appointed in 1959 to the Literature Committee to set up the first Festival, which was due to take place in 1960. Bishop suggested to me that since my mother was a very old friend of the Premier, Sir Thomas Playford, I should be one of a delegation to ask Tom, as he was universally known, for Government support for the Festival. Tom listened to us patiently, and heard the predictions of the advantages to South Australia that would accrue from the Festival. He then said, with the authority of one with a Master's Degree from the University of Hard Knocks, that he would put no obstacles in our way and he wished us well, but we could go out and find the money ourselves.

Well, Lloyd Dumas, Bill Hayward and others did just that. Later premiers, such as Steele Hall and Don Dunstan, had very different ideas about the relation between the South Australian Government and the Festival. Tom Playford, the longest-reigning premier in the history of the British Commonwealth, did many good things for South Australia. Personally always most agreeable, he was a model of political cunning and incorruptibility. He grew excellent cherries on his farm in the Adelaide Hills, and cultivated prize orchids. The growth of the arts in Australia was of no interest to him at all. If people wanted them, then they could have them, but it was all a waste of time to him. In any case, orchids and roses were far more beautiful than Australian wildflowers. His attitudes were, alas, typical of his time.

With the exception of Professor Bishop, the Governors of the Adelaide Festival were strictly businessmen. Some, like Bill Hayward, knew quite a bit about some or one of the arts; most of them were the sort of people who have antiques in their homes and consider themselves cultured. Bishop had a hard time getting them to think beyond the Adelaide plains. I attended some of the Governors' meetings as a representative of the Literature Committee; Colin Ballantyne did the same for the Drama Committee. Sometimes it was desperately difficult to keep a straight face, as when "Hack" Hayward, Bill's brother, declared that the knock-out climax of the first Festival would have to be the march down North Terrace of the 10th Battalion, AIF brass band.

The Administrator of the Festival was a retired Major-General called Hopkins, an amiable old chap but with no knowledge of the ways of the arts or of artists.

Robert Helpmann wanted to visit his homeland from Covent Garden, and direct a new Australian ballet he had created. General Hopkins addressed the Governors. "I've heard a shocking rumour. They say this fellow Helpmann is a homosexual." "Good Heavens," Colin Ballantyne interrupted in tones of the utmost sincerity. "Not possibly. I've never heard a word of it." "Well that's all right then." General Hopkins looked much relieved. He went on with other business. Turning to Colin, he said, "I still haven't had an answer from this fellow Eugene O'Neill". "No, General, he's dead." "Oh. But I've read his play. It's got a murder in it." "Yes, General", Colin soothed him. "Murders are all right on the stage, it's rapes that you are thinking of." "Yes, of course, rapes."

General Hopkins and the Board of Governors refused to allow the official staging of the première of Alan Seymour's *The One Day of the Year*, because its treatment of Anzac Day would give offence to the Returned Servicemen's League. The Adelaide Theatre Group went on to stage the play anyhow, without official sanction or support, launching it on its career as one of the best and most successful of Australian plays.

The Literature Committee, chosen by the Governors, consisted of General Hopkins, Professor Bishop, two librarians, a representative from the Workers' Educational Association, Warren Bonython (a businessman brother of Kym), Ian Mudie and myself. At the first meeting I suggested that, as Robert Speaight was coming out to recreate his original role as Beckett in *Murder in the Cathedral*, the Festival should ask T.S. Eliot to be a guest. "Good God," Hopkins exploded, "but Eliot's that chappie who writes that modern verse that nobody can understand. What do we want him for? Dorothy Sayers wrote *Murder in the Cathedral*. I think it would be much more suitable to ask her."

On a visit to Sydney I thought how distant, in more than miles, our cities were from each other. Sydney was the centre of professional literary life. We had dinner with Doug and Margaret Stewart, in their house which was full of their idol Norman Lindsay's paintings, some of them of appalling vulgarity. Doug was one of those little, dark Scots — dry, sceptical but enthusiastic, a very characteristic mixture; he reminded me of different animals and birds, with his anteater's nose and his heron's stoop. Margaret had been one of Norman's models, and had obviously been beautiful, and still could be, but didn't worry much about her appearance any more. As Margaret Coen, she was quite a talented watercolour painter, but I found it hard to forgive her for being a leading player behind the court case involving William Dobell's Archibald Prize portrait of Joshua Smith.

The next night there was a party at Beatrice Davis's house. Beatrice, bright-eyed, with an odd mixture of nervousness and confidence, was a very handsome woman of great style and elegance; there was nothing bourgeois about her. She did not force her intelligence upon you, but quietly brought out a pungent remark about an author or a merciless assessment of a book. She was already famous as Angus & Robertson's senior editor, having tamed wild men such as Xavier Herbert, but she would never, and never did, talk about her relations with her authors, which at that time included most Australian writers, so pre-eminent was Angus & Robertson. She also liked a drink. Kylie Tennant used to call her the bottleneck of Australian Literature.

Dal Stivens was there, with his wife Winifred, both of them affecting a very surprising English accent and manner. "Bloody pomposity," Doug whispered in my ear. D'Arcy Niland had just had a triumph with the film of his novel *The Shiralee*, but he was looking uncomfortable in his dark-blue suit, and stayed quietly in the corner.

The one I was most pleased to meet was Ken Slessor, plump, neat, clubbable, white and pink, rosy-cheeked with a bow tie, his oiled hair brushed down tight above his Germanic face. His blunt manner of speech reminded me of Roy Campbell, except that he did not say "Man". Doug and Ken and I talked of Roy; we all loved his poems, the shape of them, the passion, the imagery. At the end of the evening I drove Ken back to his house in Billyard Avenue in Elizabeth Bay, while he talked about his cat. He invited me in for a nightcap; the interior of the house looked like the lounge of an English country inn. But outside the windows the lights and little swells of the Harbour were shining, and the rocking buoys were flashing red and green.

The Commonwealth Literary Fund Advisory Committee had a meeting in Adelaide in 1958. Doug, Ken, Max and I had a good dinner and then we went grimly along to a meeting of the Fellowship of Australian Writers. Ken in a flat voice read a desperately boring lecture on anthologies which he had obviously written many years before. Then there was iced claret cup. Doug murmured to me, "FAWs exist for the Flexie Hudsons of the world."

The next day I drove Ken and Doug up to Anlaby for lunch. On the way up, Doug was saying how good it would be to see the landscape of the Barossa, and the old buildings at Anlaby. Ken made an effort to agree. But when he saw the library his spirits soared. We had lunch, and then retired to the library for port and cigars. After a while I offered to take them for a drive around the station. "If you don't mind, Geoff," said Ken, "I've seen the memoirs of my old friend William Hickey over there, and I'll join him for another glass of port." Doug and I returned an hour later, our cheeks tingling from the icy gale; it was blowing so hard that six black ducks could scarcely make it into the wind as they took off from the Fox's Pool on the River Light. Ken's cheeks were rosy from the port.

After his return to Elizabeth Bay Ken wrote to me: "I was most interested in the Barossa landscape — but I was nothing less than enraptured by the glorious library at Anlaby."

* * *

When my brother John was in the Western Desert with the 9th Division, AIF during the war, he had an idea, which he discussed with his friend Jimmy Gosse, in the way soldiers like to talk about what they will do when the war is over. John proposed to overhaul the old Talbot at Anlaby, the car in which my father had made the first overland crossing of Australia in 1908, and take her across again on her fiftieth birthday.

He kept his word, and for many months the old Talbot was in Alby Fahlbush's garage in Kapunda, being completely stripped down and rebuilt for the journey. John generously asked me to come too; the idea was that our wives, in my Peugeot station wagon, would come along with the Talbot, bringing the food and the camping gear. John, Jimmy and I would take it in turns to drive the Talbot; as there was only room for two in the Talbot, we would also take turns for one to ride in the Peugeot. It was not as male-chauvinist as it sounds; the Talbot needed a strong man to manage the steering, gears and clutch.

The car was ready on time, but the arrival of our son Francis caused the expedition to be put off for a year. When we finally set out, we allowed a fortnight for the Talbot to complete the two thousand miles from Adelaide to Darwin. She made it in time, but only just. The worst hazard for most of the journey was the hospitality of the bush people, who had no idea at all of time, or any concern for the dangers of driving when full of alcohol. Some of them came from hundreds of miles away to stand by the roadside and cheer and offer a couple of cases of beer. We did manage to keep going, but when we were just one day out of Darwin, in the only hilly section of the whole trip, the Talbot lost power, and could not make it up one of the hills. A valve spring had broken. It was no trouble to verify this, as in the Talbot the push-rods bounced up and down outside the engine block, in full view. Jimmy and I left John to extract the broken spring, and drove fifty miles into Pine Creek. It was Saturday night and the bar was full and so were the customers. The publican finally managed to silence the mob, and I called out, "Has anyone got a valve spring for a 1908 Talbot?" This request produced the expected pandemonium, but a few seconds later a tough character in khaki shorts and a blue athletic singlet came up and introduced himself as the local foreman of the Public Works Department. He invited us to come and have a look through a big box of bits and pieces at his place.

We poked around, using a couple of torches,and found the box. "Watch out for pythons when you lift the lid," he warned. We began to hunt through the assortment in the box. Suddenly Jimmy turned to me. "What do you reckon, Geoff?" He held up a spring that looked exactly the same size and strength as the broken valve spring. "Good spring, that one," said the PWD man, "it's out of an old pram." Four hours later, about 2 a.m., the spring was installed and the Talbot running like new.

We made Darwin on time, to drive behind a posse of outriders through crowded streets and be given a civic reception by no less than three mayors, all fat and perspiring. There had been a disputed election, so we were welcomed by the outgoing mayor and both the hopefully incoming ones. It was a very Northern Territory occasion.

A few weeks later, I was due to give a lecture in Melbourne, and Andrew Fabinyi and Elizabeth asked Ninette and me to dinner with Maria and Pat Donovan; Maria, under her own name of Koszlik, was writing cookery books for Andrew. Pat, now Professor of Commercial Law at Melbourne University, was as nice, as floppy and scruffy as he had always been, but it was obvious that Maria was going to smarten up the Queensland lad. In time she certainly succeeded. The next time I saw Pat and Maria was in the rigid splendours of Harry Seidler's Australian Embassy in Paris, where Pat, in dark suit and waistcoat, was Australian Ambassador to the OECD.

While in Melbourne we were heading one day for Clifton Pugh's home, Dunmoochin (that dreadful pun), in the bush near Cottles Bridge, just outside Melbourne. Clif had asked me if he could paint my portrait for the Archibald Prize. Clif's house was a crazy castle, which he had built himself, and was constantly rebuilding. At that time he was still living with the incomparable Marlene, of whom he painted some of his best portraits.

Clif loved endless philosophical discussions, in which, as Lawrence Daws described it, Clif was always "stumbling towards a conclusion". He seldom actually reached one, but that would have spoiled his fun. That night he had invited for dinner David Armstrong, a professional philosopher, Frank Dalby Davison, the author of *Man-shy*, with his wife Marie, and Noel Macainsh, a poet. A discussion raged about the D.H. Lawrence version of the mediocrity of Australians (Armstrong), the good-bloke syndrome (Davison) and the subjection of Australian women (Marlene, who said she was an outcast because she didn't like housework). These subjects are perennial, but Australian attitudes to them are much less rigid now.

Next morning in the studio, Clif, in a few minutes, roughed out a masterly portrait of me, using Dulux and big brushes. Then he decided it was not right. While he worked, he continued an argument he had had with me in Adelaide. Academics cannot be writers, and I had become an academic. "I know you don't look like an academic," said Clif, "but I'm going to alter you to suit my painting." He spent two days altering me, then after I had left, dressed me in a dark suit with a pale sweater, two items which I would never wear together, which went with the droopy, intellectual look he gave me. The painting did not win the Archibald, but was bought by the Art Gallery of New South Wales, which thankfully never seems to hang it.

In Melbourne we visited Deasey, who had set up house in Melbourne with a French wife, Giselle; she broadcast for Radio Australia. The visit was rather depressing. An improbable bourgeois respectability seemed to have settled on the wild Irishman. But a flash of the old Dease returned when he started to talk about a new comedian who was also a mad Dada artist, by name of Barry Humphries. Dease had a record, which he played, called "Wild Life in Suburbia". Not only was it one of the funniest things I had ever heard in Australia, but it was entirely new and yet unmistakeably old; this was Australia, but a region now visited for the first time by a comic genius. Scarcely anybody had heard of Humphries; I asked Dease, who had met him on several occasions, to write a profile of him for *Australian Letters*. Clif Pugh had done a dank, rather stricken portrait of Barry which would go perfectly with the profile. Dease's article appeared in the next issue of the magazine; it was one of the first public tributes to Humphries. Clif's brilliant portrait showing Barry in his contemporary persona of Transylvania sex-fiend, was later lost; the finding of it, many years later on a pile of junk in London, is one of Barry's best stories, a real spook-story.

When the new term started, I was back at the grind in the English Department in Adelaide. Derry's successor, Colin Horne, had settled into the job and was busy abolishing institutions such as the morning coffee sessions where students mingled with staff. Colin and his wife were preparing to go camping. They asked my advice, saying they couldn't go anywhere too far away from a hot shower. I suggested the Coorong. "What do we do for water there? Oh, would we have to take some with us? What will we do after dark?" I refrained from suggesting anything. "Well, we've got a bicycle torch, I suppose we could read by that."

The remoteness of many academics from ordinary life never ceased to amaze me in my years at universities. With someone like Jack Bennett it was endearing, genuine eccentricity, although it was sad to see his innocence being bossed by his Schools Inspector wife. With others, life was supposed to adapt itself to their needs. One day when I was having lunch with the Jeffares, another Professor came in — Bert, a British bachelor in his thirties whose father was a very distinguished scholar in Scotland. He was fuming with indignation, because he had taken a girl to Brighton and she had refused to go in swimming with him. "Perhaps it was the wrong time of the month?" suggested Jeanne. "What do you mean?" asked Bert suspiciously. So Jeanne explained the monthly facts of female life to him. "Well, all I can tell you," Bert spluttered, "is that nothing like that ever happened to my mother."

In 1959 Derry wrote to me from Leeds to say that he was able to offer me a visiting lectureship for three months as a Commonwealth Fellow, to give a course of lectures on Australian Literature. There was enough money to make it practicable. Adelaide University was prepared to give me leave, so in January 1960 Ninette, Francis and I flew to London in a Comet, my first experience of a jet.

I have never been so depressed by a city as I was when we drove into black Leeds, with its back-to-back slums. I had never seen such barbarous housing before. The terrace houses just backed onto each other, and there was a communal lavatory and wash-troughs in the street. Not a tree, a shrub, a flower, and everything covered in black grime. But, to my astonishment, Yorkshire people turned out to be much more agreeable and less snobbish than any of the southern English I had met in my years in Oxford and London; and as soon as you got out of the cities, the countryside was the most beautiful I had seen in Britain. The dales were quite unspoiled in 1960, and real farmers lived in the farmhouses instead of stockbrokers.

On a visit to London I found that there was general dismay when I said I was teaching at Leeds. "Leeds! But, my God, that's in the North. Civilization stops on the north side of Oxford Street." Another voice chimes in: "My father always used to say that the train takes a lot longer from London to Leeds than from Leeds to London — it still does." We had dinner with Austen Kark, now a senior BBC executive, who had remarried, to a writer, Nina Bawden; she was definitely London and not Yorkshire, formidably English and on her guard with colonials. There was a white tablecloth and heavy silver. "I've got very bourgeois," said Austen. It was true, but he was still able to laugh at himself. He had also developed heavy jowls and a paunch, but he explained that the paunch was due to a truss for his slipped disc.

We went to Oxford and had lunch with Tom Boase at Magdalen. In the thick, warm air inside the walls of the President's garden he spoke about his glass eye, which was the result of being hit by shrapnel in World War I. He said English people could not bear him to talk about it. I sometimes think he felt more at home with his many Australian friends than with a lot of his own people. He had come to stay at Anlaby about a year before our visit while he was on an official tour of Australia, from which he had managed to detach himself to see something of the country. My mother, who always referred to Tom as "The President", asked me what were the things he liked best to eat. "He likes very simple things," I answered. "He told me once that his favourite meal was mince on toast." My mother was appalled. "No guest of mine is going to be given mince on toast. I've ordered a sirloin of beef. Make sure when you carve that you give The President the undercut."

Derry had found us a house in Leeds, and Jeanne an old Yorkshire nanny for Francis. From the distance of 1993 I cannot see why we needed one, but I meekly went along with it. Jeanne's Scottish mother, Dot, described the nanny as looking like Harpo Marx.

My course was the first ever given in Britain on Australian Literature; Derry had done wonders in assembling some books for the students to read. They were a very rewarding group, all British except for a rather eccentric but very amiable Indian. Several of them went on to distinguished academic careers; one of them, Norman Talbot, who teaches at Newcastle University in New South Wales, is a poet with a good reputation. I enjoyed my time with them.

Ever since I had last seen him, I had been keeping up a correspondence with Richard Aldington. He was one of the last great letter writers, making jovial comments on every imaginable subject, with pen portraits of people he had known or just met, and talk of food and wine. Thanks to Alister Kershaw, who with his second wife Sheila had bought a house near Sancerre for Richard to move into, and various friends (including myself) who had paid his debts, Richard had a new lease of life. Publishers had even accepted some of his new books. Now he wrote to say we should pop over to France and go for a little tour in his Simca, which was roomier than my Renault. He suggested that we start by visiting H.D. and Bryher in Zürich, then call on Lawrence Durrell near Nîmes, turning back to Sury-en-Vaux.

As soon as there was a break at Leeds, we set off, Richard in the back seat commenting on everything we passed, while I drove. Going across a stone bridge: "We're now entering another Département, the Allier. How curious that there are many more vipers in the Allier than in any other district of France." We stopped for a beer. Richard produced a card of a miniature of the Queen of Sheba in the Hermitage Museum. He told us negotiations were under way for the Soviet Writers' Union to ask him to Moscow and Leningrad for his seventieth birthday; he was one of the largest selling foreign authors in Russia, but never received any royalties because the Russians had at that stage not signed the international copyright agreement. Handing over his postcard he said, "Solomon was a cad. He put a sheet of glass across a stream and hid behind a bush. Sheba, thinking she was going to get wet wading the stream, pulled up her dress and Solomon saw that she had hairy legs."

Richard had the *Michelin Guide* with him, and decided where we would eat. He always chose well, and we had wonderful wines and food, but I found it difficult to keep up with two enormous meals a day. We stopped in Colmar for the best *choucroute garnie* I have ever eaten, and to see the ferociously wonderful altarpiece by Grünewald. Richard disagreed with Aldous Huxley's claim for Piero della Francesca, and gave the title of greatest painting in the world to the Grünewald. It was an odd choice for an atheist; but Aldous, at that stage, was also an atheist.

We arrived in Zürich, and Richard kept giving me confusing directions to the private hotel where H.D. and Bryher were staying. He was obviously very nervous, for he and H.D. had not met for many years. Their last times together had been very difficult. When Richard was in the trenches on the Western Front, she had had an affair with the musicologist Cecil Gray.

Richard, returning on leave, found that she was pregnant, and not by him. She had a daughter, whom Richard accepted as his own, but the tensions grew too sharp and they parted.

Richard suddenly said, "Oh let's go back to France." A moment later he said, "Shit, we just passed the hotel."

We were shown in, and waited in the lobby for H.D. She appeared at the top of the stairs, tall and majestic, but uninhibitedly screeching "Welcome!" and waving her arms and the sticks that supported her when she walked. She and Richard embraced, both in tears. Behind all this drama was little Bryher, neat and tidy and anonymous in a tweed suit. In contrast, H.D.'s long dress was stylish, and she had taken great care in making up her face.

There was a fuss about champagne, of which there were half a dozen tiny bottles; H.D. had already opened one and was worried because it had not gone pop. Richard explained the difference between a seal, which these had, and a cork. Bryher refused the champagne and drank mineral water. She said she had been put off champagne for life as a child, when on a trip up the Nile with her father the drinking water had run out. Her father, unperturbed, had given orders that champagne should replace water, even for tooth-cleaning.

H.D. settled down and talked acutely with me about Patrick White; she was a great admirer of his work. She was a fascinating mixture of great dignity and gaiety, dragging on a cigarette as she talked. She urged Richard to come and live in Zürich; I could see him backing away from that one.

We returned to France, and drove down to the south along minor roads, which are one of the joys of France. Richard was so exhausted by the visit to H.D. that he slept most of the first day, and we did not have our usual accounts of the various regions. After visiting some old haunts we stayed at Nîmes, and went to have dinner with Lawrence and Claudia Durrell. It was a pleasant old farmhouse, bulging with books; I noticed a complete set of the old Mermaid edition of the Elizabethan dramatists, and rows of Victorian novels. Durrell was a little man with a neat head, sparky with humour and word-play. It was obvious that he venerated Richard. He talked about the characters of the *Alexandria Quartet*, Pursewarden and Scobie, as if they were friends of the family. He fished out a guitar and sang some songs he had written for Scobie, the sort of music-hall ditties the old reprobate would have enjoyed. He had written them out in a little book, which he had illustrated himself, with great talent. Durrell was passionate about what he called the tremendous exfoliation of English-language literature outside Britain, especially in America, and now it was happening in Australia. Like H.D., he admired Patrick White; "Such great conceptions in all the novels. It's nothing to do with their length, but they are big books."

Leeds was a bit grim after all this, especially the food. Derry was interested in Durrell's idea of the exfoliation of literature in English, as it was exactly that which he was aiming to encourage in inviting Commonwealth writers to Leeds. Wole Soyinka was one of these writers, a most genial companion and a man of wide reading. Wole was best known then as a poet. I was later able to have him invited to Writers' Week at the Adelaide Festival. These contacts, in many cases well before the writers became famous, were one of the most valuable achievements of Writers' Week.

Derry was also editing a series of small books, called "Writers and Critics", for publishers in Britain and the USA, and he asked me to write one, giving me the choice of Walt Whitman or Scott Fitzgerald. Rather to his surprise, I chose Whitman. He warned me that Whitman was very unfashionable. It was 1960, and amazingly enough what he said was true. Whitman was anathema to the tightly buttoned English poets of The Movement, as also to the academics of the time who were laying down the law, splitting American writers into two camps, something like classics and cowboys. They seemed unaware of the fact that Henry James and Edith Wharton used to read Whitman to each other in the evening. So in my spare time I was reading Whitman, with ever-increasing awe and love.

In some ways, the best thing about Leeds was meeting Ruth. Annie would have approved of her directness. I had the temerity to say to her that she was the first English girl (the word that was still used in those days) that I had found attractive. "That's because we're both foreigners," she answered. "I'm Welsh." She was more intellectual than Annie, but that was just part of her, not to be emphasized. She was also without emotional ploys or sexual guile.

Flying back to Australia and rereading Whitman I discovered that Walt had described Ruth:

> The continual changes of the flux of the mouth,
>   and around the eyes,
> The skin, the sunburnt shade ...

In Leeds poems flowed out of me, and when I returned to Australia, I sent some to Doug Stewart. He accepted them for the *Bulletin*, but said some of the images were so sexual that he did not know whether he would be able to get away with it. This had not occurred to me when I was writing the poems, since most of them were "landscape" poems, and Ruth was firmly in the background, I thought.

Nineteen

Back in Adelaide, I stumbled on, looking for direction, pursuing several affairs, playing otherwise at being the Solid Citizen.

When I was in Leeds, one of the most dynamic members of staff had been a Jamaican, Fernando Henriques, Professor of Anthropology. He was regarded with suspicion by his more dreary colleagues, because he had written a bestseller, a history of prostitution. We were chatting away affably over a drink one day, when he abruptly said, "Why did you send us that bastard Eyre?" I vaguely knew that the Australian explorer, Edward John Eyre, had later been Governor of Jamaica. "But he's one of our more authentic heroes," I protested, "and not only for his explorations, but for his exemplary treatment and support of the Aborigines." "He was a right shit with my people." Fernando was not going to give up.

This crux of hero and murderer had sounded promising for a new biography, something I had been casting around for, but without success so far. So from Leeds I went down to the London Library, and studied everything I could find about Edward John Eyre. I soon realized that the opportunity for a really thorough treatment of Eyre's controversial life was there, wide open. So now I began the long task of writing another Australian biography.

After being blamed for putting down a minor uprising in Jamaica with great brutality, Eyre had been the cause of an intellectual civil war in England, with Carlyle, Tennyson, Ruskin, Charles Kingsley and others on his side, and the Jamaica Committee, consisting of John Stuart Mill, T.H. Huxley, Herbert Spencer, T.H. Hughes and others, against him. Private proceedings were brought three times against him for murder, but he was acquitted each time. He retired to Devon and lived out the rest of his long life in silence.

Shortly after my return to Australia Lloyd O'Neil, a young independent publisher, asked me if I would like to edit for his Lansdowne Press a series of booklets on Australian writers and their work. Lloyd, tall, fair, with a high domed forehead and a handshake that would have done justice to a wharfie, had done well with what was called "Australiana", in other words books about our environment and our traditions, themes that publishers had hardly touched in the 1950s. It was very courageous of him now to launch into a strictly literary field, and he had no grant or other money behind him. The only stipulation Lloyd made was that I should write the booklet on Patrick White myself; everything else he left to me. I was determined that the series should not be imprisoned in any literary dogma, and a variety of excellent people, from James McAuley to Max Harris, agreed to write on the various authors.

I had first corresponded with White in 1957, when I asked him to write the "Prodigal Son" article for *Australian Letters*. In agreeing, he had written, "I must warn you in advance that I have never written an article in my life", and he added "I enjoyed your paper, particularly the articles by foreigners, and hope you will continue to call them in to ease the parish constipation". So much of Patrick was already in that first note: his modesty, his willingness to take a chance, his scorn for the parochial, and his interest in the bodily functions.

Over the next twenty-five years, until our final falling-out, Patrick wrote me over seven hundred pages of letters. I kept his, although he often asked me to burn them; he destroyed all mine, as those of his other correspondents, who of course also kept his wonderful letters. So only his voice remains. When we were friends I sent him a copy of Francis Steegmuller's translation of Flaubert's letters. He said it meant an enormous amount to him. He seemed unaware of the contradiction, that people must have kept Flaubert's letters, and indeed on Patrick's shelves were a number of volumes of letters.

We seemed to be friends well before we met. I turned out to be one of only six Australians who admired *The Aunt's Story*. He had met Ursula Hayward once or twice with William Dobell and liked her very much. He even thought (erroneously) that we might be related, through some New South Wales Duttons. Our only genuine link seemed to be that our great-grandfathers had arrived in Australia in the same year, 1826, to begin lives on the land breeding sheep, a life that we had both escaped.

He invited me out to Castle Hill, where he and Manoly Lascaris were living on a little farm, Dogwoods, but they went overseas before I was in Sydney again. He wrote from Greece, and from London, where he hoped the Royal Court might stage his play, *The Ham Funeral*.

After his return he wrote to say he had bought and enjoyed my *Antipodes in Shoes*, and would like to use a stanza or two from my poem "The Lament of the Bulldozers" on the title page of a new novel. This seems never to have been written. In the same letter he asked if I could help find employment for a Greek couple from Alexandria with the formidable names of Panayota and Socrates Joachimidis. They were fifty-eight and sixty-eight, but "very vigorous". Panayota had worked for an aunt of Manoly's, and was apparently an excellent cook. Some pungent comments followed: "They are the type of Greek of whom there must be very few in Australia — proud and correct — not the kind of upstart Dodecanesian peasant who has done well in a milk-bar, and absorbed all the worst that our 'culture' has to offer".

I had been trying for a long time to persuade my mother to take on some help at Anlaby. She would eat alone in the vast kitchen, the two tables gradually being covered with books and magazines and newspapers until she had finally exiled herself to one corner of a table, surrounded by piles of print, like a desperate soldier in a foxhole. She always refused, saying a cook would be more trouble than she was worth. It was hard to argue with her on this, since she had had two bad experiences. The first was with an ex-London policeman and his wife, whom I interviewed in London for her in 1955. I thought them a bit stiff, but reliable. They turned out to be useless. The wife was an atrocious cook, and the husband, supposed to be working in the garden, used to drive my mother mad by coming up behind her when she was on her knees digging, and saying, in the voice of a London Bobby addressing an old lady at an intersection, "Can I help you, Madam?"

They were followed by a Dutch family. On the day of their arrival, my mother cooked a large meal for them, but they ignored it and disappeared into their sitting room. After a while Fritz, the husband, emerged and said, "My vife, she go flop." She remained flop for several days, while my mother cooked, and then emerged to live a very delicate life, while Fritz pulled up flowers instead of weeds.

But Greeks, I thought, Greeks will be different — in her mind compatriots (actually they were from the island of Imbros) of KG (who of course was not from Greece at all), and descendants of Pericles and Sophocles. What could be more promising than the husband's name, Socrates? I thought it well worth a try. My mother was captivated by the idea.

These two tiny little creatures arrived, and were an immediate success, especially Panayota. My mother had great trouble in pronouncing her name, so Panayota suggested she call her Mary, as *panayota*, meaning "sacrosanct", is one of the epithets applied to the Virgin. Mary had almost no English, and my mother no Greek, so they got along famously, either shouting at each other or smiling, or getting by on my mother's few words of Italian, in which Mary was fluent, or French. Mary was indeed a wonderful cook; Socrates did not do too much damage to the garden. He used to hide behind the door in their sitting room to have a smoke, but as the sitting room was the first room along the corridor from the kitchen, the reek of his pipe used to betray him. But my mother did not roar at him. Mary did. "Socr*a*tes", she would shriek, with a long "a", and he would step out into the garden with guilty speed.

I had sent Patrick (we still had not met) a copy of *Founder of a City*, and he admitted he was appalled at the thought of reading a book "on such a subject". But he found he enjoyed it: he had had no idea that Australian history contained such people. He wrote a letter full of ideas for making a novel, play or film from the women who followed Wellington's army in the Peninsular War, or a play from the mix of personalities involved in the founding of Adelaide. However, he added characteristically, "Have you anything of the theatre in you, or aren't you sufficiently dishonest?"

Patrick was a good friend for a writer, always full of suggestions for following up ideas or books, offering to introduce me to literary people in London, and himself the model of a true professional, a writer of integrity. He was one who saw how little time a writer really has, because a writer needs so much time, that society, other writers and writers' organizations must be kept at arm's length.

At times I might well have taken more heed of his advice and example, but so much needed to be done. One piece of Patrick's advice I did eventually take was to get myself a literary agent. Patrick suggested the excellent Tim Curnow of Curtis Brown. Now, twenty years after signing on with Tim, I regard him as not only an efficient and knowledgeable literary agent, but as one of my old friends. This is more remarkable than it sounds, as I've given Tim a lot of problems to deal with over those years, some of them personal rather than professional. During these crises, Tim remained reliably unflappable, unendingly helpful.

Patrick was not a recluse; he had a wide circle of friends. Later, when he and Manoly moved to Centennial Park in Sydney, he loved giving dinner parties, which were preceded by a sweating, pale figure darting around the tiny kitchen of Martin Road, having another swig from the whisky bottle. Then he would emerge to the guests. Nor did he flinch from large parties; one New Year's Eve he had twenty to dinner. But all those people mattered to him, while too frequently Ninette and I seemed to spend time with people I was not really interested in at all.

I wrote to Patrick that Lloyd O'Neil wanted me to write on him and his work, and asked if he would cooperate. He replied that he was pleased I was taking him on. "One could have fared badly. I wonder, for instance, who will get the Arch-Bitch Leonie Kramer … As poetic justice I hope you will bring Kramer and Hope together; it should be a devilish partnership." He invited me to stay for a few days at Dogwoods, assured me that he was not a bad cook, and said that all he would ask of me was to make my own bed.

It was luck that I had caught him on a lay-off period before his revision of *Riders in the Chariot*. When I finally met him, on 24 August 1960, he had a gentler and more humorous face than I had expected, under a jaunty beret. Soft-voiced Manoly had met me at the airport and driven me up to Dogwoods. Now, peering through his glasses more from habit than from not knowing the way, Manoly took me to my room, and then we had an excellent salad for lunch and talked about Greece, monarchists and republicans, the goats and schnauzer dogs they bred, the nightly chore of deticking the bitches, the eccentricities of his family, an uncle who never spoke to his mother again after she wore a sleeveless dress. His father never read a book. His mother did. Patrick had just read *Lolita, Dr Zhivago,* the novels that were available of the *Alexandria Quartet*, and liked them all. Patrick said to me once that one should have two lives, one in which to write books, the other in which to read them. Actually he read a large number of books all the time; it was Patrick who introduced me to Edna O'Brien (*The Country Girls*), and Yevgeny Yevtushenko (*A Precocious Autobiography*). But there were enormous holes in his reading, sometimes deliberate, on other occasions through ignorance. He would often be delighted at being put onto something good which he had never read. On one occasion I mentioned Lermontov's *A Hero of our Time*; he had never heard of it, but immediately said, "Oh I shall read that; Lermontov, I like the sound of his name." Critics who snuffle after "influences" often do not realize how much better read they are than those they are writing about. Many writers are not at all widely read.

The next morning, when we were to begin talks about my research on his life and work, Patrick was ill in bed with bronchitis and probably an attack of flu. Manoly was told to take me for a drive. I was dismayed, thinking my journey was to be a waste of time, but as we chugged around the district in their awful Standard Vanguard Manoly told me not to worry. Patrick, he said, was just nervous of having to talk about himself to me. He would recover. Manoly had a lovely sense of humour, and his contacts with the local people brought a lot of life home to Patrick. He told me that their part-time gardener had come in one day and said, "The gentleman who drives the shit-cart would like a cup of tea, not for himself but for his fiancée who is taking a drive with him, but is feeling crook." I often thought that Manoly had a better ear for Australian idiom than Patrick.

By the time we returned, Patrick seemed to have recovered, and I sat by his bed drinking cups of tea while we talked. During the next couple of days we spent many good hours talking together while Manoly, as usual, worked in the garden and with the animals. I persuaded Patrick to send me a copy of *The Ham Funeral*, which had been turned down by the Royal Court. I thought it might have its premiere at the next Adelaide Festival. He promised to "try to find it".

On 25 May 1961 our second child, Teresa Rose, was born. We called her Tisi after Francis's first attempt at saying Teresa, and Tisi she has remained.

Max and I were doing well with *Australian Letters*, and the "Artists and Poets" series was particularly warmly received. We were also publishing a number of new writers, although I found there were difficulties with Max about the more experimental ones. He was still suffering from the trauma of Ern Malley; in fact, he never quite got over it, however often he was vindicated over the years by the growing number of those who admired

Ern's poems. I think in some obscure way Max now rather resented the freedom of those who wanted to try something new. It was ironic and sad that he, who had done so much for new writers, was now suspicious of them, even hostile; over the years I met several young writers who had approached Max at the bookshop and had been rubbished, even cruelly, for Max had a tongue that could get out of control. Perhaps he was like my mother had been in Florence — the old person — and resented others their youth and experimentation.

So now I had to use some cunning with Max, and not push too obviously. An unknown writer called Peter Carey sent in some stories, which Max without hesitation classified as bullshit. I thought the young Carey had some talent, and talked Max into publishing a short story; it was the first Carey story to appear in a magazine.

Frank Moorhouse, also almost unknown, presented even more problems than Carey. I had seen something of his in a university magazine, and suggested that he submit some stories to *Australian Letters*. A large bundle arrived, all of interest, but nearly all absolutely unprintable under the censorship regulations of the time. They were both explicitly homo- and heterosexual, not only full of the dreaded four-letter words, but involving some very interesting situations indeed. Finally I found one that I thought not too outrageous, and went to work on Max. The first Moorhouse story to appear in a literary magazine had been in *Southerly* in 1957; it was remarkably chaste. I think we were the first to take a chance on these disturbingly sexual stories.

Australian Letters had remained determinedly non-academic and eclectic, and seemed livelier than the sober *Meanjin* and *Southerly*, perhaps because of the amount of red wine that lubricated our editorial sessions. Now Max came up with a new idea: a monthly to be called *Australian Book Review*, which would review all new Australian books. It would also each year contain a children's supplement and an educational supplement, as well as a regular survey of the quality of production of Australian books. The latter came to be anxiously awaited by publishers, for it was obviously written by someone with excellent taste and a profound practical knowledge of book production. The author's pseudonym, "Peter Pica", proved impregnable, amazingly enough; it disguised the quiet skills of Andrew Fabinyi. He was no less honest about Cheshire's books than about those of other publishers. The magazine itself appeared in a large format on good paper. I was co-editor with Max.

Australian Book Review (ABR) filled a vital need in the Australian book world, and from the beginning was well supported by publishers; their advertisements enabled us to pay five pounds for a thousand words, which was not at all bad by 1961 standards. As with *Australian Letters*, neither

Max nor I took any salary. It was pleasing that the first issue coincided with the publication of *Riders in the Chariot*, which was the lead review.

For a while Max and I were the sole editors, and we were later joined by Rosemary Wighton. After a while our solicitor, Robert Clark, himself a poet, who had been editing our annual anthology, *Verse in Australia*, gave us as his legal opinion the warning that a magazine such as *ABR* ran a risk of being sued for libel if some unscrupulous person thought there was some money to be made out of it. I appeared to have considerable assets (in fact, of course, this was far from the truth), and Bob thought it best that my name should no longer appear on the magazine as Editor. I agreed, and from then on Max and Rosemary were officially the Editors, although I continued to work for the magazine. The original *ABR* closed down in 1974, and Max later gave permission for the name to be transferred to a new publication, which of course is still going strong.

In 1961 I met a young accountant from Melbourne, Brian Stonier, who had spent some time at Harmondsworth with Penguin Books, bringing them up to date with some aspects of the new computer technology, in which he had just done an advanced course. He told me that Allen Lane, the founder of Penguin Books, wanted to start an Australian publishing programme, and there was talk of its being set up by Brian, Max Harris and myself. It seemed an exciting prospect. The three of us were invited to Sydney in July to meet Lane. By a lucky piece of timing, I had been asked to give a Commonwealth Literary Fund Lecture at the University of New South Wales in early July.

I did some research on Eyre in the Mitchell Library, and then collected Max at the airport. We went to call on Tom Fitzgerald and George Munster (who could have been an equally scruffy brother of Wally Robson) in the dingy little office from which they ran the fortnightly *Nation*, which with its opposition, the *Observer*, had since 1958 livened up the dissemination of ideas in Australia to an extent unimaginable a few years before.

When people talk of the 1950s as being a dull and slothful period when Australians pottered around the fenced-in workplace under the managerial eye of Bob Menzies, they can never have read an issue of the *Observer* or of the *Nation*.

Fitzgerald, who was also the Financial Editor of the *Sydney Morning Herald*, had a red, rounded faced and a jolly manner, but you were immediately aware of his acuteness in anything to do with politics, the arts or economics. We were urged to turn up late that evening at Vadim's, a restaurant in Potts Point run by a Russian, which was the regular meeting place for any *Nation* contributors who happened to be in Sydney.

We then went to call on Donald Horne at the *Bulletin*, the very new *Bulletin*, which now incorporated the *Observer*. It had been taken over by Frank Packer, and Doug Stewart and the old gang had been sent packing.

Fortunately Doug was not long out of a job, and was very soon installed as Editor at Angus & Robertson. Donald Horne's first act was to remove the slogan "Australia For The White Man" from the *Bulletin*'s masthead. He had written to me in March, asking Max and me to write for him: "I do hope we can rely on the support of people like yourself. If we can I think we shall be able to revolutionise the *Bulletin* within three or four months. It's losing five hundred pounds a week at the moment but we hope to have solved that problem by March or April of next year."

Donald's great virtue has always been that he is not only intensely practical, an excellent journalist and expository writer, but that he also has a wild streak, especially when he has had a few drinks. He does not conform; he is game, on for a go. So he confronted Australian racism in the 1950s, and later lent his voice for the republic when most journalists ran, and many of them still run, that tired soulless line that there are other more important matters to be attended to first. Donald was also sceptical about the trendy left when it was fashionable to be one-eyed about communism.

We retired to a pub which was full of lively people like the novelist Hugh Atkinson, writers of criticism such as John Rorke and Gus Cross, a skinny, bat-eared young spark, Robert Hughes, who did cartoons and wrote art criticism, and Donald's associate, Peter Coleman. It was the first time I had met Hughes, who was to become another lifetime friend, and within two minutes he had talked me into driving him out to the University of Sydney to collect his girlfriend. There has always been something irresistible about Bob, and he would be the last to deny his talent for getting his own way. The girlfriend later went off to act in some play, and eventually Bob, Max and I arrived at Vadim's, which we did not leave until nearly 3 a.m.

I rose at 7.30 a.m. to prepare for my lecture, leaving Max fast asleep in the other bed in an apartment some friend had found us in a grand old house in Rose Bay. At Kensington the atmosphere in the English Department was hospitable but heavy, definitely not like Vadim's. The Professor of English, in a blue suit, with a nice smile but no imagination, talked vigorously about university politics. I gave my lecture, and then went to lunch at the Professor's house, amidst walnut veneer and cut moquette, with painted plates of pictures of Mediterranean ports on the walls. Leonie Kramer was there, with a death-ray eye, but very charming and pleasant; I kept away from subjects like the writers Stow and White and Harris.

That night Max and I went to dinner with Ken Slessor at Billyard Avenue, an old-style English roast-beef dinner excellently cooked by Ken, who lived on his own, having parted from his second wife, Pauline. The whisky and wine came in copious quantities, and Ken opened up, rather to my surprise, about his childhood expeditions to country towns with his father, who was a mining engineer. I had asked Max to write on Slessor for the Lansdowne series, and Ken suggested that we spend the morning with him before going to lunch at the Yacht Squadron with Allen Lane.

We surged off to the Yacht Squadron in the little car I had hired. Lane was neat, smooth, clean and quiet, and nothing escaped him; anyhow, in most matters he had tied everything up beforehand. Thanks to Ken's cognac and our natural Australian brashness, we cheeked him, and gave the impression that he did not impress us all that much, which obviously delighted him. Although he knew the ropes of the circus of English society, he strongly disliked the class system and British conservatism; he really enjoyed Australians who thought it all a pain in the arse and said so.

We were bidden to lunch the next day at Newport, at his sister Norah's house; his brother, who also lived in Australia, would be there too. In front of a wonderful view over Pittwater and the untouched bush on the other side, he still confined himself to oblique hints. Finally, over the port, he said he wanted to inaugurate a Penguin Australian publishing programme. He would like Brian Stonier to be Managing Director of the whole Penguin Books organization in Australia; I was to be editor of the new publishing series, and Max would be editorial adviser as well as overseeing the promotion of the Australian books.

I drove Max back to Rose Bay in high spirits, so high that I drove the wrong way down the Cahill Expressway by the Art Gallery. The cars rocketing towards us were all blowing their horns, and Max and I thought New South Wales drivers were damn rude, until I suddenly realized what I had done. Somehow I got us out of it. Whichever of the gods it is that looks after publishing must have wanted Penguin Australia to succeed against all odds.

The next day we went out to Dogwoods, where Patrick White had organized a large lunch. John Tasker was there, and David Moore the photographer, and Alan Seymour, whose *The One Day of the Year* had moved from Adelaide to a very successful season in Sydney. I had a fierce argument with Seymour over some lovely poems of David Campbell's which we had published in *Australian Letters*, the series later published in his book, *Poems*, as "Cocky's Calendar". They remain some of the best poems ever written by an Australian, but their subtle and deceptive country simplicities enraged the urban Seymour.

In the 1960s, there was among Australian intellectuals a revulsion against the country and the bush that I always found baffling. True, too much emphasis had been placed on siting the Australian tradition in the bush, but this was no excuse for now pretending that our country links did not exist. I still vividly remember the lean and bespectacled Seymour quivering with venom as he recited David's blameless quatrain, which he had firmly by heart:

Sweet rain, bless our windy farm,
Stepping round in skirts of storm:
Amongst the broken clods the hare
Folds his ears like hands in prayer.

"Fucking Dürer, he pinched the image from him, and what the fuck does a praying hare have to do with Australian life?" And so it went on.

Patrick, who knew better, joined us and we talked about Australian pessimism, so deeply ingrained in the Australian character, although I would maintain that it is more of a sardonic scepticism than pessimism. Seymour was again keen to indicate the wide range of his cultural references. "Would you say," he addressed Patrick and me, "that Australian pessimism is more akin to that of Chekhov, or to that of Sophocles?" "Both," answered Patrick and went off to get another bottle.

Those days in Sydney had been so intoxicating, and the future was so full of promise that I returned to Nonsuch on the Sunday night on the crest of a wave; but I was quickly pushed off it by Ninette, who seemed to think the whole Sydney visit had been a waste of time. At one moment she seemed to be saying that I should have been asked to run the whole of Penguin Australia single-handed, and in the next that the venture was doomed to failure anyway.

There was a truce until Wednesday night, when she attacked me again, this time for sleeping in the same room as Max. Why did we have to go to this house at Rose Bay and not take two rooms at a hotel? I kept wondering who would be the more astounded, Max or myself, to find ourselves off on a homosexual assignation.

In August I gave some lectures on Australian Literature for the Council for Adult Education (CAE) in pleasant, if freezing, Victorian country towns like Benalla, Beechworth and Mansfield; I was driven around and looked after by an agreeable man from the Council. In those days there were no motels, and one had to suffer the traditions and discomforts of country hotels, which were often fine old buildings, but with a ten-watt globe in the one light in the middle of the high bedroom ceiling, and a hundred-yard walk to the bathroom. When we signed in at Benalla I was asked, "Would you like a cup of tea in the morning?" "No, thank you." "Would you like a paper?" "Yes, please." "Well, you can't have the paper unless you have the cup of tea."

My companion told me that on a previous tour he had been accompanying a Viennese opera singer, who gave talks about opera and then sang arias. At breakfast at this hotel the waitress asked her whether she wanted tea or coffee. "Coffee, please. But is it real or essence?" (In those days before instant coffee there was a thick liquid in a bottle called "Coffee and Chicory Essence".) "Sorry, dear, I don't follow you," replied the waitress. "Is it made with freshly ground beans or does it come out of a bottle?" "Christ, I dunno, dear, it comes out of a forty-four gallon drum."

At the end of the tour, Ninette joined me in Melbourne, where Dease had become a meek, school-teacher husband, fussing over what turned out to be an excellent baked fish — "Shall I slit the foil, dear?" Bert Tucker was there, very friendly, but like me exasperated by a school-teacher friend of Dease's who was intolerably solemn and kept asking questions like "Albert, do you think that all Australian artists ought to go to Paris to study?" Indecipherable noises from Bert. "But, Albert, it is the artistic capital of the world, don't they say?" Bert, who had once lived in a little caravan on the banks of the Seine near Notre Dame, managed to change the subject.

There was no solemnity in Bungendore, staying with the Campbells. We then moved to a motel in Canberra as we had to leave early the next morning for Sydney. David came to guide us to the Clarks', where we were going to dine with Manning and Dymphna; David said there was sometimes no grog at Manning's, so we'd better have a slug first. Instead, Manning, presiding like a benign Lenin, turned on bottle after bottle during Dymphna's magnificent dinner. Alec Hope was very amiable, if a little parsonical in manner. The two of us, and David, were in the midst of what I thought was a rather enjoyable discussion of the refugee status of all writers, the mental exile most writers live in (a favourite subject of Patrick's), when Manning turned on the gramophone triple forte with the Bach "Magnificat".

Dymphna, pretending to collect some empty glasses from the living room, turned it off. By this time Manning had found the conversation interesting, and had joined in. Suddenly Ninette tapped me on the shoulder and said she had a terrible headache and we should go to our motel. When I finally found it, through the maze of Canberra, she was quite distraught. She said she could not stand being with so many people and was going to go away on her own. I hid the keys of the car. I began to realize that her often-repeated talk of going mad was really a generalised plea for my sympathy and understanding. Rather than rail at me about my affairs, she railed about something safe, and something that would end with her being comforted by me.

This was a different problem from the one that had greeted me when I returned from the Penguin meeting in Sydney. This now was part of a strange repeating pattern, that dogged our marriage. Perhaps the first time it had happened was in Melbourne, in our first year together, when she insisted on going home when a good evening was developing with Sid Nolan and Max Harris. In the middle of our first lunch with Richard Aldington, at an excellent restaurant in Le Lavandou, she had made me take her home, to Richard's dismay, just as the main course was being brought in. When Netta Aldington asked us to dinner at her flat in London with Dylan Thomas, she had pleaded a sick headache just when the conversation was soaring.

It was a manifestation that only happened when she was straining too hard; to Annie, say, this would not have mattered in the least, she would have simply moved with the flow. It never happened at Colebrooke, because the atmosphere was so like Anlaby. It never happened at Nonsuch or Rocky Point, because there she was in control. When it did happen, I think she had a vision of herself standing, a forlorn figure on a rock, watching me sail off into the distance. So I always turned back, took her home and blamed myself for being inconsiderate.

In Sydney she went to see some friends, and I had lunch with Patrick, to bring him together with Max Harris and Harry Medlin; Harry was Professor of Physics at Adelaide University, bearded and muscly, and Chairman of the Theatre Guild. At long last, after much prodding, Patrick had sent me the typescript of *The Ham Funeral*, as promised. I was very excited about it, although I thought it was a bit mannered, in the style of the Auden-Isherwood plays. Max was also enthusiastic, and had passed the script on to Colin Ballantyne, Chairman of the Drama Committee of the Adelaide Festival. David Marr has expertly summarized the ensuing drama of its rejection by General Hopkins and the Governors. Now the Theatre Guild wanted to produce the play after all.

Max was now entering a new phase of sophistication which involved a silver-topped cane and a coat with a beaver collar; they made him look a Jewish diamond dealer from Amsterdam, but did wonders for his shaky confidence, hidden under his cut-and-thrust conversation. The beautiful, swaying John Tasker was also there; Patrick had chosen him to direct the play. Patrick's infatuation with Tasker surged up and down in the troubled waters of the stage.

The Governors' rejection of *The Ham Funeral* had driven Patrick into a fury of creativity; he completed a new play, *The Season at Sarsaparilla*, almost immediately, and two more plays soon after that. Despite the excitement of all this activity, I have often wished that I had never asked him to send me that script of *The Ham Funeral*; the theatre, as he had told me before we met, is a dishonest business compared with writing novels. In many ways the frenetic activities of the theatre brought out the worst in Patrick, various outbursts of hysteria about a world of plots and intrigue, venomous gossip, manipulations and a series of infatuations.

His reputation as a novelist had been growing steadily in Britain and the USA, and since *Voss* he had been a world success. But none of his plays, into which he poured so much precious energy, ever achieved successful production outside Australia. The virus of the stage had entered his blood as a young man in London, and, as Manoly shrewdly if sadly remarked, John Tasker brought it back again. "Drug" would perhaps be a better word, for it was self-administered. He was not at the mercy of a virus, but of his own indiscretion.

The pianist Mitsuko Uchida once remarked that "Life has so many rules which the outside world enforces; the difficulty is sorting out which of them will work for you". As a writer of fiction, Patrick, unlike myself, had sorted them out very well. But now, in the theatre, he was enmeshed in another set of rules, which the playwright, unlike the novelist, has to observe, for he is not a lone operator. In the theatre, as with film, Patrick was always trying to break those rules, and to exercise too much control; that is why there is no major film of any of his novels, although on several occasions the possibility was quite close. Of course, the theatre is a heady, almost sexual, excitement, which comes from being involved in a mix of talented people and seeing the play emerge as a combined effort. But I think it was a bad drug for Patrick, and did him a great deal of harm.

However, all was sunny at this lunch in Sydney. Max and I teased Patrick, which he liked, and he was happy holding court, being the key figure in a little circle. It was not as lonely as writing novels.

After dinner with Tass Drysdale, we went on to Mervyn Horton's; Mervyn was an art collector and founding editor of *Art and Australia*. There were some society women there, one of whom, on being introduced to Tass, said, "Oh you must be the Drysdale who went to Geelong Grammar with my brother." She had never heard of Drysdale the artist. Tass was particularly keen to accompany me to Vadim's, and meet Tom Fitzgerald. When we arrived, Harry Kippax was also there; Harry, a colleague of Tom's on the *Herald*, was writing under the pen-name of Brek as the drama critic of *Nation*. *Nation* was at the peak of its vigour, attracting the best of writers, people like Manning Clark, Sylvia Lawson and Cyril Pearl. Tom and Harry would arrive at Vadim's about 11 p.m. and the sessions around the big table would sometimes go until 4 a.m.; Vadim would often lock up the restaurant and toss the keys to Tom. Now Tass bought drinks all round, but talk was the thing rather than drink; Tass himself was one of the best conversationalists I have ever known, at home in so many subjects beside art.

There was nothing elsewhere in Australia like these sessions at Vadim's. Clem Christesen, on a visit from Melbourne, attended one and wrote to me: "No discussions of that kind in bloody Melbourne". Patrick, whose round of phone conversations every morning gave him an astounding intelligence survey of what was happening in Sydney, wrote to me that he had hoped Clem would get in touch with him, as he would have liked to meet him. He was obviously disappointed that Christesen had ignored him. It was sad that the grumpy persona Patrick cultivated to keep what Ursula Hayward called "costly casuals" away, also scared off the people he would have liked to see.

In Sydney I was still also moving in what Patrick considered the enemy camp. Doug Stewart came in our car with us up to Springwood to see Norman Lindsay, Doug's great hero. Lindsay was a tiny, frail, intense man bubbling over with enthusiasm for what he considered the Australian literary renaissance. (I kept off the subject of art, knowing his hatred for any serious art since Rubens.) He himself was still hard at work painting and drawing his awful leering nude women and rapacious pirates. But his support for a lot of new Australian writing was genuine and whole-hearted, as it had been with Kenneth Slessor. He admired not only David Campbell, Rosemary Dobson and Kenneth Mackenzie, but a difficult new poet like Francis Webb as well. I was most gratified when he told me that *Founder of a City* was the best Australian biography he had read. For all I know, other writers might have had a similar accolade, but all the same, it did me good.

Patrick was never one to let an enmity cool; he once wrote to me that he had taken out all the reviews Douglas Stewart had ever written about his books (mostly unfavourable), and reread them all. Of course he had never met Doug. One day he did, and wrote to say he rather liked him. There must have been something about Doug that made us all think of the animal kingdom, because Patrick later described him as "a strange-looking little man, like a hairy mosquito".

Max Harris and I went to Melbourne on 11 December 1961 for our first Penguin Editorial Meeting with Brian Stonier. Allen Lane was a publisher of genius (he and Billy Collins remain the two most impressive publishers I have ever met) and it was his instinct that this was the right moment to launch Penguin Australia. The trouble was that his minions at Harmondsworth lacked his feeling for Australia. His chief editor, Tony Godwin, was a brilliant but very busy man; from the first he resented being bothered by this colonial outcrop of Penguins. A couple of years later, when he came to stay at Anlaby, I proudly handed him our latest Penguin and he looked at it and said, "Dammit, it looks like a real Penguin!"

We had been told by Lane that we would be able to keep our costs down because Harmondsworth would take ten thousand or more copies of each of our books. We carefully chose many books that would sell in Britain, but Godwin never took one of them. Even Donald Horne's *The Lucky Country*, our best-selling book, which would have appealed to a wide audience in Britain, was ignored until Lane himself forced Godwin to take fifteen thousand copies; even then Godwin changed the title to the boring *Australia in the Sixties*.

We had trouble not only with new books, but with any book by an Australian, even an expatriate like Christina Stead. I commissioned Bob Hughes to write *The Art of Australia* and John Manifold to make a collection of Australian folksongs (which were only then beginning to be rediscovered by Australians). Both books sold enduringly well. Our other authors included Randolph Stow, Robin Boyd and Martin Boyd, and we wanted to do a collection of Patrick's plays. Patrick was unequivocally enthusiastic about the Penguin enterprise: "It is wonderful to think you have landed the Penguins. Surely the biggest publishing coup ever in Australia ..."

Closer to home, Doug Stewart was furious and told me that we were a bunch of pirates; this was because he was now working for Angus & Robertson (A&R) and considered that all Australian books should be published by the Old Firm. Our chief difficulty with him and his firm was that a very large number of Australian books had been published by A & R in hardback. When Max and I would think of a book which should be reprinted (some of them many, many years out of print), I would usually have to write to Doug asking for the rights. After a while we could picture the scene at A & R — Doug: "These Penguin pirates want the rights for X. It'd obviously be a good seller. Let's do it ourselves." We ended up being talent scouts for A & R's own rather tatty paperback series.

However, there was one notable coup. I wrote to Doug asking for the rights to Judah Waten's *Alien Son*. He wrote back to say I was welcome to that communist crap. Twenty years and tens of thousands of copies later, *Alien Son* is still selling.

Brian Stonier had turned out to be not at all the chilly accountant, but a young man of verve and humour. (Brian was almost ten years to the day younger than me, still in his twenties in the 1960s.) He said that Lane would allow us 10,000 pounds for commissioning and producing six or seven books, a modest enough sum. The Lane parsimony was legendary; it also extended to my retainer, 250 pounds a year, plus a fee of 100 to 200 pounds for any books I edited myself. I was allowed travel expenses, but nothing for secretarial services. But we were all carried away by the general enthusiasm for the Penguin Australia imprint.

Twenty

In November 1961 Patrick arrived to stay with us for the opening of *The Ham Funeral*. Beyond Nonsuch, at the bottom of the hill, was another little cottage of pisé and stone, built about 1880, with fourteen acres of untouched bush with noble, tall trees. I had bought this, and connected the electricity, and water from our bore, and it made a comfortable little home away from Anlaby for my mother, who took great pleasure in immediately planting what soon turned into a very pretty garden; fortunately our bore was a good one, for the sprinklers ran incessantly. Chibs and Dick and their children were only about a mile away up the hill. This was not always a happy arrangement; although Chibs was now in her forties, her mother still often treated her as a wilful child.

When the cottage was vacant, it was an excellent home for visitors, who could be away from the racket of our children and make their way up the hill whenever they felt like a drink or a meal. Tass Drysdale came for a week or so. Donald Friend, a humorous troll with a marvellous wit and fund of gossip, came to do the drawings for the anthology of Australian children's writing, *Kangaroo Tales*, which Rosemary Wighton had edited for us for the Penguin list. Bob Hughes came for *The Art of Australia* and did a lot more than just study the collection in the Art Gallery of South Australia.

Now Patrick came. I told him I had left a selection of food and drink for his breakfast, but he said, oh dear, no, he would like to have breakfast with us, no matter how early we ate. Just something simple, lettuce and garlic and molasses and a few more items. Before breakfast he would stand at the marble-topped table chopping up all his ingredients, and gossiping to the three-year-old Francis.

On the first night of the play he seemed very calm but, typically, got the hiccups. *The Ham Funeral* was an enormous success. The Adelaide Establishment was routed, the most influential critic, Harry Kippax, loved it, all was well.

The next night we took Patrick to dinner with Ursula. Among the guests was Michael Scott, at that time the head of Aquinas College at the University, a good friend, a most sensitive Jesuit who knew a great deal about art and was instrumental in founding the Blake Prize for religious art. I was sure he and Patrick would get on well. Instead, they both froze.

Another guest was Arch Harrington, the Admiral in command of the Royal Australian Navy, who had married Chibs' childhood friend, Janet

Winser. Arch was unbearably pompous, and thought he was displaying his sophistication by telling painfully sexist and racist stories about Josephine Baker. Patrick commented on these with exquisite muted irony, which Arch completely missed but Ursula and Michael relished.

The ice between Michael and Patrick was melted at dinner. The Haywards had a full staff including a butler, Aidan, and a ravishing Spanish maid called Soledad. She tripped as she was serving me and dropped the entire contents of a silver dish of boiled potatoes in sizzling butter into my crutch. Clasping my scalded balls I rushed to the lavatory, threw down my trousers and chanelled cold water onto my cock and balls. Aidan rushed in and said, "Are they all right, sir?", and handed me a new pair of trousers and underpants. By the time I returned to the dining room, Patrick and Michael were chatting happily.

A few days later, on my way home, I called in on Ursula for a drink. She was going to Sydney shortly. Hannah Lloyd-Jones had rung her and said, "Come to lunch on Friday and we'll get Paddy White." I have often wondered whether Hannah was the last person to use Patrick's childhood name.

I went to Melbourne for a Penguin meeting. Brian told me that Steve Murray-Smith had kept me a seat for a dinner in honour of Clem Christesen and the twenty-fifth anniversary of *Meanjin*. I agreed to go, not knowing that there was waiting for me at home, unopened, an abusive letter from Clem rejecting a poem I had sent and calling me a viper for the last editorial in *Australian Letters* (actually written by Max) which had suggested that some reforms were needed in Australian literary magazines.

This dinner was my first experience of how Melbourne looks after those of whom it approves. It is an enduring tradition, and there is a lot to be commended in it. But there is also a solemnity about the adulation on such Melbourne occasions which would not survive long in Sydney. There is an earnest rising above the vulgarities of commerce, a praise of high principles which is blind to prejudice and paranoia, a respect for a past which is more idealized than accurate. All this is accompanied by speeches with a portentous delivery, often of platitudes, and a funereal diction.

Professor Maxwell, of the English Department, said, "We hope and pray that *Meanjin* won't become part of the Establishment" — Clem had just been awarded an OBE. Arthur Calwell lumbered to his feet and said, "Indeed it is a good thing that we should have a native LiteraCHOOR." A.A. Phillips orated, "If a journal has paid its way it has fatally compromised its true purpose." (*Meanjin* had grants from the Commonwealth Literary Fund and the University of Melbourne, which also gave it accommodation and secretarial assistance). Judge Barry spoke of cultural aims that seemed so close in the 1930s but had receded since.(I cannot think what they were.) Finally, Clem rose to prolonged applause and said, "More than to my contributors, I owe everything to my wife." Steve Murray-Smith then revealed that the three guinea charge for the dinner was to help pay for a portrait of Clem. Clem had refused to be painted by Clifton Pugh or Noel Counihan, and had chosen William Dargie.

Clem and many at the dinner suffered from a lack of what W.B. Yeats, speaking of George Eliot, called "a springing foot". Of course George Eliot was a great novelist, and there are many who lack that springing foot. Pushkin had it, Dostoyevsky did not. The greatest of all geniuses, Shakespeare and Mozart, had it. Patrick had it until he drove it back as he imposed on himself and the world the image of the monster; however, David Marr tells me it was there at the end, in the personality if not in the writing.

It is not quite the same thing as a sense of humour, although the two are certainly compatible. After a visit to Melbourne, Patrick wrote to me mentioning Christesen: "There isn't a great deal of humour in him ... He is an absurd old thing in some ways, but I'm rather fond of him. I also like his wife very much. She reminded me of a good apple."

A capacity for sheer pleasure, an instinct for fun, is essential to most writers and artists. The high seriousness recommended by Matthew Arnold and, in a slightly different style, F.R. Leavis, was not at all shared by most of their exemplars. And even Henry James, than whom no one had a loftier or more serious brow, wrote to his brother about the very serious Charles Eliot Nortons, with whom Henry and his sister Alice had been spending some time in Paris: "I feel less and less at home with them, owing to a high moral *je ne sais quoi* which passes quite above my head. I went with Charles the other day to the Louvre, where he made some excellent criticisms, but he takes art altogether too hard for me to follow him ... I daily pray not to grow in discrimination and to be suffered to aim at superficial pleasure."

There was always something heavy and unrelentingly serious about *Meanjin*. Nevertheless, Clem was an excellent editor, if paranoid about a number of issues, not to mention other literary magazines. He always used to refer to *Australian Letters* as his "Reptile Contemporary". But he cared strongly about his contributors, as Doug Stewart had in his *Bulletin* days. I remember sending Clem a longish poem, "Abandoned Airstrip, Northern Territory", and he returned it with some suggestions which led me to improve the poem. In the end it was a poem that appealed even to A.D. Hope.

Clem's remark at the end of his speech, about his wife meaning more to him than his contributors, was certainly true, and also in the financial sense. Nina, a remarkable woman in her own right, was Professor of Russian at Melbourne University, and one of the many unsung heroes of

Australian Literature who have, with their incomes, kept their writer spouses afloat more reliably than any series of grants.

All this time, my own life was undergoing some changes. Below the rocks and flowers of the ordinary day the subterranean flow of poetry was still running, in which my secret life moved towards some mysterious sea. Early in 1962 there was a small end of an era: the row of little old terrace houses in Grenfell Street was pulled down to make a used-car lot. They would, with very little restoration, have made excellent lodgings for students, being only two minutes walk away from the University and the Royal Adelaide Hospital. But it was during the twenty-seven-year reign of that old barbarian Sir Thomas Playford, and the buildings of Adelaide's heritage were there to be knocked down.

Protests were in vain. The beautiful little Theatre Royal was demolished to make a car park, despite powerful local pressure and appeals from Laurence Olivier and Vivien Leigh, Ralph Richardson, Sybil Thorndike and Lewis Casson and many other famous actors who had played there and been delighted with it. The old Dutch-style stone-and-brick Police Barracks behind North Terrace also disappeared. My mother, who had known Playford since his childhood, appealed to him that the Barracks would make a wonderful Historical Museum, which Adelaide did not have. He laughed at her.

Meanwhile, another era had begun. For several months I had been sharing Grenfell Street for many hours with Ilse, a Viennese woman who ran a flower shop. She had a disturbing passion for perfection, a touching seriousness, a good knowledge of Rilke and Schubert. Although in some ways she was childlike, it was I who was living out in her my childhood dreams of Europe. She was in exile from Austria, but had no illusions about Old Vienna, the faded waltzes and the schmaltzy tenors.

I translated three of Rilke's poems for her: "The Girl in Love", "To be said before going to sleep" and "Parting". They seemed to me exactly like her, an uncertainty, a reaching towards a new world, a vulnerability, the sadness waiting to be liberated into joy. I really did love her, and it lasted, more or less, for six years. It was no straight path but a series of violent zigzags of jealousy, despair, rapture, sulks, gaiety, suspicion. At times it was very exhausting.

Sometimes I think I was living out with her, not only what was for me a mystic quality of being European, but the personification of all the youthful German romanticism I had shared with Deasey, the heavy sighs, the dream of death, the sadness of tears, despairs and longings, *Sehnsucht, Weltschmerz, Tränenflut*. With her I was far from Australian pragmatism and "She'll be right, mate"; the trannie playing the popsong in the street had become *ein Nachtigallenchor*, a chorus of nightingales.

In February 1962 Max and I were in Melbourne for a Penguin meeting. Harmondsworth had sent out two young Englishmen to help Brian in sales and accounting. They were pleasant and willing enough, but terrified of Australia. There was no clear class system, the rules were different, the climate was too hot, nature was too violent. Both the boys, as we called them when they weren't there, were moving house; they liked their houses, which were in attractive new developments, but they were scared of bushfires. One of them confided to me that the main reason for moving was not this at all, but that his wife hated the kookaburras so much; she was convinced they were mocking her. "Do you think there'll be kookaburras in Blackburn South?" he asked piteously.

It was no use explaining to him that kookaburras treat Australians just the same as they do Pommies. They really are extraordinary birds. Birdsong is solitary, or answering, but the kookaburras' performance of laughter is a duet. They seem to be speaking as well as laughing. "Ho ho ho! What's this? What's this? 5 a.m. and you're still asleep? Ridiculous!" And then they go off to another tall tree to persecute someone else, and maybe later return to your tree as a reminder. I wished we could send a kookaburra to laugh at Tony Godwin, who was obstructing us with his usual lack of enthusiasm.

After the meeting we went out to the new Monash University to see Jock Marshall, who was now inaugural Professor of Zoology, and also Scientific Adviser to Penguin Australia. He showed us the new buildings; somehow or other he had persuaded those in charge of Monash's finances to buy a fine selection of modern Australian paintings, and to commission a mural from Clif Pugh. Alas, the books he planned for us came to nothing, through no fault of Jock's.

An interesting problem came up early in 1962 when a Sydney critic, J.V. Byrnes, sent *Australian Letters* an article, "Patrick White's *Voss* and T.S. Eliot's *Four Quartets*". I liked the article, which seemed to me a legitimate study of influence, whether conscious or unconscious; Max agreed with me. So I sent it over to Patrick for comment. He replied, "I find the enclosed most interesting, scholarly, and extraordinary — I say extraordinary because I have never read *Four Quartets* ...[he went on to list the Eliot works he had read] it seems to support my favourite theory that our books are poured into us from some other source, and that a supernatural one." We thought it best not to publish the article; Mr Byrnes was flabbergasted.

Perhaps the high points of provincial comedy in Adelaide over these years were the dinner parties at Government House. The incumbents at this time were, of course, British: a retired Lieutenant-General, Sir Edric Bastyan, and his wife Victoria. We used to call him cocksparrow; he fancied himself as a painter of landscapes. She had a tight little governessy face and was quite intelligent under the ermine mantle of representing the Crown. On one occasion we filed in, arm in arm, all twenty-two of us. The men had been told to wear white tie and tails, but then this was countermanded to dinner jackets as the visiting English dignitary had not brought his tails. The Adelaide doctor's wife next to me at dinner told me, in great detail, about the time she had met the Duke of Bedford. She then switched to painting, confusing Canaletto with a Frenchman among other outrages.

The ladies left and the port and brandy went round. Sir Keith Angas, Colin's uncle, ("Keith Fungus", Ursula used to call him) was tugging his forelock and saying Their Excellencies must visit him at Lindsay Park: "The beds are made up, but of course the place is not looking at its best with this drought." "Ah," said Sir Edric, "but you and I have different standards. I see things as an artist." He caught me looking at him with what must have been a tremor of disbelief. "Well," he corrected himself, "a sort of an artist." We joined the ladies, spread upon sofas and chairs in three rooms, Lady Bastyan's eyes flickering around. Every forty-three seconds the men would have to move and each couple would have to crank up another conversation.

Shortly after this agonizing evening I was in the Mary Martin Bookshop in the Da Costa Building, asking Max how my book of poems, *Flowers and Fury*, was going; it had recently been published by Cheshire, elegantly designed by Robin Wallace-Crabbe. Max's assistant said to me that a customer had bought a copy that morning. The assistant had said to her, "You're in luck, there are a few signed copies left." "If you don't mind," the customer replied with severity, "I'd rather have a clean copy, please." Just then two heavily built, grey suited men came in; it was obvious that neither of them would have known Hans Andersen from Schopenhauer, but they walked around the shelves peering at the books. I asked Max what he had done to have the cops after him. He didn't know.

The next day he did. The two men were Commonwealth Police, sent by ASIO. There had been a complaint from Government House. Max's last issue of his witty *Newsletter* had the name and address and hours of trading of the Mary Martin Bookshop at the head of the first page, and, immediately below it: "After Hours, Government House, North Terrace, Adelaide". Max had to make a public apology or face ten years in jail.

I made the mistake of telling my mother this story. She looked sternly at me and said, "You can't have a sense of humour about Government House."

In late March the second Adelaide Festival surged over the town; it really was getting under way as a national occasion and drawing people in from all over Australia, not to mention the overseas performers. The Commonwealth Literary Fund (CLF) had a meeting to coincide with Writers' Week, so Ken Slessor and Doug Stewart were there. So was Xavier Herbert. I had written a disrespectful review of his novel *Soldiers' Women* in *Nation*, and had also commented unfavourably on his grotesque statement in an interview that learning to fly an aeroplane was more difficult than writing a book. I wrote not only as a pilot but as an ex-flying instructor. Xavier announced publicly that he was coming down to Adelaide "to knock that bastard Dutton's head off".

The inaugural party for Writers' Week was in a dingy hall at Belair, in the hills above Adelaide, near Wykeham, where I had gone to Preparatory School. I tried to remember Mr Hutchinson's instructions about straight lefts and uppercuts. "There he is, Geoff." Doug pointed out an old chap with a big moustache. I thought I had better get the confrontation over, so with Doug I walked across the room and Doug introduced us. I was a lot taller than Xavier, but he looked fairly tough. "I came down here to knock your block off," Xavier said, "but you look a pretty decent sort of a bloke. Put it there." We shook hands and had beers thrust upon us.

Writers' Week, like most other writers' meetings, was mostly given up to the financial iniquities suffered by all the then Australian writers except Morris West and Nevil Shute. Hal Porter, drunk as usual at such gatherings, livened things up. An extremely boring local writer called H.A. Lindsay was first on his feet at Question Time. "Now I wrote an article and sent it to a leading national paper and they paid me three pounds ten shillings for it." "What for?" shouted Hal.

There was then a poetry reading by the bank of the River Torrens, the best moments of which came when Bill Harney read an elegy for a mate of his who had done a perish and had then been eaten by a dingo and passed through its arsehole and fertilized the desert.

Donald Friend was staying at our cottage down the hill, and was joined there by Tass, who had come over for a meeting of the Art Advisory Board (AAB). Thirty came to lunch on Sunday, and at about ten o'clock that night Ninette and I were doing the clearing up from the lunch, which had only just ended, when in from Adelaide stormed Tass, Snow the Commonwealth driver, and Jim McCusker, who was the Secretary of both the CLF and AAB. Snow seized Ninette by the waist and removed her from the sink, Tass grabbed the towel off me, and Jim started putting plates away in the wrong places. Shortly afterwards Tass took up two spoons with which he beat on the marble-topped table while singing one of Louis Armstrong's blues, Jim peering from side to side of his nose like a crow in a cartoon. At 3 a.m. I threw them out.

The next morning there was an official opening by Sir Robert Menzies of the first exhibition of the treasures of the Nan Kivell collection of the

National Library. I had recently published, with Rigby, a small book on the paintings of S.T. Gill; there was a limited edition, and a general edition. I had been asked by Sir Lloyd Dumas, Chairman of the Festival, to present copy number one of the limited edition to Menzies, a painful duty for one who felt about Menzies as I did. After fulsome speeches from Menzies and others I made my presentation. Then the Governors and librarians withdrew with Menzies for sherries; I was neither introduced to Menzies nor offered one of the no doubt awful sherries. Such was the status of writers in Adelaide during the Menzies years. I should have said I was an OAF (popular acronym for Old Adelaide Family).

In April we had another member of the art world, Bob Hughes, staying again at the cottage, with his puma eyes and cascading talk and hands looking for a cigarette. Ninette did not want him to come. There was a rerun of the drama about Max and me in Sydney. She had noticed that Bob had come up from the cottage to talk to me when I was having my shave without any clothes on. I said I'd rung and asked him to come up whenever he wanted breakfast. But I was supposed to be talking to him about the Penguin art book. And on it went. I could not quite see Bob, any more than Max, as a homosexual partner.

If anybody has a springing foot it is Bob. It was wonderful to have someone so quick, witty, inventive and affectionate in the house. He reminded me of the old days with Kershaw, smoking all our cigarettes, popping full packets into his pocket if you didn't watch him, leaping to help and knocking something over. Ninette asked him for a match to light the gas stove. He looked through a box. "All dead-heads," he said, and turned back to talk to me.

He roared off in a hired VW to meet a girlfriend, who was in some Festival play. About midnight the phone rang. It was Bob, staying at a city motel, in a dreadful state of agitation. His girlfriend was in an appalling condition, death seemed to be imminent although he didn't specify what the trouble was, and please did I know of a doctor close by. I gave him the number of a doctor who would go at this hour to Bob's room.

Later Bob, with the original of that cliché "an infectious grin", confessed to me what had happened. It was in the pre-pill days when some women, before fucking, used to insert a contraceptive cream with a plunger. Bob had gone to the bathroom, leaving the girl lying on the bed, screwed in the tube and filled the plunger. The cream was inserted, and the moment of truth came. But instead of passionate embraces there were screams of pain and fright from the girl as foam poured out all over the bed. The diagnosis was simple and no harm was done, for when my doctor friend arrived he found that Bob had filled the plunger with shaving cream.

My mother had asked Sir Edric and Lady Bastyan to lunch at Anlaby, and they were due to come on 12 May. For a while there was some uncertainty about arrangements, and she gloomily said the Bastyans probably wouldn't come because they would have found out that I was a friend of Max Harris. But all was finally arranged; Chibs was ordered to come up on the day before the lunch with the crayfish and other food, so she asked us to have her two children, Charlotte and Tom, for the night.

On the evening of Friday 11 May I drove up to Nonsuch after a late lecture, feeling very tired. With me I had two beautiful large flounder for dinner, the genuine flounder of the southern coast of Australia, bought from my friend Melva at Cappo's fish-shop. One of the dogs had been sick, and I started to ask Ninette about him when she interrupted me, to say my mother was dead. Chibs had just arrived at Anlaby, and was unpacking the car, when Mary found my mother on the floor by grandfather's pedal organ, at the entrance to the library.

The great solemnities of death are always accompanied by trivialities, by fiddling arrangements which have to be made. I rang Mavis, who helped in the house, to ask her if she could come and mind Chibs'and our children. Dependable Mavis said immediately, "If we can't help each other out in trouble there's something wrong with us."

And what to do with the flounder? It seemed foolish not to eat before driving off into the country, but it seemed disrespectful; a monkish fasting would be more appropriate. To hell with it, Mum would have wanted us to eat the flounder. We had just finished them when Chibs' husband Dick arrived, and we drove with him to Anlaby in silence, the car full of thoughts.

The last fortnight of my mother's life had been perfect, the mid-May weather warm and sunny by day, and cold at night, just as she liked it, the garden at its best. We had been there to stay with her for a week, and not a cross word. She had not had a row with anyone at Anlaby, not with John, nor with Robbie the manager, who one day had collected her to drive around the station and said, "Well, are we going to be polite today, or shall I come back tomorrow?" She and Chibs, who had lately been at war, had not fired a shot at each other, and she was thrilled that Chibs had won the Women Pilots' Cup. And how typical of her to die when preparing for a Government House visit, and thus having the house and garden spic and span for her own funeral.

She was a most remarkable, unforgettable woman, no doubt of that. Patrick had seen her quality immediately, and her failings, when he came to stay at Anlaby. He told me that Elizabeth Hunter, in *The Eye of the Storm*, had elements of my mother in her. And he got her exactly in the description of Ursula [note also the Christian name, Patrick liked to mix his sources] Polkinghorn in "The Letters": "Whenever she made her entrance, at weddings, for instance, smoothing the long kid gloves, a hand barely passing through the faint effulgence of her pale hair, everybody forgot the bride".

But what a sad life, with all those natural and social advantages. An alcoholic husband. More than thirty years a widow. An alcoholic son, dead in his thirties. Her eldest son neither rich nor famous, who in truth had a deep revulsion against her; there was something in the past he could never forgive her for, although he never told me what it was. He did once say to me that she had no sense of humour. She could laugh, often bawdily, which those who did not know her well could not believe, but basically, yes, her view of life was mostly serious, tragic, noble. There was no gravedigger in her *Hamlet*. She would have agreed with Dr Darling, who once told us at school that Australians place too much importance on a sense of humour. There is hardly a photograph of her smiling, let alone laughing, throughout her seventy years.

She had told her only daughter nothing about the facts of female life, but tried, outrageously, again and again, to organize Chibs' life. Once when I was still a schoolboy, driving Chibs and her home to Anlaby, I stopped the car and said I was going to get out and walk unless they stopped fighting. She provoked Chibs beyond endurance, again and again, and did her best to ruin her life by pushing her around those schools in England and Europe when she was a child. I often thought that Chibs had the most amazing strength of character, to have survived so well.

I tried to analyse her character. I knew every one of the photographs, in their sleek leather frames, sitting up like stuffed dogs on the lid of the Steinway. KG at the front, with the simple signature "George II". Were they physical lovers? I think not, she did not care for "that sort of thing". She used to say of a certain woman, "Oh, she's very highly sexed", as if she was sniffing a leg of mutton that had gone off. KG, reputedly a longtime lecher, might have found it soothing to be close to a woman who did not go to bed with him.

Behind KG were the signed photographs of the Gowries, the Pembrokes, the Spencers and other lords and ladies, usually taken by Lenare. She had been close to the Gowries, but most of these other people she had met only a few times. She thought that their photographs were a kind of proof that she was an honorary member of that distant society. It was all so false, especially as in her normal life she was intensely proud to be Australian.

My mother always liked me to give her a cuddle, and there were all those happy memories of being in her bed while she read me stories as a child. And her garden, wildflowers, native trees, these were true and enduring loves, as were the beauty both of nature — of clouds or hills and of created things — a statue or a piece of music. When I was younger I found it difficult to forgive her for her narrowness of taste. She responded to the excesses of Wagner, but once in the smoking room when I put on a record of Mozart's K595 Piano Concerto, she conducted with her finger, and then, when the lilting last movement began, said, "Tinkly tinkly." But the tastes of each one of us might seem atrocious to others.

She had almost no close friends. Hundreds who admired her. "Oh your mother is a wonderful woman." "Mrs Dutton is a great lady." That sort of thing. But no one with whom she could weep or be just plain silly, except Nell Wynyard, whom I remember as vapid, and with whom my mother and father once danced on the sand in the shallow sea, near Victor Harbor. She never had more than a glass of wine; if I offered her another she would say, "Do you want to get me tiddly?" This was not altogether because of Dad; the wine would have sapped her control, and she always had to be in control, even in the most trivial situations. She used to drive John and me mad by asking one of us to load her car, when she was going down to Adelaide or up to the cottage in the hills. Whichever of us it was would carry out the heavy suitcases and boxes that always accompanied her, even if she was only going to be away a night or two. Just when the hapless son had finished loading the boot of the old Buick, she would charge out the door and say, "Oh, I'm the only one round here who knows how to load a car, now put that case there and that box there. Really, men are useless."

Perhaps she was happiest when the Buick was new, when after the outbreak of war she drove thousands of miles to every corner of South Australia working for the Red Cross. Sometimes Mick, the station mechanic, would accompany her, but usually she was on her own, even when petrol rationing forced a gas producer to be fitted to the Buick, a huge contraption out of which flames roared when it was time to refuel. On these journeys she was fulfilling that higher duty, to King and Empire, for which she always longed.

I realize too, now that I was older, that with my father an alcoholic, it was no wonder she needed to escape. She hated it when he was affectionate at times when he was drunk. In a rare reference to him on such occasions, she said to me with loathing that he was "sawney" — a Scottish dialect word which means "foolishly sentimental". On the other hand, she never completely lost her tender feelings for my father. Many years after her death, I took the back off the photograph of him in a leather frame, which used to be in the library. There inside was a folded sheet of paper on which, in his beautiful handwriting, was copied out a passionate (and not very good) poem by the American James Whitcomb Riley, headed "When She Comes Home", inscribed "From Harry to Emily the beloved". In my mother's writing is "Written to me to Melbourne the day before I returned from my holiday in Melbourne and Sydney, December 1931".

Now at Anlaby, when everyone else had gone to bed, I went in to the big spare room, the room into which she would not move because it was always kept ready for the Governor or some notable. There she was, on the smaller bed, not on the four-poster. I pulled back the sheet, below her sleeping face.

She was so exactly like herself, looking indomitable, her chin and nose daring the world. I leaned down and kissed her, and was shocked, physically, by the marble cold of those cheeks that had been so soft in Florence. No, she was not sleeping.

The next day, the day before the funeral, the comedy began. Kon Pfitzner, the undertaker, arrived with "the casket"; how she would have snorted at its frills. "I'll go and see how Mother is," said Kon, and then stopped to mention that he had brought "a portable wreath-rack" for the Buick. Peg came over from the cottage, her mind already full of the wording of the obituary, of who was getting what jewellery, and whether we should sell up.

The day of the funeral was cold and blowy. The old Buick was full of flowers, and the portable wreath-rack too. Marc, the gardener, drove it behind the hearse, and someone said it looked like the General's charger. We huddled around the grave. A child scuffled. As the parson droned on, I watched some cattle drifting along by the trees in the paddock next to the cemetery, and then half a dozen draught horses, an odd piebald one nipping and nuzzling the brown mare beside him. Suddenly they tossed their manes and galloped up to the skyline. The coffin was lowered into the grave above my father's coffin.

Back at the house the refrigerators were bulging with food for the Viceregal visit, crayfish and other good things. "Mum would have wanted us to eat them," said Chibs, echoing my sentiments about the flounder. We all tucked in and I brought up a lot of wine from the cellar.

I had agreed some months before all this to give the Commonwealth Literary Fund lectures in Brisbane at the University of Queensland, and left to drive up there, towards the end of May.

It was at about this time that "primitive painters" began to be known as "naive painters". One of the very best of them, Henri Bastin, originally from Belgium, by this time had become a good friend of all my family. Henri was stocky, with a square face and white hair, and immensely strong. He had been trained as a toy-maker, and with those big hands made all sorts of delicate and ingenious toys. He did not care at all for being called a "naive painter"; he certainly was not naive in any respect. He announced proudly, "*Moi*, I am genuine *primitif*."

I had first heard of Henri when I was writing art criticism for the Adelaide *News* and the Sydney *Bulletin*. An antique dealer rang to say he had a small show of paintings by a Belgian primitive painter, an opal miner called Henri Bastin, and please could I come to look at them and review them. I had finished my reviews for the week, and was about to post them, and thought it would be a waste of time to go to look at some rubbish at the back of an antique shop. Fortunately, more conscientious thoughts prevailed, and I found a kind of Aladdin's cave in the little room. There were landscapes of the far country of his opal mines, that remote region where South Australia, New South Wales and the Northern Territory meet, creeks and red plains and rocky hills dotted with coolabahs and leopard gums with their separate leaves painted one by one, white cockatoos tumbling in their branches, and one of a young Aboriginal woman in a lusher setting, called "Hommage à Rousseau".

The prices were absurdly low, mostly five to twenty guineas. I persuaded the antique dealer to charge twice as much, and rang Kym Bonython, the Wrefords and other collectors, as well as Patrick. The show was an immediate sell-out. From then on, Henri regarded me as his protector, and would send me everything he painted. I was able to arrange exhibitions for him in Melbourne, Sydney, London and Texas. I never asked him for any commission, and simply took out the expenses of sending the paintings. When he came to stay he would arrive with the most exquisite and ingenious toys for the children. When Henri's business affairs became too much for me, Kym agreed to take over on a professional basis, and Henri used to arrive with toys for the Bonython children.

One day at Anlaby Henri startled John and Robbie and me by saying he was going to make a bank across the dry Waterloo Creek which, when rain came, would divert water to make a large dam. He set off with a pick and shovel and a bottle of brandy "to keep off the flies". His levee was washed away in the next flood.

Henri spoke in a mixture of French, Flemish and English, with a few Aboriginal words thrown in. His speech was fairly easy to understand, but his letters took rather a lot of deciphering. Here is a sample of one of them: "Sinn arrived breck in Queensland have lurne from the ranchies lott of Wais of growing fautte fort Stoct. Pour hexemple ..." (Translation: "Since arriving back in Queensland I have learned from the station owners lots of ways of growing food for stock. For example ...")

He had jumped ship in Port Pirie in the 1930s and walked up to Broken Hill to find work in the mines; with him were two Greeks and an Englishman. "Now the Greeks own many cafés in west Queensland, and eighty thousand pound motel in Brisbane, the Englishman the biggest department store in Newcastle, and *moi* — I own my bicycle! *Mais*" — a favourite word — "*je suis toujours heureux.*" He patted his hip. "And plenty *monnaie*!" He would then add that he spoke the purest French, because he came from Charleroi.

Now when I told him I was going to Brisbane he asked me to take him along, with his bicycle, and he would show us his opal mine near Eromanga, in the corner country. So we set off in the Peugeot station wagon, Henri's bicycle on the roofrack, his new pick and shovel and modest swag in the back. As we drove along he didn't respond to anything we said, but talked at length, most entertainingly, about the back country, its plants and birds, and most of all about opals, "opaals", and opal miners, people like Canny Jimmy who buried all his opals and then died and no one knew where to find them, and another miner who hid his pipes of opals in champagne bottles. Some old timers, he claimed, used to bury their opals in a grave and put a cross and a name above it. Henri said that when he was short of water and didn't know where to look for it he would feed his dog a lot of salt beef, then rub washing blue on his paws, and then follow its track.

He commented on all the different trees we passed, saying, "Those artists in Melbourne, Sydney, Adelaide, they all paint the same tree." Suddenly, east of Balranald, he tapped me on the shoulder. "Geoffroi, stop. I smell mushroom." I had hardly pulled up when he was limping off to a stand of peppermints, his right foot splayed out. He had been shot in the ankle in the First World War, and a German doctor, amazingly enough, had rebuilt his ankle with silver. He would often pull up his trouser leg and knock his pipe out on the skin which had grown over the silver ankle. His hat was soon full of mushrooms.

We made a lovely camp by the Lachlan River. At bedtime Henri raked all the coals back from the fire, laid green boughs over the hot earth and unrolled his swag on them. He was gone when I woke not long after dawn, but came limping back, saying, "Good mushroom here, what for we pick them and then we have good breakfast." We filled the washing-up basin and a piece of curved bark Henri had found with delicious mushrooms.

We had some delectable camps, fishing with Henri's grubs and catching yabbies and listening to one of the most beautiful birdcalls in the world, the lingering purity of the call of the butcher-bird of evil habits.

Then, alas, it began to rain, and the faithful Peugeot slithered through the mud to Charleville; it had been too wet to camp, and we arrived at Charleville very early in the morning. Henri assured us we would get a good, hot breakfast, as one of the Greeks who had jumped ship with him owned the Bunch of Roses café. Henri was as good as his word. His Greek friend embraced the three of us, and then brought huge steaks smothered with eggs. "Geoffroi, what for we stop here three-four days, rain finish, then we go Eromanga for opaals." But I had to be in Brisbane to give those lectures, so we left Henri, with his bicycle, his pick and shovel and his swag.

At Mount Tamborine we called on Judith Wright and her philosopher-husband, Jack McKinney. Judith sat up very straight and her eyes were deep behind her glasses; her deafness gave a characteristic timbre to her voice which shifted between sharp and flat. She spoke sardonically about the tough mountain people around Tamborine, who had burnt down a doctor's house after he won a law case against them. She said she was a bit nervous herself, though she didn't sound it, because of a letter she had written to the paper about the trapping of birds for sale.

In Brisbane Wally Campbell was on his steady ascent to the top, one of

Brisbane's leading QCs, and later to be Chief Justice. I have never known a man and his wife less spoiled by success than Wally and Georgie.

Brian and Marjorie Johnstone's art gallery had had a prodigious effect on the Queensland art market; Brisbane people bought far more modern Australian art than their counterparts in Adelaide. Brian told me of another side to Henri's character. Having seen some of Henri's paintings, Brian had offered him a small exhibition, and had lent him a hundred pounds so he could take the time to paint. The pictures were hung, and a number had been sold, when Henri limped into the gallery one day, seized the best painting off the wall, and bolted with it. When Brian tried to stop him, Henri grabbed him round the neck and said he would kill him.

We drove out to Wynnum and had lunch with John Manifold and his wife Kate. John was well ahead with his *Song Book* for Penguins. He played a tape of his band, the Bandicoots, and the items at the last Ballad Night, with sounds from all sorts of home-made instruments. John was a born teacher. He loved working with his young friends and the whole atmosphere of "joining in", as he would say in his rather English voice. He and David Campbell had been at Cambridge together, and it was really thanks to John that David began to take writing poetry seriously. John's and Kate's communism seemed very earnest and naive; most of his bad poems are political ones.

On our journey to Queensland and back Ninette and I spent many hours talking about what we would do now that my mother had died. In her will she had left me most of the contents of the big house at Anlaby; Chibs was to get all the Australiana in the library and John all the first editions of writers like Dickens and Thackeray. (Later, when the Australiana was sold, Chibs bought herself a Cessna aeroplane with some of the proceeds, and gave a most generous share of the remainder to me.) My mother knew that no one but me would consider living in the big house; John refused to, and neither Chibs nor Léonie (my dead brother Dick's only child), who was now a quarter owner of the Anlaby Pastoral Company, would ever be able to, because their husbands' careers meant they had to live in or near a city. It was definitely not a house for weekends.

My mother had always warned me that if I went to live at Anlaby everyone would think I was rich. This had always amused me, because she and my father had continued to think of themselves as rich long after most of the money had dribbled away. She left me no money. She didn't have any; all that she had was tied up in a mortgage over Anlaby. Of course everybody thought she had left me a packet, and that I was now rich.

And yet I decided to go and live at Anlaby, Ninette enthusiastically agreeing. I would resign from the University, and we would sell the two houses and land at Mount Lofty. I still cannot think why I made such an absurd decision. I knew there was no money; yet I gave up my job. I was behaving as if I were rich, ensuring ultimate financial disaster. My legacy from my grandfather had been seriously bitten into by my purchase of the cottage down the hill at Nonsuch, and the fourteen acres of land behind it. The loss of my salary as a university lecturer would further reduce my income. I think I was impelled, not by *folie de grandeur* so much as by a kind of crazy sense of duty to keep beautiful Anlaby going. Because my mother had left me all the furniture, pictures and such like, I believed I had to go and live in the house. I was not worried about any injustice in her leaving me most of the contents of the house, as she had many times told Chibs and me that John and Dick had had large amounts of money when Grandfather was still alive, and later in the 1920s, the equivalent of which Chibs and I had never had. She had also already divided up a lot of furniture and silver.

We all needed money, so I thought I would suggest that we sell Uno. The two stations were very inefficiently run. John, as General Manager, had an excellent eye for sheep but no training or ability as a business manager, and no capacity for handling all the personal problems that face efficient pastoral management. His and Peg's own property, Burleigh at Mount Gambier, was a success because it was small and simple, not over-capitalised, Peg was shrewd, and it was their own. He could never stand up to our mother, and should never have exposed himself to living next to her at Anlaby. He was a charming old country gentleman, and that was that. Bill Hayward once said caustically to me that he wouldn't let John run the sock department at John Martin's.

Yet I was going to take my family to live in the enormous house, and sink all the proceeds from the sale of Nonsuch into the repairs that desperately needed doing to it. My quarter-share of the Anlaby Pastoral Company's profits would be next to nothing, as any profits had to go into paying off some of the hefty overdraft. I had a new, and very good accountant, Eric Cox, who tried to make me see sense. "Look, Geoff, you're a writer, and I know from doing your tax returns how little writers make. Why don't you sell the lot, Anlaby and Uno, and just have the postman drop a regular cheque into your mailbox? After all, you've got a lovely place to live in, up there at Nonsuch, and those twenty-three acres are going to be worth a great deal of money in twenty years if you want to move to town." He looked at me, and shook his head, and said ruefully, "I suppose Anlaby is a way of life." Would that I had listened to him. And would that he had not been a polite Adelaidean, and had said instead, brutally, "You silly bastard, you can't afford it."

We finally had a family meeting, which was as fraught with explosions as such meetings usually are. I proposed selling Uno. Léonie said that her "advisers" (actually Ian McLachlan, father of the present MP) had said to her that it would be more sense to sell Anlaby and keep Uno. Ian was absolutely right, but the suggestion was treated as sacrilege by the rest of us. It was finally agreed that I should move my family to the big house, do it up and pay a peppercorn rent to John, Chibs and Léonie, who were of course still the other three part-owners with me of what was left of the property.

Patrick had said many times how much he liked Adelaide and hated Sydney, and that he and Manoly had seriously thought of moving there. I asked him if he would like to buy Nonsuch. He replied from Dogwoods: "It made me feel how much younger you are than ourselves [only ten years, actually]. I feel that when I do move I will want something much smaller and more compact even than this." It was hardly a preview of the house at Martin Road that he was soon to move into.

In September Nonsuch had its last fling. Patrick came over for the premire of *The Season at Sarsaparilla*. The extent of the Adelaide Establishment's collapse can be gauged by the fact that the Governor and his Lady attended the first night, and dinner jackets were required. Patrick refused to wear one. The Bastyans disapproved of the play.

The Season was a sell-out, and Zoe Caldwell's Nola was the star performance. The laughter ran in waves through the theatre, and the big scene between Zoe and Cliff Neate brought the hankies out. As Patrick wrote to me aferwards, it made him cry, and "Where I have my cry I know I have got my audience! You see I am really very Common Man inside, perhaps even Common Housemaid."

The only trouble was that Patrick, like the bitch in his play, was in season. He had fallen madly in love with his leading lady. Zoe was tiny, but as powerful off the stage as on, and relishing the genteel absurdities of Adelaide, about which she was quite uninhibited. Patrick danced around her, giggling. Up at Nonsuch he was on a high and over-chatty, following Ninette or me around with a whisky glass, chattering. Zoe could not have been unaware, but she didn't give a damn. She was in the midst of a violent love affair herself, but the lover was in Queensland. She asked Patrick to stay in her room at the Botanic Hotel after the first night, instead of driving with me up to Nonsuch; she said there was a spare bed in the room, and she knew Patrick would stay in it. She also said she was never disturbed before 1 p.m. He stayed, and at 9.30 a.m. the door burst open and the entire staff came in singing "Happy Birthday to Zoe".

A few days later the dog-minders changed guard, and Manoly came over to stay and see the play. He very much liked both the production and Zoe, but broke down and wept later in the night, talking about Patrick's infatuation. He had put up with Tasker, but this heterosexual passion distressed him dreadfully. Later, during the Melbourne run of *The Season*, Patrick stayed with Zoe and her parents, who delighted him with their views on life.

I sold Nonsuch for thirteen thousand pounds and in the end spent the lot shoring up the ruins of the Anlaby homestead. We left Nonsuch in October and moved into the big house.

Twenty-One

Before I resigned from the University, I had done a lot of research for my biography of Edward John Eyre, but now realized that it would be impossible to write the book unless I went to libraries and Public Record Offices in New Zealand, where Eyre had been Lieutenant-Governor under Sir George Grey, and in Jamaica and in London; I also needed to absorb some of the background of the places I had not been to. New Zealand was relatively easy to reach, but I could not afford Jamaica and London. After all the research I had already done, it was depressing to reach a dead end.

There were no grants available to writers, and even had I still been a member of the university staff I could not have expected any help — I was in the English Department, and a biography of a non-literary figure belonged to History. That a biography or a work of history might also be literature was not acceptable, and among most of those who study Australian Literature is no more acceptable today.

Enter, once again, the element of chance. I had often talked to Patrick about the syndrome of coincidence, chance, luck, fate and all the inexplicable random elements of life. Neither of us having any competence in mathematics or physics, we could not enlarge the discussion by hints from probability theory or non-Euclidean geometry, although later on I thought I caught a glimpse or two in James Gleick's account for the layman of chaos theory. Patrick often said that if he dared to put some of the coincidences he had encountered in life into his fiction the critics would tear him to bits.

Although Patrick was very sensitive to poetry, he often said he could not understand how it worked. He wrote to me: "It is the technical side of it which always stands finally between me and complete understanding and enjoyment". But he was already halfway there, with his use of metaphor in his fiction. This he certainly understood, and until the end of his middle period his prose is continually enriched, and often strained, by what is basically a poetic use of metaphor.

Beyond technique, it seems that chance or coincidence can bring life and death together in the most outrageously irrational way, like Dr Johnson's famous denigration of the wit of the metaphysical poets where "The most heterogeneous ideas are yoked by violence together". Chance can both destroy and save, as it so capriciously did when Geoff Tuck and I crashed on our way back from the volcano in Bougainville. It was by chance that we were at the right height and time to fly into the invisible wall of hot air that broke the wing of our aircraft; but it was also by chance that our other wing hit a high tree, causing us to spin safely to the ground; again it was by chance that the aircraft did not catch fire and that I was not trapped in the wreck, and was able to pull Geoff out.

And it was chance that now offered me the possibility of doing what I had thought impossible. At this time there was an American Professor from Kansas, Earle Davis, visiting Adelaide on a Fulbright Fellowship. Earle was one of those agreeable, easygoing Americans with a good sense of humour. He was trying to break himself of the need to smoke cigarettes, and had the strange habit of nearly always having one in his mouth, and slowly eating it. I invited him for a picnic at Anlaby. He knew about my research on Eyre, and asked me how it was going. When I told him I had reached a dead-end, he swallowed what was left of another cigarette and said, "Come to Kansas for a semester and teach, and we'll pay you enough money to go round the world and take your family too." I didn't think he was serious, but laughed and said of course I would enjoy going to Kansas, while privately thinking Kansas would be even more provincial than Adelaide.

A couple of days later Earle came to my room, holding a cable. It was from the President of Kansas State University, Manhattan (yes, Manhattan!), offering me the post of Visiting Professor for a semester, with a fee of US$10,000. With this offer, I didn't care how provincial Kansas might be.

Meanwhile a team of builders moved into Anlaby and stayed for weeks. Yet again, for me, they shattered the myth of the beer-soaking, philistine Australian. Ron, the painter, sculpted, read the *Connoisseur* and had travelled all over Europe; Roy, the bricklayer, used to come in in the evenings and ask if he could listen to my classical music, and had been to Europe where he had pursued opera from country to country; Ted, the carpenter, was also keen on sculpting, and modelled some new heads for the eroded concrete lions over the water-spouts around the terrace. When the builders and painters had finished, the old house looked as it never had in my lifetime. But all the money from the sale of Nonsuch had gone into the restoration of the house.

In the course of doing up the old house I opened one door that had always been locked. Downstairs, near my father's bedroom, was the shower he used; in one corner of this room was a pine door that led, I had been told, to his darkroom. He was a talented photographer, as demonstrated by his photos of the 1907–8 Adelaide-Darwin trip in the Talbot.

I found a key and opened the door. The darkroom was panelled in pine, with a bench running round it as high as my waist, with a porcelain sink and taps. There was no photographic equipment there, but under the bench along the wall were stacked about a hundred and fifty empty whisky bottles. At right angles to them, neatly piled against the pine boards, were some thirty sets of first editions, many in two or three volumes, of the journals of the Australian explorers, duplicates of those that had been in the library. Those hard, thirsty journeys over deserts and gibber plains were all there: Sturt, Eyre, McDouall Stuart, Forrest, Giles, Mitchell, Leichhardt. The pencilled prices were still in them, mostly under ten shillings.

The thirst represented by those bottles was never slaked at a muddy waterhole. I wondered who his accomplice had been in getting him those bottles. It had obviously been harder to get rid of the empties. Poor old Dad.

In 1962 Richard Aldington died, in his seventieth year. Ironically, the old hater of Communism had gone out on a high, having returned from being fêted in the Soviet Union in celebration of his seventieth birthday. In the Soviet Union he was one of the most popular novelists in translation from English. He took Catha with him, and had a wonderful time being spoiled, especially after his rejection by the British literary establishment. Although he had refused the vodka and brandy, keeping up his pretence that he did not drink, it could almost literally be said that the Russians killed him with kindness.

In recent years there has come a strong impetus to revive Richard's neglected work, mostly coming from America, and there are now disciples around the world, and seminars in his honour, and his work is getting back into print again. In his wars with the British literary establishment, he was usually traduced as a surly, suspicious character. In my experience, over many years, he was one of the kindest and most generous people I have ever met.

Sid Nolan arrived not long after we had moved into Anlaby, quiet, steady-eyed, with a nose that was looking more and more like a gherkin. I told him about the interests of our builders; he also had been having some experience of the ways in which Australian attitudes differed from the clichés about them. In Perth he had seen his father, the ex-tram driver, who after all these years had told Sid that his grandfather had painted pictures. Sid's father had said, "I might have a go myself." Sid did not seem to be in the least spoilt by his growing fame. He had been to some strange places in Ethiopia, and hinted that he had been lucky to escape with his testicles intact.

That summer Patrick and Manoly came to stay at Rocky Point. With them in the house were Bob and Val Southey and their four boys. Patrick gossiped away in the little kitchen non-stop, about war crimes, society ladies, Schubert, food and again about food. He always wanted to wash up, but we had to try to circumvent this, because he took so long and rinsed everything several times in our precious tank water.

On their way back Patrick and Manoly stayed with Max and Von Harris in their lovely old stone house which was called Voss; the Harris poodle was called Mrs Lusty, and slept on Patrick's bed. He said they were "perfect hosts".

Max was very odd about his domestic affairs; in all the years, twenty or more, that we were closely associated in various literary ventures, I was only once asked to a meal at home with him and Von, although they frequently visited Anlaby.

Patrick had enjoyed the Southeys, "from the beginning to end of their rather long family. I feel I understand all about them — their sexy relationship, and the anxious little boys."

He wrote a story, "Dead Roses", that is partly set at Rocky Point. As he often did, he used a name from one of those present, Val, but the portrait is not of Val Southey but of Ninette. On the other hand, Val's husband, Gil, is more like Bob Southey than me. The other characters in the story are unlike anyone in the house party, except for the light sketch of the little boys.

Patrick wrote later that he could well understand how much I loved Kangaroo Island, because it was the way he felt about Mount Wilson, where he had been happy as a child. "The first day was particularly wonderful, and one clung on to it as long as one could." That made me remember bumping down the limestone road in Dad's Buick, waiting for the first sight of the house on the cliff above the sea, with the rocky point stretching out into the bay, black-and-white shags draped around the rocks. Patrick, back into the intrigue of the theatre, where talented and beautiful John Tasker was now "the Tasker", "slithering" through every kind of infamy, ended his letter: "Why don't we all live on an island, become fishermen, and reject all such dishonesties?".

The purity and honesty of Rocky Point flowed through so many magical years; perhaps the best one of all had been when Chibs and Sandy Dey and I were down in 1940, and my mother was at her best, looking after us. But immediately so many other years assert their claims, especially the years when the children were growing up. The constants remained, unspoiled nature, fishing, mucking around in small boats, swimming and snorkelling, eating and drinking with no planes or buses to catch in the morning.

In the early days Kangaroo Island and the escape from the mainland really began with the voyage on the old *Karatta*. Lawrence Daws and I sampled the little steamer again in the summer of 1960, when we took the Peugeot station wagon down on it, to get everything ready for Ninette and Francis, who would fly down.

Jimmy the Steward entertained us. Before a recent voyage, Jimmy told Lawrence and me, he had gone down to the wharf to check the supplies. There seemed to be one extra box. It was quite small. Jimmy opened it; it contained some sort of white powder. He licked his finger, put it in and tasted it. No, it wasn't flour. It wasn't icing sugar. It wasn't salt. Just then Captain Pearson came down the gang-plank and asked if there was an extra package. It was the ashes of old Mr Sanderson, who had made dozens of voyages on the *Karatta*, and wished to be buried at sea. So in the middle of Backstairs Passage the *Karatta* came to a halt, and Captain Pearson read the service and committed the ashes to the deep. "The passengers were quite affected by the occasion," said Jimmy to Lawrence and me, "and they came down to my bar to fortify their spirits. One of them said to me, real lugubrious, 'I suppose, Jimmy, you knew Mr Sanderson real well?' 'Know him?' said Jimmy. 'Christ, I tasted him this morning.' "

When we reached Rocky Point we stood on the veranda and looked at the dark trees on the pale hills, the light across the bay, and Lawrence said, "And they say the English watercolourists were romantics." Later I wrote a longish poem, "Night Fishing", and Lawrence did a series of paintings and drawings for it, some of which were published in *Australian Letters* in our "Artists and Poets" series.

The peace and isolation of Rocky Point were then secure, as they had been in my childhood, for Kangaroo Island was difficult of access for the motor-car. Now there is a huge roll-on, roll-off car ferry, and houses are bobbing up behind the sandhills all around the bay, that was once almost empty. And the fishing has gone off, especially the delectable whiting.

The dominant themes of Rocky Point were the sea, the beach, and the scrub that came up to the back door. But those themes were subject to endless variations of wind and light. Even the bush, that from the distance all looks much the same, actually varies from the vertical, pale nude trunks of the mallee to the dark, twisted tea-tree. And, in spring, the wildflowers! Ninette and I once counted twenty-four different kinds in one square yard. As with the flowers, so with the shells washed up every morning along the curve of the white beach, unmarked by any human foot, but bearing the different traces of wallabies, goannas and lizards, which for their own mysterious reasons came down to the beach at night.

There are no foxes and no rabbits on the Island, and very few feral cats around Rocky Point, so the little birds are there in myriads. The base of an old Coolgardie safe made an ideal bird bath, below the kitchen window and under the shelter of a myoporum bush. As many different little birds as there were shells on the beach would come to this pool of water in the dry scrub, a dozen kinds of honeyeater, robins, blue wrens, firetail finches, then the bigger birds like wattlebirds and occasionally a clumsy currawong with his glaring, yellow-ringed eye.

Over in Australia, as the Kangaroo Islanders say, the peace immediately evaporated with the last-minute rush before leaving for Kansas. Ninette said she would need a Nanny to come with us; because of my peculiar upbringing I did not know how normal Australian families operated, so accepted this. Fortunately Mary Black was available and said she would come; Mary was the perfect country girl, strong, practical, patient, unflappable, overflowing with laughter. As a trained Mothercraft nurse, she had looked after Francis when he first came home to Nonsuch from hospital. Everyone who met her liked her.

There were last frantic consultations with Brian and Max over the Penguin programme. Our new books were on the way. I was responsible for all of them, but the two I was most closely involved with were *The Literature of Australia*, which I had edited, and Bob Hughes's *The Art of Australia*. I had been determined in commissioning writers for *Literature* to avoid factions, as I had been with the Lansdowne series. So I asked Manning Clark to write on Lawson (which launched him later to write a whole book on Lawson), Leonie Kramer on Henry Handel Richardson, James McAuley on Douglas Stewart, David Campbell on Francis Webb, Ian Turner on "The Social Setting", and Katharine Brisbane on "Australian Drama". They were all professionals in their field, and I had few worries from them.

With Bob Hughes, in his way more brilliant than any of them, there were endless dramas. Bob was twenty-four, and as he cheerfully admitted about his career as art critic for the *Observer* and then *Nation*, was educating himself as he went along. This is one reason for the sparkling freshness of the book. He also had, and still has, a wonderful instinct both for quality and for falsity, unhampered by dogma or a dominating theory.

Now he was learning about the whole history of Australian art on the run. I had to keep hounding him to ensure that he would meet his 1963 deadline, so he used to send me chapters as they were completed. The trouble was that he would then start to rewrite them as he learned more about the particular artist, usually from Daniel Thomas, who was a great help to him. This was especially so of contemporary artists. Bob would write his summing-up of, say, Lawrence Daws, as a painter of the outback, extending Drysdale's themes into new areas of technique and thought. Then suddenly he would ring and tell me to cancel the pages on Daws; he had just seen his new "Mandala" series. A totally different assessment would arrive. But often it did not arrive, because he would be pursuing some other fresh design. Sometimes it was impossible to raise him by letter or phone. I once sent him a telegram: "BOB ARE YOU DEAD?".

Of course, what did eventually come in from Bob was livelier than anything previously written about Australian art. *The Art of Australia* is a classic. Its publishing history passed out of my hands when everyone resigned from Penguin Australia and we founded our own paperback publishing firm, Sun Books. It was eventually published in 1965. Almost the entire edition was immediately pulped, on instructions from Harmondsworth. It was, in a way, Tony Godwin's revenge. He blamed Griffin Press, for faulty production. Griffin immediately sued Penguin and won the case. The book was finally printed in Hong Kong and published in 1966, and has been through many editions. *The Literature of Australia* appeared in 1964, and was also reprinted many times, as well as appearing in a revised and enlarged edition.

It is impossible now to realize how much books like these, and John Manifold's *Australian Song Book* and Russel Ward's *The Penguin Book of Australian Ballads*, and Roger Covell's *Australia's Music* (which I commissioned before I left Penguin), meant to the self-awareness and national dignity of Australians. The ten-volume *Australian Encyclopaedia*, published by Angus & Robertson, had led the way in 1958, and was followed by Bernard Smith's *Australian Painting* in 1962. The first volume of the *Australian Dictionary of Biography* appeared from Melbourne University Press in 1966. Sidney Baker's *The Australian Language* had been first published by Angus & Robertson in 1945, but a much more handsome, enlarged edition appeared from Currawong Press in 1966. G.A. Wilkes' *Dictionary of Australian Colloquialisms* did not appear until 1978; Stephen Murray-Smith's *Dictionary of Australian Quotations* in 1984; *The Oxford Companion to Australian Literature* in 1985; Oxford's *Australian National Dictionary* in 1988.

Before these books there was something inchoate about our cultural history, just as it was not taught to children. Now the evidence of it is there, solid on the shelves. But the books that took off in the greatest quantities from the shelves were the Penguins, the affordable ones, the ones in the reach of the general public.

We left for Kansas near the end of January 1963. Patrick cooked a delicious lunch for us, and what with the lunch and the talk we very nearly missed the plane. In the middle of lunch, Patrick announced, in his most oracular style, " 'Loneliness will never have a child' is quite wrong." In the stunned silence I could not for a moment place the quotation, and then remembered it was from my poem "Abandoned Airstrip, Northern Territory". He continued, "Artists all produce their works from loneliness, and at the other extreme all those lonely soldiers fathered those poor little unwanted bastards." Out of context, he was, of course, quite right; Patrick's vehemence was nearly always personal, the context wrenched to his way of seeing things. A few lines further on, my poem spoke of "The sharing and the loneliness of love". Beneath his words, spoken above the heads of the two small children at his table, was the knowledge that he and Manoly would never have a child, and the equal certainty that he had both fathered and mothered all the books he had written. It was another case of the artist as hermaphrodite, a theme Patrick was to embody in *The Solid Mandala.*

America. The taxi driver taking us out to the airport at San Francisco asked where we were going. "Kansas, eh? You'll see more darkies out there, they get cheeky but they keep them in their place down there."

Two very nice members of the English Department, John Noonan and Rolf Soellner, had driven 126 miles into Kansas City in two cars, to pick us up and take us to Manhattan. "Earle's got you a kinda unusual house." They both giggled. "He said it had to be out in the country and it had to have a grand piano."

Eventually out of the snow and darkness a tall stone farmhouse emerged into the lights of the cars, looking like Wuthering Heights. Inside, it was almost too hot; the kind landlady had not only lit the central heating but made up five beds.

Despite the manifest cruelties of life in America, no people are kinder than individual Americans. Rolf said he had realized it would be difficult for us out at Cedar Knoll Farm, even when I had bought a car, and maybe lonely, so he was lending us his Volkswagen and a cat. I was instructed to pick up the cat the next day. They went off into the night in John's car.

I was to find teaching in an American university in the Mid-West quite different from anything I had known in Australia or England. In the English Department there were thirty permanent staff and thirty-five casual, offering one hundred and sixty optional courses. My first shock was to find that I would not be teaching Australian Literature, as I had thought, but "instructing" (there was a new vocabulary to learn) a sophomore class of about twenty-five in "Dr Johnson to the Romantics", and a postgraduate class of about ten in modern English and American poetry. Thinking I would, as at Leeds, be bringing Aus Lit to a virgin land, I had arranged for my *Australian Encyclopaedia* and all the basic texts and criticism to be sent to Manhatttan. None of this had arrived, but now it would not be needed. At least, having lectured on the other subjects, I would be able to improvise.

In 1963 there were all sorts of restrictions in Australia on buying hard currency, especially the American dollar. The bank manager in Adelaide had advised me to take a minimum of traveller's cheques, and get an advance on my salary as soon as I arrived.

Here the other side of the kindness coin emerged. The University flatly refused to give me a cent in advance; I would receive my first payment in a month's time. I appealed to Earle, than whom you couldn't have found a kinder man, saying I had no money and five mouths to feed, not to mention Rolf's cat. But the Bursar, said Earle, was in charge of finance. Very sorry. I went to the bank that corresponded with my bank, but was turned away, even though I had a note from the Dean to confirm that I was a Visiting Professor on a salary of $10,000 for the semester. I shot off a desperate cable to my bank manager in Adelaide. I don't know how he did it or where it came from, but $1000 arrived in a few days. I went out and bought a 1955 Ford with a powerful Mercury engine for $395, and was able to leave the VW with Ninette.

A further horrifying discovery was that Kansas, although not a dry state, discouraged drinking by putting a heavy tax on liquor. The University itself, one of the so-called Land Grant Universities established across America in the 1860s, was totally dry on campus. Even the President was not supposed to serve liquor in his Lodgings. And the only bread you could buy in Manhattan tasted like Kleenex. In the staff common room was a blackboard where people contemplating a visit to Kansas City would put up their name and the date of the visit. Orders would then be placed by members of the staff for liquor and bread. The state of Kansas and the state of Missouri joined in the middle of Kansas City, and in the insanity of government, a bottle of whisky on one side of the street cost ten dollars and on the other forty dollars. (You were thought to be an alcoholic if you asked for wine in either state.) There was a small but excellent Jewish bakery in Kansas City.

So when we first went to Kansas City it was as well that the Ford had an enormous engine and a vast boot; we returned with a dozen cases of whisky and beer, and about fifty loaves of bread.

Another insight into the American Way of Life came when I first parked in the University. I was stopped and made to pay three dollars by a parking guard who had a .38 on his belt. There were fines of sixty dollars if you overstayed the three hours granted by your ticket. There was no parking space reserved for staff; most of what was available was taken up by students, who all seemed to have huge cars.

Soon after arriving, I had my first meeting with my students. Classes were called "instruction". At ten minutes before the hour, buzzers sounded in all rooms. When the second buzzer sounded on the hour the students immediately got up and left, even if someone was in the middle of a sentence. At midday and again at 1 p.m. a foghorn roared over the whole campus, but by 12.50 a.m. the teaching staff had already bolted for their cars and raced off home for lunch.

The temperature had shot up from 15 degrees Fahrenheit to 65, and there was glorious sunshine, but in every "office", as our rooms were called, the blinds were down and the lights on, and over in the students' magnificent Union building the students were sitting around, even in the window seats, with blinds down and lights on. One day one of my colleagues said to me, "Do you remember when there was that craze for fresh air and people used to sleep with their windows open?"

My sophomores looked vacuous, the graduate students intelligent. I soon found out that the sophomores were almost totally ignorant; anybody could enrol, because it was a free Land Grant University, and the average standard of these students in their second year was about that of Year 10 schoolchildren in Australia. When I marked their first papers I could see the reason for the popularity of the book *Why Johnny Can't Read*.

One day members of the staff had a meeting with some of the most esteemed English teachers in Kansas high schools. One of them said to me that she was advising her brighter students to write their assignments, and then get a good dictionary or Thesaurus and rewrite them using longer words for all the short ones. She was quite serious about this.

Rolf had warned me about the ignorance of the students. He said that it was a good idea to give them a quiz from time to time and toss in a couple of very easy questions so that the bad ones could at least tot up a few marks. But even this could backfire. He had recently given as one question: "What was Elsinore?" One student had replied "The wife of Sir John Falstaff".

The graduate students, on the other hand, and despite the fact that at twenty-two or so they all seemed to be married with one or more children, were really interested. To my embarrassment, everyone called me Dr Dutton, even the Dean. When I said that I was only a humble B.A., he said, "Hell, it was Oxford, wasn't it? That's as good as any Ph.D."

By far the prettiest of my graduate students was called Barbie (Bahrrbee), but, despite having a degree, she was not all that bright. When I handed back one of the assignments I thought I had been generous in giving her a C. But Barbie waited behind after the class and then dashed over to the desk and flung her arms around my neck and burst into tears on my shoulder, sobbing, "Doctor (Dahcta) Dutton, why do you hate me? I've never ever been given a C!" I disengaged myself, thankful that the door was open and so nobody could accuse me of harassing her, but at the same time conscious that it was open and someone passing could see us. For once I thought of the right retort. "Tell me honestly, Barbie, what do you think it's worth?" She giggled. "Probably only a D."

A couple of weeks later Barbie came into the class with her arm in a sling. I commiserated, and asked her what had happened. She said she had dislocated her shoulder. "We went to a drive-in and my boyfriend went to sleep with his head on my shoulder and that kinda did it."

My troubles in finding I was not to take classes in Australian Literature were as nothing compared to those of the Australian poet R.D. FitzGerald, who had been invited to the University of Texas at the same time, also thinking he was to be talking about the literature of his own country. Fitz was a very sturdy character, but when he rang me there was anguish in his voice as he informed me that he had been told he was to give a series of classes on "Great Minds from Montaigne to Rousseau". "They must think Sydney's in France", he groaned, adding that he had never made any systematic study of Montaigne or Rousseau, let alone what lay between. Fitz was a surveyor by profession. It was relatively easy for me, having studied literature and lectured on it, to handle my classes, but he just did not know what he was going to do. All that I could suggest was that, since he was undoubtedly wiser than anyone in his classes, all he had to do was to be one day ahead of them in his reading. The first and only time either of us was asked to talk on Australian Literature was when Fitz was asked up to my University in Kansas, and I was asked down to his in Texas.

What I found most alarming about Kansas was the way the Mid-West of America was prepared for war. Fort Riley base was not far from Cedar Knoll Farm, and jets used to scream over every day dropping practice bombs. There were big armament factories at Wichita and other places in Kansas, and the whole state was dotted with minute-men pointed towards Russia. Many houses had bomb shelters in their back yards. One of the professors said to me that America 1963 reminded him of the England of Disraeli's *Sybil*, except that the gap was not between rich and poor (although that would have been bad enough) but between those who wanted peace (and were not communists) and those who seriously talked about sixteen million casualties being "acceptable", and who had machine-guns ready by their bomb shelters, not to fight off the Russians but their fellow Americans who did not have bomb shelters. Of course, thousands of Kansas homes already had cyclone shelters; for the coming war these were given extra protection and stocked with food and drink for several weeks. Cedar Knoll Farm had a cyclone shelter, and I was advised to stock it up.

We were bidden to have drinks with the President and Mrs McCain; apparently he had obtained a special licence to give us sherry, a most peculiar drink for Americans, but maybe the authorities thought it less dangerous than martinis, or else *de rigueur* for Oxford graduates. Mrs McCain told me that she had met "some Russian woman" (actually a famous Soviet scientist) who was visiting the University. When the Russian heard that both women had seventeen-year-old daughters, she suggested that they correspond and talk about what life was like in their respective countries. Mrs McCain said to me, "I had to say yes, even though I was not at all in favour of the idea." She continued that several months later the FBI man had called, "just making his regular visit to the campus, checking out this and that around the University", and as he went out the door he had turned and said to Mrs McCain, "By the way, did your daughter hear from her friend in Russia?" She waited a moment. "I know they can't check up on all the mail, but it's kinda reassuring and comforting to know that they must be reading quite a lot of letters."

From time to time we invited a few of my colleagues and their wives (there were no women professors) out to Cedar Knoll Farm, which was a really lovely place, with the woods around it from which the coyotes would stream past the house at night on their way to Wildcat Creek, and the big empty wooden "ghost house", and the red barn that had whole pine trees as beams.

Mary Black was the great success of these gatherings. Mary enjoyed reading, although she was no literary scholar, but it soon became obvious that, with her Australian freshness and humour, she was cutting a swathe through the angst-ridden professors. Little Rolf, with his toupée that was made all too obvious by a sort of plastic strip between it and the top of his forehead, took me aside and said, "Geoff, I know I'm no Adonis, but I'm going to propose to Mary. I mean, she's the sort of girl a man like me *ought* to marry." He did propose, but he didn't succeed in keeping Mary in Kansas. And before the end of the semester, another bachelor professor proposed to her — again without success.

In February the University celebrated its Centennial; I was asked to "present congratulations" on behalf of the University of Adelaide. I told the Dean that I had no gown with me. He said it would be no trouble to get me an Oxford gown, there were several Oxford men in the University; it would be waiting for me in the Robing Room just before the ceremony (which was to be held in the enormous basketball stadium). When I went in to the Robing Room I was handed the gorgeous scarlet gown of an Oxford Doctor of Philosophy. I rushed over to the Dean and explained (not for the first time) that I was only a B.A.; B.A.s were only entitled to a black gown with a bit of rabbit's fur around the collar. "Oh Hell, Dr Dutton, an Oxford degree is an Oxford degree. Here, take it."

At the ceremony we had to walk in two by two, and as (amazingly enough) the University of Adelaide was the second oldest of those universities represented, I found myself near the top of the procession, alongside the Catholic Archbishop of Kansas in his full splendour. The colour clash was sensational.

On the next day a photograph of me appeared on the front page of the town paper with the caption "Professor Dutton presents congratulations from England". I was heartily sick of this kind of thing, and of people saying to me, "It's a real pleasure to hear that English accent of yours, even if it is a bit hard to understand".

Far away from my native land, I sat down and wrote an article called "British Subject" for Tom Fitzgerald's *Nation*. (In 1963 we were still "British" on our passports). In the article I confirmed my republicanism and said that Australia should rid itself of the monarchy. It was the first such article of its time.

In the same article I mentioned that a Professor of Physics and another of Chemistry had called on me to talk about Australia, where they had each spent a year working. They said it had been bizarre, but they had often found themselves defending Australia from attacks by English migrants. One Englishman and his wife took the chemist for a drive up to what they said was "the only beautiful country in Australia". It turned out to be Mount Wilson, and my American colleague said to me, "But Goddam, it looked like England or maybe New England, not Australia — nothing but oaks and elms and suchlike. I told them to take me to some real bush."

Patrick could have shown him that the bush, the sassafras and lyrebirds, were only a short walk away from the oaks and elms. I often think that Patrick's love-disappointment relationship with Australia partly stemmed from his loss of that childhood paradise, where the English and the Australian coexisted and there was no dust or heat. When he saw the *Nation* article he wrote to me: "I still think Mount Wilson the most beautiful place I have seen in Australia — possibly because I grew up on it more or less, and know every inch, not only the elms and maples, but the sassafras, blackwood and scrub".

One gem of comedy emerged from the republican soil. Tom Fitzgerald rang me from Sydney and asked if there was such a person as L.M. Dutton. I said it was my sister-in-law Peg. He said he had received a Letter to the Editor, and was checking that it was not a hoax. So in the next issue of *Nation* there appeared a letter from my true-blue sister-in-law Peg (President of the Liberal Country League of South Australia), dissociating the Dutton family from my attitude to Our Queen.

I had already learned about the hardness of America's financial heart when I was refused an advance on my pay. Now I learned about American "efficiency", which is rather akin to German efficiency in that it strangles itself with rules. When the first official month was up (we had arrived a week before the start of the semester) and I was entitled to my cheque, I went to the pay office to collect it and was told that I could not have it, as my social security number was not available. I told them I had applied for it four and a half weeks earlier. Five days later, the social security number arrived and I rushed to the pay office. I was blandly told that the cheque would now be "processed" and I could have it at the end of the next week.

My thoughts were turning more and more to Australia. After I wrote the article for Tom Fitzgerald I began to write a novel, based on life in the RAAF. The hero was partly modelled on my old friend Geoff Cornfoot, my fellow double-OGG. (Old Boy of Geelong Grammar and of Geelong Gaol.) There was an empty room in the big farmhouse, and I got up early and wrote, and removed myself from the University as often as I could to write more. It roared along, the sound of Air Force Australian idiom sweet in my ears, Geoff's irreverent attitude to authority soothing my feeling of frustration on campus. The first section of the novel, which I called *Andy*, after the name of the hero, or anti-hero, was set in the gaol. The experience of being locked in a stone cell is agonizing; the deprivation of liberty as the door clangs shut and the bolts and locks close has to be experienced to be fully understood, but Geoff taught me that it can also be a kind of freedom. Although some of the subjects of the novel were very painful, it was turning out a comedy.

In March Ninette went to the doctor who confirmed she was pregnant.

Francis and Tisi were very pleased at the news, and for some obscure reason both were convinced that it would be another boy.

While we were at Cedar Knoll Farm Ninette, with Mary to look after the children, and a VW at her disposal, had time to look around. She found that there was an enamelling workshop at the University, and managed to make contact with a teacher to give her lessons in enamelling. She became expert in the technical aspects of enamels, and later on in Australia had many successful exhibitions.

In April our household was enlarged by a visit from George Bailey with Ariane, his daughter who, to my astonishment, was already turning into a woman. George had a great bushranger beard; as usual, he was bursting with song and story. He read the typescript of the first section of *Andy* with great approval, but said I must watch out against making it too damn literary. He was right, and I made some cuts. Working in a university is dangerous for a novelist, it makes you want to play word-games.

We flew up to Chicago with George, where he left us, and then on to Ohio where Robie and Anne Macauley had asked us for the weekend. Robie was editor of what was probably America's most prestigious literary review, the *Kenyon Review*. Kenyon College was small, quiet and sophisticated after Kansas State; it seemed like paradise. Robie, himself a talented writer of fiction, was one of those Americans who can be both efficient and easygoing, genial but far-seeing. He was an ideal editor of a literary magazine, and he and Anne were excellent hosts, but marvellously vague. Robie and I went to town to do some shopping for their party; at about ten to five Robie suddenly asked me whether the party was at five or five-thirty.

Robie had assembled a kind of a reunion for the weekend; the major occasion was to be a lecture and poetry reading by Robert Lowell. John Crowe Ransom was there, the founder of *Kenyon Review* in 1939, when he was Professor of Poetry at the College. Poet and critic, originator of "The New Criticism", Ransom was seventy-five, gentle but very sharp. The last thing Robert Lowell brought to mind was the New England aristocracy; he was big, untidy-haired, gangling, with a sunken gaze that could almost mean he was falling asleep, but then he would suddenly seem to wake up and talk, gesturing with the effort, and with an oddly southern cadence to his speech. A friend of all of them, the writer Peter Taylor, was there, a quiet man with a kind of bent face. The poet and critic Randall Jarrell was also one of the guests; like Ravel and the "Bolero", Jarrell now hated "Death of the Ball-Turret Gunner", the poem that had made him famous.

It was a refreshing atmosphere after Manhattan, where I was getting depressed by what seemed the pointlessness of it all, although grateful of course for the money. And at least I had been impelled to begin the novel and write the republican article. As well, the physical climate at Kenyon was much more agreeable. The climate of Kansas was not only harsh but deceitful; in late February it was 50 degrees Fahrenheit one day and 5 the next, a cheery sun making pretence the temperature was the same.

The group were all very interested to hear about Penguin setting up in Australia, which rather surprised me; most Americans seemed to think of Australia as being somewhere a few miles west of London, England. They all urged me to reprint in Penguin Australia Christina Stead's novels, especially *The Man Who Loved Children*; Robie suggested that Randall Jarrell would be the person to write an introduction, and Jarrell said he would be pleased to do so. Jarrell and Elizabeth Hardwick, Lowell's wife, and Lowell himself, had long been champions of *The Man Who Loved Children*. It seemed that the novel, published in 1940, although set in Baltimore and Annapolis, was actually based on Stead's childhood in Sydney.

I felt ashamed that I had not read the book; the only works of Stead's fiction I had read at that stage were *The Salzburg Tales* and *Seven Poor Men of Sydney*. Her books were out of print and not otherwise available in her native land, a situation typical of the literary scene in the early 1960s. Robie lent me his copy; I thought it an extraordinarily impressive novel, and immediately wrote to Brian Stonier saying we should reprint it, with Jarrell's introduction. Brian got in touch with Harmondsworth but Tony Godwin torpedoed the idea before it was even launched, refusing to take an English edition. Of course it was impossible for us to publish such a very large book in Australia without Harmondsworth support for sales in Britain. Harmondsworth eventually published it in 1970, after its great success when reissued in New York in 1965, with Jarrell's Introduction. So much for Godwin's belief in his Australian colleagues.

However, through Robie and Randall I was able to get in touch with Stead, and we were the first to publish her novella, *The Puzzleheaded Girl*. It appeared in *Australian Letters* (Vol. 7 No. 2, March 1966); Lawrence Daws did a drawing for it. With three other novellas, its title was given to the volume published in New York in 1967.

Lowell's lecture was enthralling, although it was a kind of stumble from theory to personal reflection. Like so many major poets, he was a bad reader of his own work, but it was still more rewarding to hear him than some actor sprucing up the shaggy lines. He had an odd trick of throwing away the ending of a poem; it reminded me of the way Australian Aboriginal dancers just stop playing and singing and walk away.

There was a party afterwards at the University; unlike Kansas, Kenyon was obviously not dry. Over a lot of cognac Ransom and Lowell were arguing about involvement in wars; in World War II Lowell had of course been put in gaol as a conscientious objector. The argument seemed to be something about the excitement and genuine life in fighting at the top of the hill, but I lost it. Or maybe they did. At about 2.30 a.m. Ransom rang Robie and asked him to come and collect Lowell and me.

When I went downstairs at about ten in the morning Robie was getting his son Cameron breakfast. I settled in with them and asked Robie if he would consider coming to Writers Week at the Adelaide Festival; he would indeed, so for the next few months we set about raising the funds to pay for his visit.

Not long after our return to Kansas, R.D. FitzGerald and Marjorie arrived for him to give his lecture. Gentle and shabby, they had lost their luggage somewhere en route from Texas. After the gathering at Kenyon, they seemed very provincial, although there was no doubt about their integrity. Marjorie said she didn't approve of segregation, yet she understood — you wouldn't want your daughter to etc. etc. Fitz said that Americans were physiologically just the same as us, so why didn't they eat mutton. She didn't approve of *To Kill a Mocking-Bird* because you wouldn't find a town like that, and kids wouldn't be allowed to walk home at night by themselves. She said Patrick was wrong about Himmelfarb's crucifixion in *Riders in the Chariot*, that Australians wouldn't do such a thing; I agreed with her about that.

Some restive academics had joined the students for Fitz's lecture the next day. But the lecture was a great success, with his gritty emphasis on the thing, the substantive noun, the old virtues which were not the classical ideal. Unfortunately he also said that Norman Lindsay was the greatest Australian artist. He hated Tom Fitzgerald and what he called Black Australia, meaning what he considered the favouring of the Aborigines above white Australians.

Fitz's reputation as a poet was secure (or seemed so then), with poems like "The Wind at your Door" or "Bog and Candle". He was to take a stand in the protests against the Vietnam War; in that and other ways he was no conservative. Yet, fourteen years younger than Ransom, he seemed much older and more fixed in his thinking than the American.

A week later I went down to give my lecture at the University of Texas at Austin. Joseph Jones, the head of the English Department, had been for decades a champion of Australian Literature in the USA. He took us to a baseball game. He pointed to Fitz and me and laughed: "How's that for two Aussie poets, sitting watching a baseball game and licking frozen Raspberry Sno-Cones".

The FitzGeralds now said they believed in the town in *To Kill a Mocking-Bird*; they had gone back to Texas through Arkansas. I was pleased to hear the conservative Fitz praising Max Harris; he said he had behaved like a man over the Ern Malley affair. I particularly liked Fitz's enthusiasm for Byron; he said he considered him the greatest genius. They had seen some odd things in Texas, such as a man who went for a leak at a baseball game and returned to find his seat taken — so he pistol-whipped the usurper. Putting away his pistol in its holster he had then turned to Fitz and said, “It’s sons of bitches like that give Texas a bad name.”

By the middle of May we were all feeling gloomy in Cedar Knoll Farm, even Mary. By this time it was very hot and appallingly humid, and a wind that affected one’s nerves like a north wind in South Australia blew ceaselessly, bending flat all the irises and peonies in the garden, blowing dust into the old house which was now hot inside, despite the thickness of its stone walls. Finally our time was up, and we packed our belongings.

It poured with tropical rain in Jamaica — we streamed with sweat — but somehow the climate was preferable to that of Kansas. I spent a fortnight in the Institute working on Eyre. There was no air-conditioning, and many documents were rotting away, in particular the 1865 newspapers with accounts of that year’s riots which Eyre had disastrously misinterpreted as a rebellion. The first time I turned the page of the newspaper I was reading, it simply disintegrated. I then worked out a system of turning the pages, holding them between two sheets of heavy paper. None of the attendants seemed interested in the fate of their precious documents.

After I had collected the material I needed, we all flew on to London, via New York, and arrived there on 24 June 1963.

Twenty-Two

In London Allen Lane had arranged for us to have his flat in Holland Park. I was really impressed at this generosity to his Australian editor, who was in fact not very high in the pecking order.

The flat was very comfortable, with pleasant furniture and some quite good pictures on the walls. It even had a grand piano. We were just settling in when there was a knock on the door. I opened it to find a little man in a dark suit, wearing a bowler. He had a foolscap folder in his hand. "Good morning," he said, "I've come to collect the rent. It's twenty-eight guineas a week and will you please give me one month in advance." This was rather more than five times as much as Allen Lane was paying me as his Australian editor. Still, that is how millionaires stay millionaires. I can't imagine why we didn't move out into something cheaper; but we didn't.

A few days later I went out to Harmondsworth to have lunch with Godwin and the Penguin editors and designers. Godwin was a beaky, intense person, with sideways looks and narrow smiles, who shook my hand with too much emphasis. However, he did have a proposition for me. Penguin were commissioning a series on New Writing from various countries, and he wanted me to edit one from Australia. The book would emanate from Harmondsworth, but I thought it would provide an excellent outlet for Australian writers, and immediately agreed to do it.

He then introduced me to some underlings and dashed off to another office. Nobody knew who I was or wanted to know. The only one with any warmth was Kaye Webb, the founding editor of Puffin Books, who had no idea why she was there, but when I told her about Penguin Australia she was then full of good ideas for cooperating with us. At lunch Godwin answered, or failed to answer, my queries with endless evasions. He then excused himself and said he had to rush off to a conference.

I had been bidden to take afternoon tea with Allen Lane at his farm near Harmondsworth. In his clipped, quiet way he said: "You should know about my private life. Lettice, my wife, comes here and lives in the flat you are occupying in Holland Park, and we go to Spain together, where I have a house. My girlfriend and I live at Drayton and then we go to Ireland, where I have a castle." All this seemed sensible enough, given Lane's character.

Later a friend of Lane's in London told me one detail which Lane had omitted. Apparently the girlfriend, Susanna, was the mistress of a German publisher. He and Susanna had come from Germany to stay with Lettice and Allen at the farm. Driving them back from the airport in his Rolls,

Allen stopped at a tobacconist's in a small town and said he wanted to buy some cigars. He suggested to Susanna that she might be amused to see a small English tobacconist's shop. He went out the back of the shop with her, found a taxi, returned to Heathrow, took her to Portugal and did not return for fifteen days.

I have often wished I had a tape recording of Lettice and the publisher's conversation in the Rolls while they waited. The pauses must have got longer and longer.

I was rather pleased to have arrived at Lane's farm in my own Rolls-Royce. Derry Jeffares, always a car enthusiast, had suggested that the way to solve the problem of buying a car in England and not losing money on it when you sold it on leaving for home, was to buy an old Rolls or Bentley, for they always kept their value. There were in fact a couple of garages which sold you these cars and guaranteed to buy them back again. So I bought an enormous twenty-five-year-old Rolls for a modest sum and had much pleasure from it. The area behind the front seat and the back was so vast that Francis could run his toy cars around it. The man who sold it to me told me always to be sure to unscrew the naked-lady mascot when leaving the car at night, otherwise it would be stolen. I remembered to do this every night I was in England, except on the last night, when I was so drunk I forgot. It was gone in the morning.

A Rolls, even an old one, is a good means of measuring the prodigious snobbery of the English. A lot of my research had to be done in the Public Record Office (PRO). There seemed to be a large space for parking cars in its courtyard, and always plenty of room, so to avoid walking to and from tube stations in the usual London drizzle, I asked the guard at the high wrought-iron gates whether I could park my car there. "Oh no, sir," he said, "this 'ere courtyard is only for the 'igh-ups." The next time I went I took the Rolls. The guard sprang out of his shelter box, swept the gates open and waved me through. After that I always went to the PRO in the Rolls.

Some of the most interesting people in London were old friends, Australian artists and writers. Lawrence Daws was there, and Sid Nolan, Arthur Boyd and John Perceval; Patrick and Manoly arrived from Greece to take up residence for two and a half months. Patrick's mother Ruth was dying. I had a dismal day with him and Manoly while the London rain came greyly down. "God how I hate this country," said Patrick.

Sid, as if he were arranging an assignation with a lover, would ring me from a public phone and ask could I have lunch with him at Quo Vadis, but be sure not to breathe a word to Cynthia. Cynthia, at the other extreme, gave Ninette their silent phone number and said, "Be sure not to tell Geoff what it is."

Sid and I had a long lunch together, and I was as baffled as ever by the contradictions in Sid's character. He was so tough and resourceful, and yet gentle, modest and generous. Although he did not drink anything alcoholic himself, he insisted on buying a bottle of wine for me. He talked of Australia, his passion to return, and of Cynthia's nervousness and suspicion that they would both be savaged. "By whom?" I asked. He was vague. "Oh, you know, critics and other people." I told him that if they did go back, in that sort of mood, it would be as it is with dogs when they can smell the scent of fear: one of the critics would bite them. He took another glass of tonic water and poured me another glass of wine; I had resigned myself to drinking the whole bottle. "It's not only me," he continued. "Australians don't like Cynthia or her writing." Suddenly I remembered that I had written, maybe in *Nation* or the *Bulletin*, an unfavourable review of a very bad book by Cynthia.

He said that living the past ten years in London had been like living in a vacuum, and it was true of Arthur, Lawrence and Charles Blackman as well. He had never wanted to paint England or London, the light had never meant anything to him. But this did mean that he could work at his painting without any kind of interference, his imagination was free. He thought what Australia needed now was a period of consolidation, a building up of criticism and critical responses. This was far-sighted of him, and I was able to tell him that the process was already under way with Lansdowne Press and Penguin Australia. He had been very wounded by an article of Max's which had accused him of carefully planning his career. "No one is that shrewd planner of Max's imagination — well, no genuine artist."

We laughed together over Patrick's hostility towards various people we happened to like. After leaving us at Rocky Point Patrick had met Jock Marshall and his family, on the way to stay with us, for two minutes at the Kangaroo Island airport; he wrote to me "that Jock Marshall is awful, but awful". We compared notes about Patrick's elephant's memory for bad reviews, his transparent candour about telling you what he liked or did not like. Sid said that after Patrick had outlined to him his plans for his next twenty years of writing, that he (Sid) had gone home and thought of the things he intended to do, but suddenly felt a bit tired, so went to bed early and slept like a child for ten hours.

That night C.P. Snow and his wife, Pamela Hansford-Johnson, came round for drinks after dinner; they had asked to come then. A bottle of Scotch disappeared in a few minutes; fortunately I had another. After initial snorting from him, and vowel-bending from her, they loosened up, especially when they heard that we had stayed with Helen and Lydig Hoyt in their house by the Hudson. They were terrible snobs and name-droppers. But they were much better on their own than in larger gatherings, where they played a sort of idea-pingpong with each other, tossing half a sentence for the other one to complete. They were great supporters of Sid and other

Australian painters. I had some of Henri Bastin's paintings with me, and they immediately bought one. They had just returned from Moscow, where they had met the young poet Yevtushenko. They liked him very much, full of gaiety and abandon, a bit of a show-off but at the same time very vulnerable.

A few nights later Arthur and Yvonne Boyd, John and Mary Perceval and Max Nicholson came around to dinner. Max had, to my astonishment, just driven in an M.G. "B" from Bagdad, where he had been teaching English, to London. He talked, sending himself up with gusto, of the ferment of the 1940s in Melbourne, the prissiness and anti-Australian prejudices of the English Department at Melbourne University. He asked about Deasey, recalling how he had once rushed out to Deasey's house after Deasey's girlfriend Pat Gray had found a suicide note from him on her table. When Max arrived panting, Deasey was reading a book; no doubt he had hoped Pat would rush over.

Perceval was rude and determined to annoy somebody. I showed him and Arthur what Bob Hughes had written (at that stage) in his Penguin art book, sections of which kept arriving. Although Hughes had praised Perceval he had also pointed out some weaknesses. Perceval, at this stage of his life and alcoholism, expected nothing but praise; he was furious, and announced that all art criticism was inaccurate and irresponsible.

Arthur looked up at me from under his eyebrows and said, "Do you mean to say that Rolls out there in the street is yours?" I nodded. He asked me what I was going to do with it when I returned to Australia, so I told him that the man I had bought it from had promised to buy it back. "Do you think we could do a swap?" asked Arthur. "I've just done some big new tiles you might like." Then, typical Arthur, "But it would be fairer to offer you two tiles, I mean ... I mean they're only tiles. Maybe a painting?" I said one, repeat one, tile would be more than enough. Arthur had met Patrick and had asked him what he thought of enamelling, as Ninette had done a course in Kansas and was keen to follow up when she got home. Arthur whispered to me: "It was a bit embarrassing, Patrick said 'Oh they're all doing that, it's a lot of crap, worthless'." Arthur said, with one of his mock-satyr grins, that the standard joke about Australian artists in London was that they were imparting virility to the tired English.

What a contrast it was to go the next night from real, working artists to John McDonnell's flat in Belgravia. John was an art collector and connoisseur, one of the original partners in the Macquarie Gallery in Sydney, and since 1947 buyer for the Melbourne Gallery's munificent Felton Bequest; he had bought some wonderful works of art of various kinds for the Gallery. John was charming and courtly, what Patrick would call an old queen. In his elegant aesthete's house not a thing was out of place, the Tanagra statuettes in their perspex boxes, the Tiepolo sketches and a meaningless little squiggle by Salvator Rosa; there were double locks on the windows and the triple locks on the door of the lift which opened directly into the sitting room.

A few days later I had a doleful lunch with Sid and Patrick. Sid was very hurt by some more scornful comments Max Harris had made about him in an article. Sid said Max's *Nation* article had been the worst attack ever made on him. He would never ever go back to Australia now. His mood had completely collapsed since our lunch at Quo Vadis; he had a crumpled look. "It's all on again," he said, "the sniping, the knocking, the in-fighting. Max is now the reactionary, the equivalent of McAuley in the Ern Malley affair." He had another tonic water, and added, "That was the time Max ran away to Adelaide and hid." I didn't recall Sid turning up for Max's trial. Max had an extraordinary ability to wound Sid, going back to the early days at Heide, and he could not resist using it. Yet before long they were on friendly terms again. This sort of drama was essential to Sid and Cynthia; they always had to be fighting their way through a forest of conspiracies.

Sid said that with the Tate Gallery show of Australian art it was all finished for Australian artists in London; he thought he'd go to America. Patrick said that at least Max had been on the right side as far as literature went. In fact he had done more than anyone else to make him (Patrick) a success in Australia. (I was a bit miffed at this.) Patrick had been looking at an exhibition of Francis Bacon's paintings; he had met Bacon many years before, through Roy de Maistre. "Bacon's paintings," he said, "are the true image of England: he hates art, he hates life, he hates himself." Just then we were joined by Tom Rosenthal and Trevor Craker from Thames & Hudson, the art publishers. As Tom in a review in the *Listener* had said that Sid's were the best paintings in the Tate show, Sid was able to brighten up when Tom told him not to take it all so seriously. The person who should have been told that, of course, was Cynthia, who always had to keep the pot of anguish on the boil.

I had wanted to go down to Walreddon Manor, near Tavistock in Devon, to see where the unfortunate Eyre, exonerated but shattered after his third trial for murder, had spent his last thirty years, in total seclusion. It was a beautiful old grey stone sixteenth-century house, on a slope overlooking a river, completely tucked away. The owner, Major Jack, was very helpful. I visited Eyre's grave in Whitechurch, the stone saying simply, "Australian Explorer and Governor of Jamaica".

Lawrence Daws and his first wife Dilys met Ninette and me in Exeter, and we pottered along in the Rolls until evening, when we stopped in a small village at a beautiful old hotel with a stone courtyard. One of the two bedrooms we were offered contained six beds, and had just been used by members of a visiting cricket team. At dinner a choleric maid abused us for sitting down at 7.20 p.m. instead of 7 p.m., and shouted with relish that everything was off except the roast pork. Dilys was Jewish, and Lawrence asked politely if she could have something else. We heard the maid yelling in the kitchen, and then she came back and said, "My gentleman says you can have gammon."

I asked could Dilys have an omelette. Certainly not. I was so annoyed that I went into the bar and asked to speak to the landlord. I heard him roar: "Who's he? Tell him to wait." I charged up to him and said that Dilys was not allowed to eat meat for medical reasons. He was one of those bullies who collapse immediately when confronted. "Tell her the omelette's on the way." I thought that it would never have happened in Yorkshire. But even southern English hospitality could not spoil our leisurely trip back to London through the lush summer landscape.

Tom Rosenthal asked me to come round to Thames & Hudson; he and Trevor Craker had a proposition to make me. It turned out that they wanted me to write a book about Russell Drysdale for their series on Australian artists. The first one, on Nolan, had appeared in 1961; they were also commissioning one on Arthur Boyd. I was pleased with the idea, in fact so attracted that I agreed to a ferocious deadline so that they could publish in 1964. I very much looked forward to seeing a lot more of Tass.

I went over to Arthur's house in Hampstead and chose a lovely greenish-grey tile to swap for the Rolls; it reminded me of a poem I had written for his paintings many years ago, "Hound and Lover". I arranged to leave the Rolls for him at a garage in Holland Park. As I have mentioned, on 7 September, our last night in London, I got drunk and lost the naked lady. It cost me eighty pounds to get a new one.

At Heathrow we said goodbye to Mary Black, who was going to stay on in England for a while longer. For the first time, her monumental calm shattered and she cried. All of us did.

Anlaby was in the midst of a flood when we arrived home.

Then coincidence again. Shortly after our return, on a visit to Melbourne for Penguin, I went to get a taxi at Melbourne airport. The driver was reading my article on the republic in *Nation*. I asked him whether he liked it, thinking that if he hated it, I needn't confess I'd written it. He said: "It's bloody beaut. At last someone's said it. But we're all so bloody lazy. How do we get there? Politics?" He shook his head. "Propaganda?" When I told him I'd written the article he took one hand off the wheel and shook mine. He kept talking about the subject all the way into Melbourne.

It seemed I'd scored a hit with this article, except at the cottage at Anlaby, where Peg asked had I turned into a communist in America, and in the Adelaide Club, where there was a deep freeze when I walked in the door. Indeed I wondered why I wasted my time (and money) belonging to such a hidebound institution. I could see why Judah Waten, in an article, had referred to Harris and me as "Slapsie Maxie and Dutton the Adelaide Club poet".

At dinner at the Balzac Steve and Nita Murray-Smith seemed not only genuinely pleased but a bit surprised, making me realize how much my origins, and signs like the Adelaide Club, had typecast me as a sort of literary country gent. Steve's Lansdowne booklet on Lawson had been well received, *Overland* was flourishing, and Steve was pleased I had asked his friend Ian Turner to write the opening survey for the Pelican *Literature of Australia*. Unlike Clem Christesen, he wished us well for *Australian Letters*. One of Steve's most appealing characteristics was his fairness, which went with a gutsy enthusiasm for our writers and our country; he was always ready to throw his big frame behind them and push like hell when needed.

The Balzac was run by Georges and Mirka Mora; Georges was a good friend and patron of young artists. Colin Lanceley and the Annandale Imitation Realists had stormed in from Sydney to Melbourne with an exhibition early in 1962, and Georges had kept the three artists in food and wine in return for the murals that now gave an added zest to the Balzac. This was the first time I had met Mirka. Like everyone else, I was captivated by this small, dark European-Jewish woman, who still looked like a girl of nineteen. Her delicious accent, her apparent naiveté, her impulsive humour projected a plausible persona that in no way revealed the subtleties underneath. Mirka was in fact deeply read in French and English, of formidable intelligence and acuity, and of a temperament that was wickedly satirical one moment and kind and affectionate the next. Her murals were also on the walls of the Balzac, as unmistakeable, droll and tender as herself.

She said she was always home in the mornings at her flat at the top of Collins Street, so after breakfast a couple of days later I called on her. The front door was down some steps and along a corridor; it was set inside some panes of glass. I knocked and waited. No one came, and when I peered through the glass I could not see anybody. But I was sure I had heard a movement. I knocked again, but without success. So I wrote her a short poem and shoved it under the door. Later Mirka confessed that she had been home; she had hidden behind a curtain and watched me. She was very pleased with the poem. So began our long friendship, always sexy but enduringly platonic, a typical Mirka paradox.

At Penguin's Bob Hughes' typescript had come in, more or less complete, but many more months of correspondence lay ahead. A new book we were particularly interested in had not yet been written; it was to be published under the title of *The Lucky Country*. This had been Max's idea. Before I went to Kansas he had suggested to Donald Horne that he write a Penguin

Special, as Lane's original series had been called, about Australia today. At one of our regular long lunches Max had told me this, and suggested I follow up by writing to Donald, who by this time had left Consolidated Press.

These many and most productive lunches were at this stage usually in the Da Costa Restaurant under the Mary Martin Bookshop. The restaurant was run by a man called Fuss who was not only an excellent chef himself, but would get in special food to tempt us, such as a goose or a Murray cod, a delicious fish that is almost unprocurable nowadays because of the ravages of the European carp. I, it seems, was the reliable one who kept notes. "Write that down, Dutton", Max would say with a flourish which spilled some more claret over my piece of paper, for we never had anything dignified like a folder or file. The ideas behind *Australian Letters*, Penguin Australia and *Australian Book Review* were fuelled by these claret-stained scraps of paper. Fortunately Brian Stonier, while managing to remain clear-headed, also enjoyed such sessions, which are so much more productive than earnest gatherings round a table in an office, lubricated by Nescafé.

Now in Melbourne we had a long synopsis from Donald and a promise that the 70,000-word book would be promptly written. We were all strongly in favour of the book, provisionally entitled "An Anatomy of Australia". Brian sent the synopsis off to Tony Godwin; we needed his support to print a big enough run to keep the price down. But Godwin was not impressed.

Within five months I had the first draft of the manuscript. I wrote to Donald that I thought it was going to be a winner, and that the title of the book should be the one he had used for the last chapter, "The Lucky Country". Donald replied "The title The Lucky Country is OK by me". I sent the manuscript off to Godwin. His reply was dismally tepid; he said there was "a lack of concrete examples". Donald said to me, "It's a book of ideas and imagination, not facts."

For the next two months letters passed between Godwin and me, getting nowhere. We decided to go it alone; Brian ordered a run of ten thousand, and wrote to Harmondsworth asking if they would take even three to five thousand copies to help us. Not only did they reject that, but they refused to sell any copies of our edition; they had given the same negative response to Robin Boyd's *The Australian Ugliness*. We finally published *The Lucky Country* in December 1964; the first edition sold out immediately, and of course hundreds of thousands of copies have been sold since.

Lane had told me when I first met him not to be afraid of having a row; he enjoyed them, and they showed spirit. So in August I had written him a strong letter saying that he was the only one at Harmondsworth who understood Australia and Australians, and he had better pay us a visit and do something to rescue the Australian operation from the dead hand of

Harmondsworth. Brian found Lane a good excuse for a visit in the opening of the new Penguin building at Ringwood.

Lane came out with his most trusty lieutenant, Harry Parroissien, and opened the building. They then came over to stay with us at Anlaby. The cellar still held some precious bottles from previous generations (my mother kept the key from my father), and I gave them a 1909 Chateau Lafite and a 1937 Chateau Yquem, as well as a liberal amount of good Australian wine. I was not going to let Lane get away without his supporting *The Lucky Country*.

Two days later I was able to write to Donald: "I am happy to say that *The Lucky Country* is now to go to the UK in a big way". Lane forced Godwin to take fifteen thousand copies. Godwin was such a bastard that in revenge he changed the title of the Harmondsworth edition to *Australia in the Sixties*. At the same time he again knocked back *The Man Who Loved Children*.

In Melbourne I called on Deasey. The Delage was mouldering away in the street; he was waiting for some part for the Cotal electric gearbox to arrive from Paris. I suspected it would never arrive; meanwhile he was driving a Holden. He seemed to be surviving quite well in his unlikely profession as a schoolmaster. Kershaw had gloomily written from France: "Deasey is dead".

Meanwhile I had completed the editing of the collection of Australian New Writing which Godwin had commissioned me to do. When I sent it off in April 1964 I felt rather pleased with it, and how it demonstrated the strength of Australian writing. It included prose by Patrick White, Randolph Stow, Patricia Rolfe, Peter Mathers, Elizabeth Harrower, and Robert Hughes, and poetry by A.D. Hope, David Campbell, Judith Wright, Francis Webb, Gwen Harwood and the young Les Murray.

After three months silence I had still not heard from Godwin. Then Brian Stonier sent me a copy of a letter to me from Godwin, enclosing a copy of a report made by Francis Hope, Assistant Editor of the *New Statesman* and *Nation*, which, to summarize, said the collection was inferior and not worth publishing. He also said that the best Australian writers were the expatriates like Colin MacInnes and Peter Porter whom I had not included. (Actually Peter Porter was there with "Phar Lap in the Melbourne Museum"; perhaps Hope had flipped through the collection so fast he had galloped past that one.)

I was so disgusted with the report that I sent it, and Godwin's letter rejecting the anthology, to all the contributors. One of them was Max Harris (who of course knew, in any case) and in buoyant style he wrote a piece about it in the *Australian* which was picked up in London by the *Sunday Times*, and a fine old row erupted. The outcome was that Billy Collins and Ken Wilder published the anthology in Fontana paperback and in Collins hardback; it was a great success. Charles Higham was commissioned by Godwin to edit an anthology more along the lines he wanted.

Meanwhile I was getting on with my book for Thames & Hudson on Russell Drysdale. He had asked me to come over to Sydney for a few days so we could talk, and had agreed that it would be a good idea for me to bring a tape recorder.

I arrived at the flat in Potts Point and rang the bell. Tass's wife, Bonnie, opened the door, tough and untidy as ever, and looked me up and down. "You are pretty, aren't you?" (I must say that no one else has called me that, before or since.) "Yes, a pretty man. I always distrust pretty men." She let me come in. "Oh what an old port you've got! I thought a moneyed man would have something better, but I quite like it that you haven't." She kept on needling me as she shut the door. When Tass came down from his studio she said to me: "You know, you've got no aggression in you, none at all."

Tass and Bon talked simultaneously on different subjects. Tass was trying to tell me that he had booked me a room in a nearby private hotel in Macleay Street. Bon was asking me (as if I would know) why Tass had phoned James Fairfax from Donald Friend's and not from a phone box? Tass advised me to go and talk to Donald about him, as nobody knew more about him than Donald. "Yeah," said Bon meaningfully, "Tass and Donald lived together, you know."

I really enjoyed Bon, she was full of spirit, despite being not at all well, and having suffered the blow of their son Tim committing suicide. The world as a whole did not impress her overmuch, and she was not in awe of anyone. She also had a deadly sense of irony. Tass told me how on one occasion when they were with Menzies, the great man had asked Bon what she thought of his new Budget. She looked innocently up at him and said, "Now why would a great big man like you want to be asking a little woman like me a question of that sort?"

Tass and I did a great deal of talking, drinking and eating; I had spent some time with his old teacher, George Bell, in Melbourne on my way to Sydney, and there was a great deal of mutual respect there. But it was proving very difficult to get Tass to talk for the tape; he wasn't against it at all, but just kept putting it off.

I took up Tass's suggestion and went to talk to Donald Friend. Tass' procrastination with the tape didn't surprise Donald. He said a key to Tass's character was his laziness, and his inability to start a painting. Donald was very critical of Tass's obsession with psychiatrists; one of them had even told him he should stop painting. Taking a risk, one day when Tass was up the street, I asked Bon about Tass's difficulty in starting painting. She said it was because of his passion for standards, for always wanting to be better, unlike Donald who just painted and drew for fun.

Then, in the early hours of the morning, after we had finished one bottle of whisky, Tass suddenly said it was time to record the tape. We would do it in my room so that Bon would not barge in. He said, "Geoff I haven't known you for all that many years, but I feel you are part of the same sort of life as me, I feel quite at ease with you."

He talked, wonderfully well, for the next three hours, and at about 4 a.m. he said he must go to bed. His flat was only a few hundred yards away, but I thought I'd better accompany him. We made it to his front door, but he simply could not get the Yale key into the lock. I said I would do it. Finally, by sitting on the ground, as the lock was rather low down, I managed it. "Geoff old boy," said Tass, "are you all right down there? Would you like me to walk with you back up to your room?" I managed to make it on my own.

Back home at Anlaby a little over a fortnight later, I was hard at work on the final chapter of my book on Tass when the phone rang. It was Ursula. Bon had killed herself. Tass had been out, and returned to the flat late at night to find the paper and milk still on the step, and the door locked and bolted. He had had to break the door open. Bon had known she was dying; she hated doctors and hospitals, and she had the guts to do it. But her suicide was terribly hard on Tass, who had already been through his young son's suicide. Fortunately, Tass still had his daughter Lynne and her husband Bill, two very sturdy characters who could help him. But Bill also was soon to die, from an illness, at an early age.

At least in South Australia joyful things were happening. Sam, who had started life in Kansas, was born on 5 December. A week later I had a final meeting with Tass in Sydney about the book. He met me at Mascot in the Landrover in which he looked like a bushie, his favourite persona in Sydney. The set of his jaw was the same, but his skin was blotchy and his one good eye seemed at times to jam in his face. He was living with Bill and Lynne. We had a four-hour lunch at Watson's Bay. He said he'd spent so many years painting people of determination and guts that some of it must surely rub off on him.

Sam was christened on 1 March in Grandfather's little church at Hamilton. Patrick was there and fully acted out his duties as godfather, even holding the baby by the church door, looking simultaneously nervous and proud. Before the ceremony the parson came up with the jug of christening water, which he had just filled from the rainwater tank by the vestry. He held it up and said, "I don't suppose a few wrigglers in the water will impair the efficiency of the sacrament."

Patrick went back to Adelaide to rehearse his new play, *Night on Bald Mountain*. It was being given its première by Harry Medlin's Theatre Guild, again after appalling troubles with the Festival Governors, who had not only rejected it but in the end would not even grant it Fringe status.

Patrick stayed at a motel in Adelaide, and settled into the last stages of his bloody battles with the now despised John Tasker.

We had visitors — David, Bonnie and their daughter, Raina Campbell, Bob Hughes, Kaye Webb, Jean Battersby and Peter Sculthorpe. The first arrivals made the best entrance, Tass, Sid Nolan and Hal Missingham surging up in the heat to the peppertrees by the Anlaby front door in Tass's father's Rolls. The three of them were lads on the loose, roaring old songs. Hal, apart from the great contributions to art in Australia which he made while Director of the New South Wales Art Gallery, was a most genial, totally unpompous individual. He was the catalyst that routed Sid's nervous suspicions and lifted Tass from his grief.

Tass wanted to go to the nearest pub. It was an old coaching inn, the Wheatsheaf, reputed to be the oldest licensed hotel in Australia still owned by the original family. The publican was a little old man, like his pub, the chipped skin very tight-drawn over the bones of his face, with enormous hands and nails as big as his eyes. Tass noticed the hands immediately; the hands are always very closely observed in his paintings and drawings. He said to me, "It's an occupational development with publicans, like the feet in a fast bowler."

They purred off to Adelaide in the Rolls; Tass was very pleased with the air-conditioning, which most cars did not have in those days. Sid and Tass both had exhibitions at the Festival.

Bob Hughes was busy at Anlaby doing big pen-and-ink drawings as illustrations for some verse satires I had written on various groups such as graziers, academics, leisured ladies, good blokes. Chortling with the pleasure the pen was giving him, he completed the set and urged me to write more. We planned that they would be made into a booklet, but, alas, too many other things intervened. He had to go down to Adelaide to cover the art shows for *Nation*.

At that time we had half a house, in Curtis Street in North Adelaide, which I used as an office, and where we could stay if we had a late night in Adelaide. It was what real estate people call a semi-detached; in other words, a little old stone house built with a wall down the middle, and four rooms on either side, with an outside dunny. The salt-damp came at no extra charge, from the stone walls having been built in the 1880s with no damp course.

We left the Campbells and Tass there, and returned to Anlaby for the night. Next afternoon, when I parked the car outside the Curtis Street front door, Tass came bursting out and said, "I've buggered up your wall, but I'll make it all right again." What had happened was that, late at night and well into the whisky, David had recited a new poem (now Part One of "Chansons Populaires"), beginning "Hey Jack, give the grog and the women a rest", and Tass had immediately seen the need for a mural on the white wall of the sitting room.

At first he could find no suitable drawing pencils, so he began with Raina's eyebrow pencil. Then someone runmmaging in a drawer found a selection, and Tass was away, his hand as sure as ever, despite the hour and the whisky. David then wrote, in his fine, strong sloping hand, the words of the poem. So this was the buggered-up wall. Would there were more like it.

Back at Anlaby I had been thinking of the contrast between these happy boozers who had cast off their various loads of personal anguish: Tass, David, Hal, Bob — even Sid, who was not a boozer. Art took Adelaide by storm in 1964, for there was a delectable exhibition of Arthur Boyd's work as well as those by Tass and Sid. And there, fighting miserably in the theatre with the hated Tasker (now always referred to in letters to me as "Tilly"), was Patrick, a bigger boozer than any of them, incapable of forgetting his anguish for more than a few minutes. Where they were rejoicing together, he was alone and angry. His play, *Night on Bald Mountain*, had at its centre an alcoholic wife, and it was a play about the destruction of love. On the perimeter of the play, but actually meant to hold the play together, was one of Patrick's "good" people, the goat-woman Miss Quodling. It is by far the weakest of Patrick's plays, and a demonstration that a playwright needs more than a number of fixed ideas and a dominant will.

The atmosphere at the exhibitions was enthusiastically amiable. But Patrick later wrote to me: "It isn't an exaggeration to say I experienced moments of pure fright, the worst of them being at the Nolan opening. I couldn't get away fast enough from that."

His own opening was not quite the success as depicted in David Marr's biography, although the run developed well. I felt a lot of hostility on the first night, and nag, nag, nag at the interval; people like David Campbell let it flow over, and waited for it to sink in, but the critical minds weren't giving it a chance. The second night was much better.

After the Festival, I went to New Zealand to carry out more research on Edward John Eyre; Eyre had been Lieutenant-Governor there after leaving Australia.

In Australia the ferment of artistic ideas and production in the 1950s and early 1960s was exactly that, a ferment, not a consciously directed operation nor a connected web of influence. Rather it was a burst of rays of individual enlightenment and discovery which, as they mixed, opened up new landscapes and cast beams into shady places. The mistake people make nowadays when writing about the 1950s and early 1960s is to think that because Menzies was in control from 1949 to 1966 that Australian life corresponded to his conservatism. In the realm of ideas, almost no leads came from the top, from Right or Left. Labor, apart from the eccentric art-loving Bert Evatt, the goodwill towards literature from the clumsy Arthur Calwell, and the odd miracle like Cahill commissioning Utzon to build the Sydney Opera House, was as stultifyingly narrow as the Liberals. At the top you had Menzies boasting about being British to the bootstraps; at the bottom you had Alan Seymour's Alf boasting about being a bloody Australian and proud of it. Both of them were keeping out what was new and invigorating. Both had differing but equally narrow ideas of patriotism.

Perhaps the most misunderstood of all popular quotations is Dr Johnson's "Patriotism is the last refuge of a scoundrel". Johnson made the remark, on 7 April 1775, at a dinner with "numerous company" which included Edward Gibbon and Sir Joshua Reynolds as well as the recording non-angel, Boswell. He was pouring scorn on scoundrels, not on patriotism. As Boswell said, "he did not mean a real and generous love of our country, but that pretended patriotism which so many, in all ages and countries, have made a cloak for self-interest". It was such scoundrels that always drove Patrick to fury, precisely because he was a fanatical idealist. Tass, Sid, Arthur, Hal, even Bob in lighter measure, were genuine patriots.

They were all explorers, they wanted to lead Australians, in the isolation of our enormous island, into new countries of the mind. At the time, the ways ahead were wide open to those with sufficient talent and vision. Patrick was the only one among them, cursed by his temperament and burnt soul, to be incapable of "a real and generous love of our country". He might not have been lacking in what the King James Version of the Bible calls "charity", but his greatest contempt was for himself. He had a marvellous eye for reality, and he was one of the most generous people I have ever met, but his failure to fulfil Christ's injunction, "Thou shalt love thy neighbour as thyself", was crucial. This rendered him incapable of avoiding destructive outbursts. He was branded with the impossible ideal, like that terrible destroyer, Hjalmar Ekdal in Ibsen's *The Wild Duck*, who says, "In certain cases it is impossible to overlook the claim of the ideal". All too conscious of his own faults and mistakes, Patrick could not forgive those of other people or of his own country. But unlike those in control of the country, whether in Canberra or in Sydney or Adelaide, he was always, at least at this time of his life, open to new ideas, and his passionate feelings about Australia were based on the need to impart these ideas to his countrymen and women.

The others were much more easygoing, less destructively idealistic, in their feelings about their country. Sid said to me one day, "Tass is the most Australian of us all." If he was right, and I think he was, it was because

Tass was the one who felt the most easy with Australia. Drysdale and White were both from pioneering Australian families and were both born in London in 1912. Nolan's paternal grandfather was a poor selector, his father a tram driver; he was born in Melbourne in 1917. All three, the two artists and the writer, were rebels in their different ways, and yet, without being conservative, were faithful to certain elements in their background. And none of them wanted to leave Australia as he had found it.

Tass, although deeply complex, was happy in the company of stockmen or graziers. Patrick, descended from graziers, and once, improbably, a jackeroo, was not at ease with stockmen and was hostile to most graziers. Sid, with his Irish charm, could get on well with stockmen, tram drivers or graziers, but his thoughts were elsewhere, full of his plans; Sid (with Cynthia watching him) had to beware of himself, knowing he was dangerously gregarious. He could see how Tass wasted his time in company.

Although all three were basically very solitary people, neither Tass nor Sid could live without a woman, nor Patrick without a man. Of them all, the two who were probably closest in spirit were Patrick White and Cynthia Nolan, burnt souls both of them, as profoundly suspicious of other people as they were ruthless in manipulating them for their own advantage. Maybe one basic element of Drysdale's Australianness was a rather naive inability to make use of other people.

In some respects the 1950s and early 1960s were a season for solitaries in the arts, a time for explorers in the near-desert of both Australia and the individual mind.

PART 5
Sun Books and Russia 1964–67

Nor would he be surprised at all
To watch the stars of Europe's wisdom fall
East, west and south. He would certainly try
To make room for them in our hard, glittering sky.

"Thebarton Hall, 1955"

Twenty-Three

I returned to Anlaby on an idyllic day in April, driving in past the mad white scribbles of young lambs chasing each other up and down the banks of the dry creek bed. I went over to the office to see Robbie. He came down the hill in his ute, took something out of the back and walked over to me, his usually cheery face taut. In his arms he had a lamb. A fox had eaten off its tail and half its backside, and also its entire nose and tongue; it was still alive, and made clucking noises through the stump of its face. I went into the office and got the rifle and shot it for Robbie, who still did not want to speak. He said that in more than thirty years on the land he had never before seen this particular horror. I remembered a line of David Campbell's (of whom Alan Seymour had complained to me that he was too joyful): "crows take the eye first (foxes the tongue)".

After New Zealand, my pace was frenetic in these years. I don't know where the energy came from. There were more trips to Melbourne, for Penguin Australia was up and running, and my Pelican *Literature of Australia* appeared in 1964. Also in 1964 Andrew Fabinyi published my next book of poems, *Flowers and Fury*, with Cheshire. Then a big, handsome hardback arrived from London, an advance copy of my *Russell Drysdale* from Thames & Hudson.

Another project came to fruition — a series of twenty-one large full-colour reproductions of modern Australian paintings; I selected the paintings and supervised production, while Bob Horgan, who ran a wholesale paperback bookstore in Adelaide, ran the business side. Beautifully printed by Griffin Press, these reproductions were the first series of such works produced in Australia. The artists included Dobell, Drysdale, Nolan, Arthur Boyd, Tucker, Daws, Blackman, Pugh and Len French; they were all astounded when we paid them royalties. We called the series Artists of Australia.

Patrick's collection of stories, *The Burnt Ones*, dedicated to Ninette and me, appeared in that year, with the Rocky Point story, "Dead Roses", in it. Patrick's mother, Ruth, had died in 1963 and he and his sister Suzanne had inherited a great deal of money; he was now a rich man from that alone. Patrick was always generous with his money, but he could never quite understand what people without money had to do to keep going. I remember once, when I was with him and Elizabeth Riddell, he made an acid remark about a woman journalist in her fifties who worked for Consolidated Press, something like, "She ought to be ashamed of herself, working for that fascist shit Frank Packer." Elizabeth stopped him in his tracks by saying, softly, "But Patrick, she needs the money. She hasn't any."

He wrote me a letter in May, which began with a defence of the story "Dead Roses", which I did not think a success. He then went on with "a word of criticism":

> all this commerce — flying about — Melbourne twice — Kangaroo Island almost immediately after — and the Festival before that — how is it all going to affect your work, the work that really matters. I wrote some time ago that I had seen signs of deepening and maturing in your criticism, and when you settled at Anlaby I hoped you were going to give more time to this. Now I am beginning to have my doubts. It is very difficult to write this kind of thing without sounding pompous and awful, but I feel that you and I can quite easily get sucked back into something from which we thought we had escaped. I know I have to sit down to a serious stocktaking. I feel just about clapped out creatively — partly through the recent critical battering, partly through the temptation to become a sort of social flibbertygibbet. I've got to humble myself, and more or less start painfully all over again.

The letter was well meant, and contained much truth, but Patrick as usual did not understand about money (or the needs of children on holiday). Patrick's despised "commerce", Penguin and the art prints were financially helpful, as were lectures. Patrick never took it in that I had not inherited money, as he had. And once again those warning words of my mother were being proved right: "If you go to live at Anlaby everybody will think you are rich".

Patrick did what was best for him — he wrote. Unfortunately he did not confine himself to fiction, but wasted his time, genius and emotional energy on the stage. Maybe I was wrong, but I thought I could manage other roles, following such masters as Dickens and Trollope or even Flaubert — committees, publishing, literary magazines, "commerce", all things which were totally alien to Patrick's temperament. I was not being scoundrelly-patriotic, but I did strongly believe that it was my duty to do all I could to help in what seemed to me to be the great breakthrough of Australian art and literature in the 1950s and 1960s. He, often to his fury, felt the same, but at this stage took no part in public life.

He was right, of course, about the dangers of being a social flibbertygibbet. He had recently written a very funny letter about going to what was referred to in the papers as "the social high-light of show week", a dinner at Hannah Lloyd-Jones's Rosemont; the only good things, according to Patrick, had been "a conversation with Sid on the veranda, with the moon coming up behind some tall gums, and a good gossipy gin-up with Ursula". (He had just found out that Ursula was also a Gemini, which further explained their rapport.) Such occasions did in fact fuel Patrick's own fiction, but they did nothing for my writing.

There were also other diversions, mainly theatrical. The Beatles came to Adelaide, and Bill Hayward, who was the sponsor and had centre seats in the upstairs section of the huge old Centennial Hall, asked us to join him and Ursula. Like flocks of birds that wheel together, the teeny-boppers seemed to know when they should all scream, a noise that rattled the ears, while on the stage the Beatles themselves seemed quite dignified, with their page-boy haircuts. Then the fans started to beat their feet and the whole upstairs span started to creak up and down; it was quite scary. When it was all over one girl just behind me hissed to another one, "You didn't scream — you must be senseless." Later I was surprised to hear from Patrick that he was going to the Beatles in Sydney. He said it was "a dreadful prospect, but I feel one ought to see what really goes on".

I was asked to deliver the CLF lecture at Townsville, and decided to take as my subject "The Vision of Evil in Australian Literature". The idea had been rattling around in my head ever since I wrote the short book on Whitman; W.B. Yeats said that Whitman "lacked the vision of evil". I think Yeats was wrong, but Whitman's determination to keep on hoping seemed to me very characteristic of a lot of Australian writers, although of course not Patrick. Having just finished writing about Drysdale, I found Tass's work almost devoid of such a vision of evil. He certainly had it, but kept it to himself.

In July, on the way to Townsville, Ninette and I stopped in Sydney for a couple of days so I could do more work on Eyre in the Mitchell Library. I rang Dogwoods to confirm arrangements for Manoly and Patrick to come to dinner with us. Manoly told me that Patrick was in hospital with a very bad attack of asthma; but he sounded relieved to be able to come to dinner alone and talk. Things had been very low indeed between them. There had been another theatrical love affair, but Manoly had been told that infidelities did not count, Patrick had more than enough love for more than one person. I did not say anything; at the time, I shared the same belief. And Manoly was unhappy about the move to Sydney. In May Patrick had bought a house in Martin Road, Centennial Park, and they were hoping to move in September. Manoly loved Dogwoods, where he had created the garden and planted so many trees; he dreaded the jangling life that might surround them in Sydney. Now he thought Patrick might die and he was overcome with love for him.

Old friends knew just how foul Patrick could be to Manoly. I was staying with them once when Patrick had invited half a dozen people to dinner; in front of all these guests, he said such wounding and insulting things to Manoly that Manoly's face crumpled and he went upstairs to his room in tears, while Patrick stamped out into the kitchen. I was so disgusted with this entirely unprovoked attack that I went out and told him he should be ashamed of himself. "Oh, Manoly," he snorted, his face grey with sweat, downing a drink, "Greeks are all fucking masochists."

Now in July I went to see Patrick in his house of winds, high in the hospital. He looked and talked as if he were right on the edge, hanging on with his finger-tips, breathing too quickly. His eyes had strange rings around the pupils like the stone eyes in some statues. But I was sure that he had no intention of dying.

In September we went down to Rocky Point for the children's holidays. I already had a bad cough, and almost immediately started to run a high temperature and had to go to bed. I couldn't put up with staying in bed all day, so carried a cane chair and a file of paper down into the scrub, where I set the chair on the green moss in a little grove of native pines, sheltered from the northerly wind. I wanted to write some poems about the island for the children. I wrote thirty-six poems in ten days, between eleven and one o'clock each day; at the end they were coming, in full rhyme and structure, at the rate of about five a day. "That's the way poems ought to come," replied David Campbell when I sent them to him.

John Perceval liked them and agreed to do some drawings for them, to appear in a new series Andrew Fabinyi was planning. He and Mary were living in Canberra, where I called on them. Mary told me that John's drinking was now so bad that it seemed he would never paint or draw again, but something had appealed to him about these poems, perhaps because of his love for children, and doing drawings for them had given him a new lease of life. The drawings are a bit mad, but very evocative of childhood, and not from a cute, grown-up point of view. Andrew published both poems and drawings in a very handsome book called *On My Island*. Not long after this, John worsened so hopelessly that he voluntarily went into hospital, and did not work again for many years. Happily, he did then come out and paint again with some of his old freshness.

In 1964 I had had an idea for what I thought would make a children's book; this involved using photographs, which were acceptable in children's books in those days, and having three-year-old Tisi as a model for the central character in the story. Dean Hay, an old friend, who was both a successful businessman and a very fine photographer, agreed to cooperate on making the book, which I called *Tisi and the Yabby*. I thought it might have quite a good sales potential, and also that it might appeal to readers in Britain, so next time I was in Sydney I gave it to Ken Wilder, then managing Collins in Australia. Ken was most enthusiastic, and soon reported that Billy Collins agreed with him. The book was scheduled for simultaneous publication in Britain and Australia in 1965.

In October I agreed to serve on the Literary Committee of the *Encyclopaedia Britannica* Australia Awards; these were, at the time, the most valuable awards for the arts and sciences in Australia, being for five thousand pounds each. An engaging Hungarian called Gabriel Carr managed them, and made sure we were treated extraordinarily well. We were put up at the Belvedere, a rambling, eccentric old hotel in Kings Cross that has long since been demolished. The main building had only two storeys and the bedrooms were scattered around the extensive garden. The public rooms and bedrooms were jammed tight with comical furniture and statues perched in windows and made into lamps; there were battered watercolours and greasy oils of Europe on the walls, and all night long outside the bedroom window camphor laurels rustled like stiff silk dresses in the wind. Gabriel saw to it that the meals and drink were of the finest quality; the meetings went on for many hours after the business had been concluded.

As at Writers' Week in Adelaide, some old suspicions and hostilities were healed at the awards, and new friendships made. When we first assembled I noticed Vincent Buckley and Clement Semmler glaring at each other, so I introduced them and tried some diplomacy, but to no avail. Then Clem suddenly said, "Excuse me for a minute, I just want to go and listen to the next race at Randwick." Vin's Irish face lit up. They were immediately united in a common love of horse racing. I had been deputed to sound Patrick out as to whether he would accept that year's Award; as I had expected, he refused. Also expected was some abuse from Patrick for going on the committee and wasting my time; I pointed out that as well as the benefits for Australian writers, it meant a free trip to Sydney and Canberra, where I could do more research on my biography of Eyre. But this was the sort of grubby necessity he could not understand.

We recommended Judith Wright for the prize, although Vincent Buckley argued hard for Francis Webb. Webb certainly deserved it, but I, with the rest of the committee, thought it a waste for the permanent inmate of a mental hospital to be given five thousand pounds.

A first-class row was to erupt three years later, in 1967, when we unanimously recommended Christina Stead for the Award; *Cotter's England* had been published in New York in 1966 and in London in 1967, but of course we considered the Award would be given for her life's work. This was in May. The General Council for the Awards, which were for several other fields as well as for literature, met in October. They ruled that she was not eligible because she "had not lived in Australia for forty years … and it was also doubtful whether the proposed candidate's contribution to literature was of sufficient and specific relation to Australia to satisfy the importance attached to this qualification in the Awards Constitution". Actually our decision was perfectly in accord with the Constitution. Unfortunately our Chairman, Clem Semmler, was overseas at the time of the Council meeting.

This was a disgraceful decision on the part of the Council; no Award was given, and the prize money was not used. I had known the Chairman of the Council, Sir Leonard Huxley, for many years; he had been Professor of Physics at Adelaide University. I rang Len and told him what I thought of the decision, and that Stead was a writer of world fame who had spent the first twenty-six years of her life in Australia; she was a wanderer, not an exile. Len was both apologetic and evasive, and more or less told me that his Deputy Chairman, the scientist Sir Macfarlane Burnet, had been the leader of the opposition to Stead. Burnet was politically very conservative; the parent company was American. I have always thought that Stead's links with communism — she was to the end of her days an unregenerate Stalinist — were the real reason for the Council's shocking decision.

Patrick of course fumed and roared and said that I should resign from the Literary Committee. The truth was that he had always loathed the whole idea of the *Britannica* Awards, considering it a form of American imperialism; he didn't need the money, so why should anyone else have it. He also hated most of those to whom we had given awards, especially A.D. Hope and Hal Porter.

But to get back to my own work. With the Eyre biography, one of the problems was that I felt I could not write the book properly unless I had seen the country around the Bight across which he and the Aboriginal boy Wylie had walked, nearly dying of hunger and thirst; the cliffs near which Baxter had been murdered; the bay where, miraculously, a ship was at anchor and the captain gave them food and drink. But I had neither the time nor the stamina to walk like Eyre from Streaky Bay to Albany.

Chibs came to the rescue. She was an excellent and very experienced pilot, and owned her own plane, a four-seater Cessna 172. She suggested that we fly together around the Bight and back again. We filled the back-seat space with extra petrol and water and food, and set off early in November 1964. It was pleasing to be doing things together again, just the two of us, as we had all those years ago at Anlaby and Rocky Point.

It was an adventurous flight, replete with marvels. The Nullarbor Plain stretches desolately out of sight, and at the coast the land abruptly ends at cliffs which rise vertically four hundred feet from the ocean. Every now and then there is a giant slab of rock that has broken away from the edge but is still poised above the water; an old bushman said to me, "A dog's bark would set 'em rolling."

In the Cessna we flew two hundred feet above the water, and were still two hundred feet below the top of the cliffs. An albatross provided some scale to the vastness, the giant bird just a speck between the ocean and the cliffs. Suddenly the cliffs stopped, and the sandhills began, some of them six hundred and fifty feet high, moving inwards over the land, the posts of the old telegraph line disappearing into them. Then came the delectable Recherche Islands with their little bays, in one of which the ship of Eyre's saviour, Captain Rossiter, had been anchored. Eyre and Wylie were on their own by then, Baxter having been murdered by the other two Aborigines in Eyre's party. Baxter's monument at the murder site must be the loneliest memorial in the world. Then what fortitude it must have taken for Eyre and Wylie to leave the safety of the ship and walk on to Albany. I have always thought it most unfair that Francis Webb's long poem is called "Eyre All Alone".

Two days after making it back to Adelaide at last light in the Cessna, I was flying in the commercial airliner to Melbourne for the opening by Allen Lane of the new Penguin building at Ringwood. The contrast was unnerving. I had rapidly to regain my equilibrium in tackling Lane, after the rows with Godwin over *The Lucky Country* and the anthology he had rejected. We got over the latter, and its removal to Collins, in twenty seconds. Lane later complained to me that there was not enough excitement and temperament at Ringwood, so he had enjoyed our encounter. So much for Brian Stonier's efforts to make everything run smoothly.

We retired for a five-hour lunch and then Brian and I taught Lane and Parroissien "The Wild Colonial Boy" as we drove in a taxi back to the hotel.

In January 1965 I began the actual writing of the Eyre biography, feeling like a single-handed sailor going off around the world in a boat stocked with provisions. Of course, a biography never quite works out so simply; new material is always turning up and demanding room, sometimes too late. But it was to be a long, slow haul.

My novel, *Andy*, which I had begun in Kansas, was still on hold; I could not work out how to structure the last section of the book. At least, that's what I told myself; the real reason was probably that my last two attempts at fiction had been failures, and I was woefully underconfident about this new one, even though I was sure that what I had written was good. But writers' blocks may only be with one book, not with the ability to write; the answer is to start work on another book.

In April, Billy Collins and his wife Pierre (pronounced "Pier") arrived to stay at Anlaby. (Her real name was Priscilla but she was always known as Pierre.) With them were Ken Wilder and the head of sales in Britain, Ian Chapman. Billy was tall with bushy black eyebrows, very direct, like Lane, but much more open. You could imagine him with the heroine of his current bestseller, *Elsa the Lioness*, but you certainly could not imagine Lane. You could trust Billy, and he was much more generous with money. Pierre I had imagined as gaunt, intense and spiritual, but she turned out to be more like an English country aristocrat, an indomitable like Cynthia Brooke, though much cleverer. Billy, more or less to keep her out of the way, had allowed her to set up Fontana Religious Books; instead of being a quiet little lady-chapel, this imprint had become more like Lourdes, and the books were selling in tens of thousands.

The Collins entourage came with advance copies of *Tisi and the Yabby* and predicted good sales. They were right, as Collins usually were in matters of sales; they were not like those publishers who produce a handsome book and then have no idea how to sell it. *Tisi and the Yabby* not only sold until children's picture books using photos as illustrations went out of fashion but, amusingly enough, became quite a cult. Mothers who had had it as children read it again to their daughters, and when Tisi was a strapping woman of thirty she was still getting fan letters from children who saw her as a little girl.

Like a comic turn in vaudeville, Tony Godwin turned up a few days later, endearing himself to us by immediately launching forth on a tirade about how second-rate everything was in Australia, as if we were English. The next morning it was scaldingly hot, and after breakfast he changed into Bombay bloomers, and announced that he was going to go for a long walk, at least five miles, in "the bush". I told him that if he did so, he was likely, in the Australian phrase, "to do a perish". He insisted; we made him take a water bottle.

I drove him out to the Waterloo Dam, which was only about three miles from the homestead, and told him to be sure to follow the creek back again. Some hours later, at about 1.30 p.m., when I was thinking I should go to search for his body, he arrived back at the house. By this time the temperature had reached 105 degrees Fahrenheit. Instead of returning directly from the dam, he had followed the creek north for a couple of miles, then turned back. He was red-faced, streaming with sweat despite the dryness of the air, and slightly delirious with the joy of showing Australians how tough he was.

Shortly after this visit Brian Stonier and I decided we could no longer tolerate working with Godwin and resigned from Penguin to start up our own paperback publishing company, Sun Books; we were joined immediately by Max Harris and George Smith, our production manager.

I wrote to Lane saying I had always enjoyed working with him, unlike some of his underlings, and that I hoped he would not be bitter at our mass defection. He wrote back cheerily saying it was the sort of thing he would have done himself. "Having tasted blood, you want to be on your own." He was a ruthless old pirate, but a very likeable one, and one of the greatest of all publishers.

It was exhilarating to be our own bosses, although slightly daunting in that we were now ourselves responsible for financing the books. Brian and I managed to borrow enough money to launch Sun Books; the remainder of my grandfather's bequest was used as security. Max never put any money into the venture, but was paid a retainer to help with editorial and marketing. Despite the lack of big money, and thus, little promotion, there was something about Sun being Australia's only paperback publishing company that appealed to people. This was most true of those working for us. George Smith would have been making more money if he had stayed at Penguin. Lee White, who managed the office, and was soon learning about editing, was an honours graduate with the highest qualifications who could have been making twice as much as a private secretary to a big businessman. Brian Sadgrove, who became one of the most succesful Australian designers, created our distinctive house style of black and gold, and all our covers, for almost nothing. Sadgrove worked on Lawrence Daws' original design, based on the Aboriginal Wandjina-head, to create our logo.

Brian Stonier's wife Noel made a brilliant coup by finding us a magnificent office for a minimum rent because it was in a building in Little Collins Street that was due for demolition. She had been tipped off that it would be a couple of years before this happened. Noel and Brian cleverly used cheap but bold materials to make the huge rooms look extremly chic. Other publishers, like Andrew Fabinyi and Douglas Stewart, came from their squalid burrows and went away sighing that they wished their firms had the money that was obviously behind Sun Books.

When we got under way with Sun, Australian paperback publishing was, apart from Penguin, in a bleak way. What should be the strongest link between ordinary readers and Australian writers was at that time inadequately served by the likes of Pacific Books and the Horwitz list.

Our first books were an odd mixture, of necessity mostly reprints, for our planned Sun Originals would take some time to produce. Our early titles included Christina Stead's *The Salzburg Tales*; Henry Handel Richardson's *Maurice Guest*; *Gary Player's Golf Secrets*, not a book of the highest literary merit but a much-needed money-spinner; Jack McLaren's *My Crowded Solitude* (like *Alien Son* a forgotten classic); Ian Mudie's *River-Boats*; C.P. Mountford's *Brown Men and Red Sand*; David Martin's novel *The Young Wife*; Maie Casey's *An Australian Story*. Before long we had also published Patrick White's *Four Plays* and commissioned two poetry anthologies — David Campbell's *Modern Australian Poetry* and Tom Shapcott's *Australian Poetry Now*. Our best seller was to be Geoffrey Blainey's *The Tyranny of Distance*.

We published other poetry, such as Michael Dransfield's *Drug Poems*, and a collection of poems from Papua-New Guinea edited by Ulli Beier. We also published a number of books which were not by Australians: poetry by Yevtushenko, Vosznesensky, Bulat Okhudjava, Robert Rozhdestvensky, James Dickey, Alan Ginsberg and Lawrence Ferlinghetti, all to coincide with their visits to Writers' Week at the Adelaide Festival of Arts. We published *The Ecstasy of Owen Muir*, by Ring Lardner Jnr, which had appeared first in East Germany as Lardner had been blacklisted by

Senator McCarthy. We were the first to publish David Foster and the first to reprint Janet Frame, with her novel *Owls Do Cry*. I asked Patrick White if he would write something for the covers of both books, which he generously did, saying with a sigh, "You do know that if ever I recommend anything it always kills sales." What he wrote about *Owls Do Cry* is a fine and far-seeing tribute to Janet Frame: "The most considerable New Zealand novelist yet. Her innocent eye can show one the commonest object for the first time, and her sensibility can convey, and has perhaps experienced, the bloodiest tortures of the mind." This was written some sixteen years before the publication of the first volume of Janet Frame's autobiography; it shows, yet again, White's extraordinary sensitivity.

There were some entertaining oddities in Sun Books, such as a reprint of Jules Verne's crazy 1891 novel about Australia (which of course he had never visited), *Mistress Branican*. I commissioned Lucy and Caroline Moorehead to make the first translation of Celeste de Chabrillan's novel about the Victorian goldfields, *The Gold Robbers*; de Chabrillan was a real live Countess much sought after by Melbourne society, which did not realise she had been the famous courtesan, La Mogador.

We still seemed to be acting, as when we were with Penguin, as talent scouts for Angus & Robertson. Various titles we asked for were, we were told after a few weeks, just about to be republished by Angus & Robertson. We bought the rights to Christina Stead's *The Salzburg Tales* from Peter Davies and published it in 1966. Since Penguin days, and then with Sun Books, we had been trying to buy the rights to *For Love Alone* and *Seven Poor Men* of Sydney from Angus & Robertson. Perhaps our applications jolted them into action, for they themselves republished the two books in 1965 and 1966.

It was an exhilarating, if daunting, time to be publishing paperbacks in Australia. It really was pioneering: apart from Penguin and the lurching programme of Angus & Robertson, there was no local paperback publisher of serious work, and at that stage the big London firms were interested only in their own home-published paperback lists, where these existed.

It amazes me now when I think how blithe we were. But Brian managed to keep the banks at bay and somehow or other, after Max's and my claret-fuelled brain storms, I commissioned the books and edited them, and George Smith prepared them for printing.

In April 1965 we spent ten days at Rocky Point; Alan Moorehead and Lawrence Daws were among the visitors. I had previously met Alan in London and then in Melbourne; he was enormously successful as a journalist and as the author of books about the campaigns in the Western Desert in World War II; biographies of Churchill and Montgomery; and books about the Nile, and Gallipoli. I liked him very much. He was a small, neat man, mild, almost English at times in a clipped style, but with eyes that burnt from within; here, you knew immediately, is an individual who would make up his own mind after going through all the evidence with immense thoroughness.

Before he left London, I had written to Alan to tell him about Sun Books. He was immensely enthusiastic, and immediately offered us the paperback Australia-New Zealand rights to his new book, *Cooper's Creek*. This was exactly what our young firm needed: a ready-made bestseller. But English colonial attitudes soon stopped such nonsense. Alan's agent, Lawrence Pollinger, and his publisher, Hamish Hamilton, would not allow him to do what he wanted. They insisted that the paperback should have an English publisher who would have what were still called British Empire Rights. So *Cooper's Creek* appeared in a dingy format and made more money for an already rich English publisher, appearing long after we would have published it.

Most people came to Rocky Point to fish, swim, lie in the sun, eat and drink and talk, although some, like Lawrence Daws, did not care for swimming or sunbaking. Usually no one worked. But Alan did, setting up a chair and table at the far end of the veranda, overlooking the blue bay. Each day, he would do four or five hours work on his new book, *The Fatal Impact*, his account of the white invasion of the Pacific which began in the eighteenth century. Only then did the bay tempt him. Meanwhile, Lawrence speared a giant cuttlefish, Aboriginal style, from the rocks of the Point.

Alan later told me that the next book he had intended to write was a biography of Edward John Eyre. He had heard in Melbourne that I was already under way with my biography, so he signed off, which was very generous of him.

At about this time an extraordinary invitation arrived from the East German Writers' Union. For some mysterious reason they were inviting about ten Australian writers to an international conference in Berlin and Weimar. Most of those asked were, of course, communist-minded: people like John Manifold, Frank Hardy and Judah Waten. But the Union also asked Clem Christesen, Max and me. Both fares and accommodation would be paid for. It was obviously a propaganda move, but Max and I discussed it and decided that we ought to go; being uncommitted, we could give an honest account of what we saw. We were well aware that Cold War warriors like Frank Knopfelmacher ("Knucklefucker" as Tom Fitzgerald always called him) would abuse us for naiveté. Ninette was to accompany me as far as West Berlin, where George and Beate Bailey were living.

For various complex reasons we were stuck in Central Australia in May, and unable to leave until the middle of the month, so I only caught up with the Conference in Weimar. East Berlin had looked grey and depressing, and the driver sent to meet me in a Russian Volga was a gloomy fellow, though amazingly outspoken. "*Berlin ist tot*" ("Berlin is dead"), he said as we drove through the half empty streets. As we lurched along in the Volga, which reminded me of Patrick and Manoly's old Standard Vanguard, he hit the steering wheel and cursed, "*Schwer wie ein Panzer*" ("Heavy as a tank").

A late party was still going strong when I reached Weimar; it is always painful to be sober when everyone else is pissed. I don't know how reformed alcoholics like Barry Humphries can stay so cheerful at such parties. I did my best to catch up on the unexpectedly good Armenian brandy.

John Manifold was very genial. He put his arm around me and introduced me to two Cuban poets as "Our best poet". The Cuban, one enormous and one tiny, responded by stuffing my pockets with Havana cigars and then proposed a toast to eternal friendship because "Cuba and Australia are both islands".

My suitcase had been lost somewhere along the way and the Armenian brandy helped me to resign myself to this most atrocious of traveller's dilemmas. But when I eventually went to bed, there it was in my room, with a note which read: "*Grüss ihr Fahrer mit dem Panzer*" ("Greetings from your driver with the tank").

Returning to Berlin we went to the best production of Brecht I have ever seen. It was just as well, as we had been taken that afternoon to the blood-chilling Wall and given a lecture about how necessary it was, to keep out West German speculators who were destabilizing the currency.

On this, my first visit to a communist country, I was surprised at the number of people of different nationalities everywhere, not just at the Conference. It was clear from talking to these people that communism was not the monolithic structure portrayed (of course in total ignorance of first-hand experience) by Senator McCarthy or Robert Menzies. It was also obvious that East Germany's was one of the most rigid forms of communism; John Manifold was urging the Russians at the Conference to invade East Germany and liberate it.

As far as I was concerned, by far the most momentous event to come out of the Conference was the result of a simple query from Frank Hardy. He was going on to Moscow. Was there any Russian writer I could suggest who might be able to come to Writers' Week at the Adelaide Festival? Some time before, Patrick White had sent me a slim Penguin, *A Precocious Autobiography* by a young poet called Yevgeny Yevtushenko. I liked it so much that I bought a book of poems, also in Penguin, *Zima Junction*; despite the drab translations, I thought the poems were electrifying. I urged Frank to ask the Russians to send us Yevtushenko. As soon as I returned to Adelaide I would organize an official invitation for him. Frank promised to make this approach, and added that if anybody could bring it off it would be Frank Hardy.

The invitation went out in June; the next Festival was due in March

1966. I did not hold out much hope that the Russians would send Yevtushenko, especially as they would have to pay for the airfare. I had been surprised when Max Lamshed, the new Administrator, who was even more conservative than General Hopkins, and the Governors had agreed to ask a Russian poet, but not surprised when they said he could pay his own fare. At least they would look after him in Australia.

To my astonishment a cable came from Moscow saying that Yevtushenko would come, accompanied by Alexei Sofronov, Editor of the magazine *Ogonek*, and Oksana Krugerskaya as interpreter. The Writers' Union would pay all fares. Shortly after this Frank rang to say Yevtushenko had given him a heap of poems which he hoped we might be able to translate and publish in time for his visit. The heap turned out to be a long work made up of many shorter poems, called *Bratsk Station*, which was the name of the huge hydro-electric station in Siberia. Yevtushenko's letter accompanying it said that it had been published in a magazine in the Soviet Union, but that it was banned from being published as a book. He would also send some unpublished lyrics and shorter poems. He very tactfully implied that *Bratsk Station* was to be read allegorically rather than as a Stakhanovite glorification of heroic Soviet labour. I was to learn that Russian readers were expert at deconstructing texts, and that the truths revealed in this way by the poets helped explain their enormous popularity. New books of poems by people like Yevtushenko or Vosznesensky appeared in Russia in first editions of more than a hundred thousand.

Brian Stonier and I agreed that if I could find a Russian to help me translate it, we would publish both it and the shorter poems in Sun Books for the Festival. Since my Russian was minimal, I would try to make an acceptable English version from a translated prose version.

I knew that Tina Tupikina-Glaessner, the wife of the Professor of Geology at the University of Adelaide, was not only Russian but very well read in poetry, and I asked her if she would help me in this giant task of translating five thousand lines of poetry, to a ferocious deadline. She agreed, although it was clear to both of us that it would be impossible to reproduce the variety of styles and diction that make up *Bratsk Station*. Yevtushenko is a great master of his craft.

In the meantime I asked Rosh Ireland, a Cambridge graduate who had served in the British Embassy in Moscow and was now teaching Russian at the Australian National University in Canberra, if he would write an introduction. This was essential for most people, who would be unaware of the dangers and complexities of being a poet in the Soviet Union, even after the death of Stalin. Yevtushenko, whose two most famous poems, "The Heirs of Stalin" and "Babii Yar", were highly critical of certain aspects of Soviet history and present-day life, had got away with it for a while, and was allowed to make foreign tours. But in November 1962 Khrushchev visited the pioneeering exhibition of modern art at the Manège, and launched a violent attack on modernism that soon extended to poetry. Poets were told they were losing touch with the workers. Russia's two most popular young poets, Voznesensky and Yevtushenko, were forced into a kind of internal exile, and left to wander around the Soviet Union. Yevtushenko went as far afield as Bratsk in Siberia, where he was born. "Bratsk" means "brotherly", and he was trying, metaphorically, to rediscover his extended family. He was still very much out of favour when he was writing *Bratsk Station.* This long and uneven poem series attempts to relate the problems and personal history of the Soviet poet, then thirty-two, to the history both of Russia and of its literature. Rosh Ireland took as the epigraph to his introduction two of Yevtushenko's lines: "Lord, let me be a poet / Let me not deceive people".

It soon became obvious to me that Tina, who had a fine knowledge of and feeling for the Russian classics, was hopelessly out of touch with current idiom. While we battled on I tried to find someone who could check her prose versions, which I was attempting to make into something vaguely resembling the original, an impossible undertaking in the time available.

The project was saved by a member of the Russian Department at the University of Melbourne, Igor Mezhakoff-Koriakin. Igor paid regular visits to Russia, and kept in touch with contemporary life. Endlessly patient, thorough and good-natured, he became the ideal partner in this most difficult of tasks, the translation of poetry. Together we were, later on, to translate other works by Yevtushenko, as well as those by other poets such as Yevtushenko's first wife Bella Akhmadulina.

It is obvious that translating poetry is a task which cannot entirely, or often even partially, succeed, but it is essential to try. And when bowed down by the difficulties, or abused by those superior souls who think the whole exercise a waste of time, one can only repeat to oneself that Chaucer was called "grant translateur", and take heart from the names of those who have translated poems of other languages into English: Wyatt, Campion, Jonson, Milton, Dryden, Pope and all the rest. It is, one must conclude, a desperate but worthwhile cause.

I was to find out that Yevtushenko himself is a translator of genius, brilliant at using the wealth of rhymes available in Russian. I will never forget him reciting his versions of Kipling's "Boots" and Verlaine's "Chanson d'Automne". I had always thought the latter untranslatable into any language, with its languorous intimacy of vowels and rhymes: "*Les sanglots longs / Des violons / De l'automne / Blessent mon coeur / D'une langueur / Monotone*". But Yevtushenko's Russian version sounded exactly like the original, while preserving the sense.

At last Yevtushenko's shorter poems and lyrics arrived through another messenger; they had never been published inside or outside the Soviet

Union. Most of them were far superior to *Bratsk* as poetry, and with Igor to work with, I was able to make much better versions of them than I had of *Bratsk*, keeping some of the tempi and cadences of the originals. Igor came to stay at Anlaby, and we worked fourteen to sixteen hours a day.

In July Patrick came over and stayed for a week at Anlaby. He was more at ease than I had ever known him, and liked by everyone — the children, John and Robbie. Everyone but True-Blue Peg; he and she took an instant dislike to each other. He told me he thought Anlaby was the most beautiful house in Australia; I suggested that he had not seen all that many, but he stuck to his opinion.

We went down to town to dinner with Ursula, and she told me of a couple of incidents at Hannah Lloyd-Jones's dinner party. Two society ladies had said that Nolan's new paintings were only fit for a second-class railway carriage, and Patrick had caught fire: "It's people like you who make me want to leave Australia tomorrow — here, I suppose you'd better have another brandy." Someone else had daringly suggested that the trouble with John Tasker was that Patrick was in love with him. "Oh dear, how modern," he sighed.

A couple of months later Manoly came for a fortnight, during which he worked hard all day in the garden. One evening he said that the heads of private schools, whether men or women, should all be English. "No Australians are fit for the job. They are so naive. They just lack the sophistication to understand children." This reminded me that Manoly was often an instigator of Patrick's scorn for so many Australians.

On 17 December 1965 I finished my biography of Eyre, which I had begun writing on 14 January. It was about 180,000 words, and I prepared myself to battle against cuts, for most publishers seem to complain that books are too long. *Eyre* was going to be published simultaneously by Collins in Britain and Cheshire in Australia. Andrew Fabinyi's halo would be tarnished in the process; he fussed and fiddled and argued over endless details with Billy Collins, insisting for far too long that the book should be printed in Australia, when it was much cheaper to print it at Collins's printing works in Glasgow. The book did not appear until 1967, eighteen months after I had finished it. At least it was a very handsome book. I dedicated it to Patrick and Manoly.

When I wrote to ask their permission for the dedication, saying I had finished the book, Patrick wrote back: "I certainly never thought we should see the Eyre book finished after you got caught up in all the other activities". He continued on an old theme: "Perhaps you will even write an Eyre play, but I don't think you could turn dishonest enough, even temporarily, to make a playwright".

Soon after the book was finished I had to fly to Sydney to discuss it with Ken Wilder, before it went off to Billy Collins. I stayed with Patrick and

Manoly; Patrick looked at the typescript and said darkly, "Biographies could become a habit — look at Hesketh Pearson." Indeed. Who remembers Hesketh Pearson?

As the 1966 Festival approached and the cables flew to and from Moscow, the pace of translation got hotter and hotter. *Bratsk Station* went off to Griffin Press. Igor came again so we could work on the shorter poems, sometimes for twenty hours a day. We gave this collection the title of one of the poems, *The City of Yes and the City of No*; there was no time to publish them as a book so they appeared in a typed booklet, which would go through eight editions in the next year. Printed and published in less than a week, it was one of the first examples in Australia of desktop publishing for serious literature.

In March I was down at the airport to meet Yevtushenko, as were officials from the Festival in black cars. He was unmistakable — tall, slim, his skin pale among the late-summer Australians, walking stiffly from exhaustion and the tension of waiting for the usual hostile TV questions. Suddenly he rushed towards me, away from the official party, and said with certainty, "You are Geoffrey Dutton." I nodded and he kissed me on both cheeks.

I was introduced to huge, lumbering Sofronov and tiny, dark, spider-like Oksana Krugerskaya, and they drove to Griffin Press in the black cars while I followed in my old Peugeot station wagon. We reached the production line at the exact moment that finished copies of *Bratsk* were rolling off the press. Zhenya — as I came to know him — seized one in both hands and kissed it and said in triumph, with tears in his eyes, "The first copies in the world!"

He rejoined the black car. When it slowed down as it approached the gate the back door suddenly flew open and Yevtushenko ran over and jumped into the Peugeot with me. "I talk to you in private, away from my big child [Sofronov] and that Stalinist [Oksana]." His English was not very grammatical but it was remarkably fluent; on official occasions, he explained to me, he would have to talk Russian. "You think a lot of *Bratsk Station* bullsheet?" I was familiar enough with the unevenness of the poem and was too embarrassed to answer, but he was continuing, without waiting for reply, to tell me that bits of *Bratsk* were written to show the party and Writers' Union officials what sort of writing their demands would lead to. Banal. "Is necessary in our small country." This, I found, was a favourite phrase.

I also discovered how those living in a country where any room or car or train may be wired by the KGB, will not talk unless they know they are in a safe space, like my Peugeot. Zhenya begged me to take him to Anlaby, another safe space, although he said apologetically that his big child and Oksana would have to come too.

Lamshed, whom Zhenya was already calling "Lambshit", was furious, as I knew he would be, but I told him that Yevtushenko had demanded to go into the country and have a rest before his recitals. Lamshed had to give in. But he was to try his best to sabotage this rotten Communist Russian poet's visit.

Already there were moments that were not so serious. Zhenya fished around in his wallet and pulled out some cards he had had printed in New York. They were set out like a poem and read: "Only French Champagne / Only Standing Up! / Only One Night / Maybe Not On Time!"

Fortunately he quickly developed a taste for Australian champagne. He hated vodka, which of course he was always being offered in foreign countries.

Twenty-Four

For Yevtushenko's readings it was arranged that readers would present the translation first, and Zhenya would then recite the poem in Russian. Nothing like this had previously been attempted in Australia, although of course Yevtushenko had given immensely successful readings in the United States, Britain and other countries, using the same strategy.

The two readers engaged by the Festival authorities were Dame Judith Anderson and Peter O'Shaughnessy. I arranged a preliminary meeting between them and Yevtushenko at the Haywards' house; Dame Judith was accompanied by her very pretty niece Jenny. A few seconds after the introductions were made, Zhenya urgently signalled me; we withdrew into Ursula's library. He put his hand on my shoulder, looking as ferocious as if he were defending himself against Stalinists at the Writers' Union, and hissed, "I cannot have my poems read by that" — he groped for a word — "old crow." I was well aware that Dame Judith was sixty-eight, but tried to soothe Zhenya down by explaining that she was a world-famous actress on a return visit to her native land. "I would prefer the daughter," he added with a grin. I finally talked him into accepting his fate.

There was no trouble with Peter, who was not only an actor but a creator, the sort of original who immediately appealed to Zhenya. I knew he would not only read well but act as an intermediary between Zhenya and Dame Judith.

Dame Judith and Peter left to study the poems we had selected, and I drove Zhenya, Sofronov and Oksana up to Anlaby. Zhenya and Sofronov had to share the billiard room; at least there were two beds. It seems absurd that with such a big house there were so few rooms available as bedrooms, but it so was. Part of the problem was that each of the three children had a room, and my secretary, who also looked after the children, took up another. Zhenya was appalled. He said to me, "My God, when my friends at home hear I slept with *Sofronov*!"

Sofronov, one of the biggest literary *apparatchiks* in Russia, had a big body and smooth skin plumped up by a thousand committee meetings sustained by brandy, vodka and many courses of food and wine. His bluff manner was sustained by his beliefs and hid any number of crimes. He said to me, genially, "And what is it which is most important to Australians?" Such seemingly innocent questions are of course the hardest to answer. "Freedom," I said. I saw Oksana wince, Zhenya roll his eyes, but Sofronov beamed on. "Ho, freedom!" he answered me. "Just to be able to do what you like? No, I mean, what is it that matters most to Australians?" I suggested something along the lines of being happy, to have enough money to have (if only on a mortgage) a house and a block of land and a family. Sofronov would not let up. "I mean belief. In the Soviet Union we believe in state socialism and the ideals of Lenin." Zhenya lit another cigarette. I was getting desperate. "In Australia we believe in freedom, democracy and what we call a fair go." Sofronov shook his head and turned to Oksana, who did her best to switch a fair go into Russian.

I was saved from further solemnities by the arrival of John and Peg for dinner. Peg's curiosity had got the better of her, overcoming her horror at having to meet Russians. Zhenya took one look at my brother and whispered to me, "The Moustache!" I recognized the reference to Mandelstam's famous underground poem about Stalin; the dictator's discovery of it ended in Mandelstam being incarcerated in a camp. "I really mean it," Zhenya continued. Turning to John he said, "Please no offence, but you look exactly like Stalin." John did not know whether to accept this as a compliment or not. He was equally baffled when, during the usual Russian toasts during dinner, Sofronov proposed a toast to John as "Chairman of the collective farm".

We had to have a very early lunch the next day, as it was essential that we be present at the opening of Writers' Week in the afternoon. The British High Commission's Rolls had arrived in the morning with Sir Charles and Lady Johnston and Frank Hardy, a combination to be relished. In fact there was a genuine reason for the Johnstons' presence. Charles was a Russian scholar, and his translation of Pushkin's *Eugene Onegin* has a good claim to being the best translation of it ever made into English; Natasha was a princess from one of the most famous Georgian families, and Zhenya, like his friend Pasternak, was passionately devoted to Georgia.

I finally managed to push everyone off for Adelaide, and was much amused when the pace caused the Rolls to break down and arrive late, whereas the old Peugeot kept going. Writers' Week was to be officially opened by the guest of honour, who was not Yevtushenko but Angus Wilson. Zhenya, always surprising, turned out to know Wilson's work well, and was an admirer. "Good English tradition of Jane Austen, eh?" was his comment. The Opening was to take place in the courtyard of the Students' Union at the University. There was a big crowd, and several television camera crews were in waiting.

Angus spoke very well, but not a TV camera whirred. Then Yevtushenko was asked to say a few words, and the cameramen sprang into action. It was very embarrassing, both for Wilson and for the Russian; Wilson was so peeved that he did not speak again to Yevtushenko that day. The episode was in no way Zhenya's fault, and he was distressed by it.

That night I had been ordered to take him to the special performance of the ballet for the Festival. He refused to go, saying that he loathed ballet. I sympathized with him, but explained that it was his duty to go and there would be an international incident if he didn't, and finally persuaded him. He was looking very elegant in an Italian suit. At the interval he immediately jumped to his feet and said he could not take another minute of ballet, and rushed up the stairs of the dress circle. After him, from different areas of the audience, raced three women. I have never known any man who was so attractive to women, not with screaming fans but with mature, intelligent women. At the top of the steps he looked quickly behind him, seized the arm of one of the women, and disappeared into the night. I knew her, and that she worked at the ABC; she did not go to work for four days, and moved in with Yevtushenko.

About 9.30 the next morning I went to the Hotel Australia where both Wilson and Yevtushenko were staying, to collect them for a session of Writers' Week. Wondering how I was going to keep the peace, I went first to Angus's room. He was dressed and ready, and immediately started to tell me what had happened. "I was fast asleep," he said, "when at about half past four the door opened and in came" — his voice rose in pitch — "this Russian *bear*. He was going to *rape* me. I screamed." He smiled. "But he had only come with a bottle of champagne, to apologize for the TV cameras, which episode of course was not his fault at all. Oh he is *such* a nice man!"

Asking him to wait for me in the foyer, I went to Zhenya's room. He too was ready, and grabbed my arm. "Djeff! I go to have a drink with poor Angus, who is insulted by the TV people. I open the door, with my bottle of champagne, and he sit up straight in bed and scream! He think I am going to rape him! But all is well. Oh, he is *such* a nice man!"

Meanwhile I had found out that Lambshed had altered the venue for Yevtushenko's third reading. The first two were to be in the old Regent cinema, a good choice. Now Lamshed had moved the third reading to the Centennial Hall at Wayville, the terrible old barn in the Showgrounds where we had heard the Beatles. It held about two thousand and its acoustics were suitable only for a rock group. The Regent, to everyone's astonishment, had been booked out. Lamshed's official excuse was that Yevtushenko needed the vast space of the Centennial Hall, but of course his real reason was that at the best it would be only about a quarter full, and the famous Yevtushenko would be humiliated by the relatively sparse audience. Lamshed had already said to me, brandishing a copy of *Bratsk Station*, "This stuff is Bolshevik propaganda!" He assured me that the Governors agreed with him, and Yevtushenko was lucky not to have all the readings cancelled. There was no time to give him a little talk on the complexities of being a poet in the Soviet Union.

At this very moment there was a big Russian ship at Port Adelaide, with several hundred crew and passengers who were immensely excited at the coincidence of Yevtushenko's also being in Adelaide; they asked Lamshed to make a block booking, which would have been a great help in populating the steppes of the Centennial Hall. He told them the wrong date. Not one of them heard Zhenya recite.

Lambshed's hatred of Communism went with a fear of all things Russian, which was typical of Australian conservatives. I was reminded of a poem I had discovered in some researches in the Barr Smith Library. In 1883 there was a panic in Adelaide that Australia was going to be invaded by the Russians; a fort was built at Largs, near Port Adelaide, to stop them landing. A lady called Hannah Fry was inspired to write, to the tune of "God Save The Queen", "O God of truth and might! / Keep Thou the Muscovite / Far from our shore! / And may the nations see / That we are kept by Thee / From Russia's tyranny / And Russia's power". God not being available, Lambshed was now standing in for Him.

The poetry readings were, apart from the venue of the third one, the most extraordinary success. No one who heard them will ever forget "Babii Yar", "The City of Yes and the City of No", and "Sleep, my Beloved". Yevtushenko did not recite like an actor, but he had all the great actor's sense of drama and control over his audience. In his few rehearsals with Dame Judith and Peter, they began to read like actors; he skilfully redirected them to the way in which he wanted his poems to be read.

On official occasions Zhenya mostly refused to talk English, and communicated through Oksana. She was a brilliant interpreter, but Zhenya never trusted her. I took them out to the ABC studios, where a long interview was recorded. The ABC gave me a tape of this interview. When I later played it I heard Zhenya rap out in English in the middle of Oksana's translation of his answer to a question. "I did *not* say that!"

When the interviews and recitals were over Zhenya had a little spare time, so Chibs flew us down to Kangaroo Island. He told her that the last private pilot he had flown with was Fidel Castro. She was pleased when he added, "You are much better pilot."

It was a perfect day, and Rocky Point was sublimely solitary in the middle of the green-and-blue bay. Zhenya peeled off his shirt and trousers and ran down to the beach in his underpants. He was wearing a small gold cross on a chain around his neck. I was just going to tell him that we usually swam in the green, over the sand, and not out beyond the blue line of weed in case of a cruising shark, when I saw his body, pale as ivory after the Russian winter, splashing out into the water. He swam straight out, beyond the blue line, as if he were heading for Siberia.

That evening, back in Adelaide, there was a large party at the Haywards' house. I saw Barry Humphries with Peter O'Shaughnessy; Barry was in Adelaide for his new show, *Excuse I*, in which, for the first time, Edna waved the gladdies. At this time of his life Barry was still swerving alarmingly between sobriety and Johnnie Walker and had not yet achieved the teetotal miracle. Of course he still had his long, dank black hair, and on this particular evening he had been unable to resist the copious supplies of Bill Hayward's Black Label.

He had noticed Yevtushenko, and lurched across the room towards him. Before I could introduce them he had seized Zhenya by the Italian lapel and was giving a devastating imitation of a long-haired pansy (no other word will do) critic lost in a Soviet hydro-electric station. It was certainly a brilliant performance, but Zhenya had absolutely no suspicion that it was not real, while Barry, scenting success, made this mincing character, long hair falling into the whisky, flaunting his exquisite sensibility, more and more appalling. At that time to be homosexual in the Soviet Union was inviting twenty years in the Gulag, and despite Zhenya's travels around the world it was still an area in which he was uncertain. And who could have doubted the reality of this character Barry had invented?

Fortunately at this moment Dame Judith Anderson entered with her niece Jenny, and in an instant Zhenya was talking to them. Afterwards he took me to task for exposing him to this dreadful critic. It was the only time I have ever seen him discomfited. Two geniuses together.

On Barry's next visit to Adelaide, with *Just A Show*, he invited Ninette and me to the theatre and then to supper with him and his second wife, Rosalind, at their hotel, the South Australian. The show was a great success, but it was a mystery how Barry managed to keep it going, and the marriage was almost gone. Rosalind had been sent downstairs with instructions that he would be there in a minute or two, so the three of us went into the dining room and sat down. The terrible old trio on the platform, piano, violin and cello, were still churning out ancient melodies and signature tunes. After about twenty minutes of stilted conversation at our table, Barry made his entrance, to some clapping from the diners who recognized him. It was obvious that there must be an empty bottle of Johnny Walker in his room. The conversation at the table spurted and stopped like a car running out of petrol. Lewy, the old head waiter and tyrant, was watching Barry anxiously with an expert eye. The elderly trio came to the last chord of their number, and suddenly Barry pushed back his chair, walked across the room and onto the little stage, waving a hand towards the piano. The pianist had recognized him and vacated his seat with a smile.

The dining room fell silent as Barry sat down and extended his hands towards the keys. He held them there for a moment, quite still, and then his head crashed to the keys. The guests clapped and whistled, thinking it a brilliant performance, and continued to clap as Lewy and I heaved him to his feet and helped him out of the room.

In Barry's autobiography, *More Please*, he has given a painfully honest account of his battle with alcohol. Those who were familiar with him in his drinking days will know what a terrible battle it was. Barry's history makes one think that Montaigne was right when he wrote: "We must be besotted ere we can become wise, and dazzled before we can be led".

It was remarkable that Yevtushenko never showed any sign of becoming an alcoholic; when he was in the mood, which was mostly all the time, he could put away more than anyone I have ever met, yet still remain apparently sober. Perhaps it was because he did not drink vodka, the downfall of his fellow countrymen, preferring champagne.

Later he was to tell me that on his way back to Moscow he stopped in Paris, where some fans took him to dinner at Maxim's. They asked him which champagne he wanted to drink, and the *sommelier* brought him a wine-list "the size of the Holy Bible". Zhenya looked through it, and said, "The champagne I want is not here." The *sommelier* was stunned, but rallied and asked which champagne Yevtushenko wanted. Zhenya said firmly, "Australian Great Western". Maxim's immediately despatched a runner to the Australian Embassy to ask if they had any Great Western. Some years after Yevtushenko told me this story, it was confirmed when I met a man who had been one of the secretaries at the Embassy, and was detailed to get a couple of bottles for Maxim's.

According to Zhenya, when the messenger came back and handed over these bottles, a little man dining by himself at one of the other tables called the *sommelier* over and said he would like to try a bottle. The *sommelier* regretted, but this was impossible. Zhenya, on hearing this, asked the man over to have a glass. It was Aristotle Onassis.

Yevtushenko's visit to Adelaide was to be followed by readings in Melbourne and Sydney. When he left for Melbourne, he swore that I would receive an invitation to visit "his small country". This seemed an attractive proposition, but I thought nothing more of it.

In Melbourne the Jewish community, always at the heart of culture in that city, had organized tremendous publicity for him, and the venues were packed. He was not only the poet of "Babii Yar" who had a street in Jerusalem named after him, but an untiring opponent of Soviet anti-semitism, and defender of the rights of the Jewish citizens of the Soviet Union. The long poem in *Bratsk Station*, "The Light Controller", is about a Jew, Izzy Kramer; as he sits at the giant control panel of the hydro-electric station he is remembering his time as a boy in a German concentration camp. The poem ends with the poet's prayer that "the word 'Yid' will disappear forever / not degrading the word 'man'."

Yevtushenko had told me that he had a great admiration for Patrick White; he had managed to read some of his work, even though none of it had been translated into Russian, and was especially impressed by *Voss*.

Zhenya had an extraordinary gift of being able to recognize quality, and detect the phony, even when offered it by prominent critics in other countries. He was absolutely certain that Patrick was of the first rank. He was determined that Patrick should be read in the Soviet Union, while fully aware of how ideologically unsound most of his books were. But he thought, quite rightly, that *The Tree of Man* would be the novel with which to start in the Soviet Union. He knew how the system worked, and laughed: "This novel all about farm workers".

After Melbourne, and managing to avoid Canberra, Yevtushenko went on to Sydney, where Patrick had arranged to have a party for him, and with typical thoroughness and generosity had invited painters, composers, architects, potters, silversmiths, an anthropologist and a teacher to meet him. Patrick did this because he thought Zhenya must have had "a pretty unattractive diet of Australian Writer in Adelaide". Patrick spent days cooking for the party. Moreover, he told me, "I have worked out my plan for rushing Yevtushenko into hiding if there should be any hint of his wanting asylum." In fact I had already been approached in Adelaide, on behalf of "Canberra", asking me to let them know if Yevtushenko wanted asylum. Zhenya spoke to me at length on this subject, saying that it was impossible for him to live anywhere but in the Soviet Union, however often he might wish he could leave that glum country. He said he could not live in exile from the Russian language. In any case, he thought the best way to reform the country was to stay and fight; besides, as he says in his poem, "It would be a bit boring ... to live in that shining, multi-coloured City of Yes". He was committed to his own country, people and language.

David Marr has given a rather misleading account of Yevtushenko and White in Sydney. In fact they had two meetings, not just one, and Patrick was most attracted to the new poems we had published in *The City of Yes and the City of No*. He said he thought "Sleep My Beloved" was "one of the most beautiful poems I have read". As I had expected, he did not care for *Bratsk Station*; of course, he did not understand the complexities behind it.

Yevtushenko and Frank Hardy managed to get away from Krugerskaya and turned up at Martin Road the Sunday before the big party so they could talk openly. At this stage Patrick was a supporter of Frank's; many times I heard him defending Frank's work, especially *Power Without Glory*, despite its manifest stylistic faults. Patrick and Zhenya had a good talk, without any inhibitions. Yevtushenko told me afterwards that he thought Patrick and he had understood each other, and that he had convinced him that he (Zhenya) would do all in his power to ensure that Patrick's novels were translated into Russian, and not by someone like Krugerskaya. Patrick felt about her as I did: "Doesn't she remind you of a big black velvet spider?"

Marr makes the party seem like a disaster, dominated by Yevtushenko's egotism. In fact Patrick wrote to me that "All went very smoothly, except that at one point" there was "an embarrassing tirade of hate against America". This might have embarrassed Patrick (who was never chary of delivering tirades himself), but it did not represent hatred of America so much as hatred of America's war in Vietnam, in which we were participating. Zhenya had spoken to me about this almost as soon as he arrived in Australia, and was amazed at what seemed to be the general Australian approval for the war. In my own case, and Patrick's, it was more like apathy. We needed waking up; Yevtushenko certainly helped me to wake up.

In 1965, following my *Nation* article about the need for an Australian republic, Sun Books had commissioned me to edit a book to be called *Australia and the Monarchy*. I thought at this stage it was best to present a balanced argument, so the contributors were by no means all republicans. They were: Jock Marshall, Zelman Cowen, Rohan Rivett, Donald Horne, Max Harris, Richard Walsh, Don Whitington, Stephen Murray-Smith and Peter Coleman; I wrote the introduction. Les Tanner contributed a brilliant cover drawing of a Dinkum Aussie holding a beer glass, wearing a crown that contained two bottles of Foster's. Even before publication of the book, there was an upsurge of interest in the republic. In Melbourne I gave a lecture on the subject for the Fabian Society; the meeting was chaired by John Button. Before the lecture, I had dinner with Robin and Patricia Boyd, in the house he had designed. Yet another brilliant member of that astonishing Boyd family, Robin was the son of Arthur's artist uncle, Penleigh, who was killed in a car smash at a tragically early age. Robin, with his very pale skin and blond hair, was courtly and precise. Patricia was formidable, handsome, very intelligent and in control; I was a bit scared of her. Robin seemed to have forgotten his father's fate, as he drove us at high speed to Kew in one of the most beautiful cars ever made in America, the Studebaker Hawk designed by Raymond Loewy.

The lecture went quite well, but I was rather peeved that an academic, Noel McLachlan, had been allowed to see a copy of my text and immediately after I had finished launched into a long attack on republicanism. The Boyds, Jock Marshall and others were not at all happy with the way this attack had been engineered; I hadn't been asked to take part in a debate. But it was a useful foretaste of the monarchists' fury that the sanctity of the crown was being questioned, and a reminder that there were a few monarchists among the intellectuals.

I was shocked to see how ill Jock Marshall looked, although I knew that he had cancer. Now Janey told me there were heart troubles as well.

I was writing to Alan Moorehead shortly after this, and mentioned the bad news about Jock. Alan replied: "How abominable about Jock. The thing I mind is that his sort of spirit is so needed all the time and everywhere if the bores and the play-safers are not going to take over." How right he was; Jock always routed the bores and play-safers. Alan went on to say, in lighter vein: "Edna O'Brien has just been on the phone — will I be sure to come to the party tomorrow night? Like a lunatic I probably will. But that wise man Sid Nolan with whom I lunched yesterday and who lives next door to her, said NO, not for me. It is that marvellous restraint of my friends that baffles me. I only know how to live like a hermit or a rake, nothing in between."

Australia and the Monarchy was published in June. The response was very pleasing, and I was dashing around various cities appearing in TV and radio discussions about the republic. In Melbourne a Toorak lady in the audience told me I had been very entertaining, and asked was I really serious. Everyone under twenty-five or so seemed to be solidly pro-republic.

In the Adelaide Club, however, and around the antique-laden houses of the Establishment, and at True-Blue Peg's on the other side of the Anlaby courtyard, loyal monarchists were coming to the boil. In July I received a letter from one Collier Cudmore, a curmudgeonly old Adelaide lawyer, who had rowed with my father at Oxford, and had actually put me up for membership of the Club at some early age, like birth. Although I had known him for forty-four years, his letter began "Dear Sir". The gist of his letter was that the Adelaide Club was indissolubly linked to the monarchy, that I was disloyal and therefore should resign at once from the Club.

I wrote back to say that I was loyal to Australia, not to the Queen, and that I was appalled to think of continuing to belong to a Club with members who thought like him, and therefore was writing to the Chairman to tender my resignation. I felt a sense of relief; I had wasted too many hours in the place, not only for the excellent food and wine, but foolishly thinking I could be a bridge between the Establishment and new ideas. Years later, Donald Horne lamented to me that the myth that I had been kicked down the stairs of the Club and out into North Terrace for my republican beliefs was not true.

I too would love that myth to have been true, but what actually happened was that before the next committee meeting of the Club, the Chairman, Ian Thomas, had already written to me accepting my resignation. Chris Legoe and my brother-in-law, Dick Blackburn, although both monarchists, immediately resigned from the committee, saying that my resignation should not have been accepted before a full committee meeting had taken place. I was interested in the letters and phone calls from those who supported me, among them Archie Price, Charles Fisher (son of the Archbishop of Canterbury) and various businessmen. Rich doctors and lawyers were monarchists to a man.

Until 1963 I had been more or less apolitical, and even after my *Nation* article I still had not thought clearly enough about Australian politics, or our policies on such matters as Vietnam. But I should have been alerted one evening at the Haywards when, after the ladies had retired and the men were into the cigars and brandy, the other five men (probably the richest in Adelaide) began discussing their contributions to the Democratic Labor Party (DLP). (This was the right-wing, anticommunist, breakaway Labor group that in effect kept the Labor Party out of power from 1957 to 1972). There was an election coming up in December 1963, and these Menzies supporters were agreeing to make some very large donations to the DLP, simply to keep Labor out of power. Suddenly Tommy Barr-Smith, Ursula's younger brother, a creature somewhere between a coathanger and a lounge lizard, said, "I hope young Dutton can be relied on to keep his trap shut." Bill Hayward winked at me and said, "Old Geoff's all right."

Now in July 1966 someone (not me) leaked the Adelaide Club row to the Adelaide *News*. A furious correspondence erupted between monarchists and republicans; people would stop me in the street and wish me luck. Deane Toseland, an old racing cyclist who ran a bike shop in North Adelaide, told me his family was split down the middle; he supported the republic, his wife the Queen.

Of course I was already regarded in staunch Adelaide as a communist because of my enthusiasm for Yevtushenko. A *News* billboard screamed "R.S.L. PRESIDENT: SEND DUTTON BACK TO RUSSIA WHERE HE BELONGS". Ninette went to call on her parents. Madam Vitriolle (as I now called Clarice behind her back), after saying that they had known all along that I was a communist, said, "Oh well, Geoffrey can be a republican as long as he stays loyal to the Queen." Donald Horne wrote about the state of our republican cause in Sydney, saying that while I was resigning from the Adelaide Club he had been dining at Admiralty House with the Governor-General, Lord Casey, and Maie Casey.

People were very muddled about communism and republicanism. I was in Sydney in July, staying with Patrick and Manoly; one of the dinner guests was Patrick's good friend, Margery Williams, wife of the director of the British Council in Australia. I found myself in an argument with her when she said that Angus Wilson had been insulted at having to sit on a platform at the Adelaide Festival with a communist, and that she didn't blame the Adelaide Club for booting me out.

In the midst of all this upheaval Mick Stow came to stay at Anlaby, an apolitical person if ever there was one. He was still a silent stalk in any company of more than one. He had been out in the semi-deserts of the West, the country of his novel *Tourmaline* and some of his best poems, and slowly came out with stories of suicides and solitary drinkers, Jimmy Woodsers, and of one man he had met in a pub, who had come in from a long spell in the far outback and talked in perfect rhyming couplets.

I had suggested to Sid Nolan that he would enjoy Mick's poems, and might like to do a set of paintings or drawings for our "Artists and Poets" series in *Australian Letters*. Sid had managed to escape from Cynthia and meet Mick in London; they got on very well, and the set of paintings and poems is one of the best in the series, and formed the basis of *Outrider*, a handsome new book of Mick's poems.

Alan and Lucy Moorehead also came to stay, with their two children; Alan was writing a story about Anlaby for the London *Sunday Times*. I had not met Lucy before and liked her very much; she was a great admirer of Richard Aldington's poems, novels and biographies. She recited one of his poems, "Evening":

The chimneys, rank on rank,
Cut the clear sky;
The moon,
With a rag of gauze about her loins
Poses among them, an awkward Venus —
And here am I looking wantonly at her
Over the kitchen sink.

While the Mooreheads were at Anlaby a cable arrived from Zhenya in Moscow saying that I had been officially invited by the People's Republic of Georgia, all expenses paid, to the 800th birthday celebrations of the national poet, Rustaveli, at Tbilisi, the capital of Georgia. He went on to say that I was to come for an extra week so that he could show me his small country himself. Alan and Lucy were as excited as I was, but Ninette was not pleased. She said it was not right that I should go away on my own.

I thought I would be mad not to go, and said unhappily that I intended to. The arrival shortly afterwards of the official invitation did not raise the temperature. I sent a cable to the Writers' Union asking if she could come if I paid all her expenses. After a few days a cable came saying that it would be in order for me to bring her.

I wish I could have gone on my own, for a number of reasons, one sordid one being a lack of money. It was proving very difficult to survive at Anlaby, where the expenses included the secretary-child-minder and a permanent help in the house. Sun Books was doing well, but most of the profits had to go into paying the interest on the money Brian and I had borrowed. I was being widely published, and appearing on TV and radio, but very little money came in from it all. I was to have an interesting correspondence with Cyril Pearl about the small returns in Australia for the years of work that go into writing a biography.

After finishing *Eyre* I had taken up *Andy* again, and Billy Collins seemed happy with the finished version, if a bit shocked with some of the language of the RAAF. I was hoping to make some money from it, but had no other lucrative prospects.

Ninette's enamelling was going very well, and she had had exhibitions in several states and a number of commissions. She did not work full time at it, and her materials (copper and the enamelling oxides) were very expensive, so that there was little profit.

My quarter-share of Anlaby and Uno brought in depressingly little, as most of their profits (not high in the 1960s) went into paying overdrafts and mortgages. I had at least succeeded in talking the rest of the family into selling Uno, although, as Léonie's advisers had said, it really would have made more sense to sell Anlaby. If the Uno sale went through, it would provide a much-needed injection of capital, although no great riches as the Anlaby debts would swallow most of it. The overseas trips were another drain.

When word got around that I had been invited to Russia, people like Peg and Brigadier Eastick of the RSL took it as further proof of my communism. The Adelaide storm in a teacup continued to bubble. One day I went to lunch with Chris Legoe at the Chesser Cellar in Adelaide. An old man of whom I had been fond since childhood, Hugh Gooch, was having a drink by the bar. He had been one of the husky bachelors who stayed with Bill Gunson in the house on the beach below Rocky Point when I was a child. I had often enjoyed having a drink with him at the Adelaide Club in more peaceful days; he always used to say, pouring his fourth gin before lunch, "Gins don't count, Geppie m'boy". Now, as I went up to the bar to order drinks for me and Chris, he turned on his heel and faced away from me, as gentlemen in romantic novels do when a cad approaches. I realized that for the first time in my life I had been "cut".

An hour or so later he came over to our table and asked could he buy us "a good port". He returned with the ports, sat down beside me and with a tear in his eye said, "Good health! England for St George and St Pancras for Scotland!" What a strange divided world those old boys of the Empire lived in. I was reminded of Patrick White's response when I sent him a copy of our Sun edition of Maie Casey's *An Australian Story*, which he liked very much. He wrote: "The book has also solved something of my own puzzle, I feel. It is not that I am not Australian, I am an anachronism, something left over from that period when people were no longer English and not yet indigenous." People like Hugh Gooch, and there were lots of them, and not only in Adelaide, hadn't even got that far; they were still basically English.

Under all these exterior activities the secret river of my extramarital affairs was still flowing strongly. Whether, like Keats' "muddy stream" it was bearing "along my soul to nothingness", or whether it was more like Coleridge's "Alph, the sacred river", I don't know, but many poems came of it and I could not live without it.

My affair with Ilse lasted six years, and for three of these we were meeting regularly. I must have been insane to put up with her imagined insults and injuries, and not call the affair off. I am amazed now to read in my notebooks how, if we had two hours together, one and a half would be spent in a recital of her woes. What should have been a rapturous meeting would degenerate into a ritual of pain and tears.

At boarding school in the absences of my mother, in the discipline of the RAAF, during the rationing of postwar Britain, even in the pain of earache or of a carbuncle being lanced without local anaesthetic, life seemed to me to demand an enduring stoicism. One just had to put up with things, even the financial ruin that Anlaby promised. So I put up with Ilse's hysterical changes of mood.

I had never at any time seen my mother in tears, nor had Chibs. Their furious fights left Chibs weeping, but not my mother, whose jaw would set ever firmer. I accepted such violent emotional upheavals as normal, but also thought I should emulate my mother's iron control. Even when I was not in control at all, I felt I had to appear so, and keep calm and sympathetic. This situation was as true with Ninette as it was with Ilse.

In 1966 Ilse returned to Vienna, where she lived with her father and found a job in his business. For many months I wrote to her every day. When I finally met her father he said to me, "You must love my daughter very much to have written to her every day." So I did, or, perhaps more accurately, so I had.

In several letters she said she expected I would find someone else when she was away; she even urged me to do so, saying she would not be jealous, which she admitted to be her worst failing. Perhaps I had already begun to move away, and my letters were an amalgam of guilt and stoicism. I did not think she would come back to Australia, and even if she did, I didn't want her to come back into my life.

At a party in Adelaide I met a woman in her late twenties, a lawyer who was doing very well in her profession, at that time an unusual one for a woman. Joanna had striking film-star good looks and glamour, not altogether an advantage for a professional woman in the Adelaide of the 1960s. However, she was not afraid of making her own way, and her success commanded general repect, even from men who had failed to seduce her and women made nervous by her glamour. We began an affair because we enjoyed each other's company, not because we were in love. She had had for some time a still attentive lover in Sydney; she said disarmingly that it would be kind of rude to the poor bastard not to go to bed with him when he visited Adelaide from time to time. I didn't mind; she amused me and I liked her honesty.

When we could take enough time off, she would make me lunch in her flat in the city. Despite my ardour I used to wish I could teach her how to cook fish. She would buy beautiful fillets of St George whiting, one of the best fish in the world, and cook them until they were curly, brown and dry as cardboard.

Then she went overseas for three months. This time I did fall in love. She could not have been more different from Ilse, or, indeed, Joanna. She was tall, blonde, alarmingly (but not oppressively) athletic, and very French, always singing Jacques Brassens' or Charles Trenet's songs (Ilse hated French music). Her name was Dominique. Her father was a Professor at the Sorbonne, and her mother ran a very chic interior-decorating business in Paris, but Dominique was neither intellectual nor businesslike. She was, however, naturally very stylish, in a grand, careless, what-the-hell way. Her miniskirt, new to Adelaide, might well have caused several deaths in the Adelaide Club when she walked down North Terrace. Perhaps it was a mutual love of her country that brought us together, but she retained a fierce independence that had nothing in it of Ilse's perpetual attempts to uphold an independence she really didn't want. Nevertheless, there were little spurts of underconfidence in between taking the world on, anywhere, any time. She did not need to work, but had a job teaching French.

She came up to Anlaby and loved the house and garden but was not impressed by us as a family. "It's all too pleasant, *trop agréable*, everyone is too damn nice, *trop friand*", as if she was telling the waiter to take a dainty dish away and bring her something with more flavour. Her English was perfect, but she liked from time to time to make little emphases in her own tongue.

She was right about my family life. To outsiders Ninette's and mine was the perfect marriage, yet a perceptive observer could see how much energy went into keeping up appearances. Hence the polite pleasantness that Dominique deplored. I could not afford to quarrel, or else the edifice we had built would crumble.

Dominique and I made certain firm agreements, such as a pact that we would not use those three fatal words, "I love you", to each other. Not long before I left for Russia, she said she had a suitor flying out from Amsterdam to see her. She was going to dispose of him, and then go up to Queensland and get a job as a waitress at one of the Barrier Reef islands. She told me she had no intention of getting involved with anyone else, she just wanted to be alone and remove herself from Adelaide. I sympathized. I wished I could do the same.

I had found over the years, whether justly or unjustly, that it was my affairs which kept the marriage going, not the other way round; the affairs were part of my core where the marriage was not. I had fallen out of love with Ninette fairly early in the piece, despite the carved-in-stone façade the marriage presented to the world. Falling out of love happens in many marriages, and is nobody's fault. Usually there is enough to be getting on with for it not to matter too much.

Igor and I had translated one of Yevtushenko's poems which begins: "I fell out of love with you — what a banal denouement ...". He refuses to become a sentimentalist, to drag out the last act. The poem ends: "I no longer love you; for that I do not ask forgiveness. I did love you; that is what I ask forgiveness for."

I find it hard to write of my marriage because it had two faces: a very public face, assiduously cultivated by Ninette, and in which I colluded, and a private face with elements of suppressed tension and anger which occasionally emerged, to be thrust back under control again. Only the most acute and perceptive observers ever saw beyond the façade of the public image.

I have said that I chose to escape aspects of my marriage in affairs, but I had goodwill and affection towards Ninette and saw my life with her and the children as central to day-by-day existence; the affairs, hidden and seemingly peripheral, were, like poetry, tokens of a secret sun.

Twenty-Five

The Soviet Union, September 1966.

To have a new car is an achievement here; Zhenya has one, a little Moskvich, sturdy and out of date, typically Russian. "First we go to Peredelkino." He turns off the main road in from the airport onto a winding road through the woods. In the snow-leopard shadings of a birch forest you are truly in Russia.

Ninette and I walked to Boris Pasternak's grave. Like many graves here, it has a little fence around it, and there is a wide seat where you can sit and talk silently to the dead. There is a woman already sitting there, and we join her under two interlocking pines. All around the plain stone, with just the name and a bas-relief, are wildflowers, violas, cowslips, clover, and vase after vase of cut, fresh flowers around the grave. Across the valley is the green roof of Pasternak's house, where fifteen thousand people had come for the funeral, although there was no word of it in the press.

* * *

Spartak, Moscow, versus Dynamo, Kiev. There are eighty thousand people in the stadium. The red-and-white players on the brilliant green grass are surrounded by the muted colours of the spectators. They are nearly all men — lots of soldiers and sailors, lots of drunks (although drinking is allegedly illegal in the stadium), plenty of vodka, beer, sausage, pickles. *"Davai! Davai!* (Let's go)," they yell. "Abolish all Ukrainians! Send them to Siberia!" Zhenya is jumping up and down, yelling "*Davai*!" A solid fellow in a corduroy cap and a raincoat sitting next to him looks up at him and shouts, "You're Yevgeny Yevtushenko!" It's unbelievable, but he actually has in his raincoat pocket a battered copy of one of Zhenya's books. "Here, sign it, sign it," he says, and whips off his cap and puts it on Zhenya's head. It's a new one, too, with "Made in Glasgow" stamped inside the rim. Then he uncovers a bottle of vodka and offers it around.

* * *

This is what happens everywhere. The Russians are crazy about poetry. Zhenya's new book, the first he has been allowed for four years, has just appeared in an edition of a hundred thousand but is sold out already. He has been paid twenty-two thousand roubles for it (one rouble is equal to one Australian dollar). Zhenya has translated four poems of mine which have appeared in his big child Sofronov's *Ogonek*. I have been paid four hundred roubles for them, more than my whole last volume, *Poems Soft and Loud* earned. Zhenya has been paid the same, as translator. When he recites them they sound a lot better in Russian than they do in English. And he has kept all the rhymes and the rhythms.

* * *

Zhenya has found me an English translation of Rustaveli's epic poem *The Knight in the Tiger's Skin*; the eight-hundredth anniversary of his birthday is the excuse for the celebration in Tbilisi. Even in the dreadful translation you can sense what an extraordinary poem it is. How to describe it? A mixture between *The Romance of the Rose,* the *Morte d'Arthur, the Chanson de Roland* and *The Faerie Queene*?

* * *

A party in Zhenya's apartment, which is in one of those skyscrapers in the Stalinist-Baroque style. Zhenya's wife Galya is a strong, handsome woman, a translator from English into Russian. Around the rooms and on the walls are icons, and a Braque, a Chagall, a Max Ernst, and a Sidney Nolan. There is an exquisite thirteenth-century ivory statue of the Virgin. Zhenya tells me that when he was leaving Madrid after a reading the daughter of a Spanish Duke gave him a parcel and told him not to show it to the Customs or to open it until he was safely back home. In it was this ivory statue, which she had lifted from the family palace.

There is a powerful painting by a Russian artist, who is not allowed to exhibit, of soldiers cutting a watermelon with bayonets as if it were human flesh. Zhenya says he will take us out to meet the artist. The guest I like most is the playwright and fiction writer Vasha Aksenov, solid, wary-eyed but friendly faced, bubbling with anecdotes. His father was a member of the Central Committee of the Communist Party, and was liquidated by Stalin. His mother, Evgenia Ginzburg, spent ten years in solitary confinement. Vasha was separated from his brothers and sisters and brought up in a Home for Children of Enemies of the People. And yet here is this jolly man, telling a very funny story.

Zhenya says that Vasha's mother, despite everything, is still a Leninist Communist, an idealist who thinks that it could all come right in the end. He lifts his eyebrows. He says she has written the most important book yet about the Stalin era, and that it is about to be published by Mondadori in Italy. [An English translation, *Into The Whirlwind*, appeared in 1967, published by Collins Harvill.]

I have already noticed that often, when Zhenya introduces someone, he says that he or she spent ten, fifteen, twenty years in the camps. He wants you to know, and so do they.

* * *

When Zhenya's high spirits crack they crack like the ice on Lake Baikal; down below are endless black depths. He drives us way out into the suburbs to a dingy block of flats where the plaster has split, the paint has peeled and the lift has broken down. His friend the artist Alexei Selkov, who paints the watermelons, lives there with the unforgettable paintings he is not allowed to exhibit. He lives by designing for the theatre, but is very poor. In the West he would be a millionaire.

Driving back, Zhenya says he has lately felt so melancholy he has thought of committing suicide, but too many Russian poets have done that already. "Why are men such bastards?"

We are driving down a wide road into the centre of Moscow. Four cops on motorbikes, occupying the whole road, are advancing towards us. Behind them are about twelve more motorbikes, escorting six big black limousines full of VIPs from some foreign country or other. The private cars and trucks in front of us swerve off the road and stop on the gravel. Zhenya keeps driving. A huge cop bears down on us, waving us furiously off the road. Zhenya keeps driving. I wait for the shots. Zhenya stops, but still on the tarred road. The cop brroom-brrooms up beside us.

He must be one of the few people in Russia who do not recognize Zhenya. But Zhenya is not interested in recognition, only in his rights as a Soviet citizen under a constitution that has been flouted ever since it was proclaimed. I am only interested in getting out of range of the cop's truncheon, which is now swinging in his hand. The ZIM limousines roar past. Khrushchev is in the first one with Ceaucescu, the flag of Romania flapping. "Ceaucescu! Shit!" Zhenya spits. The cop is baffled. This bloke isn't behaving like an orderly Soviet citizen, but he is obviously not a hoooligan and he has a new Moskvich. He scratches his head as Zhenya explains the constitution to him. In despair he waves us on our way and speeds off to catch his convoy.

* * *

Bella. At last I meet Bella Akhmadulina, Zhenya's first wife, and the greatest woman poet in Russia since the death of Akhmatova a few months ago. Bella, born in 1937, the terrible year of the Moscow Trials, the bombing of Guernica, the Japanese invasion of China and the establishment of Buchenwald concentration camp. Bella, tragedy in her veins but fire in her eyes as well as in her red hair with its curling fringe. She is fresh, beautiful, fun, affectionate. She smokes jerkily with her fingers stretched straight out.

I am promised a book of her poems to translate with Igor Mezhakoff-Koriakin. Zhenya will write an introduction. One of my official duties is to ask her to come to Writers' Week at the next Adelaide Festival. She laughs.

Of course she will come, if she is allowed to. Bella is very unpopular with the committee deadheads of the Writers' Union.

In the taxi Zhenya asks what is her latest poem. It's called "Adventure in the Antique Shop", and she begins to recite all two hundred-odd lines of it. At the centre of it is a woman who dies in 1937. We have long ago reached our destination, but the taxi driver is as rapt in her poem as we are, and waits until the end.

Bella at the Writers' Union. Zhenya says he is going to invite an older poet to our table. Bella says no, he is a Stalinist. Zhenya says he wants Djeff to hear what they sound like, and brings over a grey-haired man who smiles too much. "Oh yes," he is saying, "they were difficult times, yes, people were killed, my own brother, but one must try to understand how difficult it was, the international situation, bad people here, yes, thousands of people were killed, but Stalin did good things."

Suddenly flame-haired Bella fires up, jumps to her feet. "It is impossible to forgive a man who has killed *one* man, let alone thousands." She storms out.

"Ah yes," says the Stalinist, still smiling, "it is good for a woman to react thus, to show female tenderness. For her it is like Stendhal, red or black, but there are so many colours now."

As he walks away Zhenya says, "Not stupid, but poison." He empties his glass. "You know what our poet Yesenin wrote? 'We are rowing to the land of the future with oars of chopped-off arms.' "

* * *

I used to think I liked my booze, but in Russia I am as a baby. Official meetings in the Writers' Union or in a publishing or magazine office begin at 11 a.m., and all down the table are bottles of vodka and Armenian brandy. They are not there for decoration. Breakfasts with Zhenya are always of caviar and champagne. Even at the airport the Red Army lieutenant and his girlfriend at the next table have a bottle of brandy for breakfast.

When Zhenya says, "Exists dangerous possibility of big drinks party", you get ready for a serious occasion. You learn not to worry too much about time. He rings to say he is coming to pick us up. "I come after twenty minutes, maybe five, maybe seven minutes late, no more than ten." Forty minutes later, if you're lucky, he arrives.

* * *

We fly across Russia and Ukraine. Suddenly the flatness is broken by the shock of the Caucasus, great, crumpled bare-pate peaks rising beyond to snow, dense forests full of bears and chamois. Zhenya points to the mountains. "Pasternak said the Caucasus looks like a bed after love." Right below the mountains is the Black Sea, ringed with beaches and towns. Zhenya is triumphant at having shaken off Krugerskaya.

We land at Sukhumi in Avkhazia, a beautiful little country lying betweeen the snow-covered peaks of the Caucasus and the water, dark as blackcurrant juice, of the Black Sea, named by the Turks who were no sailors and frightened of its storms.

We spend most of our time, here and in Georgia, in the company of the local poets, their wine and their sumptuous food. There is an apricot-coloured white wine, and a red they serve chilled, like a beaujolais; both are delicious. The danger is that you are handed a goblet with no base, tapering to a point, so you cannot put it down without draining it. And there are endless toasts at every meal. The position of toastmaster, or *tamada*, is one of great responsibility and skill. When you respond to a toast you are expected to talk for at least five minutes, and then drink to it.

The food is marvellous, great cuts of meat and vegetables with herbs I have never tasted before, and all sorts of just-picked fruit. A Georgian poet says to me, "Never eat grapes when you are drinking wine, it is like sleeping with the grandmother and the granddaughter at the same time."

One party is at a collective farm ("All Georgian farmers are black marketeers," whispers Zhenya), where a statue to Rustaveli is to be unveiled. It has been commissioned by the collective farm. Poetry and drinking go on from lunchtime into the night. I go for a piss and realize I am very drunk. I crash through the rows of sweet corn which will not keep me vertical and trip over some melons and collapse onto a row of aubergines. There lurches into my vinous brain a couplet of great purity:

Stumbling on melons, as I pass,
Ensnared with flowers, I fall on grass.

I am mortally ashamed for the honour of my country and realize I have also squashed some tomatoes. Zhenya and a Georgian poet are looking down at me, laughing. They help me to my feet and half-carry me back to the table. Everyone seems delighted that I am drunk.

Looking at the wine stains on my trousers the next day, Zhenya says, "By the time we leave Georgia we'll be able to drink those pants."

* * *

Back in Tbilisi again, Zhenya takes us to meet the famous Georgian artist Gudrashvili, in his lofty apartment with great chandeliers flashing above the creaky parquet floor. He was a contemporary and friend of Braque and Picasso in Paris before the Russian Revolution. But when he returned to Georgia, he soon fell out with the Soviet state, and has long been in disgrace. But he remained so popular with Georgians that he was allowed to restore the decaying frescoes in one of Tbilisi's ancient churches. While carrying out that task, he insisted that a curtain be drawn across the church so no one could watch him working. On the day of the unveiling of the restored frescoes, in front of a large crowd and all the Communist Party dignitaries, the curtain was drawn. There was the Virgin Mary, with the face of Gudrashvili's mistress, and Judas Iscariot, with the face of the Commissar of the Communist Party of Georgia.

As we drink his wine, he suddenly presents Ninette with an original watercolour, and me with a whole portfolio of prints. Zhenya's eyes are out on stalks. He says to us, in Rustaveli's words from his epic, *The Knight in the Tiger's Skin*, "What you give, you keep; what you keep, you lose."

* * *

Georgian wine seems also to have intoxicated Furtseva, the Soviet Minister of Culture, who comes to open the plenary session of the conference. Her speech is very emotional and she weeps at the end over the glory of Rustaveli. Grim Party people with faces of cement or dough growl their approval. She is a big, blowsy blonde whom Zhenya tells me everybody has slept with. When we are introduced she invites me to visit her at her home in Moscow. I decide to stick with Yevtushenko.

* * *

Aksenov tells me about John Steinbeck's visit to Russia. He wanted to wander alone around a hooligan district of Moscow. Vasha told him that if he got into trouble to say he was a famous American writer. "There are many things wrong with our country, but we do respect writers." Steinbeck does get into trouble. He wakes up in the gutter, cuddling an empty vodka bottle, being prodded by the boot of an enormous militiaman. Steinbeck remembers what he should do, sits up and says, "I am a famous American writer." "Ah," says the militiaman, "of course, Mr Gemingway", and calls a taxi. (Russians can't sound "H"; it took me some time before I realized who this unpopular fellow Gitler was.)

* * *

After Georgia Leningrad, and then Moscow again. On our second-last day, 13 October, there is a poetry reading, Zhenya, Bella and me, in the Polytechnic, organized by the engineering students — yes, engineering! The reading is for 5 p.m.; at 3 p.m. the doors are closed. Even the standing room is gone. There are two thousand in the hall. Bella recites her poems standing with her legs slightly apart, her arms sometimes held out, sometimes by her sides, her head slightly tilted back. She recites that complex poem about the antique dealer. Tremendous applause.

Zhenya recites two of the translations he has made of my poems and then I read them in English. I am the goose with two swans.

Bella kisses me goodbye and hugs me. *"Djeff, ya lyublio."* ("Geoff, I love you.")

At the airport the next morning Zhenya says the same, kissing me on both cheeks. Nothing cold about Russia except the weather, already chilly in October.

Ninette flew back to Australia. I went on to Switzerland, London and New York on Sun Books business and to see my own agents and publishers. There was an American sitting next to me in the Swissair plane. We had a couple of bourbons. He sighed with content. "You're damn right to take a few days off in Switzerland. It's like coming up from a deep dive, leaving Russia. You need time to decompress."

Switzerland might be neutral but it was not to be free of stress.

Coming to Switzerland now, after Russia, was like my first visit to it in 1947, after the destruction of the war elsewhere in Europe. The colours of fresh paint, shops full of food and clothes, streets full of cars, churches still open, the sound of an organ playing. Papers on the airport bookstall in six languages. Freedom.

After the desperate seriousness of Russia, everything seemed trivial. And yet all these trivialities were what the Russians were denied and longed for. Zhenya's "City of Yes". Is neutrality, non-involvement, the price of peace? The absence of tragedy, instead of being liberating, was almost oppressive. Against twenty million dead in World War II alone, the accidental bombing of Schaffhausen. Against the Stalinist saying the killings were necessary, millions of them, thousands of silent bourgeois hatreds. No haunted memories. What happened in Switzerland in 1937 — an increase in the price of mousetraps?

Ilse was there to meet me, looking more at home in Zürich than she ever had in Australia, but still anxious. Our reunion was that of lovers, rapturous, but alongside even the mere memory of Bella, Ilse seemed trivial.

But there she was, in the death-in-life dead centre of Europe, representing the unbroken continuity of European poetry and ideas, something which in Australia we were denied, something which the Russians had desired and imposed by force, like Peter the Great's St Petersburg. They could only achieve it by denying their own heritage; in the nineteenth century the upper classes spoke French. Here in Zürich the burghers not only spoke German but their own brand of it, the hideous vowels and cadences of Schweetzer-Dootsch. There were no Gulags to be sent to, but in this country, in the block of very comfortable apartments where Ilse was staying with a friend, you were only allowed to use the washing machines once a week, and women were forbidden to hang their underclothes outside on the line.

We had three days. It was going to be very romantic. We were going first to a little island on a lake, where the old monastery was now a small inn; then to the south-west, to follow the valley of the Rhône between the mountains, up past Sion to the village of Raron, where Rainer Maria Rilke is buried.

I had been reading a crude, typewritten English translation of Pasternak's *An Essay in Autobiography* that I had been given in Russia. In it Pasternak speaks with profound admiration of Rainer Maria Rilke, and translates two of his poems. Having so recently been at Pasternak's grave, this was a further continuity for me when we stood in front of Rilke's headstone, in the churchyard high above the village of Raron, by a sun-warmed wall beyond which was the valley of the Rhône. A rose branch curved over the enigmatic epitaph on the headstone. One of Rilke's uncollected poems, it read:

> ROSE, OH REINER WIDERSPRUCH, LUST NIEMANDES SCHLAF ZU SEIN UNTER SOVIEL LIDERN. (Rose, oh pure contradiction, delight to be no one's sleep under so many eyelids.)

There is also a play of words, "Lidern" meaning "eyelids" and "Lieder" meaning "songs".

We had one more night. Then I had to fly to London. The town where we had decided to stay was in the throes of some festival, and the only room we could get was in a motel outside the town. The motel and the room could have been anywhere in Australia. But I was too tired to go on to another town. The decompression the American had spoken of had not been without other pressures. The rewards, the exaltation even, of Rilke's grave and the island, the continuity of poetry, had lifted me above the ground, as in one of Chagall's paintings, and Ilse was my surreal partner. It would have been cruel to bring her down to earth and look at her, but in a sense she did not matter at all, only what I had met through her.

When we went to bed, after a lot of good wine, I felt very peaceful. She asked me, with a laugh, if I had been faithful to her in Australia, adding that of course she had released me from such bonds, and hoped that I had found someone. I was in that flux of being which is beyond caution, and told her about Joanna. (There must have been some residual caution, because I never mentioned Dominique, the one that really mattered.)

She exploded in fury, called me faithless, trivial, unworthy of her love, a philanderer, I lacked the true soul of a poet, and so on, *und so weiter*, for we were in bourgeois German Switzerland with a vengeance, *und so weiter*, *und so weiter*. Glass by glass over the next three or four hours I drank the carafe of water by the bed. Every now and then I would fall asleep in the middle of one of her harangues but then be shaken awake again. I would feebly say, "But this is our last night." I longed for take-off but had to wait.

In the morning I was so exhausted I could hardly climb the steps into the plane. Of course I had to turn and look, and there she was at the airport window, giving a little wave, sad I was going, but happy to have made me unhappy, and even happier that I had been soft-hearted enough to turn and look at her.

London, grey but, compared with Zürich, flowing over with life. Patrick had written to Edna O'Brien telling her to expect to hear from me. "I think it will be an interesting experience for you both," he said, an unlikely pander. Perhaps it might have been, but on the next day Edna was leaving for Dublin and I for New York. "Where shall we meet?" I asked. "At the Ritz," came the splendid reply.

Edna, at thirty-four, was five years older than Bella, but they had a lot in common besides beauty and talent. They were both, in the title of Patrick's story, burnt ones. They had both, like Yeats, been hurt into art by their countries, both of which they loved while hating what had been done to their people. Edna said that she would dearly love to come to the Adelaide Festival. I thought what an occasion it would be if she and Bella could be there together.

Through the usual subterfuges I managed to see Sid Nolan, who knew when I would be arriving in London. We had tea at Fortnum and Mason's, one of the odd arrangements that Sid liked to make. He had written to Robert Lowell about me. "I didn't know you'd met Cal," said Sid, slightly peeved that his lion had already been stroked. I explained about the gathering at Kenyon. Sid was doing some paintings for a book of Lowell's. One sure thing about Sid, evasive in so many ways, was his love of poetry and poets. He wanted to know every detail of what had happened in Russia and Georgia, and was delighted that I had seen his painting hanging in Yevtushenko's apartment. He said to me, in almost exactly the same words that Zhenya had often used with me, that there were people around the world who were lighthouses, mostly writers and artists, people who could trust each other, who were available to each other, who could tell the truth to each other without fear of betrayal. I too believed this, and still do, despite some grievous blows.

Zhenya had said he thought of Lowell as a lighthouse. He admired his poetry but had reservations about his angst, while recognizing the pain involved in his precarious hold on sanity. "But," Zhenya said to me, "he talked to me for two hours about suffering, and I don't doubt he has suffered, and even been put in gaol for a little while for being a conscientious objector, but it's not supportable for a man like Lowell to talk to a Russian about suffering. That novelist we go to see, Smelyakov, he spent sixteen years in the camps. He can tell you about suffering. It makes me a little cynical, this American suffering." His mood changed, and he laughed,

"Do you know, Lowell tells me he is mixture of Saint-Just and Dostoyevsky's Alyosha!"

Lowell's apartment was much larger than Zhenya's, and the paintings and artworks were not as good, but like Zhenya's it was the ambience of someone you could trust, whose preferences were all around you in the bookshelves and on the walls. Preferences, of course, that were also those of his formidable wife Elizabeth Hardwick. I asked them both to come to an Adelaide Festival, hoping there was truth in the strong rumour that the American State Department's Australian agents were so vexed at the success of Yevtushenko's tour that they were going to finance the visits of American writers and theatre companies.

After a couple of those horribly dangerous American martinis Lowell signalled that he and I should move out for lunch. As I had noticed in Kenyon, he had a strange face and manner, obviously patrician but not very successfully put together in the womb. He peered at the world with a mixture of censure and hope, every now and then letting slip a very sweet smile. He wanted to hear all about Russia. He knew a lot about what was going on there; he liked Yevtushenko and his poetry, but his favourites were Voznesensky and Akhmadulina. We laughed at the well-promoted rivalry between Yevtushenko and Voznesensky. When I arrived in Moscow Zhenya had said, "It is a pity, but Voznesensky is in South America. He had to flee the country when he found out that the print run of my new book was bigger than his."

We shared our detestation of the literary hangers-on, critics and faint poets, who attend functions like the Rustaveli Festival. Lowell said, "They expect the privileges and inside information of being with writers, but don't accept the hazards; they don't get drunk, they don't fuck, they don't fight. The worst are usually English." I told him there were two particularly choice examples, both English, at Tbilisi. One of them had said to me, after a session in which there was a speech about Walt Whitman, "Why do the Russians waste their time on a second-rate poet like Whitman?" Nevertheless, Lowell obviously had a deep love of England. I told him he ought to go to Yorkshire.

We talked about Vietnam, and I admitted, with some shame, that it had needed Zhenya's visit to jolt me out of my apathy about what was really happening there. He said I must read the latest publication from *Ramparts* magazine, *A Vietnam Primer*. After lunch we walked to a bookshop and he bought me a copy; I bought another one to give to Patrick. On the jacket was a photo-portrait of a Sergeant who had won the Congressional Medal of Honor; he looked the fresh-faced, All-American boy. When I commented on this, Lowell told me that his testimony against the war was the most powerful piece in the magazine. And so it was.

In New York I had an appointment with an editor from Doubleday, who had had a set of galley proofs of *Andy* from Collins, and was interested in the book. In London I had had lunch with Billy and Pierre, and Billy had warned me about American editors: "They all want to rewrite every author's book. Don't you let them." Since Billy was one of the two shrewdest publishers I knew (the other was Allen Lane), I kept my appointment, at the Harvard Club, in a sceptical frame of mind. The Club was one of those typically American male institutions with lots of dark panelling and deep armchairs with the leather beginning to crack, all extremely comfortable and the perfect setting in which to get drunk on bourbon. The editor was in a wheelchair; he was a most delightful, intelligent and unbossy man. He said he loved *Andy*; it was happily in *Catch-22* territory without being in the least derivative. He said it had a great potential. I warmed even more to him, not to mention the third bourbon. He then wheeled his way to our table, and ordered a starter of those delicious little cherrystone clams, and some good east-coast white wine.

Then he said he would be very pleased to work on the book with me, if I would not be dismayed if he suggested some radical restructuring. Billy Collins' warning flashed on my private screen. He talked on, while I made non-committal remarks. At the end of lunch, I agreed to ring him the next day.

I rang Billy first. He said "There, what did I tell you? Damned Americans, what cheek." So I declined the editor's proposition, and made the worst mistake of my career as a writer of fiction. Despite my Oxford degree in English and years of teaching, in the business of writing fiction myself I was a first-year student, not even a sophomore (which comes from Greek "sofos", meaning "wise", something I was not). That editor and I would have made something good out of *Andy*, it would have had an American edition, and he might have helped me to make something much better of my later novels than I did by myself.

Although I would have indignantly denied it, I was still under the potent influence of the Mother Country, although in Billy's case it would be better to say "Father". What was maddening, and further confusing, was that I had an excellent editor at Collins, Philip Ziegler, later to achieve fame as a biographer. But Philip, in the British tradition, restricted his always helpful comments to relatively minor matters, and never suggested what the American editor had seen was necessary, a major restructuring.

Of course, Billy was right about some American editors. A couple of days later I went to a literary party in New York where I was introduced to one of America's most eminent editors. I forget which publisher he was working for at the time, but he said to me, "Hey, you've got a writer of real promise down there in Australia, Patrick White. I hear you know him? Well, if you could persuade him to come to me, I could make a real success of him. Clean up his style, for a start."

When I returned to Australia I told Patrick the story, which provoked a strangled laugh, and I gave him the copy of the Ramparts *Vietnam Primer*. A week or so later he mentioned it at the end of a long, gossipy letter. "Haven't yet read the Ramparts which no doubt will reinforce my 'black reactionary colonial' attitude. That model sarge on the cover is just a bit too clean-cut to convince."

A week later he had changed his mind. "I have now read the *Vietnam Primer* & see that I have been wrong, chiefly through ignorance. I am writing to Ramparts for more copies ... The 'model sarge' is the one who impresses me most as being first-hand and sincere." When the copies arrived he sent them out, including one to Harold Holt, who was then Prime Minister. He also started to involve himself deeply in activities against the war.

Somewhat different attitudes to knowledge were revealed shortly after my return to South Australia, when a well-known and very rich grazier and his wife told me, without any shame at all, that they had bribed their god-daughter with a six-month overseas trip to stop her enrolling at the University to do History and Politics.

The year 1967 was one of enormous upheavals. Uno was sold, and at last I had some capital to pay off some of my debts. It would also enable me to go back to Russia under my own steam and not as an invited guest. This was because I had the idea of writing a book about Yevtushenko and the young Russian writers. I had discussed the idea with Billy Collins in London. Billy was very interested in Russia, especially from his partnership with Harvill, the English publisher of *Dr Zhivago*, and thought there was a big potential in such a book. I had guardedly mentioned the idea to Yevtushenko and had got an equally guarded reply which I interpreted as approval. He always took great precautions with the post. Any letters that spoke frankly he would give to a reliable foreign visitor to post outside the Soviet Union. Sometimes he would be openly ironic, irony being quite beyond the grasp of the KGB.

Like all the younger Russian writers he loathed Sholokhov, who had been a good writer in the days of *And Quiet Flows The Don* but had turned into a vicious reactionary. Sholokhov lived in an opulent country house and was reputed to have his own private aircraft. He frequently denounced any writer he considered subversive. So Zhenya sent me a postcard, unsealed, of a recent photo of Sholokhov, who had been a very handsome man in his youth, looking like a KGB torturer. On it he wrote, "Behold the proud face of our people!" No doubt the censor thought he was being a true patriot.

I made plans for Ninette and me to arrive in Moscow early in October 1967 and spend a fortnight there, simply as Intourist visitors. Intourist soon revealed itself as the worst hazard of travel in Russia. I could not help remembering one of Aksenov's stories, which went: "Do you know why

Napoleon retreated from Moscow?" "No, why?" "Because his visit was managed by Intourist."

In the meantime a chain reaction had been set in motion by the sale of Uno. It seemed inevitable to the family that without Uno's backing Anlaby would not survive. It was still the oldest sheep-stud station in South Australia, but John was not exactly a dynamic general manager. Eight thousand acres, only sixty miles north of Adelaide, sounds a lot, but in fact the returns from grazing and cropping were small. On top of it, of course, were huge overheads: all the buildings, a general manager, a manager, an overseer and five station hands. Grandfather would have thought all that insufficient to run the garden, but times had changed in the past sixty years, although it often did not seem apparent.

It was decided to sell Anlaby at the end of the year. Of course, I should never have moved the family to Anlaby from Nonsuch in the first place. The financial drain had been unrelenting. But it had been a marvellous place for the children to grow up in. Surely such beauty and variety would give them something to hang on to all their lives, as it had for me. And we had had very happy times there. Now it was inevitable that we should go.

There were rumours already of a big consortium wanting to buy the place, and of an English millionaire who was going to make a bid. There was even a report that Alick Downer was interested. After all, he was Grandfather's godson, and Anlaby was genuinely old by Australian standards; Downer's home in the hills, Arbury Park, looked like something out of the eighteenth century, but he had built it in the 1930s. With Anlaby, he would have some genuine heritage.

In August I wrote to David Campbell to say we had decided to leave South Australia and settle near Canberra, and asked his help in finding a block of land where we could build a house; we also needed to rent a house for the first six months of 1968. The architect Guilford Bell, when I met him in Melbourne, had said he would design a house for us. David wrote to say he would look out for a few acres for us near Canberra, and that Manning and Dymphna Clark, who were going overseas for six months, would like to rent us their house in Canberra.

David was still one of my dearest friends, but I was beginning to wish I had not commissioned him to edit *Modern Australian Poetry* for Sun Books. The terms were a hundred pounds on signature, one hundred pounds on delivery, and five per cent royalty, and he had accepted the contract in June 1965. A year later I was begging him for at least a list of contents. Seven months later I was imploring him to finish, as the Penguin anthology was not to be reprinted. We would have no competition. Six months later, in May 1967, I at least had gone through the probable contents of his selection with him, but we still had no list of contributors that we could use as advance publicity to stake our claim in the market. The book finally appeared in 1970, having taken five years. It is a very good anthology indeed, but David was simply incapable of doing anything quickly, except sweep a woman off her feet.

One achievement that I did manage, having what often turned out to be an absurd hope that my friends might like each other, was to bring David and Patrick together in July 1966. They liked each other immediately; it took David several years to read *Voss*, but he liked that too. In the 1970s he wrote a characteristic poem about the white cockatoos visiting Martin Road, which pleased Patrick.

Patrick was gloomy about our projected move to Canberra. He agreed there were good people there, David, Manning Clark, Bob Brissenden, but there were all those dreadful professors called Hope.

We left Australia at the end of September 1967, and stayed the night in Singapore, where I bought a tape-recorder for the coming interviews for my book. We flew on to Rome and then drove to our old haunts by Le Lavandou, then stayed near Les Saintes-Maries with Catha Aldington, the long-legged little girl now solid like her father, married to a man who bred cattle in the Camargue. We went to a bullfight, the South of France kind where the bull is the hero and only the bullfighters in their white trousers and sandshoes risk being killed.

We flew into Moscow on 9 October. Oksana Krugerskaya was at the airport to meet us; Zhenya was in Avhkazia. I began to realize how foolish I had been to return, how hopeless it would be to gather the material for my book.

An Intourist guide waited for us every day, an earnest girl called Ira who was doing her third year at Moscow University. We dutifully went to the Tretyakoff gallery where, in front of a painting of the Nativity, she explained to us that Mary and Joseph were the parents of Jesus.

On the way to the Pushkin gallery we passed a huge swimming pool. I asked Ira whether she liked swimming. She replied, "No, I do not like to swim, but swimming is interesting. Especially interesting in the winter." We went on to an appalling exhibition of Fifty Years of Soviet Art in a huge pavilion near the Kremlin. The whole visit was turning into a disaster, the official Russia by courtesy of Intourist and a lot of foreign exchange. I just wanted to talk to my writer friends.

At last I was allowed to go to the Writers' Union. Bella was there, fresh and sweet, with straight-into-the-arms hugs at meeting again. She said that Zhenya had "problems", and might stay in Avhkazia. She also said that Galya would not be with him. More problems. She introduced me to the sculptor Ernst Neizhvestny and his shy young wife. He was stocky and strong with vast shoulders; the marble would have cringed in front of him. He was famous not only as a sculptor but also for his outburst at the first exhibition of genuine modern Soviet art at the Manège in November 1962.

Neizhvestny had been deputed to show Khrushchev around the exhibition. Khrushchev stamped around, glaring, and then said, "This is horse-shit." Neizhvestny squared up to him and said, "That's what I'd expect an ignorant peasant like you to say." There was the original of all stunned silences. Then Khrushchev, clapping Ernst on the shoulder and laughing said, "I have always admired courage." Unfortunately this episode did not change Khrushchev's view of modern art, and a period of repression followed, of literature as well as art.

Aksenov turned up in a roll-necked sweater, looking as cheerful as ever. Then Zhenya arrived, in a blue-striped suit with a blue shirt and a white collar; there was a blonde girl with him, whom he introduced as Natasha. Despite the smart clothes he looked scraggy, his face drawn. There were obviously problems. Oksana was whispering about him to a very correct poet from Estonia.

Zhenya pulled me aside and pointed to Natasha. "Is ugly but is good girl and good actress." To add to his problems he had forgotten to take off the windscreen wipers on his Moskvich before he went to Avhkazia, and both of them had been stolen. Impossible to buy new ones. I promised to send him some, if I could buy them in Europe.

We all went out to a restaurant for lunch. Ernst flagged down a van, an illegal manoeuvre known as hiring a "left" taxi. There were so few official taxis that dozens of people with cars or vans cruised and picked up passengers who hailed them with the left hand.

I said I had been to the art exhibition celebrating the fiftieth anniversary of the Revolution. Zhenya snorted. "Is fifty times worse than the original one." I tried to have a word with him about my idea for a book; I said I had brought a tape-recorder and could do some interviews. "You are stupid bloody great Australian bastard," he said affably, and changed the subject. Of course the sight of a foreigner with a tape-recorder was enough to make even the most loquacious Russian immediately dry up. I should have realized that.

I could make no arrangements with anyone. Zhenya told me to get Ira to take me to the Foreign Languages Library — "our only source of good reading". I did, and was amazed at the library. There were, for example, first and second editions of the English and American editions of all Patrick White's novels, and a vast collection of essays and reviews. They even had some journal reviews of my books, as well as the books themselves.

We returned to the old Metropole Hotel, and I found out how true it was that there were no telephone books in Moscow. I asked the Service Bureau for a phone book. "No, we don't have one, but try the Information Desk opposite the lift. I believe she had some numbers once." I went there and said, "I want to find out the telephone number of a friend." "Is impossible."

Then there was a phone call from Oksana to say Zhenya had gone back to the Black Sea.

Interviews had been arranged for me with the editor and staff of some of the leading magazines, and some of the lecturers from the Literary Institute, and people from radio and television. The same complaint about Yevtushenko kept coming up: "You see, he is too popular".

Suddenly, after I had returned to the hotel, the phone rang. "You recognize my voice?" Zhenya was back in Moscow again. The champagne flowed. He had got us into the Circus, despite the impossibility of buying seats — he was good friends with the famous clowns, Karandash and Popov, and many of the other performers; we would be allowed to sit on the steps.

After one terrifying acrobatic act Zhenya said, "These people are honest, they can't fake, they have to be courageous." We went on to the Actors' Club, where Natasha was waiting for us; we ate huge dishes of freshwater crayfish. I said we called them "yabbies" in Australia. Everyone laughed uproariously. Zhenya leant over to me. " 'Yabby' is 'fuck' in Russian."

Natasha was not beautiful, but was memorable, uninhibited and reckless. Zhenya was subsiding into melancholy: he was not getting on with Galya; he was having great joy with Natasha, but this was also causing misery. "Galya hates the world, maybe Natasha loves it too much." Natasha was mocking him. Turning to me, she said, "It is his Roossian soul", and then to him, "You mustn't think of iron hooks." "What iron hooks?" "Well you think how good it is to make love, then maybe I would like you to make me a baby, then a beautiful baby comes, then we have a house together, then baby takes his first steps, then falls down trapdoor into cellar and hangs himself on an iron hook." That broke up Zhenya's melancholy. When, some hours later, it looked like returning, she called out, "Iron hooks!"

Cheering up, Zhenya told me some stories about Bella. She had been reciting her poems in Tbilisi, the only woman with four men on the platform. A Georgian poet read a poem praising Stalin (who of course was a Georgian). At the end of it the audience cheered. Bella took off her shoe and hit the poet twice, hard, in the face. And a few weeks ago Bella had gone to the railway station to see off the poet Bulat Okhudjava (a jongleur-poet of great originality and character whom I had met on my last visit and had invited to come to Adelaide), who was going to Bulgaria. She was having a drink with him in his compartment when they realized that the train had started. So she stayed on it for two days until the frontier. There she found that the frontier guards were fans of hers, so she stayed with them for two days. Then she met a Georgian poet, a very old friend, who was on his way home, so she went with him to Tbilisi. There she met a group of old friends and they all went to Novosobirsk. She arrived back at her flat in Moscow two weeks after she had left to go to the railway station.

Zhenya fell into the glooms again. "She is being stopped going to Rome.

All tickets were sold for her readings. Now Simonov and another are going without her. They will never let her go to Australia."

I saw Ninette off at the airport, for her return to Australia, and went to the Writers' Union, where I spent the rest of the morning with the bureaucrats, discussing which Soviet writers would be coming to the next Adelaide Festival. Maybe Rozhdestvensky and Okhudjava. More brandy and vodka and caviare were consumed. "And Akhmadulina?" I asked, and invented an elaborate story of how many thousands of fans she had in Australia and what credit she would bring to the Soviet Union. "Maybe none," one grey man in a grey suit filled up his glass again with neat brandy. "She drinks too much. And her poems are too personal, neurotic even." "But all Australian poets drink too much," I said, "she will be among friends. And they probably drink much more than she does." The best I could get out of them was that she might be able to come. I knew of course that it was only an excuse. Bella drank, indeed, but she was not an alcoholic, and she was a totally reliable performer of her work.

I left Moscow for Prague with very little achieved, and one useless tape-recorder. I also had a hangover and the night before had had no more than two and a half hours sleep. Barry Humphries had a friend in that city, still so beautiful albeit with the paint peeling. Theo Wilden was a best-selling writer of high-class thrillers; he had been in gaol for some time for his political views.

Theo looked very formal, but clearly was not. "Tonight I will show you Prague. We will have five courses for dinner and eat them at five restaurants." He was as good as his word. When I woke up next morning in the quiet and comfortable intimacy of my room at the Esplanade Hotel, I could remember nothing after the second course.

At his apartment the next day Theo introduced me to his charming wife and then to his study, which must have been the most remarkable room in the country. In front of his desk was a large panel which looked rather like the cockpit of an old DC-3. There were switches and flashing lights and a big red button. Theo explained that it was basically a radio system which enabled him to talk to his friends without involving the telephone exchange and its unwanted listeners. He pressed a button and a voice answered. "Just testing," he said to the microphone, switched off and said to me, "That was my private chauffeur. He does hire work when I don't need him." He pressed another couple of buttons and talked to friends. I asked him what the red button was for. "To rupture the eardrum of the secret police." He pressed and a piercing squeal like that of a dying pig erupted from the loudspeaker. He pressed another button together with the red one. There was silence. "When I wish to make an interesting call, I press both buttons and only the police get the squeal."

I mentioned that I had a brand new Sanyo tape-recorder which I was hoping to sell. He pressed the button for the chauffeur, and I was assured of a deal that afternoon. If I approved of the price quoted, then he would like to suggest that he despatch his chauffeur to a castle a few hours out of Prague, where he knew of some eighteenth-century Bohemian glass that would be a nice present for my wife. By this stage I would have agreed to anything. The chauffeur was despatched.

After leaving the amazing Theo I flew to West Berlin where I had my own good deed to do. I went to a large motor-car spare parts warehouse and bought four Moskvich windscreen wipers and had them sent to Yevtushenko. Later he wrote that they were the best present anyone had ever given him. I was pleased, but didn't myself think they quite matched up to the Spanish Duke's thirteenth-century ivory.

When I arrived home in early November, an advance copy of my biography of Edward John Eyre, *The Hero As Murderer*, was waiting for me. It was a handsome book and it was well received; it later went into a Penguin edition and was in print for many years. I liked many of the reviews and comments, but was most pleased when Patrick said he and Manoly thought it was "a noble book".

Towards the end of the year Max Harris and I decided that *Australian Letters*, which had published much of enduring merit, should now come to an end. Rosemary Wighton, who had been helping us in editing the magazine, needed all her energies for the very busy *Australian Book Review*, but that was only one of the considerations that helped us towards the decision.

In our final editorial we suggested that ten years was enough for a literary magazine, which provoked rage in Clem Christensen and genial laughter in Steve Murray-Smith. After several years of *Australian Letters* we had managed to get a small grant from the CLF, all of which we used to pay contributors. Otherwise we survived by advertisements, donations, subscriptions, and sales through the Mary Martin Bookshop in particular. When I was teaching in Kansas, Max had sent over issues of *Australian Letters* and *Australian Book Review*, and my American colleagues were amazed when they heard of our piddling finances. They told me that it would cost at least fifty thousand dollars a year each to produce such magazines in the United States, money that could come only from a university or something like the Ford Foundation.

In 1968 Sun Books published a hardback selection from the magazine, elegantly designed by Alison Forbes, called *The Vital Decade*. Looking back through the issues of the magazine, and also being a veteran of the Ern Malley wars, I find it amusing that there are some innocents who think the world began in 1968. But of course, every generation thinks it is vital and that it is wielding the original new broom.

One manifestation of this is the belief that you and your friends are at last sexually liberated, not like your poor old straitlaced parents. In the 1970s I went to a very grand wedding in Melbourne, and found myself sitting next to Dame Mabel Brookes. We were publishing her autobiography, and Brian Stonier had asked me to remind her that she was running somewhat behind schedule. I did this, as tactfully as I could, and she replied, "Well, Geoffrey, the trouble is, I keep having to cut things out that might turn out libellous. I mean, they talk about this being the permissive society nowadays, but compared with our generation they're just a lot of puppy-dogs and pussy-kittens."

Twenty-Six

At Anlaby everyone was busy sprucing the old place up for the sale. What real estate people call a brochure had been produced by Elders, under the black capitals: "HISTORIC ANLABY STATION/ HOME OF SOUTH AUSTRALIA'S OLDEST MERINO STUD/ 8184 ACRES 8184. Possession by 1 March 1968." Only the weather did not cooperate, the drought year continuing with only a few miserable sprinkles of rain.

The best description of the reasons for the sale is in a letter I wrote to Chibs and her husband Dick Blackburn. The problems were insuperable. If any one of the four owners died, death duties would force a sale. Léonie might want to sell anyway. I continued: "You know how we have always stuck out to stay here, and how much of everything we have put into making Anlaby our home, and how much we love it — but I can see no certainty, however modestly one should hope for small certainties, in our future here. To flourish as it ought to, Anlaby needs one owner, a millionaire, or else a powerful group of people or a rich company. For me, it used to represent a hope of permanence, but it doesn't any more." Ninette and I had been away, "and we waited for a few days till the joyful warmth of the immediate homecoming had worn off (I don't mean that home is cold now! — only that one is always at one's most sentimental coming home). And we are sure we are right. Oddly enough, I think she is more distressed now at the thought of moving than I am ... I feel that at this stage we are the lynchpin or whatever the technical term is and that if we are removed the whole thing falls apart. But of course we want everything to be done by common consent."

The sale was due to take place on 1 December 1967. Elders were gloomy because the rich British buyer had pulled out. At the sale there were no bids for the property as a whole, buyers obviously being scared off by all the houses and buildings. Elders then asked us if we would allow the property to be offered in lots. We agreed to this, and Frank Mosey, a local grazier, bought about five thousand acres, the manager's house (where he intended to live) and the woolshed. Mosey also took over the Anlaby merino stud, and was allowed to retain the name of Anlaby. Brian Shannon (brother of the painter Michael) bought the paddocks along the River Light. This left about fifteen hundred acres around the homestead, with the big house, the "cottage", and all the station buildings except the woolshed.

The family gathering after the sale was very melancholy, none of us knowing how we would ever sell the homestead block. I could not help thinking of the thirteen thousand pounds (not dollars) we had sunk in refurbishing the big house. John and Peg were moving in any case to their new property at Clarendon.

We all had dinner together and then Ninette and I set off to drive to what was not going to be home. Suddenly, as we were coming up the straight past Parafield, we both decided to use my share of the two blocks that had been sold, and buy the homestead block from the other members of the family. I turned the car round and drove back to Adelaide, resolved to see Elders and the family in the morning.

One should never underestimate one's ability to attempt to cover up one's mistakes, but nothing can justify this absurd decision. It was as if the car were no longer running on the tarred road but being swept along in a warm flood of sentiment. We were immersed in the very sentimentality about coming home which I had cautioned myself against, and mentioned in my letter to Chibs. Ninette was ecstatic, and kept saying how wonderful it would be for the children.

A quarter of a century later, and I hope a wiser man, I am still baffled by my stupidity. If, as truly outlined in my letter to Chibs, Anlaby was only viable for a millionaire or a company, the whole 8184 acres of it, how on earth was I going to make it work with 1500 acres? I loved the place; it (and Rocky Point) had been the one constant in my life, my family loved it. But that is no excuse. Perhaps there was vanity in it, for I did enjoy the style of living there, even though I could not afford it. Ninette certainly enjoyed it, and had modelled herself on my mother. I averted my gaze from the truth and looked instead on the sad probability of some hard-headed buyer taking it over and bulldozing the big house and many of the other buildings. Now it was up in big letters on my mind's screen: "Anlaby Saved". But what I should have seen was that that was only the beginning of the film.

In the morning the deal was done. We would call our homestead block Old Anlaby, so that Frank Mosey could retain Anlaby for the name of the stud. My final act of insanity was to pay the other members of the family cash, borrowing most of the money while having to wait three years before we got our money from Mosey and Shannon. So I started off in the red. And now I had to pay the wages of three station hands, a secretary-nanny and a girl who helped full time in the house, run the property without any real experience, and continue in my career as writer, publisher and member of various committees and organizations to do with Australian writing.

I decided that there would have to be some more intensive farming on such a small acreage in that type of country, so asked our employee Marc Schutz if he would take charge of a piggery. We would build it from the mile-long avenue of jarrah posts put up by Grandfather, with their white paint that had long since been flaking. Marc, good Barossa-Deutsch, knew little about pigs but enthusiastically agreed to become a pig breeder. I was to find out that, no matter how conscientious and hardworking Marc was, and no matter how all the family cleaned the piggery and fed the pigs at the weekend, that these jolly, intelligent and surprisingly endearing animals needed constant expert management. No matter how hard we tried, the pigs never reached the target below which they became a liability which devoured dollars as the pigs did pigfood.

Manning and Dymphna Clark were extraordinarily forbearing in having to find a new tenant for their house, as was David Campbell in having to look for a new buyer for the forty acres by the Molonglo he had agreed to sell us.

One undercurrent running steadily and strongly below my activities throughout these years was the growing of my children. There were infinitely rewarding years: whatever else was falling apart, and whatever misjudgments I made on so many levels, nothing disturbed my bonds with those children.

The other always-positive element in our lives was Rocky Point, which we visited whenever we could. I had begun to prefer it when there were not so many visitors, although some visits were to be treasured. It was also a wonderfully tranquil place for work, although I insisted that work and holiday should never be mixed. Only Alan Moorehead got away with doing that.

Sometimes, however, I felt I was the manager of an exclusive holiday resort. One of the most rewarding events at Rocky Point was to go night fishing, drifting backwards along on the glassy water under the stars in the big clinker dinghy, with a pressure lamp on the stern, someone with a spear on one side, someone with a dab net on the other, looking for the iridescent gleam of garfish or the pale thrust of a squid. But too often now such expeditions were not poetic at all, just another duty. I remember rowing softly, almost asleep with exhaustion, in the early hours of one morning, when the man with the spear turned around and said, "Dutton's a top ghillie." Too often Rocky Point seemed like an obstacle race of unending chores, and too many people, people, people.

A welcome visit was that of Patrick and Manoly who, in the New Year of 1968, came to stay for a week; as a result the world was nearly deprived of Patrick's last eight or nine books. Patrick's skills, since his horse-riding days as a jackeroo, had not extended outside his study and kitchen; he could scarcely change a fuse or mend a puncture. The only fish he caught were those determined to catch themselves, and the boat always lurched alarmingly when his leg, encased in a gumboot, came over the gunwale.

Our most exciting fishing at Kangaroo Island was for an elegant, hard-fighting and delicious fish called "sweep", which we caught off the rocks on the South Coast. It was only possible to fish for sweep on a low tide, and on a north-wind day when the seas coming in from Antarctica were temporarily levelled. Even so, there was often a swell still rolling in, and the golden rule was to keep one eye on your line and the other on the open sea. If a big wave was coming, you either retreated from your spot on the edge of the reef, or joined arms with those alongside you, and leaned into the swell.

On this particular day we went to a recently discovered place, reached by scrambling down a cliff and walking out across the reef until you came to a little promontory. Here the water went straight down for about twenty feet, and, most exciting, in the crystal clear water you could see the big sweep drifting in and out from under the ledge of the reef. There was one hazard, as well as the usual ones, about this spot: a blowhole, about four feet across, through which you could see the glitter of the green sand below the underside of the reef. The best place to stand and fish was around the seaward edge of this blowhole.

The little sandy cove at the bottom of the cliff was always rich with shells, especially the south-coast cowries, and I suggested to Patrick that he should collect shells rather than fish in this rather tricky place. No, he insisted on fishing, and on wearing his accursed gumboots. I always asked guests to wear sandshoes, or some other flexible shoe, to protect their feet from the very sharp rocks, but Patrick was determined to stick to his boots.

Four of us went out, Ninette, Patrick, Chris Legoe and myself. The day was perfect, with the occasional swell, and the fish were there in hundreds. Everyone was so intent on hauling in the sweep that no one noticed a large wave advancing. Suddenly I saw it coming, and yelled for everyone to link arms. When it came, in its oh-so deceptive gentle, slow, blue curve, it was up to my waist, and I am six foot three. All would have been well except for Patrick's gumboots. They filled with water; Patrick stumbled, and was sucked straight down the blowhole. Ninette, alongside him, threw herself down across the edge of the hole so he could grab hold of her, while Chris and I swished through the water to either side of the hole and caught his arms. Above his mute mouth his blue eyes, alarming at any time, had the look of a man being buried alive. Chris and I managed to heave him out against the suction of the sea hissing down the hole.

From then on, that spot was known as Patrick's Hole. Typically punctilious, he arranged with Chris Legoe to send us down a rod to replace the one he had lost. However, a few days after the incident there was a freak glassy calm, and I put on snorkelling gear and dived under the reef and recovered the undamaged rod, which was jammed between sand, kelp and rock. Even on this dead calm day, there was something very scary about the dark under-ledge of the reef, and the shaft of blue light coming down through the sunlit water slurping in the blowhole. Sucked under there, Patrick would certainly have drowned.

We were back at Rocky Point again some months later, just the family, while I began a new novel, based on my journeys to Russia. Like a dreadful tap on the shoulder from all that was most vile in the Soviet Union, at the very time I was starting to write my novel, we heard on the radio that Russia had invaded Czecho-Slovakia. Amazingly enough, a day later the Adelaide *Advertiser* printed the text of the public telegram Yevtushenko had courageously sent to Kosygin and Brezhnev protesting against the invasion. A Russian friend later gave me the *samizdat* text of Zhenya's poem about the invasion, a poem which in Russian hammers out the thump of the tanks on the cobblestones: "Tanks are rolling across Prague / in the sunset blood of dawn / Tanks are rolling across truth / not a newspaper named *Pravda*". (The word *Pravda* — also the name of the Communist Party's newspaper — means "truth".) Apparently tens of thousands of people knew Zhenya's poem by heart.

And while this was all taking place, only five months after My Lai, my family and I were wrapped in the peace and beauty of Kangaroo Island. Patrick wrote in deep gloom from London: "Surely there is nobody ridiculous enough still to think human beings can make any progress".

Meanwhile *Andy* had appeared from Collins, with the jacket of the hardback featuring a Lawrence Daws print. On my way back from Russia in 1967 I had been looking through his work in his studio in London, and there found a print with a biplane above a big grey building in the jungle. My novel involved Tiger Moths, the jungle, and the gaol. By one of those strange coincidences, they were all there in Lawrence's print.

But for the paperback, a different cover was used. Billy Collins, a sensitive, almost proper, man was nervous that I might be shocked by it. It showed a naked woman, high in the sky, astride the shoulders of the pilot of a Tiger Moth; it had also been enlarged into a sensational poster. Maybe because of this, the book sold thirty thousand copies in paperback, with all its chronic faults as a novel. More than twenty years later I completely rewrote it and it was republished as *Flying Low* by University of Queensland Press.

Fortunately the copy I sent Patrick had the Daws cover. Even so, he didn't like it, which was what I had expected. What he wrote to me (from London) is revealing of our different experiences of life in the Air Force.

> We found the copy of *Andy* waiting at the Bank, and here comes the difficult part of this letter, but you wouldn't want me to gush and pretend. Perhaps it just is that I'm allergic to aeroplanes. After those miserable years in the RAF, I decided never to think about the damn machines again except when forced to travel in one. I was never able to take an interest in them, & found I couldn't get on with your book — a distressing state of affairs as I had been looking forward to it all this time. It was not only the Air Force theme, I didn't like the tone of it. By that I don't mean the four-letter words, which I use myself with

the greatest pleasure. I had the feeling that a hearty young philistine had been buried in you all these years, and suddenly felt the urge to expiate your devotion to literature (just as I suspect some Elinor Glyn deep in myself may some day dash off a novelette to shatter the world). I hope I am wrong about *Andy*. You remember how I was unable to read *Catch 22*, which everyone else seems to think a masterpiece. But factual books are, I think, your line. *The Hero As Murderer* was a noble work, and I hope you will write others in that vein.

I was later to think, especially after reading David Marr's biography of Patrick, that "those miserable years in the RAF" had actually done him a lot of good. For one thing, he was out of range of his mother. He particularly liked the South Africans he was stationed with in the Western Desert, and joined them in singing filthy songs, like my characters in *Andy* or in the real life of Tasmania. One would have thought that Patrick would have been pleased to be spending nearly all his time in the exclusive company of young men. But the truth was that he was frightened of them. All his life he suffered from what Max Nicholson, years ago in Melbourne, used to call "Fear of the world, dear boy, fear of the world". I had the opposite experience; I found my four and a half years in the Air Force cured my fear of the world.

Philistinism in fact takes a bash in *Andy*, which sometimes goes too far the other way. Some of the writers I admire most are those who as well as having exalted imaginations are very worldly, like Chaucer or Shakespeare or Byron. This applies even to Flaubert, Patrick's soul mate in many ways, who, despite his ideal of an "austere life of tranquil art and long meditation" was very familiar with the bad smells of the world and detested notions of "the sensitive artist". Patrick was always protesting that he loved vulgarity and had a hopelessly vulgar nature himself. But his attempts to express this in his books are nearly all self-conscious failures.

The artist must not be afraid of philistines, but philistines are the enemies of art because they have no dreaming. I found in the Air Force that an acceptance of the vulgarity around me gave greater vitality to my dreaming, which was immune to philistinism. I really began as a poet not in the beauty of the Anlaby library but in a noisy hut full of young men. And even in a walk to the latrines the sky and stars were above you.

I had already taken Patrick's advice about writing factual books. When I finished my novel about Russia, *Tamara* (most of which I now find embarrassingly bad), I resumed work on a biography. When I was in London after my second trip to Russia, my old Magdalen College friend Charles Monteith, now a director of Faber & Faber (along with T.S. Eliot) and eventually to become Chairman, had asked me if I would write a biography of Ernest Giles for a new Faber series about world explorers. After Eyre, I did not really want to write about another explorer, but Charles's commission was for a book of only about fifty thousand words, and Giles, humorous, poetic and the greatest bushman of all Australian explorers, had long attracted me. I called it *Australia's Last Explorer*, a phrase he used about himself. In three months I had finished the book and Charles Monteith had accepted it for Faber & Faber.

Doug Stewart, now at Angus & Robertson, rang and asked me to write a biography of Kingsford Smith. I followed this up when in Sydney, and then went to see the old *Southern Cross* in Brisbane. I liked all the flying but thought the man himself unattractive; perhaps I would come round to him when I found out more about him.

In 1967 Barry Humphries had suggested to me that there might be an anthology for Sun Books in the naive Australian poems he had been collecting for some time. He had noticed some gems in the section in *Australian Letters* called "The Stuffed Galah" in homage to *The Stuffed Owl*, that inspiring British anthology collected by D.B. Wyndham Lewis and Charles Lee. Barry had also profitably consulted Douglas Stewart's *Book of Bellerive* and Nancy Keesing's collection of Elsie Carew. Mary Durack offered Barry her gathering of such gems, and I contributed a few items. *The Barry Humphries Book of Innocent Austral Verse* came out in 1968. The naive painter James Fardoulys executed an eye-catching cover depicting a long-haired Barry improbably sitting on the trunk of a dead gum-tree in front of a windmill, a dam and a friendly koala. It is a marvellous, or maybe dangerous, book for reading out aloud.

Gough Whitlam is usually given the credit for establishing the Australia Council and giving it enough money to make it the greatest patron of the arts in Australian history. He deserves great credit, and is a genuine lover of the arts and an omnivorous reader. But it should not be forgotten, as it often is, that John Gorton in 1968 set up the Australian Council for the Arts, under the Chairmanship of Nugget Coombs, to advise the Government on the performing arts and distribute the funds available. In 1973 Whitlam brought all the arts together, but they were still under the umbrella of the Australian Council for the Arts until the *Australia Council Act* was passed in 1975.

Early in June 1968 I received a telegram from Dr Coombs in Canberra, asking if I would accept an appointment to the new Australian Council for the Arts. Coombs said, in his usual way, that I would have to make up my mind quickly. Having just taken on so much additional responsibility at Anlaby, and with the biography of Giles to write, I was loath to be involved in more work, but Brian Stonier sensibly pointed out that I would save Sun Books a lot of money by being able to stop off in Melbourne for a Sun meeting, on my way to Canberra or Sydney.

Without wishing to sound pompous, I did also feel that a writer, or any artist, ought to give up some of his or her time to help other artists. Drysdale, for instance, was on the Art Advisory Board, as Slessor and Stewart were on the CLF. I sympathize with those like Patrick White or Barry Humphries who are temperamentally incapable of sitting on committees, although, to my astonishment, Patrick once wrote to say he had agreed to go on a committee for the New South Wales Government to award literary grants. It was not for long. But I think that the rest of us, who are not geniuses, should for a while at least take on these boring jobs, even though they do keep you away from your work. And this new Council for the Arts was potentially an enormous step forward in Government patronage of the arts.

There was also a powerful hidden, almost unconscious, reason for me to accept the offer. This was the strange compulsion, through all these years, to get away from Anlaby and indeed from South Australia. I felt stifled by domesticity and by provincialism. On the literary front, almost everything that was really happening emanated from Melbourne and Sydney, and I could regularly see stimulating friends such as David Campbell and Patrick White. So I accepted, and a few days later a letter arrived from John Gorton confirming my appointment.

Actually I was amazed to have been asked by a Liberal Government to accept the appointment. Surely they must have known of my republican sympathies, my fracas with the Adelaide Club and my friendship with Russian poets. Nugget must have recommended me. As Chairman of the Reserve Bank he had been a notable patron of artists, and encouraged Australian playwrights through his association with the Elizabethan Theatre Trust. He was now also Chancellor of the Australian National University. Nugget, as small in physical size as he was big in ideas, imagination and sheer brainpower, is one of the most remarkable people I have ever met. He was also the most skilful Chairman, even of the enormous ANU Council of which I was later to be a member. Expert at cutting off bores and ruthless in keeping to the point, he made brilliant use of his slightly rasping voice to make people laugh and also to sort out what was serious and what was trivial. His darting looks missed nothing.

I was somewhat dismayed when the full membership of the Council was announced. I seemed to be the only practitioner of the arts. Judah Waten, by now a good friend of the Former Adelaide Club Poet, and as passionate about the arts as he was about politics, wrote a caustic letter:

> When I look down the list of your colleagues (Coleman, Mrs Erwin, Barry Jones etc.) I am appalled that the Gorton Government considers such people to be the most suitable custodians of Art in Australia. Happily you are on it too and you certainly have a big job ahead; and plenty of responsibility on your shoulders. But stay on at all costs and don't let anyone push you off and never resign even if you are called awful names such as ... [I dare not mention them]. At all costs

don't lose your nerve. You might even win a few sinners: Miss Archdale for instance. If I remember rightly she was a good cricketer. Is that a qualification for the Arts Committee?

I had a letter from Athens from Patrick, who as usual was *au fait* with the latest gossip from Australia. The composition of the Council, "looks pretty dreary to me, the emphasis as usual on Edgercation. Apart from yourself, I shouldn't think anyone on it has any taste, or any idea how to encourage creative imagination in the arts. Certainly not old Betty Archdale; you ought to see her house. But she's in because she's a headmistress, can speak English, and quote Shakespeare." Patrick obviously was not as well up in cricket as Judah. Actually Betty was an excellent Council member, both shrewd and enthusiastic.

Nugget alarmed me by setting up a Drama Committee and making me Chairman of it. I loved going to the theatre, but my experience of the stage was minimal; Ah-timid-dormouse was hardly a recommendation. Thanks to Patrick, I did know quite a bit about theatre intrigue, but it seemed my non-involvement was exactly what Nugget wanted. I had no favourites. My committee was an odd mixture: John Sumner, the director of the Melbourne Theatre Company; the critic Katharine Brisbane; a conservative Melbourne academic, Professor Macartney; Mary Houghton, a theatrical producer from Tasmania; Marlis Thiersch from Adelaide; my old classics master, Professor K.C. Masterman; a wild young man, 23-year-old Jim Sharman; and short-story writer and journalist Patricia Rolfe, who was and is a beacon of sanity in the sometimes murky atmosphere of Australian literature.

Amateurism is the curse of the arts in Australia; fortunately we were all agreed that the emphasis on funding should be towards professional theatre companies. Many years later I was told that we had made the right decisions, but at the time I found presiding over this committee to be one of the most exhausting of commitments.

I continued to work on the Council committee. The exciting developments in the arts in Australia were mild and gentle compared with the violent pressures then being inflicted on my poet friends in Russia. In this respect, some Australians had not been helpful. In a series of articles in England and Australia Frank Hardy had obtained a lot of publicity for his own perturbations about Communism and Russia, but his disclosures harmed people like Yevtushenko, Voznesensky and Akhmadulina. I myself had been clumsy and naive in some notes to poems of Yevtushenko we had published, and in my references to Sofronov. Then a row erupted in England over the nomination of Yevtushenko as Professor of Poetry at Oxford. He had great support, especially from the students, but a ferocious assault on him was launched by Kingsley Amis and others, reactionaries who knew nothing and cared less about Russian poetry or the troubles of its leading lights.

In December 1968 my old literary colleague Max Harris strained our friendship by writing a crude attack on Yevtushenko in the *Australian*. That deadly journalistic lure of controversy, of stirring the pot, can sometimes lead to a useful reconsideration of an issue; in other hands it is just a cheap personal ploy, and I regret to say that on this occasion that was all it was with Max. He was consumed with jealousy over not being involved in the triumphant success of Yevtushenko's Australian tour. He had given no help to the Adelaide Festival since its inception, and had gone out of his way to attack it as often as possible. Now, having read about the row in Oxford from his airmail copies of the London *Sunday Times* and *Observer*, he realized that he could stir up argument in Australia by attacking Yevtushenko. What I think was deplorable was that he was not in the slightest degree interested in the young Russian poets. And I knew from Patrick's letters that Max was already spreading malicious gossip about Yevtushenko. The whole incident provides a footnote to the Cold War.

Towards the end of 1968 I had a sturdy letter from Judah Waten, a master of the subtleties needed in handling the Russians.

> This note arises from Max's attack in yesterday's *Australian*. I really cannot understand why Yevtushenko should be attacked by people of good will. In London he is being attacked by Kingsley Amis & Co, inspired by the Congress for Cultural Freedom, in Australia by P. Morgan & Co, supported by the same agency. What is the purpose of this onslaught? Is it to discredit all Soviet writers? Is it purely cold war? I think it is. The very writers who taunt Yevtushenko are the very people who suck up to the Establishment in their own countries. Not one of them makes as much as a whispered criticism of the great of his own country. Yevtushenko knows the situation in the Soviet Union and has used his influence whenever he deemed it wise, just as we try to do here on all sorts of issues. If we are sincere about better relations with writers in the Socialist world we will not doubt the motives of those in the Soviet Union who also work for a cultural debate, and that includes Yevtushenko.

A few months later Yevtushenko wrote to me; the letter was posted by a friend in Paris, and is headed "Very personale". It was, and I have never shown it to anyone, but now that the situation in Russia has completely changed I think it is legitimate to print it as an example of what writers went through under the tyranny of Communism. The reference to "mustash of your brother" is of course to Stalin and his heirs. I reproduce the original spelling and grammar because it is so vivid.

> My life is funny — rather, rithm is broken — in Russia we have again mustash of your brother — but this is truth. I stay in very bad situation. NO big catastrofs, but big shit, and seems to me will be very long shit. Now BASTARDS are

Kingsley Amis and company — for me it [Oxford] was only possibility to go abroad. From August I wrote about 70 poems and published only 2. My book is stopped. My Readings of Poetry are forbidden. I really don't know what to do.

Unfortunately Frank's articles about our conversations were held against me. Dont say him, because it will be disgrace for him. But he was very uncareful about another people. We are living in compleatly different conditions. You was also uncareful — I mean your small notes before my poems and "Ogonyok". Now our big child behave himself very bad with me and in general. He gave me back about 20 poems. But I dont worry. I hope in general the Lord loves me and will help me. My consciense is pure — it's principal thing.

I am sure my english is somethink unsuportable.

PS the content of this letter — between us.

Love

Genia

Following the arrival of this letter I consulted with Brian Stonier, and then spoke to Peter Karmel, the Vice-Chancellor of Flinders University, saying that Sun Books would provide $4500 to finance a Visiting Fellowship for Yevtushenko. Peter agreed on behalf of the University, and a letter of invitation was sent off to Yevtushenko. No reply was ever received. Someone else must have got the letter.

One unofficial benefit of being on the Council for the Arts was that I was able to meet Dominique in Sydney; in a miracle of timing, she managed to escape for a couple of nights from the Barrier Reef. "I look like a *putain,*" she said, waltzing into the hotel in a pair of blue jeans and a red shirt, and with wild blonde hair. The hotel was in Kings Cross, but I had seen nothing on the streets that looked like her. She had no city clothes because of working on her island, so we went out and bought some. She still did not look like a *putain*.

She said she had been very afraid of death lately, not of dying but of being caught without ever having done anything good in her life. I refrained from saying that I thought she was doing a good deed now, simply by being in Sydney, but suggested that goodness was the sum of many tiny actions, not of a big Albert Schweitzer kind of action.

At our picnic by the harbour, we looked out at the boats on their moorings. One had a sign on it: "For Sale $6000". I said if I had $6000 in my pocket we could buy it and go away together. It was the first, and for another fifteen years it was to be the only time that I ever spoke to any of my lovers about leaving my marriage.

The worst part of illicit love affairs is not only that meetings are so short but that there is a violent banality in the return to ordinary life. To leave Dominique in the hotel room and go to a committee meeting! I was reminded of an occasion when I was still lecturing at Adelaide University. I was in an Arts Faculty committee meeting in a room at the top of a

University building on North Terrace. While the meeting droned on I looked out the window and saw that on the flat roof of the building opposite there were two lovers who thought no one could see them. And there we were in our committee, talking about timetables.

In July 1969 I had lunch in Sydney with Tass, who was now a knight, rueful not in countenance but in having accepted something so un-Australian. Tass was not a hypocrite; he was no republican, although of course he knew that many of his friends were. I think the answer was that despite being a very complex man, Tass was in some ways very simple; he really thought the knighthood was good for the status of art in Australia.

Tass arranged another lunch, for two days ahead, this time with George and Charmian Johnston. At breakfast the next morning he rang to say that Charmian had committed suicide during the night. It was hard that he, of all people, should have had to tell me about a wife's suicide.

Towards the end of August I also had bad news from London. Alan Moorehead had been operated on for a blood clot, and the operation had induced a stroke, which left him unable to read or write, and able to muster only a few words of speech. Bob Hughes wrote from London: "Alan is well — insofar as the word 'well' has any meaning in his case any more. At times he is crucified with boredom — as well he might be, locked up in his body and unable to express himself adequately — and subject to deep depressions. But his courage is amazing, and so is Lucy's — it is like watching a man trapped in a glass room, mouthing and struggling."

In October Sid Nolan came to stay, after accepting the *Britannica* Australia Award in Sydney. He was as gentle, rich and easy in conversation as always. You could see him drinking in the Australian presence, if not the wine. (Sid was still a teetotaller.) Each evening, when thousands of galahs came in to perch along the great white trees of the avenue, he would walk by himself for an hour or so, listening to the music of the magpies and the clang of the galahs. I had told him of the difficulties in taking over Old Anlaby. Not having to pay the bills, he was sure we had done the right thing.

He told me that every afternoon in London he would take the car into town, park it near the National Gallery, and spend a couple of hours in the Gallery, and then potter around the bookshops. He had got the idea for his great "River Bend" paintings from a Cézanne in the National Gallery. I told him what Gino Nibbi had said: "It is impossible to live anywhere!" The galahs? The National Gallery? Sid laughed, and said he had spent some time in Sydney with Patrick and Manoly, and that Patrick was busy declaring once again that it was impossible to live in Australia. Yet in London the year before Patrick had admitted to Sid and me that he was homesick for Australia.

I told Sid that not long before his visit I had been staying with Patrick and Manoly at Martin Road. At dinner Patrick had been carrying on about the awfulness of the world in general and of Australia in particular. Finally he had shouted, "I'm not an Australian!" Then he quietened down and said he had seriously been considering committing suicide. He would take an overdose of pills like Charmian Clift. Manoly laughed. "There's not enough pills made to finish you off."

I began to feel that some malign force was trying to finish me off. I had been at the top of a ladder one day, painting the high ceiling of the room above the station office, with Tisi and Sam painting the walls, each wearing old shirts of mine that trailed along the floor after them. Suddenly the old ladder collapsed; my wrist jammed in the rungs and broke, and several ribs cracked as I fell on the wreck of the ladder. On such an occasion one is disgusted with oneself; for a moment or two I was unable to do anything but lie and moan, with the two children mutely watching. Tisi raced off for help. Marc came and fussed about washing the brushes, but then got one of the shearers' mattresses and laid it in the back of the station wagon. Ninette drove me into Kapunda, where the doctor set my wrist and kept me in hospital for the night. Every hour on the hour a man in a room down the corridor roared like a bull. At first I was alarmed, but the nurse said it was just old Mr Pfund, he always did that. So I went to sleep.

Just a month later, at the end of October, I was watering the back garden of our little house in North Adelaide, standing on the wooden cover of the old car pit inside the back gate, when the planks collapsed and I fell five feet down the pit, landing on the wrist and ribs I had broken before. I couldn't believe the malignancy of it, the damned meanness, as I lay powerless in the grease in my suit, with the hose squirting over me.

Then Dominique came back to Adelaide. She told me she had decided to get married. I let her go. She let me go. That was so for that day. But of course we saw each other again, while trying to move out of each other's lives.

I must have looked haunted by all that was happening. Lawrence Daws, on a visit from England, came to stay at Anlaby. When he left, he wrote to me, "In the light of my present thinking hang-up, your multi-faceted activities would seem to be in the TOP VULNERABILITY bracket".

I felt that at forty-seven I had reached some mysterious watershed of life, but didn't know what it was, and couldn't see the landscape below and in front of me. I thought 1969 had been the worst year of my life. I wrote to Doug Stewart and said I couldn't write the biography of Kingsford Smith, that I found the man repellent, however brave he might have been. I had done some preliminary work on a history of the Germans in Australia, so I thought I would go back to that and finish it off. But for the moment I wanted to do nothing but laze, read books, think.

PART SIX
Endings and Beginnings
1967–83

But I am committed to motion, and memories deeper
Than the cold centre of the seasonless spring.

"Anlaby"

Twenty-Seven

Montaigne's "Of Experience" is the last of his essays, and one of the most complex. What is so enchanting about Montaigne is that everything he says is, in Keats's words, "proved upon our pulses". He welcomes life in order that he might understand its variety, and hates neither himself nor the world. But he is not a foolish optimist, and has a profound knowledge of physical and spiritual pain. Would that he could have been a visitor at Anlaby in 1969!

Although my mind had been highly trained, and my body had not been short of experiences, at midlife I was woefully short of knowledge, especially self-knowledge. Not of experiences, even that of being close to death, but of the sort of experience from which one can learn. Montaigne is immune to clichés; old tags like *experentia docet* just set him thinking. He knows there is no book of rules. So he begins "Of Experience" (which, unlike many of his essays, is about what the title says it is about) thus: "There is no desire more naturall, than that of knowledge. We attempt all meanes that may bring us to it. When reason failes us, we employ experience. Which is a meane by much more, weake and vile. But truth is of so great consequence, that wee ought not disdaine any induction, that may bring us unto it."

The greatest source of knowledge for ordinary people is that of family life, however "weake and vile" the experience might have been. I had had almost no early family life, and boarding school was no substitute. I had to wait until my four and a half years in the Air Force to be exposed to the sort of experiences I did not know as a child.

Some natural sagacity, of which I have never had a lot, enabled me to sniff out the falsity and hypocrisy of the rules for life laid down by schoolmasters like Jennings. I had sensed what Montaigne says so unforgettably: "A young man should trouble his rules, to stirre-up his vigor … For, there is no course of life so weake and sottish, as that which is managed by Order, Methode and Discipline … Let such men keepe their kitchin." In my pantheon of wisdom, this ranks with William Blake's "The man who never alters his opinion is like standing water, and breeds reptiles of the mind".

Floundering through 1969, I certainly could have done with some "Order, Methode and Discipline" in my financial affairs, to sort out what was really going on with Anlaby and the pigs. But in my personal life I needed to "stirre-up" my "vigor", to reach towards some kind of deeper knowledge, not to be afraid to alter my opinions and start again.

At least I had helped Ilse to start again. She had returned to Australia a year after the debacle of our visit to Switzerland, and I had brought her together with a friend of mine, an architect, a widower with two children who was yearning to marry again. We asked them both down to Rocky Point, being sure that that would bring them together, and it did. They were married in 1969.

Not long after falling off the ladder, I had written Patrick a very peculiar letter. As far as I remember (I have no copy, and he always destroyed other people's letters), I wrote to him that I was profoundly depressed, that, in the old phrases, my soul was afflicted and disquieted within me. But I felt guilty about these feelings, because (so I wrote) I lived in a beautiful place with a loving family, and, when not falling off ladders, I enjoyed excellent health. So why should I not be happy? I put it down to self-pity, which my mother had told me was the curse of the Duttons.

I could not have been more foolish, first in ever asking Patrick for help with such troubles, and second, in not taking sufficient notice of the implications of his struggles with his latest novel, *The Vivisector*, the harshest and most revealing of his methods of all his novels. It was like asking a python to examine the character of the piglet he is about to swallow.

Patrick wrote: "I don't know why you should be plunged in such gloom & remorse for having it good in life and an amiable character thrown in. There are so many depressive, violent, irritable, sleazy, destructive people about, it's a relief to think of somebody attractive and enviable. So relax and enjoy your spiritual status."

In other words, here I am, Patrick, this awful person (all those adjectives, except "sleazy", apply to him) and there you are, this happy fortunate person, so get on with it. The paradox was that I, the healthy person, was asking advice of the sick, one who was more and more suffering from the worst of all sicknesses. Montaigne puts it succinctly: "And of all the infirmities we have, the most savage, is to despise our being". I should have written to David Campbell, not to Patrick; and Scottish-Australian farmer David would have been able to give me some good advice about Anlaby.

What my letter to Patrick was really asking, and I lacked the experience to understand, was the true reasons for my guilt at my unhappiness amid such apparent good fortune. There were no flaws in my relationship with my children. The falsity was in my relationship with my wife and with the whole construction of living at Anlaby.

My love for Dominique was genuine; I still loved her, despite our determination to move apart. The pain was quite physical, like that which followed falling off the ladder; it hurt, as when I breathed with my cracked ribs or when I tried to grip something with my left hand and broken wrist. When I was reading medieval and Renaissance poetry in my student days, I used to think the poets exaggerated in their descriptions of the physical symptoms of lovers in distress. But they were true, for the body is in all ways as much a part of love as the mind and soul, or wherever is the seat of passion in our make-up.

At the end of 1969 I decided I might be able to improve my life if I resigned from all my committees, except that of Writers' Week at the Adelaide Festival. So I left the Council for the Arts, suggesting to Nugget Coombs that Kym Bonython take my place, which he did; I also said goodbye to the wonderful lunches at the meetings of the *Britannica* Award Committee, and to these of the Ampol Arts Awards. Of course I did not abandon Sun Books.

One positive event for me in 1969 was editing, with Max Harris, a book on censorship in Australia, which we called *Australia's Censorship Crisis*. The imbecilities of Australian censorship, unknown to present generations, were all too familiar to us. As a student of English at the University of Adelaide I had to obtain a signed chit from Professor Stewart to read the copy of *Ulysses* which was kept in the strongroom. As a Lecturer in English at the same university, twenty years later, I was in Professor Jeffares's room when an exasperated bookseller, Harry Muir, rang Derry from the Customs Office at Port Adelaide, asking him to confirm to the Customs Officer that the *Autobiography of A. Trollope* was a reputable book and not a saga of whoredom. During this period, Bryn Davies and I set *The Catcher in the Rye* for English I, only to be told that the book was banned. I wrote to the Minister of Customs (books were banned by the Customs in those days), Senator Henty, a shopkeeper from Tasmania, saying that he would be made to look an idiot if he banned Salinger. Rather to my surprise, he replied that he would be in Adelaide in a few days time and asked Bryn and me to come and meet him. When we met, I asked him to tell us where and how the book was obscene. When he said it was about male vice Bryn and I laughed. "No, it's true," he said, taking up his copy of the book. "Look, here on page 4, it says 'My brother then went and prostituted himself in Hollywood'." I had to explain to the Senator that this referred to the brother becoming a hack script writer. Senator Henty lifted the ban. Other recent books Australians were not allowed to read, apart from hordes of classics, included *Portnoy's Complaint, Couples, Myra Breckinridge, The Spy Who Loved Me* and Steven Marcus' scholarly *The Other Victorians*.

Censorship was not only of books, but of films and plays, provided complaints were made to the police. *The Boys in the Band*, a play about homosexuals, ran into a lot of trouble, and Alex Buzo's *Norm and Ahmed* was successfully prosecuted for the words "fuckin' boong". Amazingly, the objection was to "fuckin", not to "boong".

Our book consisted of nine essays on various aspects of censorship, and then extracts from the banned books that have been mentioned, plus *Tropic of Capricorn* and *Fanny Hill*; an extract from *Gulliver's Travels*, was thrown in to show how "obscene" Swift was. The book also contained the judgement of Mr Justice Stable, rejecting the appeal in the *Norm and Ahmed* case. As both editor and publisher, I was told by my lawyer friends that I might well end up in gaol as a result of printing these extracts.

In 1970, it being an even year, it was time for another Adelaide Festival. The real achievement of Writers' Week was twofold: it brought together Australian writers who had never met, and now found each other to be human (in most cases); and it brought overseas writers to Australia. The latter was doubly beneficial: it broadened our horizons and, on their return, these writers brought news of faraway Australia and its writers to the rest of the world. Unfortunately there were always a few Australian writers whose parochialism remained unshaken, and who resented the foreigners; what these writers really wanted to do was to sit around with other Australian writers and grizzle about Angus & Robertson (also known then as Anguish and Robbery) and Clem Christesen.

Edna O'Brien was coming that year, and she had written to say she very much wanted to see something of the Australia beyond the capital cities. I arranged for her to leave the plane in Darwin and stay with Chibs and Dick (who was now Chief Justice of the Northern Territory). Chibs very generously offered to fly Edna to some remote regions in her Cessna. This plan fell through, and Edna asked instead if she could arrive early and come up to Anlaby for a couple of nights, to recover from the flight and see something of the country.

Edna, thirty-eight in 1970, was of course beautiful, full of genuine Irish charm and extraordinarily intelligent, and, like Bella Akhmadulina, she never seemed to allow terrible experiences and alarming talent to interfere with the living of the moment. Without pretension, open and kind to young and old, Edna was always herself.

She was dreading Writers' Week and I was worried that the Festival authorities had, as always, asked the visitors to do too much. I promised to try to rescue her whenever possible. A fellow guest was Anthony Burgess, who was accompanied by his wiry Italian wife Liana. Edna and Anthony each had to give a long solo address in the University's Bonython Hall. Edna managed it well; Anthony was quite extraordinary, talking non-stop for an hour, without any notes, to a riveted audience.

The next evening I picked her up at her hotel and brought her into the old South Australian Hotel for one of the Festival's gatherings. It was in the so-called lounge, where there were white, fluted, square pillars between the two open halves of the room. Just as we entered and I was signalling the waiter for drinks, Liana charged up and started, in her rich

Italian accent, to berate Edna for seducing Anthony. Horrified, Edna retreated until she was backed against the pillar, while Liana continued with her accusations. Anthony finally managed to remove her. Edna, really shaken, said to me, "I can't imagine anyone I would less like to sleep with than Anthony Burgess."

As I had feared, Edna was beaten off her feet by Festival duties, although she seemed always to come back softly, like a wave. It is always a mistake of these festivals not to give guests some time to be solitary. She went on to Sydney, where she had lunch with Patrick and told him that she had loathed most of the time she spent in Adelaide. I couldn't blame her.

Cynthia Nolan was a very different visitor. A few weeks before the Festival, she rang from London to say that she and Sid would be arriving with Benjamin Britten and Peter Pears, and someone called Princess Margaret of Hesse. Hastily placating the republican, Cynthia said that the Princess was in fact Scottish, and a major patron of Benjamin Britten's Aldeburgh Festival. Cynthia went on: "Now, Geoffrey, Ben and Peter and Peg would very much like to have a few days with you at Kangaroo Island, and of course Siddy and me too. Is that all right?" I explained that it was, most emphatically, not all right. It was impossible to open up the big old house for a couple of days, and in any case we were much too busy to go down there. There was no alternative but to ask them to Anlaby for two nights. I remembered Ursula's favourite phrase, "Costly casuals".

In fact, the visit was a sucess. Cynthia looked as much like a vampire as ever, but she was at her best, and particularly amiable with the children, rather to my surprise. There was a very kind, under-confident and slightly childish person buried under that scheming, suspicious exterior. I was a bit embarrassed about meeting Peter Pears, as there was some quality about his singing voice that I had always found repellent. However, he turned out to be a large, comfortable fellow, a good foil for his lover, thin, intense and rather nasty Ben. Princess Margaret ("Call me Peg, but please don't let anyone call me 'Princess Peg' ") was the biggest surprise, a plump, sweet-natured Scot. I put a copy of *Australia and the Monarchy* by her bed, as I knew that her late husband had been closely related to Queen Victoria, and that Prince Philip (better known in my circles as Phil the Greek), had spent a lot of his very unfortunate childhood with the Hesses at Wolfsgarten. She read it avidly, and said that although for her the monarchy was A Good Thing, she could see that Australia would inevitably become a republic.

We took them all for a picnic by the River Murray, on the straight reach of the river where Edward John Eyre had lived at Moorundie. Peter wrote from Singapore, on their way home, "There was nothing in Australia more happily unforgettable than those days at Anlaby".

A week or so after the Festival Dominique was married. There was a whole row of failed suitors in the church. She was so late that I wondered whether she had fled. But eventually she arrived. The guests and the newspapers would say she looked beautiful and radiant. I thought she looked determined. It seemed to me that the parson paused for an uncomfortably long time after those words beginning "Therefore if any man can show just cause ..."

Nature and a focusing of the mind are usually the best remedies for a confusion of the soul. I turned to my history of the Germans in Australia, on which I had already done a lot of work, especially in the Mitchell Library on visits to Sydney.

I felt personally involved in the subject, partly because of having been born and raised in country farmed by old German-Australians whose families had emigrated over a hundred years ago, but also because of my own family links with Germany. My great-great-grandfather, the father of the four boys who had emigrated to Australia in the 1820s, had been British Vice-Consul and Agent for Packets (a nice old phrase for Shipping Agent) in Cuxhaven, the seaport of Hamburg. My great-grandfather had been consul for Hamburg, the first consul for a foreign power in Australia. And I, after studying German at school, had planned to attend the University of Freiburg when I left school.

Of course, it was essential to spend some time working in the various archives of the city-states of old Germany. Friends suggested (rightly so, as it turned out) that I would receive support from both the West and the East Germans.

For some mysterious reason, but probably connected with my activities in Writers' Week and our translations of Russian poetry in Sun Books, I was also invited to visit Romania. Ninette and I spent a fortnight in that beautiful but depressing country, and then flew to Munich. It was interesting to compare the levels of support given to a visiting researcher by the two Germanys. West Germany had an agency called Internationes; on arrival I went to its office, in this case in Munich, where I was handed a huge bundle of marks to cover a fortnight's living and travel expenses. Once I had been given them, I could have taken the next plane out of Germany and had a spending spree and no one would have been the wiser. I was told I could travel by rail or hire a car, whatever pleased me.

That was the democratic way, but in the cynically named German Democratic Republic I was met at Checkpoint Charlie in the Wall by a driver (an employee of the secret police) in another of those dreadful Volgas, and an interpreter guide. They accompanied us everywhere. The guide paid for everything. Of course, I was welcome to change any hard-currency traveller's cheques for the outrageous official rate of exchange. The only time I did so was to buy a lot of incredibly cheap and very good gramophone records.

Our guide, who answered only to Herr Major, was quite unlike the thug of a driver, Wolfgang; Herr Major was a gentle, sensitive little man with a lot of poetry in him. He had undergone a terrible childhood during the war: his father had disappeared in the army in Russia, his mother had been removed to work in a factory; and he, aged three, with his sister of two and brother of one, had been herded into a camp for children. For five years he had had to look after his sister and brother, and make sure they did not lose their armbands with their name and date and place of birth, the only clues to their identity. He was never to know where he had been during those five years. After the war the Red Cross tracked down his mother, who was working in Halle; she had assumed that they, like her husband, were dead. He told his story without self-pity, and said, "It doesn't matter, there was nothing we could about it, then or now". I remembered the story a friend in East Berlin, the embattled novelist Stefan Heym, had told me about a little lost child in Berlin, who either would not or could not tell the police anything about himself or who he was. Finally the policeman said in desperation, "Can't you remember *anyone's* name?" "Yes, Lenin", was the reply.

Perhaps Herr Major thought that we innocent Australians should be made more aware of suffering. In one unforgettable day he instructed the driver to take us to the brutal memorial, erected in 1913, to the dead of the 1813 Battle of Leipzig, where 111,000 men were killed in three days. Then we drove to the memorial at Lützen, where in 1632 in the Thirty Years War Gustavus Adolphus of Sweden and thousands of Germans and Swedes were killed. On a beautiful evening we arrived in Weimar to stay the night — Weimar, the lovely old city of Goethe and Schiller. But as soon as we had checked in at the Elefant, we were told to get back into the car again, and were taken up into the hills and the forest to Buchenwald. No one else was there, the sun was setting over the wide, deep valley, the forest in shades of green through veils of mist, the sparks of an electric train dotting a message between the trees, and then the slow-travelling sound of the rumble of its wheels.

We wandered through what was left of the concentration camp, and past the chimney of the gas ovens. "Fifty-five thousand died here," said Herr Major. Another train went by, going the other way. Somehow one of the worst things to me was that those prisoners of misery would have been hearing the sound of the train wheels disappearing into the distance towards which they would never again be able to travel.

In a great cathedral like Chartres, one is profoundly moved, even if one is not a Christian, and not only by the beauty of the building. There is a sense of the community of belief, the anonymous builders, the many congregations of worshippers. In Buchenwald I felt a similar awe, not from any presumption of trying to imagine the lives and deaths of the prisoners behind the electrified wire, but for the essential holiness of life, here, where it had been daily violated. The ugly slabs on which the huts had stood, the chimney, were as moving as great works of art. Little Herr Major had worked his crescendo well, Leipzig, Lützen, Buchenwald, a day of death. The dead soldiers of the two battles made one think of the futility of war, but Buchenwald, far more evil, made one cherish life and peace. It was a paradox that could not be explained by logic.

After we returned to West Germany we went to stay with Peg Hesse at Wolfsgarten. She took us to lunch with her friend Tatiana Metternich at Schloss Johannisberg, where the splendid Tatiana produced some unforgettable wines. She knew Yevtushenko, and he had taken her to the Writers' Union in Moscow in 1968. She told us of a French student there who was excitedly telling an admiring audience about the riots in France. "It was a revolution!" he was shouting. "We stopped the whole nation!" Zhenya went up to him and put his hand on the Frenchman's shoulder. "My friend," he said, "you are wasting your time telling us all this. We did it all fifty years ago. We stopped everything. Please go and tell some other country, not us. We have had all the benefits."

After we returned to Australia, I waited until the school holidays and then took everyone up the Birdsville Track in the Toyota, to the ruins by the dried salt lakes of the German mission stations at Kilalpininna and Kopperamanna. The mud-and-straw walls were crumbling, sand was halfway up the door frames, the roof timbers were still twisted as when they were cut from the mulga. There is endless debris in all such deserted settlements in Australia — flakes of rusted iron under stoves and pumps and curving bed-ends, fragments of china, blue, white and milky mauve, the deep shining green of a thousand broken bottles. Francis found one perfect, unchipped bottle of something called Row's Embrocation.

And of the Dyeri blacks, from whom the missionaries had had to be protected by police? Nothing, except chipped stones. What had they done to deserve being offered Jesus? Nothing. They had been at home in what looks like desolation, the plains of little gibbers furring the sand like iron filings on brown paper over a magnet, the polished shine of the big gibbers, the odd purple flowers and yellow daisies, the harsh cane grass. Only the crows and the dingoes seemed to be of a family living then and now.

Back at Anlaby, I was still in my regular routine of getting up at 5 a.m. to work on whatever I was writing. At 6.30 I would wake the children, who would all three hop into bed with me while I read to them. At 7.30 I would go over to the station courtyard and discuss with Marc and Harold their work for the day. The other farm worker, Allen, had left us for a job in the winery at Yalumba, just after I had bought a prefabricated wing for his house, to make room for his expanding family. Allen was ruthless but sensible; he saw the hopeless nature of the financial basis of Old Anlaby. The "cottage" had been done up for Chibs and Léonie as a holiday house; they did not pay rent, but paid for repairs and for Marc to work one day a week in the garden. So four of the six houses were more or less occupied; there were also many empty rooms in the buildings around the courtyard and behind the stables.

I was desperately tempted to give up everything and live a country life at Anlaby. But it was impossible to live there inexpensively, and I could not give up writing, so the best I could do was to try to live a more simple life. But I find written in my notebook at about this time: "There is nothing so spiritually debilitating as constantly worrying about money".

At least I had, more or less, my sanity. I began seriously to be alarmed at Patrick White's state, or rather, states of mind. *The Vivisector*, allegedly the life of an artist, has some great moments but is a most unsatisfactory attempt by a writer to enter the world of a visual artist. Among my artist friends I have never found one who thought the book rang true. What it is, like so much of Patrick's work, is an allegory of his own state of mind. *The Solid Mandala* represents the two sides of his nature, destructive and regenerative; *The Eye of the Storm* is about the life and death of a woman but it is really about himself. *The Twyborn Affair* is about himself as man and woman. All these books are great constructions, of varying artistic success, but although he could write and rewrite them, and still wrote wonderful letters, the pressures he was forcing on himself were from time to time unhinging him.

His tragedy was not to have listened to what he himself wrote in *Voss*, about the battle between pride and humility. Voss's God despises humility, but Voss knows the destructive power of the ego, and in fact drives himself to death along this path. He says, "To make yourself, it is also necessary to destroy yourself"; he succeeds in destroying himself and others, except Laura who stays apart, but his tragedy is not cathartic. Addressing Voss, Laura speaks the truth about Patrick when she says: "Everything is for yourself. Human emotions, when you have them, are quite flattering to you. If those emotions strike sparks from others, that is also flattering. But most flattering, I think, when you experience it, is the hatred, or even the mere irritation of weaker characters." Weaker, of course, in the estimation of Voss's ego. It is a deadly analysis of White — maybe it came from Manoly? — which is amplified in *The Vivisector*. Manoly's enormous strength of character, and Patrick's desperate need for him, enabled them to survive as a couple, but only just. Several times Manoly nearly left Patrick.

It was most distressing to witness the erosion of Patrick's sanity, the self-destruction of flattering himself with hatred. And it was often women who provoked his worst outbursts. Some were sturdy, and stood up to him, like Elizabeth Riddell and Maisie Drysdale, Tass's second wife; Maisie was the widow of Peter Purves-Smith, that very fine artist and close friend of Tass's youth. Patrick had both written and spoken to me of his admiration for Maisie; he liked her character and spirit and was amazed at the extent of her reading. It was not long, however, before he was trying to find means to make her hate him, and reasons for him to hate her, as was happening more and more in his relationships with people.

I was at a dinner for nine people at Martin Road; Tass and Maisie were among the guests. I could see Patrick was working himself up to an outburst. He achieved it by a ferocious attack on the composer Peter Sculthorpe. Maisie interrupted him by saying, "Stop trampling on my friends." With that sickly grey of fury that was so characteristic of him, he shouted at Maisie, "But you trample on mine, look what you've said about Cynthia Nolan." He stamped off into the kitchen for half an hour, soothing himself down with a brandy bottle. I went out to try to be a peacemaker. I reminded him of his several declarations of respect for Maisie. "That barmaid," he snorted, pouring himself another slug of brandy. I laughed. There are all sorts of barmaids, but Maisie is like none of them. Patrick fed himself some of the hatred that was part of the ingredients for dinner, but Maisie was too tough for him, and she had Tass behind her.

Not so with the gentle, beautiful wife of another artist. Only a month later, I was again staying with Patrick and Manoly. There was another dinner for nine. (This number enabled Patrick to sit at the head of the table.) This woman was a favourite of all who knew her; her house was always full of visitors and friends, and she was a superb cook. She was intelligent and sensitive, but without any artistic gifts or pretentions. Her husband was a genial Pole. On this particular occasion, she made a harmless remark advocating tolerance and patience in some issue; what it was I cannot remember. Patrick once again went grey, his eyes bored into her and he shouted, "That's what a stupid, gutless woman like you would say. You think it is enough to waft around being nice to people and trade on your looks. It's because you're too stupid to see how people despise you and make use of you." It then got much worse, and her husband pushed back his chair and walked out of the house. She wilted in the silence and then the false chatter that followed Patrick's exit into the kitchen for another rendezvous with the brandy bottle. She excused herself to Manoly before Patrick returned. Her husband had gone home. This time Patrick had really succeeded in helping to destroy an already eroded self-confidence. A few months later, she cut her throat.

What I thought unforgivable was that so many of Patrick's so-called friends allowed him to get away with this sort of behaviour. Maybe he put up with my counterattacks on him because he had not yet finished using me and my family. All the clues to his use of people are there in *The Vivisector*. But, as Manoly said to me, "He needs people, he needs friends."

Patrick spent a great deal of time and money, and always with success, in choosing the right individual birthday and Christmas presents for my three children, and was always issuing invitations for Ninette and me to stay with him and Manoly when in Sydney. His visits to Anlaby and Rocky Point were almost his only expeditions into the Australia outside Sydney and the Blue Mountains, although at one stage he used to stay with his friend Freddy Glover, a Rural Bank manager, to get the feel of country towns.

It is a truism that in a general sense genius is close to madness. But also, in Patrick's case, there was an increasing individual dementia that was fuelled not only by the old simplicities of love and hate but by the feeding of his vanity with hate. There is a nauseous tendency among people who have claimed his friendship, and critics who claim to understand him, that his moral purpose and idealism were so high that we all, and indeed Australia as well, disappointed him. There is no high morality in such idealism, which is poisonous because of its lack of humility, which Patrick knew only too well to be perhaps the greatest virtue, as pride is the deadliest of the sins.

When Blake said Milton was of the Devil's party but he did not know it, he was referring in powerful measure to the core of Satan's pride, which was a sense of injured merit. Patrick's destructive vanity came from such a pride; he really believed he knew, in respect both of Australia and of his friends, what was best for them. He had a tremendous sense of injured merit because the world went along on its sinful way despite him, and his work degenerated when he displayed this injured merit in public, taking on the role of Jeremiah. He devastated himself by feeling superior in judgement, if not in life, to ordinary Australians, which was a matter of indifference to them. With individuals the devastation was more dangerous.

When he hated others, and wanted them to hate him, it was because he hated himself. The reason White's style is so difficult (less so in his later books, perhaps), and that most people find his books hard to read, is that they are muddied by his own involvement in his characters. To speak clearly it is necessary to think clearly. When Flaubert said, "*Madame Bovary, c'est moi,*" he humbled himself into her; his art was no more arduous than that of White, but it was more pure and detached. He purged himself of that murky involvement from which White could not extricate himself.

Patrick's physical decay and violence of mind might have been due to the number of drugs he took for his asthma, especially cortisone. His use of this drug, over twenty years, would account for his final bone decay, but prolonged cortisone treatment also causes severe changes of mood. He was always irritable and often irrational, but from the 1970s on there were increasing outbursts that could only be called mad. Many times these were exacerbated by drink, for he put away an alarming daily quantity of spirits and wine. Every now and then he would write to say he was on the wagon, but he would soon fall off it again. Later on, there was another element of disintegration. Margaret Fink, the film producer, has a theory which I share — it had already occurred to me — that Patrick was chronically changed for the worse by the extraction of his teeth. The false teeth altered the shape of his face and thus mortified his vanity, and also prevented him from eating what he wanted to, and eating was one of his few genuine, unalloyed pleasures.

When, at this time, I was depressed by my own inadequacies and the madnesses of my friends, I would try to draw sustenance from nature, what Diderot called "the Whole", which is uninterested in such foolishness. Even a walk in the chook-yard to collect the eggs was rewarding. One swishes through the knee-deep grass, one's senses electric for snakes, catching the turkey chicks that freeze dead silent in the green stalks, like little heaps of dried yellow grass, while the mother turkey, having heaved herself up onto a dead tree, burbles with alarm. The chicks, once caught, have to be put into the safety of a fox-proof enclosure. There is interest, too, in the differences in breeds of ducks: the Khaki Campbells round and down to earth, the lean Indian runners up and springing. The gobblers thundering, the chooks flapping and charging off with that hunkery run, and the cursed egg-stealing crows somewhere else. All this life goes on, and is before one's eyes.

Like Montaigne, I had a tower to work in. In my case it was Grandfather's Folly, the water-tower, with a room on the ground floor, another room with a balcony on the first floor, and above that a water tank six feet deep, hidden behind beams and plaster below the tiled roof. Because of the huge tank, it was cool in the tower even on a heatwave day. In earlier days, my mother used to practise her violin and piano on the ground floor, and dusty heaps of her music were still lying around, and the music-hall songs my father liked to sing.

Kaye Webb, of Puffin Books, came up to lunch, and talked about the whirlwind romance she had had with Tass before he married Maisie; it was the year he and Sid and Hal Missingham came over for the Festival. She had walked down through the garden with him, and up to the water-tower, where on the balcony he put his arm around her and said, "Nah, wot abaht it, luv?"

One person I could always draw sustenance from was David Campbell. In November, I was having dinner with David and Judy in Canberra, and Les Murray turned up. I knew David liked his poetry, but I hadn't met this big, fat man with his successful tough act. No Canberra charcoal uniform for him. I liked the way he obviously had the deepest respect for David, but didn't act respectful at all.

In 1971 the anti-Vietnam movement began to gain strength and I was spending a lot of time with the committee in Adelaide, and taking part in various activities which were not for tender souls. We got used to being called traitors or, of course, communists. It wasn't a bad idea to wear one's war medals. On one occasion I was with a group reading anti-war poems outside a shopping centre in Elizabeth. While I was reading, a particularly vociferous short-back-and-sides RSL type was hurling insults at me, so I made up a new poem as I went along, really enjoying pouring scorn on him in rough iambics, and raising more and more support.

Brian Medlin, Professor of Philosophy at Flinders University and quite a talented poet, was the chairman of our committee. At a previous march through the city streets I had been particularly impressed with Brian. The famous firebrand from Monash University, Albert Langer, had come over to inject some fire into us. While we were all assembling by the City Bridge, Langer was shouting through a loudhailer that it was time we stopped pussyfooting around and got stuck into the pigs. His message was that only when we had knocked a few policemen down and got ourselves arrested would we make any impact on the inert and bourgeois populace. Brian Medlin grabbed the loudhailer from him and said that was not the way to do things, and that we had good relations with the police. Langer was disgusted.

But at the planning of the Moratorium for 30 June Medlin was a changed man. He was now the complete radical, rushing around and denouncing Don Dunstan as The Enemy. He had adopted the Langer line, and was determinded to force a confrontation with the police. He and his group of supporters were longing to become martyrs. I said I thought we should oppose the war, not the police. Neal Blewett (then lecturing at Adelaide University) and I and others were dead against violence, saying we would lose the very people we were trying to bring around to our way of thinking. A big, slow, solid Vietnam veteran, who had been discharged after being wounded, agreed with us that it was essential to keep the demonstrations as broad as possible, and not antagonize open-minded people. But Brian was determined to have his way, and I refused to go to the Moratorium. Brian succeeded in having himself arrested, and there were photographs of him lashing out at the police.

Meanwhile protest was not the only thing that had been happening to me. One day when I was working at the table by the front window at Curtis Street, in the company of David Campbell's barmaid and Tass's mural, I looked up just as a girl was walking past. It was only four or five paces, but her walk seemed to go into my being in slow-motion, a progress that swayed her long blue corduroy jacket and her black skirt and her long dark-brown hair. She looked vaguely familiar. Then I saw that she was coming in the gate.

I could not say that it was love at first sight, because Poppy had been a student of mine, one of the most intelligent, ten years before. She was now a tutor at Flinders University, and had been on that anti-Vietnam march from the City Bridge. She had heard that I was looking for a research assistant with my German book; she could read and speak German.

She was either pregnant or she had a figure like one of those Graces painted by Lucas Cranach that have the beauty of a pear. She told me she was pregnant with her first child. I told her that when writing my novel *Tamara* I had been going to make my heroine pregnant but thought that it might offend my readers to have my hero making love to a woman carrying a child that was not his. She laughed and said she hadn't realized I was so old-fashioned, having such an idea and still using terms like "hero" and "heroine". Poppy was to be my education in the world of the early 1970s. Later on, when Mirka Mora met Poppy in Melbourne she said to me, "At last I have met Modern Woman." It was not without that delicate touch of satire in which Mirka has always been so expert.

To celebrate the tenth anniversary of Sun Books in July Brian Stonier arranged a dinner in the Atheneum Club for as many of our authors and Sun staff as could be rounded up. It was a comical and notable evening. The Caseys were there, of course, Maie's *An Australian Story* being one of our most successful books. Dick in his capacity as Lord Casey proposed the health of the Queen. I then proposed the health of the republic. Maie talked to me about the sexual adventures of her generation, confirming everything that Mabel Brookes had told me. Jock Marshall had, alas, died in 1967, but Jane was there; the paperback of Jock and Tass's *Journey Among Men* was one of our most handsome books. Geoff Blainey was there, author of our best bestseller, *The Tyranny of Distance*, and Judah Waten, the communist, hitting it off splendidly with Casey. Lee White, who had started as Brian's secretary and was now our senior editor, said everyone who worked for Sun Books had to have a private income. She was right; we never had enough money to pay our employees, let alone ourselves, what we all deserved. It was enlightening to be both publisher and author. And all this was taking place in the formal suroundings of the old Atheneum Club.

Towards the end of 1971 the ABC commissioned the composer Nigel Butterley and me to put together a cantata based on Walt Whitman's poems. I met Nigel in Canberra and liked him immediately, a musician who was also deeply read in poetry. I had made some possible selections, and suggested the title "Sometimes with one I love", from one of the poems, which appealed to him. We were later to work on the piece at Rocky Point, where the beach with its drifts of weed was exactly right for Whitman's sea poems.

David Campbell and I had both been corresponding with a young poet called Michael Dransfield. At twenty-three he had published one book of poetry and a lot of other poems in the journals; we were to publish his *Drug Poems* in Sun Books. He had a marvellous ear and a headlong style, and his work appealed very much to David and me. He had several times asked us both to stay with him at his house, "Marchpane", in the town of Cobargo, which is between Bega and the coast. Not without some hesitation we finally decided to accept his invitation and set off from Canberra, with Ninette, in David's battered Fiat 850 on which scarcely any of the instruments worked, a door was liable to fly open, and the tyres were never too good. David was very hard on cars, especially across open paddocks.

He also liked to tweak a nose or two from time to time. I was once driving into Canberra with David in the Fiat when we got a blow-out in a rear tyre; it was rush hour and we had to stop just by the Manuka turn-off. I was loosening the wheel nuts when a police car pulled up alongside us and two large policemen sauntered over. The gist of their conversation seemed to be that we were a great danger to traffic. "Well, is that so, Officer?" said David with a slow smile. "My friend Geoff and I" — he gave me, crouched by the wheel, an expansive wave as if I were the American Ambassador — "we went to a great deal of trouble to make sure that the tyre would blow out exactly on the Manuka corner. Wouldn't you agree that that was no mean feat?"

The two cops didn't know what to make of this; it reminded me irresistibly of Zhenya and the policeman from the VIP procession in Moscow. There was a similar look of bafflement on the police countenance. David kept slowly on while I tried to hurry. "Now I expect you officers have stopped especially to help us, and I thank you for your courtesy, but my friend Geoff is one of the most skilled wheel-changers in Australia. When there is a Grand Prix he is in demand at the pits." "Well, thank you, Sir," the police were retreating, "but be as quick as you can, won't you?" David watched them drive off. "Well, Geoff, we won that one, wouldn't you say?" I was also reminded of my old friend Deasey. David and he both had the capacity to go through with some outrageous routine without, as I would have, ever getting the giggles.

I wasn't sure whether we were going to win in getting to Cobargo alive. But somehow we did, and found the rambling old wooden house. Michael emerged, looking like a telephone pole with a magpie's nest at the top. Hilary, Michael's girlfriend, was blonde and rather sweet and vague, and as soon as we were inside she offered us coffee, teacakes she had made herself, and pot. Best quality pot, Michael assured us. The house seemed to contain more spiders than furniture. I wondered what might be resident in the beds. David declined the pot, saying the booze was enough for him. I never seemed to get a flicker out of marijuana, but thought I should try once more. After a while the gleam on the coffee jug seemed to get a little brighter, but that was about it.

Then, like old Air Force times, Michael suggested that the blokes should go down to the pub and leave the sheilas for a chat. We talked about poetry which was easy because we mostly shared the same enthusiasms and dislikes. The stumbling block was A.D. Hope. Dransfield said he hated him. David said he was rather a good bloke as well as being a good poet. Dransfield said that he was horrible, both as a man and a poet. So we drank a toast to Ken Slessor, who had recently died and whom all three of us respected.

Twenty-Eight

Back at Anlaby it was perfect spring, the thrush's rounded notes drifting over the crab-apple blossom and the sun-filled magnolia flowers and the burgeoning dahlias. And in Adelaide Poppy was flowering. She looked a real seventies hippy in her flowing Indian dress with its tiny mirrors. But I was feeling suicidal; my pattern of life seemed hopeless. In such depressions trivialities loom enormous. I tried to restore some humour in myself by remembering a letter from Alexander Pope to Jonathan Swift, in which he said he had been in town with a companion when, just in front of them, a servant emptied a jerry into the street. Pope said, "It would vex one more to be hit over the head with a pisspot than a thunderbolt". It was a time when even Poppy was feeling low. Her domestic situation was not the best, and, like so many women, the only money she had was that doled out to her by her husband. She bought a lottery ticket under the name of "Black Pit".

I only survived an enormous Christmas party of people who had come to stay by remembering how, two days before, I had wheedled my way through a phalanx of matron and sisters to the room where Poppy was with her baby boy, strong and smiling.

People were coming to stay, and, as so often at Anlaby, the ancient sewerage blocked up. Marc and I had to dig down about six feet through the hard soil and free the old earthernware pipes from the knotted mass of peppertree roots. Then one of the septics overflowed; the girl helping Ninette in the house had ignored instructions and put her sanitary pads down the toilet. One of the most hateful of sensations is to have to thrust your bare arm above the elbow into a septic tank to free a block.

One of our houseguests, a big wheel in Government, brought his transistor into breakfast and listened to his Christmas speech on the ABC. Charles Fisher, the headmaster of Scotch College at the time, told us that in these 1970s there was a need for a redefinition of the three Rs. He had told the boys the new three Rs should be Reason, Restraint and Responsibility. What had happened to the imagination, the spirit, humour?

I had come to hate Christmas, the excess giving of presents to those who already had so much, the ritual guzzling, the carols that after a month in the shops and streets were worn beyond repair — and all to celebrate the birth of a child few people believed in any more.

A few days later I rang Poppy at the hospital on a grey day of surly clouds. She was depressed as her little boy was being circumcised; she did not want to have it done, but his father insisted. She suddenly laughed and said, "It's just the day for losing a foreskin."

Things looked up in 1972, as they always did at Kangaroo Island, where we spent part of the school holidays. Sun Books had paid a dividend, and instead of putting it all in the bank to reduce the overdraft, I had bought Francis a little fibreglass sailing boat. Its class had the ridiculous name of Sparrow, so he called it *Spoggy*, slang in South Australia for a sparrow.

David Campbell and his second wife Judy, blonde like David but definitely not bony, came to stay, and tiny *Spoggy* went bending across the bay, Francis at the helm, with David and Graham Brookman, another solid man, leaning out over the water. Francis had a feel for the little boat, and somehow or other they never tipped up. When David returned to his property by the Molonglo, he wrote to say that of all the good things that had happened at Rocky Point the best was sailing in *Spoggy*.

For once I had to break my own rule and work on what was supposed to be a holiday at Rocky Point. The reason was that Andrei Voznesensky was coming to Writers' Week at the Festival in March, and we were going to publish a selection of his new poems in Sun Books. Igor Mezhakoff-Koriakin had just sent me his meticulous preliminary translations, with their multiple suggestions for nuances of meaning, and a fully phonetic rendering of the subtleties of sound in the original, and charts of the rhythmic structure — in fact notes on anything which I might miss in following the Cyrillic script.

At Sun Books we had for some years been filling a gap by publishing new selections of poems by poets visiting Writers' Week. The poets usually went on to give readings in other states. These books were very popular, especially with the poets, whose work was often unobtainable in Australia. We did it with James Dickey in 1968 and with Allen Ginsberg and Lawrence Ferlinghetti in 1972. For 1968 Igor and I had made translations of collections by Bella Akhmadulina, Robert Rozhdestvensky and Bulat Okhudjava. The fiery individuality of Bella's poems was of course anathema to Soviet orthodoxy, although rooted in the great Russian tradition of poets like Akhmatova and Tsvetaeva. And at times she could also be playful and delicate as Pushkin. But as with Yevtushenko or Voznesensky, it was hellishly difficult with her poems to give any idea in English of the subtleties of sound, rhyme, assonance and rhythm in the Russian.

Bella, as she had predicted, was at the last minute not allowed to come. Protests were made at Writers' Week by Steve Murray-Smith and others, but although invited time and time again, she was never allowed to come to Australia. At least she sent us more poems, particularly fine ones, and Igor and I had time to make them into tolerable, properly finished translations, which were published in London and New York as well as by Sun Books.

Now there was a mad panic with Voznesensky, as Igor's prose drafts had arrived. David was fascinated with the process and the poems, and this led him later to join with Rosemary Dobson and a Russian expert in Canberra to make some fine translations, especially of Akhmatova.

In February 1972 I had received a letter from Peter Howson, inviting me to join the Advisory Board of the Commonwealth Literary Fund; Howson was Minister for about ten departments in the McMahon Government, including the unimportant Arts. Still in my mood for being free of all committees, and not being impressed by Peter Howson, I at first refused. Several people I respected urged me to join, and I remembered Ken Slessor saying he hoped that I would succeed him on the Board, and so eventually I accepted. I was in excellent company. Geoff Blainey was Chairman, and the Board members were Alec Hope, Kylie Tennant and Douglas Stewart; our recommendations went to the three politicians who controlled the Fund, Billy McMahon, Gough Whitlam and Jack McEwen, the Leader of the Country Party. This mix presented some problems, although there was no longer the gross political interference of Menzies and Fadden.

I am not very good on committees, despite the years I have spent on them, but I think I did make one genuine contribution when on the CLF. This was to suggest that we should not only give fellowships and grants to established writers, but make more effort to take a punt on young writers, and try to encourage them at the crucial stage of setting out as writers. This was predictably denounced by some hostile witnesses, including my old friend Max Harris, as a waste of money — "Who are these so-called writers? How do you know they're going to turn out any good?"

The Festival was approaching, the Voznesensky book was finished for Sun Books and printed, as was the ingeniously designed book of Ginsberg's and Ferlinghetti's poems — printed back to back in the one volume with a photo of the poet on each cover. But it seemed none of the three might be coming. They were all scheduled to give readings in the Town Hall on different nights and most seats were already sold.

The Americans were holding out for some enormous fee, which the impoverished Festival simply could not pay. Both poets had recently been visited by Yevtushenko, and had translated his poems, so I sent them a long, emotional cable that they should lower their demands and come for Zhenya's sake. It seemed to do the trick, as a phone call from Ferlinghetti followed, saying they would come. They came cheaper, but still not cheap. Louis van Eyssen, Administrator of the Festival, later said to me, "Of all artists coming to the Festival none drove a harder commercial bargain than the transcendental, possession-rejecting Buddhists Ginsberg and Ferlinghetti."

The trouble with Voznesensky was not the size of his fee but the Soviet

Writers' Union. The grey Stalinist bureaucrats were still shilly-shallying over whether he would be allowed to go. In a last-minute drama his friend and admirer, the great prima ballerina Ulanova, intervened directly with Brezhnev. The impresario Michael Edgley, who had been bringing major companies from the Soviet Union to Australia, paid his fare and provided an interpreter.

Voznesensky was slight and pointy faced, nervous but also charming. He lacked the physical presence of Yevtushenko but recited his poems with tremendous panache and emotion. In the middle of his recital, when he was pausing between poems, a man rushed up onto the stage, shouting abuse, and tried to knock him down. Colin Horne, the Chairman of Writers' Week, and I jumped up after him and grabbed him. I felt rather as I had all those years ago when forced to box at Wykeham Preparatory School. The man was smaller and much less strong than me and I certainly didn't want to hit him. Fortunately a couple of police arrived and he agreed to go back to his seat, as Voznesensky did not wish him to be charged.

The attacker was a Ukrainian, an anti-communist Christian. I felt desperately sorry both for the Ukrainian and for this Russian poet who, like Yevtushenko, was always in trouble with the authorities at home. Neither poet, of course, was a member of the Communist Party, yet often in foreign countries they were attacked as communists or communist agents. In the case of Voznesensky's visit, the attacks were being orchestrated, and Voznesensky was to have an even worse time in Melbourne and Sydney.

Voznesensky came up to Anlaby for the night, with his interpreter, a young Australian woman. Although remaining nervy, he did relax in the country and during dinner. The two guests' rooms were at opposite ends of the long corridor. At bedtime Andrei walked with Mary and us to her room, looked around it and said, "And where am I sleeping?" I explained that he was sleeping in the billiard room, where I had carried his bag. "Mary is not sleeping here," he said, grabbed her hand, and walked off with her to the billiard room.

Andrei was due to give a recital in Melbourne, and then one in Sydney; the latter had been arranged by Grace Perry, Editor of *Poetry Australia*, a very forceful and opinionated woman, a medical doctor of repute but a very bad poet. She had once asked Kenneth Slessor whether she should be a doctor or a poet, and Slessor had replied, in a delectable, unpublished letter, that poetry was much more difficult than medicine, and from the examples of her verse she had sent him, he recommended sticking to medicine. Now she had lined up a number of other functions for Voznesensky, in addition to the reading, although I had warned her not to make too many demands on him. He was not a big, tough person, but nervous and shy, and his health was precarious; he had been very shaken by the incident in Adelaide.

Andrei rang after his recital in Melbourne, where there had been another demonstration, and said that he was absolutely exhausted and ill; did I think he could be released from the Sydney obligation? He had no official contract, as with the Adelaide Festival, and I advised him to do what he thought best. Of course I knew how disappointed his Sydney audiences would be. But we had often had to cancel Festival readings when overseas visitors let us down for one reason or another, and I had become philosophical about it. His health and safety were the most important things to be considered. He sounded relieved.

The next morning the phone rang. It was Andrei again. He was almost hysterical, weeping. He had told Grace Perry he was going to cancel the Sydney visit. "No you're not," she said, and rang the Russian Embassy in Canberra to say that Voznesensky was about to disgrace the Soviet Union, and that he must be made to come to Sydney. Shortly after, Andrei said, two KGB thugs had come into his hotel room and said they were going to escort him to Sydney. His story was confirmed by Mary. I immediately rang Grace Perry and asked her if she realized what she had done; had she any idea what an incident like this would mean to Andrei when he returned to Russia? I couldn't believe it when she said, "I don't care what happens to him, I've arranged a big reading and several functions, and he's not going to wriggle out of them." I lost my temper and told her she was every kind of stupid bitch, and ought to be ashamed to call herself a poet.

Andrei was escorted to Sydney, where there was a most unpleasant demonstration in the course of his two recitals, and he had to be taken off to safety. The repercussions, of course, did not help him when he returned to Russia.

There had been difficulties too with Michael Dransfield who had also been asked to Writers' Week. I had met Michael and Hilary at the airport and taken them to my old friends Nancy and Dean Hay's house at Seaton, where they were going to stay. They had asked not to be in the centre of things. They were both looking well. Hilary remained with Nancy while I drove Michael to the State Library in North Terrace for the afternoon session in which he was one of a panel due to talk about poetry. We were just about to get out of the car when he asked me who else was on the panel. I mentioned a couple of names, and then Alec Hope. His awkward, long frame twisted back into the car and he slammed the door. "I'm not appearing with Hope. He'll rubbish me." I explained that Hope might say anything in print, but would never be rude to a fellow poet on the same platform. He would not budge. I drove him back to Seaton and then rushed back to the session. Later Nancy Hay told me that Michael was utterly distraught, and that Hilary had taken him into their bedroom where they both spent the rest of their time in Adelaide, on heroin.

As usual, some of the best moments in Adelaide were still in Ursula

Hayward's little library-sitting room, now rebuilt since the fire that had ruined Dobell's Joshua Smith portrait. Although many of her incinerated books had been irreplaceable, attempts were being made in London to restore Dobell's Archibald Prize portrait of Smith, but Ursula did not think the damage could be repaired. (The painting was later disposed of by the Haywards, having been most unsuccessfully restored.) She was suffering a lot of pain from her back at this time, but her wit was as jaunty and sharp as ever. Then soon after, she suddenly died. Bill was left rattling around in Carrick Hill, the enormous house they had built to house the children that never arrived. There was no one like Ursula in Adelaide, or, indeed, anywhere else.

In mid-year Manoly came to stay for a week or so, gentle and witty as ever, and confiding. He said that Patrick would never carry a lot of money because he couldn't bear taking notes out of his wallet; Manoly had accounts at the shops but paid in cash, never by cheque. Patrick would niggle over buying more than one tin of Carnation milk at a time (Patrick and Manoly never had fresh milk, always diluted Carnation); yet the other day, Manoly said, he had paid $189 for a valve grind for the Rover without a murmur. (Oh that Rover, what a dreadful car!) At one stage Patrick had made the house and everything in it over to Gillian, his niece. Manoly protested that half of it belonged to him. "Nonsense, she's your niece too," Patrick replied. Then he took a dislike to Gillian and her boyfriend and remade his will. After one really terrible row Manoly had said he was leaving; he went and packed his bags and said he was going to get a taxi and go. Patrick's comment was, "Well, fuck off and go." He walked into the kitchen and came straight back again. "No, you can't go. You are my eyes." Manoly continued, "It's true. Patrick can't see things and people, he can only see into them. He cannot recall a landscape or features or clothes."

When I talked about Patrick's intolerable prejudices, Manoly said, "No, he hasn't any prejudices, he has fixations." Manoly recalled the agony it had been to carry out Patrick's instructions to burn the manuscripts of *Voss* and *Riders in the Chariot*. He had longed not to do so, but Patrick had trusted him. It occurred to me that Patrick could have burnt them himself — had he really hoped that Manoly would not obey his orders? Manoly described the manuscripts, how they were all in neat copy books, with corrections and notes in the margin, and Manoly's notes as well. I have since wondered whether in the destruction of his manuscripts Patrick was ensuring that the world would never know how much Manoly had helped in the shaping of his novels.

Manoly told me that Ralph Smith had sold to Heywood Hill Bookshop in London all the letters Patrick had written him. Margarete Forbes had kept them all, unread, at the bookshop, and gave them back to Patrick when he was in London. Patrick burnt them all.

Earlier in the year I had a letter from the London publisher Tom Rosenthal. He had been with Thames & Hudson when they commissioned the Drysdale book, and was a great supporter of Australian artists, especially of Arthur Boyd. Tom had now moved to Secker & Warburg. He had had some preliminary discussions with me about a composite biography of the Boyd family, that amazing collection of artists which also included an architect and a novelist. Now he was writing, offering a contract, including an advance, and suggesting that I come to Europe as quickly as possible to talk with Martin Boyd in Rome; Martin was very frail in body, although still quick in mind. His knowledge of the family, apart from his own achievements, would be essential for the book. Then later, in England, I could discuss the book with Arthur and Yvonne, and Mary Perceval; Arthur was very keen that I should write the book.

One good thing the CLF had done, was to give Martin Boyd a thousand dollars and a lifetime pension of thirty dollars a week; this was just before I joined, and was due to the efforts of Gough Whitlam, Patrick White, Barrie Reid and others. Until then the old man had been supported mainly by his nephew Arthur. When Martin got the news of the CLF grant he wrote to Arthur and Yvonne: "I feel like Danae or whoever it was in the shower of gold".

I decided that this would be the only opportunity in my life to take the whole family to Europe. The advance gave me the foolish illusion that I could afford it. So on Anzac Day 1972 off we went; Francis was thirteen, Tisi ten, and Sam seven. We had an excellent farewell dinner with Patrick and Manoly in Sydney, and they very generously cleared out the other half of their double garage so that our car could be stored there while we were away.

In Rome on 15 May Ninette and I went to see Martin Boyd at the *pensione* where he lived, the Alto Adige. When we arrived he was seated in the *padrone*'s private sitting room, in a rectangle of sunlight in front of a window, his white legs bare under rolled-up trousers, his arms also bare, trying to get some sun. In a high clear voice that did not run evenly he said, "You'd think the sun would make me feel stronger, but I seem to be so weak, weaker." He said he used to walk a hundred steps a day, but couldn't now. He rang the bell and two women came and helped him to his room, where we were bidden for tea.

He received us in his bed, so thin and tufted and white, as if he were made from pipe-cleaners, yet with such a bright eye. He talked about the betrayal of youth by intellectuals and politicians, and was glad that his last short book, *Why They Walk Out*, was going to appear in Australia. He rang for the tea. After the maid had brought it he said, "They will make tea in these teabags, they don't understand how to get out the flavour." He tried to squeeze the bags in the pot with a spoon, but was too weak, and I had to do it for him.

I thought that it was a great privilege to talk with a dying man. Patience is also needed, as with children. I asked if we were tiring him. "No, not at all. Don't know why I'm so weak. Never been so weak. The Signora thinks I'm dying." He paused to have a sip of tea. "I was doing fine after a recent operation, but then the night the Americans exploded their H-bomb in Alaska there was a terrible storm and I got sick again." He said he was touched but ironically amused when the English Ambassador brought along a copy of *Day of My Delight* for him to sign for presentation to the Eton library — "You know what I think of English public schools." He believed that the reason for the success of his reissued books was that they had a message of hope for the young, some positive values. John Murray refused to publish *Much Else in Italy* because it was blasphemous. Then when Macmillan published it the best review it got was in the *Church Times*. He approved of the idea of my book about the family, and said he was leaving all his papers to his nephew Guy, the sculptor.

I was sure I would not see him again. We were in fact to be his last non-family visitors at the *pensione*. His niece Mary Perceval arrived from London that same day, and on the next day she went with him to the Blue Nuns' Hospital, where he died on 3 June.

We came back to Anlaby to drought, day after clear, hot day, the crops, only a few inches high, already being cut for hay. At this time of year, October, drought is so deceptive, for the stunted crops are still green.

Patrick's cousin Peggy Garland came to stay; she is the mother of Nick, the cartoonist, Barry Humphries's collaborator in *Barry Mackenzie*. Although she has a round, smiling face, pulled-back hair and a vaguely tweedy academic look, she has the piercing eye of her cousin and comes out with similar cut-through comments. We mourned together over the failure of so much of the old life of England, the greyness, every sort of evil that follows on overpopulation. Peggy recalled Patrick as a young dandy in the South of France with an opera cloak and a gardenia. She considered Manoly to be becoming very bossy now that he had come into his own money and was financially independent. But it was about time, she and I agreed. We also agreed about Patrick's outrageous prejudices, or fixations, the latest being to despise Solzhenitsyn's great book, *The First Circle*. No budging him. The Greek singer Theodorakis was also a current hate.

Peggy cared deeply for Patrick and understood him very well — if that were possible for anyone. She said: "He misses out on a lot of things. But maybe it's deliberate, not to complicate his life, to leave him undisturbed by too many things." She had said to him one day that she thought he was a good man. "Oh no," he interrupted, "oh no, I'm not good. But I understand about goodness."

In my absence overseas, some high Russian comedy had been enacted at the Writers' Week Committee. I had suggested, as a visitor to Writers' Week, the name of a very interesting Romanian writer I had met; the Romanians were willing for him to come to the Festival, and to pay his air fare. When on my return I went into the office to look at the minutes I found that the suggestion had been knocked back: "It was generally agreed by the Committee that it would rather spend money on someone better known. Dr Whitelock suggested Solzhenitsyn. Mr Steel [the new Director of the Festival], who would be in Moscow next month, offered to approach Solzhenitsyn through his friend Rostropovich. Sholokhov was suggested as an alternative, a Soviet writer not frowned on by the Kremlin. Mr Steel agreed to make private enquiries about Solzhenitsyn and public enquiries on Sholokhov when in Moscow." I could hear the sad laughter this display of provincial ignorance would have provoked in Zhenya or Bella. Solzhenitsyn had been in the deepest disgrace since the award of the Nobel Prize in 1970; he was to be expelled from the Soviet Union in 1974. There would have been absolutely no hope of his being allowing out to Adelaide. As for Sholokhov ("Behold the proud face of our people!"), he had become an arch-reactionary and was universally detested by all genuine writers.

Adelaide's provincialism was still having trouble with the protests against the Vietnam War. Bill Hayward had, very sensibly, married again after Ursula's death, to a pleasant woman totally unlike Ursula. There was a real Adelaide Establishment party for him and his new wife at his nephew Ian's house. One old codger bailed up a friend and me and said something would have to be done about those students sitting on the steps of Parliament House with placards and pamphlets about stopping the Vietnam War. "We're too soft on those young buggers, they'll have no respect for us if they're not beaten. You two young fellers ought to do something about it!" I was fifty at the time, and of course I had been one of those handing out such pamphlets.

I had been having discussions with people at the Adelaide Gallery about an idea for an exhibition of white artists' paintings and drawings of Aborigines, from early white settlement to the present day. The Board of the Gallery now commissioned me to make an inventory of such works, and to write a book about them. The result was the book, *White on Black*, and a travelling exhibition. I was fortunate enough to have the help of Ron Appleyard, a curator and art historian of profound knowledge, and a most agreeable man to work with. We went together to Tasmania, and later to Sydney and Canberra in search of material.

I thought the book and exhibition, apart from their artistic value, would be important as something that would help give a face to Aborigines, who were still very much the hidden people of Australia. There have been so many dramatic changes since then in white Australia's consciousness of black, that it is very difficult now to imagine the ignorance of earlier times. I can recall, to my shame, that when I first met Derry Jeffares, in 1951, and he asked me about the future of the Aborigines in Australia, I had nothing coherent or thoughtful to say.

In Sydney I stayed with Patrick and Manoly. We talked about the Garland family. Peggy had mentioned to me that her handicapped son was the model for Waldo in *The Solid Mandala*; Patrick remembered giving him a record of Mozart's First Symphony, which he played over and over again. He said Peggy's son used to come out with some very pertinent remarks.

Patrick's mood degenerated at dinner at a Chinese restaurant. He began to shout curses on mankind for being so evil, about the modern world being so intolerable. I told him that he was being dishonest — in which century were things better? — and that he spent too much time reading the newspapers. I reminded him of all the progress there had been: that there was, at least in the so-called West, no more slavery, no child labour; that women seldom died in childbirth; that polio and smallpox and so many other afflictions were no more. He drank another glass of wine and said, "But there it was, in the *Sydney Morning Herald* this morning; three small children poured petrol over an old sleeping drunk in the park and set fire to him."

For many years it had been a recurrent failing of mine to think it was a good thing to bring writers together, although I suppose it had sometimes been proved well worthwhile in Writers' Weeks. I should have remembered, though, that Patrick adamantly refused ever to go to a Writers' Week. Anyway while I was in Sydney I asked Patrick and Manoly and the poet Les Murray and his wife Valerie to dinner together. Patrick suggested a new French restaurant in Surry Hills. The food was indeed good, but the restaurant very noisy and cramped. Les is a very big man and could scarcely balance on the little iron chairs. It was a terrible evening, not made any better by Les, who could not disguise his dislike of Patrick and all his works. Worse still was the arrival of Frank Hardy, who in the middle of our dinner swept through the door of the restaurant with a girlfriend (always later referred to in Patrick's letters as The Radical Chick). Frank saw Patrick and swerved over towards our table. I saw the look in Patrick's eyes as Frank leaned over the table, ignoring the rest of us, stuck out his hand and said, "I'm Frank Hardy!" "Yes, I know," replied Patrick wearily, leaving his hand on the table. Yet I had many times heard Patrick defending Frank as a writer, especially with reference to *Power Without Glory*, and also for his campaign for land rights for the Aborigines at Wave Hill.

Everything seemed to be going well in 1972, except for the never-ending financial drain at Anlaby and my own passivity in the face of it. My book on the Boyds was prospering, with some very rewarding sessions in Melbourne with Guy and other Boyd and a'Beckett relations. Meetings of the CLF were taking me to Canberra where there was always a reunion with David Campbell, often joined by Bob Brissenden, a rare example of a man who was both an academic and a genuine poet. Bob's gusto and humour made him immune to pedantry or fashion or the freeze of theory. Absurdly enough, our friendship had begun in hostility. Max had asked him to review for *ABR* the latest batch of my Lansdowne monographs on Australian writers. He had taken me to task for the sloppy general editing of the series; it was not long before I began to think he was quite right, but at the time I accused him of academic nitpicking. David Campbell rang me and said the cure for this nonsense was for Bob and me to have a long lunch with him next time I was in Canberra. The cure worked to perfection.

And, best of all, at least for me, was that poems were pouring out of me. David Campbell was the one of all my friends to whom I could talk about love and poetry. We never needed to explain what we meant or justify ourselves. I told him about Poppy; he had a similar story to tell me. He liked the poems I showed him, and made a couple of invaluable suggestions for improving them. We talked about the Muse, and the woman who is the Muse and who cannot be possessed. Dear old Richard Aldington, who knew a great deal about love and suffering, was wrong when he wrote: "I must possess you utterly / And utterly must you possess me".

David and I both took love poetry seriously; he has written some of the finest, in so many moods, of the twentieth century. Back in the 1950s I had written an article for *Australian Letters* called "The Bashful Bloke", about the paucity of love poetry in Australia, and the fact that most of it that had any passion had been written by women. This gave rise in the 1960s to Max Harris's suggestion that I edit a book of Australian love poetry. I did, but it was slim. Even among literate Australians, the reaction if you published some love poems was "You're a bit of a sentimental old bastard, eh?" Well, David and I thought it good to be in the company of Sappho, Catullus, Donne and Yeats, however far behind we might be.

I had found a high-ceilinged room where Poppy and I could meet, in an old hotel in central Adelaide, a hotel where only the bar was still used. Down the stairs, at the back entrance, lived an old pensioner who kept up a tiny garden. The street outside the three big front windows with their bamboo blinds was a thousand miles away.

I sometimes thought curiosity was Poppy's true passion. She was curious about every aspect of love, curious about how far her violent husband could be provoked or restrained, curious about my attitude to her taking other lovers, curious also about how endings can be woven into beginnings. She made me a small rug of thick wool she had spun and woven herself, to keep my feet warm at my desk. I was thus always conscious of her presence-in-absence.

But 1973 started badly; it was as if a giant front-end loader had come along and taken a huge bite out of my normal landscape. For some days I had been feeling terrible; our usual doctor was away, so I went to the locum, a trim little person who said, "Go home and let nature take its course." Fortunately, Ninette had more sense, and drove me over to the doctor in Eudunda, who took an X-ray and found that I had double pneumonia. I had never been so ill, and while being conscious of that, I found it fascinating how visual the experience was. I felt I was in a velvet tunnel sloping down to a bottomless pit of black swans' feathers. The black curtain of my closed eyelids gave onto endless swirling forms like the fine detail in a Doré engraving of Hell, or an enlargement of the fur (but black fur instead of cream) on the belly of a possum, or the hair and winking eyes and scruff of a banksia, of May Gibbs's bad banksia men whom I had never had as a child but my children enjoyed.

The very day I was sent to bed Patrick had arrived to stay for a week. Kindly he sat with me, but the effort of talking to him was for me almost as difficult as was Martin Boyd's in lifting his teacup. But a day or two later, when I felt better and Ninette was in town with the children, I enjoyed his company more and more as we talked and gossiped. He loved the talk of servants in old English houses, the world of Henry Green's novel *Loving*; he had some relations in England — were they cousins? — who had two old servants who had been in service at the Dorchester in London. They were full of jokes and dirty stories and libellous comments about the guests and their sex lives. He said he was not afraid of dying, but would bitterly resent it if he was carried of in the middle of a novel, or on the day before the weekly house-cleaning. He was fascinated by my activities. When I rang Brian Stonier about Sun Books or Geoff Blainey about the CLF, he would say, "This is a *very peculiar* pneumonia". He was rivetted by the advertisements on TV; needless to say, he did not have a set, and Manoly was not permitted one.

The last time Patrick had come to stay at Anlaby had been two years before. In the long letter making arrangements when and how he would come, he had offered some fatherly, or perhaps big-brotherly advice. I was only ten years younger than he, but he was always carrying on about how old he was. 'In my old age', he wrote in one letter that year (he was 59). "You amaze me the way you rush from one holiday to the next with hardly a breathing space between," he now wrote. "This would be none of my business if your every other letter didn't come up with the cry of poverty and what-will-become-of-Anlaby-and-the-children? I should have thought if you dug yourself in at Anlaby for two or three years you might improve the situation. When the pre-Revolutionary Russians were hard up they retired to their estates. Certainly they drove themselves mad with boredom in most cases, but you, like Pushkin, have your 'embroidery'. Because Manoly & I are fond of you all, & wonder what will become of you, I felt I had to make these remarks." His advice was obviously well-meant, although, being childless, he didn't understand that I considered I should make time to spend some of their holidays with my children.

It was also very sensible advice, except that Patrick, like many others, fell into the category of those, who, in my mother's warning words, thought I was rich because I lived at Anlaby, or who thought that Anlaby kept us. It was in fact I who kept Anlaby more or less going, while the property slipped further and further into the red. Patrick certainly knew I wasn't rich, but he was so canny himself he had no idea how disorganized I was about money, and how little I had.

Now, sitting by my bedside, he didn't read me any lectures, although my finances were in fact even worse than they had been two years before. By this time, though, I knew better than to mention the fact.

A week later the doctor allowed me to go down to Kangaroo Island, on condition that I only sat on the veranda. But this was a hopeless ideal. Even the journey from the airport had its problems when a wheel came off the old Volkswagen Kombi on the way to Rocky Point. It bowled off down the road while we skidded to a halt an inch or two away from a fifteen-foot culvert. A number of guests came to stay, amongst them Poppy and her surly husband, who clamped his jealous eye to the telescope watching Poppy sail in the bay with Francis in *Spoggy*. At midnight Poppy and I would meet in the total darkness of the old boatshed, and lie on an ancient sail on the sand.

In 1973 the CLF was amalgamated into the Literature Board of the Australia Council, and became responsible to the Council and not to three politicians. By 1973-74 its budget was seven times that of the CLF in its last year. If a committee can ever be exhilarating, this one was, with Geoff Blainey as Chairman, and Manning Clark, Judah Waten, Nancy Keesing, Tom Shapcott, Alec Hope, Elizabeth Riddell, Dick Hall and Richard Walsh as members. Geoff, Alec and I had been members of the old CLF Board, so had what was jokingly but accurately called inbuilt memory, a great help to the new members.

I particularly admired the style of Manning and Richard Walsh. Manning used to fall asleep after lunch, his beard sinking onto his tie; this had nothing to do with the drinks we were allowed at lunch in those far-off days, for Manning did not drink. When a discussion arose, Manning would suddenly erupt from sleep and make an acute comment on what the last speaker had said. Richard always looked crumpled and never wore a tie, as if he had just come from an all-night pot-smoking party, to which his grey face always seemed to bear witness. But he was probably quicker and more eloquent than anyone. Always at the end of a session, while the rest of us were gathering up the minutes and all the other papers, he would be off out the door, unencumbered by a single page.

Our first two meetings were held in a tiny room in Sydney; we had no staff, and Geoff recorded the meetings. A month later we got a paragon of a secretary, Joan O'Donnell, who had been private secretary to Arthur Calwell. We desperately needed an executive officer, and Judah Waten (with typical lack of prejudice) recommended a Catholic ex-priest, Michael Costigan, for the job. He was to be the mainstay of the Literature Board for ten years; his position was later known as Director.

By July we were meeting in slightly better premises in Melbourne, at 4 Treasury Place, but we also met in other cities. We had all assumed our home would be in Melbourne, and approved of our being distanced from the main body of the Australia Council in Sydney. But Nugget Coombs, as Chairman of the Australia Council, and Jean Battersby, as Chief Executive Officer, did not like our being in Melbourne. They thought, perhaps rightly, that it made for extra expense and gave opportunities for failures of communication. Geoff Blainey and Jean did not get on, to put it mildly; as I knew them both well, I sang the praises of each to the other, but to no avail. In December 1975, by which time Nancy Keesing had succeeded Geoffrey Blainey, the Board's office moved to Sydney.

There was a lot of work involved. In the first year there were 1,147 applications for grants. We had no outside readers, and went through them all ourselves. I was pleased that the Board was unanimous in wanting to continue to support younger writers, despite the risks involved. All these writers' manuscripts, whether any good or not, represented possible new directions for the Australian tradition as well as interpretations of what had already happened in this country (not that all of them had to be set in Australia).

At Anlaby money was still running away. A friend suggested to me that instead of selling the wether lambs off-shears, often for very little money, I should buy some cheap land on the Murray River flats where the rainfall drops to about eight inches a year but there is good grazing, and keep them for their wool. We found two thousand acres divided into four paddocks, with water from the main pipeline, with bluebush and saltbush and seasonal grass, myall and mulga. When we went to look at it a mob of eight hundred to a thousand budgerigars rose from the long grass and formed themselves into a kind of whirring ball, like those intricate Chinese spheres carved inside one other. There were rather too many kangaroos, but very few rabbits. I bought the land for eleven dollars an acre and to pay for it sold my parents' four Baines oils of the Gregory Northern Territory expedition to the National Library. They are now in the National Gallery. I have a pang every time I see the postcards that have been made of them.

Actually, it would have made far better economic sense to keep them and not buy the land.

Of course there were hidden traps. The most physically painful one was the bindii burr in the wool; even the tough old Mallee farmers who came to help with crutching and shearing used to wear gloves. The worst problem for the sheep themselves was that so many of them became flyblown, even after frequent crutching. The helpful neighbours mulesed them for me, a painful operation, but as they said, not as painful as being eaten by maggots.

We called the place Cassia; lots of those lovely yellow-flowered bushes grew there. The ones who enjoyed Cassia most were the children, who rounded up the sheep on the three ag-bikes. They never got lost in those nearly dead-flat identical paddocks.

Randolph Stow came to stay at Anlaby on a visit from England, which was now his permanent home. He was looking bony, grizzled and distinguished, wearing a black jacket with silver buttons. He was as silent as ever, but somehow I deduced he would never come back to live in Australia. Nevertheless, when we took him out to Cassia, it obviously appealed to him greatly; he said it reminded him of Uno. I could not imagine living, as he did now, in dank, flat East Anglia. But he was happy there.

I too responded to Cassia, but before long I was realizing what a mistake it had been to buy it; I already had too much to worry about. Perhaps symbolically, fate one day might have been telling me what a trap it was. I was alone at Anlaby in late summer, and decided to go out to Cassia by myself in the afternoon to spread some lucerne hay for the sheep. A contractor had delivered and stacked the bales. I was on top of the stack throwing down some bales onto the back of the truck when the bales suddenly opened outwards and I fell ten feet or so onto the ground between the bales. When I had partially recovered my wind I started to move my limbs to find out which of them were broken, but I was most nervous about my back. Finally I sat up very slowly, squeezed between the bales. Neither back nor bones were broken. I was badly bruised all over, and it took me a while to burrow out between the bales. I wondered what would have happened if I had been immobilized in the middle of the stack. No one could have heard me shout for help, the nearest house being about five miles away. I suppose in the end they would have come from Anlaby and seen the truck.

In August I had my fiftieth birthday. I had written a poem about ripeness and rot. Poppy laughed. She was nearly thirty. "I'm almost full ripe, you're on the edge of rot." But neither she nor I believed in this theoretical nonsense. Age seemed to me irrelevant, and still does. She had what was basically a hopeless relationship with her husband, although in many ways they really liked each other. When we were first meeting, she came one day with a deep blue-black bruise on her hip. She said she had walked into the kitchen table when carrying her son in her arms. But later there were more bruises, and she gave up pretending.

Sometimes, because she was a country person trapped in the city, we would drive up into the hills where we had found a secluded clearing in the bush. Back in the room in the city it was also good, but she talked of parting, because there was no future for us. This is the trap that waits for all illicit lovers. Robert Browning had it right: "The old trick! only I discern — / Infinite passion, and the pain / Of finite hearts that yearn".

Twenty-Nine

I was in Sydney at a dreary motel on the North Shore for another meeting of the Literature Board when Richard Walsh rang me to say Michael Dransfield had died of tetanus on Good Friday — a conjunction Michael would have sardonically relished. He wrote too much, but at his best, which is how writers should always be remembered, he was a true poet who wrote like no one else. He also looked only like himself, with his wispy tall elegance, even when in acute disarray, a leafy sea-dragon breathing air. He lived with a death wish for years — and then died by accident.

I was staying in a room high above the railway lines, overlooking the giant cloverleaf crossing of the expressway. "Cloverleaf", what an inappropriate name for a cluster of tarred roads! Clover, symbol of luck, sign of good green feed for stock, of subterranean survival waiting to show a sprout. How could a poet be of this era? How could he see a cloverleaf as anything but green?

Michael liked to be on the edge of a country environment, close to green shoots or pale summer grass, and he liked to look like a cocky farmer with a white shirt and dark waistcoat, and black shanks tapering to boots that could have held their own in wet cattleyards. But he could not surrender to slow country rhythms. He had a sweet ear for cadence — no Australian poet is more musical — but the broken rhythms of our era made his life jagged and his movements jerky, and too many of his poems fragmentary.

Michael's mother said to me: "He had to have this terrible crutch to get through life." Heroin made his frequent crashes on motorbikes seem flower-fresh, the snapping of limbs no more painful than the cracking of stems. Again and again Michael's frail organism came up for more, responding to accidents as the excess of life, even though the accidents were the fallout of a death-wish.

Michael's death came just when he was cheerful and working well. A recent letter to me had said he was about four-fifths through the first draft of a novel; "that CLF Fellowship really saved me".

Michael wrote his own epitaph, in a poem called "Fugue in G Minor":

A last fuck, and then away, the next planet
waits ... Let someone else
carry the torch ... Such a drag being dead tho',
confining as the cells, tiresome as genius ...

From time to time Patrick had mentioned, with some embarrassment, that he was being considered for the Nobel Prize, and in late March the Swedish Ambassador rang him to say that an eminent Swedish man of letters, Artur Lundkvist, was visiting Australia and would be having dinner with Patrick; Patrick wrote that Lundkvist would like to see something of the Australian countryside, and wondered if he could visit us at Anlaby? It was obvious what the visit was about, and Patrick confirmed my suspicions. Lundkvist was a charming man with a wide-ranging mind; he was Patrick's greatest supporter on the Nobel committee. He came to lunch and was given the ritual drive around the station and through the paddocks. We talked at length about Patrick and his books. I was very respectful, and hoped I was seeming respectable. The word "Nobel" was never spoken.

In October 1973 Patrick was awarded the Nobel Prize. He always maintained that accepting it was the greatest mistake of his life. But when we spoke on the phone after the announcement he really was excited, as well as being amused, sardonic and harassed. It was as if the Prize provided him with some certainty of recognition that he still needed.

At Sun Books we had been working on plans to bring Yevtushenko to Australia again, and in 1973 we succeeded. He sent the typescript of some new poems, *Kazan University*; unfortunately Igor was not available to work on them with me, so an Adelaide Russian-speaker, Eleanor Jacka, and I translated them. Kazan University is a safe-house for the allegory of the poem; it is where Lenin went as a student. From that secure base the poet can begin to talk in his own language; this is the way understood by readers living under tyranny. The dialogue in one of the poems encapsulates the difficulties of being a poet in Russia betweeen 1968, the year of the invasion of Prague, and 1973. " 'Sometimes it is wiser / to retreat / Posterity glorifies / only the one / who knows how to retreat. Stubborn rashness is senseless ..." / "But often / when we rationalise / the beautiful word strategy/ is only a pseudonym for cowardice ...' "

I flew to Sydney to meet Zhenya, although there was the usual confusion as to how and when. Then by chance a friend saw a telegram lying on the airport manager's desk. "Sydney Airport — if Geoffrey Dutton or anybody from Sun Books coming to meet me I arrive BOAC Tuesday. Russian poet E. Evtushenko."

After six years he looked older, more wary about the eyes, skin tighter drawn over the cheeks, after Prague and a poem of his that ended "A Russian writer crushed / by Russian tanks in Prague". After being virtually silenced. After marital upheavals. His letters to me in those years were often despairing. One of them, posted in Paris, said about his homeland: "Living in this country is like swimming through a sea of used toothpaste". But then his face lightened, to be back in the freedom of Australia, with friends. He pressed a parcel into my hands, saying, "Is one kilo of caviare."

It really was, jar after jar of it. I have never, before or since, held a kilo of caviare in my hands.

The reading that night was in the Town Hall. I had arranged for a young poet, Richard Tipping, to read the translations. No Dame Judith this time. The great space of the Town Hall was almost empty. Then suddenly people started to pour in. In the end it was three-quarters full, but still Zhenya, used to standing room only, said, "My greatest defeat."

When we returned to the hotel after a party, at about 2 a.m., there was a girl on the carpet in front of his door, curled up like a dog, with a bunch of flowers pressed against her. Zhenya woke her and opened the door for her. A few minutes later he knocked on my door. "Is a university lecturer, very nice girl. Please give me one jar caviare."

Zhenya told me sadly that he had had rows with Voznesensky and Aksenov. "Bella?" I asked. "No, not Bella. I have never been betrayed by a woman." He said that Khrushchev, just before he died, had asked him to come and see him. Khrushchev had apologized for his bad behaviour to Zhenya and other artists and writers.

After a reading in Melbourne, well-attended, he came to Adelaide for another reading and then spent a few days with us. He had asked me to take him up into "the outback", so I had arranged to drive him in our Toyota Landcruiser truck to Arkaroola in the Flinders Ranges, where we would stay in the motel. The children got a couple of days off from school so they could come too.

It was a pity he would not have enough time for a proper camping trip. Camping was one of the great joys of life with the children. I had had a steel frame built to fit in the back of the Toyota, with weldmesh around the sides to keep everything in, and a canvas top that could be rolled up around the sides and at the back in good weather. Harold had made a padded back-rest which swung down from the top, and the children sat on four or five old shearer's mattresses between it and the tailboard. There was room there for five or six. In this truck we would go to remote areas, especially of the Flinders Ranges, up faint, dust-lifting tracks over the bony hills and down into a valley with a running creek in all that dryness. For the days we were there we would see no other living creature except kangaroos, wild goats and goannas, which were not afraid of us, and myriads of birds. Ninette was at her very best out camping, expert at provisions and able to cope with all difficulties. We had a big French tent and a smaller one, but mostly slept under the stars, Ninette and I on separate stretchers and the children on stretchers or inflatable mattresses.

In Adelaide Zhenya wanted to go to the bank where he was expecting some hard-currency royalties. I was very proud when he told me that a couple of years before, when he was in Santiago, he had sent cables, requesting royalties owed him, to his publishers in several hard-currency countries. (Soviet writers always asked such publishers to hold their earnings, they were immediately confiscated if sent to the USSR, and the author received only a few roubles.) Sun Books had not only been the first to reply to his cable from all the publishers around the world, but had also paid immediately.

Now we went into the bank, and Zhenya was told by the cashier that the bank was holding about fifteen hundred dollars for him, and how would he like it. "Cash," said Zhenya. He was wearing only a grey shirt and jeans, and stuffed the money into his hip pocket. I asked him whether he would like me to arrange for it to be put into an interest-bearing account until he wanted it all. He simply replied, "And what is wrong with money?"

He stayed a night at Anlaby before we headed north. I was showing him some bird books, looking out the various birds we might see on our trip, when he said, "I hope once in Australia it is possible to publish as beautiful a book about poets as about parrots."

The next morning we set off for Arkaroola in the faithful Toyota, probably the most reliable vehicle ever built. Zhenya insisted on riding in the back under the canopy, with the children. By the time we reached Terowie, almost a ghost town, there was such a bad petrol blockage that I could only just keep the Toyota moving. There was a garage, but the mechanic was out on a job. An hour later he returned. He looked like a Mexican, but amazingly turned out to be a German who had been a POW in the Soviet Union and could speak quite good Russian.

The Toyota was still sick when we reached Hawker. Fred Teague eventually came to his garage, saying he had vowed to watch the Davis Cup at home and stir for no man, but he felt sorry for us with a Russian poet on board. He blew the tank out; it had been filled from a dirty pump. By now we were more than two hours behind schedule, with a long way to go around the edge of the Flinders Ranges. Near Wilpena a tyre blew out. A few miles further on the steering felt very odd. I stopped and found the wheel-nuts on the replaced wheel were almost undone and nearly worn through. (I found out afterwards that the spare, which had not been used for months, had a coating of dried mud in the holes for the bolts, so when the wheel seemed tight it was in fact up against a layer of caked mud.) I protested to Zhenya, cross my heart and die, that I had been all over Australia in this Toyota and nothing had ever gone wrong; I had never even had a puncture. It was true. But he was throughly enjoying himself.

Near Wirrealpa we had another puncture. I always carried an extra wheel and tyre when out in the bush, but had not bothered to put it in because we were driving on well-used roads. Fortunately I had a spare tube, but it was impossible to lever the tyre off the wheel rim. I remembered an old trick Mick Ridge had showed me when I was a boy, and, to Zhenya's fascination, applied it. It consisted of driving the truck across the edge of the tyre; the weight of the truck sprung the tyre free of the rim. Then, to get the tyre on again, Zhenya and Francis and I linked arms and jumped on the tyre, Zhenya roaring out some Siberian convict work song and saying, "Is a poem, dance of poet brothers on rubber."

Away we went again, and it was soon dark. We had gone about sixty miles, and were ten miles south of Arkaroola, when — unbelievably — the other rear tyre went down with a puncture. There was nothing for it but to camp, just off the road. I was appalled at the series of misadventures, but Zhenya was laughing his head off. "KGB have been sprinkling nails all the way up Flinders Ranges!"

At dawn a bus came by, and promised to radio for help. What happened next pleased Zhenya most of all. Almost simultaneously, after half an hour or so, two Toyotas approached in clouds of dust, one from Arkaroola and the other from Wirrealpa, with bread and hot soup and thermoses of tea and first-aid kits. They had heard on the radio that a vehicle was broken down with lots of children on board. Yevtushenko had seen the outback radio network of instant communication in full operation. He thought it was marvellous.

He had also learnt something more about Australian life. To improve his knowledge of foreign languages, he always travelled with a dictionary of the language of the country he was visiting, and would ask people to comment on words that were new to him. In the back of the truck with the children, he had also asked them to teach him some useful phrases of Australian idiom. They told him that an invaluable one was "She bangs like a shithouse door". He duly wrote it in his notebook.

When I saw him off in Sydney, on his way home, he told me that he had had dinner in Canberra with the Prime Minister and Margaret Whitlam. Gough had asked him whether he had met a well-known female academic. "No," answered Zhenya innocently, "but I believe she bangs like a shithouse door." He asked me to thank the children for teaching him such a useful phrase.

Zhenya had an enormous capacity to drink and be none the worse for it. But he did not drink spirits. Not so the next poet to visit Anlaby, Laurie Lee. He put away a whole bottle of Scotch between arriving at midday and leaving at five, as well as plenty of wine for lunch, showing no more sign of it than if he been drinking water. I knew his brother Jack, the film-maker, but gathered the two did not get on. Laurie had a crumpled look and an amiable manner, and obviously enjoyed the opportunity to get away from the cities. He thought the lyric was still alive and well in Australia because we were all close to the country even if we lived in the city — there was something of the bush in or near every Australian city. This is still true of Australian cities. He said, surprisingly, that the Oxford meadows and the English countryside had invigorated Auden. I suggested that there was not much meadow in that lovely lyric "Oh lurcher-loving collier, black as night / Follow your love across the smokeless hill ..." He laughed, but he might have been right about Australia in the Seventies; the lyric is now almost dead in Australia, and most of our poets, even those who come from the country, with the obvious exception of Les Murray, are unremittingly urban, and don't write lyrics.

Laurie said, as Patrick had often said to me, that we had a hard lot as writers, our tools of trade were so drab, unlike those of artists and musicians. But we have one great advantage: a lover may say our lines to his mistress, and we keep our poems, we don't sell them like paintings and they're gone. This conversation took place after lunch and the whisky bottle was well down. He asked did we have a fiddle. I went and fetched my mother's old violin; only two strings were left whole. He tuned them, and then played it remarkably well. I could imagine him wandering around Spain with it, and thinking, "Two strings will do".

Like David Campbell, Laurie is a poet who is not scared of love poetry. In my case, things were not good with the relationship that had, to use Yeats's phrase with due humility, spurred me into song. I thought I was only compounding the difficulties of Poppy's life, especially since her husband had broken open a locked drawer and found some letters of mine, although he said he bore me no ill will.

We decided to part, and then allowed ourselves one more meeting. And the affair went on and on. I have wondered since about the origins of this repetitive pattern, this courting of pain, of the harsh rhythms of parting and reunion, abandonment and reconciliation. It happened, until everything changed many years later, with all the lovers I was closest to: Ilse, Dominique, Poppy, even Annie who by comparison was such a messenger of wholeness.

By my involvement in these tempestuous and ultimately hopeless situations, I was probably also exposing myself to the possibilities of fiction, by learning about lives so different from my own, outside my own intensely ordered home life. Dominique, on her visit to Anlaby, had been appalled at the ceaseless control, the calm and the politeness of my marriage which disguised the real life tumbling around underneath. Poets and writers of fiction have to be honest. I could be that with my lovers, however inept I was in managing these affairs.

Love may be foolish, but if it is felt deeply it is not trivial. Nadezhda Mandelstam, widow of the poet Osip, writes in her great autobiography: "Love is not merely a source of joy or a game, but part of the ceaseless tragedy of life, both its eternal curse and the overwhelming force that gives it meaning". But of course it is, even in the worst of times, also a joy and a game. A game that is a joy. But a game for two, not for one person playing games, which is something quite different, and not joyful. I had begun to suspect that Poppy was playing games, although I could not quite understand what they signified.

By 1973 Sun Books was getting beyond the financial resources of Brian Stonier and me, even allowing for the fact that we had sold some of it to Paul Hamlyn to give us an injection of funds. It is always the way: when a business succeeds, more money is needed for it to expand, and without expanding it will collapse. So, by some brilliant wheeling and dealing, Brian sold Sun Books to Macmillan in London. In return we more or less took over Macmillan Australia, which was guaranteed independence from London in the production of its Australian books. Brian became Managing Director and I became Editorial Director; George Smith, who had been with us since Penguin days, brought all his talents to being Production Manager; Lee White came as Senior Editor, eventually to become a freelance and President of the Society of Editors. Max Harris continued as Adviser.

Amalgamation with a big publisher would mean changes. I would be relieved of a lot of work, as well as of financial responsibility. Sun Books had been exhilarating in spite of the time spent reading incoming manuscripts and commissioning them, communicating with the authors, editing their work and even writing the blurbs for the books. I thought it was all worth the sacrifice of time because it was helping to establish a sound base for Australian writing, especially with the help that was being given by the greatly strengthened Literature Board. Someone like Patrick could never understand my enthusiasm; secure in his private income, personally doing a lot to help writers and artists, he could still not admit much worth in the cause. He wrote a withering letter to me about the expanded funds of the Literature Board. "The CLF has been doling out for years without improving the standard of literature. Perhaps this new body could pay writers to go away for years, if not for ever, like Henry Handel Richardson, Martin Boyd, Christina Stead, Peter Porter, Randolph Stow, Shirley Hazzard, and Sumner Locke Elliott."

It is certainly a formidable and daunting list. But he could not understand that what was needed was the creation, or development, of an Australia where people like all these talented writers did not need to become expatriates. They could come and go and please themselves, because home was no longer a desert for people like them. The talent nourished by the CLF and the Literature Board varied in quality, but every nation needs a large number of writers of the second rank in order to give body to what the nation's readers can feed on. The odd genius like White doesn't make Australian Literature, although it gives it inspiration, status and impetus. Open the review pages of the Sunday papers and weeklies in London (which Patrick devoured as if he still lived there), or of papers like the *New York Times*, and there are dozens of books that will probably be forgotten in a year or two. But in the meantime they provide an invaluable cash flow for publishers and a supply of books both for buyers and for the library users who are the backbone of literary consciousness. And who knows which books, that have seemed failures, will surge back into demand, like the novels of Christina Stead?

Patrick's mention of Sumner Locke Elliott is a case in point. Here was one of Australia's finest novelists who was scarcely known in his own country since he had left Australia in 1948 for the USA, to become a succesful writer for film and television. All I knew of him was that his wartime play, *Rusty Bugles*, had been acclaimed by audiences and had fallen foul of the censors, and that I had read his first-class novel of his childhood, *Careful, He Might Hear You*. In Zürich in 1972, desperate for something to read in English, I had found in a second-hand bookshop a scungy American paperback of Locke Elliott's novel *Edens Lost*. I thought it was so good that I rang Brian Stonier and urged him to buy the paperback rights for Sun Books — the book had been almost unknown to the general public in Australia since its publication in the USA in hardback in 1969. It turned out to be the old story. No paperback was planned, but the publishers refused to sell us the Australian-New Zealand rights.

In the meantime I thought that at least Sumner could be invited to Writers' Week at the 1974 Adelaide Festival. I had alerted Patrick, who asked his friend James Allison, the admirable Woollahra Librarian, about *Edens Lost*. James had no less than five well-read copies of the book in the Library, a remarkable achievement. Patrick wrote: "I agree that this is one of the best Australian novels. Why has one not heard about it? I can't remember seeing reviews in English or Australian papers ... I've written to Sumner & said I hoped he would be coaxed out here for the Festival." Despite his oft-repeated scorn for Writers' Week, Patrick really knew how useful it could be.

Sumner did come, quirky and gentle under his bald, mottled dome, but deadly witty if aroused, and he was a great success with everyone. What was more important was that the whole experience of his youth in Sydney and the Blue Mountains was reopened for him. He went back to New York and wrote *Water under the Bridge*, which, with *Edens Lost*, was made into a TV serial; *Careful, He Might Hear You* was made into a film.

Sun Books never did get the rights to any of these books, but Sumner was so grateful to us that he insisted that we (as Macmillan) be given the hardback rights for Australia and New Zealand for another of his books. I was most touched when he told me that the whole course of his life was changed by my writing to him about *Edens Lost* and bringing his name before the Committee of Writers' Week. I mention this only to demonstrate how flimsy the links of Australian Literature were in the early 1970s, and how the old British Empire Rights system of publishing did so little in

Australia for Australian writers living outside their own country, unless someone or some organization got in there and pushed.

Some academics have been a great help in this process of making Australians aware of their own writers, and little-known ones from overseas, especially the younger ones of the Association for the Study of Australian Literature. But that was not founded until 1977. Meanwhile, it is to be regretted that some academics of great potential influence did at that time so little to encourage or help living Australian writers.

In 1974 Barry Humphries brought a highly succesful one-man show to Australia, with the typically ironic title of *At Least You Can Say You've Seen It*. The film of *Barry Mackenzie* had been a rousing success, despite or perhaps because of the censors giving it their most restrictive classification. At Sun-Macmillan we also risked a wrestle with censorship by publishing in Sun both *Barry Mackenzie* and its sequel, *Bazza Holds His Own*, with the Humphries text and Nick Garland's drawings.

It was almost uncanny to be with a Barry Humphries who now did not touch the amber fluid, or any other colour of alcohol. The only thing that worried me about his teetotalism was the boredom we boozers must now induce in him as the evening wore on.

Barry is, of course, a very complex character, but many people who know how funny he can be, and how fierce, might not know how kind he can be, sometimes in the most discreet and unexpected ways. Ninette and I had an example of this in August when we were in Melbourne for the wedding of one of the Sun-Macmillan staff. The day before the wedding also happened to be my birthday, and I went with Ninette to dinner at the Florentino. Barry and a serious-looking man with the appearance of a tax lawyer were sitting at a nearby table, and Barry came over for a chat, and wished me a happy birthday. He left the restaurant, with his sombre companion, before we did. When we had finished I asked for the bill, only to be told that Mr Humphries had already paid it.

The sale of Sun Books was no sudden source of affluence. The small amount that was left over after paying Sun Books' debts went into paying some of mine. Anlaby continued to be a constant drain, stemmed when desperate by the sale of a painting or books, and then, worst of all, by the sale of a couple of paddocks. The contemplation of past stupidity is only slightly less depressing than thinking about present idiocies, but I still cannot understand why I did not take some advice about Anlaby, not of a general kind such as that offered by Patrick, but of a practical nature. Apart from David Campbell who could have given some, an even more obvious source of good advice would have been Colin Angas who lived less than thirty miles away. Colin was not only a succesful farmer and an experienced member of the boards of several large companies, but a sympathetic, honest character who would have told me a few home truths about hanging on in the old family home. Collingrove, the old Angas family home where Chibs and I used to go as children, was now a National Trust property. But I blundered on, selling a couple of my father's Rowlandson drawings, or one of my own Arthur Boyd landscapes, when the bank manager lost his patience.

And my writing was also in trouble. I was bogged down with the German book. I had written some of it and then lost my way with the enormous amount of material available. Whatever happened in private, Poppy was a very efficient and imaginative research assistant; she knew how to follow up hunches, and had the imagination and intelligence to have hunches in the first place, which is essential for writing history or biography. But I could not find a thread which would join it all together. Once again, I might have taken some advice, although writers can really only help themselves. I had also been planning an Edwardian novel, something of my father's generation, but I could not make that take shape either.

Worst of all, because it was a good idea and money had been paid, was that I had had to abandon the Boyd-family biography. I still had the warm support of Arthur and David, the dying Martin's blessing and Robin's widow Patricia had promised any help that was needed. But I had run into implacable opposition from Guy and his wife, and the elder sister Helen. It was also strongly conveyed to me that the a'Beckett side of the family was against the book; this was easier to understand in those days, because the founder of the family fortunes had been a convict. This didn't seem to worry the senior member of the a'Beckett family, when I talked to him, but I supposed others might have brought pressure. Guy, who had originally been so helpful, now said that all the younger members of the family, most of whom seemed determined to become artists or sculptors, would somehow be spoiled by the publicity. A deeper reason was suggested to me by a friend — namely Martin's homosexuality which, it was true, would have had to come out. However, in his book *Much Else In Italy* Martin himself had already made it pretty clear to any percipient reader.

You cannot write a family biography and become involved in a family fight. And Guy was Martin's literary executor and could refuse me access to vital documents. So I wrote to Tom Rosenthal and told him I had had to give up the book, and I returned the advance, a very painful procedure.

All in all, apart from poetry which flourished on both joy and pain, my writing career was in a very bad way, littered with abandoned manuscripts like the shells of rusty cars beside the road. Fortunately, at this moment I was again unexpectedly rescued. Brian Stonier rang from Melbourne to say there was an offer of a book which would lead to a movie, and at last there might be some money in writing. Brian had been approached by some acquaintances in Sydney, Colin Chapman and his son Rob. They had by various means learned about the extraordinary story of a woman in the late nineteenth and early-twentieth centuries, who was known throughout the South Pacific as Queen Emma. She was half Samoan, half American, and had with one of her husbands founded a commercial empire based near what is now Rabaul. She had had a really wondrous love life, and her abilities as a business woman were astounding for the time and place. Her story had been briefly told by R.W. Robson, a pioneer in writing about the Pacific, and founder of the *Pacific Islands Monthly*, but his book was both dry and short, and there were many hints and sparse accounts to be followed up. For instance, Emma's sister Phebe, a most attractive personality, had been the subject of a long, and published, interview with Margaret Mead.

The vital figure in all this was Emma's great-nephew Bob Schultze, a man in his seventies who lived in Sydney and had made friends with Rob Chapman and his father. He not only had photographs and letters and printed records, but had lived in what is now New Britain for many years.

I met the Chapmans at the Macmillan office in South Melbourne, and agreed to write the book, which would have to take the form of a novel, for there were many gaps where the imagination would have to build on the meagre facts. Funds were available for me to go to Samoa and then to Germany, where there were members of Emma's family; and the centre of her empire had been in what used to be German New Guinea. Bob Schultze was agreeable to coming to Anlaby to stay for several days and talk about Emma and the family.

At the end of February I met Bob Schultze at Adelaide airport; he was a splendid-looking man with a high forehead and what would once have been called a noble countenance, with just enough of the Polynesian to give him a beautiful skin of a glowing brown. We walked over to the car with his bags, and as I was unlocking the door he said, in his deep and sonorous voice, "Geoffrey, before I come to stay in your house there is one thing you must know. I am a convicted felon, convicted of attempted murder."

This was the most potent stopper of polite conversation I have ever encountered. What could one say? — "Don't worry, Bob old chap, lots of my best friends are ..." or "Bob, of course I don't mind, things like that mean nothing". Or perhaps, "Oh Bob, the children will be thrilled". In the event, I think I just mumbled and smiled and opened the car door for him.

As we drove up to Anlaby he told me what had happened. Of German and Samoan origin, Bob had been a wild young man in New Guinea after World War I. He had gone with two Australians into country never before visited by white men, to recruit labour for the plantations around Rabaul. They had run into an ambush, arrows flying everywhere, and had opened fire to defend themselves. One of the tribesmen had been badly wounded. The court case came at a time when the Australians were very conscious of their situation as trustees of the Territory; there was also a lot of anti-German feeling remaining from the War. Bob had been made the scapegoat; he was convicted of attempted murder, and the two Australians were discharged.

In his years in gaol he had learnt accountancy, and was now a respected and successful accountant in Sydney. Bob was a flower of the old German civilization. He could quote Horace or Sophocles in the original Latin or Greek; I played the accompaniment (more or less) for him as he sang Schubert or Schumann in a beautiful bass voice. His aristocratic education in Germany showed in his impeccable carriage and manners, but he was totally devoid of any militarism.

The world he unfolded to me was quite new, and quite unlike the crudity of my own experiences in New Guinea and Bougainville. His memories played around the photographs of Emma and Phebe and the children on the verandah of the huge house above the bay by Rabaul, elegant in their long white dresses, their Polynesian-European faces glowing. Phebe was married to a famous German botanist; Emma put up with a variety of husbands but was more interested in her lovers.

Late in March Ninette and I arrived in Western Samoa. We stayed in Apia at the famous Aggie Grey's sprawling, flower-strewn hotel. I had never encountered Polynesian directness before. Aggie was a majestic old lady, allegedly seventy-six, still with a wicked glint in the eye, and on dance nights was out on the floor with the best of them. I gave her my card (specially printed for this trip). "Ah, Dutton," she sighed. "On the boat to New Zealand I was loved by a man called Dutton." Another sigh, and a sparkle in the eyes. "Ah, lovers!" Aggie spoke of her troubles with various "guvments" over her boundaries. Finally her friend in the Treasury had rung up and said, "Aggie, you got the Guvment by the balls."

Aggie told me that Samoan women are very intelligent. We were to go to dinner with Taisi Tupuola Efi, the Prime Minister, a lawyer educated in Auckland. "His wife Filifilia is a big reader, very bright, you watch out! Myself, I confess I have just been reading Germaine Greer, *The Female Eunuch.*" A sigh. "Ah, it is a very male world here."

Efi was a majestic but affable man, and Aggie was right about Filifilia. Efi apologized for his big house, which looked like something out of *Gone with the Wind*, built by the trader Hank Nelson, who had adopted him. Efi was from one of the Samoan royal families, of which he was now head, or Taisi Tupuola.

Polynesians are immediately physical. When I was due to meet one of Emma's relatives the next day, the handsome girl at the front desk put her arm around me, whirled me up the front steps and introduced me to him, saying, "How you like my new boyfriend?" The waiter put his hand on my shoulder to see if I had finished, saying, "I like your hair." The hotel was rich with music and flowers. Two young men played guitars by the courtyard, while one of the two waiters who brought us a plastic bowl for the flowers Filifilia had given us held it upside down and played it like a drum.

The Samoans I talked with all mocked Margaret Mead, telling me she had only been in American Samoa, that she did not know the language, that she had had her leg pulled. And this of the author of *Coming of Age in Samoa*, one of the most influential books in the Western world in the 1960s and 1970s and everybody's bible of promiscuity. All lies, said Efi and Filifilia and their friends; Samoans are very physical but very strict. All this was later to be discussed by Derek Freeman in his book on Margaret Mead, which provoked attacks on him by those who had made their reputations on her shaky foundations. In New York, on the way to Germany, I was to meet Margaret Mead in her fortress on top of the museum by Central Park. In her mid-seventies, she was a tiny little figure in a blue embroidered smock, treated like a goddess by her many assistants. She was very helpful to me about Emma, and about Phebe whom she had known well; Phebe worshipped her big sister. Margaret Mead said interesting things, such as how the Samoans looked down on the black New Britain natives, and how Emma always had a bodyguard of natives from Buka, the island off Bougainville.

In Germany I was pleased to be able to reopen communication between Bob Schultze and his aristocratic relations, who had refused to have anything to do with him after he had been sent to gaol. One old Baroness, the Samoan blood apparent in her lovely skin and regular features, told me how she had been educated by the nuns in Sydney and had then done medicine, something daring at that time for a woman, and of course unheard-of for a Polynesian. She said that when Emma moved into her mansion at Vaucluse she used to sweep into town in her four-in-hand, with two Buka "boys" seated in splendour on either side of the driver. But White Australia would not allow her to keep the Buka boys, nor her New Britain maids.

My next Literature Board meeting was in Canberra, and David Campbell asked me to stay for a few days. He was waiting to meet me at the airport; he had a new little Toyota, but I noticed it was already slewing to the left. When we reached the entrance to the property there was a ford over the creek; to maximise the car's ground clearance, David's stepson David Jones and I had to get out and walk across over the stones, while David in the Toyota crawled crashingly from one rock to the next.

David and Judy were happy and secure together. David showed me to my room, which was freezingly cold. He said "When you build one of these houses that come in sections, you lose your privacy. A fart in the bathroom echoes round the whole house." It certainly did, as I soon became aware — my room being next to the bathroom.

We drank and talked late about Yevtushenko, a great admirer of Daiv (as he spelt David's name). We agreed that we were not happy with Solzhenitsyn's religious truculence; the dangers inherent in the Old Believer's faith seemed to have as destructive a potential as communism. In Australia it was possible for life to be personal, for desperation to be individual, but in communist societies the individual is a potential traitor. In 1974 there had been bad news from Russia. Solzhenitsyn had been expelled from the USSR, branded as a traitor for writing *The Gulag Archipelago*. Yevtushenko and Solzhenitsyn by no means saw eye to eye, although Yevtushenko told me that when he read *The First Circle* in *samizdhat* typescript he thought it made Solzhenitsyn the greatest Russian novelist since Tolstoy. Now Zhenya had not only refused to give a public denunciation of Solzhenitsyn but had made an 1800-word protest to Brezhnev, which had been released in the West.

On the eve of his programmed gala reading from twenty years of his poems, due on peak viewing time on TV before an audience of tens of millions, the reading was cancelled. He described the reprisal as "immediate, crude and humiliating", and the situation as one where "Truth is replaced by silence and silence is actually a lie".

He was now a long way from flat tyres at Arkaroola. But he would never have gone into exile, here or anywhere else, because, as he said when we were camped by the road, "Without the Russian language around me I would die."

The Adelaide comedy continued. A woman rang me, saying she was secretary of the Christian Writers' Fellowship, whatever that was. She wanted to write a letter to the paper about Solzhenitsyn, and asked me, "Is he a Christian or an Orthodox Church?" I suggested they quote some of his own words about Christianity. "Oh, I've never read anything by Mr Solzhenitsyn," she replied sniffily.

In the morning it was so cold that there was frost right up the trees to their top leaves, and then the fog came down. Whatever was going wrong at Anlaby, I thanked fate that we had not moved here. Judy hacked the ice off the windscreen with a carving knife, and I hunched in the back of the little car on frozen toes.

It was the last day of my term on the Literature Board; all the "old guard" were leaving, which would make things very difficult for the new Board. Nancy Keesing was to succeed Geoffrey Blainey as Chairman; the inept official handling of this change led to Blainey's blaming Keesing, with unfortunate results. I had very much admired Geoff as a Chairman, but he was then, and is now, a puzzling character. He is also given to doing good works in secret. Joan O'Donnell told me that he had sent his own cheques to two Literature Board Fellowship holders in desperate straits, whose cheques had been delayed by the bureaucracy.

The next day I asked David Campbell, Humphrey McQueen and David Foster for lunch. I was pleased that I had launched David Foster, as a novelist with Macmillan, and recently as a poet in the new series Max Harris and I were publishing; Fay Zwicky's first book was in that same series. David, who had given up a prestigious scientific career for a life of poverty as a writer, was, as always, dark, shy, and elliptical, but available if he trusted the company. He was genuinely very modest about his poems; David Campbell liked them. Humphrey was sometimes confused in his thinking but attractively enthusiastic, especially about his students. In the current academic upheavals he was firmly on their side; quite rightly, he maintained that the teachers needed to learn. His boss, Manning Clark, had been unable to come to the lunch; we drank his health. Manning was much loved by all of us. Manning and David Campbell each had a very wild, unpredictable side to his character; each relished it in the other.

As so often when I returned home from such trips, I sailed straight into emotional storms with Ninette. This time it was not so much about my going away, but about the impossibility of continuing to live at Anlaby. The new girl helping Ninette in the house was hopeless; the house was just too big. But she didn't want to live anywhere else, and we didn't have the money to build a smaller house. Francis had had his first party, where one of the boys had vomited over the carpet, and a carload of gate-crashing girls had arrived. I didn't think these things worried Francis, any more than they worried me; it all seemed fairly normal teenage behaviour. But Ninette said that at that age (fifteen) "everything should be beautiful". Romantic idealism is terribly destructive, and not only for the idealist.

Thirty

In 1974 my book *White on Black; The Australian Aborigine Portrayed in Art* was published, coinciding in Adelaide with an exhibition in the State Gallery of some of the works reproduced in the book, which later went on tour to other galleries. It was the first exhibition to be composed entirely of portraits, by white artists, of the Australian Aborigines and the way of life under the impact of the white invasion. It was, in a way, symbolic of an awakening in Australian whites, that at last the Aborigines were becoming visible.

Prince Philip was paying a visit to Adelaide at the time, and I was asked to take him around the paintings and drawings. I could see that he was not particularly interested in them, but suddenly he stopped, jerked his jaw towards me and said, "You're the republican chappie, aren't you?" I congratulated him on his intelligence network. He said abruptly, barking out the last phrase, "Well, we'll go when you want us to, just tell us and we'll go!"

But what a slow business it was for us republicans, getting the message through to our fellow citizens that it was high time we told them they must go. I thought that another Sun Books symposium might help. Brian and Max were in agreement, so I set about sending letters to potential contributors. This time the tone would be more urgent.

I did not have to go any further than my own children to find how Australians needed educating about republicanism. Before our second book on republicanism appeared, there was a TV programme on the occasion of the Queen's fiftieth birthday. Apparently in the course of this programme there had been a reference to me as a republican. Sam (aged twelve) told me that after this he had had a rough time from his fellow students at Pembroke (a particularly enlightened school in many ways). They told him that if Australia left the monarchy and became a republic there would be nobody left to defend us. Francis (aged seventeen), who was listening, said, "You want to leave that subject alone, Sam, you'll never get anywhere with it. When I was at boarding school [at Scotch College in about 1972] they held me down in the street and rubbed cigarette butts out of the gutter all over my face because my old man was a republican and a communist." The parents who had given these children their ideas were from affluent, middle-class Adelaide, and no doubt all supporters of the Vietnam War.

Looking through my notebooks of the time, nearly twenty years later, I

Bryn Davies, Max Harris and Geoff at the launch of *Australian Letters*, Adelaide, 1957 (Adelaide *Advertiser*)

Jim Gosse, John and Geoff Dutton, 1959, at Alice Springs Telegraph Station, during fiftieth-anniversary trip from Adelaide to Darwin in Harry Dutton's 1908 Talbot

Patrick White, Kangaroo Island, 1963

Jock Marshall, 1965

Bella Akhmadulina, Tbilisi, 1966

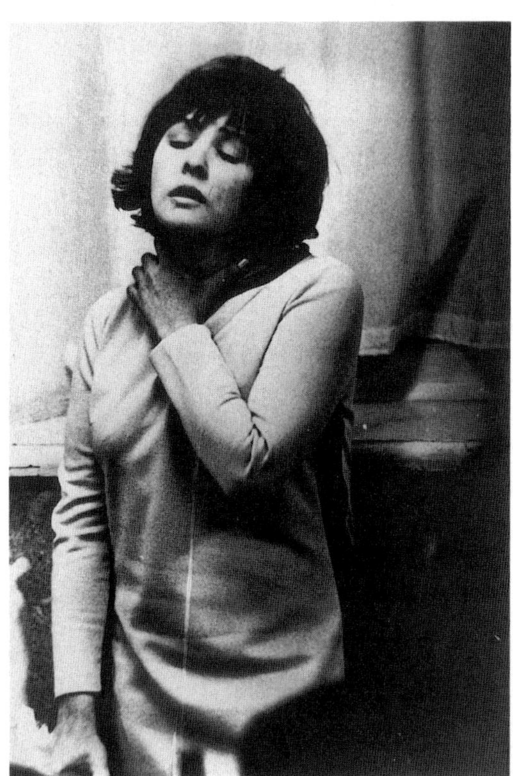

Yevgeny (Zhenya) Yevtushenko, Anlaby, 1966
(Igor Mezhakoff-Koriakin)

Zhenya with Geoff at Anlaby 1966 (Igor Mezhakoff-Koriakin)

Barry Humphries, Brian Stonier and Geoff, 1968

Geoff, 1968 (Mark Strizic)

Igor Mezhakoff-Koriakin, Stockholm, 1970 (Igor Mezhakoff-Koriakin)

Chibs and Dick Blackburn, Darwin, 1971

Lawrence Daws and Edit Richards, 1971 (Lawrence Daws)

Zhenya at Arkaroola, 1973

Zhenya and Patrick White, 1973 (John Fairfax & Sons)

Bob Brissenden, left, and David Campbell, c. 1975 (Rosemary Brissenden)

Henri Bastin, 1979 (Harri Peccinotti)

John Dutton by Barry Humphries
(Barry Humphries)

John Olsen, 1981

Robin, Pearl Beach, 1983

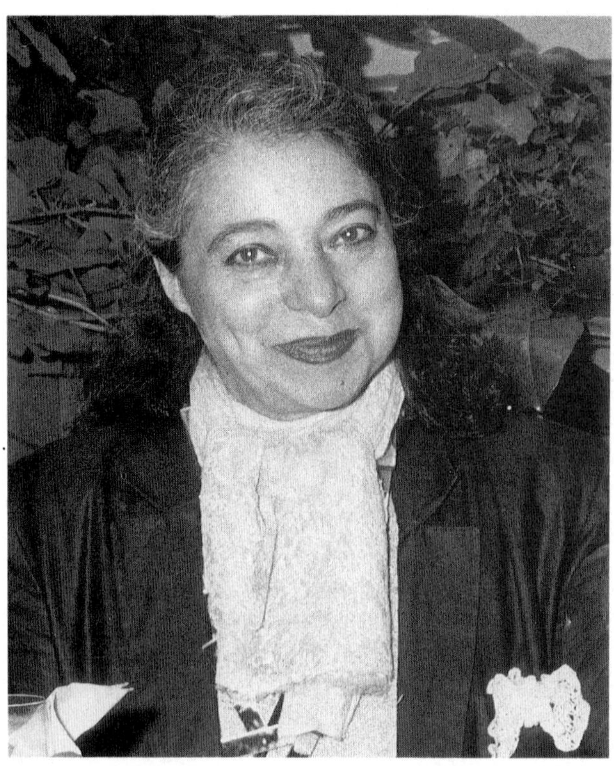

Mirka Mora, 1985 (Jon Lewis)

Colin Lanceley, 1985 (Jon Lewis)

Kay Lanceley, 1985 (Jon Lewis)

Bob Hughes, Rocky Point, 1988

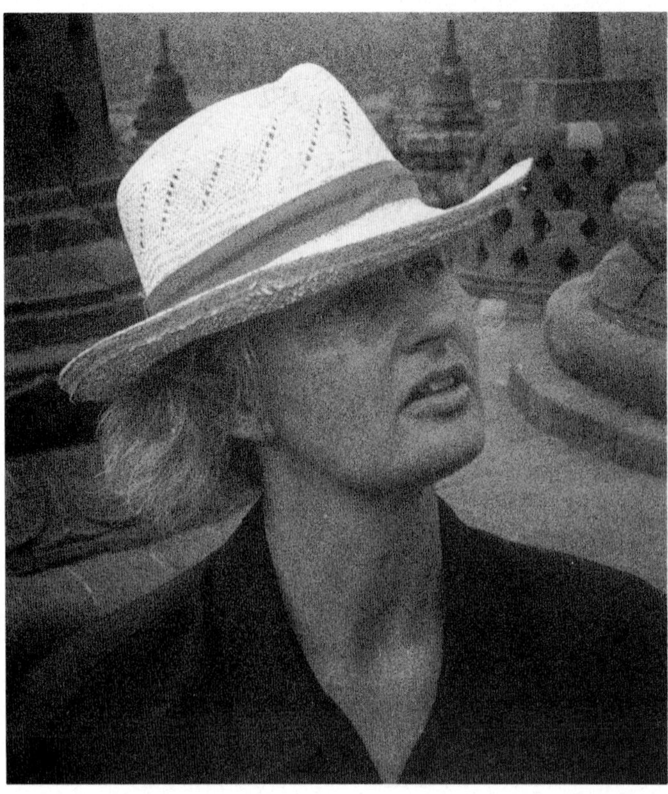

Robin at Borobudur,
Indonesia, 1989

Tenth anniversary of David Campbell's death, Canberra, 1989, left to right: Bob Brissenden, Alan Gould, Rosemary Dobson, Manning Clark, Alec Hope, Geoff, Geoff Page, David Brooks (National Library of Australia)

Arthur Boyd and Barry Humphries, Bundanon, 1990

Yvonne Boyd, Bundanon, 1990

Peter Carey and son Sam, Mudgee, 1990

Initial Committee of Australian Republican Movement, left to right, from end of table: Donald Horne, Harry Seidler, Neville Wran, Franca Arena, Jenny Kee, Franco Belgiorno-Nettis, Colin Lanceley, Geoff, Faith Bandler (absent, Geraldine Doogue, Tom Keneally, Malcolm Turnbull, David Williamson)

Lawrence Daws, Geoff and Oscar, Glasshouse Mountains, 1993

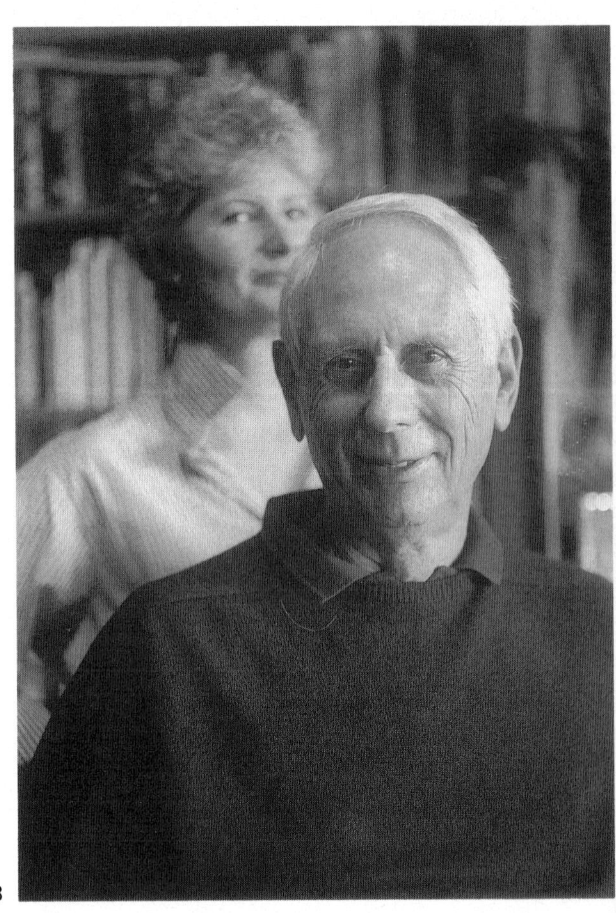

Robin and Geoff, 1993

am appalled to see how many pages record desperate depressions, fits of black melancholy, some to do with Ninette's own depressions, some of them to do with the on-and-off relationship with Poppy, some to do with money and Anlaby, perhaps the worst to do with my own inability to snap out of it. Some days I felt as if a great growth inside me had been torn out by the roots, but instead of my being made whole again, another was growing as fast as an Indian magician's mango tree.

I had been rereading *Anna Karenina* and responding to Levin's agonies of doubt and melancholy, which almost lead him to suicide. But he is like Hamlet, thinking makes it so; when he stops this sort of thinking and changes to action and goes and works on his property, the agonies disappear. As I checked the water troughs at Cassia while the children went round the paddocks on their ag-bikes, I thought such certainties were available to me, like Levin's mowing, albeit less poetic — in my case feeding the pigs or lamb-marking with Harold and Marc. But Levin's next step was not available to me. No peasant would unwittingly bring my lost soul to God. I felt no bond with Christianity. Perhaps a lack of religion was the trouble. I could hear Poppy laugh at such self-deception. But perhaps another sort of self-deception was the trouble.

Levin's answer does not stop at the certainties of action, but goes on to religion. Levin, despite having so much of Tolstoy in him, is a landowner, not a writer, and it is legitimate for him to be a man of action. An explorer or a soldier may write a book, but the professional writer cannot be a man of action. I was always seduced by wanting to do as well as write. It's a dingy life being a writer; look at Patrick's, and he also steered clear of most writers. I tended to be guided by a dangerous remark of Byron's: "One hates an author that's *all author*, fellows / In foolscap uniforms turn'd up with ink". It is a useful warning, but not true that writers who are all writers miss out on life, which is supposed to be their subject. It is a mystery, but writers both cease to be all writers, and are writers more than ever, when like Hopkins they look at a hawk, when like Kenneth Slessor they look at the waters of Sydney Harbour, when like Elizabeth Bishop they look at an old fishing shed, or when like Yeats they simply look at "that girl standing there".

Yeats's cry, "But O that I were young again / And held her in my arms!", is pure sex, the way we were as young men in the Air Force, with all those fuckable girls who lusted after us as much as we lusted after them. For a writer, especially for a poet, both sex and love can open the door to life. For lovers, life is no longer dingy, and lovers can both do and be. There are two dominant dangers, among many more. One is of triviality, of the predator snapping up the sexual snacks. The other is of playing games; lovers can be manipulated in a destructive obsession, as it was with Poppy and me. It was off, and then it was on again. Alexander Pope, physically incapable of a boisterous life, knew exactly what tyranny can rule a lover: "Beauty draws us with a single hair".

As a writer, I could not complain at being obsessed, because my attempts to understand such a tortuous and painful and then rewarding love led to poem after poem. A hundred other poets had cursed their weakness and then drawn strength from it. I turned to my old friend, the wise Montaigne, who was always quoting poetry but was not a poet. He gave me good advice about Poppy. " 'If your affection in love be over-powerfull, disperse or dissipate the same', say they; and they say true, for I have often, with profit made triall of it: Breake it by the vertue of severall desires, of which one may be Regent or chiefe Master, if you please; but for feare it should misuse and tyrannize you, weaken it with dividing."

Poppy had a blonde, witty, cynical friend, Jill. One day the three of us had lunch together in a restaurant not far from my room in the city. After the food and wine Poppy went to the library to work on her research on *Queen Emma*. Jill and I went to the room. No talk of love, no anguish, a lot of laughter. Maybe this was another of Poppy's games. Maybe she had set it up — both of us researching.

One aspect of living where problems could not be weakened by dividing was money. Somehow or another I had to find at least twenty-five thousand dollars to appease the bank. Arthur Boyd's beautiful *Lucerne Field*, one of his best Wimmera landscapes, the one I had bought when I opened his exhibition all those years ago, went off to Joseph Brown in Melbourne. There was a horrible gap on the wall where it had hung, over the fireplace in the dining room. I found another painting downstairs, to hang in the space, but its inadequacy was almost worse than the blank space. I began to feel that if we stayed at Anlaby we would end up living in empty rooms.

Ninette was also depressed. Suddenly during dinner one night she said she had spent an awful day convinced of her total inadequacies, thinking she must be going mad like her mother or her old friend May Osborn, wife of the Professor of Botany at Oxford, who had been so good to her when I was living in college. Motherly but brilliant May, who had been Howard Florey's most valuable assistant in his researches, later suffered from Alzheimer's disease. Abilities were no defence. Ninette seemed really to mean it. "I'm going mad." I tried to convince her otherwise, by many different examples of her control of life and people, but there was not the usual flood of giving in to what I was saying.

I began writing my novel on Queen Emma on 8 February 1975, on one of those days in a prolonged heatwave, when the landscape seems to be holding its breath lest it breathe in flame, when there is the faintest rumble of thunder and promise of rain, but nothing comes. But I began to write, it flowed, and I was full of hope. I remembered Patrick telling me that he had written his best in his worst bouts of asthma.

Queen Emma was eventually published in London and Melbourne in 1976. I wrote it as the memories, and in the different voices, of twenty-two different characters. Most reviewers did not like this approach, although I recall with gratitude the young Marion Halligan's enthusiastic review in the *Canberra Times*. She recalled T.S. Eliot: "He do the police in different voices". Meanwhile, the movie kept disappearing over the horizon. Rob Chapman and his wife went to live in Hollywood, and the names of famous directors and actors kept flashing onto my horizon, and then the money would fall through and the whole process would start again. At one stage I was asked to write quickly a bit part for Laurence Olivier, who was very keen to play Emma's near-neighbour, Eduard Hernsheim; Hernsheim had loved to declaim Shakespeare in German, which he said (as a number of Germans do) sounded much better than the English. I longed to hear Olivier intoning, "*Sein, oder nicht sein …*".

But one plan after another fell through, until finally, many years later, Emma appeared as a TV mini-series, with an ageing Hollywood sex-symbol playing Emma in one of the worst, and certainly most embarrassing, productions I have ever seen. As I was stupid enough at the time of the original contract not to have an agent, I was to find that I had been trapped, and thus had no say in the butchery of my novel, with all the work that had gone into it. Tim Curnow, when he came on the scene, did his best for me, but was unable to do anything about that original contract.

March lurched along in a series of minor disasters. One of them might have been major. We were burning off in the paddock west of the mile-long avenue leading to the house when a willy-willy came out of nowhere and picked up some flaming stubble, taking it right across the avenue, with its road and double row of trees, and dumping it in the adjoining paddock. In a moment flames were stealthily moving across the paddock towards the group of trees by the fence. Marc and I hurried around with the tractor and water tank and pump on the trailer and sprayed across the front of the fire. Suddenly we were trapped, caught between the flames and the trees, and we could not get out. Neither Marc nor I could see; I had never fully realized the denseness of fire and smoke — you can't see or breathe. Fortunately we emerged through a gap in the trees, singed but safe. I was glad that the tractor was a diesel. By this time the wind had freshened, and the fire was fanning it, and I was afraid it would jump the main road and set fire to our neighbour's late crop. But we managed to hold it at the road.

I have found that I can usually talk more easily with women than men — I mean those long, desultory, uninhibited conversations where neither is putting on an act. In Adelaide there were few men with whom I could have such talks. There had been Lawrence Daws, but he and Edit Richards had taken off for Queensland after stirring Adelaide with a double marital break-up. Although I had friends, and plenty of acquaintances, Max Harris was the only person left to whom I could really talk.

In one of those great *aperçus* which can cut two ways, like Blake's "Energy is Eternal Delight", Byron suggested that "Man, being reasonable, must get drunk". This can mean that man, being sensible and rational, must think it a good thing to get drunk. It can also mean that man, cursed with the limitations of reason, must get drunk. The next line is also double-edged: "The best of life is but intoxication". Max and I frequently got drunk, at long lunches that ended dangerously with a bottle of port. It was all very well for Max, he had his chauffeur waiting with the Daimler to take him home; I usually had to drive sixty miles. Fortunately, although I was not a believer, St Christopher must have been looking after me, and I always got home safely.

Max when young had been the champion of new and often difficult writers. After the Ern Malley affair he became very conservative, especially with new poetry, although he rightly never abandoned his stance over Ern. But around 1975 he seemed to have taken on more confidence, and in a new series we published first books by Fay Zwicky, David Foster and others. The books were well designed and printed, and we could never have produced them without Max's Mary Martin Book List, which by now had subscribers not only all over Australia, but in Papua-New Guinea and places further afield as well.

Most important of all, for me, was that Max and I could talk about poetry without prejudice. He had even written some new poems himself. Only with David Campbell could I talk at a deeper and more satisfying and critical level than with Max. So wrong-headed and crudely journalistic in many of his pronouncements in his column in the *Australian*, he preserved his integrity with poetry, and he was honest and helpful with my work.

Like thousands of other people, I was profoundly moved by the end of the Vietnam War. In one way or another, against the French or the Americans, it had gone on for over thirty years; only those of us over forty-five could fully remember the story. I could never quite feel the same again about otherwise good, sensitive, honest and liberal people, men and women, who never protested against Australia's shameful involvement in the later stages of the war. These middle-aged people in the professions or in business were not prepared to alienate their clients. It seemed an added insult that it was by a lottery that their sons were selected for a war very few of them believed in.

At the beginning of 1976 everything was happening at once. After four years, and all those partings which had seemed so real but were not, Poppy and I were not seeing each other any more. I wrote in my diary: "She says I know her better than she does herself, and in many ways it's true — but at the deepest level I don't understand her at all".

As the Anlaby crises became more frequent, I enlisted the aid of an adviser from the Department of Agriculture. He said that with our small acreage I was on the right track with the pigs, and that I should build a big new piggery and dramatically increase the numbers of breeding sows. Special low-interest agricultural loans were available for such projects, and he would recommend me for one. To fill some of the debt hole, we sold Cassia, to the sadness of the family.

I was also, as Chairman of Adelaide Festival Writers' Week, involved in some desperate dramas about visitors from overseas. Alberto Moravia, James Baldwin, Erica Jong, Kurt Vonnegut and several others had accepted invitations but in the last few weeks they began to drop out. Anthony Steel, the Festival Director, had actually been to Baldwin's house in the South of France and given him his air ticket to Adelaide, but a week before the Festival a cable arrived to say he could not come. Kurt Vonnegut rang me from New York and said his literary agent had just got him a contract so valuable he had to begin work immediately. Moravia cabled from North Africa to say he had pleurisy.

The press always picked up those who weren't coming, and did not mention those who did come, writers such as Wole Soyinka, Shirley Hazzard and her husband Francis Steegmuller, and Robie Macauley, who were of the front rank anyway. That most appealing Maori writer, Hone Tuwhare, said to me on arrival, "It makes one feel guilty not to be James Baldwin."

He need not have felt that way. One of the most valuable achievements of Writers' Week was to bring to Australia writers from the Commonwealth like Soyinka and Tuwhare and the many who came from Canada, Samoa, India, Japan, the Philippines and the West Indies, all helping to dislodge the stiff old London-New York axis and replace it with a flexible global community of writers in English. The history of the Booker Prize in later years demonstrates how powerful this movement has been. Lawrence Durrell was right when he spoke that night at his house about the exfoliation of literature in English.

The Festival was early in March, and it was very hot. I felt terrible, with what seemed to be some sort of flu, but kept going. By the poetry reading in the tent in the late afternoon of the day after the opening, I was on fire. I went to the doctor; I had a temperature of 104 degrees, and another attack of pneumonia. I spent the rest of Writers' Week in bed at Anlaby with more whirling black visions. I also missed the launch of *Queen Emma*.

A week later, and a stone lighter, I began to feel human again.

One of the genuine achievements of this particular Writers' Week was the tent. It took proceedings out of the stuffy and crowded rooms of the State Library into an independent and stylish ambience. The only writer to disapprove of the tent was the poet Les Murray, who wrote a most offensive article about it, which claimed that Rosemary Wighton (who took over the Chair when I went down with pneumonia) and I were demeaning writers by putting them into a tent. I have always thought that the real reason, or irrational cause, for this outburst from the usually amiable Les was that as a child, going to country shows, he was used to seeing the permanent galvanized-iron sheds used for the prize stock, while the sideshows were under canvas.

You need a strong stomach to be a farmer. That year one of our sows had a bad sore on its shoulder; Marc rang the vet who told him what ointment to put on it. Marc kept her in for a couple of days, and when it seemed to be better, turned her out into the paddock. The next day he saw her walking around with a crow on her back, and the crow was hauling meat out of the hole it had made in the sow's shoulder. "He was going so deep you could see the strings coming out," said Marc.

Cassia was sold and the stock had to go, even though the season was so poor and wool prices so low that we could not expect to get more than forty cents each for the three hundred ewes. The proceeds would scarcely pay for the truck to take them to the abattoirs. The shorn ewes stood with drooping heads and hipbones high as the Himalayas. Young Kleinig, the truck-driver, cursed their weak stubbornness and his over-excited dogs and "those bloody city bastards that get fifty dollars a day for handing the tea around. I've worked both city and country and I know where the bludgers are." There was a little lamb (born after shearing) with its mother, and he said, "Can I have that one? My little boy loves to bring 'em up. He got two dollars for the wool off the one he has now." He popped it into the cage on the side of the semitrailer with the sheepdogs, Trixie and Jake. "They won't do it any harm, keep it warm." City people can never understand the tension between cruelty and kindness in the country.

In the spring of 1976, the Anlaby garden foaming with blossom, a totally unexpected ray of light suddenly appeared through the financial gloom. Rigby, the old Adelaide-based publishers, had asked me to edit an anthology of Australian poetry from the beginnings to the present day, which was to be a large hardback. It took a lot of work and research, but I was rather proud of the result, as it covered the whole period of verse in Australia. It was quite a handsome production, except that the jacket, to my annoyance, bore an Australian flag of which by far the most prominent feature was the Union Jack. I didn't expect to make any money out of it, but suddenly a cheque for $2,500 arrived. I was ecstatic. Max said to me "I suppose you realize that's about an academic's salary for one month?" The anthology was later taken up by Lloyd O'Neil and reprinted with an enlarged text — but with a very different jacket.

In September Ninette and I were asked to a surprise party for Don

Dunstan's fiftieth birthday. Don had done great things for South Australia, especially for the Aborigines and the Arts, and in general dragged South Australia out of its torpid sloth, and away from the deadening influence of the Establishment and the Adelaide Club. His predecessors Tom Playford and Steele Hall had put some of this process into motion. Playford was regarded in the Adelaide Club (of which, of course, he was never a member) as being a damn Commo for taking over the electricity company and making it a state enterprise. Steele Hall had restructured the electorate, thus abolishing the gerrymander that had kept Playford in power all those years, and ensuring his own defeat. He had also supported the Festival and begun the Festival Centre.

Don had been Playford's most redoubtable opponent, and it was good to see Playford at this birthday party; he was looking scrubbed and shiny, and said, "I won't have to worry about the breathalyzer driving home, not like you mob of youngsters." David Williamson, at this other Don's party, towered over Gough Whitlam who loomed over Don and made the expected good speech, but with an unexpected generous reference to Playford. Don was in tears, his arm around his beautiful Chinese-Malaysian wife Adèle. Although most of us did not know, she must already have been very ill; her early death was a tragedy.

Towards the end of the year I was staying with Patrick for the first performance of Nigel Butterley's *Sometimes With One I Love*, for which I had made the selections from Walt Whitman. (I was later to find out that Patrick had financed the production.) We had an argument that raged, quietened while he had his evening bath, and then started up again, like a bushfire that has crept under fallen leaves.

We put away a couple of bottles of red before dinner, with some snacks. He accused me of "running away to the country", "false innocence"; I should have been sticking it out in the city where I'd find out how awful life is. He was feeling guilty that he had been conning his niece Frances, who was living with them, by telling her she should be optimistic. I said I thought he was in a bad state if he could not encourage a teenage girl to think optimistically, it was like shitting on flowers. He began to weep, pretending that he had flipped a piece of cheese into his eye, and said, "But I love the flowers." I said I wanted him to understand that flowers and shit can happily coexist. He said he was looking forward to being dead. After his bath it all started up again. He said he did not mean he wanted to kill himself, no, he had too much still to say. But he envied the peace of the dead.

I noticed the paintings in the house had been rearranged. Patrick explained that he had presented a number of them to the Art Gallery of New South Wales. Patrick's opinions about art were not always based on aesthetic judgement, as exemplified in the case of John Olsen. Patrick had told me that in his opinion Olsen was the best of the younger painters, and he bought some of his work, including the very fine painting that hung in the place of honour on the wall at the head of the table in the dining room. But, later on, when Olsen became a Trustee of the Art Gallery of New South Wales, he and John Coburn ("Laurel and Hardy", Patrick called them) rightly criticized the poor quality of many of the paintings Patrick was presenting to the Gallery. This immediately got back to Patrick, as things invariably did, and from then on Olsen was OUT. Patrick thereafter referred to John's painting as "brown knitting", and got rid of his Olsens.

The ABC had been in touch with me about a TV history of South Australia, which they wanted me to write and narrate to camera. It was to be a six-part series. This seemed like a worthwhile challenge, and it would also bring in some money, if not very much. The producer was to be Paula Nagel, a very capable woman I had known for some time; she was both a trained historian and an experienced performer on radio and TV, so admirably suited for the job. I was also lucky enough to have Warren Seip and Mike Piper, both first-rate professionals, on camera and sound. To my astonishment, Warren, a big, tough, thoughtful man with tattoos on his arms, the best and most unmistakable type of Australian, was a monarchist. I soon realized that he, like most Australians, had never thought seriously about the country becoming a republic. I was rather pleased that by the end of the filming I had converted him. But he wasn't sure what his wife was going to say.

I hadn't realized how much work the series was going to take, both in research and in shaping the text so that it could fit in with the camera. And of course I had to learn it all off by heart. The experience itself of recording the programmes was fascinating, if exhausting. For programmes such as these there are several factors which have to be absolutely right: the weather and time of day; the level of noise, especially traffic; the holding at bay of the groups of spectators which always gather, regarding the filming as a free show and calling out comments that immediately stop the take. The narrator has then to remember what he was saying, and crank himself back into the same tone of voice as before the interruption.

On one occasion we were in the lovely old town of Gawler, my mother's birthplace, outside the gate that is all that remains of the Martin Engineering Works that had such an influence on the history of the town. There had to be five takes of a simple short scene; two were caused by voices from the spectators, two by a motorbike and a truck, and the fifth by a dogfight.

We drove out to the far west to film the Nullarbor Plain and the great cliffs by the Southern Ocean; it rains about six inches a year out there, if the farmers are lucky. It rained all those six inches the night we arrived. We had to stay three days in a fairly primitive motel, drinking brandy and playing canasta, until the mud hardened.

The most exhausting day of all was at Blanchetown on the River Murray; the temperature was 110 degrees Fahrenheit, and just when I was near the end of a long take a car-full of yobbos went past and yelled into the microphone.

Back at Anlaby I blessed my ancestors for the underground rooms, one of which I used as a study. The thermometer by the front door, in the shade, read 109 degrees. Down in my study it was 66 degrees. The grotto with the mirror where the thrush had sung to himself, and the arches outside my window, were black with thousands of blowflies; I could always tell when it was going to be a hot day as they were gathering there in clouds even when I began work at 5 a.m.

At 8.30 a.m. on Boxing Day morning Ninette, Tisi, Sam and I fed the pigs, and I returned still smelling of them, something you have to get used to if you keep pigs. It is just like it is in Elizabeth Bishop's poem "The Prodigal": "The brown enormous odor ... with its breathing and thick hair". Suddenly there was a sound of a vehicle coming up the avenue, and then a taxi came in the gate and pulled up in front of the house. A taxi! Sixty miles from Adelaide? It was Henri Bastin.

Henri had recently had a succesful show in Sydney, and sixty miles in a taxi was nothing to him. Out of the back of the car and out of the boot came all his presents: a huge brown-paper-and-bamboo kite for Sam; five life-size cardboard cats to hang from the fruit trees to keep the rosellas and starlings away; ingenious ashtrays made from his tobacco tins. He picked up a small dry gourd and said, "Geoffroi, how you call this one?" A few minutes later he handed it to Tisi; it was now a beautiful dragonfly. He was brimming with suggestions for growing avocados under the rose-arches. "What for you no grow avocados here?" Under his silver ankle he now had a specially made shoe with a sole about two inches thick, and he hardly limped any more.

Kangaroo Island still remained a mighty fortress. In recent times there had been some notable occasions at Rocky Point. Arthur and Yvonne Boyd had come down, and Arthur had made some drawings from the ink of the squid we had netted when night fishing. He sat on the veranda drawing, not in the least minding the group of children watching him. Manning and Dymphna Clark came; Dymphna went for enormous walks along the beaches while Manning, needless to say, indulged in his favourite occupation, fishing. Manning sometimes lost his balance, and was not always very sure on his feet, and when we were fishing for sweep in the South Coast surf I could see he was not too happy about going right out to the edge of the reef. So I found him a more sheltered spot, where the fish were biting, not wanting to risk losing him as well as nearly finishing off Patrick White.

In May we went with David Campbell down to Manning and Dymphna's beautiful beach house at Wapengo, in the bush and spotted-gum forest.

After lunch Manning said we should all go fishing off the rocks. It seemed much too rough to me, but he was the local expert, so we went. He said the best spot was down on a ledge near the water, where there was just enough room for three to fish. He went to another spot, further up the cliff. We had caught only one fish, in the boiling water and foam, when a wave came straight at us. Being on a ledge, we had no way to retreat, as we had on the Kangaroo Island reef. We linked arms and it hit us green in our faces. Somehow we were still there, drenched, when the wave retreated. Manning waved cheerfully from above. It was some strange test, the Dionysian side of Manning.

Returning home, I started once more on the book about the Germans in Australia, and it seemed at last to be coming into shape. But Manning's giant wave was not the only one threatening me. I was having recurring dreams of surfing on the South Coast at Kangaroo Island, at Pennington Bay where I had gone since childhood. A lovely big wave was coming up, and I was preparing to catch it, when suddenly it kept on and on, growing until a hundred feet of bottle-green water was gleaming above me. Other dreams were about seeing the children being swept into a giant whirlpool the size of the Anlaby house. It did not need Carl Jung to tell me what was causing the dreams, but I had pinned my hopes on the new pigshed to restore our fortunes. The shed was certainly big enough, and Marc, from being a kind of Sergeant-Major of pigs was now a Major at least, with two hundred sows in his command.

In the meanwhile, a partial rescue operation had been launched from New York, of all places. Some years ago I had become good friends with Greg Vitiello, a wiry, humorous New Yorker of Italian descent. He was editor of a very handsome magazine, *Pegasus*, which was published in about five languages by Mobil; it was not for sale, but sent around the world to Mobil's customers and others worth impressing. It was one of capitalism's little incidental benefits for writers, as it paid very well; it was also very elegant in the use Greg made of artists and photographers. Greg had enlisted the services of a brilliant designer in London, Derek Birdsall, to handle the production and artwork. Each issue had a theme; Greg would invite me to contribute an essay on any subject I liked which would fit in with his theme. It was most enjoyable work.

Greg was also in charge of Mobil's publishing programme, and had been responsible for some magnificent books about various regions of the world. He now wanted me to do one on Australia, a kind of historical and present-day discussion of how Australia came to be the way it is, with a firm background of the land and the cities. I would work with Harri Peccinotti, one of the most talented English photographers, based in London and New York. Harri, whose main source of income was fashion photography, later told me with relish that his real name was Harry Peck. The fashion houses were much more impressed with the Italian label.

I asked Greg how much interference I would have to put up with from Mobil management. He promised me there would be none, and the book was to be subtitled "A Personal View". In the event he was as good as his word. The only interference I received was an appeal from Jim Leslie, Chairman of Mobil in Australia, asking me if it would be possible to cut my five anti-Joh Bjelke-Petersen anecdotes to two or three.

Money was at that stage no object with Mobil. Greg suggested Cairns for our preliminary discussions, as it was winter. I told him and the Mobil-Australia representative, Jim Cass, that the only major region of Australia with which I was totally unfamiliar was the north-west of Western Australia. So it was arranged that a hire car would be made available in Perth so that Ninette and I could drive up to Broome and into the Kimberleys, and on to Darwin. When I had completed the first draft of the book, Harri would make a journey right around Australia following my tracks.

Patrick exploded when I told him about the book. How could I take money from a multinational, especially an American one, etc. etc. No mention of my successful insistence on independence, nor of my financial need, of course. I was much amused when, some time later, he was involved in the establishment of the Belvoir Street Theatre in Sydney, a co-operative theatre company. Esso contributed a large sum towards the company's first production, Patrick's play *Signal Driver*. Unfortunately, such hypocrisies under the guise of integrity were becoming more and more frequent with Patrick, and he was surrounding himself with admirers who thought he could do no wrong. What he really needed was the presence of a few friends who would not be afraid to give him a kick in the arse from time to time. As it was, a recent letter had said, "I grow more embittered every day". And more determined to keep it that way, I thought to myself.

Another card at much the same time said, "Wrote you a long letter in reply to yours about the good that is to be found in country life and turning one's back on public causes then I felt it was too savage to send!" I wish he had sent it. Maybe I could have drawn up a chart to see who had supported the most "public causes". His periodic madness, for want of a better term, and his egotism disguised as public virtue, was becoming worse and worse, exacerbated, as always, by his dealings with the theatre or cinema. The film of *Voss* was now definitely off, and his producer, Harry Miller, had, according to Patrick, turned into a complete monster.

I found it amusing how our roles seemed to have been reversed. Originally it was I that was the flibbertigibbet, running round on public affairs when I should have been sitting at home writing. Then I had been told that, like the Russians, I should retire to my estate. Now I was spending most of my time at home working, while Patrick was leading marches or going down to Melbourne to make speeches, always saying what agony it was for him, but in fact adoring being a public figure. Various people whom he had despised were now in postures of adulation, espousing the causes he expoused, and so in his opinion they had become very serious and worthwhile citizens.

I had lunch with Tass Drysdale in Sydney, who suddenly started talking about his paintings of years ago; this was something he rarely did, but he was prompted by my mentioning Oscar Wilde's crack about nature imitating art. Tass said that *Moody's Pub*, in the National Gallery of Victoria, one of his most famous paintings, was based on some vague memories of a pub at Seymour in Victoria. Now the pub had been altered, and given verandahs, to make it look like his painting. For another painting, *Mullalloona Tank*, he had made up the name. This painting was in an exhibition in Adelaide, and Robert Campbell, the Gallery Director, had rung up to ask him where Mullalloona was; Tass wriggled out of that one by saying, "Oh, up north". Campbell then asked him how to spell it. "Geoff," Tass said, "I had to think quickly. I said, 'Doubles all the way'. 'Like Woolloomooloo?' Campbell asked. 'Yes, that's it,' I said." In fact, Campbell left out one 'l' as in Woolloomooloo, and it appears in catalogues as "Mullaloona".

In another case of art and life, I remembered Tass telling me, when I was working on the book about him, how he stopped for a drink at Mullengandra, near Albury, on his way down to Melbourne. He had done a painting of the landlord standing outside the pub, and called it *George Ross of Mullengandra*. A yellowing print of the painting was pinned above the bar. Tass said to George Ross, "George, I'm sorry I had to leave out the beautiful elms outside your pub." George replied, "Don't think about it, Tass, them elms were buggers to sucker anyhow."

Drysdale had a most complex relationship with nature. Being a countryman at heart, he did not sentimentalize it. Being a scientist by inclination, he loved to examine its particular details, although he never painted them. When he put a figure into the landscape he did not tell a story, but provoked a mystery. I had been reading Ruskin before this meeting with him, and found a passage which I thought very relevant to Drysdale's ability to see, albeit with only one eye. "The greatest thing a human soul ever does in this world is to see something, and tell what he saw in a plain way ... To see clearly is poetry, prophesy and religion ... Nature is never distinct and never vacant, always mysterious but always abundant, you always see something, but you never see all." (Of course, "abundance" is not quite the word you would use about nature in Drysdale's landscapes.)

For many years I had liked Jeffrey Smart's paintings, but had met him only briefly, as he was living in Italy. Ursula often spoke of him, and was obviously very fond of him as well as being an admirer of his work. Now at last I met him on an occasion when there was time for talk. I had opened an exhibition in Adelaide of Fred Williams's paintings, and then gone on to dinner with Dee Jones, herself a successful painter. Jeffrey was there, and I soon realized how witty he was, and what a wonderful raconteur. He had known and enjoyed my mother's style, and had some classic stories about her which only he could tell. He had also been a very close friend of Mic Sandford, that uncharacteristic Adelaide man who had been one of those mysterious wartime army officers who were not at all army types, but were probably in some sort of Intelligence outfit.

Barry Humphries was back in Australia for another of his one-man shows; as I was to be in Sydney in a couple of days at that time, he suggested we might have lunch together, and invited me to see the show. He went on, rather diffidently, to say he would very much like to see Patrick again, and perhaps I could arrange that the three of us have lunch together. Patrick, always an admirer of Barry, had often said how much he would like to see him again, so I rang and asked if he would come along to the lunch. There was a long pause. Then Patrick said, in his slowest voice, "Oh no, dear me, definitely no. It would take me at least a fortnight to get my act together for Barry Humphries."

Barry was disappointed when I rang him. I was disappointed for another reason, as I thought it was yet another example of Patrick's increasing tendency to want to be in control. He knew very well that with Barry there would not be the faintest chance of that. Barry was one person he would never be able to bully. Innocently I did not look at the ticket waiting for me at the box office, and I was led to a seat in the third row. At the end of the show, at gladdie-time, Edna suddenly peered in my direction and screeched, "There's a dear old silver-haired senior citizen", and threw me a gladdie.

When the magnificent new pigshed was built, and it was full of clean, contented sows, and the first sales began to come in, it seemed that at last Old Anlaby might be going to pay its way. In the 1975–76 financial year it had lost $26,000. In the last six months of 1976 the loss had been cut to one thousand dollars.

But the upward trend did not continue. Despite the strictest hygiene, the best feed and Marc's loving care, our litters that began so well were nearly always decimated by the dreaded scours or some other disease. Experts came in and said we were doing all the right things, but we never achieved the unnervingly high survival rates which are essential to commercial pig farming.

More and more the only viable option seemed to be to admit failure, and sell Old Anlaby. Marc was not dismayed. Joan had her job at Kaiserstuhl winery, and they could retire to their little farm outside Kapunda. "I'm not going to have a bludge, there'll be plenty for me to do," said Marc cheerily.

Harold had his trade of cabinet-maker to fall back on, and was confident of getting plenty of jobs around Kapunda.

The worst difficulty was going to be in telling the children, for whom I had thought living at Anlaby was going to be such a positive experience. And so it had been, in many ways, and not only because it allowed them to grow up in such a beautiful place. Whether children are going to remain on the land or not, a country upbringing makes them immensely practical and self-reliant. Francis was away in New South Wales now, but Tisi and Sam could be relied on to go out on the bikes by themselves and bring three hundred sheep into the yards without a dog. They could cope with all manner of fair and foul practical matters. Sam was already an expert vegetable gardener. They had gone to primary school with the local kids; there was no local secondary school, but in their holidays from the city they learned all sorts of useful and useless things from Marc and Harold which were definitely not on the curriculum in town.

But the disadvantages had been profound when they were old enough to realise that the apparent stability and continuity were an illusion. They were also living a life far removed from that of their own generation.

By the end of February 1978 the sale of Old Anlaby and most of the contents was over. Buyers came from all over eastern Australia for the 1299 lots in what the *Sydney Morning Herald* called the greatest junk sale of all time. The most amazing items did emerge from dark and cobwebby corners where they had been for a century or so. For instance, there was a station medicine chest, from the 1850s, about five feet square, with dozens of the original bottles and jars. There was my father's model yacht, from the 1880s, about six feet long and three feet deep, all beautifully carvel-built from thin, separate teak planks. There were all the glass jars and rods and other equipment from the days when the station made its own electricity. There were oddments such as leather muzzles for the horses of Grandfather's Clydesdale stud. There was a galvanized-iron camel water can, and emu eggs and Aboriginal weapons given to my father on his motor trip across Australia in 1907–8. There was a bag of old fine-leaf gelatine and two tins of Bombay Ducks, which the auctioneeer took the precaution of advertising as "not sold as suitable for human consumption". Tisi was selling catalogues, and one old Greek buyer asked me if she was for sale too.

With what was left of the proceeds Ninette and I bought a block of land on the hills above the Barossa Valley, where we intended to build a house; there were outcrops of huge granite boulders, so we called the property Piers Hill. (Piers, my second name, comes from the Greek *petros*, meaning "a rock".) We built the house down in the valley, where it would be easy to make a large dam which the front windows would overlook. On top of the hill there was already a small prefabricated house, and I asked Harold if he and Aileen would like to live there; he could work a couple of days a week for us and keep an eye on the small flock of sheep we could run on the paddocks. He agreed to come, and would be able to get more work in the Barossa Valley.

While the house was being built my old school friend Bob Fisher lent us a house on Waverley Ridge in the Adelaide Hills, overlooking Nonsuch and the valley beyond. The house of Nonsuch was still there, but a dozen or so large houses now stood in what had been empty paddocks. The man who bought it from me had made a small fortune by subdividing it. I tried not to think of how I had buggered things up.

That year I had been invited to give three public lectures in Canberra on the theme of "The Credibility of Australian Literature". Richard Walsh, who was now running Angus & Robertson, asked to see them with a view to publishing them. A few months later he asked me to come to Sydney to discuss a book that might arise from them, on what he said could be called the ecology of Australian Literature. In May I went to Sydney and agreed to do the book. He suggested that I apply for a Literature Board Senior Fellowship to enable me to take time off to research and write the book. I did eventually receive a two-year Senior Fellowship, which was an enormous help, but the book shaped itself differently from Richard's conception of it, and he no longer wanted to publish it. I took it to Penguin/Viking, who published it in 1984 as *Snow on the Saltbush.*

I went on to Canberra, mainly to see David Campbell, who was in hospital with lung cancer. He was very ill. Above the anonymous mound of sheet and blanket, his noble head lying on the pillow looked irrelevant to his surroundings. His body was listless but his eyes electric, a red flush on his cheeks. He had conned the nurse into letting him have a bottle of Gewurztraminer smuggled in by his son-in-law, Guy Baring. Despite everything, he was still writing; "Mosquitoes", written then, is one of his best poems. I never saw David again. He died not long after my visit.

Of all my friends since the early days with Deasey, David was the one I most enjoyed talking to, partly because of the pleasure of yarning, spiced by his endearing sense of humour, but mostly because the talk teased out the threads of ideas, especially about poetry, that were still tangled inside me. There was no forcing, or hectoring, or justifying. Lots of gossip, but no needling malice. Most of all, perhaps, talking to someone whose knowledge of poetry was not academic or even all that wide, but very deep. What he knew he knew to the sound of every syllable. I miss him more than anyone else.

On 14 December 1979 I finished the first draft of the Mobil book, early in the morning of the day we moved to Piers Hill.

Thirty-One

With the expansion of Sun and Macmillan, I was no longer seeing all the books that were being published, although they were all sent to me on publication. Sam opened a parcel of new books one day, and after a while said, "This one's pretty depressing". The book was on mental illnesses. I looked through it and decided I probably had about six of them, including both depression and being manic-depressive.

Travel was always a palliative. Nugget Coombs had asked me to join the Council of the Australian National University, of which he was Chancellor, and in 1979 I accepted, as I admired him so much, and also because Judith Wright who was also a member. Nugget said it was a help for him to have people like Judith and me who were not part of the academic structure. It was a very large council, and I felt inadequate, especially as so much of the agenda was quite beyond my comprehension. But I soon realized that the experts in one university department could not understand the experts in another. What was sad was that often their written English was so bad that nobody could understand it except themselves.

It was always a pleasure to talk to Bettina Arndt, who was elected to the Council by the students; her father, Heinz, was also a member of the Council, but that never inhibited her. At that time she was always in trouble with the censors with her magazine, *Forum*, which dealt with people's sexual problems. There was absolutely nothing salacious about the magazine, but many of the subjects it dealt with were new to print in Australia.

My brother-in-law Dick Blackburn was also a member of the Council (he was later to be Chancellor). One day, when I was sitting next to Tina, Dick proposed what seemed to me to be a very sensible motion. However, it was then attacked by a particularly pompous member I will call Smith. Dick politely replied to him, saying how much he agreed with several of his points, but went on to make clear, just as politely, how completely Smith had been confused. Tina turned to me and whispered, "What a brain, what a lovely man he must be to live with. Brain is what really counts."

On the way home I stayed with Patrick and Manoly at Martin Road. Betty Riddell was also there for dinner. Patrick grumped at everyone and everything, and berated Betty and me for writing for the *Bulletin*. I was dismayed by a new development in Patrick's catalogue of hates. He, who had created Himmelfarb in *Riders in the Chariot*, was now coming out with a variety of anti-Jewish remarks. Zelman Cowen, then Governor-General, was always referred to as "Cohen". "What was the name of that Jew with Thames & Hudson who used to like my books? He doesn't now." This was a reference to that admirable man, Tom Rosenthal, who had been an early champion of Patrick, and Australian artists such as Arthur Boyd. According to Patrick, of course all the Sydney Jews were rallying around the despicable Harry Miller, and of course Miller would get out of all his gaol business unscathed; this was after all happening in Australia. Mirka Mora got on so well in Melbourne because they were all Jews down there. He had been taken to dinner at the "Balls-ache" and the food was disgusting. I told him to lay off Mirka. Then he turned his attention to gentile Australians; he had been visiting some dreadful relation. "Actually he's a very nice man," said Betty, sturdily. As the evening wore, or rather gurgled, on, he suddenly became his old self, finally quite giggly, and saying, "Please don't go. Have another whisky."

The *Bulletin* had also been mentioned because Trevor Kennedy, then its editor, had asked me to compile a large literary supplement to help celebrate the magazine's centenary in 1980. He had particularly wanted me to try to get a contribution from Patrick. A few days later Patrick rang me at Piers Hill; he began gloomily with the news of a friend's suicide, but soon cheered up. Then he switched to anger, saying he definitely would not give me anything for the *Bulletin*; didn't I remember how often they had attacked him and rubbished his books, and there was that dreadful David McNicoll and that awful Ron Saw. And on he raved. I told him he would be almost the only major Australian writer not represented; the response had indeed been terrific. But he had his integrity and he was going to keep it; bugger them.

In June I was in England and France for a short time. At that time my old Magdalen friend George Bailey was associated with the editing of *Kontinent*, the magazine of Russian writers in exile that had been started by Solzhenitsyn. The editor at this time was a talented novelist, Vladimir Maksimov. In Paris George took me to see him, and we had a most interesting conversation that lasted several hours. We spoke for a long time about Yevtushenko. Maksimov said Yevtushenko had been unjustly attacked by Russian writers in exile (himself included), but now he and many of the other writers (including Solzhenitsyn) had realized, from further information, how much Yevtushenko had done to help the cause of Russian writers, and what dangers he had exposed himself to. I wished Kingsley Amis and his friends could have been listening.

George and Maksimov told me about their efforts to arrange a meeting between Nabokov and Solzhenitsyn, something both writers had asked for. The intermediary had been William Cody III, Buffalo Bill's grandson. Finally a meeting was set up to take place in Nabokov's rooms in his Montreux hotel. George described the hotel as being quite revoltingly luxurious. They had waded through the deep carpets and knocked at the door. Nabokov greeted George as Maksimov. When they had sorted that out, he demanded to know where Solzhenitsyn was; why had he not kept the appointment? So George and Maksimov went to see Solzhenitsyn in his house.

It turned out to be a small, drab house; George said that every room looked like the Rome Post Office. A thin track meandered through the piles of unopened letters and telegrams to the great man's study. Solzhenitsyn said, yes, he had agreed to go to Nabokov's hotel. But Nabokov had not confirmed the appointment. Maximov then asked if he could ring Nabokov. Yes, said Nabokov, he had confirmed the appointment. "But if so," said Solzhenistyn indignantly, "what could have become of his letter?"

On my return to Australia I tried to organize a lecture tour for Maksimov; for a while it seemed that funds would be available, but then it all fell through, which was a great pity. He was a man of great integrity.

The Twyborn Affair arrived from Patrick and for the first few chapters I did not like it, then suddenly warmed to it more and more, and in the end found it one of Patrick's best novels. By "coming out" with his homosexuality he seemed to have found a new freedom of expression.

At the end of October Patrick came to stay at Piers Hill. He was pleased with the new kitchen with its high bench, and enjoyed leaning on the huge granite slab which our Barossa-German builder had found in a monumental mason's yard. I still had some pink Georgian vodka I had been given in Moscow, and he liked drinking that. He enjoyed helping me with the chooks and ducks and geese. As we walked up to their yard through the deep clover I said, "You must have had fun writing the brothel bits in *The Twyborn Affair*." "I never have fun writing. It's always hell." I mentioned Kenneth Slessor's "Writing is a pleasure out of hell". "He had the sense to give it up." I went over to a farm near Tanunda to get some more geese, while Patrick had his after-lunch snooze. I returned with two grey geese with their orange bills, and he came with me while I let them loose in the yard. "Mmm, there are a number of girls in Sydney who have just that look."

When we were walking back to the house he suddenly said, "I'll let you have a piece for your *Bulletin* supplement. Something from the autobiographical thing I'm writing, called *Flaws in the Glass*."

A week later I was in Sydney. My stocks were high with Trevor Kennedy and the other people at the *Bulletin*; even without Patrick, the Centenary Supplement was shaping up very well indeed. I went to lunch with my old friend Patricia Rolfe, the magazine's literary editor. She is well known for her history of the *Bulletin* and other factual writings, but has never had sufficient credit for her own low-key but highly observant fiction. She is one of those shy people who are frightened of no one, but quite incapable of promoting themselves. It is another matter when it comes to helping other people, but with her that is never obviously done. At lunch that day I had my first opportunity to get to know Edmund Campion, whom I had previously met only briefly. A most witty and civilized man, he was at that stage obviously fond of Max and Von Harris. Max had bought a house in Cascade Street, Paddington, and was going to move to Sydney. Ed thought the move would kill Von. In the end they never did move, Von's health being given as the reason. But I think the real reason was that although Max liked hopping from time to time out of his little pond in Adelaide into the great big one of Sydney, he always needed to hop back again. Unfortunately, in one of Max's typically inexplicable changes of mood and trust, he took Ed to court over a legalistic quibble about a sentence in a review by Ed, and was awarded damages. The law can frequently be not only an ass but a friend to those who are not in need.

As well as being a good historian Ed is an untiring friend to all manner of Australian writers, not only as an honest reviewer and in his term as member of the Literature Board, but in hidden ways he does not allow to become general knowledge. What a shame that Harris, who in totally different ways has also done so much for Australian writers, should have turned on someone of such good will as Campion.

I had been having further discussions with Mobil and Greg Vitiello, who wanted me to do another book for their series, also with Harri Peccinotti, this time on Singapore. The subject, and indeed Asia in general, had interested me ever since my research for the biography of William Light whose father had founded Penang. Raffles, who after his work in Java founded Singapore, his "almost only child", had always seemed to me one of the most fascinating characters of the time, a fine example of the old learned breed of English imperialists, who had a deep feeling for the peoples of the region where they were living. And although my hair was maybe a bit long at the time, I had some admiration for Lee Kuan Yew, as anyone must who has studied the history of modern Singapore. Lee would have heartily agreed with Raffles: "Our object is not territory but Trade; a great commercial emporium".

In my case too, the money would be very welcome. True to my usual hopeless pattern, I had allowed the building at Piers Hill to run way over budget. So I agreed to write the book. They suggested that I fly to Singapore for a week of preliminary discussions with Greg and one of Mobil Singapore's senior executives. I was to leave on 10 December.

Most unsuitably, a week before I was due to leave, I could not resist beginning a new novel, a satire on Adelaide and the Festival. It was also to be based on two extraordinary cases of confidence men who had taken in the South Australian Establishment and the social ladies. I began it on 3 December, and continued writing it in the airport lounge in Melbourne, where I had to wait for four hours, in the plane going there and back, and at night in the hotel in Singapore. I finished the first draft on 3 January 1980. I called the book *The Eye-Opener*. It must have had something going for it, for when it was published it appealed equally to two of my old friends, Bob Southey and Barry Humphries, who in most of their tastes could not have been further apart.

When the shops opened after New Year 1980 I went to buy some oddments at the North Adelaide hardware shop. I asked the assistant whether she had had a good New Year's Eve. "Well, I sat up till 11.30, and then said, 'Bugger you, 1979, you've been a lousy year, I'm going to bed'." My sentiments, exactly.

Later in 1980 I was to go to Sydney and rang Patrick to ask him and Manoly to have dinner with me. We had a long telephone conversation which, as usual now, lurched between calm and storm. He had liked Mick Stow's new novel very much. So had I, so I relaxed. But he was furious at not being sent a copy after Mick had been given the Patrick White Award. "Those bloody dishonest publishers, they put on the cover 'Winner of the Patrick White Award', when it's not for a book but for a life's work. Just like you bloody people at Macmillan and Sun with that novel of Sumner's you published." "But," I said, "they put 'Winner of the Nobel Prize' on your books". "Oh … oh … so they do." "How's Manoly?" "Oh, sore wrist, sore toe, sore back, didn't enjoy Athens." "Well, I suppose Greece isn't a very happy country for him." (At that time Greece was under the Neo-Fascist regime of the Colonels.) "Nowhere is a happy country, certainly not this one."

When we met for dinner he was more cheerful, but only after attacking me for living in a place as beautiful as Piers Hill; according to him, I was clutching at innocence, hiding from the world. (He had begged me to do just that some years earlier.) I suggested that it was odd that so many great minds of earlier centuries had thought that nature was the source of reality, and retired to the country to look for the truth in their writing or thought — shouldn't one follow their example. Patrick, on the other hand, wanted to rub his nose in the shit and treachery of the worst human beings and make that his standard for judging the world.

I had lunch with Barry Humphries the next day. He told me that he had loved *The Twyborn Affair* so much that he had read it twice. He had tried three times to write to Patrick about it, and had in fact written three long letters, but couldn't send them as he thought it would look as if he were offering literary criticism. So he had just sent a note. Maybe that was wise, given Patrick's deteriorating state of mind. But what a pity.

Barry did a wonderful imitation of his interview with the millionaire impresario Robert Stigwood, with Barry wringing his hat between his hands. He finished the story, and then reflected, "Why do the very rich make us so nervous?"

Patrick had asked me if I would like to walk with him and the new dog,

Eureka, in the park in the morning at 7.30. Eureka was a jovial mongrel, leaping around on the end of her leash. Patrick appeared in gumboots, overcoat, scarf and beret, carrying a stout stick. "What's that for?" I asked. "Oh, we were nearly raped by a Labrador the other day. Got to be ready for them."

Everything seemed to be going well. Rob Chapman rang to say that Bryan Forbes had agreed to direct *Queen Emma* and various astonishingly eminent stars were interested in appearing in it. Max was keen to do some more titles in our new Bibliophile poetry series. The Centenary Issue of the *Bulletin*, with its large Literary Supplement, was a great success. For months I had been delicately asking Trevor Kennedy if he would give me a couple of pages every now and then for new verse and prose, so that the *Bulletin* could in a small way continue its original commitment to encouraging Australian writers. Now Trevor called me into his office, glared at me and said he understood nothing about literature, and those fucking bastards on the Literature Board needn't think he was doing it to be in sympathy with them, but he was giving me thirty-two pages, quarterly, for a *Bulletin* Literary Supplement of new prose and verse. The sum of thirty-two pages in the format of the *Bulletin* was equivalent to two or three times that in one in the literary quarterlies.

This enlightened decision led to a magazine that was to last for five years; it gave Australian writers regular access to a couple of hundred thousand readers, and paid them well, all at no cost to the Literature Board. Moreover, it did a great service for those thousands of readers who had no ready means of keeping up with new Australian writing. In the 1970s Michael Wilding and Frank Moorhouse and others had had a considerable success with *Tabloid Story*, some pages of prose and verse which were inserted into various journals; but contributors to *Tabloid Story* were always paid with funds from the Literature Board, and there was no regular service to a large number of readers. I have always thought that most academic critics, assiduous readers of the literary magazines with their tiny circulations, have given insufficient recognition to Trevor Kennedy and Consolidated Press for their support of the *Bulletin* Literary Supplement; I suppose they were frightened to write or say anything that might look like praise for Kerry Packer.

Editing the *Bulletin* Literary Supplement was very hard work. Contributions came in by the sackful, and I had no secretarial or editorial assistance. But it gave me great pleasure because most writers were so pleased that the Supplement existed. I persuaded some of our leading artists to make drawings to accompany some of the stories and poems; Arthur Boyd, John Olsen and Charles Blackman were among the artists who took part. Brett Whiteley said he would like to join them, and I sent him a story I thought he might enjoy.

The next time I was in Sydney for the *Bulletin* I called in on Trevor Sykes, the new editor. Trevor and I always got on very well; he was, perhaps surprisingly for a financial journalist, very well read, especially in Shakespeare, and a lover of poetry. He received me with a torrent of four-letter words (oaths were very much in the *Bulletin*'s editorial tradition). The gist of it all, when I could calm him down, was that I was trying to corrupt a decent family magazine and turn it into a porno rag. I simply could not think what he was talking about. Then he opened a drawer and pulled out a black-and-white drawing. "Just fucking look at fucking this." For once the adjectives were apt. Brett Whiteley's drawing for this magazine catering for a couple of hundred thousand readers, was a virtuoso drawing of a man and a woman having a sensational fuck, with the penis in full stroke. When I mildly told Brett that his drawing was not exactly suitable he (sounding like Sykes in reverse) went off on a tirade about censorship of sex and how disgusting it was, fucking interfering with fucking artistic freedom.

When he settled down, Brett told me he was having troubles with Patrick. Twice a week they used to go for a two-hour walk together in Centennial Park with the dogs. One day recently Patrick had suddenly stopped and shouted, "There's no one I can trust, except Manoly." He spoke so violently that, in Brett's words, "all the grass in a two hundred yards' circle turned a bright cerise and the dogs ran for shelter". Patrick didn't elaborate then, but a couple of days later Brett received a letter listing nineteen points telling Brett exactly what was wrong with his life and work. At least half a dozen of them, Brett said, were quite insane. Brett said it was like getting a parcel bomb.

A few days after my fifty-eighth birthday Jim Leslie and Mobil turned on an enormous launching party for *Patterns of Australia* — "The Knitting Book", Patrick called it — at a huge old house, Rippon Lea, in Melbourne. Room after room was filled with dreadful nineteenth-century paintings of which my favourite was *The Poet Being Touched By Inspiration.* Doug Nicholls' son (actually an aeronautical engineer) played the didgeridoo, and the rest of the noises off came from The Bushwhacker's Band, and then from a string quartet playing Mozart. There were mountains of prawns and Moreton Bay bugs and cold fillet steak and champagne. It was all most unlike the usual literary launch. Geoff Blainey made a generous speech.

As soon as I could get away I went out into the garden to have a pee. I was just finishing when I heard footsteps crunching on the gravel; in guilty haste I did up my fly, only to find it was Geoff on a similar mission.

In many ways the most interesting person there was Greg Vitiello's wife Jane. She was a Jewish social worker in one of the roughest regions of New York. She found that her life with her extended family and her clients involved a seven-way language connection: English, Yiddish, Russian,

Polish, Hebrew, German and Italian. Widening the circle, Greg's sister had recently married a black academic. Jane and Geoff Blainey might well have had a good chat.

A series of interviews followed in Melbourne and Sydney. The worst was with Mike Walsh on the "Mike Walsh Show", my introduction to the plastic, analgesic society of these TV programmes. Walsh never looked at me while I answered his questions, but waved to members of the audience and mouthed instructions to the camera crew. It was unnerving to talk animatedly to someone off camera, whose face was going through these antics.

It was all a learning experience outside the cosy society of writers' groups and the cold isolation of the writer's own room. It had nothing to do with poetry. But neither did Wallace Stevens's insurance company. I don't think it does writers any harm to be roughed up a little by the philistine world of commerce, as long as they remember D.H. Lawrence's advice to a correspondent: "Business is No Good".

The Mobil book and the *Bulletin* Centenary Supplement provoked two of the most vicious attacks ever made on me, both on ABC radio, one by Humphrey McQueen (whom I had always liked) and one by an academic called Reid. They were both basically trying to politicize me as an apologist for big business. As one who had always voted Labor, I found this imputation of being a lackey for big business very annoying. But, of course, for people like McQueen Labor was worse than Liberal. I remembered an anti-Vietnam march in Adelaide, when we were being led by Gough Whitlam and Don Dunstan, when there was a huge placard held aloft by some Maoists in the crowd, with the words "DUNSTAN, STOOGE OF THE RULING CLASS".

Lawyers rang me on behalf of Mobil, Macmillan and Consolidated Press asking me if I wanted to sue, and saying that in both matters I had a watertight case; but I don't think writers should invoke the law. Trevor Kennedy suggested that I write an article in the *Bulletin* about the McCarthyites of the left, but then shrugged his shoulders and said it wasn't worth it; he had been similarly denounced when he left the *National Times* for the *Bulletin*. If anyone wants to look up this dreary business, all the evidence is in my papers in the National Library.

Patrick had been rumbling for some time and I thought it would not be long before he blew up like one of those geysers in Rotorua or Yosemite that from time to time wake up and spew steam and mud. In September a letter arrived from him, the first typewritten letter he had written me for more than six years, making me suspect that he had kept a copy. It began amiably enough; I had subsidized Francis and Sam to take Patrick and Manoly out to dinner, and that had been a success. Then he got down to business; he had received the copy I had sent him of the Mobil book.

I found the photographs in the Mobil epic very beautiful and original. I've only flipped through the text because I've had so little time for reading, and anyway some of your statements froze me and made me realise how far apart we are in our beliefs, and how little of me you understand. (This of course is why I am writing *Flaws in the Glass*; even those I have known for years know very little about me.)

That bit about the "aristocrat" was particularly blood-curdling. You can't have met many of my family — Somerset farmers who came here early in the piece, got hold of a lot of land, made money by hard work, but have remained most of them pretty crude. We were the new-rich of the turn of the century. Hardly aristocracy. If I am anything of a writer it is through my homosexuality, which has given me additional insights, and through a very strong vein of vulgarity. All of this I hope to bring out in *Flaws in the Glass*.

The first letter you wrote me after the publication of *Voss* froze my blood in the same way as the statement in this book. I have tried to shove the memory away, but it pops up again in moments like these. You complimented me on Voss and said you were so glad Australia had another writer who was also a gentleman. [The other writer I referred to was, of course, Martin Boyd.] I found this remark so vulgar, in the colonial sense, as opposed to the vulgarity which strengthens creativity.

I'm sorry to dredge this up [after 23 years], but now that I am losing faith in almost everybody in this two-faced jingleland I might as well try to explain a few other things which have contributed to what must seem like churlishness, or at least coldness, after years of friendship.

When you had to leave Anlaby you had all our sympathy. We were glad to hear you had found somewhere else which pleased you and were building a house. However, we were rather surprised by accounts of the Altman-style house-warming you gave to the Adelaide establishment and your remark "the children have to show the flag". Then when I went to stay with you in what is certainly the most beautiful house in the most idyllic landscape, I was even more surprised considering the times and what we understood had happened to you. But what really shocked me was to arrive back in Sydney and read the day after that you had been given that enormous grant by the Literature Board, particularly when you had been jetting around the world with Mobil, helping them tidy up their Australian image, and living it up in the old Dutton funster fashion. Australia disgusts me more and more, but what really shatters me is when those I have loved and respected shed their principles along with the others.

No doubt you'll think this is all fatuous and humourless, and carry on as before. But for some time I've been screwing myself up to say it. Now it's said, and you can destroy the letter.

His signature at the end of the letter, usually so firm and flowing, was jagged and wobbly.

I do not make copies of my letters, but in this case I did, as I knew Patrick would destroy the original, ensuring that my side of the argument would never be heard. (He knew very well that I did not destroy his letters, despite instructions; as well as I knew how much he enjoyed reading the letters of Flaubert or Chekhov or whoever.) So here it is.

For the last few months I've been waiting for some such letter from you, and wondering what form it would take. I find I have anticipated most of its contents. Even so, there are some surprises.

It's time you recovered your sense of proportion, your sense of humour and most of all your sense of humility, which once long ago you declared to be the most essential thing of all. Since those *Voss* days you have succumbed more and more to a moral megalomania, which is having a destructive effect upon you. I'm sorry to be blunt, but I can't regard trust and affection as commodities, something to be abandoned.

To take first the most astonishing and impercipient of your charges — for that is what they sound like. How after all these years you could impute a snobbish vulgarity to me, I simply can't understand. Of course I know your ancestors weren't aristocrats. (Neither were the ancestors of most of the aristocrats in England.) All those years ago, when I wrote to you about *Voss*, I meant to say that your birth and your upbringing gave you the inestimable advantage of being able to write about "society" in Australia, knowing just how far from high it is or was, as no other writer except Martin Boyd has been able to do. As we had more or less the same backgrounds, I never dreamed that you would not understand what I was saying. As my father would have put it, a gentleman can say things to a gentleman that he would not say to others. Another point which you shouldn't forget is that social changes happen, up or down, with great speed in a colonial society. It needs to be pointed out to ordinary Australians that people like you or David Campbell, are, whether you like it or not, the equivalent of aristocrats in this country. As for the vulgarity you say is basic to your writing, I have always enjoyed it and admired it and have frequently referred to it in writing about you. It is also well-known that it is the middle classes that are genteel and afraid of vulgarity, whereas the aristocracy and the lower classes are not.

To set you straight on a few misconceptions. I'm glad you think Piers Hill is beautiful, but you should remember that the whole thing cost less than a modest house in Paddington or Woollahra. I forbear to mention Centennial Park.

Mobil. Well, I think it is depressing that one of your stature should think the same as Humphrey McQueen. We live in a capitalist society where it is still possible to vote Labor. As one who has been on several occasions to Communist countries, as you have not, I much prefer to live in a society where everything is not run by the State. Mobil is a great patron of the arts all over the non-communist world. We should encourage patronage of the arts from both private companies and the State. As for the patrons themselves, one may or may not approve of them. One could argue that neither the Medicis nor the Esterhazys were morally estimable, and no doubt it could be argued that socialists in the opera or theatre or literature should not take money from the Fraser Government.

Which brings me to the Literature Board grant. I don't want to be harsh about your own personal situation, but you have no idea why I applied for that grant. The project for which I was given it is one that would normally be undertaken

> by an academic (although in this case most important that it should not be undertaken by an academic). He would be on a salary of about $30,000 [three times the Literature Board grant], plus secretary, research assistants, travel grants, free phone calls, postage, etc. To do the job properly, I have to have (and do have) research assistants working for me in Australia and London. I have to pay for everything myself, including travel — which is why I always try to carry out some of my own work when travelling on behalf of the *Bulletin* or ANU or even Mobil.
>
> It is profoundly depressing to have to spell all this out to someone I have always loved and trusted. Your moral megalomania is getting worse and worse — what right have you to pontificate about other people's lives? You should reread King Lear, for more than one reason — "who should 'scape whipping?" Despite your extraordinary insights, your genius in fact, you have not enough contact with the ordinary world since you left Castle Hill. 20 Martin Road is more of an ivory tower than Piers Hill. Your homosexuality, since you mention it, has indeed given you great insight, but it has also denied you the give and take, the interaction of love with human frailty, that comes not only from one's own life with wife and children but from those of the children's friends. Your private income has enabled you to write and you have had the strength of mind to devote yourself to writing, a grim hair-shirt that causes irritations that sometimes make you oblivious of what other writers have to do to keep going.
>
> You say we are apart in our beliefs. Basically, I do not believe this to be so. As I have already said, your misconceptions of my ideas about aristocracy are absurd. It is a case of what you want to believe I believe, rather than what I believe.
>
> But it is really intolerable when you take this assumption further and talk about "those you have loved and respected shedding their principles along with the others". It is time you examined your own motives and principles a little more closely. The way you are going at the moment you are destroying both yourself and your friends. Unfortunately, perhaps, love cannot be destroyed, and I still feel it for you.

By one of those ironies, all the time I was typing this letter, maybe half an hour or more, a thrush sang and sang outside my window.

As professional writers we both should have known to hold off, not to write when the accelerator of the emotions was flat to the floor. Anger does not refine words, it just throws them.

How extraordinary, but how typical of him, that Patrick should have nursed that remark of mine about *Voss* and the gentleman for twenty-three years. Perhaps he thought I considered myself to be the other gentleman. Surely not. David Campbell would have understood what I meant; if he hadn't he would have asked me what I was on about. Actually at the time of *Voss* I was working on a lecture "Gentlemen vs Lairs — The Decline and Fall of the English Gentleman in Australian Literature". Hence my use of a rather dangerous word. The material was so abundant that it should have been made into a book rather than a lecture. Its theme could more or less be encapsulated in a sentence from Furphy's *Such is Life*: "There is no such thing as a democratic gentleman, the adjective and noun are hyphenated by a drawn sword". I wanted to show how true in some aspects, and how false in others, Furphy's remark is of Australia and, by extension, of Australian Literature. No one knew better than I, if only from observing the members of the Adelaide Club, how limited and often absurd Australian "gentlemen" were; and, incidentally, how often cruel to their sons. Patrick knew the breed too, and quite rightly wanted to steer clear of them.

But at the same time, Patrick and I often talked of our mutual hatred of the Australian love of levelling down, of tall-poppy slashing. This tendency was very much in evidence in the work of writers of essays or articles or books in the 1950s and 1960s. The issue was well expressed by H.L. Mencken, writing about the United States: "The curse of this country, as of all democracies, is precisely the fact that it treats its best men as enemies".

White, though, was being less than fair, to put it mildly, about his family. As a whole, they were certainly not "pretty crude" — for example, his uncle, H.L. White of Belltrees, was a famous ornithologist, flower-grower and collector, especially of books.

Patrick was always trying to get away from his ancestry, and yet he was trapped by it. He considered that one reason for the initial attacks on his books in Australia was that he came from a squatting family. On his return to Australia he had tried to set up with Manoly at semi-suburban Castle Hill as a kind of cocky farmer, as far removed as possible from the wide acres of the grazier Whites. As they scratched away at the dirt and deticked dogs, all the farmlet did was ruin Manoly's back; Manoly of course did nearly all the work on the place. By 1980 Patrick had become a socialist, an anti-nuclear protestor, the thinking man's demagogue, the ragged idol of young theatricals. In the 1950s and 1960s he used to dress with restrained elegance, as he lived. No dinner jackets, no crystal chandeliers. Now he shambled around like someone auditioning for *Waiting for Godot*. It was determination as well as the loss of his teeth that forced his face, that had been so attractive, even handsome, into that scowling gargoyle beloved of some intellectuals and photographers.

He went to appalling lengths in *Flaws in the Glass* to prove that his friends did not really know him, that he was in fact a nasty person and emphatically not "a gentleman". As proof, there were such insensitivities as the portraits of Manoly's family, especially of the father, which he knew would wound Manoly. But perhaps the obsession is most obvious in the minor, totally unnecessary, attacks, such as the one on Joan Sutherland, someone he should have respected as a great singer, whatever her tastes in reading. But no, it was as if he were lurking somewhere in Clubland, waiting and praying for the members to say, "That Paddy White just isn't a gentleman to say that sort of thing about Dame Joan".

Patrick let three weeks go by, and then replied to my letter. If my charge of megalomania had needed proof, he supplied it, beginning his tirade with: "If I'm a moral megalomaniac it's from living in this increasingly corrupt colony".

Poor Australia! Texas Guinan said that fifty million Frenchmen can't be wrong, but to Patrick seventeen million Australians were always wrong. If there were no living balanced and humane human beings he would listen to, then he might have taken some regular dose of people like Montaigne or Dr Johnson. Montaigne he had had to read at Cambridge, but he put him aside. When, on one occasion, I praised Dr Johnson, he snorted in disgust. No one could have expected Patrick to become humane and balanced, but he need not have been so proud of being the opposite.

The extract from Boswell I had asked him to read, when praising Johnson, was from a 1788 conversation with Edmund Burke and others. Burke had said, "From the experience which I have had — and I have had a great deal — I have learned to think better of mankind."

> Johnson: From my experience I have found them worse in commercial dealings, more disposed to cheat, than I had any notion of; but more disposed to do one another good than I had conceived … And really it is wonderful, considering how much attention is necessary for men to take care of themselves, and ward off immediate evils which press upon them, it is wonderful how much they do for others. As it is said of the greatest liar, that he tells more truth than falsehood; so it may be said of the worst man, that he does more good than evil.

Dr Johnson suffered as many if not more physical ills than Patrick, and suffered even more terrible depressions, while the life around him in London was that illustrated by Hogarth.

Patrick had a remarkable ability to infect otherwise good people with his own churlishness. One day I rang a mutual friend, someone I have admired for years, who said, "I've just been talking to Patrick. He said that Australia is a piffling country. Isn't that a good word, piffling?" She was quite upset when I indignantly said I thought exactly the opposite.

One more point, which refers to Johnson's phrase about "warding off immediate evils". Apart from his health, Patrick had a dream run in life. He always had a private income, which expanded into wealth (a lot of which he mostly generously gave away). In 1965 he wrote to me, "*The Burnt Ones* hasn't paid off the E & S [his publishers at the time, Eyre & Spottiswode] advance, and I don't suppose, by this time, ever will. How disgusting all this money for writing sounds! I have never written with that in view, and don't intend to begin, although it is lovely when it comes — all the paintings it will buy." For the rest of us, the money "when it comes" has to pay some of the bills. When Patrick's father died in 1937 he received, in addition to what he already had, 10,000 pounds and an annual income from a trust;

he and his sister Suzanne would inherit the lot (about 250,000 pounds in 1937) on their mother's death, which happened in 1969.

Though much has been made of how deeply affected he was by the terrible developments in Europe of the 1930s, he was never (as emphasized by his cousin Peggy Garland) spurred into any kind of action by the rise of Hitler, Mussolini or Franco, or by the state of the poor of Europe and Britain. When the war came he was in the United States. He returned to Britain but did not volunteer for the services; he knew he would be called up within a year. So, wartime and all, he returned to his lovers in the United States. The fall of France made him feel guilty, and he returned to England in June 1940. He was finally accepted by the RAF as "suitable fodder for the war machine" in November 1940, and was made an Intelligence officer. He was shot at a few times, but never suffered hardship, let alone a calamity like being taken prisoner by the Japanese.

Finally, for forty-odd years he had the most loving and devoted companion anyone could have, of great intelligence and humour, who put up with innumerable insults, even in front of other people, and who in many ways was Patrick's eyes and ears. Patrick also drew a lot of hidden comfort and confidence, especially in Europe, from Manoly's distinguished ancestry.

After fifty years of more or less sheltered life, he should have been making joyful noises unto the Lord. He supported, in many cases with great generosity, a number of good causes, both with his voice and with his pocket. But it is intolerable to hear him being idolised as a moralist. His morality was all too often based on a rigidity of mind which in turn was often based on egotism. It made him feel better about himself.

Other great writers have lived more deplorable lives than Patrick, but none, I think, reached the destructive depths of his megalomania in his later life.

In his letter of reply, he quite rightly attacked me on my inadequate remarks about his homosexuality, their inadequacy being mostly the result of the words having been set down in anger. I had said that his homosexuality denied him the give-and-take of ordinary family life. "My God, if you knew!" he replied. In fact, I knew very well, from years of watching, and listening to, him and Manoly. He went on to say, "And as for missing the give and take provided by children and their friends, I have a whole clutch of younger friends, middle-aged today, but young enough to be my children ..." This was true, but Patrick had never changed their nappies (there is an episode in *Voss* where the action of cleaning up another man's shit is almost sanctified), he had never had to comfort a child come weeping home from school or waking from a nightmare. Most of all, he could dispense with any of his "children" when he got fed up with them. And children do not suck up to their fathers, as some of his "children" expertly did.

Where I was totally inadequate in my remarks was in not allowing for his imagination, which was, after all, the imagination of a genius. Although he did not mention it in his letter, in some ways dogs were his real children. His letters, like his conversation, face to face or over the telephone, were again and again concerned with mating or whelping or the illnesses of the dogs. The dogs, and Manoly, were the only creatures he truly loved. But I never heard him speak with cruelty to the dogs, as he so often did to Manoly.

In January of 1981 Barry Humphries came by himself for a weekend at Piers Hill. He had brought his painting materials and, despite the fierce heat, spent hours outside the house painting the dam, which was full, the cloudless blue sky reflected in the gunmetal water. In a long-sleeved shirt he had borrowed from me, and a big hat, he turned to me and said, "How lovely to be doing something at which you don't have to excel." In the evening he was full of stories about the infamies of the film world, how Bruce Beresford had had to pay for his wife and himself to fly tourist class to Cannes while the two producers flew first class, at no charge to themselves, and then accepted congratulations for Bruce's film. The producer of another film was getting ten thousand dollars a month for post-production expenses while Bruce was getting nothing. I listened with some anxiety; everything now seemed to have fallen through with the film of *Queen Emma*.

Barry said that a strange thing had happened to him when he was on the stage recently in Melbourne. "Edna was rabbiting on and suddenly I heard her talking about an obscure little bookshop, not at all the place she'd go to, and I got a bit alarmed — then a little old woman in the audience was holding up her hand, and she said, 'I'm Dora, remember me, I work in the bookshop'. Cheers from the audience. I must have seen her in the audience, not registered consciously, and then away Edna went."

A few days later in Melbourne for Sun-Macmillan I bumped into David Martin, the novelist and poet whose *The Young Wife* had been one of our first Sun Books. Apparently there had been another review, which I had not yet seen, politicizing *Patterns of Australia*, this time by John Hooker. David said he was so incensed by the review that he went out and bought the book. "You made the mistake of saying you love Australia. I can say that and just get away with it because I'm a reffo Hungarian Jew and allowed to be a bit sentimental." I wondered yet again why so many Australian intellectuals made such an issue of hating Australia, of being "alienated". Patrick, of course, was their patron saint, the one who preached "This fucking awful country".

David said he could not make me out, was I a poet, historian, publisher, editor etc. etc. It was a complaint I was used to, but I was surprised to hear it coming from someone of his background. Judah Waten, of comparable origins, or Steve Murray-Smith, as Australian as could be, liked it that I spread my efforts. But on many occasions I have been well aware of how in Australia writers are pigeonholed, popped into a box like those above the old silky-oak station desk in the bookkeeper's office at Anlaby, safely marked "Poet" or "Novelist" or "Editor". I have always been unable not to have a go at whatever seemed worth doing; perhaps it's an indication of shallowness of mind.

It was a melancholy time for old friends; Tass was now dead, in the year after David Campbell, and Patrick half-mad. One very alive old friend arrived for a short visit: Bob Hughes. He also had recently been savaged by Humphrey McQueen. How could anyone not be who worked for *Time* magazine? Bob was full of all his old charm and zest, but he had grown heavier, not so much from the sign of a slight paunch as from a look like a later Roman Emperor who has had trouble keeping down the barbarian tribes. He had been filming in France, at the Norman tower of La Roche-Gruyon, for *The Shock of the New*, and in a lunch break a *chasseur* approached and sat down for a chat. He asked Bob about his accent. "Ah, Australian — then you must know the celebrated Australian author, Alister Kershaw, author of *A History of the Guillotine*. He is a drinking companion of mine." Alister's *Guillotine* must be one the of the least-celebrated books of the twentieth century; in an effort to get its merits more widely recognized, I had asked Lawrence Durrell to review it for *Australian Letters*. He had liked it, despite its subject, but I don't think his review led to enormous sales. Alister had been living for many years now in France, in the house he had bought for Richard Aldington, near Sancerre.

It was inevitable that Bob, like Alister Kershaw, Alan Moorehead and Clive James, should have lived permanently overseas. It is not a question of talent driving them out of their homeland. Talent is (or was, alas, in the case of Moorehead) abundant in all three of them, but Australia was unable to supply their particular needs. Peter Porter is very much an exception, and now often comes to the land of his birth, even though it could no longer be called his homeland. The same is true of Barry Humphries. The important thing is not, like some Australians, to adopt a kind of jilted sniffiness about expatriates, but to make sure they are given plenty of opportunities to visit, and make them welcome when they do come back.

Thirty-Two

A quiet event in 1981 changed the course of my life. It was not a *coup de foudre*, the dawn did not come up like thunder. It was more classical, a soft entrance of new light, Homer's rosy-fingered dawn. Nor did it fit in with that other dead poet's saw; it was not quite love at first sight. Yet there was a tremor, a hint of vibrations that were soon to make a whole and answered chord. The literary allusions have their relevance, as I will show.

During the children's holidays Ninette, Tisi, Sam and I had been to Robe, a little fishing port about 250 miles south-east of Adelaide, where we camped in the scrub a few miles out of the town. One afternoon we were having a drink in the town with some old friends and their neighbours, Geoff Baulch, and his wife Robin. Geoff was a farmer who had land by the Coorong where he ran cattle; he flew up there in a Piper Arrow which he kept in a hangar by the Robe airstrip. Robin was an attractive, intelligent woman in her early thirties, with short curly hair that was, rather fetchingly, just beginning to go grey. She was very quiet, and I did not have much opportunity to talk to her.

A few months later Ninette and I and another couple were again in Robe, this time staying with the same friends for the weekend. Robin joined us for dinner, by herself. Geoff had flown to a cattle sale somewhere in New South Wales. (Our hostess's sister said to me, "He does that all the time; he's never home.") Robin was sitting next to me at dinner, but long before that she was next to me in some more intimate way than physical closeness. As soon as she came in, very clearly defined, with cool grey-blue eyes, a modest person making no claims on the little gathering's attention, she completely captured mine. Perhaps that old dead shepherd was right; this time I had clearly seen her, as it were for the first time, and I loved her.

Such feelings must, of course, be mutual, the electricity must connect; in some unscientific way, lovers each manage to be the positive pole. I cautiously misbehaved myself during dinner at the large table; I slid my hand down inside her leather boot to a slim ankle. But we chattered away innocuously, with all the desperate attention to other people of lovers longing for each other.

I was tortured that night by not knowing where she lived. Had I known, my bare feet would have hurried across the sandhills to her door. Later, she wrote to me about that night: "I surfaced from conversation with you and returned slowly to the so-called real world to find everyone else obviously waiting for me to shut up and go home — I suddenly realised I was the only one who wasn't staying the night and that the others had all run out of conversation. But the return to the real world couldn't have been complete because I went home and quite seriously and calmly prepared for your arrival. I don't mean I thought: 'Wouldn't it be nice if' ... I really expected you. Sanity returned slowly, I was a bit odd for a few days."

So was I, but couldn't think what to do about someone 250 miles away. Then a large envelope arrived, with a bundle of poems and stories, under her maiden name, Robin Lucas, asking whether any of them were suitable for the *Bulletin*. When I read them I found that a lot of them were eminently publishable, wry, witty, economical, with a strong current running under a limpid surface. I rang her and suggested, still being very correct, that next time she was in Adelaide she might be able to have lunch with Ninette and me at the little town house we had bought after selling Curtis Street. She came, in not too much of a rush, a couple of weeks later, early in October. After lunch Ninette left to do some shopping, and Robin and I sat down to discuss her work.

Excellent though the poems and stories were, it was impossible for either of us to concentrate on them. Leaping over all those usual preliminary fragments of looks and touches, messages of the moment that lead to future hours, I invited her to come to my room with the high ceiling in the city. There I found that she was devoid of pretence or games-playing or manipulating. We were complete immediately, with that marvellous completion only possible to lovers, but also with the surety that this was only a beginning.

After she had driven away on that long journey back to Robe, I wrote to her: "I was thinking afterwards. A miracle suddenly changes the pace of the world, but in a way miracles are always expected, however unbelievable their possibility seems beforehand. In other words, miracles only happen to believers! The vibrations already exist, at first sight."

Although parted by distance, we were lucky in a way to get to know each other by letters, in which there was nothing tentative but nothing taken for granted. Letters flew across the difficulties of distance, the other commitments of the busy lives we both led. I became aware that the bond between us, amazingly already existing, was made up of threads which I had been trying to find all my adult life. On the face of it, our two lives could not have been more different, although the difference was not in the twenty-five years between our ages — that never mattered. Her maturity and apparent calmness came from what had been demanded of her. As the oldest of a family of five children, one sister twenty years younger than her, she had always accepted the responsibility of looking after others. Then, at the age of twenty, she had married Geoff Baulch, a widower with two little girls of seven and five, Libby and Kate. She brought them up and they call her "Mum". This frequently astonishes me today, when these two accomplished women in their thirties call this youthful woman "Mum". She and Geoff then had Emma and Michael — thirteen and ten when we first met. Robin also had parents who enjoyed life to the full; it would be impossible to imagine two people less like Dr Trott and Madame Vitriolle. Her large, vibrant family life was quite different from anything I had known in my own life.

The bond between us was a blend of passion and intellect, poetry and wit, imagination and worldliness. When Robin came in the door, out the window went all those romantic demons that had sunk their claws into me in my youth, *Wehmut, Seufzer, Schmerz, Traurigkeit*. They were still outside, of course, melancholy, sighs, pain, sadness, but they were not made welcome in Robin's clear light as they had been in that murky fog of German romanticism in which I had pleased myself to be lost, or in that *Sturm und Drang*, that tumult and distress, in that earlier life with my mother and most of my lovers. With Robin there was no pretence that the winding tracks and sharp rocks did not exist, but there was the surety that we would get through them, with no pause for masochistic tears. But German was still a link. There was an added pleasure for me in her knowledge of German poetry; in her very first letter she sent me the gift of her heart in a German folksong of pristine clarity. I soon found that she also united two strains in my own development, for she was also a devotee of French literature, and in herself expressed that clarity, wit and logic which are so characteristically French.

We were modest enough, neither of us wanting to destroy the other's domestic environment. Yet we immediately saw ourselves as remaining there for each other. Like Donne's lovers (he was another mutual favourite), we "watched not one another out of fear". Robin, a committed feminist, jokingly allowed herself to be TOM, The Official Mistress. The appointment was for ten years, subject to renewal; no less. With this jokey contract we were signalling to each other a kind of commitment. We were avoiding that "there's no future in this" ending of an affair, which I now realised really meant, not that there was no future, but that the relationship had run its course.

From a kind of inertia, I continued to see, occasionally, an old friend, and told Robin about it; she called her TOF, The Old Friend. Robin's response, again not hurried, was simply to send me a tape of one of Paul Simon's songs, "Fifty Ways to Leave Your Lover", with its various telling phrases: "Just slip out the back, Jack / And make a new plan, Stan / You don't need to be coy, Roy / Hop on the bus, Gus / Drop off the key, Lee / and get yourself free". I laughed. It worked. Exit TOF.

Patrick was in Adelaide in 1981 for the opening of his new play, *Signal Driver*. He refused the offer of our town house in North Adelaide, saying he wanted to stay with the cast. But would I buy a big bunch of flowers for him to give to the leading lady, Kerry Walker. I delivered them to him at the boarding house where they were all staying; he came to the door, a bit giggly, almost like a naughty boy, and took the flowers in his arms, asking how much he owed me.

The play was not very good, but he was so popular with Adelaide's theatre audiences by then that it got a very good reception. He came onto the stage after the curtain, and had to motion with his hands for silence in the applause before he could say his few words. He was laughing. It was obvious that he was very happy with the young cast and director, that he had made them into a kind of family. Almost at the exact moment of the end of his speech, there was a stupendous crash outside, as the Festival fireworks began to explode along the River Torrens.

A couple of weeks later, Robin was in town and we escaped for a day from the city and drove down to Second Valley, the tiny bay with a jetty where the little steamer *Karatta* used to come in to take us to Kangaroo Island. There were only a few people about, and a short walk over and between the big, round rocks brought us to an inlet of complete privacy. Above us and the bare-breasted hills two wedge-tailed eagles circled, in front of us an occasional puff ruffled the burnished water, and the clarity of the light under the sea softened the basalt to a pale blue. There was a rift in the rocks near the dip where we lay on our towels, and as each of the slight surges came in, the rock itself seemed to breathe and sigh. It was our first whole day together; it was a kind of confirmation point.

We were to meet again at Robe, in the same group as before, when Ninette and I went to stay again at our mutual friends' house. We were all asked to lunch with Robin and Geoff at the house they had built when they moved from the Western District of Victoria and bought the property on the Coorong. It was a pleasant two-storey house, nothing luxurious, but as soon as I walked in the door and up to the living room, with the kitchen overlooking the blue bay, I felt at home. This was a woman who liked the same books, art, plates, glass, furniture, whatever, as myself, and who cooked the sort of meals that were just right. I remembered that unfortunate lunch with Joanna, and the overcooked whiting. It was a question of atmosphere in Robin's house, not that "Taste" which is written about in magazines for design and living, and always makes me squirm. The English wit and artist Osbert Lancaster called it "ghastly good taste". What is indefinable is the subtlety of the atmosphere of someone's house and food, where the taste behind it is like your own, which doesn't mean it's better than anyone else's. The glossy magazines might not approve of it at all, but for the two people involved, the vibrations are in tune. If they are not, that is a sign of the ultimate fragility of the relationship.

Robin would have been anathema to Madame Vitriolle. While she was getting lunch I was, no doubt unhelpfully, leaning against the refrigerator.

Something came up for which my two hands might be useful, so I put my drink down on the top of the machine, which was about level with my shoulder. It was very dusty. For some absurd reason, I found this very appealing.

After lunch Geoff took me up in his Piper Arrow and very sportingly handed it over to me and let me land it. In tune with the rest of the day, it was a good landing, the first time I had landed an aircraft for thirty-six years.

Not long after this I had to go to Sydney on *Bulletin* Literary Supplement business, and Murray Bail asked me to have lunch with him; there was something he wanted to discuss with me. Soft-spoken and elegant (but no dandy) as ever, Murray this day had that unmistakable look of very quiet triumph which means a writer is doing well. Murray was much too wary to be hearty about it, and anyway not given to expansive gestures, but he had some of the confidence of an impresario in offering himself, but very restrained. Writers operate against such odds, they work so hard and silently, alone, that they may be allowed a little celebration when they are made publicly welcome. Needless to say, Murray never mentioned his successes to me, that his novel *Homecoming* had won two major awards the year before, and his excellent monograph on the painter Ian Fairweather had just been published to applause. But he smiled with pleasure when I congratulated him on them.

I could see Murray had a plan. He reminded me that Patrick would be seventy in May the next year, and said the event should not go unacknowledged in Australia. Of course Patrick would hate any sort of public occasion, but Murray wondered whether he might not be pleased to be offered a *Festschrift*, a book of essays on his work, for the occasion of his birthday. He thought I might be able to organize it. I agreed it was a good idea, but pointed out that we would have to work very fast to get all the essays done and achieve publication by May. But we thought it could be done, so we began to draw up a list of contributors from around the world.

A few days later, back at Piers Hill, when I had done all the homework and spoken to a few friends, it did not look good at all. Brian Stonier had agreed that Macmillan would publish the book, but allowing for production and something extra for strikes (the curse of Australia at that time), he would have to have the manuscript by February at the very latest. Murray had left all the editing to me, but the essays would still have to go to Sydney and back for him to see them; I would never be able to achieve the world round-up in time.

More important than anything else, however, was that I was sure that there was no possibility that Patrick would approve of all fifteen essays. He was so cranky by now that at least half a dozen of the writers, unknown to me, would be certain to have done something to mortally offend him.

The *Festschrift* would be an *Unglückschrift*, a calamity, a disaster, an unhappiness.

I phoned Murray and said we should call it off. He reluctantly agreed. "But we must do something," he said. "The occasion mustn't be ignored in Australia. How about you write something in the *Bulletin*?" I said I would think about it. So I rang Trevor Sykes and he said it was a good idea. A long article about White and his work. But not bloody literary criticism. Keep it personal, something about an old friend.

When *Flaws in the Glass* was published, I praised it in a review for its good points, which were many. In private I took Patrick to task for his attacks on Sid Nolan and Joan Sutherland. But his egotism, his self-endowed entitlement to dictate to others or comment on their lives, was no longer capable of restraint. He wrote back but refused to back down. Sid was now a "weak and devious man" who had "thrown himself on the other one". "As for Joan Sutherland, I pay tribute to the voice while depressed by the Ocker in her. Just as Melba was a prime vulgarian with a miraculous voice. (Did you ever hear how an interested admirer asked her what she thought of her fellow artist Caruso, and she replied 'the best semen I ever gargled with')." He was now exhausting himself by becoming a public figure, appearing in political rallies and marching in antinuclear marches. I once asked him why these marches were always clamorously anti-American, and ignored the Soviet Union, which had as many nuclear devices as the Americans, but he only snorted in reply.

I tried hard in this article to show the kindness, the affection and the concern behind the scowling mask he so assiduously cultivated. But if I had been sensible enough to have aborted the *Festschrift*, why was I so bereft of sense as to agree to write this article? Knowing him so well, I should have realised that by making the article so personal I was making it certain that he would hate it, and in trying to make it so personal, I had used many anecdotes from my family's experiences with Patrick, which tended to make the article look as if it were as much about the Duttons as about Patrick. It was not my best effort, not well thought-out, and hastily written.

It was a total disaster, an *Unglück* that acted as the fuse to blow up a friendship of over twenty years. He wrote to me on 1 June 1982:

> I was amazed by your effusion in the *Bulletin*, as were any of our friends who have read it. I am told you wanted to organise a *Festschrift* and were choked off by those who knew I would dislike any such carrying-on. But the unexpected alternative ... Manoly and I squirmed all the way through it, not only for the inaccuracies, but for its silliness and vulgarity. Perhaps you did it out of pique because there wasn't reference enough to the Duttons in *Flaws in the Glass*, when the book really only dealt with those who were of influence in my development. If I had been writing an autobiography I expect I should have made more of the rich and famous I have met on social occasions around the

> world. But *Flaws in the Glass* is not an autobiography, and you I should have thought would never have sunk to the level of Andrea and Nola Dekyvere [social-notes journalists of the time]. No doubt the *Bulletin* was thrilled: those dames were pillars of the Packer press, and here is Geoffrey Dutton upholding the tradition.
>
> I'm sorry, but I've had enough of Duttonry, and ask you not to ring me when you fly from capital to capital for what I can't see as any good reason. And please let there be no correspondence. As you know, I don't keep letters, but this one will be an exception — to show the curious why our relationship ended.

To which I replied in a typed version, having censored my earlier handwritten letter:

> Your notion that I wrote that *Bulletin* article out of pique that I wasn't mentioned in *Flaws in the Glass* astounds me. What a vain prick you are! You of course have chosen to forget how I praised the book when it was published. I have a private and public life sufficiently full not to leave any little vacuums longing to be puffed into by P. White. My sole aim in writing that article was to try to show that you were once a humane, generous and even good man as well as a complex artist. I realize now that unconsciously I was writing an elegy.
>
> In recent years it has been painful to observe you becoming ever more vain, intolerant and authoritarian, even descending into rabid anti-Semitism.
>
> I thought it the duty of a friend to stick by you, but your last letter has certainly cured me of that. You say you will keep that letter; I too will keep this one. I intend never to write or speak to you again, and as for telephoning, I wouldn't waste the ten cents on you.
>
> P.S. The idea of a *Festschrift* was Murray Bail's, not mine. He suggested to me that I should organize it, and after discussing the idea with a few people, and realizing it wouldn't work, it was I, not anyone else, who "choked the idea off".

I never saw him again, which was sad, because he had been a good friend. I was more sorry for my guiltless children, who were genuinely fond of him and believed he was fond of them; but they were tainted by the sins of their father, and total silence descended on them.

Popularity is a strange two-headed monster and comforter, especially in the arts. The popularity of the gold-embossed novels in airport bookstalls means lots of lovely money for their writers, but not even a toehold in the future of literature. On the other hand, many of the greatest novelists continue to be popular — for example, Dickens, Balzac and Tolstoy. Even poets qualify; the Penguin translations of Homer were best-sellers, and thousands still want to read Keats and Burns, as millions read or recite Pushkin in Russia.

Whatever writers may say, I have never known one who was truly indifferent to popularity — or who did not read reviews. Patrick read and kept every review of his books, and desperately wanted to be popular, but knew he never would be, even after winning the Nobel Prize; he would never be popular like writers such as Graham Greene or Evelyn Waugh.

The theatre, and his public political appearances, gave him the warm (a word he hated!) glow of being popular, without having to consider what a small audience it in fact was. A full theatre every night for a season at the drama theatre at the Opera House did not compare in numbers with the readership of one of his novels in Australia, for books reach more than one reader and go on and on. And, of course, the plays never reached overseas audiences. But I can see that the theatre gave him a "family", a sense of belonging in a community totally committed to an activity that had always meant so much to him.

Some twenty years earlier he had suggested to me that some episodes in my biography of William Light would make a good play, but that "I was not dishonest enough for the theatre", while saying, about himself, "I am very tired of theatre intrigue". His advice to me about the theatre was sound, but he was unable to take it himself. He was to return again and again in letters and in conversation to the theme of dishonesty in the theatre. Unfortunately, the theatre made him dishonest with himself as an artist. He might have been, in different aspects of his psyche, many of the characters in his novels, but the big concepts of his novels, which Lawrence Durrell so much admired, prevented him from using them as vehicles for uninterrupted direct preaching in his own voice. Nevertheless, the extent to which he allowed himself into his novels would have shocked Flaubert, whom he thought closer to himself than any other novelist. As Flaubert wrote to George Sand: "Don't put your own personality on stage. I believe great art is scientific and impersonal. What you have to do is transport yourself, by an intellectual effort, into your Characters — not attract them to yourself."

By decades of doing the opposite, of attracting his characters to himself, Patrick had come to think of real people as his own characters. They had to reflect his own views, to live up to or fall short of what he thought of as his own standards, however little he lived up to them himself. What should have been the impersonality of his art became the personality of both art and life. What was thought of as his "morality" was in fact inflexibility. And all this was much more tempting, and possible, in the brevity of a play and on the platform of a stage.

For the corruption of his artistic standards by the theatre one need go no further than those pitiful pages, near the end of *Flaws in the Glass*, when he writes of the failure of *Big Toys*. "It upset the vulgarian shyster rich ..." and the television version "made no great impression on those who watch in the glass towers and the lounge-rooms of their homes". Patrick never saw that the failure of *Big Toys* was not from its neglect by the hated rich or the equally despised suburbanites, but from the lack of control in his own writing. A friend of Manoly's once said that Manoly probably thought the theatre was "a sort of virus" for Patrick. Manoly was, of course, justifiably jealous of Patrick's reversion, remarked on by Barry Humphries, to the stage-door Johnny, for the Patrick he loved was the great novelist.

What the theatre eventually gave Patrick was warmth, that hated word. He basked in the glow of admiration which radiated from Jim Sharman and the young actors, male and female — so much so that he suffered amnesia, as David Marr puts it, or told lies, as others might term it, in saying in *Flaws in the Glass* that Sharman's production of *The Season at Sarsaparilla* was "the success it had not been in Adelaide, Sydney and Melbourne fifteen years earlier". On the contrary, it had been a smash hit in Adelaide and Melbourne, and as he wrote proudly to me, had even made money. In Sydney it survived a five-week run, but was not a great success, and was rubbished by all the critics except Harry Kippax, the best of them. To succeed in Sydney, with Jim Sharman directing, was what mattered, and to hell with the truth about the rest.

So the theatre gave him warmth but dishonesty to his own artistic conscience, which was already weakened by his all-inclusive egotism. After *Big Toys*, he wrote three more plays but only one short novel, the self-indulgent *Memoirs of Many in One*.

By June 1982 the cracks in our friendship had long been evident, and I was not surprised when the end came. Perhaps, unconsciously, I had brought it to an end by writing that stupid article. There were some friends he had used and then cast off when he had no more use for them, as to his shame he did with his Jewish friends. I do not think he used myself and my family, nor some other old friends, although he got a lot out of us; he also enriched our lives. Barry Humphries truly said that we disappointed him, and he disappointed us; we disappointed each other. But his decline as a writer, and the ever-worsening degeneration of his health, saddened both new friends and old.

Another sadness of this time was the death of my old friend Deasey, from cancer. In these last Melbourne years of being a respectable schoolmaster, he had become very touchy; worse, even a bit boring. But he had been my oldest close friend, and I will never forget those teenage years when we poured out our souls to each other, both ludicrous and touching. He was an original who never had the organizing talent to make something permanent of his brilliance.

In the many areas of discussion with Dease over the years we had often wandered into the dangerous world of Friedrich Nietzsche. The oracular pronouncements in *Also Sprach Zarathustra* had both fascinated and alarmed us. Then Hitler's war seemed to us to have put paid to Nietzsche and Wagner. Yet there is, of course, a great depth of poetic intuition in the words of Nietzsche that continues to be relevant to one's inner life. One such gnomic utterance is that one ought "to become what one is", by which he meant that one's life as well as one's art is there to be created. Until I met Robin I tried to be true to what I thought I was, often a disastrous recipe. I should have looked clearly at what I really was, and set about creating what I could become by stripping away the inessentials. With Robin I began this difficult and often painful process of creation, and began to become myself.

During 1982, when I was working on the book that became *Snow on the Saltbush*, the letters were flowing between Robin and me, and I was writing poems for her that were emblematic, metaphysical, accessible on different layers of meaning. Not so our letters, which were unashamedly direct, from the heart, yet giving us both marvellous opportunities to get to know each other's minds, for lovers who have only a limited time together never have time to say all they want to say. In our letters we both created our love and opened our lives.

We were also always copying out poems for each other, as if the poets had written especially for us, a harmless illusion that lovers have; thankfully we sent their messages to each other in our letters. They came from every age and language into all the situations in which we found ourselves. I sent her Sir Philip Sidney's "The Highway" after driving down the main road to meet her, for the road he had addressed was also my road. "Now blessed you, beare onward blessed me / To her, where my heart safeleft shall meet ..." There was never any doubt about that "safeleft". And when we parted we did not really part, as in yet another poem by that inexhaustible poet, Anon.

Wee must not parte as others doe
with sighs and teares as wee were two,
though with these outward formes wee parte
wee keepe each other in our hart,
what search hath found a beinge where
I am not if that thou be there,
true Love hath winges and can as soone
survey the world as Sun and Moone,
and every where our Triumphes keepe,
over absence which makes others weepe,
by which alone a power is given,
to live on Earth as they in heaven.

Then she was reading Byron's letters and copied this passage out for me about absence: "The only thing that consoles me during absence is the reflection that no mental or personal estrangement, from ennui or disagreement, can take place; and when people meet hereafter, even though many changes may have taken place, in the meantime, still, unless they are *tired* of each other, they are ready to reunite, and do not blame each other for the circumstances that severed them".

We would both analyze our own faults, and ask what it was in us that appealed to each other. I wrote to her that this was my first adult relationship, and it was true, as far as she was concerned, for I myself still had a long way to go in becoming myself. She wrote: "The things you like about me are the things I've always liked about me too, but had been persuaded they weren't valuable".

We could be absolutely honest with each other because, in Byron's word, the discernment was there on both sides. Neither pretences nor apologies were needed, and certainly not any manipulation or playing of games. Yet we thought we would have to remain peripheral to each other's lives, and this would be made bearable by the fact that we both knew we were at the same time at the centre together. Like the old poet Anon and distance, we could keep each other in our hearts.

In 1982 John Olsen came to see me to tell me that Allen Christensen, an eccentric American billionaire, wanted to send him and me, with Mary Durack and Vincent Serventy, to the north-west of Western Australia for an extensive journey that would result in a book; John would contribute paintings and drawings. Christensen was an extraordinary man who had made a fortune out of mining, in America, Australia and elsewhere, and had a passion for Australia and for art. He had already presented several state galleries with valuable collections of early art and artefacts from South-east Asia, and modern Australian works. Now all the writings and art works from this journey would also be presented, in this case to the Art Gallery of Western Australia. Mary, Vin, John and I were already friends, and I could not think of better travelling companions. The man organizing the whole concept was a large, jovial Australian of Italian descent, Alex Bortignon, who ran a gallery in Perth and dealt in South-east Asian art works.

No expense was to be spared for this expedition. Apart from the four-wheel-drive vehicles provided, fixed-wing aircraft and helicopters would be available to get us into areas of the Kimberley, such as the mouth of the Prince Regent River, which were inaccessible by land. We would be away for about ten weeks from August to October, and would return again to the north-west at Easter, to an area which at that time was almost totally unknown, the Bungle Bungle Ranges.

I had interrupted *Snow on the Saltbush* for this trip, and there was another break for the Bungle Bungles, but by working hard I managed to finish it on 13 April 1983. By 31 May I had finished my 10,000-word share of the text of *The Land Beyond Time*, and revised the fifteen poems I had written on the journey. *The Land Beyond Time* was a beautiful book, and all our friendships survived intact. It was a great privilege to have taken part in the expedition, which enabled us to go to places we could never have reached on our own resources.

As for the poems, Stendhal said that love is an exquisite flower, but one must have the courage to go and gather it on the brink of a dreadful precipice; so must poetry be gathered. Through many months of travelling in remote regions, in the north-west and then on the other side of the continent, the poems came, obliquely or directly always for Robin. I wrote them at dawn or near dusk at halts in strenuous days of travel, sitting on a log or on the red sand. I wrote ten 16-line sonnets, in the form Meredith used for "Modern Love", about Byron's life (actually in some ways symbolic of my own) in two days cooped up with John Olsen in a motel room in Broome.

This was at Easter, on our way back from the Bungle Bungles, but in the previous September, Ninette had opened a letter from Robin. If I had been honest, I would have left then, although I did not know whether or not Robin would have come with me. She and Geoff Baulch had that rare thing, an open marriage in which they remained good friends. But her younger children were fourteen and eleven; mine were all grown up.

Neither Robin nor I made a move, nor any claim. And so it went on, month after month. Robin and I tried to remain light-hearted. I asked her what she thought a new life together would be like. "Bloody hopeless," she said. "You pour salt over all your food and I cook without it." In summer at Kangaroo Island, with fourteen people staying at Rocky Point, I carried an old cane chair down into the scrub, where the dried moss on the sandy soil was sheltered by native pines and wattles, and wrote a series of poems for Robin on absence, based on the complex forms of that Elizabethan master of poetry, music and love, Thomas Campion.

Ninette wanted to do a book of paintings of wildflowers, so took me away with her to the far north of South Australia and into western Queensland and New South Wales. In a little tent zipped up against a million flies, I translated French poems for Robin, accepting the challenge to reproduce the original structures of rhyme and rhythm. It was an odd thing about all these poems, both my own and the translations, that the more difficulties they were written under, the more complex they became technically, as if the desperate challenges of rhyme and rhythm were parallels to what we must go through to stay lovers.

I had a virus before the wildflower trip, and camping in the bush, normally so recuperative, became more and more difficult. To carry a can of water from a creek to the campfire totally exhausted me. I never normally need a lot of sleep, but on 10 June, after a couple of days at the first camp at Sturt's Preservation Creek at Depot Glen, I went to bed at 4 p.m. and slept for fourteen hours. I have never felt so ill. But we went on, through Queensland and New South Wales, until finally I could take it no longer and we returned to Adelaide, arriving on 20 July. Without being melodramatic, I thought this deadly exhaustion meant that I was going to die. The doctors took X-rays and said the virus had affected my heart, and that in turn had affected my liver and kidneys and God knows what else. As a *memento* of near-*mori*, my heartbeat is still absurdly irregular. "It *would* be your heart," said John Olsen.

I finally got my priorities sorted out and decided to leave. Robin did not hesitate. She would come with me. In the ensuing awful days, before we left, I was most of all amazed that I had actually made the move; I should have made it years before, when I went to Oxford. In fact, Ninette and I should never have married in the first place; we were too young, we were not really suited. After I had been to Bougainville, and had nearly been killed, I should have looked hard at myself and at both our futures. We were to have many good times together, long before the children came, but I was basically still Ah-timid-dormouse, as stoical-passive as I had been when directed by my mother. At boarding school and in the RAAF I had developed a secret life, of poetry and love, although in the RAAF it was sex rather than love. For many years, although committed professionally to literature, for most of the time I approached it in the spirit of one who will not forsake the world for art, seduced by Byron's prescription that a writer should not be all writer.

Ninette took over, as my mother had done, devoted to keeping things on an even keel and presenting the façade of the perfect marriage. I hypocritically went along with this as long as I could continue with my "secret" life. In the years when I should have been creating myself, I was in fact preserving the image of a self which was someone not true to my real self.

In my last year at school, home for the holidays, I once picked up one of my mother's books, an anthology of modern poetry. She had a bad habit (I think only after my father died — perhaps it was an unconscious token of freedom) of underlining certain passages in pencil, or marking them in the margin. Here, in Roy Campbell's "Horses on the Camargue", she had underlined and marked in the margin the opening line: "In the grey wastes of dread". My father had been dead for at least six years before she bought the book, but that line must have brought back the desolation of being married to an alcoholic who went on benders. So the surface of life had to be unruffled; she had to be the grim guardian of her children, as in those photos, first of her with John and Dick, then, fifteen or more years later, with me and Chibs, where she wears the identical expression.

For long periods of our lives, John and I were stoic-passive. He came back to Anlaby when he should have put a thousand miles between him and his mother. Even after she was dead, I repeated the pattern. I escaped to my love affairs and in my writing and all those other activities which should have been basic rather than escapist. Not until my life with Robin, not until we began to live together, did I get my priorities right. Since I have been with her I have never had another lover, and never wanted to.

Marriage break-ups are very painful to all concerned. Robin's came after sixteen years of marriage, mine after nearly forty; between us, we have seven children. Anyone who has left a marriage will know how distressing those last few weeks are, and how out of misguided guilt and pity we do and say things we later regret. It is a time of great opportunity for the so-called "guiltless" parties, and a measure of their character as to how much flesh and blood they demand in return for the humiliation of being left. The "guilty" party always acquiesces in the most outrageous demands at this time. Now, from a distance, my advice to others would be to get out as quickly as possible and let the lawyers sort out the details.

By the time we left, Robin and I were only just afloat on the tide-race of emotion. Fortunately, perhaps, the tragi-comedies of love are as old as love itself. True lovers must have a sense of humour. I drove in Tisi's usually reliable Renault to meet Robin at her house in Norwood. Geoff Baulch had tactfully gone to the farm; Robin's children, Emma and Michael, would be at school. But Emma and Michael firmly declared that they wanted to be there and say goodbye to both of us. They said they didn't want to miss out on the fun. Then the Renault broke down, in the outskirts of Adelaide. I had to hire a car, and arrived more than an hour late. Just as we were packing my gear in Robin's Fiat, Geoff arrived back from the farm. To his eternal credit, he laughed and brought out a bottle of champagne.

John Olsen had said to us that we would be too physically exhausted by emotion to set out to drive to Sydney; we should come down to his house at Clarendon and stay the night, and leave, refreshed, in the morning. John was being a true and generous friend. He offered us his beach house at Pearl Beach, so we would have somewhere to go when we arrived in Sydney. He even asked if he could lend us some money.

Not long before we left, Richard Walsh had commissioned me to write a book for Angus & Robertson. It was to be a monster, in size and in the effort required to write it in time for his savage deadline. His idea was that I should select a book each from a hundred Australian prose authors, from the beginnings of white settlement to the present day. I should take a typical extract from each book, and write two short articles, critical and biographical, about each book and writer. It would all then be very handsomely packaged, with suitable period illustrations, as a book to help people who wanted to know more about Australian writers and writing, as well as being a notable possession in itself. It was a bold concept, an attempt to reach the middle Australia which both Richard and I thought was rather nervously longing to expand its sense of belonging and knowledge of its literary heritage. It was not to be a lowbrow book, but it was certainly not to be written for those who already knew a lot about the subject. And I, who had been writer, publisher and editor, and lecturer, knew how relatively few people were familiar with all those hundred books of fiction and non-fiction, not many of them in the accepted and endlessly repeated academic canon.

At the last minute (after I had done the work) Morris Lurie and the executors of Alan Marshall's estate for various but equally disappointing reasons, refused permission for Lurie's and Marshall's books to be included, so the volume deals with only ninety-eight works.

For Robin and me, our "honeymoon" at beautiful Pearl Beach included all those things that honeymooners usually do, but also consisted of a fourteen-hour working day for me, and a long day for Robin editing my chapters and managing the contributions to the *Bulletin* Literary Supplement. Walsh wanted to set the book and assemble the art work as I wrote it, so that he could publish it as soon as possible; this meant working under extreme pressure. But he paid me on a regular basis, month by month, so we called The Monster our running-away book.

Pearl Beach was beautiful and peaceful, but only temporary. Fortunately we were soon able to find a flat in an old house in Rose Bay, so we moved to Sydney.

Sydney had always been very exciting to visit, after the doldrums of Adelaide-between-Festivals. (Many people have an erroneous notion that Adelaide keeps up the sparkle of those weeks for the rest of the two years between Festivals.) There were old friends and new friends who lived in the city, and friends on visits to Sydney. Colin Lanceley we met in the deli at Pearl Beach, and he and Kay became two of our dearest friends. There was Ed Campion; Patricia Rolfe; Russel Ward down from Armidale — so strange to think that he had taught me at school, and introduced me to *The Waste Land*; Patsy Zeppel; Brian Johns; Olsen coming-and-going; Barry Humphries being manoeuvred by his disastrous wife Dianne into spending a fortune redesigning and re-redesigning several floors of beautiful flats in the Astor in Macquarie Street; Noel and Sue Ferrier — after one of their lunches, which ended after dark, Robin and I went for a night surf at Bondi and nearly drowned ourselves; Judah Waten and David Foster on visits to Sydney; the vivid young poet Dorothy Porter.

It was an odd feeling, and very good for me, to be living in this huge city where no one gave a damn that my ancestors had been pioneers and I lived at Anlaby. But there were to be some odd repercussions from this family connection. When we moved into Rose Bay I thought we should insure our meagre possessions, or at least the books and the few pictures we had. So I rang the insurance company my family had dealt with in South Australia for the past hundred years or so, pointing out this fairly long association to the clerk who answered my call. Obviously not impressed — he might well have asked me where Adelaide was — he said that he supposed they would consider the matter. A few questions. I answered them, until he said, "Are you married to this Robin Lucas with whom you share the house?" I suggested that it was none of his bloody business and that I would like a word with the manager. He said that was not possible, but that he would speak with the manager, if I would hang on for a moment or two. He came back on the line and said, in an equally insouciant voice, that as Robin and I were not married, they could not insure the contents of the house. Company policy. I told him what I thought of him, and changed insurance companies on the spot.

That night, Barry Humphries came to dinner. I told him the story, thinking it would amuse him. But, to our astonishment, he seemed to take the situation quite seriously. He said, in a very restrained voice, "I think, Geoffrey, you should write your insurance manager a letter: 'Dear Sir. I am writing to apologize for my intemperate language to a member of your staff today. I realize that I strayed from my usual polite discourse, and regret that I may have offended your employee. In conclusion,' his voice suddenly turned to steel, 'you can stick your insurance policy up your arse'." Barry looked thoughtful for a moment or two, and continued, "A last nice touch might be to tie up all your insurance policies with his company in red ribbon, and forward them to the manager, together with a jar of Vaseline."

There were comic interludes in our new life together, but for Robin there was a constant undercurrent of sadness which came from parting with her younger children, Emma and Michael. For her older children, and for mine, who were well into their own lives, it was not so difficult, though not easy. But Emma was only fifteen and Michael twelve when Robin and I left. She told me not long after we met that she was a bad wife but a good mother. Whenever I was with her and her children, the strong links between them had been clear and sound. Now they were parted, at least temporarily. We had an arrangement with Emma and Michael that, if ever they wanted to come and live with us in Sydney, they could. But they decided to remain in Adelaide where they had a network of friends and familiar schools. As it was, they spent most of their school holidays with us, either in Sydney or at Rocky Point. In her more anguished moments Robin reasoned that this arrangement was no worse than if they had been at boarding school, but she found the separation hard.

I gradually got to know Robin's parents, Grumpy and Claire; it would be impossible to imagine a couple less like my first in-laws. Robin's father was christened Harold and known as Tom, but he acquired the nickname Grumpy in the RAAF, in which he was a fighter pilot in Kittyhawks. He was called Grumpy because he was so good-natured. This was typical of the RAAF; I had a friend who was six feet eight inches tall and was called Shorty, and another, almost an albino, who was known as Midnight.

Robin and I went to stay at Rosebank, Grumpy and Claire's beautiful old stone house in Victoria at Koroit, on the edge of the extraordinary Tower Hill volcano crater. Henry Handel Richardson's poor, mad father is buried in Tower Hill cemetery; her mother was postmistress at Koroit. Frank Hardy was born at nearby Southern Cross. Hal Porter often came over from his sister's farm at Garvoc to stay at Rosebank.

But the associations were not all literary. I went out barracouta fishing at five-thirty in the morning with Grumpy and his mate Donny, in Donny's battered couta boat. "Fishing's like the grog," said Donny, "it makes men boys." We pulled in seventy couta in an hour. As we drove home Grumpy said a morning with Donny made him decent to live with again.

Libby and Kate, Robin's older girls, came to stay with us in Sydney, and then, in another South Australian school holidays, which by luck were after the New South Wales ones, I hired a cabin cruiser and we chugged up the Hawkesbury for a couple of utterly peaceful days with Emma and Michael. The river was so beautiful that we didn't bother to go very far, but just tied up by the bank under the steep, dark hills. We prised oysters off the rocks and ate them; Michael doesn't like oysters, but he opened dozens for the three of us who do. Emma and Michael rowed around in circles in the dinghy and swam. We got to know each other. It was good.

PART SEVEN

To the Glasshouse Mountains 1983–93

Yet we're not like ants
In the grey mountain's
Daunting presence.
There's no fear in the forest.
We might even be blest.

"Mount Coonowrin"

Thirty-Three

Although thousands of Sydney dwellers never see the Harbour for most of the year, it is still at the centre of the city's life, making it like no other city in the world. The Harbour is not only beautiful but changeable, moody, unlike all those suburbs that are as determinedly and cheerfully the same as a row of red bottlebrushes. And of course, neither the Bridge nor the new tunnel will ever heal the gap between the central city, with its eastern suburbs, and the North Shore.

From Rose Bay it was only a short drive to Nielsen Park. We would take a bag of prawns and a bottle of wine and have supper on one of those patches of grass between the boulders above the water, from which you can watch the sun go down through changing veils of light behind the Harbour Bridge and the towers of the city.

In Sydney you have to be very disciplined in your work to resist the seductions of good company. By rigorous effort, and the discovery of a wonderful stenographer, Ros Deanes, I finished The Monster on time. But we were so broke that I had to start immediately on another book, one about the Beach, which by then had taken over from the Bush as the central myth of the Australian experience.

Despite the rigours of work, Sydney seems to give you extra energy to see your friends. Sydney is vulgar, maybe, but never genteel, plodding or grey. It's not what John Olsen calls "boojy".

One asset of coming to live in Sydney was that we were able to see more of Chibs and Dick, who were living in Canberra, where in time Dick was to become Chief Justice of the Federal Court and Chancellor of the Australian National University. One of my greatest pleasures was that Robin got on so well with both of them.

Shortly after our arrival in Sydney, Bill Reed, who was then Publisher at Macmillan, came up with what seemed like a good idea for a book. Richard Haese's *Rebels and Precursors*, about the development of modern art in Australia, had been a useful book in many ways, but it had perpetuated the old split between Melbourne and Sydney. Haese, following John Reed, seemed to think that everything had happened south of Albury. It was the opposite attitude to that of Sydney Ure Smith, whose *Present Day Art in Australia* had managed to avoid mentioning any of the Melbourne painters. Bill Reed now suggested to me that I write a book about the growth of modern art, literature and ideas in Sydney, provisionally to be called "The Sydney Alternative". (It was published under the title, *The Innovators*.)

So began the slow task of research and of interviewing the artists involved. Renewing an old friendship with Donald Friend, I went to see him at his little house in Belmore Place, Paddington. The house looked like a Sali Herman painting, standing perkily separate from the surrounding terraces, enclosed in its garden. Donald was digging among his vegetables, old and sick with chronic emphysema, but still chain-smoking cigarette after cigarette down to the edge of the cork filter, and as genial and witty as ever. No other Australian artist has been able to equal Donald's mastery of the spoken and written word. He opened a bottle of excellent dry sherry and we settled down to the first of many talks, including a long interview on tape which fortunately preserves the sparkle, mockery and enthusiasm of his voice.

Every now and then Donald would say, "Let's turn that tape off for a while", with a roll of eyes in his satyr's face. Armed with another cigarette and another sherry he would say, "Thelma Clune had a boyfriend, a very glamorous, sort of loping boy — God is not kind to make them loping — like a meringue, you know, but lacking in crispness". Thelma had told Donald she was the classic shy, lonely girl; he had never realized how deaf she was. Frank Clune, as no one who heard it could forget, had a very loud voice. Thelma said to Donald, "Frank was the first man I could hear, so I married him."

The republican cause was still very low-key in the 1980s, occasionally erupting in scenes that demonstrated some of the prejudices of the monarchists. I took part in a radio debate on the issue, chaired by Margaret Throsby, with Franca Arena, Max Teichelmann and me versus John Howard, Sir William Keys (of the RSL) and John Paul. At question time a woman got up and asked Keys why he opposed a referendum on the republic. She was an Australian who had recently returned from living in London for three years. Whenever she had mentioned her republican views her English friends responded with enthusiasm: "So you're at last growing up out there".

Keys's notion of a reply was to call her a troublemaker and a stirrer who wanted to betray the flag Australians had fought under in two world wars. She furiously replied that her father had been killed in World War I, and her husband wounded in World War II. She said she thought Keys was just a rat. Keys jumped to his feet and shouted, "There, that's proved it, you're a dreadful woman." Such were the monarchists in 1984.

Brian Johns, a friend who was then head of Penguin Books, came to see us one day when in Sydney on a visit from Melbourne. He asked me if I, with Robin, would come out to Ringwood for lunch one day, after which I could talk to the staff about the foundation of Penguin Australia. This invitation was typical of the imagination and thoughtfulness of this remarkable man, who had come to Penguin with almost no experience of publishing, and had made a tremendous success of the job; he wanted his staff to have an idea of the history and continuity of Penguin Australia. When I talked to them, I found them a most responsive audience. Such a sense of the whole, of what is distinctively Australian and how it is developing, is typical of Johns, and emerged again in his later work at the head of SBS.

In September I was asked by the Australia-Japan Foundation and NHK (the Japanese national broadcaster) to go to Japan to advise NHK on a big TV series the company intended to make in Australia. Robin and I went — our first visit to Japan, after years of reading its books and looking at its art and film.

The top people at NHK were enormously impressive; I could not help comparing them with some of our own TV executives. One had an honours literature degree. He had wanted to be a concert violinist, but unable to reach the top as a violinist, he now contented himself in private with his talents as a pianist. Another was a philosopher, another a scientist. After some very strenuous hours of discussion they took us out to dinner. I had not realized how the Japanese love puns. They thought the link between "Datsun" and "Duttonsan" was hilarious.

I was nervous of going, fearing Japan would be like a sort of frenzied United States, ugly, crowded and ruthlessly commercial. Robin believed otherwise, as she had Japanese friends and had read widely in what contemporary Japanese literature was available at the time. The ugly elements existed, certainly, but Japan is a country where a rubbish bin is hidden in a beautiful wooden chest, and the bedroom in a simple inn is in itself a work of art.

After our business was concluded, Gilbert George of the Australia-Japan Foundation, took turns with two excellent young interpreters, to show us a lot more of Japan than Tokyo. I already knew something of what is absurdly called "Asia", especially from that intensive time in Singapore, but Robin's enthusiasm for the region urged me on. She instinctively responded at first hand to what I had absorbed through books. Monkey, Arthur Waley's translations of Chinese poems, William Light and his father in Malaya, Raffles in Indonesia and Singapore, Conrad among the islands, all these had enthralled me, but at a distance. But Robin was of the new wave; the distance from Australia to Jakarta or Tokyo was in fact far less than to London or Athens, and she relished the complexities of unravelling the cultural distance.

We were to pay many rewarding visits to these northern (from Australia) regions, and it was good that they were not just holidays but that we were working as well. Later, we were both asked by the Australian-Indonesian

Institute to lecture in Indonesia. I was asked on one occasion to lecture in Singapore, on another to be one of the judges of their first literary competition. We made good friends with Edwin Thumboo and Kirpal Singh, both poets as well as academics, and came to feel at home there, especially as our Singaporean friends introduced us to corners and aspects of the country we would have had no chance of learning about on our own.

In Indonesia we were lucky that Robin's daughter Emma was working there over a long period; she was impressively fluent in Indonesian and had a working knowledge of Javanese. Robin said that seeing your child functioning and communicating in another culture and language was like meeting her for the first time as a different, adult, person. The last time we visited Emma there she was having trouble with her English, being out of practice. "Oh, what's the word?" she would groan in frustration. "Those things that ... " (furious hand and arm gestures), "I know! Windmill!"

Emma, so slim and pretty and quick, fitted in perfectly among her Indonesian friends. We did things with her that we would never have done as tourists, following Emma and her friends down dark streets to local restaurants or humid, sunny streets to markets and unmarked antique shops. We went to a remote sandy beach on the Java Sea where a narrow fishing boat came in, its floorboards flapping with fish; we selected one each, and Emma arranged for a tiny nearby bar to clean and charcoal-grill them for us. Spiced with chillies, they were delicious, and as we were eating them a man came jogging down the hill with a python in a bag over his shoulder to sell as bait to the fishermen.

These working visits extended my knowledge and understanding far beyond the old familiar boundaries of Britain, Europe and the United States. Those long car journeys from London to Colombo and from Cape Town to Tangier had given me access to all sorts of riches, but they were temporary, those of the traveller. In contrast, this new focus brought journeys of discovery that related to me more permanently. I have said there is no such thing as "Asia", but a knowledge of the region, whatever we are going to call it, is firmly hooked to the experience of being an Australian in the last two decades of the twentieth century.

Towards the end of 1984 our landlady, who lived in America, decided to sell the house, so we moved to Surry Hills. Before long we had also to move from there, so, with the help of an enormous mortgage, we bought a terrace house in Paddington.

One day Trevor Kennedy asked me to have lunch with him, and after the second bottle and an excellent meal told me that everyone in the *Bulletin* office except himself found the Supplement boring and often unintelligible. They were all in favour of "cutting its throat". Other readers seemed to enjoy it, but I have found over the years that many journalists do not like "creative" writers or what they write. They think that writers of fiction and poetry are a pack of bludgers and they hate the Literature Board or any other organ of patronage. And yet in a journalist like Trevor Kennedy, and in many others who often talk as if they value ephemera more than writing which takes its chance with the future, there is buried a deep respect for novelists, poets and historians. It is a strange and apparently insoluble paradox.

I was sad to see the Supplement go, thinking of all those writers who would no longer be reaching the large audience of the *Bulletin*.

Enter once more fate, chance, destiny, or whatever it is that periodically takes charge of our lives, if we have the sense to let it. Less than a fortnight later, on a Monday, Brian Stonier was in Sydney on a visit from Melbourne, and Robin and I had lunch with him at a small French restaurant in Cleveland Street. Brian asked how the Supplement was going. I told him it was dead; that I had a whole new issue ready to go to press, and wished I had somewhere to take it. "What about the *Australian*?" asked Brian. He said he was seeing Les Hollings, editor-in-chief of the *Australian*, the next day, and would suggest that the *Australian* take over the Supplement. On Wednesday Les rang and asked me to see him in his office at 3 p.m.

There, in the dingy surroundings brightened by the presence of three of Sid Nolan's paintings, Les spoke as if it were all fixed. The Supplement would appear quarterly, inside the *Weekend Australian*. He finished by saying, "I'll discuss it with Finance and write to you tonight." I thought Finance would be sure to kill the idea, but no, in the morning Robin went out to get the paper and found a letter under the door, making a formal offer to me to edit the *Australian* Literary Supplement. Part of the deal was that the technical production of the Supplement, and its finances, would be managed by one of the *Australian*'s original journalists, now an executive, Arnold Earnshaw. I was delighted with the arrangement, and Arnold, with his unreconstructed Yorkshire accent and sense of humour, was always helpful. This Supplement was fuelled by gin. Every Friday afternoon, at about 5 p.m., Arnold would arrive at our house in Surry Hills, or the one we later bought in Paddington, and we would discuss the Supplement and almost everything else in the wide world. The *Australian* Literary Supplement reached even more readers than the Supplement in the *Bulletin* had, and was always very handsomely presented.

Robin and I had decided that our lives and those of our former partners would be tidier if we were divorced, and then Robin and I would marry. Harold and Betty, who had lived above us in Rose Bay, said, "If ever there were two people made to be married to each other, it's you two." We felt the same. Our divorces eventually came through in February.

In the meantime I had been engaged, with daily anguish, in another kind of wedding. Robin had finally talked me into buying a word-processor. Bob Raymond had shown me how these magic machines may be tamed, and had helped us in choosing one that would be reliable and practical. The only hidden snag was that, unbeknown to us, the people we bought the computer from had not only sold us one with a fault in its hard disk but had subsequently lost the agency for that machine.

I was faced with another terrible deadline, this time for *The Innovators*, which I had begun writing a week after our divorces went through. I was getting up at 4 a.m. and finishing at 7 p.m. This was endurable, but what was intolerable as well as nerve-shattering was when the printer started to spew out pages of the letter "s" instead of my script. The people from whom I had bought the computer, still not confessing that they had lost that agency, sent around a willowy young man who wasted my time and did nothing to rescue my files.

They sent me to a place that serviced computers, way out past Parramatta. Then the computer went wrong again. A nervous breakdown was imminent. Finally a message arrived to say that the American manufacturers of our computer had set up their own agency. It was a long drive away, in some obscure suburb of southern Sydney, but these Americans were princes, angels of light. They found the fault in my hard disk and copied all my files onto a new hard disk. I had lost about thirty pages, but soon rewrote them.

On 31 March I finished this 90,000-word book. But then there was the revision to be done. A few days after I had finished this, on 4 April 1985, we were married. Anders Ousback organized a magnificent wedding breakfast. The furniture in our one big room was turfed out into the backyard and a long table and chairs were installed. Somehow in our tiny kitchen Anders and Sarah de Teliga cooked a superb meal while we drank the five different wines he had chosen. Robin and I left the guests, including the five of our children who were in Australia at the time, to finish the wine, and went to the Regent for the night.

Fortunately for our very frail finances, offers of work for both of us kept pouring in, even though it sometimes took big bites out of the day and night. I wrote a script for a film Tristram Miall was making for the BBC, which towards the end was calling for an eighteen-hour day. Tris went on from strength to strength; later he was the producer of *Strictly Ballroom*.

I was working one day in the Mitchell Library and there was Bob Hughes in the next bay, pounding away furiously on his laptop; he was working on *The Fatal Shore*. He was even more solid now and a bit flushed — he had changed from the lithe puma to the bull. I rang Robin and we all went to a nearby restaurant that used to be very good, and had a terrible lunch. As usual, the stories were pouring out of Bob. Degas to Whistler: "Monsieur Whistler, why do you paint like a professional and comport yourself like an amateur?" I am always suspicious of writers or artists who dress for the part. We talked about the swing towards an Australian republic; Bob's long residence in the United States had not diminished his republican enthusiasm, nor his scorn for the scare tactics of the ancient monarchists. The next evening we went to a party given by his niece Lucy, who is married to Malcolm Turnbull; everyone was urging for the republic.

We were seeing Barry Humphries quite often; he was never quite at ease when Dianne was also there, his iron control on the stage fumbling into uncertainty. What can you do when it is obvious that an old friend has made a disastrous marriage? Especially when it is his third. At times the two little boys, whom Barry loved, seemed to be the only bond between them.

Barry told us about an episode when a nut forced his way onto the stage where Barry was being Lance Boyle. "Edna would have disposed of him in a few seconds." But Lance being a monologue character of a totally different kind, Barry had to juggle it along for a few minutes, while holding the stagehands back from a rescue.

Margaret Jones, with a mind as formidable as her physical presence, had come back from very difficult times as *Sydney Morning Herald* China correspondent during the Cultural Revolution. She was now Literary Editor of the *Herald*, and asked Robin to write a weekly paperback review column. Robin kept it going for seven years, never missing a week, until the post-Fairfax-crisis management dispensed with the services of their freelance writers. The weekly cheque, though modest enough, was an enormous help to our finances. Soon after, Arnold Earnshaw, who was baby-sitting Sandra Hall's literary pages in the *Weekend Australian* while Sandra was in France, suggested to us that what the pages needed was a kind of literary gossip column, and that Robin should take it on. It would bring in some money, and might provide some entertainment. Rob Drewe heard of the project, and told Robin he thought it was a good idea, but she should ring Sandra and explain the situation to her. It was very good advice, and saved any possibility of a rift in a friendship.

The only problem was that Robin was in effect moonlighting from the *Herald*, and did not want her name to be used. The people at the *Australian* suggested Robin Dutton, but neither Robin nor I wanted that. Then I remembered that one of Arnold's first jobs on the newly founded *Australian* had been to write a page of gossip under the name Martin Collins, the name being based on two streets in Sydney and Melbourne. So I suggested that the author of the new column should be Elizabeth Swanston, after two more streets. When the name first went to print the subeditor, obviously not a Melbourne man, thought of Gloria, so Robin became Elizabeth Swanson. It was a well-kept secret.

In 1986 we spent three months at Rocky Point, from April to July, from warm days to winter gales when the prevailing wind goes round to the north and hits you in the face when you open the front door. Robin said something that had never occurred to me in sixty years of going down to

Rocky Point, that it was like a ship, sea on both sides, the point going out into the sea like a bow, and the weather greeting you as if the front verandah were the bridge.

One week Grumpy and Claire came, with Emma and a boyfriend. Sue and Noel Ferrier were also there, having driven from Sydney, Noel claiming that the boredom of the Hay plains had nearly killed him. Sue has such style, such a noble carriage, such skill in dealing with Noel. Noel has many faces: the Oxford don with his glasses off, reading close to the book; Billy Bunter from the front, the eminent actor from the side; the comedian when, as Sue says, on goes the red nose, and his mouth and chin pop out from his jowls like the telescopic lens on Sue's automatic camera. In the car he sings and accompanies himself in the style of a muted trumpet. Like Barry, he is a reformed alcoholic who patiently puts up with the rest of us boozers.

He and Grumpy have discovered a great bond — they are both Merit Boys, which means in Victoria that they left school at fourteen, too early an age to sit for any exams, so they have something called a Merit Card. Noel gives Grumpy hell when he starts up on a war story about the old Kittyhawk days. He calls him Kitty Lucas. Grumpy takes no notice and keeps right on with his story.

Grumpy and I were out fishing for whiting one morning and suddenly saw what looked like a nest of sea-snakes on the surface of the water. It was a giant octopus. A couple of days later Michael and his friend Willy Hay found it inside one of the beautiful new crab pots Grumpy had had made for us at his bus workshop in Warrnambool. They heroically killed it and got it out of the pot, and then carried it up to the house. From tentacle tip to tentacle tip it was over eight feet across. I tried to tenderize a tentacle with a hammer, and then with the flat end of the Canadian wood-splitter, and marinaded it for days, but it was still too tough to eat.

After three years of emotional dramas, the move to Sydney, the divorces and the mad pressure of several books and scripts, even winter storms at Rocky Point were wonderfully soothing. Between occasional visitors, we both had work to do, but it never ground us down.

A few months later, Sandra Hall wanted to resign as Literary Editor of the *Australian*, in order to get on with her own work, and our good angel Arnold Earnshaw asked me if I would be interested in the job; Les Hollings was in favour. I agreed to do it, and for the first time in my life, after writing innumerable pieces for newspapers, found myself actually working for two or three days a week inside the madhouse of a newspaper office.

For the one and only time in our lives, we now had quite a good income coming in, from Robin's two columns and my two jobs at the *Australian*, and my various literary earnings. It made it easier to keep up the payments on the mortgage, but, typical Sydney dwellers, we seemed to spend all the rest, mainly on meals. I cannot understand how anybody manages to live sensibly in Sydney.

Working alongside journalists sharpened my perceptions for a new project on which I made been doing preliminary research. This was to be a biography of Kenneth Slessor. Slessor, within his range probably the finest of Australian poets, and certainly the greatest technical master, was an engrossing challenge for a biographer. Here was a man of the utmost refinement who at the same time had been a brilliant journalist all his life, and especially in the knockabout world of *Smith's Weekly*, that vulgar but always readable paper of which he finally became editor. From the ambience of whipping up copy to meet deadlines, and boozing in pubs or the Journalists' Club with his tough colleagues, Slessor retired to his study to become the meticulous poet who, as his manuscripts show, worked through seventeen pages of alternative readings until he got right those two lines in "Five Bells" that sound so spontaneous:

Deep and dissolving verticals of light
Ferry the falls of moonshine down ...

He was a very private man, and much research would be needed to flesh out the portrait. Fortunately I had a lot of help from his younger brother, Robin, who was in his eighties and had an excellent memory.

I spent a lot of time trying to trace the woman Slessor lived with after the death of his wife Noela. Her name was Kath, or Katey, or Kathy McShine when Ken knew her. His last published poem, "Polarities", was written for her. Finally, after a series of sleuthings that almost qualifies me to shake the hand of Sherlock Holmes, I found her, now the widow of a Qantas pilot, living on the North Shore.

Kath, whose name by now was Myers, agreed to come to have a cup of coffee at our house in Regent Street, Paddington. She was in her eighties, still very handsome, her trace of West Indian blood giving her face an enduring strength. At first she was very suspicious of me; then Robin came in, and she began to relax. By the time we switched from coffee to whisky she was quite happy to talk, uninhibitedly, into the tape-recorder, about the wild times she had had with Ken at Elizabeth Bay. Instead of the usual car burglar alarms of Paddington, we seemed to be hearing the splat of crashing crockery. It was easy to see how Ken fell in love with Kath, after the gentility of Noela, although, despite everything, he never ceased to be in love with Noela.

I wanted to show my gratitude to Kath, so asked her to lunch, telling her I would also ask an idol of hers, Noel Ferrier. She was thrilled, but said: "Will it be all right if I wear slacks? I used to have legs like a racehorse, but one of them's larger than the other nowadays." At lunch at an Italian restaurant she fittted in immediately with Noel and Sue, Grumpy and

Claire. She flirted with Grumpy and looked adoringly at Noel, who basked. Noel was in top form, on a high from being such a success in a revival of *My Fair Lady*. When she left she told me she had had more fun than at any time for the past thirty years. (She died in 1990; she was very pleased with my account of her relationship with Ken in my biography.)

One day Peter Carey called in with the manuscript of his new novel, *Oscar and Lucinda*, which he wanted me to read. I remembered the excitement when I launched *Illywhacker* for him at the Powerhouse Museum, right under the Blériot monoplane which his father had flown. Robin and Peter had lots in common in their memories; their fathers had both run used-car yards in Victoria. Peter shared the same school with me, Geelong Grammar, and the same dislike of it and of the bare Western District landscape and its rows of pine trees. There is something enormously appealing about Peter's pointy pixy face, his receding chin, his long lips over his buck teeth, his quizzical, shy smile. His occasional sharp remarks don't make him prickly. When something in the conversation distresses him, say some memory of injustice to one of us at school, his anguished face looks even more pointy and skinny, and he looks up sideways at you as if he were lifting a weight with his nose. He told me he went to Monash University to do science because of Jock Marshall — he was different, offering something not hackneyed.

On another occasion we dined with Peter and Alison at a little Vietnamese restaurant in Glebe; he was going to give a reading at Harold Park, and was terribly nervous. He had given only one reading before, when he got very drunk and hashed it, so this time he didn't drink. Nor did Alison, because she was pregnant. So Robin and I got drunk instead. A few months later their son Sam was born, and we had lunch at their house in Birchgrove, a modest house in what has become a rich street. Janey Marshall, Jock's widow, lived across the road. What a pleasure to be with a young couple who adored their baby and really shared it! When we arrived, Peter said, "It's Alison's turn to change the nappy, so she's upstairs." Peter was interesting about the message of optimism at the end of *Bliss*, a novel he had written in bad times. He said that when he was young, in times of full employment and easy days, he wanted to read the blackest books, authors like Beckett, and write about the worst possibilities.

On a less happy day, Chibs rang to say Dick had died; we had paid two sad visits to him as the cancer got worse. Dick's death came when he was loaded with honours, just when Chibs and he were going to enjoy the pleasures of retirement. Dick was one of that rare and valuable breed, a conservative with an open mind. Chibs sounded drained but relieved that it was all over.

Jeffrey Smart had an exhibition with Rex Irwin, and he and Ermes came to lunch. Jeffrey is so entertaining and witty; it's always good to gossip with him about Adelaide, and remember so many happy days with Ursula Hayward. He told us about his last dinner with Patrick White. Patrick was holding forth on Piero della Francesca, for whom Jeffrey has a passion, claiming that Piero was an artist of pure form, which was why he had influenced the moderns so much. Jeffrey told him he had it arse up: Piero was as devoted a Christian as Fra Angelico, and the paintings are full of emotion and are in fact very romantic, though of course expressed in that pure form. When Patrick, undeterred, went on in the same vein, Jeffrey told him he had no right to talk to him like that — Jeffrey had spent a lifetime studying Piero, and he lives near Arezzo, right in the middle of Piero's territory. "If we were talking about nineteenth-century novels, I'd listen and be taking mental notes, it's your territory. But I am an artist, you're not a visual person, you should keep quiet and listen to what I'm telling you." Patrick sat white and dead silent and never asked Jeffrey to dinner again.

The best place for a total break from Sydney was Rocky Point, both when Robin and I were alone and when the old house was bursting with talk and awash with wine: once (the only time we had a lot of guests) we had Grumpy and Claire, Robin's old friends (and my new ones) from Ballarat, Mary and Michael Rasmussen, John Olsen, Bob Hughes and his wife Victoria. The little kitchen never had so many simultaneous cooks as on this occasion. Bob used to get out of bed before anyone else and empty the pots of the crabs caught during the night. He would then prepare them for lunch with Japanese trimmings, while Mary and John discussed what they were jointly going to cook for dinner; meanwhile Claire quietly prepared a salad and Robin checked her homemade bread. I, who am usually the cook, was delighted to do nothing except keep the glasses filled.

Other artists were more full of plans. Sid Nolan rang from England to say he was coming to Sydney and would like to discuss with me an idea he had for a book. Over the years Sid could have written a thousand letters for the price of his phone calls, all at odd hours. The strange thing is that he wrote so well when he allowed himself to. He met me at the Intercontinental, where he and Mary were staying; for many years Sid always did himself well when travelling. He was looking old and frail, but his charm was undiminished; Sid could have talked the Ayatollah Khomeini into reading Rimbaud. As if to make up for age, his suits (this one a kind of purple) and ties (in this case hand-painted by Mary's daughter by John Perceval) were, if not quite successfully youthful, at least from another age.

We got into a taxi and went out to Bay Books together. Sid had discovered the joys of drawing with a computer; he was taking his old photographs of drought-stricken Australia and drawing human figures over and around the skulls of bullocks and the taut hides and rigid legs of sun-dried cattle. It was to be a satirical series, *Nolan and the Ironic Tradition*. It is true that

Sid always had a masterly sense of irony, but I was not confident that it would be possible to write a suitable text. Besides, I was working on my biography of Kenneth Slessor, and would have had to drop that temporarily and meet an impossible deadline for Sid; that wouldn't have worried him in the least. The problem was that he wanted the book to be published to coincide with a retrospective exhibition of his work in Melbourne.

Robin was very sceptical about the project, and, as it turns out, rightly so. But as Colin Lanceley says "Sid is a genius, and you can't write him off". But the man at Bay Books could. Even if I had been able to meet the deadline, and Sid to make all the art work available immediately, the book could still not have been ready in time. The meeting ended, as the publisher had to catch a plane to China or somewhere.

We retired for morning tea at the Intercontinental with Mary, who had had the flu and was looking very pale, though as beautiful as ever. Patrick's attack on her in *Flaws in the Glass* had been unforgivable — and had not been forgiven, especially by Sid. But Sid's counterattack, the huge painting of Patrick and Manoly, which I saw in Perth, was equally disgusting, making the blameless Manoly into a kind of cockroach. It was a feud that diminished them both.

By the middle of 1988 Robin and I were becoming more and more exhausted by Sydney. The city was exhilarating, we had lots of good friends, there were invaluable resources, such as the Mitchell Library, our terrace house (albeit still with a huge mortgage) was always a pleasure to wake up in. And with our four jobs, we had, for the first time in our lives, quite a good income, apart from sporadic royalties and the ever-welcome annual payment from Public Lending Right. But we never seemed to save any money to pay off some of the mortgage. We discussed moving somewhere not too far from Sydney where we could save money and spend more quiet time together. Then one day Robin came back from having a haircut in Woollahra. She had seen photographs of a house in the window of a real estate agent's office in Queen Street. "It's in a place called Mudgee," she said. "Where's Mudgee?" I replied that it was in Henry Lawson's country, a couple of hundred miles west, over the mountains. That's about all that I knew about it. Later, a friend remembered a line from *Seven Little Australians*: "One more word out of you, my girl, and you'll be on the first train to Mudgee".

Robin insisted I come with her, immediately, to look at the photographs.

It was an enchanting long, low brick house with a loft running the length of the building; built in the 1840s, it had been completely renewed by the owners, who were highly skilled in the arts of restoration. So we got into the car and drove to Mudgee and dined with the owners, Simon and Susan Pockley, and agreed to buy the house. Real estate was booming in Sydney and in the mad euphoria of falling in love with this Mudgee house we were sure we could sell the Paddington terrace.

It was a classic example of that banking nightmare of buying the new house before you've sold the old one. But fate and the market were kind to us. At the agonizing auction we sold the Paddington house so well that not only could we pay off all the mortgage but had something left over after paying for the Mudgee house. The latter, being in a country town, was ridiculously cheap by Sydney standards. And it had been meticulously restored, in perfect harmony with its original design. Simon was a maker of outdoor furniture from native woods, and a master craftsman. He had, for instance, installed new floors throughout, of waxed cyprus pine. There was even a new damp course.

I resigned from my job as Literary Editor of the *Australian*, handing over to Barry Oakley. Barry, one of the wittiest men I have met, was capable only of desperate, self-deprecating jokes when he came to the office to find out how to run the literary pages. The Literary Editor's reviews come into the *Australian*'s computer, where you call them up to edit them. In front of the green glare of the computer, Barry was like a Roman Christian facing his first lion. A kindly subeditor paused and patted his shoulder, and said, "Don't worry, it's as easy as driving a car." "But I don't know how to drive a car," Barry mumbled. Nevertheless, in a remarkable display of fortitude, Barry has not only mastered the computer but has gone on to make a very good job indeed of running the literary pages.

Robin also resigned as Elizabeth Swanson. I was still editing the *Australian Literary Quarterly*, but our income had plummeted. Our theory was that, by leaving Sydney, our expenses would also drop dramatically.

Thirty-Four

There are fresh landscapes to be learned all over Australia far outside the familiar environs of the major cities or the red centre from Alice Springs to Ayers Rock: the gorges of the Kimberley, the plains of the Mallee, the rainforests of Queensland — dozens of them, all different. But there is one basic Australia, the primal pastoral country that was shaped by white settlement, of grazing paddocks shaded by giant gums, which many Australians immediately respond to. There is no finer example of this country than that which lies between Lithgow and Mudgee. After Sydney, and the slog through the towns of the Blue Mountains, it was a joy to drive through it.

We moved to Mudgee in the spring of 1988, and the big garden, though somewhat overgrown by now, was flowering with old roses, daffodils, plums and peaches and apricots, and over the fishpond the new willow leaves were pale, translucent green. The peace of Mudgee was there, especially after the traffic and the burglar alarms of Paddington, but it was not quite as peaceful as we had expected. We were a couple of streets back from the main road coming into the town, but from 5.30 a.m. onwards, the house shook from the clatter of the empty trucks and trailers going back to the mine near Gulgong, or the roar of an old truck with a load of pigs. There were dogs which yapped for hours, literally for hours, one at the front, the other out the back, in exactly the same high tenor. Then there were the dear old neighbours, Eric and Joyce — you couldn't find kinder, nicer people, but they had no idea that writers who work at home are not doing nothing. Working at home is a great trap; people who would never dream of interrupting you if you worked in an office drift in and out with a jar of marmalade or two slices of a fresh-baked pie or to borrow a hammer.

Robin's study was in the house, and I appropriated a lovely old wooden hut in the garden to work in. I could hear the clang of Joyce's gate, and then see her advancing across the lawn. If Robin didn't answer her knock she would walk in and shout, "Yoo hoo, Robin." If Robin still lay low, she would potter across the lawn to my hut. "Oh, you're not working are you Geoffrey? Sorry to interrupt, but ..."

Henry Lawson spent his early years at Eurunderee, a few miles to the north of Mudgee, and at one time rode his horse to the Mudgee school. It is a crime against our national heritage that the childhood home of our greatest writer of short fiction no longer exists. It was demolished in the 1950s on the mad whim of the new owner, almost as if he had a grudge against Lawson. He then built a "Lawson Memorial" that looks like an overgrown barbecue and gave a patch of land around it to the state. Buses stop here, and bewildered tourists look at this strange object in crazed stone, shake their heads and are driven on to Gulgong, a pretty little town where the Lawsons lived for a short time, and where there is an interesting Lawson Museum.

In between chapters of the Slessor book I began to read Lawson again, admiring the great stories more than ever. But it seemed to me now that a lot of his work in his last years had been grossly underrated, and I decided to make a new selection of his work which would give it the emphasis it deserves. I wrote a longish introduction, when I had finished the Slessor book, and my selection and introduction were published by Picador not long after Penguin had published the Slessor biography.

There were other literary treasures, as well as gold, in the district. Over the range and near Scone, an awkward English lad named Havelock Ellis had, in 1878, been the sole master at two little bush schools; on set days during the week he would hike over the hills and through the bush from one school to the other. On his first night, under a roof missing a few shingles, a possum curled up and went to sleep in his top hat. We spent a day over there; the farm and outbuildings where he went to draw his water from the well are still exactly as they were more than a hundred years ago.

Ellis wrote a most attractive novella about his experiences, with an imaginary love affair as well, when he was back in England, living with the South African writer Olive Schreiner and embarking on his great studies in the psychology of sex. He called the book *Kanga Creek*. I had been wanting to reprint this book ever since the beginning of Sun Books, but it was a little too short on its own. Now I had the idea of combining it with his diary of the time, which is in the Mitchell Library, and the account of the same period in his published autobiography. Thus there would be a triple version of the same story. The resulting book was also published, with my introduction, by Picador.

About the same time as I finished my biography of Slessor I read the very uneven collection of prose pieces called *Patrick White Speaks*. I decided to write to him, not with any intention of reopening either friendship or correspondence, but to tell him how my life had changed since living with Robin. It was a short letter: "I've been reading the collection of your prose pieces, and thought that I would write to you, but not intending that you should answer. The book brought back a lot of memories. I am thinking in particular of the letter you wrote me which resulted in the end of communication between us. I was enraged at the time. Now I think you were quite right. My life was all wrong, and you had been trying to tell me so for some time." I went on to mention, in a few words, that I had finished the Slessor biography, because I knew how much he admired Slessor's poetry and treasured his review of *The Tree of Man*, in which Slessor called it "a timeless work of art". I ended the letter: "His was a sad life like that of most writers in this country".

The Mudgee district is rich not only in literary associations. At the Huntington winery near the town, Bob Roberts has established the Huntington Music Festival; for this occasion he clears out the central building of his winery, which has near-perfect acoustics, and some of the finest performers in Australia play among the wine barrels to a large audience. Nowadays it is almost impossible to get tickets, so popular is the Festival in Sydney and other places far from Mudgee. When I met Bob an amazing coincidence came to light: he is related to Queen Emma, the subject of my book of that name.

From another world, Peter Carey rang, still on a high after winning the Booker Prize. He had just had a fax from the London *Independent*; they had asked Dorothy Green for an opinion and she had said: "I don't care for Peter Carey's work. He is a creation of the capitalist press." I remembered Patrick White, before Dorothy Green was elevated to P. White's private literary sainthood, saying that she had got everything wrong about his novels.

John Olsen, who was living at that time in the Blue Mountains, was another visitor at Mudgee, sweeping in with a bottle of champagne in each hand, saying he was restoring his eye by getting out of Scotland into Australia. He went off painting, and in the evening came back with another couple of bottles, saying it was not just the landscape that had refreshed him, it was the whole of nature, surrounding and nurturing.

One day I had a phone call from Bernd Benthaak, an opera director, husband of the book designer and publisher Barbara Beckett, for whom I had written the *Beach* book. They had an idea to discuss. So the next time we were in Sydney we had lunch with them. Their idea was to mount an Australian version of Mozart's *The Magic Flute*, not just to have a few Australian animals cavorting around the stage, as in a production I had seen in Melbourne, but to set the whole strange opera in a part-mythical, part-historical Australia. They proposed that I should translate and modify the libretto. The idea expanded as we discussed it and became full of possibilities. They suggested that either Sid Nolan or Arthur Boyd might be interested. Arthur was the one I wanted. I rang him in England and he was immediately enthusiastic.

Then I had a startling vision which I was a bit nervous of imparting to Bernd and Barbara: Barry Humphries as Papageno. "But he's not a singer," protested Bernd. I assured Bernd that, in fact, Barry has a true and very attractive voice, even though he can't read music. I reminded Bernd that Schikaneder, author of the libretto of the opera, had not been a professional singer, but had played the first Papageno. So I rang Barry in London. He thought it a marvellous idea, and said he would certainly like to be in it. He and Arthur had always been mutual fans. Then Bernd got in touch with his agent, Greg Hocking, who, after some thought, said that not only did he think it a good idea, but that he was sure Yehudi Menuhin, whose recent Australian tour Greg had managed, would like to be Musical Director. I knew that Menuhin had for many years been fascinated by this country, and it was not long before Greg reported that Yehudi would love to do it. There was already a magic about this *Magic Flute*.

So I settled down to the work of translating and modifying the libretto. It proved to be one of the most difficult tasks I have ever undertaken. Not only do you have to try to keep the sense, which is often closer to nonsense, you have to keep the metrical form and the rhymes as well. Most difficult of all, perhaps, is to keep the right vowels in the right places, for a singer cannot take a high note on a thin vowel. Robin had given me a piano at Mudgee, which was a great help now. I would also, of course, always have the musical score as well as the libretto beside me when I was working out in my wooden hut. On one occasion I was singing a line, realized my translation wouldn't work, and yelled "Fuck!" at the end of Mozart's phrase. There was a noise of startled movement and I realized that my neighbour had been mending the fence alongside my hut.

The Magic Flute is such a strange mixture of mystery and comedy, idealism and earthiness, that it is infinitely adaptable. Even so, a totally new Australian production sounded bizarre. How could such a new culture cope with such an opera? In fact, the natural world of prehistoric Australia, the home of the Aborigines, with its unique flora and fauna, and the contrast with the settlement of Australia by the British with their convicts, could provide a wealth of symbols from which the opera could take on a fresh meaning.

The Australian setting would bring out the contrast between the two different basic themes of *The Magic Flute*: the mysterious world of magic, night, fairytale, nature and Aboriginal environment; and the realm of Sarastro, which, although ostensibly that of the sun — enlightenment, wisdom, forgiveness and magnanimity — is in fact founded upon slavery and is maintained by force.

All this might seem far from Freemasonry, but it is not. In Aboriginal culture there exists the most profound engagement with the wholeness of things, that nature and mankind are as one. As Freemasonry is concerned with those fundamentals of all religions common to all men, so it is in harmony with the Aboriginal belief that all people are brought together by the common bond of their natural background, its flora and fauna, rivers, waterpools and mountains, even fire, in its capacity, in Australia, to renew the environment after apparent destruction.

Arthur Boyd's magnificent property by the Shoalhaven River, Bundanon, which he has given to the nation, was a magical setting for the development of our ideas for the opera. As Bernd and I drove in through the bush four black cockatoos came out of the trees, with the slow flap of their big wings, and crossed right in front of us, immediately suggesting the Queen of the Night. And in Arthur's imagination she had already emerged from a mysterious, black pool among the dark trees, to which he took us soon after we arrived.

We sit with Yvonne and Arthur under the flame-trees in front of the stone house, the occasional red beak-like flower dropping into our coffee cups. ("Dreadful old cups full of cracks," says Arthur of the beautiful tree-pattern Minton, "they're so old, that's the trouble".) Up among the red flowers the rowdy friar-birds clatter and chatter at each other, fight and flip and nip, and occasionally let their droppings fall on our shirts or manuscripts. We have an idea that the three boys should be kookaburras, and right on cue, after a long silence, three kookaburras laugh as if they have been listening. There is an old wooden settler's hut on the green slope leading up to the tall bush, receding into darkness beyond its verticals, birds all around it, and this, we think, could be Papageno's home ... The whole ambience of Bundanon seems to be in harmony with our ideas.

We retired into the house and played more records of the opera. Arthur remembered someone saying "Mozart was the voice of God".

It is such solitary work, writing or painting. How good it was to be working in conjunction with other people! I thought more understandingly of Patrick in his forays into the theatre. Bernd was stimulating and humorous, with a profound knowledge of music; Arthur was not only endlessly visually imaginative, but daring in all his concepts.

By early 1989 I had finished the first draft of the libretto, there had been more meetings, and now Arthur and Yvonne, and Barry Humphries and his bride Lizzie all came to stay at Mudgee. At last in Lizzie Barry had found the right woman; she accepts him without any nonsense. Stephen Spender's daughter, brought up with people like W.H. Auden and John Huston, she does not, unlike Patrick White, have to get her act together to cope with Barry. As for Barry, after the first discussions about the opera, he was out in the garden with his easel and brushes, painting our long, low old house. Arthur lent a hand. "Not too many painters," said Barry, "have their palette prepared by Arthur Boyd."

A couple of weeks later we all came together again, with Bernd, at Bundanon. The weather was hot and clear, and we all swam in the Shoalhaven. Back at the house again, Bernd was getting more and more anxious that he had not auditioned Barry. I practised a few of Papageno's arias on Arthur's Steinway, but Barry was more interested in painting, having set up his easel in front of the valley and the slope with the settler's hut. Arthur and Yvonne had rigged up a canvas to shade him, and he was painting in his bathers and an old shirt. Finally Bernd was so insistent that I went out and told Barry he would have to come in and sing.

Barry cannot read music, but he knew the melodies and peered over my shoulder for the words. Bernd had been worried that Barry's voice would lack volume, but when a forte was needed, my eardrums rattled. Barry had just got through that passage where Papageno repeats "Pa-Pa-Pa" when Bernd stopped us. He explained to Barry that he must not just rattle the Pa-Pa-Pas out like machine-gun fire, but modulate them. "Oh, I get it," said Barry, and we did it again. He was perfect. Bernd had heard all he needed to, and Barry rushed back to his easel. Bernd told me he had rehearsed that passage with various famous tenors, and it had sometimes taken a quarter of an hour to get it right. Barry had done it first time, in about thirty seconds.

Meanwhile Greg Hocking had been negotiating with Yehudi Menuhin's agent, and amid general enthusiasm there was talk of bookings in Yehudi's home town, San Francisco, as well as in Sydney, New York and London. "It seems doomed to succeed," said Greg cautiously.

I had sent the libretto off to Yehudi, and now received an enormous fax from Hawaii, where he was on holiday, with useful suggestions he and his wife Diana had made for improvements to the text. Meanwhile Greg, and Yehudi's agent Eleanor Hope, had been working on the basic showbiz problem of raising money. By mid-1990 it seemed that a Japanese backer had been found, and it was arranged that Yehudi, Arthur, Barry, Bernd, Greg and I should all meet in London. At the last minute Bernd was unable to come. Unfortunately, as we were paying for ourselves, Robin and I could not afford her fare, let alone the holiday we would have liked to have after the meeting. Apart from this, I was pleased that I would have the opportunity of seeing Tisi and Sam, who had been living in London for some years.

On 8 June we met at Yehudi's house. One could say that he is irresistible, but that is the wrong word, for he does not set out to conquer. He hardly needs to; but, like Arthur, he is all modest, although one is aware of the steel underneath. I had met him and Diana some years before, in Adelaide, but had forgotten that his modesty also extends to his height. He looked even smaller now, as he was in his bare feet, walking on those orthopaedic plastic sandals that look so painful to anyone who has never worn them. Greg had told me that when he was managing Yehudi's last tour in Australia, he had flown beside him from Perth to Melbourne. When the plane had settled down at cruising altitude, Yehudi had quietly stood on his head for ten minutes or so, practising his yoga contemplation.

Diana is like his partner in a ballet with words, always moving towards or away from him, then charging right across in front of him. It is not a surprise to find out that her father commanded a battleship.

Yehudi asked me to sit beside him on the sofa, with his huge score of *The Magic Flute*, and we went through it with all the suggestions he had made for slight changes to my libretto. I told him about the first time I heard him play, when as schoolboys Deasey and I had stood in the garden of the Nicholas house in Toorak, while he practised a Bach Chaconne.

He then took us all, including his elegant agent, to lunch at a nearby Chinese restaurant. Without at any time taking over the conversation, Barry was so funny at lunch that he reduced the unflappable Eleanor, and Greg and myself, to convulsive giggles, while Yehudi sat, quietly smiling, as if he were conducting a concerto and had laid down his baton to listen to the virtuoso going through his cadenza.

Despite having no naval blood in his veins, Barry could also outmanoeuvre Diana. Yehudi had recently returned from Budapest, where he had conducted an enormously moving concert with a famous Hungarian orchestra, the Philharmonia Ungarica, which had been in exile for some thirty-four years. We were all listening, enthralled, when Diana cut clear across Yehudi's bows and said, "Of course, most of the original dear things are dead, and these are young replacements." Whereupon Barry, deploying a loud murmur, cut across her with, "Just like the Inkspots."

There is, in Barry, the great comic artist, an intense seriousness of mind. When I was on the Board of the Art Gallery of South Australia we made use of his expertise to get advice on possible purchases of European and English art of the forty years or so from the early 1890s to the late 1930s. From sales in Belgium, France and other places, he found us a number of treasures. I was also well aware of his knowledge of certain periods of literature, but had not realized the range of his interest in music until I heard him discussing with Yehudi some fairly obscure violin concerto, by someone like Moeran. "Heifetz recorded it in 1943, and Izaak Perlman in, I think, 1972, and of course, Yehudi, you played it in New York in 1966." (Yehudi delightedly nodding his head.)

Later in the day, we were at dinner at Lizzie's house when Jeffrey Smart, who was urging me to see a visiting exhibition at the Tate Gallery while I was in London, said, "There's that wonderful tiny little Picasso of the two women running by the sea." "Yes, wonderful," said Barry immediately, "the one Diaghilev used as a backdrop for *Le Train Bleu*. When I was playing at Drury Lane, the old technician, knowing I was interested in art, unrolled for me the original backdrop, signed by Picasso, Diaghilev and Fokine — it's too big to hang in the Tate, where it's owned, so they keep it in the theatre."

Jeffrey began to talk about my mother, of whom I already knew he had a wonderful fund of anecdotes. "Apart from being so beautiful she was intelligent and interested, a truly cultured woman. And the poor darling had to stick it out in Adelaide."

In the morning I went to the Marlborough Galleries to see some of the paintings Arthur had completed as studies for the backdrops to be used in *The Magic Flute*. They were marvellously evocative of the strange but in some ways familiar world, in which our version of the opera would take place.

After a few more days I returned to Australia, and to that waiting for financial news which is the most tedious side of show business. Greg seemed optimistic, but suddenly there was some obscure upheaval in the Japanese stock market, and our backer retired. By this time the mania of the imminent Mozart bicentenary had made it almost impossible to find room for any new production, and the various bookings at opera houses and theatres could no longer be held open for us while we looked for a new sponsor. So that was the end of our *Magic Flute*. "Don't worry," said Greg, "things always go on like this in show business. It'll happen." But I don't think it will. Arthur's paintings and drawings have been exhibited. My libretto, product of so many hours of wrestling with rhymes and singing of syllables, remains in my filing cabinet, while Yehudi and Barry are as busy as ever. *In Memoriam* it is, indeed: "O last regret, regret can die!"

In 1990 the parliamentarian Franca Arena asked me if I would join the committee of a new organization, the Australian Republican Movement. I gladly accepted. The first committee consisted of Franca Arena, Faith Bandler, Franco Belgiorno-Nettis, Geraldine Doogue, Donald Horne, Jenny Kee, Tom Keneally, Colin Lanceley, Harry Seidler, Malcolm Turnbull, David Williamson and Neville Wran; Denise Darlow-Ng was our secretary. In view of consistent monarchist disinformation, it is interesting to note the minimal Irish element in the committee. The aim of the committee was to urge for the creation of an Australian Republic by 2001, and that support for it should be politically non-party.

I could never have anticipated, after nearly thirty years of involvement in the cause, how the wave would suddenly start to run. What is amazing is that the monarchist opposition is still bringing out the same clichés they were voicing in the 1960s, apparently still unaware not only of the need for an Australian republic which was being voiced by Henry Lawson in the 1890s, but of the composition of Australian society in the 1990s, and the mood of the people. They still exemplify the old way of thinking in Australia, when an open mind was thought to denote an absence of principle. Even when a majority thinks differently from them, they still talk about discussion of republicanism, or the flag, or whatever, as being "divisive". Reactionaries always uphold the status quo, but what they don't realize is that in a democracy the status quo is not sacred; it must be reshaped when people no longer believe in it.

Australian attitudes are slow to change, and I think this is a good thing, and makes for a stable society. But looking back, I'm amazed at the rhythm of initial slowness and final speed in which attitudes do change: think of attitudes to the Aborigines; the White Australia Policy; censorship; care for the environment. There were even those who thought we should still be "British Subject" on our passports; then, suddenly, we were allowed to be Australian. A lack of faith in their fellow Australians is the hallmark of those who have wanted us to remain British. As the poet Charles Harpur said, about one hundred and fifty years ago, "It is not in the nature of things that men brimful of Englandism can ever do us any real national good".

Nor can the attitude, common to monarchists, that Australians who want to disturb the status quo are naughty children. Way back in the late 1970s, when we published our second book about the possibility of an Australian republic, a Melbourne Collins Street/Toorak magnate said to a mutual friend, "Geoffrey ought to have his bottie smacked." I was fifty-five at the time. Now, fifteen years later, I read in Brisbane's *Courier-Mail* an article by their London correspondent. It ends: "When, or if, the flags fly for a Republic of Australia, few tears will be shed in Britain ... It is all seen here for what, perhaps, it is: naughty, noisy, harmless schoolkids beating drums."

One of the inevitable results of getting old, in years if not in oneself, is that friends start dying off. For some people, this is a kind of triumph. My great-aunt (by marriage) Mollie, in her eighties, positively glowed with youth when it was reported that yet another old lady had died. Later at night, of course, she might have wondered how much longer she herself would last, and have felt a twinge of loneliness. For those still living, death always makes a comment on life which is often sardonic, especially in the case of friends who are no longer friends. Death makes quarrels and estrangements absurd.

On 1 October 1990 Robin and I were asleep at Mudgee when the phone rang at 1.30 a.m. It was someone from the *Australian* asking if I could confirm the report that Patrick White had died. I replied that no one was less likely to be aware of it than myself. We were leaving to drive to Queensland later that morning, and just as I was about to lock the front door the phone rang again. It was Andrew Olle from the ABC asking me to talk about Patrick, who had indeed died the day before. I tried to be honest and not just *nil nisi bonum*. I had loved the man and then been disappointed in him; his books had meant so much to us all, but now I was nervous of rereading them lest they also disappoint. But there is no doubt of his greatness.

Six months later Bob Brissenden died in Canberra, and I went down to be a pallbearer. I was asked to read something at the graveside. After a lot of thought I decided on the first verse of Byron's Incantation from *Manfred*,

"When the moon is on the wave". Apart from the beauty of the lines, I thought them relevant to Bob and Rosemary's love for each other. I hoped that not too many people would realize how much I had taken them out of context. Bob, who loved Byron as much as I do, would certainly have known, but I think he would have approved. Bob was not only a good critic and scholar but a true poet; some of his poems will certainly endure. Bob himself was a lovable person, full of humour and camaraderie, despite suffering from grievous physical ills.

Bob had a splendid funeral, which he would have enjoyed, especially in some of the unforeseen accompaniments. From my motel in Canberra, the morning of the funeral was warm and sunny. But by the time I reached the cemetery at Queanbeyan a giant black cloud was hanging over the landscape, looking as if it were about to disgorge a snowstorm. We pallbearers set off for the grave beside the coffin, which was in a fine old Cadillac hearse, led by a band of Bob's favourite trad jazz musicians, four brass (including a tuba) and a clarinet. It was hard to walk sedately to such an infectious rhythm.

Before the final approach to the grave, the coffin was slid out and we took its weight on our shoulders, left hand on the handle, right arm around shoulders of the opposite bearer (in my case, Tim Curnow). A huge red sun faced us, and the black cloud thickened. Down the avenue of tombstones, at the exact centre of distant perspective, there was a man on crutches, watching. With the coffin by the side of the grave, we gave our readings, and then at the precise moment the coffin was lowered into the earth a huge streak of lightning went right around the landscape and a gigantic peal of thunder cracked the black clouds above our heads. The red sun still gleamed through the pale western clouds, and as the coffin came to rest a silver jet aircraft, with the sun full on it, flew over the line of the hills. A great movie director, someone like Fellini, could not have staged it more dramatically. I noticed Manning Clark among the mourners, looking rather frail, but before I could reach him he had gone.

A few weeks later, when I arrived in Canberra to give a paper at a seminar on Kenneth Slessor, I heard that Manning had died. Robin, who was in Queensland, urged me to stay on for his funeral. But then she rang again to say that the young son of two of our dearest friends had committed suicide in Brisbane, so I flew back to support them at the cremation.

There was Manning Clark the great historian, Manning Clark in prophetic role thundering against the backsliding of Australia into materialism, Manning Clark the teacher, but my favourite memories are of Manning the fisherman. This was a Manning Clark standing on a reef at Kangaroo Island, or perched on a rock ledge near Wapengo, his line in the often alarming ocean, his beard twitching, and the light of hope in his eye that this time the sea would send him a big one.

Of the same calibre are many hours spent on many occasions with Manning and David Campbell, of whom Manning was to write so eloquently in the last volume of his autobiography. Although he did not write poetry, and no longer drank, Manning relished the company of poets and drinkers. The reason for this, apart from human affection, was that he had a poet's imagination and capacity for metaphor in thinking as well as in language, and the drinker's capacity to let go. At the same time, he had a lot to hang on to. His beliefs and loves were sturdy, but they went with a hint of desperation, of a ceaseless consciousness of a cauldron below the walkway, the suck of the ocean below the reef.

W.B. Yeats once wrote of Walt Whitman that he lacked the vision of evil. Yeats was wrong in this; he was not a particularly wide reader. But the phrase could be used of many Australian writers and artists. They did not let on about the black holes in the sunburnt country. When the English historian Froude said of us that it was hard to quarrel with a people whose aim in life was to be innocently happy, he didn't intend to insult us. After all, it is a noble aim. But when Manning came to think about Australia, which, as he often said, was not all that early in his life, he found that in Australia, as anywhere else, human nature does not allow for too much innocence or happiness, and that there is such a thing as evil. There were peculiar evils in Australia's past, particularly to do with the Aborigines and the convicts, and too many seeds of evil in Australia's present. Manning longed to believe in the Enlightenment, that by reason and just laws man has the ability to banish evil, but, although not a Catholic, he was haunted by the possibility, maybe certainty, of some original sin.

The oracular, prophetic note in his prose, with more than a hint of it in his appearance, never intruded on his conversation. His soft voice, sometimes hard to hear at a party, made its mark without any drama. This was because his ego did not crave a pulpit or a mountain. My favourite portrait of him is the one by Arthur Boyd that hangs in the Clarks' dining room, complete with wide-brimmed hat, dog called Tuppence, and the Australian bush.

Manning never ceased to have the honesty and courage to denounce a man of evil, but, unlike Patrick White, he did not detest himself or think he had the right of moral disposal over other people. Like some other eminent figures, he enjoyed the company of sinners, but his capacity for forgiveness never made him any easier on himself. Manning possessed genuine humility, which is one of the reasons that he was such a profoundly important and successful teacher.

His beliefs, and in the case of his visit to the Soviet Union, his wish to believe, as well as occasional errors of fact in his books, led to some ferocious attacks on him. He never bit back, simply carried on. Manning was vulnerable, of course, and he had a great satirical sense of humour, but he was never snide or vindictive, and in fact was extraordinarily generous to his enemies as well as to those he admired.

Manning was not just the scholar in his study. He paid Australia the compliment of wanting to stand on the earth where the events of which he was writing took place, even if it were as far away as Dirk Hartog Island. This was not just being conscientious. It was his way of getting in touch with the soul of the country.

Manning's great *History of Australia* is in itself a kind of mini-history; the times changed as he was writing it. As he himself many times admitted, Volume One contained very little mention of women or the Aborigines. But the virtues of the man and the writer remain indestructible, the splendid sweep of his vision, the often unexpected humour, the unaffected love of his country and his people, and above all the capacity to see beyond good and evil and take pity on our human frailty.

I was alone at the time of Manning's death, and that night, over a friendly whisky, I thought how lucky I was to have known a few people who were, or are, in their personalities akin to the Geoffrey Chaucer described by John Dryden: "He must have been a man of a most wonderful comprehensive nature". Men like Manning, Arthur Boyd, David Campbell; women like Annie and, above all for me, Robin. It is sad that Patrick, for all his genius, lacked that "comprehensive nature". He could have coped with the Wife of Bath, but would have been merciless to the Prioress; he would have patronised the Knight and hated the Pardoner so much he would have been unable to write about him at all.

All these deaths made me think of those, whether dead or alive, still living on in their books, who had influenced me as a writer. Most of those who are there in one's formative years remain with one forever. For me, they included the wise poets and storytellers, Shakespeare and Chaucer; the metaphysical poets, Donne, Marvell and Herbert; the pure, and some not so pure in their lives, lyric writers, Campion, Verlaine; the wild ones, Blake and Rimbaud; the poets of love and praise like Whitman, Rilke, and David Campbell, or of love and damnation, like Baudelaire, Yeats and Akhmatova; and all the greatest novelists, who mostly for me seem to be Russian or French. The list goes on and on. One can, and should, always be reading them again.

It is rewarding to think of the links between the writers who have, in their lives, been friends of mine. The struggle to be honest which is so poignant in the lives of Richard Aldington, Roy Campbell, Yevgeny Yevtushenko and Bella Akhmadulina and Judith Wright; the audacity of imagination in Peter Carey and David Foster, and a similar capacity, allied to a deadly eye and an endless comic invention, in Barry Humphries. Patrick White I value most for his poetic sense of the eternal flux in things and in people, which is a typical paradox for a man obsessed by his own fixations.

And in nearly all of them I value their passion, and their worldliness, by which I don't mean that Wordsworthian sense of the world that is too much with us, but of enjoyment of the human comedy. Perhaps the supreme geniuses here are Byron and Pushkin. Patrick White once said to me that he thought Mozart the greatest of all because he was so unworldly; in some ways this is true, but in the operas alone, Mozart is sparklingly worldly.

All these influences have to sink in, maybe not to emerge for many years, and never, if possible, in imitation, although there is a great scope for imitation in the various forms of translation. It is notable how many of the writers I have just mentioned have been involved in direct or oblique translation from writers in other languages, sometimes, as in various poems of Ezra Pound and W.H. Auden, from Old English.

The one attribute they undoubtedly do all have in common is a zest for life.

Thirty-Five

In August 1991 Robin and I went to Brisbane for Writers' Week at the Warana Festival, only just getting out of Mudgee, which a day before had been cut off by floods. We went to lunch at Government House with my old RAAF friend Wally Campbell, by then for many years Governor of Queensland, and his wife Georgie. Both of them had managed to stay exactly as straightforward as they used to be, uninhibited by job or surroundings. In the sunny afternoon Wally put on a beret and drove us around the 42-acre grounds, which include areas of pure bush, in a converted golf buggy. He was still as disconcerting a driver as he had been when we had the old Dodge at Western Junction.

The next day we had lunch, again in that wonderful winter Brisbane sun, in a restaurant on the river bank; the banks of the Brisbane River have been transformed from the muddy squalor that I first saw during the war. A thought was stirring in my mind — why are we living out at Mudgee, where the frost is still on the lawn at midday, and it is fiercely hot in the summer, and a draining four-hour drive over the Blue Mountains to Sydney, when we could be living up here? But I didn't say anything.

We then went to stay for a couple of days with Lawrence and Edit Daws in the Glasshouse Mountains. Robin and I were sitting on their verandah looking at that wondrous view of all those dramatic peaks, when she suddenly said to me, "Why don't we come up here to live?" The best relationships are those in which mutual thoughts precede words, so that what is spoken is only a confirmation.

A few days later, we were home at Mudgee when Edit rang to say that we should come and look at some land a real estate agent had shown her. So we got into the car and drove right back to the Glasshouse Mountains, and there, under the great thrust of the volcanic plug of Mount Coonowrin, the most dramatic of all the Glasshouse Mountains, we found twenty-four acres of untouched bush, a Queensland bush of tall trees, black, white, grey, smooth and rough, where we could build a house.

Thanks to Philip Bacon, Lawrence's dealer, we made contact with Geoffrey Pie, a brilliant Brisbane architect, and at his first visit to our land he knew exactly what we wanted. He designed us a long, low house, very simple, that fits perfectly into the bush. We sold the house in Mudgee, and settled into an apartment in Caloundra while our new house was being built. From the apartment's windows we could watch the huge container ships thrusting up the channel between Bribie and Moreton Islands; they would seem to be almost coming in our window when they would swing round ninety degrees and follow the channel. The sun shone through winter as the house went up, and on our frequent visits we became good friends with all the builders. There were so many surprises. The man who drove the bulldozer that levelled the site took enormous care not to damage the big white gum that would be near the front door. The chief builder on the site, Terence, was a New Zealander who seemed to have an instinctive understanding of the requirements of this site in the Australian bush. His young brother, Bruce, an Adonis with genuine muscles, not those deformed weight-lifter's excrescences, raced around without a shirt, despite Robin's pleas to him not to invite skin cancer. The foreman, Greg, a carpenter, was a native-plant enthusiast, and brought us trees and shrubs from his nursery.

Then two pardalotes made their nest in a little tunnel in the heaps of topsoil near the entrance. As the bobcat whined around, or the men clattered and clanged with wheelbarrows and hammers, these tiny birds popped in and out of their burrow, quite unconcerned. When the time approached for spreading the topsoil, strict instructions were given by the builders to the bobcat driver not to disturb the pardalotes. However, most accommodatingly, the babies hatched and the family moved out just before the topsoil had to be spread.

We moved in on 1 October 1991. On our first morning the birds were so many and so loud that they woke us in the false dawn, their notes sounding from all the bush around us. It is remarkable that some of the strongest songs come from the smallest birds. One wonders about the dramas of bird life. To the west a butcherbird calls, the most beautiful notes of all, beginning with short, interrogatory notes, liquid as a flute but purer, yet carrying like a trumpet; across the valley to the east another bird answers. The calls sound closer as the two birds fly towards each other, until they are both singing in the same tree just outside the house. Then suddenly one flies off, and the other bird's insistent calls are not answered, no matter how often it tries. Meanwhile a whipbird, interested only in listening to himself, thrashes them both.

Grey kangaroos go through the dark trees; a little echidna, with golden tips to his almost-black spines, comes right to the door, snuffling up ants; and two fat quail walk across the bark right outside our bedroom window. Robin must have a goanna totem, there are so many of them. These south-east Queensland goannas are very handsome, with lemon-yellow tails and yellow streaks under their chins. The biggest, six feet long, slowly and sinuously climbs the bloodwood tree in front of the house, probably to rob a bird's nest or look for ants; if you go out the door it hides behind the trunk, and then its head slowly sneaks a look at you. With goannas, we have witnessed two remarkable scenes. The first time, the biggest goanna was about five metres up the bloodwood tree when suddenly a kookaburra, making a hooting noise quite unlike the usual cackle, shot like a rocket between the tree and a close-by sapling, and gave the goanna a glancing blow with its great beak. The goanna reversed, shot down the tree, and raced into the long grass to hide. On the second occasion, a similar attack was launched on one of the smaller (but still quite large) goannas, but by an exquisite little azure kingfisher. This time the goanna hung on.

We learn how violent Queensland can be. In December we had twenty inches of rain in thirty-six hours; in February twenty-two inches in three days. The house stood firm while the iron roof thundered; even in Bougainville I had not seen rain so heavy.

Before the February rain we had a bushfire; two fire brigades came, one from the fire service at Beerwah, gleaming red truck and brass helmets. The other was local, blokes in thongs and athletic singlets with the World War II ten-wheeled Studebaker truck they use for spraying pineapples; the truck looked like something out of a Mad Max movie.

We learned that south-east Queensland bushfires are, fortunately, not like those in the south, although terrifying enough. The fire runs up the bark, but the trees do not explode, the fire thrusts on but does not leap. Our fire was started by neighbours clearing bush; by nightfall it seemed to have been contained. But next afternoon it surged back into life, and this time advanced right towards the house. Waiting for the fire brigades to arrive, clutching our puny little hose, Robin said to me, "Do you think we ought to go?" Just then the local fire-truck arrived and blasted thousands of gallons of water across the face of the fire. The boss bounded into the house to ring for more help, saying out of the corner of his mouth, "This is a real fucking fire this time."

Within a few months you would not have known there had been a fire; all the lower growth was up green again, and none of the big trees had died. The birds and animals were as plentiful as ever.

Working here is working in paradise. Interruptions and repetitive noises — noise is one of the worst of pollutions — are minimal. I can work anywhere, but the Glasshouse Mountains and Rocky Point are the two best places I have known. I always find it interesting to talk to my writer and artist friends about their work habits. About the only thing we seem to have in common is a perennial compulsion, or rather, need, to work; there are of course some exceptions, like Tass Drysdale, who procrastinated so much. Some of us are night people, some day; some insist on regular meals, others go right through the day or night without eating more than a snack. Most of the artists I know like to have music playing while they work. For most writers, any sort of music is a distraction, and anything with an insistent beat is sheer torture.

My writing day often begins at about 3 a.m., if I have to get up for a pee

— one of the curses of age. I start to think about what I'm working on, and sentences come into my mind. I resolutely do not write them down, but try to remember them, as I want to get to sleep again. I get up somewhere between five and six, depending on whether it's summer or winter, pull on what Robin calls my possum suit (a track suit), cut a slice of pineapple (here in south-east Queensland at the moment you can buy five pineapples for a dollar), and turn on my computer. I have breakast about eight, then a shave and shower, and then drive into the village to get the mail and papers. I read what I can of them in the time it takes to have a cup of coffee, then go back to work. Robin and I have a good lunch, and maybe a beer or a glass of wine, then we go for a walk through the bush, on the firebreak right around our twenty-four acres. It's extraordinary how different the perspectives of the tall trees are in a right-hand and a left-hand circuit, and the varying aspects of the mountain through the leaves.

I work until about four, then have a cup of tea before doing the garden or other physical work for a couple of hours. I think it is important not to sit hour after hour at one's desk without a break. Our near-neighbour, Lawrence Daws, leaves his studio for half an hour each morning and afternoon to work in his vegetable garden, which with its burgeoning terraces looks like something out of Italy, except for the avocados and pawpaws at either end.

After the gardening comes the best part of the day. We have a whisky in winter, a gin in summer, we put on a CD and I prepare the dinner. Cooking is a great relaxation for a writer. You have dealt all day with black words on paper or green words on a screen; now you are dealing with the shapes and colours of nature, scaling a fish or topping and tailing beans. Cooking, in a humble way as I do it, is a tiny act of creation which can go just right or be a disaster. And you have a trip around the flavours of the world, from Italy to Thailand.

With the meal, depending on our finances, we either have a bottle of wine, or from a cask fill a *pichet* which carries the inscription *"L'eau fait pleurer, Le vin chanter"*, and talk. The talk frequently leads to a little more wine. After ten years we haven't run out of talk.

My day sounds monstrously regular, I know, almost like nine to five at the office, but I find that no matter what I am writing, whether this long book or a short poem (for which I usually have scrappy notes in my pockets), I must sit down at my desk and work. I can't write poems on the computer, I have to write them out in my lousy writing. Waiting for inspiration is strictly for amateurs.

I agree with Flaubert in that advice of his to a young artist: "Be regular and ordinary in your life, like a bourgeois, so you can be violent and original in your works".

I have found that one of the most useful pieces of advice ever given me was when I was at school. J.R. Darling encouraged us to think about our essays at any time or place, even sitting on the lavatory. I am furious with myself if I'm in the car or walking and haven't got a bit of paper and a biro to hand. I often wonder whether doctors or lawyers or tycoons have always to be open to stray ideas or phrases or whole sentences.

As for reading, I think that for all writers, it operates on two levels, one belonging to the book that is being read, one to the books or poems that are not yet written, impulses flashing on the always open screen of the mind. For some mysterious reason this does not interfere with one's concentration or enjoyment in reading.

Growing old has some drawbacks, certainly, but it is sad when people become decrepit through not looking after their bodies. I don't mean that people should be health freaks, but only that they should care for this beautiful and intricate piece of life that we are born with, if we are lucky and there is nothing fundamental wrong with it. People who say old age is humiliating and disgusting may of course have been unlucky, inflicted with disease or chronic troubles, but mostly they remind me of people who say their car is unreliable and falling to bits, when it has never been regularly maintained.

I think there is a beauty and a kind of dignity to most machinery, which merits care. I hate to see someone cleaning a stainless steel saucepan with steel wool, or forcing a delicate piece of equipment. This is not puritanism; I don't care how often or seldom they wash their car or clean their house.

When you reach seventy you are entitled to make some sort of assessment of your life and career. My greatest practical mistakes have been connected with Anlaby. As Barry Humphries said to me after writing his own autobiography, "It's as if you're going down a river and you see this great big rock in front of you and you want to shout to yourself 'Turn left! Left!'. But you just go on straight ahead."

Apart from beauty, it was the secure base of my early years, and I was still under its spell when I made the fatal error first of returning to it, then later of buying the homestead and surrounding area from my relatives. Compounding the consequent financial ruin was the drain on my own time as a writer and editor and publisher, my true activities. Farming is a highly complex business, involving years of training, and I had had plenty of opportunity to know the truth of this. Why then, did I try to set up as a farmer? I can only think that Anlaby was a kind of neurosis — in my mind it corresponded with aspects of myself. My early and long-lasting insecurity about myself, that familiar Ah-timid-dormouse, led me to think that Anlaby would provide security. Of course I was financially quite incapable of enabling it to play any such role; in fact I, with ever-dwindling means, tried to give Anlaby security. In Nietzsche's sense I began to recreate myself when I left South Australia and shed all that baggage of ancestors and roots, and the decayed grandeur of the buildings of Anlaby.

I can now concentrate fully on what I love most. Central to my life's work, and most important, are my books, though I have no illusions about their claims to immortality. I am a professional writer, responsible for more than fifty books. I have had a go at almost anything, except pornography and other easy profit enterprises. Poetry is my first and last love. Many of my books correspond to a kind of journalism, professionally done and suitable for their purpose, but not destined or even intended to last. I think it is essential for a healthy literary community that a number of professional writers do this kind of work with books.

I am uncomfortable talking about my achievements; my prose is betraying that discomfort. But I am pleased with the help I have been able to give Australian writers and the cause of Australian literature, through being a publisher and editor of magazines and books, and from working on committees such as that of Writers' Week in the Adelaide Festival. After Brian Stonier and I left Penguin we founded Sun Books with our own money. So it was not only my time I was giving but my money, which I could ill afford, although of course I didn't always face up to the fact that I couldn't afford it. I was passionate about Australian literature and bringing books into print. Unfortunately when this was accompanied by the splendid façade of Anlaby I was, by this behaviour, reinforcing other people's perception of me as "the smiling Maecenas of Australian Literature", as one misguided commentator described me. I was in a sense trapped again by my upbringing; I must still have been cocooned from reality not to have overcome it.

Also intimately connected with publishing is something I am certainly proud of, which is that I have been an active republican for thirty years. At the beginning of Donald Horne's recent book, *The Coming Republic*, he writes: "The modern Australian republican movement began with an article by the Adelaide writer, and at the time university lecturer, Geoffrey Dutton, that appeared in the intellectual fortnightly, *Nation*, in April 1963". Because of this I feel part of a great movement in Australia's history, and I look forward to the exciting outcome that I had hoped for all those years before.

On a more personal level, it is a daily joy to me that at seventy my body is still good to live with. I am — touching wood, for I'm incurably superstitious — in full enjoyment of all my senses. I never think of being seventy, or indeed, any particular age at all.

There is no fixed colour to life, and life cannot be tied to one mood. I am reminded again and again of this when I look out from our living room at the bush. In this region of Queensland the trees are very tall, and their great trunks differ widely; some are dazzling white, others elephant-grey, others verging towards black.

The biggest, whitest, smoothest gum tree below us has a long curving branch that makes it look like one particular painting of Matisse. When there is a little rain the trunk and this bough are flecked with pink and apricot; when there is heavy rain the bark turns through tan to a glowing ochre. Yet I know that after a day of warm sun it will be back to the purest white.

Love itself may have "an ever-fixed mark", but there is nothing stationary about it. It is infinitely flexible, and responds all the time to nature and partakes of these shifting colours.

For many years I was undermined by the cry of a classical queen in an obscure Elizabethan play, as she prepares to meet her death: "Happiness makes us base". At seventy I am no longer vulnerable to her despairing stoicism. I am well aware of the dangers of hubris, but I think it is safe to say one can be in daily touch with happiness as long as one gives thanks for it, no matter to whom or what, and as long as one does not forget the misery in the world. Then happiness is not a kind of candied state, like swimming in honey, but an act of awareness, like swimming in the sea, and of infinite possibility.

Epilogue

Little Testament 1991

The Heart should have fed upon the truth, as Insects on a Leaf — till it be tinged with the colour, and show its food in every the minutest fibre.

S.T. Coleridge, letter to Robert Southey

Ah, how delicious it is still to be alive — How premature to give up, how one wants to live!

Boris Pasternak, letter to Olga Freidenberg, 15 November 1940

In the sixty-ninth year of my age
I go north and say farewell to frost.
No more will my boots crack the image
Of crystal grass, green no more lost
In wincing white. No more the cost
Of cold, the stove hungry at midnight.
No more closing the house, bossed
By shrewish draughts, starved of daylight.

Human hours are all unsure,
Death offers no tax rebate.
Life was not meant to be dour.
Let other people rush to the gate
Under the threat of being late,
I'll rise at first light for the pleasure
Of hearing the birds, who cannot wait
To pour out what they never measure.

I leave tight arses and thin lips
To those who triple-check the bill
And then economize on tips.
To those with fingers in the till,
Ruining thousands, but who still
Have those reserves in Switzerland,
I leave them kidneys going downhill,
Whisky spilled by a shaking hand.
May their funds be transferred to Brazil.

To those who never render thanks,
Who never have lifted up their eyes,
I leave them rust in their petrol tanks
And faith in politicians' lies.
May hordes of cockroaches and flies
Invade all rooms too clean and white,
And may the untidiness of the wise
Loosen lives done up too tight.

There's no harm in wills being humorous,
Especially for those who like to be
Obsequious to death. It's serious,
But better with champagne than tea,
The bubbles will rise, if you've been lucky,
And no one luckier than I.
Fancy being absolutely happy
To live with someone till you die!

To her who shares my nights and days
I leave all that is not mine
To give, but which in so many ways
Is already, like inexhaustible wine,
Shared taste and colour, a design
Of art and nature and chemistry,
The strictness bred inside the vine,
The abandon that the grape sets free.

The mountain above us makes absurd
All differences of human age.
Often we speak the same word
At the same time, a kindly sage
Having taught us how to unlock the cage
Of time and distance, for living with her
And speaking the same unspoken language
I never need an interpreter.

I give thanks to whoever lit my fire
For making me a writer, which keeps us poor
But means I never will retire.
Never dread an open door.
Always being able to raid the store
Of words, never having to say,
Like someone totting up the score,
"Hurray! The end of another day!"

True, age does not make the words
Come easier, but they may be found.
I leave my death to the trees and birds
Where there is leaf-mould on the ground.
We're lucky, silence rings us round
As the whip-bird's crack dies.
Life can go on without a sound
As light over leaves at sunrise.

Index